PENGUIN BOOKS
VICTORIAN VILLAINIES

Graham Greene was born in 1904 and educated at Berkhamsted School and Balliol College, Oxford. His first job was as a subeditor on *The Times*, and he later became film critic and then literary editor of the *Spectator*. He established his reputation with his fourth novel, *Stamboul Train*, and has written in all some thirty novels, 'entertainments', plays, children's books, travel books, collections of essays and short stories, as well as two volumes of autobiography.

Sir Hugh Greene joined the BBC as Head of the German Service in 1940, after an earlier career as Foreign Correspondent for the *Daily Telegraph*, and twenty years later became the BBC's Director General. After his retirement in 1969 he joined Bodley Head as Chairman, a post he held until 1981 when he became Honorary President. He has compiled many volumes of early detective stories, and has collaborated with his brother once before, in *The Spy's Bedside Book*.

# VICTORIAN VILLAINIES

### THE GREAT TONTINE

### THE ROME EXPRESS

### IN THE FOG

### THE BEETLE

*Selected by Graham Greene and Hugh Greene*

*With an Introduction by Hugh Greene*

# Claremont Books
# London

PENGUIN BOOKS
Published by the Penguin Group
Penguin Books Ltd, 27 Wrights Lane, London W8 5TZ, England
Penguin Books USA Inc., 375 Hudson Street, New York, New York 10014, USA
Penguin Books Australia Ltd, Ringwood, Victoria, Australia
Penguin Books Canada Ltd, 10 Alcorn Avenue, Toronto, Ontario, Canada M4V 3B2
Penguin Books (NZ) Ltd, 182-190 Wairau Road, Auckland 10, New Zealand

Penguin Books Ltd, Registered Offices, Harmondsworth, Middlesex, England

*The Great Tontine* first published in three volumes by Chapman & Hall 1881
*The Rome Express* first published by John Milne 1896
*In the Fog* first published by R. H. Russell, New York 1901
*The Beetle* first published by Skeffington 1897
This edition first published under the title *Victorian Villainies* by Viking 1984
Published in Penguin Books 1985

This edition published by Claremont Books,
an imprint of Godfrey Cave Associates Limited,
42 Bloomsbury Street, London WC1B 3QJ,
under licence from Penguin Books Ltd, 1995

Compilation copyright © Graham Greene and Sir Hugh Greene, 1984
Introduction copyright © Sir Hugh Greene, 1984

Printed and bound in Great Britain by
BPC Hazell Books Ltd
A member of
The British Printing Company Ltd

ISBN 1 85471 011 7

# CONTENTS

# INTRODUCTION

My brother Graham and I have been collecting old detective stories since just before the war. The search through four or five decades has taken us all over the country. Some of our best hunting-grounds have been Aylesbury, Bath, Bournemouth, Brighton, Bristol, Colchester, Edinburgh, Eton, Guildford, Harrogate, Leeds, Maidstone, Norwich, Salisbury, Totnes, Watford, Wells, Winchester and Worcester, apart from various corners of London. The pubs in these towns, with their variety of beers and sausages, became as familiar to us as the second-hand bookshops. We walked for miles through shabby backstreets and usually it seemed to be raining.

In the last twenty years many of the shops we used to know have disappeared. The old-fashioned bookshops with aged proprietors as dusty as their piles of books have given way to shops with clean, well-arranged shelves presided over by bright young people who know their business. Bargains, once so easy to find, have become rare.

As for our speciality – detective stories from the Victorian and Edwardian eras – where one used to pick up a dozen one is lucky to find one: where one had to pay at most two or three shillings the prices have soared to tens or scores of pounds. The junk shops in back streets – Salisbury used to be a great place for junk shops – where old detective stories could be found in the sixpenny and shilling boxes have died with their proprietors.

Of the four detective novels we have chosen by almost forgotten writers, my copy of the first edition of *The Beetle* presented by the author, Richard Marsh, to Cecil Harmsworth, a younger brother of Lord Northcliffe, would probably fetch at least £100. The price I paid, which I find pencilled inside, was five shillings. Our first editions of Hawley Smart, Arthur Griffiths and Richard Harding Davis would be worth at least another £100 between them.

It all began with an essay by John Carter on collecting detective fiction published in 1934. He mentions *The Beetle* with particular approval and also Arthur Griffiths. More than twenty years passed after the appearance of this essay before prices really got out of hand. That was when American, and I believe even Japanese, collectors started to take over.

Now, if one is to add to one's collection at a reasonable cost, one must rely on a bookseller making an occasional mistake. For instance, there was a detective story writer at the turn of the century called Mrs L. T. Meade, who also wrote books about schoolgirls which nobody collects so far as I know. I have twice found one of her first editions for practically nothing on the wrong shelf.

It is a strange coincidence that two of our authors, Hawley Smart and Arthur Griffiths, fought as professional soldiers in the Crimean War. Both were present at the fall of Sebastopol: Hawley Smart, who had received his commission before the war from Lord Raglan, the British Commander-in-Chief in the Crimea, as a captain of twenty-three, Arthur Griffiths as a lieutenant of sixteen. Their paths, as soldiers, crossed once again. Hawley Smart also served in the Indian Mutiny and then in Canada. Arthur Griffiths had preceded him to Canada, and both were there in 1861 when war nearly broke out with the United States over the *Trent* affair, after the United States man-of-war *San Jacinto* had seized two Confederate commissioners bound for Europe off the British mail steamer *Trent*. In the very small British professional army of those days it seems very unlikely that they never met.

After Canada their careers diverged, though in the end they both became professional writers. Hawley Smart sold out of the army and became an extravagant punter on the turf. He lost so much money that he turned to writing novels. He put his experience of war and of horse racing to good account and became one of the most popular novelists of the mid-Victorian years. Between 1869 and his death in 1893 he produced two or three novels every year. Some dealt with horse racing under such titles as *Cleverly Won: A Romance of the Grand National, Long Odds, The Plunger, A Member of Tattersall's* and so on: others with the Crimean War. He also wrote a few detective novels often with a background of horse racing or betting. He was near to being the Dick Francis of his day.

Hawley Smart is still a very readable writer, who does not deserve to be completely forgotten. There is an atmosphere of reckless enjoyment and gaiety about his best books which seems to reflect the character of the man, and he catches the mood of the Victorian army and the Victorian turf. *The Great Tontine* is the best of his books with a detective interest. What a tontine is those who do not know already will discover as they read the story. Some readers may remember that a tontine was the cause of all the trouble in Robert Louis Stevenson's *The Wrong Box*, which was published seven years later.

Major Arthur Griffiths was, like Hawley Smart, a keen sportsman and, we are told, an amusing raconteur. Perhaps he was a more serious soldier. He went on to be brigade major in Gibraltar, where he was put temporarily in charge of the convict establishment. This aroused his interest in prisons and when he left the army he entered the prison service. He was deputy governor at Chatham, Millbank and Wormwood Scrubs and was promoted to inspector of prisons, which he remained for over twenty years. Even before his retirement from the prison service he had begun to write, starting with such books as *Chronicles of Newgate* and *Memorials of Millbank* and several volumes of military history. After his retirement his output increased and he wrote about thirty novels before his death in 1908, seven of them detective stories.

He made a special study of French police methods and the result can be seen in the somewhat sardonic humour of *The Rome Express*. His detective Floçon, the Chef de la Sûreté, is not treated with much respect. He is certainly no Maigret.

Richard Harding Davis was also no stranger to wars. He was an American war correspondent who, in the Victorian age, covered the Greco-Turkish, Spanish-American and Boer wars and, later on, the Russo-Japanese war and the Great War until his death in 1916. It is a reminder of how many wars were going on during the supposedly peaceful reign of Queen Victoria, and writers of detective stories often seemed to get mixed up in them. Sir Arthur Conan Doyle himself tried during the Boer War to enlist in the Middlesex Yeomanry, and finally got to the front as senior physician in a field hospital. He also invented a rifle designed to kill men under cover with dropping bullets, but the War Office was not interested.

*In The Fog* is the only novel written by Richard Harding Davis which could count as a detective story. He wrote a few other novels based on his journalistic experiences and also accounts of the wars he had reported. He was a very arrogant man, rather like some of the American correspondents I have met in other wars, and seems to have been universally disliked by his contemporaries. But he could write. *In The Fog* is one of the very best accounts of foggy Victorian London, the London which many Americans, including Ronald Reagan, believe still exists. If one said more about it one would risk revealing its very ingenious plot.

Compared with his three companions in this collection Richard Marsh was, on the face of it, a man of peace. But he seems to have been a man haunted by demons. Graham and I have long felt that *The Beetle* is a book which should not be out of print. The atmosphere of horror at the beginning when the starving tramp enters what he believes to be an empty room in an empty house is beautifully conveyed. Apart from the horror there are some fascinating sidelights on forgotten aspects of the Victorian age: the ease, for instance, with which one could hire a special train with steam up in the shed, to get to one's destination as quickly as today – if some ghastly accident did not happen to prevent one from reaching one's destination at all.

Many of Richard Marsh's other books are also haunted by figures of strange horror, and I have the feeling from the laconic accounts in the newspapers of the time that some mystery hung around his death. The cause of his death in August 1915 at Haywards Heath in Sussex at the age of fifty-eight was given as heart failure, likely enough if he had encountered the Beetle. He had been educated at Eton and Oxford and was something of an infant prodigy. He started writing stories for boys' magazines at the age of twelve. Keeping up a very high striking rate, he had written over sixty novels, of very uneven quality, by the time of his death. Perhaps the only thing he shared with our soldier authors was that he too was a keen sportsman – a lover of cricket, football, golf, chess and billiards. In view of his output it is remarkable that he described himself as 'a clumsy but enthusiastic student in the fine art of proficiency at doing nothing'.

So here we offer four examples of Victorian villainy from very rare books long out of print, fraud, murder, political intrigue in the fog, darkness and horror.

# THE GREAT TONTINE

## HAWLEY SMART

For dice will run the contrary way,
As well is known to all who play,
And cards will conspire as in treason.

# PROLOGUE

## IN THREE CHAPTERS

---

### CHAPTER ONE

## THE POOL AT ÉCARTÉ

Eighteen hundred and sixty. Twenty years ago, my brethren. Ah! what memories that conjures up for many of us. Twenty years ago, when, however reckless might have been the revel of the preceding night, we sprang from our beds no wit the worse for it; when valsing, cricketing, and racket-playing entered prominently into our lives. Now the racket-court knows us no more; we look on at 'Lord's'; and as for dancing, regard it as a weariness of the flesh past endurance.

Twenty years ago the 'pattens' were ringing over the flooded and frozen marsh-lands round about Croyland, Peterborough, and the Fen country, and in London the waters of the parks were crowded with skaters. Big scores were made amongst the wildfowl by those who embarked on the arduous sport of duck-shooting. It was a bitter cold winter, and cock, curlew, teal, and widgeon were numerous in the land.

Twenty years ago Louis Napoleon was at the zenith of his power, the Imperial court in the meridian of its splendour. The Austrian had bit the dust at Solferino but a few months before, and Europe, to some extent, regarded the third Napoleon as the arbiter of its destinies. Peace or war, it was deemed, depended pretty nearly on the dictum of the French emperor. Signs of discord were rife in the great Western Republic, though few could have imagined the stupendous struggle that another twelve-month would see her committed to; when for four years the North and the South wrestled so fiercely for the mastery, resulting in the ruin of the latter, and the doing away with the bondage of – that bone of contention – their black brother. There were plenty of clever men upon both sides who, in the words of Mr Lowell,

> Thought the Union hoops were off;

but, amazing as were the resources displayed on both sides during that terrible four years, more amazing still is it, in the present day, to see how completely the traces of perhaps the greatest rebellion in modern history have been obliterated.

Twenty years ago, and men were striving to penetrate the inscrutable mystery of the 'Road' murder – a mystery destined to be solved some few years later, and affording a melancholy instance of to what terrible lengths a morbid, hysterical temperament may carry a maiden.

Twenty years ago sporting England was absolutely convulsed concerning the great international prize fight between Sayers and Heenan. Senators and peers – and scandal even contended bishops – left their beds betimes, and were whirled down into the Hampshire country that bright April morning to witness the last great gladiatorial exhibition of the cestus, to witness the sturdy Brighton bricklayer for some two hours confront the American athlete on that little patch of grass near Farnborough – last supreme flicker of the prize-ring previous to its fading away and becoming a lost relic of a past civilization, a civilization of hard swearing and hard drinking chartered by society.

On the turf the yellow jacket and the black cap of the Grosvenors was to the fore, as it is now, although the colours in those days were not borne by any scion of the house of Westminster. Mr Merry's Thormanby won the Derby, and like a loyal representative, the member for Falkirk Burghs telegraphed the glad news to his constituents –

Three forty-two – Thormanby has won.

They were on to a man, and equal to the occasion. In a few minutes back came the response –

Three fifty-eight – Falkirk Burghs is drunk!

Twenty years ago Herbert Phillimore, fifth Viscount Lakington, found that he had reached his twenty-sixth birthday and the end of his tether. There had been no bolder plunger on the racecourse for the last two or three years. At first the London world rang with stories of the wondrous *coups* brought off by Lakington. They declared that he swelled visibly after a settling day at Tattersall's, that he was perfectly distended with banknotes, and rumour declared Coutts's Bank was kept open a couple of hours after time expressly to receive the Viscount's winnings. The turf world marvelled greatly. 'The cleverest young one that has ever been out,' muttered some. 'How on earth does he get his information?' murmured others. The bookmakers said nothing, but continued doggedly to lay him shorter odds than ever. The bubble soon burst, as it has burst many a time before. The Viscount was no more astute than his fellows, nor blessed with any extraordinary sources of information. It was simply luck. For a short time he could do no wrong, and being, as before said, a very bold better, he swept large sums out of the ring; but, after the custom of most successful gamblers, spent the money lavishly as he had won it lightly. But although not exceptionally clever, Lord Lakington was no fool. It did not occur to him to retire when the smash came, to drop Ascot and Newmarket, to turn over a new leaf, and attempt to live upon what was left of his income; but he quite recognized that something must be done, and that the sinews of war must be raised from other resources than his own in future. He fell back, as might have been expected, upon the usual expedient of unmarried and impecunious nobility – the marrying of money. A popular, good-looking fellow of six-and-twenty, who can place a coronet on his bride's brow, has not long to seek for such opportunity. The amalgamation of rank and wealth is a natural law of civilization, and the majority of coronets would look dingy and battered were it not for opportune re-gilding by intermarriage with the plutocracy. Lord Lakington was not long in finding a young lady who combined all the necessary qualifications, and once more the London world marvelled at his extraordinary luck.

'Confound it,' exclaimed Sir Gerald Fitzpatrick, who had been hawking his graceless self and baronetcy in the matrimonial market for the last five years unsuccessfully, 'there never was such a fellow; he positively can't really lose. What does it matter dropping thousands on the turf when you marry millions to wind up with?'

Lakington was indeed fortunate. He had carried off the great matrimonial prize of the season from a host of competitors. A quiet, lady-like girl, who, without being a beauty, was still quite sufficiently good-looking; but whose greatest charm, probably, in the eyes of the world was that she was the only child of Anthony Lyme Wregis, the great financier. To define what Mr Lyme Wregis was, was pretty nearly as difficult as to say what he was not. He seemed to have a finger in pretty nearly every big speculation that was afloat. His enemies – and successful men are sure to have plenty of these – declared that he was a 'salter of diamond fields', promoter of 'bogus' silver mines, phantom railways, and every description of bubble speculation that filled the pockets of those that started them at the expense of the unfortunate dupes that took shares in them. However, whatever he touched turned to gold, and in this year of grace eighteen hundred and sixty he had given a park to the people, built unto himself a palace at Fulham, and was reputed to be worth more than a million of money. The Viscount's marriage was to take place the week after Ascot, and the noble bridegroom, in conjunction with three kindred spirits as reckless as himself, was at present staying in one of those pretty little houses that lie dotted around the village of Bracknell, and which had been taken by the quartette for the races.

It is the evening of the 'Cup' day, and the party, having finished their rubber, are lounging at the open windows of the drawing-room, and languidly discussing the results of the fierce combat they have waged with the knights of the pencil the last three days. It had been a wet Ascot, and, as all racing men know, that is wont to upset the cleverest calculations. Thoroughbred horses are as capricious as fine ladies, and are, many of them, as difficult to follow in their vagaries. Some of them are not able to gallop through 'dirt', while there is, on the other hand, the 'mud-larker', who revels in it; so that upon the whole the Viscount and his friends have not been having a particularly good time of it.

'How did you come through today, Lakington?' asked Sir Gerald Fitzpatrick.

'Only so so,' replied the Viscount: 'I had a pretty good win over Brown Duchess in the New Stakes, but I knocked it all down afterwards, and a bit more besides. I am fourteen hundred and fifty out, and shall have to bet in earnest tomorrow if I am ever to get home. What did you do yourself, Gerald?'

'A poor devil like myself, you see, has to be careful, and when I plunge I want to know a good deal about it. I had one good thing this "meeting", and I went for the gloves on that.'

'Hang it, what was its name?' cried Bertie Fortescue, a captain of a Dragoon regiment, just home from hunting down mutinous sepoys through the Oude country and round about Lucknow.

'The Gold Cup. I laid seven fifties to four against Promised Land, fielding to my last sovereign. One of the best things I know in racing is, when you *do* find a speedy coward, never to miss betting against him, and that is just what the Land is. Whenever he is caught he is beaten, and I thought Rupee, or Butterfly, would get to him somehow; and, as you saw, the moment he found them at his girths back went his ears, and he cut it.'

'Then I presume you mean laying against the Promised Land tomorrow in the Queen Stand Plate?' observed Fortescue.

'Just so,' replied Fitzpatrick: 'and though I may be caught occasionally, you'll see I shall be a pretty good winner in the long run; that sort of horse is always being made a strong favourite by the public, and the thief usually lets them in, as well as all connected with him. It was Fred Chichester of your corps put me up to that wrinkle. By the way, what has become of Fred? He is not in the regiment now, is he?'

'No; he sold out and got married after the Crimea, and I believe altogether made a deuce of a mess of it. Whether fired or not by Fred's example I can't say, but his father thought proper to commit matrimony on his own account. Rather rough upon Fred, I'll admit; but he need not have complicated things by quarrelling with "the governor" about it. Whether it was sheer vindictiveness or not I can't tell, but the old gentleman succeeded in begetting a son before the twelvemonth was over; he can do what he likes with his property, and I am afraid there was considerable curtailment of Fred's resources. However, Chichester took none of his old cronies much into his confidence, but disappeared, and I believe is at present living quietly somewhere on the continent.'

'I say,' suddenly exclaimed Carbuckle, a rising barrister, who was rapidly making for himself both a name and a practice on the Home Circuit, 'have any of you taken shares in the "Great Tontine"? What does your father-in-law, that is to be, think of it, Lakington? Does the scheme commend itself to the great financier?'

'Well,' replied the Viscount, laughing, 'as it so happens I did mention the subject to him. Now, as you know, he is no racing man – never troubles his head about it, in short; but, with a view, I presume, to suit my limited apprehension, he put his opinion of that scheme into turf vernacular. He described it as backing a yearling entered for the Derby to be run when he was twenty years old, and remarked further that he looked to turning his money over a good many times, and making a good deal of it, between this and then.'

'Well, I don't know, I rather like the idea myself. It commends itself to my mind as putting away something for one's old age,' observed Fitzpatrick.

'A very broken reed to trust to, Gerald, and I most sincerely hope that you'll have a good deal more than that to fall back upon in the days to come.'

'But what on earth is it?' exclaimed Fortescue. 'Pray explain to me what is the meaning of the "Great Tontine".'

'The "Great Tontine", my dear Fortescue,' replied the barrister, 'is a scheme for the benefiting of society, as originated in the fertile brain of Mr Salisbury, the great operatic impresario. He has discovered that London has no opera house worthy of the greatest metropolis in the world. He proposes to at once remedy this state of things by erecting one completely furnished with all the newest mechanical inventions of the age. The artistes' dressing-rooms are to be boudoirs, the green-room a drawing-room, and the auditorium a paradise; stock scenery is all to be found, painted by the leading academicians; plans are to be immediately called for from all our leading architects, and submitted for approval to the Board of Direction, which will comprise men eminent for their taste and thorough knowledge of all theatrical requirements. A suitable site will be selected, and the estimated trifle of one hundred and sixty thousand pounds will be raised by the "Great Tontine", and that is simply the issuing of sixteen hundred shares of one hundred pounds apiece. For every hundred pounds share you take you must nominate a life, not less than sixty years old, that is, you must give the name of some person who has attained that age – any one you like; but he or she representing the hundred pounds share must have attained the sixtieth birthday, and a copy of the baptismal register, and the name of the place where he or she was baptized, must be stated upon application for shares.'

'And you may take as many shares as you please?' asked Fortescue.

'Quite so,' continued Carbuckle; 'and name one life for the whole lot, or give a different name for each share. Now, you see, it is considered, that as all these lives start at sixty years of age, in twenty years there will be very few, if any of them, left.'

'And the holder of the last life takes the pool,' cried Gerald Fitzpatrick. 'It's just like playing pool, you see, only you can't star; your life may be fluked out in a railway accident, or at a crowded crossing. By Jove! It would be rather exciting to find one's self one of the last half-dozen left in.'

'Don't interrupt, Gerald,' exclaimed the barrister pettishly; 'I want to make Fortescue thoroughly understand Mr Salisbury's great conception. The sixteen hundred shares being all taken up, and the names attached to them being all carefully registered, and the necessary inquiries into all the said lives being *bona fide* sixty years of age, the "Great Tontine" begins. With the capital thus acquired the opera house is at once commenced, and in about two years should be finished and in full swing. As soon as that takes place five per cent per annum is to be paid to the shareholders. This, of course, represents his rent to the lessee of the new opera house. Five per cent on one hundred and sixty thousand pounds represents eight thousand a year. As the lives lapse their nominators lose all interest in the affair, and the rental is divided amongst those shareholders whose nominees are still living; consequently, those fortunate enough to have made long-lived selections find their income increasing annually. The last eight, for instance, will be drawing a thousand a year interest on their hundred pounds share; the last two will have increased to four thousand a year; while the shareholder who has nominated the final life becomes the proprietor of the whole.'

'That is exactly what I say,' interposed Fitzpatrick. 'I call it making a very suitable provision for your old age. Any of us, for instance, putting in our hundred pounds now, there is a prospect of coming into eight thousand a year at fifty or thereabouts.'

'A very distant prospect, a very dim and hazy prospect,' said Lakington, smiling. 'No, upon the whole, Gerald, I'd rather trust to picking out the winner of the "Wokingham's" tomorrow, and put my hundred on that, than put it into the "Great Tontine".'

'Yes,' rejoined Carbuckle, meditatively; 'a hundred pounds is a good deal of money to put into such an everlasting lottery as this.'

'But,' replied the ever-sanguine Fitzpatrick, 'look what a price it is! Treble events are nothing to this.'

'I recommend you to bear in mind, Gerald, the advice of the Nestor of Danebury,' exclaimed the Viscount, laughing: 'never be seduced into losing your money by taking those very long odds.'

'Advice for advice,' rejoined Fitzpatrick, gaily. 'Keep this in your memory, never waste your breath preaching prudence to an Irishman. A hundred, as we have all in our great wisdom determined, is a deal of money. That reflection would probably have been of more use if it had occurred to us in the beginning of the week; but I cannot see what old Johnson called the "potentiality of riches" escaping the grasp of four gentlemen so eminently calculated to disburse them. I have my little scheme, and it is worthy of Salisbury himself. If one hundred is too much, as Lakington in a paroxysm of prudence seems to have determined – he will probably have a monkey on that good thing in the Wokingham's tomorrow – what do you say, my brethren of misfortune, to a pool at *écarté* for "ponies"? The pleasant but lively "pony" can hurt nobody.'

'Nonsense, Gerald, an *écarté* pool of four will last all night perhaps,' replied Lakington.

'I rise to the occasion, and will show you how to settle it in three games. We put in twenty-five pounds apiece, and run it off like a coursing meeting. Draw a card each of you; the two highest first play together, then the two lowest, and then the two winners; and I propose that whoever wins the pool be solemnly pledged to invest that hundred in the "Great Tontine".'

A roar of laughter greeted Fitzpatrick's proposition, and amidst a considerable amount of chaff the other three assented to the arrangement. That the baronet was subsidized by Salisbury to promote the 'Great Tontine' was insisted on; but his plan for curtailing a pool at *écarté* was pronounced ingenious, and, as the Viscount observed, like railway whist, had the great merit of enabling you to win or lose money considerably quicker than by the ordinary method. The first two players were Lakington and Carbuckle, and the game terminated in favour of the Viscount. Fitzpatrick and Fortescue then did battle, and the baronet holding big cards speedily disposed of the dragoon.

'Come on, Lakington,' cried Gerald; 'shake up the Saxon phlegm of you. It's your misfortune, not your fault, that you were not born with an Irishman's imagination; on me sowl, I feel I am going to play for eight thousand a-year this minute, while to your prosaic mind it merely represents a game for a hundred, I'll go bail.'

The Viscount smiled as he took his place, and it really seemed at first as if Fitzpatrick would have his hankering for a share in the 'Great Tontine' gratified. He marked the king and scored a 'vole' right off to begin with; but the next hand Lakington made the point, and continued to creep up one at a time, until the game stood three all. The next deal Fitzpatrick scored the trick, and the game stood thus: Fitzpatrick four, Lakington three; and now occurred a curious phase in the contest, in which scientific reticence on the one hand triumphed over careless confidence on the other. Lakington dealt, turning up a small diamond; Fitzpatrick took up his hand and found it consisted of queen and knave of trumps, king, queen, and ace of spades. A hand good enough to play at any time without proposing, and Fitzpatrick led, as a matter of course, with the king of spades. The Viscount happened to hold the king and eight of trumps, two small clubs, and one small spade. He of course played his small spade, and masked his king, that is to say, refrained from marking it. Gerald fell headlong into the trap; jumping to the unwarrantable conclusion, that because his adversary had not marked his king he had not got it, he led his queen of trumps, which of course fell to the Viscount's king, who thereupon led a small club. This forced his adversary's knave of trumps; and when Fitzpatrick led his queen of spades the Viscount of course roughed it with his small trump, and his remaining club was naturally good. This gave him the trick, and his antagonist having played without proposing he was entitled to score two for it, which made him game.

'Good gracious, Gerald,' exclaimed Carbuckle, 'what possessed you to fool away the game like that? If you had only gone on with the spades you couldn't have lost it.'

'Too true, too true,' rejoined Fitzpatrick, ruefully; 'but, on my oath, if any of ye had felt as near eight thousand a year as I did that minute ye'd have taken the nearest way to it, though, maybe, it wasn't the safest. Was it likely I'd get justice to Oireland setting down to play with three Sassenachs?'

'You are as hard to satisfy as others of your countrymen; you'd not cultivate the land if we gave it you. I dealt you winning cards; you have only yourself to blame if you won't play them properly,' retorted the Viscount.

'I'll say no more,' rejoined Gerald; 'but remember, Lakington, you are pledged to put that hundred into the "Great Tontine". I have the strongest presentiment that you will eventually win it. It will be so like the luck of the Fitzpatricks to have chucked eight thousand a-year out of window. Anyway, I am the first of the family who ever staked as much on a hand at cards. And now I'm off to bed; I can't do the family estates any more mischief after that. I shall dedicate the next twenty years or so of my life to the framing of a compensation bill to be presented to Viscount Lakington, the then owner of the new Royal Italian Opera House.'

CHAPTER TWO

# THE FOUNDING OF LLANBARLYM

Twenty-three years ago the now fashionable watering-place of Llanbarlym on the north coast of Wales, and somewhere in the vicinity of the Orme's Head, was nothing better than a little fishing village; but at last the great colonizing agent of our times – the railway – touched it; and then visitors, at first in twos and threes, soon to be increased to shoals, poured in upon it. Explored in the first instance by artists or by tourists, to whom well-known beaten tracks were distasteful, its fame rapidly spread as a quiet, pleasant little place in which to pass the summer holidays, and drink in the invigorating sea breezes. Soon the modest inn no longer sufficed for its requirements, and some enterprising speculator rapidly ran up an hotel, which proved so successful that he speedily followed it up by building other houses, quickly taken off his hands by that rapacious race who undertake to find food and lodging for the stranger on such seasons. Now there were plenty of quick-eyed, shrewd men in the country towns, standing a few miles inland from Llanbarlym, who saw that the place had a future before it, and was evidently well on the road to develop into a fashionable watering-place. To those who dealt in bricks and mortar it was clear that there was much business to be done, and much money to be made over its growing up. Llanbarlym the fishing-village was a thing of the past. Llanbarlym the watering-place was yet to be created. Plenty of speculation to be done in building and land was patent to all who thought about the matter, and it so happened that a good deal of the surrounding soil was the property of small and needy freeholders. Even Squire Griffiths, who was the big landowner connected with Llanbarlym, was a man who, having lived in his youth 'not wisely, but too well', found himself a necessitous person in his old age. He was usually in desperate straits for money, and infinitely preferred the bartering of his acres for a fair price now, to waiting some ten or twelve years on the probability of their trebling in value.

Amongst the little knot of land-dealers, builders, surveyors, architects, and others who busied themselves so earnestly about the development of

Llanbarlym, there were none more keenly interested than Mr Paul Pegram, a solicitor residing in a country town some twelve miles from the budding watering-place. Mr Paul Pegram, albeit a sharp and a somewhat unscrupulous practitioner, had arrived at the age of forty without in his own opinion having done much good for himself. He was not a popular man; and though the Welsh have the reputation of being a somewhat litigious people, they at all events put their litigation but sparsely into Mr Pegram's hands. He was a man of very humble extraction, his father having been a cattle-jobber, who, though with no learning, had been deemed a hard-headed, clever hand at a bargain. He died very proud of having brought up his son as a 'professional gentleman', and of leaving some four thousand pounds behind him. Mr Paul Pegram had all the old man's instincts. He was frugal, careful of money, anxious to turn his capital over, and prepared to drive quite as hard bargains as ever his father had done; and he, moreover, possessed one quality which, in his own eyes, ought to have been of material assistance to him in the acquisition of wealth. As long as he kept within the law he was not in the least particular how he should acquire riches. It was perhaps his very liberal views with regard to his moral obligations that made him so much less successful than his father. As the neighbours said, 'old Bob Pegram might be a very skinflint at a deal, but his word was his bond'. That he had covenanted to do he punctiliously performed; but with Paul Pegram the case was different. He was certain to shuffle out of his part of the contract afterwards if possible. He sold his law, too, much dearer than his brethren of the profession, and 'as long as a bill of costs of lawyer Pegram' was quite a cant phrase in his native town. He had acquired, in short, the unfortunate reputation of being a man a little too sharp to safely have much to do with. In one respect only had Mr Pegram so far succeeded in life, and that was in his marriage. Some twelve years ago he had persuaded Mrs Marigold, widow of the whilom landlord of the 'Red Lion', to become his wife. She was ten years older than he was, but she brought him a thousand in palliation of each of those extra years. She had borne him but one child, a son, named Robert after his grandfather, now about ten years of age, and destined eventually to follow in his father's profession.

Paul Pegram threw himself heart and soul into the development of Llanbarlym. This was the sort of speculation that he had been waiting for all his life. It had special attraction for him.

He had some time before stumbled across an old book which gave some curious facts on the growth of London, and the enormous increase in the value of land as the great city spread over it. He had read therein how a Grosvenor, by marriage with a Miss Davies, had acquired two farms on the Kensington road, and how those farms now constituted Belgravia, probably the richest estate in the United Kingdom. He found, further, that the manor of Tyburn was originally sold for seventeen thousand pounds, and what that veritable gold-field of the Portland family might be worth now would be difficult to estimate. Thinking over these things made him curious about the growth of cities and the fortunes that must be constantly made. Like a quick-witted speculator, he set to work betimes to buy building lots. He had read how fifty years ago Melbourne was a swamp, and now he wondered what an acre might be worth in the centre of that city. He thought of Brighthelmstone, and marvelled who were the shrewd men who, foreseeing its development into the Brighton of today, bought up the land around it. If he could but only get such a chance; and now, here it was ready to his hand. There was land to be bought now at between thirty and forty pounds the acre around Llanbarlym, which before very long might be worth, in his opinion, six or seven times the price.

He was early in the field, foreseeing what the railway would do for the place. He determined to sink all the money he could lay his hands upon in this speculation. Even if his forecast of its future should prove incorrect, the land would always remain to him, and be worth not so very much less than he should now be compelled to give for it. Before even the railway had been completed he had sought every opportunity of advancing money to the small freeholders, who struggled hard and with indifferent success to get a living out of their little properties. Cultivators of three or four acres apiece, who, though eking out their pittance by working as day labourers on occasion, yet lived a very hand-to-mouth existence, and were constantly in sore straits for a little ready money. But no sooner was the railway actually completed, than Paul Pegram lost no opportunity of tempting these poor people with what seemed to them high prices for their holdings right out, or offers of what they regarded as liberal loans on mortgage; the consequence of which was, that he had not only actually acquired a considerable amount of land right out, over which he deemed the future town of Llanbarlym must eventually spread, but was also the holder of heavy liens on a good deal more. The devouring of these unfortunate debtors Mr Pegram postponed till such time as building should be in progress upon his own adjoining property.

During the next three years Llanbarlym throve and grew in a manner that quite surpassed the expectations of those interested in its extension. The annually-increasing throng of visitors had brought settlers in their wake. Lodging-house-keepers and shopkeepers flocked from surrounding towns to start in business in the new watering-place. The first hotel was already dwarfed by a gigantic rival, which, in its turn, was about to be o'ertopped by a Limited Liability Caravanserai, now in course of erection. Bathing-machines of course made their appearance. Plans for a most imposing structure for baths of all descriptions were already drawn out. Squares, even, had been marked out, and, though as yet unbuilt, were deemed by no means visionary in the minds of Pegram and some three or four other speculators who acted with him. In Mr Paul Pegram's office at Rydland hung a map, in which the Llanbarlym of the future was depicted, in colours sanguine as those in which the famous city of Eden was exhibited in the chart of Mr Scadder. Still, arguing from the very rapid progress of the last three years, it was by no means improbable that the assembly-rooms, theatre, squares, and terraces would come with time.

Not only had Paul Pegram already made money, but he saw the land he acquired increasing rapidly in value. In short, should Llanbarlym continue to prosper, as there was every reason to suppose it would, in the course of a few years he would become a rich man. But three years of successful speculation had wrought a curious change in Paul Pegram's character. The shrewd, unscrupulous money-grubbing attorney of 1857 had developed into a daring speculator in '60. Keen to turn money he had ever been, but it had been after a careful, prudent manner, in which he ran little or no risk, but in which the profits were proportionately small. His success had given him confidence. He who, only a little while back, had deemed himself an unlucky man, now believed in his star as implicitly as Napoleon. As his money grew, so did the thirst for its acquisition. He scorned investments, the profits of which would have amply contented him but a little time back. He longed for the time when his capital should have so far extended as to enable him to pursue his speculations not only on a larger scale, but in other fields than Llanbarlym. He was smitten with the rabies of speculation, as men were in those great railway days when Hudson was king. He gloated over the record of the doings of such men as Vanderbilt and Jay Gould of New York, or of the great Mr Lyme Wregis on our own Stock Exchange, and panted to be in a corner on Erie's', or 'a big rise in the Comstock Lode'.

'Forty-two,' muttered Mr Pegram to himself, as he stood with his hands in his pockets in his office at Rydland, staring at the map of Llanbarlym with a sense of exultation. 'Forty-two; yes, it was late in life for a man's chance to come, and there is no time to be lost; but I am pretty tough, as all our breed are, thank God. Father worked hard all his life, but he saw seventy-three, and was a good man to the last. Yes; I suppose I can reckon on a matter of thirty years, and there is a deal of money to be made in that time; only let Llanbarlym go on as it is going now, and I'll have a good many more irons in the fire before another five years are over; and Bob, my boy, I will see you a country gentleman and a member of Parliament before I die. Oho!' continued Mr Pegram, with a chuckle, 'cattle-jobber, attorney, member for the county.

I wonder what grandfather was; of no great account, I fancy, so I'll not inquire.'

Another curious little bit of good fortune fell to Mr Pegram about this time; and, in all probability, led ultimately to the prominent part that he is destined to play in this history. There existed in Rydland, as there no doubt does in many other country towns in the kingdom, a reading-room. It could hardly aspire to the title of a club, but was a large room in which one might see the papers, and all the principal periodicals. It was supported by all the leading townspeople, and a sprinkling of the surrounding farmers and clergy. It was as tranquil and well-regulated a little club-room as could be well imagined. Still, it would be hard to find any such community in England in which some few of the members were not imbued with a taste for sport. No card-playing, or betting, or anything of that description ever went on there; but every year, when May came round, the members indulged in the excitement of a mild Derby 'sweep'. They were not very numerous, so that even when the sovereigns were all collected, the winner did not find himself in possession of a big sum of money. Mr Pegram knew nothing whatever about racing, nor did it interest him in any shape whatever; but he had for several years unsuccessfully put into this lottery. This identical year 1860 he drew the winner. He exulted over this in a manner quite incommensurate with his gains. He had felt a superstitious curiosity about the result. It was confirmative to him that his star was in the ascendant. Like other spoilt children of fortune, Paul Pegram began to deem himself infallible. He set up for himself a somewhat fallacious creed, that there is a certain amount of good and of evil fortune apportioned to every man in this life, and that the clever man is he who recognizes when his luck sets in.

In the beginning of June there arrived in Mr Pegram's office a dark, rather flashily-dressed gentleman, with a great deal of watch-chain and a good deal of diamond-ring about him; a dark, well-whiskered man of some five or six-and-thirty, with a very glossy hat – in fact, there was a general appearance of rather too much gloss about him altogether, which his swaggering, self-assured manner far from palliated. He gave his name as Mr Hemmingby, and curtly informed the lawyer that he had come down to see if there was anything to be done with this new place – Llanbarlym. Mr Pegram naturally inquired what did the stranger propose to do for himself or Llanbarlym.

'Well, you see,' replied the other, 'that is a thing I am not particular about. I have had a turn at a good many "specs" one way or another in my time. I have managed a theatre, and "run" an hotel, and may do either again some day. I have been in all sorts of companies. I have made my fortune, and "bust up" half a dozen times, and dare say I shall achieve similar prosperity and similar "bustings up" as often again before I die. There is often a "big stroke" to be done about a new place if a man has a head on his shoulders, and doesn't arrive too late. It's very possible I am that; but I heard a good deal about this place from a friend of mine last week, and said I would run down and look at it as soon as I had two or three days to spare; and here I am.'

'Then you have not seen Llanbarlym yet?' said Mr Pegram.

'Not I,' replied the stranger; 'not much use my going over there till I have talked over things a bit with one of the local solicitors, and, from all I hear, you are the man for my money.'

'You were not thinking of anything in the building way, were you?' inquired Mr Pegram.

'No,' replied Mr Hemmingby. 'In these days of strikes and fancy wages that game is a little "played out", I guess. I notice the big builders are rather given to "busting up"; now, I've quite tendency enough that way without going into a trade of which it is a special characteristic. No; but I tell you what would suit my book. If, when I see Llanbarlym, it looks likely to be a go-ahead place, I shouldn't mind buying up a few lots of land, if they are to be had anyway reasonable. There is always money to be made that way if, as I said before, a man is in time, and don't over-estimate the future of the town. Ah! you've got a map of the place up there, I see; I dare say you know pretty well all about my chances in that respect.'

The stranger's speech afforded a very pleasant titillation to Mr Pegram's vanity. Here was an astute speculator from London come down expressly to see if he could accomplish what Mr Pegram had been stealthily doing for the last three years.

'I am afraid,' he replied at length, 'that you will not find much to be made out of that scheme. The same idea has already occurred to a good many of the local speculators, and the landowners are getting unpleasantly wide-awake to the possible value of their property.'

'I "tumble",' said Mr Hemmingby. 'In the swim yourself, eh? Never mind, I've come down here to look at the blessed place; so I may as well do that. I'll tell you what I'll do, if you can make it convenient to slip over by rail this afternoon and just show me round, I'll stand you the best dinner to be got in Llanbarlym; if you don't name the best hotel, well, that's your fault.'

It so happened not only that Mr Pegram had nothing particular to do in his office, but that, moreover, there were one or two little matters he wished to see about in Llanbarlym. Further, he was rather taken with his voluble visitor. Just possible, he thought, that he might pick up a little useful information from a gentleman who, according to his own account, at all events, had seen a great deal of the game of speculation; so he gave a cordial assent to Mr Hemmingby's proposition – that is to say, as cordial as was within the power of Mr Pegram's by no means very genial temperament.

In due course the pair met at the railway station, and, on their arrival at Llanbarlym, the lawyer showed his new acquaintance over the place, expatiating – what was for him almost effusively – on its advantages and future prospects. Mr Hemmingby rattled away with his usual fluency, interspersing his speech with incessant questions. There never was such a man for 'wanting to know'. It sometimes occurred to his auditor that many of his questions were almost childish, though he was fain to confess that there were some very shrewd interrogatories 'scattered amongst them. He wanted to know who owned the land in all directions? what it originally sold for? what did Mr Pegram think it was worth now? who was 'running' the hotel? where did the wind generally blow from? was it a very wet place in the winter? what sort of a life was old Squire Griffiths'? and would his property be in the market when he died? &c.; but the lawyer remarked that, profuse as he might be in the matter of interrogatories, he was economical in the extreme in the expression of opinion. They re-passed the threshold of the hotel in pursuit of dinner without the stranger having expressed any judgement of the capabilities of the place, or of seeing his way to anything profitable to himself.

Mr Hemmingby was one of those clever, restless, energetic spirits seldom seen in perfection out of the United States. He had indeed lived so much in that country as to habitually use Americanisms in his talk. An admirable man of business, with a clear, cool, far-seeing brain, he had been, as he said himself, on the verge of making his fortune quite half a dozen times; but what had always brought Mr Hemmingby to grief, and what would probably be his bane till the end of time, was his craze for having too many irons in the fire. No sooner had he got one prosperous business fairly going, than it was essential for Mr Hemmingby's happiness that he should immediately start a second business, of a totally different nature, somewhere else, and as that grew up another, and so on. That they should be far apart seemed to be not so much a matter of indifference, but almost a necessity. He thought no more of going from London to New York than he did of going into the city. Running across to California was no more, in his eyes, than a trip to Brighton. The consequences were obvious. No one man could possibly look after so many varied concerns. When he said he had 'run' an hotel, and managed a theatre, it was not only true, but he had conducted them both at the same time, and one or two other businesses besides. Moreover, the hotel was in New York and the theatre in London. Even with all his ubiquity, Mr Hemmingby, it may easily be conceived, failed to exercise the necessary supervision, and things – to use his own expression – 'bust up' all round. He knew how to order a dinner, and had indeed insisted upon their making for the best hotel as soon as they arrived at Llanbarlym. By the restriction of the bill of fare to such dishes as he thought might be fairly counted to lie within the capabilities of the *chef* of the Royal Cymri Hotel, he contrived to obtain a very tidy repast; and Mr Pegram, who was not given to indulge in much luxury at his own table, was fain to confess that he had not dined so well for some time.

Although it was June, the evenings were still chilly by the seaside; and their meal concluded, in conjunction with a couple of bottles of champagne, Mr Pegram was without difficulty persuaded by his host to join him in a bottle of port, and as the decanter waned their talk became of the most confidential description. Mr Pegram admitted to his new friend that he had been one of the very earliest speculators in buying up land round about Llanbarlym, and owned that he had made a very good thing indeed on the transaction in various ways during the last three years, and that he fully expected to make considerably more during the next five or six. As for Mr Hemmingby, he told wondrous stories of successful *coups* in Wall Street, grave disasters around Gresham's statue, and darkly hinted that he guessed that there were dollars to be made in 'Frisco, only he hadn't quite cyphered out the 'hang' of it as yet. It was a good while since Mr Pegram had thawed so far as he had done tonight. He assented blandly to just another bottle of port before they started to walk to the station, and over that confidentially informed Mr Hemmingby of his confidence in his luck, how everything he touched turned up trumps for him now, and finally concluded with the story of his winning the 'Derby' lottery.

'Lotteries!' exclaimed Mr Hemmingby. 'If you are good at lotteries, guess you'll have to take a turn at the biggest thing of the kind that has been on hand in my day. You will have to take a ticket in the "Great Tontine"!'

'What is that?' inquired the lawyer. 'I never even heard of it.'

Whereupon Mr Hemmingby proceeded to explain the whole system of that elaborate lottery to the best of his ability. It took some time before he made his companion thoroughly understand the scheme. It may be that the port wine had something to say against lucid explanation on the one hand, and a clear understanding on the other, although neither of the men showed the slightest symptoms of their deep potations; but when Mr Pegram had thoroughly mastered the details of the scheme he became deeply interested in it, and finally inquired whether Hemmingby himself had taken shares in it.

'I've got one,' he replied, 'and I've a great mind to take another; but it ain't so easy to find a life of sixty that you know and can do a bit with if he gets rickety. Why, damme! if I found myself in it at last, and my man a bit ailing, I'd cart him round the world until he got the climate he wanted.'

'Ah,' replied Mr Pegram, 'I like that – capital idea – life you can watch over, keep your eye on, that's the thing. I suppose the life you have got is a man of whom you can take care?'

His host eyed him keenly as he replied, 'No; and that's just the reason I should like my second chance to be of that kind. No, I won't name him; but I'll give you a very fair "tip" if you think of venturing your luck. Do as I have done – pick out one of the most eminent statesmen of that age. In spite of the tremendous work they do, the balance of them go very near living out the time. Look at Lord Brougham, Lord Russell, Lord Lyndhurst, any one of those lives would win you a whole hundred and sixty thousand pounds were they only the requisite age; but time's up, we must be on our way to the station.'

Mr Pegram awoke the next morning very little the worse for his debauch of the previous night. Upon his tough frame and iron constitution an occasional excess of this description made little impression; but he also awoke enamoured of the scheme of the gigantic lottery. 'Ah!' he muttered, as he stropped his razor, 'this would be something like a sweep to win, or even to remain in till near the finish. There *is* money in this, and now I'm in luck, dash me, I ought to have a shy at it. Let me think – I won seventy pounds over that Derby affair, it is only putting thirty pounds more to it, and there's the money. Sharp fellow Hemmingby. I like that idea of his naming a life you can sort of watch over yourself, give change of air to, or the best advice when you think it is wanted. It's amazing what a little change of air does for old people. A little warmth and sunshine in the early spring seems to put new life into 'em. Now the question is,' continued Mr Pegram, rasping away at his chin and addressing himself in the glass, 'whom do I know who meets the case?' and here the lawyer lapsed into cogitation and wrathful wrestling with the bristles God had given him.

'By the Lord I have it!' he exclaimed at length. 'Old Krabbe's the man I want. He must be about sixty, and is as hale and hearty a man as I know. He's been clerk with me now some seventeen years and never been ailing all that time. I can't call to mind his ever being a day absent or five minutes late. Father did a good stroke of business when he got hold of him; and, to do him justice, the old dad was a mighty good judge of the points of either man or beast. He never mistook gristle for bone in either one or the other, and gauged their worth pretty accurately. Old Krabbe has been a good servant to me so far. I'll just ask him his exact age, and if that's about right, put him in. Let him live to land this stake, and he shall have a new rig-out and live like a gentleman to the end of his days; and he may take his oath I'll not see his valuable life endangered by over-work, want of change, port wine, or anything else. That's settled,' summed up Mr Pegram to himself, as he tied his cravat. 'I'll put in for the "Great Tontine", and old Krabbe shall be my nominee. I'll write about it today.'

## CHAPTER THREE

# MR CARBUCKLE ENSNARES ANOTHER VICTIM

In this same June 1860, two persons stood in the Jardin des Plantes at Avranches watching the sun sink beneath the bay of St Michel. His dying rays lit up the grim old rock, altar to so many creeds, and, if tradition tells true, once dedicated to himself. The glittering waters of the bay, the grey old mass surrounded by a faint halo of mist, and all the rich, thickly-wooded champagne country lying between the hill of Avranches and the setting luminary, made a picture wondrous fair to gaze upon. If its climate be somewhat sharp in winter-time, the elevation at which it stands above the sea level insures a certain amount of cool air in the summer. Hot it can be in those days, undoubtedly, and an apathy quite equal to the occasion then pervades it. Like most French country towns, nobody seems to have anything particular to do, and not the slightest inclination to do it if they had. A very sleepy little town, with no railway coming within forty miles of it. A little town that only wakes from its slumbers once a year, when it is positively overwhelmed by the rush of business occasioned by its horse fair; when, amidst frantic gesticulation, and much vociferation of those strange anathemas that excited Frenchmen use, scores of the big, heavy Norman horses change hands. There is a sort of festive corollary to this annual disturbance in the race-meeting which follows, when the curious phenomenon, to our insular eyes, of steeplechasing in midsummer is exhibited. There is a race ball at such times, and rumours are rife that the whist of the English, and the *écarté* at the French *cercles*, for modest stakes, have been abandoned for reckless baccarat. But, take it all the year round, it is a quiet, sleepy little place, where one may live economically, and wherein there is no conceivable temptation to spend money. It has for many years possessed a considerable English colony. Fluctuating, as a rule, it is true, but composed of people who have come there temporarily, in order that their children may learn French, or, it may be, although it is rarely advanced as a reason for sojourning at Avranches, from motives of economy. It is only the wealthy who ostentatiously preach practice of that virtue. Those to whom it is a necessity are not wont to dilate upon its advantages.

Of the two persons who stand gazing at the sunset from the Jardin des Plantes, the one is a lady, who, though considerably past the meridian of life, still bears traces of remarkable beauty. You can easily picture to yourself now what Julia Caterham must have been at her zenith; although close on fifty years of age, she has retained the tall, graceful figure of her early days. At a little distance you might have deemed Miss Caterham a young woman still. It was not till you had approached her more nearly that you saw the rich dark hair was heavily shot with silver, and that the brilliant dark eyes no longer flashed with the fire of youth. Her companion was a good-looking, blonde man, of thirty or thereabouts, with the bearing of a soldier most indelibly impressed upon him.

'It was very good of you to come, Aunt Julia; you have been an unspeakable comfort, not only to Mary, but to myself all this trying time. She has no intimate friend in this place, and in their hour of trial a husband cannot be all. A woman hungers for a friend of her own sex.'

'Tut, Fred; you know perfectly well that I have always loved Mary better than anything on earth. I had to love you in the first place because she loved you, and of course I had to love that "tot" there,' and here she pointed to a child of about three years of age, who was playing at a little distance from them, 'because you two loved her. As if it was likely that I should not come to Mary in her trouble; although,' she concluded laughing, 'if there is, master Fred, anything that would cow your determined aunt, it is the crossing of the Channel.'

'The weather seems settled,' he rejoined; 'and I trust you will have a fine crossing tomorrow. Mont St Michel is most brilliantly illuminated for you to take your last look at him; there can hardly be a finer sunset.'

'Not my last look I hope, Fred. I shall come over to see you and Mary many a time, I trust; and yet,' she continued more gravely, 'I heartily wish it were not so. This is no place for you, a man of your years, condemned to wear out his life without occupation; it is sad to think upon.'

'I know it, I know it,' he replied bitterly; 'and you know, Aunt Julia, how hard I have striven, and still strive, to get occupation of some kind. But after ten years' soldiering one seems to be fit for nothing else. Of course, if I could have foreseen all that has since taken place, I would never have thrown up the old trade; but how could I possibly guess that before two years' time he would marry a girl that could almost be his granddaughter, and that the result would be my disinheritance in favour of the new arrival?'

'Hush, Fred,' replied Miss Caterham, gently. 'It is of no use talking over what is done past redemption, though I am afraid you played your cards somewhat injudiciously.'

'Injudiciously!' he broke in hotly. 'You didn't suppose I was going to see him make an utter idiot of himself without pointing out his folly to him.'

'I am afraid, my dear Fred,' replied the lady, 'that you did not discuss the thing in quite so temperate a fashion as would have been advisable. There, not another word,' she continued quietly, as she saw he was about to interrupt her. 'Don't destroy my last evening by talking over this unfortunate subject. You and your father have quarrelled, apparently irrevocably. None of us can even suggest a fit mediator between you. There is no more to be said. We can only hope that time may eventually "right" what is now so wrong.'

'In the meantime, Aunt Julia, I must live here because it is cheap, or until I can get something to do. As soon as I can leave Máry I shall run across to London again, and see if I can hear of anything.'

'Let us hope you'll be successful; but it is time we went home. Tea time, Missy; come along,' and taking the child by the hand, Miss Caterham led the way towards the town.

Fred Chichester might well look despondingly at his prospects. His case was somewhat hard, brought about in some measure, no doubt, by his own hot temper; but the Chichesters, unfortunately, were ever a headstrong race. His future looked fair enough when, barely four years ago, he married a girl of very good family. True, they were by no means rich people, and his Mary, being one of many daughters, came to him a dowerless bride. But what did that matter? Chichester was an only son, and his father, with whom he was a prime favourite, was a wealthy man. That his progenitor, at the age of fifty-eight, should have fallen over head and ears in love with the youngest daughter of the rector of his parish was rather hard upon Fred. He remonstrated in by no means measured terms, couching such remonstrance in language very similar to that he had described himself as using. When a man of mature years has made up his mind to commit a folly, nothing irritates him more than to remind him of his contemplated foolishness; but when a man verging on sixty has made up his mind to marry for love, he is sure to be touchy in the extreme at the slightest allusion to his indiscretion. One might as well attempt to argue with a rhinoceros. Such bitter words, unfortunately, passed between father and son upon this occasion as to make reconciliation wellnigh hopeless. The old gentleman, indeed, displayed an implacable animosity that was neither just nor generous. His own son was totally dependent upon him, and at the time of his (Fred's) marriage he had agreed to increase his already liberal allowance to a thousand a-year. This allowance, being solely dependent on the old gentleman's will, he, in the tempest of his wrath, announced his intention of discontinuing; and when, in the course of the twelvemonth, a male child was born to him, disinherited the son of his former marriage, and revelled in that glow of satisfaction amply satisfied vengeance imparts to man. Fred Chichester suddenly found himself with a wife and child, without a profession, and with the interest of some six thousand or so, the proceeds of his commission, to live upon. He tried hard to make his little income go as far as possible; but poor Fred had never been brought up to study 'the economies', and he was steadily, though slowly, trenching upon his capital.

As they neared the house they were confronted by a spare, elderly man, of low stature, whose face bore a mingled expression of contrition and drollery. He opened the gate for them, taking off his hat in a deprecating fashion to his master; but Fred Chichester passed him with an indignant gesture, walked up the garden, and entered the house. The man's look of dismay was comical to witness. He was evidently conscious of crime, and felt deserving of punishment. His face bore that shy, doubtful expression that a dog which has transgressed, and fears to meet the consequences of his transgression, assumes as he sidles up to his master.

'Shure, Miss Caterham,' he exclaimed, twisting his hat slowly round in his hand, 'ye'll spake to masther Fred for me.'

'It's little short of a miracle that you are not past speaking or praying for, Terence,' replied Aunt Julia. 'Such a fall as you have had would have killed any one else.'

'An Irishman takes a dale of killing when the drink's in him; but ye'll spake to the masther just this once for me, won't ye, and ask him to forgive me?'

'You know that somebody or other has been pleading for your forgiveness any time the last seven or eight years, that you are always profuse in your promises of amendment, and that you break such promises as readily as you make them. Captain Chichester has forgiven you so often, how can you expect him to forgive you again?'

'That's what it is, Miss; it comes aisier for him to forgive me than any one else, he's so used to it, ye see. Besides, it's not my fault, it's all owing to the language.'

'Owing to the language! what on earth do you mean?'

'Ye see, Miss, I am much given to rational conversation. It's always been the habit of the Finnigans, and not being able to parleyvoo with the crayturs here, I get drinking when I should be talking, and then I feel that mad when they don't understand me that I take a drop more just to mellow my accent; and thin the cognac is a treacherous stuff. It's not like good, honest, wholesome whiskey, you know where you are getting to with that; but this French stuff, ye see, it lays hould of ye before you know where you are.'

'Well,' replied Miss Caterham, laughing, 'I'll do the best I can with the Captain for you; but you will really have to take to more sober ways for the future, or else, mark me, Terence, you will find yourself sent away in good earnest some fine morning. I only wonder you have not been killed long ago in some of your drunken freaks.'

'Oh, the Finnigans are a long-lived race, glory be to God. I am sixty meeself, and my father lived to eighty-seven, rest his sowl. If it wasn't for displeasure of the masther, no harm would ever come to me from the whiskey. If the Captain will forgive me this time, never a dhrop of dhrink shall pass my lips the next six months.'

'Mind you don't forget what you have just said,' said Miss Caterham, and with a not unkindly nod at the offender she entered the house.

This little comedy had been repeated scores of times. Terence Finnigan was an old retainer of the Chichester family; he had come into the service of Mr Chichester senior close upon forty years before as an under groom, and when Fred Chichester joined the army Finnigan accompanied him as his private servant. During his military career he developed a latent propensity for conviviality which had more than once brought him into indescribable trouble, only, luckily for himself, he was not subject to the penalties of military law. He was an excellent servant, except for this one fault. He would keep sober as an anchorite for weeks, or even months, at a time, but ever and anon his impulse became uncontrollable, and he would disappear until he had his drinking bout out; then he would return very penitent and receive his discharge, only eventually to have his offence once more condoned. He was devotedly attached to his young master, and had espoused his side in the family quarrel as violently as might have been expected from his hot-blooded Irish temperament.

'Come along, Auntie, and have your tea,' exclaimed Mary Chichester from the sofa on which she was lying as Miss Caterham entered the drawing-room. 'I know you will be glad to hear that I am feeling ravenous; and I confess I ought to be presiding at the tea-table myself, but you have petted me so much of late that I cannot bring myself to give up my invalid privileges while you are here. Sad to say, this is the last day we shall have you with us; but I shall never forget all the care you have taken of me the last few weeks.'

'Chut! nonsense, child; I should like to know whose place it is to nurse you but your mother's sister's when your mother herself can't be with you. That's what maiden aunts are meant for, to succour, as far as may be, their nephews and nieces in affliction. It was scarce likely I was going to overlook the pet niece of them all. I think you will do now, Mary, and that Fred is quite equal to the task of supervising your complete convalescence. My small household really requires my presence again. My two retainers are at daggers drawn, and each accuses the other of all sorts of petty crimes and misdemeanours. When the mistress is away the servants invariably wrangle, if they don't do worse.'

That night, after Mrs Chichester had gone to bed, Miss Caterham and her nephew had a long conversation. She pointed out to him that the result of this her second confinement would be to leave his wife delicate. 'There is nothing, the doctor tells me, to be apprehended at present; but she will require much care, and I shouldn't wonder if you are recommended to take her to a warmer climate for the winter.'

'Of course,' returned Chichester, 'if the doctors come to that decision we must go; but my means, Aunt Julia, are very scanty, and though I try hard to live within my income I cannot quite manage it. Neither Mary nor myself were brought up in economical fashion, and, as a matter of course, however we may try, we fail to make a pound go as far as a pound ought to. All my attempts so far to get employment of some kind have resulted in nothing more than the discovery of how very difficult it is for an ex-dragoon to hit upon anything he can set his hand to. The last time I was over in London I talked the thing over with an old "pal" of mine – a good, shrewd, practical man of the world too – and the first thing he laid down goes to show that he was a very fit person to take counsel with. "It's not a bit of use," he said, "your going about urging your friends to assist you in getting *something* to do; you must fix upon something definite. When you can go to people and say, I hope you will help me all you can to get this or that, if they are disposed to assist you they know exactly how to set to work. You have yourself pointed out how they can do so; but when your requests are couched in a vague form they know no more how to begin than you do." Ah, you see, Aunt Julia, although his advice was most excellent so far, yet he broke down in that great essential, the second part. Though we sat up in his rooms till all was blue, and smoked three big cigars over it, we never could hit off what I was eminently fit for, or what I was to go in for. Ah!' he continued, with a faint smile, 'it's all very well to make a jest of it; if I was alone in the world I could. I should feel no fear but what I should worry through somehow; but when I think of the wife and little one, and know that my capital is melting, it makes me pretty heartsick at times.'

'You must keep up your courage, Fred,' said Miss Caterham, quickly. 'You wait till I get back to London, and I will send for my pet young man. You needn't smile, Fred, but I have got a very devoted admirer; not that he is so very young, although he is a good many years younger than me. We met at a country house some two or three years ago, and became great allies; he is a very rising barrister, and often runs out on a Sunday to bring me all the latest town gossip. I think it is very likely that he could help us.'

'Doubtful, very, I am afraid,' replied Chichester. 'You see that awkward question of what I am fit for will arise again; and again the reply will be wanting. The only trade I know I unluckily can't resume. However, it's about bed-time; let me give you your candle.'

Miss Caterham duly took her departure the next morning, and as she journeyed back to London reflected very sadly over Fred Chichester's prospects. Of course if a man has only about two hundred and fifty pounds a year, it is his business to keep himself and his family on that; but it was quite clear to Miss Caterham that the Chichesters would spend the whole of their capital before they had learnt how to live upon that income. Then the idea of a young fellow like Fred being condemned to moon away his life in a little French country town! It was too pitiful. What a thousand pities he had left the army! And then Miss Caterham thought rather ruefully over an arrangement that she had made about five years ago, with a view to enlarging her somewhat limited income; she had allowed herself to be persuaded into sinking the greater part of her capital into an annuity. This, of course, gave her more to spend during her life, but left her very little to bequeath, and she felt just now that she should have liked to have been in a position to provide for Mary and her child in case of anything happening to Fred Chichester. In the meantime she determined to invest her savings for their benefit. They were not much, but she habitually lived below her income, and, profitably invested, she could only hope they might grow till they became a respectable nest-egg. In pursuance of these resolves, on arriving in town she sent off a note to her legal friend, requesting him to call upon her as soon as he could spare the time, and to drop her a line of intimation as to what day she might expect him.

Mr Carbuckle speedily obeyed Miss Caterham's summons, and welcomed her warmly back to London. He listened gravely to the story of Fred Chichester's broken career; but, as that luckless exile had himself foretold, almost the first question the barrister asked was in what direction he had best exert himself.

'Let me know the sort of thing he wants, and I'll engage that I'd manage to get at some of the people who have the giving away of such posts. I heard poor Chichester's story vaguely told during the Ascot week; one of our party belonged to his regiment, and gave us a pretty fair outline of the state of affairs. If you ask my advice, I should say the best thing you could do is to try and bring about a reconciliation between father and son. You see, Chichester senior is so palpably in the wrong that he will be surely willing to make reasonable arrangements with his son if the son would make some slight concession, and hold forth the olive branch.'

'I am very much afraid not,' rejoined Miss Caterham. 'I never saw Mr Chichester except on the day of Fred's wedding; but he is a very bitter, obstinate old man, from all accounts, and I am afraid Fred gave him very great provocation. You must not forget that I have asked you to help him in any way that you can.'

'I will most certainly keep it in mind,' returned the barrister. 'I can only sincerely wish that I saw my way more clearly into helping you.'

'And now, Mr Carbuckle, I want to consult you about another subject. It so happens during the last few years that I have saved a little money. I want to invest it in something that will return a very large interest.'

'That's what we all want, Miss Caterham,' rejoined Carbuckle, laughing; 'but, as of course you know, the higher the interest the more shaky the security. If this is money, the loss of which would occasion you no inconvenience, I can point you out some three or four speculations that would probably give you seven or eight per cent for your money; but you will remember, I most decidedly don't recommend them as sound investments.'

'That sounds very little to me for speculation, and, remember, that is what I want. I am quite willing to risk the loss of this money, but expect big interest in return for the risk – twenty or thirty per cent I am thinking of.'

'Then on my word, Miss Caterham, there are only three ways open to you that I know of. You must put it on a horse race, take it to Homburg, or invest it in the "Great Tontine".'

'The racecourse and Homburg are preposterous; but what on earth is the "Great Tontine"?'

Enthusiastically and *con amore* did Mr Carbuckle plunge into an explanation of what he termed Mr Salisbury's magnificent conception. 'You are probably destined, Miss Caterham,' he said at length, 'to lose this money, whatever you do with it; you might as well lose a hundred in the "Great Tontine" as anywhere else. For a lady bent upon such desperate gambling as yourself this speculation seems made for you. At the end of the first ten years you will probably be drawing a dividend of ten or twelve per cent, and from that out it must be a progressively increasing dividend. As the thing nears its end the few lucky holders of lives will be drawing comfortable incomes as interest for the original hundred they put in; and then think of the grand prize to wind up with! A property worth a hundred and sixty thousand pounds will fall to the fortunate winner; but even if you keep in the "Tontine" till at all near the finish you will have got your money back over and over again.'

Miss Caterham was very much fascinated with the scheme, and as she listened, suddenly flashed across her mind Terence Finnigan's speech of a few days ago, when he had told her that the Finnigans were a long-lived race, that he himself was sixty, and that his father had lived to eighty-seven. She determined that she would put one hundred pounds of her savings into the 'Great Tontine', and that the life she would nominate should be Terence Finnigan, Fred Chichester's drunken henchman. She accordingly gave Mr Carbuckle her instructions, who readily undertook all the necessary arrangements, merely pointing out that, as it would be necessary to obtain a certificate of Finnigan's birth, she had better write to Avranches to ascertain where that hero first saw the light without delay.

# THE DRAMA

## CHAPTER ONE

## TWENTY YEARS AFTER

Twenty years have passed and gone since Herbert Phillimore, Viscount Lakington, landed that famous pool of *écarté* at Bracknell. Twenty years brings a good many vicissitudes to most of us, and the noble Viscount had experienced as much mutability as the average of humanity. If he had been fortunate to start with in his turf speculations, he had, when the tide turned, developed a faculty for backing the wrong horse almost unprecedented. He had, as we know, got pretty well through his own money when we first made his acquaintance, and, to do him justice as an undaunted 'backer', he was quite willing to go through the accumulations of his respected father-in-law to boot; and, while he lasted, Mr Lyme Wregis proved himself a very pattern relative in that respect. He made money lightly – that is to say, he landed prodigious coups by daring speculations, and he spent his winnings freely. He behaved with loyal liberality to his son-in-law. Not only did he make the newly-married pair a very handsome allowance, but he responded in a manner beyond all praise to extraneous tugs at his purse-strings. The settlements on his daughter had been even beyond the princely magnificence that might have been expected from Mr Lyme Wregis, Jupiter of the stock market, and prominent member of the great plutocratic Walhalla of Europe. But, unfortunately, although these settlements were all agreed upon, they were not ready for signature at the time of the marriage, and, as is the case much more commonly than would be supposed, their terms having been found perfectly satisfactory, they were left for signature later on, that is to say, when the lawyers should have at last got them ready, and the principals should find time to attend to such trifles.

Months rolled on, and, though the Viscount's solicitors every now and then jogged the memory of their professional brethren who managed the affairs of Mr Lyme Wregis, and had even more than once called the Viscount's attention to the fact that these settlements were still unsigned, yet Lord Lakington, an indolent man, who never troubled his head about business so long as his pockets were kept comfortably filled, interfered no further than to once or twice mention the fact to his father-in-law. Mr Lyme Wregis in reply had always some scheme for still further increasing the liberality of these settlements, or he wanted to change so many thousands of Egyptians for a corresponding quantity of 'Guatemalas', and so the signatures necessary to make valid these deeds were never affixed. The golden age, as Lord Lakington always fondly called it afterwards, lasted for about two years, during which time the Viscount backed horses and gambled as if he held the fee-simple of the sands of Pactolus. Then came the finish. The ship was on the breakers, and the captain shifted all further responsibility by blowing his brains out.

Great was the sensation through London when the evening papers announced the suicide of Mr Lyme Wregis. That when the state of his affairs came to be investigated he should be found hopelessly and wellnigh fraudulently bankrupt was only what the catastrophe had prepared the world for. Out of the wreck of the colossal fortune, which there could be no doubt the great financier once possessed, there remained but fifteen hundred a-year, which had been settled on Mrs Lyme Wregis about the time that her daughter was born. Lord Lakington found himself in similar plight to Fred Chichester, with a wife and child, and left a beggar. How it would have fared with him and his wife had they not been fortunately blessed with a guardian angel it is difficult to say. The most impecunious peers seem to get along somehow, though I fancy they find at times the pursuit of 'that ferocious animal, the *pièce des cent sous*', as arduous as less noble Bohemians.

Lakington and his wife had so far studied nothing but the spending of money, and were as a pair of children when called upon to wrestle with the *res angusta domi*. Bur Mrs Lyme Wregis was a woman in ten thousand – one of those active, energetic, undaunted women that face ill-fortune as – theoretically, we all admit – ill-fortune should be faced. She had begun the world with a very modest establishment, and, though not insensible to the pleasures and comforts of wealth, sometimes felt that sense of ennui insuperable upon having nothing to do. A quick, practical woman, she would have supervised even such a huge domestic establishment as her husband's admirably; but, when wealth and fashion have decreed that a housekeeper is a necessary appanage for your position, what is there left for the mistress of a household to do? Nothing, or next to nothing. She had to play the fine lady although it bored her desperately; but she was a staunch and true consort to her lord, and, to gratify his ambition and interests, she bravely accepted the rôle marked out for her, and did her best to fill it. She was not a vulgar woman – no utterly unaffected woman can be that; and, though she boasted no accomplishments, had received a good, sound, plain education. She was fairly popular in society, as when you have the finest houses, horses, and carriages, give the best dinners in London, are credited with an income of about half-a-million per annum, one is likely to be; but she was a little too quick-witted and plain-spoken to make many friends on her own account. She saw too clearly through the tawdry charlatanism of society. She recognized, and let it be seen that she did recognize, that she was tolerated in society not one iota for herself, but because the wheels of her chariot were golden. Still, those whose good fortune it was to have gained the friendship of Mrs Lyme Wregis knew how staunch was the true woman's heart that she carried within her breast. She had married somewhat late in life, and was some years older than her husband. Of the four children born to them Lady Lakington was the only one that survived, the youngest, and the child of her old age, as Mrs Lyme Wregis was accustomed to say in allusions to the fact that she was turned of forty when Clara was born.

When, without a note of warning, the crash came the old lady was at first paralyzed. It was not the loss of the money that so prostrated her, but the shocking and tragical end of one who, whatever his faults, had always been a kind and indulgent husband to her. But no sooner had she recovered from the shock than she gallantly faced the storm. At once abandoning everything to the creditors, she took possession of her daughter, son-in-law, and grand-child, and explained to them that they must rub along as best they could on her settlement.

'It's bread and cheese, and a roof over our heads, at all events, my dears; and if we have to give up French cookery and take to mutton-chops, it has, at all events, the recommendation of being much better for our constitutions. I know, bless you, because I have tried it; I didn't begin the world with a golden spoon in my mouth as Clara there did.'

Wealth is, after all, a matter of comparison. It is simply income in considerable excess of what we have been accustomed to. Fifteen hundred a year would of course represent affluence to the many. To energetic, clever-managing Mrs Lyme Wregis it represented comfort. To Lord Lakington it meant genteel poverty. For his *menus plaisirs* he had now to depend upon what was left to him of his own fortune. This had not been large to start with, and the noble Viscount had as near spent it as may be before his marriage. If, thanks to his mother-in-law, he was assured of a modest home still, for the next few years, Lord Lakington knew what it was to go through dire straits for ready money. It is no uncommon case with scores of well-dressed, apparently prosperous men; they lounge about London, live in comfortable homes, and seldom have a cab-fare in their pockets. It is a curiously bitter experience at first to have no fear with regard to the necessaries of life, but to be without the means of indulging in the minor luxuries; to know that your bed, dinner, and even your bottle of wine are surely and sufficiently provided for, but to feel that you must walk because you have not the wherewithal to pay for a hansom, and cannot indulge in a glass of sherry at the club because you have not a sixpence in your pocket. No hardships these in reality; but it is open to question whether spendthrifts like Lakington do not suffer more from these minor miseries than they do from the fierce pangs of genuine poverty. The Viscount, at all events, felt these things acutely. He would willingly have ignored his position, and set to work to endeavour to earn his own living, if he had the faintest conception as to how that problem might be carried out. But the only one mode that occurred to him was, unluckily, not feasible. He certainly thought that he might successfully manage a large racing establishment. His racing friends, to whom he mentioned his scheme, thoroughly concurred with him in his opinion, but showed no disposition that he should try the experiment at their expense. For a few years he dragged on a moody, discontented existence, at the end of which time two things happened to him. His wife died, and he suddenly awoke to the fact that the annual dividend paid to him on the hundred pounds he had placed in the 'Great Tontine' was rapidly becoming a very important item when regarded as pocket-money. A hundred a-year or so may not be much looked upon as income, but it becomes a very respectable sum when viewed in the light of loose silver.

The death of his wife made no difference to Lord Lakington's domestic arrangements. He and his daughter still continued to reside with Mrs Lyme Wregis. Not only had he and the old lady always been upon excellent terms, but she was gradually assuming an importance in his eyes, which was destined a little later to become overwhelming. Hers was the life that he had nominated when investing the hundred pounds won at Ascot in the 'Great Tontine', and such was the vivacity and vitality exhibited by his mother-in-law, that he began seriously to think that it was very possible she might survive all the other competitors. He had thought but little of the great lottery when he first took a share in it, and, indeed, never would have done so had it not been rendered obligatory on him by the terms of the pool that he won; but his attention was now called to it every half-year in very pleasing fashion; and as the years rolled by, that lives originally nominated at sixty should begin to fall fast was only in accordance with the laws of nature. As the lives fell so did the shareholders diminish, and so, consequently, did the dividends increase for those whose nominees were fortunately still living. The new opera house had been built long ago, and was now supposed to be a remarkably thriving establishment. It at all events enabled its lessee, Mr Salisbury, to pay the eight thousand a-year rent, which was divided punctually amongst the shareholders. As the nominees got well past the three score and ten years ordinarily allotted to humanity, the lives began to fall every spring like leaves in autumn. The searching east wind, with its attendant demons of bronchitis and catarrh, made terrible gaps in the ranks of the veterans, and at the beginning of this year of grace 1880 Viscount Lakington found that his half-yearly dividend amounted to one thousand pounds; that, in fact, Mrs Lyme Wregis was one of the last four surviving lives in this gigantic pool, and that the possibility of his coming into a fortune of eight thousand a-year was hanging upon the life of that venerable lady.

Still, the Viscount is in a position which occasions him much anxiety. He has experienced what it is to walk about with nothing in his pockets to meet incidental expenses. He is now in the command of plenty of loose cash, but this state of beatitude may terminate any day. It depends upon the existence of a far too energetic lady in his eyes, one who refuses to admit her age, and will persist in committing what, at her time of life, the Viscount holds to be great imprudencies. She will insist upon going out in weather it would be perhaps judicious to avoid, and, laughing her eighty summers to scorn, is not to be restrained from indulging her theatrical tastes when a favourable account of any such representation in the papers attracts her intention.

On a bright June morning, Lord Lakington enters the dining-room of a comfortably-sized house in the Victoria Road, Kensington, crosses to the breakfast-table, and proceeds to glance over his correspondence. A good-looking, well-preserved man, with whom time has been so lenient that he does not look within half-a-dozen years of his real age. If he has gone through a period of despondency and depression, they are jaunty days with him now. Life, indeed, is made pleasantly smooth for him at present. In the enjoyment of a comfortable home, presided over by two women both implicitly devoted to him, he can thoroughly rely upon all those comforts which become rather dear to us as we verge towards fifty; and he has now ample resources to enable him to indulge in all such social pleasures as he may desire. Both his mother-in-law and his daughter have now for so long made him the first consideration in the house that it was little wonder the Viscount should have developed a certain indolent selfishness. It is only natural, when those immediately about us habitually regard our ease and comfort as the first thing to be thought about, that we should in a short time become also of the same opinion. On one point only has Mrs Lyme Wregis been firm. Not only has she been resolute against any encroachment upon such capital as was left to her, but she has further informed the Viscount that, though she has left all her property between him and his daughter, it is so tightly tied up that he will never be able to touch it in any way. As she laughingly told him, there was no estate in the kingdom so big that it would not slip through his spendthrift fingers; and Lord Lakington quite acknowledged the justice of the remark.

He glances over two or three letters carelessly, but at length comes to one which arrests his attention.

'Good heavens!' he exclaims, after reading a few lines. 'Upon my soul, I believe it will come off. What a most extraordinary coup if it should be so! Here is another life gone – one of the last four remaining in – and, strange to say, the nominator thus put out of it the only one I know, Hemmingby, the lessee of the Vivacity Theatre. This is getting exciting. Here I am, one of three, in a sweepstakes of a hundred and sixty thousand pounds. There is only that lawyer fellow down in Wales and a maiden lady somewhere; and, by the way, Hemmingby told me some months ago that there was a screw loose about her nominee, and that all her dividends for the last two years have remained in abeyance. Her nominee has mysteriously disappeared. She cannot show him to be alive, nor, on the other hand, can the directors in any way prove that he is dead – a most inconvenient old vagabond to go wandering about at his time of life and leave no address. His inconsiderate disappearance will probably protract the ultimate wind-up of the affair, and occasion no end of trouble. Even if my dear old mother-in-law is the last known life left in, I suppose the directors will expect me to trace out where this vagrant old sinner made an end of it.'

At this juncture his reflections were broken by the opening of a door, and a strikingly pretty girl entering the room, gaily exclaimed, 'Good morning, papa,' greeted him with an affectionate kiss, and proceeded to decorate his button-hole with a flower.

'Good morning, Beatrice,' he replied, as he carelessly returned her caress; 'and how is grandmamma after her last night's dissipation?'

'Oh, she is quite well, and enjoyed her evening immensely. You are always so nervous about her catching cold; but she is a wonderful woman, remember, and younger than many twenty years her junior.'

'I know all that,' rejoined her father; 'but she ought to avoid all risks of catching cold, and, though it is June, the night air is still chilly.'

'Ah! a letter from Jack,' exclaimed the young lady as she took her seat at the breakfast-table, and turned over her correspondence. 'He says he shall be in town today, and wishes to know if we will give him some dinner on Friday. Of course we will. Shall you be at home, papa?'

'No; I am sorry to say I have an engagement. I wish it was not so, for I am very fond of the boy, which is as it should be. One ought to be on good terms with one's heir, although poor Jack won't come into much beyond the title.'

'And not that for many years we hope, papa dear. But your affairs have come round so much of late, that in a very few years now you will be quite a rich man again.'

Lord Lakington accounted for the increase of income he had latterly derived from the 'Great Tontine' in such wise. His stepmother and daughter, although they might casually have heard of the big lottery, had not the faintest idea that he was interested in it, nor that the improved state of his affairs was based upon such precarious tenure. He was honestly fond of his nephew, and had occasional compunctions of having made 'ducks and drakes' of the property, but usually consoled himself by reflecting that, after all, his heir was not his son, but his nephew, and that Jack had no business to ever suppose that he would inherit the title; and, on his side, Jack Phillimore had troubled his head very little about such contingencies. But he had a very great liking and admiration for his cousin Beatrice.

'Well, I suppose it is nice for him,' observed the young lady, as she continued the perusal of her cousin's letter; 'but still I don't see why we should go into ecstasies about it.'

'He, I presume, means Jack,' rejoined her father. 'What has he got? What is his present cause of exultation?'

'Well, he is appointed to a ship, and of course I quite understand as a sailor that he ought to belong to a ship. I don't expect him to pass his days lounging on the beach and looking at the sea like a Dover or Folkestone boatman; but he is going to the Mediterranean on a three years' cruise, and I don't see that that's a thing he ought to be so delighted about.'

'Don't talk nonsense, Trixie,' replied the Viscount. 'Jack is fond of his profession, and has earned the reputation of being a smart officer; of course he is glad to be employed again.'

'But he says, papa, he shall be away for three years.'

'Well, and what if he is? Soldiers and sailors expect to go abroad for much longer than that. Men do not think much of leaving England for three years. There is no particular hardship in it. He is going, besides, to a lovely climate.'

'No particular hardship, papa dear,' cried the girl with a roguish glance at her father. 'You don't know what you are saying; you don't know what three years out of England involves. Why, just think, for three whole years he won't see me!'

'Ah, well,' replied the Viscount, laughing, 'I certainly did not think of that; but, hard as it will be to bear, I fancy Jack will manage to get over it.'

'It is all very well to say so,' rejoined the girl with an affected pout, 'and I dare say *you* would not mind it; but I am sure Jack will feel it acutely, at least, I shall be very disgusted if he does not.'

'You know, Trixie, I should miss you very sorely if anything should part us,' rejoined the Viscount, as he lounged up to her chair and fondled her dusky locks; 'and as for Jack, just because he has petted and spoilt you ever since you were a little bit of a thing, don't imagine he cannot do without you.'

'I think he will do very badly, papa,' replied the girl as she poured out the tea. 'I have heard somewhere that it is a necessity for all human beings to have something to love and be attached to. Jack is extremely fortunate. He has me; and, now I reflect upon it, I really begin to feel very sorry for him.'

'The old story, my dear,' observed the Viscount with an amused smile: 'you shedding salt tears by the seaside, and he wondering, ere the ship he has embarked in lies hull down, whether the Italian girls are really as handsome as he has heard they are. These sailors always do it; they forget all about the girls they have left behind them as soon as they get into blue water. The old story, Trixie – Theseus and Ariadne over again.'

'I am sure I shall do nothing of the sort,' replied the young lady indignantly. 'The idea of you pretending that the daughter of the Phillimores should be forgotten in that way. As for Ariadne, she was a mean-spirited creature, and Theseus nothing better than a mere adventurer. But there is your tea; I trust it will prevent your making any more rude speeches for the present.'

## CHAPTER TWO

# LAWYER PEGRAM BEGINS HIS GAME

Lord Lakington is at present experiencing a rather feverish time of it. This being one of the last three shareholders left in the 'Great Tontine' is the largest speculation he has ever embarked in. In his racing days he had never stood to win so tremendous a stake as this. It meant either fortune or ruin. A few months might see him in possession of eight thousand a-year, or, on the other hand, they might see him deprived of the very comfortable income his dividend from the big lottery afforded him. No wonder he feels a little restless and possessed by an uncontrollable desire to talk the thing over with somebody. The somebody in Lord Lakington's case resolves into Mr Hemmingby. The Viscount was theatrical in his tastes in his youth, and had, many years ago, made that gentleman's acquaintance when he was manager of a large London theatre. Since we last saw him, Mr Hemmingby has tried his hand at a good many things, with more or less success, and has at last once more reverted to the theatrical business, and is at present lessee and manager of the Vivacity. Mr Hemmingby was by no means a reticent man. He would always talk freely about himself, and what he was engaged in, and had rather a habit of poking his nose into his neighbours' concerns, questioning them, indeed, with much affability and freedom about how they were 'getting along' in their various avocations. Whatever Mr Hemmingby went into he went into it heart and soul. There was very little fear but what he would keep a sharp eye on the list of subscribers to the 'Great Tontine', and he, of course, saw Lord Lakington's name amongst the number; and when the list began to shrink, consequent on the death of the nominees, he always laughed over their chances whenever he met the Viscount. He contrived, too, from various sources, to pick up a good deal of information about the people left in the lottery when their numbers had dwindled down, and it amused Lord Lakington to hear the histories of his fellow competitors. That he had a share in the 'Great Tontine' was a circumstance the Viscount kept jealously to himself. He did not want the world to know that his greatly improved income, instead of being the result of his affairs coming gradually round, was due to his luck in the big lottery, and liable to vanish at any moment. Mr Hemmingby and Sir Gerald Fitzpatrick were the only people he ever talked the matter over with, and even to the latter the Viscount would never have mentioned the subject, but that Sir Gerald, when they met, invariably inquired how the 'Great Tontine' was getting on, and whether he was still in it. But, even to Sir Gerald, he never disclosed how near the thing was drawing to a conclusion, nor what extraordinary interest he had been drawing for his hundred pounds the last three or four years, answering his questions, for the most part, as vaguely as might be.

Actuated by these restless feelings, Lord Lakington made his way down to the Vivacity Theatre, and was duly shown into the manager's sanctum. 'Good morning, Hemmingby,' he exclaimed as he entered; 'I have come down to have a chat with you, because you know something about every-body.'

'Well, I can't expect you to condole with me for being at last out of it. It is too much your interest for that; and I really thought, Viscount, I should have out-stayed you. But you have of course had your letter from the Directors, informing you that my nominee has gone at last. Well, I can't complain; it has been a very good "spec", and I have had my hundred back a good many times out of it. As for you, you bid fair to take the pool.'

'I want you to tell me something about my two antagonists. I have no doubt you can.'

'I can tell you very little about Miss Caterham. She is a maiden lady living at Kew, and I know nothing further about her beyond the fact that her nominee has been unaccountably missing for the last two years. Nobody knows whether he is dead, but they can't produce him and prove he is alive. As for Pegram, he is a lawyer down in North Wales. It was I induced him to take a share in it. He made a lot of money over the development of Llanbarlym, the new watering-place, you know. But he is a very speculative fellow; believes in his star, and all that sort of thing. I have a notion that his star has taken to erratic courses of late, and he has lost a good deal of money. In one or two things that we have been in together I can vouch for it; I got scalded myself, and know it was so. In fact, Viscount, I congratulate you. I look upon it now as a match between you and Pegram. I don't believe in a nominee getting lost. Old people on the verge of eighty don't stray. Their getting out of the way means "going under". Of course, I don't know who this nominee is any more than I know old Pegram's; but, depend upon it, he will never turn up in the flesh.'

'It's a tremendous big stake to be playing for,' observed Lord Lakington; 'a hundred and sixty thousand pounds on the turn of a card, you may say, for at eighty the fall of a life takes place pretty near as quickly. People at that age flicker and go out very suddenly. It would be a deuce of a nuisance to lose this income now. I wonder whether it would be possible to compromise. You know this lawyer fellow – see him, no doubt, sometimes; you might sound him on the subject for me.'

'I'll do that for you with pleasure,' replied the manager. 'I often see him. I invested a little money in Llanbarlym, and occasionally go down to look after some house property I have got there. His son too, Bob Pegram, always gives me a look in when he comes to town. He is wonderfully fond of a theatre, and, though I can't say I ever saw him, much given to strutting his hour on the boards himself. However, it is no use talking to him about it; I must get hold of the old man. I tell you what, Viscount, I never thought of it before, but the Directors are about right to keep the nominees' names a secret. It's an everlasting big pile, and the temptation becomes rather powerful when you find there is nothing but the life of an old man of eighty between you and a hundred and sixty thousand pounds; it would be might apt to go hard with the old "crittur".'

'What do you mean?' inquired the Viscount.

'Mean? Why, that there are plenty of men wouldn't hesitate to choke the life out of the poor old chap if they got a fair chance, and could by so doing make certain of landing the lot.'

'Yes,' rejoined the Viscount. 'I quite agree with you. The temptation to bring the whole thing to a conclusion in their own favour would be irresistible. The nominees must, at all events, feel easier in their minds that their names are a profound secret.'

'Yes,' observed the manager, laughing. 'I shouldn't like in my old age to know that any human being would benefit by my death to that extent; I should feel it would be prejudicial to longevity. I only hope your nominee keeps healthy.'

'Very well indeed, thank you. Now I must say "Good morning". Don't forget to suggest the compromise to Pegram, and hear what he says about it. It is very possible he may be quite as anxious to divide stakes as I am.'

'Quite so,' rejoined Mr Hemmingby. 'It's a stake that will bear dividing, and I should think it is a matter of indifference to the Directors what arrangements you may make between yourselves. In your place I would have seen it out – had all or none; but of course the other is much the most prudent line to take. I'll not forget to see Pegram, you may rely upon it. Good morning.'

Lord Lakington walked away from the Vivacity Theatre considerably relieved in his mind by this new idea which had occurred to him. It was so clearly the best thing to do for both of them, and the more he reflected upon it the more convinced he became that the Welsh lawyer must be quite as keen to come to an arrangement as himself. It was too horrible to think of going back to those days of abject poverty which he experienced before the 'Tontine' commenced paying such great interest. Yes; it was far better to run no risk and to make a certainty of half. Hemmingby was a sharp man of business, and would, no doubt, settle the affair satisfactorily with Pegram in the course of the next few weeks, and, having come to this satisfactory conclusion, Lord Lakington made his way to his club in search of lunch.

The manager's account of Mr Pegram was correct in the main. His ups and downs during these last twenty years had been very numerous. He had more than once amassed a considerable fortune, and then lost a great part of it again by seeking to increase it. It is probable that two or three times he might have abandoned speculation, and retired with ten or twelve thousand a-year, but in his anxiety to extend that ten to twenty, he had lost the greater part of it back again. At this present moment he is a poor man in his own eyes; that is to say, upon several occasions he has possessed property of three times the value of that which he now holds. Some of his speculations have proved injudicious. In other concerns he held his shares too long, missing the chance of realizing when his shrewder *confrères* 'got out'. Mr Pegram's belief in his star of late has begun to diminish. He is fain to acknowledge that his luck seems most decidedly against him at present, and that, touch what he may, it seems invariably to turn out disastrous. The acquirement of a country seat and seeing his son a leading gentleman of the county, which had been for years the object of Mr Pegram's ambition, seem as far off as ever; and yet he has been so near to it more than once. That Mr Pegram, under these circumstances, should ruminate over the 'Great Tontine' is not to be wondered at. He has indeed strong reasons of his own for assisting the affair to a conclusion as speedily as may be, and has been, ever since apprised of the death of Mr Hemmingby's nominee, turning over in his mind a scheme which may lead to this desirable conclusion. Lord Lakington would have been delighted could he have known that Mr Pegram is very ready to hear of a compromise; but whether his lordship will be quite as well pleased with the terms of that compromise, when in due course he shall learn them, is somewhat open to question. Old Pegram has made it his business for the last two or three years to pick up all he can about the shareholders still left in the lottery. No details about their past and present lives or ordinary habits are beneath his notice, and he would willingly have ascertained the names of all the nominees had that been possible. Lord Lakington, for instance, would have been astonished had he been made aware how much old Pegram knew concerning him. The old Welsh solicitor, too, has ascertained a great deal concerning Miss Caterham. He had learnt, probably from Hemmingby, that her nominee was missing; and no sooner did he find by the Directors' letter that Hemmingby was no longer a shareholder, than he told his son, with a grin, that it was time to take steps to secure – what he was pleased to term – their share of the inheritance.

'You see, Bob,' said the old man, 'there was nothing to be done till there were only two or three of us left in. It was of no use attempting to move the pieces before; and, to tell the truth, I am main glad that this Hemmingby is out of it. He is a terrible sharp fellow, and I had just as soon that he wasn't playing against me. Now, the first thing to be done is to find out all about this missing nominee.'

'It's all very fine, dad, but that will be rather a stiff nut to crack. Why, you see, they have been two years – at least, so we are given to understand – without being able to find him themselves. Now, considering we have no idea who he is, we are starting a little in difficulties. We don't even know who to look for.'

'Quite right, Bob, you couldn't have put the thing clearer; and, having got at that, you naturally know exactly what to do.'

'No, I am blessed if I do.'

'Well, you surprise me,' replied Pegram senior. 'It's obvious the first thing to be done is to find out the name of this nominee. It is quite clear we can't move a step without that. Now, the best chance, in my opinion, of getting at it is for you to call upon Miss Caterham, boldly to introduce the subject of the "Tontine" and the missing man, of course not discovering your own ignorance concerning him. Recollect this: she is a retired maiden lady and elderly. As a rule they are talkative. Be excessively polite and quiet in manner. Old ladies are easily frightened. Say as little as may be yourself, but let her talk. I think the odds are, Bob, that she blurts out the name we want before ten minutes are over.'

'Upon my word, I believe you are right. I suppose I had better call in an assumed name, and I'll make up a bit. Let's see, what shall I make up as?'

'Do nothing of the sort; we want none of your play-acting tricks on this occasion. Just simply give your own name. The probabilities are that a quiet, elderly lady like Miss Caterham has never troubled herself to inquire the names of the other competitors. You don't suppose that there is anybody but myself who has burrowed, schemed, and worked to find out all the particulars concerning them. I know a good deal about Miss Caterham. She mixes very little with the world, and, depend upon it, your name will convey nothing to her.'

'Well, it shall be as you like,' replied Bob Pegram; 'but I think you are wrong. You had much better let me take an assumed name and go as a clergyman, or something of that sort.'

'Only to find that you are of the wrong denomination,' retorted his father.

'I don't happen to know what Miss Caterham's views are upon that point. No, do as I tell you: go in your own proper person.'

'All right, sir. I'll start by the night train, but I think it is a mistake,' and shaking his head meditatively, Mr Bob Pegram left the room. This happened to be one of that gentleman's hobbies. Mr Hemmingby was quite right when he spoke of him as passionately fond of theatricals. While he was serving his time in London Robert Pegram had been a determined patron of the play-house. He had been a prominent member in an amateur dramatic society, and, in the eyes of himself and his immediate friends, was a comedian of much talent. In fact, at one time, such was his infatuation for the profession, that he thought seriously of joining its ranks; but here the old gentleman interfered, and put his foot down in a most peremptory fashion, and Mr Robert Pegram was made clearly to understand that he was quite at liberty to make a fool of himself as an amateur as often as he liked, but that if he really went upon the stage he need never expect another shilling from his father during his lifetime, and most assuredly would find himself cut off with that oft-mentioned inheritance at his death. Such particularly plain-speaking brought Bob Pegram to his senses, and compelled him somewhat ruefully to forego his chance of histrionic bays for the more certain pudding of lengthy bills of costs; to abandon the buskin for the quill, and to quit the dubious vicissitudes of the stage for the more assured future to be found in an attorney's office.

## CHAPTER THREE

## MISS CATERHAM HAS A VISITOR

Standing off the Brentford road, and in the immediate vicinity of Kew Gardens, is to be seen a small cottage half smothered in creepers. Honeysuckles, jasmine, and all sorts of climbing plants have been carefully trained about its walls, so that in the summer it looks more like a bower than a prosaic residence of bricks and mortar. In front of the French drawing-room windows lies a small flower-garden, now all aglow with colour, bearing evidence of careful tending by loving hands. Flitting about amongst the flowers with a pair of scissors, and clipping a blossom here and there, is a young lady of some three or four-and-twenty, whose acquaintance we made many years ago when she was of considerably lesser proportions. This is Mary Chichester, whom we last saw as a child in the Jardin des Plantes at Avranches. A somewhat tall maiden now, with glossy brown hair and eyes to match, and a frank, fair countenance that intuitively disposes people to like her upon first acquaintance. Two years after Aunt Julia went to assist her niece in her trouble the doctor's fears were realized. Mrs Chichester caught a bad cold, which speedily developed the latent seeds of consumption. In vain did her husband take her to a warmer climate. Her fate was sealed; and so rapidly did she sink at the finish, that Miss Caterham only arrived in time to stand by her niece's death-bed. Aunt Julia promised before she died that she would take care of little Mary, and when she returned to England she brought the child with her.

'It seems hard to deprive you of the little one in the first agony of your sorrow, Fred; but at her age I can take better care of her than you, and in a few years I shall hope to restore her to you as a daughter, able in some wise to be to you what her lost mother was.'

'It is best so,' he replied sadly; 'the child requires that watchful care that only a woman can give, for she is delicate, and makes me tremble for fear she should have inherited her mother's terrible complaint; add to which, I must strive hard to make a living for myself and a home for her in the future, and save, if possible, the pittance that still remains for her. The capital has melted terribly of late,' he concluded, with a faint smile.

Poor Fred Chichester was not destined to realize his hopes. He said no word of his intention to Miss Caterham, but he had already made up his mind as to what he would do. Heart-sick and weary of his fruitless endeavours to obtain employment in England, he had already thought as to whether there might not be greater opportunities for him abroad, when suddenly it flashed across him that, for men of his trade, there was plenty of occupation just now on the banks of the Potomac. The great struggle between the North and South was at its height, and he had heard of more than one English officer who had obtained employment in either army. With the Northern armies especially might an English soldier, who came out properly accredited from officers high in the service at home, be tolerably sure of a pair of epaulettes.

Fred Chichester hurried over to London, made a will, bequeathing all he had left to his little daughter, put a hundred pounds in his pocket, and sailed for New York, bearing with him letters of introduction and recommendation from several of the military chiefs under whom he had served. He speedily obtained a commission, distinguished himself upon more than one occasion, and finally fell, some eighteen months afterwards, upon the bloody field of Gettysburg. His faithful henchman had begged so hard to accompany him that, conscious though he was of the utter incongruity of such a soldier of fortune as himself being accompanied by his servant, Chichester had not the heart to refuse him. The North were not very particular about what they enlisted as food for powder in those days, and as the wiry old man did not look within some seven or eight years of his real age, made no difficulty whatever about enrolling him in the same troop as his master. He was by Chichester's side when he fell, and passed scatheless through that field of carnage himself, only to shed bitter, blinding tears as he laid 'the master' in the grave.

It was he broke the news to Miss Caterham in a blurred, blundering letter, made, in spite of its queer, homely expressions, pathetic by the genuine lamentations with which it was interspersed. Writing was a matter of great labour to Terence Finnigan, and after that epistle they heard no more of him for something like eighteen months, when he presented himself at the cottage, and explained that his detention in America had been to some extent unavoidable, his master's death not freeing him from his military engagements. In short, Mr Finnigan had to serve to the end of the war, desertion being an offence checked with such stern promptitude in the Federal armies as to constitute a risk too unpleasant to be hazarded. Since that he had led a very nomadic existence. The old man was an excellent servant, and, thanks to his military experiences, a very Jack-of-all-trades. A wonderfully hale old man, who could always pick up a living anywhere; but, thanks partly to his vagrant habits, and partly to his irresistible propensity for an occasional drunken bout, he never held any situation for long. Still, in the course of the year he never failed to present himself at the cottage, and Miss Caterham always took care upon such occasions he should further present himself to the officials of the 'Great Tontine', and be properly identified as still alive.

Whether old Mr Chichester was much shocked at the intelligence of his son's death Miss Caterham never knew. She had thought it her duty to inform him of the circumstance, and received a formal letter of acknowledgement in reply, which contained no expression of feeling on the subject, nor the slightest inquiry regarding his granddaughter. Aunt Julia thought it was possible that the second Mrs Chichester might have something to say to this. It was rumoured that in this case, as has happened often before, May could turn January round her little finger; and it was possible, in the interest of her own children, Mrs Chichester was not desirous of any acknowledgement of Mary. Be that as it may, old Mr Chichester died without sign that he remembered the existence of his son's child.

And now the girl's flower-snipping is interrupted by a voice exclaiming, 'Breakfast, Mary; come in, child, and pour out the tea,' and Miss Caterham appears at the French window.

When you are verging on fifty, another twenty years do not pass over your head without leaving their marks behind them. The tall, lithe figure we saw at Avranches is bowed and sunken now. The brightness of the eyes is dimmed, and the grey-shot dark hair of those days is now almost white. Still she enjoys fair health, and laughingly says that Mary takes such good care of her there is no knowing what age she may attain.

'Coming, Auntie,' replied the girl as she moved quickly towards the window; 'only see what a lovely posy I have managed to gather for you this morning, and the beds, I assure you, bear no trace of having been despoiled.'

'Thank you, child,' replied Miss Caterham as she took her seat at the breakfast-table. 'The roses are as sweet as those of your cheeks, my dear.'

'Oh, Auntie, if I wasn't pouring out the tea I would jump up and make you *such* a curtsey. Who wouldn't get up early to be rewarded with so pretty a speech.'

'By the way, Mary, I have had a letter from Mr Carbuckle this morning.'

'And what does he say? Has he obtained any tidings of poor Terence? You told me he had promised you once more to set inquiries on foot, and endeavour, if possible, to discover him.'

'No, so far he has been unsuccessful; but I will read you his letter.'

'DEAR MISS CATERHAM,

'No news as yet of Terence Finnigan; but, at such an early stage of the proceedings, it was very unlikely there would be. We can hardly expect to find him, as he has been missing so long, without considerable trouble, and I honestly own that I think it is probable that our former search for him failed from not being so thorough as it ought to have been. The truth is, that my practice is so large that I really have not time to bestow the attention upon it that should be given. I have therefore deputed to a young friend of mine who has just joined the noble profession the care of it. His poor father did me many a good turn in my early days, and I trust, as opportunity offers, to do the same for him. In the meanwhile, like most of the "just called", he has a good deal of time on his hands. I told him all about the case the other day, and (here Miss Caterham stammered, hesitated, and apparently passed over a line or two) – and – and he seemed intensely interested. I proposed to him to undertake the management of the hunt. He jumped enthusiastically at the idea, and, as he is a clever young fellow, with plenty of leisure, I feel sure that he will conduct it better than I should under the circumstances. My brains and opinion are of course at his service whenever he requires them. He has cross-examined me as to details in a very promising manner, but is anxious to put you and Miss Mary also in the box; so I have given him your address, and you may expect him to honour you with a visit shortly. With love to Miss Chichester,

   'Believe me,
     'Yours most sincerely,
      'HENRY CARBUCKLE.'

'It is very singular,' said Miss Caterham, as she laid aside her spectacles, 'but Mr Carbuckle has quite forgotten to mention his young friend's name. Well, whoever he is, it is extremely kind of him to undertake this business for us.'

'Yes,' replied Miss Chichester, 'and we shall of course know all about his name when he calls, but I am afraid we shall never see poor Terence again. He was a very old man, for one thing, and then he would never have been so long without coming to see "Miss Mary". As you know, Auntie, all that passionate devotion he had for my poor father he transferred at his death to me. Of course he has known me from my cradle, and, as he always reminded me, has carried me in his arms scores of times. I feel sure he would have come to see me if still alive.'

'Too true,' rejoined Miss Caterham, relapsing into a brown study.

Mary Chichester's remark recalled to Miss Caterham's mind that she herself was advanced in age, and that the time, in all human probability, was not far distant when she would have to bid her grand-niece good-bye, and leave her to face the world by herself. Miss Caterham's income would die with her, but Mary would find herself in possession of a slender income all the same. There was not only the couple of thousand pounds or so that her father had left her, but every shilling of the dividends accruing from the 'Great Tontine' had been most punctiliously funded in her name, and, as we know, in these latter years those dividends had been considerable. Miss Caterham sighed ruefully when she reflected that the very big returns of the last two years had not been added to her hoard. However, she could take comfort in the recollection that she had done her duty honestly by Mary; she had brought her up, and at her death would leave her by no means unprovided for.

Miss Caterham knew, not only from her dividends, but officially, that her nominee, if alive, was one of the last three lives left in the lottery, the lapse of every life being duly communicated to every subscriber by the Directors from the commencement. Indeed, she might, had she wished it, have ascertained the names of her two remaining antagonists for the grand prize. A list of the subscribers was kept in the Directors' room at the grand opera, and it was open to any individual subscriber to see that list, corrected up to the end of the preceding year, on certain fixed days; but the names of the subscribers' nominees was a secret known only to the Directors. Mr Hemmingby, for instance, finding himself one of the last in, had taken the trouble to find out the names of his opponents, and had also, through his intimacy with Mr Salisbury, ascertained that Miss Caterham's nominee was missing; that the Directors had therefore refused to pay her dividends, and held them in abeyance until such time as proof positive was arrived at of the said nominee being either alive or dead.

Some two or three hours have elapsed, and Miss Caterham is busy at the writing-table in the drawing-room, while Mary Chichester is hard at work amongst her flowers in the garden, when the neat parlour-maid enters the room, and, presenting a card to her mistress, says, 'The gentleman wishes to know if you will see him.'

Miss Caterham glances out of doors for a moment, ascertains that her niece is absorbed in her gardening, then quietly shuts the window, and says, 'Show the gentleman in, Eliza.'

A few moments, and Eliza ushered into the room a man somewhat below medium height, with rather close-cropped sandy hair, light, quick, restless eyes, the colour of which it would be hard to determine. He advanced quietly, and with a low bow, said, 'Miss Caterham, I presume.'

Returning his salute, Miss Caterham first acknowledged her identity and then, glancing at the card in her hand, observed, 'Mr Robert Pegram. You come, of course, from Mr Carbuckle. It is really very kind of you to have undertaken so troublesome a business for me.'

Mr Pegram contented himself with another low bow.

'Pray be seated, Mr Pegram,' continued the old lady. 'I am afraid you will find the discovery of this man a very wearisome piece of work.' 'Hum!' thought Miss Caterham, 'I suppose he is a very nice young fellow, because Mr Carbuckle says so, but I cannot say I think his appearance prepossessing.'

'The discovery of missing people is usually a little troublesome, but, as a rule, it's a mere matter of time and money.'

'I am prepared to spend *some* money,' rejoined Miss Caterham; 'but you must bear clearly in mind that I am not a rich woman, and can only spend money in moderation.'

'You may thoroughly rely upon my discretion in that respect, Miss Caterham. I will be very careful not to run you into any exorbitant expense,' and a close observer might have discerned a twinkle in Mr Pegram's eye, and a very slight twitch about his lips, which he evidently laboured hard to suppress. It was, however, but momentary, and Miss Caterham did not notice it.

'You are aware that we have already had one unsuccessful search for Mr Terence Finnigan?'

'I am, now you mention it,' thought Mr Pegram; 'but I was not in the least aware of it before.' He, however, contented himself by bowing assent.

'Yes; we started from Hampstead, where he told us he was living the last time we saw him. He had been a sort of odd man about one of the inns there, but he had disappeared months before, and they knew nothing whatever of him.'

'An Irishman, by his name,' observed Mr Pegram, quietly. 'He will probably return to his own country. I presume you know where he was born?'

'Oh yes; he comes from Mallow in the county of Cork, and of course that was one of the first places in which we sought for him; but we could find no trace whatever of him in those parts. You are aware, Mr Pegram, how large the interest is I have in his discovery.'

'Alive,' rejoined Mr Pegram, sententiously.

'Well, certainly,' replied Miss Caterham with a smile, 'both for his own sake and mine I should much prefer finding him in the flesh. I can hardly expect you to take as much interest in his discovery as I do.'

'Quite as much in finding him dead,' muttered Mr Pegram to himself, 'if you only knew it;' but once more he contented himself with bowing assent.

'Still, you have promised to interest yourself on my behalf, have you not?'

'I can assure you, Miss Caterham, I shall be quite as deeply interested in this inquiry as yourself. It is one of the most exciting cases I have ever heard of for all concerned.'

'Mr Carbuckle has no doubt put you in possession of all requisite particulars connected with the case; but still –'

'Excuse me, Miss Caterham,' interrupted Mr Pegram, 'but I should like to gather all the details of this affair from your own lips. Let us put Mr Carbuckle on one side, and suppose that you just now give me instructions to find this man, Terence Finnigan, for you. Now, will you kindly answer the questions I am about to put to you?' and Mr Robert Pegram proceeded to cross-question his hostess in a manner that did much credit to his professional skill.

'Thank you,' he exclaimed at last. 'I thoroughly understand now all that is necessary for me to know. I need take up no more of your time, but when I obtain any intelligence I shall of course communicate with you again;' and so saying, Mr Pegram bowed low, and took his departure.

Mr Pegram walked away in a state of considerable elation about the information he had acquired. 'The governor was quite right,' he muttered, 'in thinking that if I called upon Miss Caterham I should get at all the facts about this mysterious missing life. That Miss Caterham's nominee could not be proved, either alive or dead, he got out of Hemmingby the last time he came down to Llanbarlym, and he guessed rightly, that the chances were an elderly maiden lady had never been at the pains to ascertain what the names of her rival competitors were. I wonder what she takes me for. That she supposed me to come from Mr Carbuckle, the eminent Queen's Counsel, was of course evident; but whether she thought I was friend, barrister, solicitor, or detective, I am blessed if I know. There is one thing certain – it is quite as much our interest to find this Terence Finnigan as it is hers. Nothing would gratify me more than to find him neatly tucked in, with a legibly-cut tombstone recording the date of his departure from this world. If, on the other hand, we find him alive, we should naturally keep that disagreeable fact to ourselves. Caterham & Co.'s business is to prove Terence Finnigan alive; Pegram and Co.'s business is to prove him dead. I flatter myself, Pegram and Co. are not likely to fall into the mistake of proving their case for the opposite side.'

'Who was your visitor, Auntie?' exclaimed Miss Chichester as she entered the drawing-room. 'I saw a little man pass down the gravel walk just as I was gathering up my things to come in.'

'That was Mr Carbuckle's young man,' replied Miss Caterham. 'He's not of distinguished appearance, but I fancy he is clever. The questions he asked about poor Terence struck me as shrewd and to the point. He knows now all we can tell him.'

'I rather wonder you did not send for me,' remarked Mary Chichester; 'not, I will own, that I could tell him anything more than you could, but I should like to have heard what view he took of Terence's disappearance.'

'He showed himself a sensible man by declining to offer any opinion or conjecture, but simply said that when he had anything to tell he would let us know.'

Miss Caterham had never told her niece anything about her connection with the 'Great Tontine', and Mary Chichester had never heard of the big lottery in her life.

## CHAPTER FOUR

## 'OH! MY LOVE IS A SAILOR-BOY'

'I shall be glad to see Jack Phillimore,' said Mrs Lyme Wregis, as she and her granddaughter sat in the drawing-room in Victoria Road, awaiting the advent of that young sailor. 'It is a good thing for him, of course, to have got a ship, although I suppose that means bidding him good-bye for a very long while. Some people at my time of life would say for ever; but I mean to live till he comes back, Trixie, for certain sagacious reasons of my own.'

The speaker was a slight, wiry old lady, with snow-white hair, and dark, bead-like eyes, that at all events betokened no infirmity of vision; and, in good truth, Mrs Lyme Wregis was little wont to overlook anything that came within their ken. Although she had entered her eighty-second year, no stranger would have put her down within at least a dozen years of that age. She was so quick and energetic in her manner, took such keen interest in all that was going on around her, that one would have been more likely to remark upon how lightly she carried her seventy summers. She was an old woman, no doubt, but so singularly free from the infirmities of her time of life that people rarely recognized how old.

'Yes,' replied Beatrice, 'that is the worst of it. It is of course very nice that he should get a ship, because I know he wants one. That people I like should get what they want is all very fit and proper; but, I must say, I don't like losing Jack for so long.'

'Pooh, child! Jack has got his way to make in the world, and that is not to be done by dangling about your apron-strings. You can't expect to have him always to tease and bully.'

'I don't think Jack minds being bullied and teased by me, grandmamma,' replied the girl with a saucy toss of her head.

'Not much, perhaps; these sailors are always given to philandering. He will probably bring home a wife from the other side of the world.'

'Jack will never marry,' replied the girl quickly.

'Ah, well, my dear,' said the old lady demurely, 'no doubt you know best; but if he *has* taken vows of celibacy, I can only say I am very sorry for *you*.'

'You are a wicked old woman,' cried the girl, as her cheeks flushed, and she threw her arms round her grandmother's neck and kissed her. 'How dare you entrap me like that? But, joking apart, three years, you know, is a terrible long time to say good-bye to anybody one likes.'

'Not at your time of life, child; and I tell you, Beatrice, that I think your cousin Jack's appointment is a very good thing for many reasons. It advances him in his profession, and it will give you both time to know your own minds. You are very young yet, and have not seen much of the world. You might fall into the mistake of believing a girlish fancy to be a serious love-dream. No, don't interrupt me. Although there is no formal engagement between you and Jack, yet you know perfectly well that you both regard matters between you pretty much in that light. Now, don't think, my dear, that I wish to oppose such a thing; but Jack must of course sail for this voyage, and I think it much better there should be no formal engagement until his return. Then you can do as you like, even go the extreme length of getting married, with nothing but love and good wishes on your old grandmother's part.'

'It will be very hard to send Jack away without a little bit of comfort, should he ask for it,' replied Beatrice softly, as she kissed the old lady. 'But you are the only mother I have ever known, and I don't think I could disobey you in this matter.'

Although she did not wish to see Beatrice hampered with a long engagement, yet this marriage was a very favourite idea with Mrs Lyme Wregis. That Lord Lakington would marry again now seemed improbable. That he had not done so, in the eighteen years that had elapsed since the death of his wife, surprised nobody more than his mother-in-law. Left an impoverished widower before he was thirty, that the Viscount should again seek to barter his coronet for a wealthy bride seemed to the world only in the common order of things. Whether he was so persistently out of luck that he failed to come across an eligible *parti*, or whether his brief experience of matrimony did not encourage him to repeat the experiment, one can't say. Mrs Lyme Wregis clung to the belief that it was his affection for his daughter – and, in his indolent, selfish way, the Viscount was very fond of Beatrice – which had prevented his taking unto himself a second bride. But some of his friends who knew him best deemed it was a mixture of pride and indolence which had restrained him from seeking to repair his shattered fortunes in that wise, the fact being, that, some years after the great crash of his father-in-law, Lakington had altogether eschewed society. He was seen at Clubs, and his usual haunts of that description; but balls, garden-parties, and such assemblages of the London world knew him no more.

But now the door opened, and Mr Phillimore made his appearance – a good-looking young fellow enough, with fair hair, bold blue eyes, and a blonde moustache. He shook hands cordially with the ladies; and his greetings made, in obedience to the announcement that dinner was ready, handed Mrs Lyme Wregis with gay courtesy to the dining-room.

'And so, Jack, you are pleased with your appointment,' observed Mrs Lyme Wregis. 'I suppose it really is a nice thing for you.'

'Great bit of luck,' he replied. 'I am going out, you see, as the Admiral's Flag-Lieutenant. Now, of course, unless I am such a fool as not to get on with him, that means I shall be always pretty well taken care of when there is anything going.'

'He does not express himself very clearly, Grandmamma, but we quite understand, do we not? That means he expects to be pitchforked into the first good berth going, to the prejudice of older and more deserving officers. Still, though the service is going – well, where the service always is going, we must congratulate you personally.'

'You are a little premature, Trixie,' replied her cousin, laughing. 'There is no war going on, and a quiet little job such as you hint at is not quite so easy to manage in these days. It is well to have the chiefs of your service at your back, but you might wait until interest has done me a good turn before you chaff me about it.'

'Oh, nonsense,' replied Mrs Lyme Wregis, 'you need not think that these days are more immaculate than those that are gone. The plums of the pudding go quite as much by favour as they did long ago. The only thing is, you must not be palpably unfit for the post, in consequence of the multiplication of newspapers. Journalists are always hungry for something to write about, and delight in a flagrant case of the round peg being adapted to the square hole; and even if we at last become a Republic, as all that Radical rubbish hope we shall, you will find the brave old trade of jobbery go merrily on. Bah!' concluded the old lady contemptuously, 'your blatant democrat, or your horny son of toil, is quite as ravenous for a snug sinecure as any one else.'

'And so you are to be away three years, Jack,' remarked Beatrice.

'Yes; but it is to be spent at a first-rate station. There is the opera, balls, and all sorts of gaiety when we are at Malta; then one is certain to get a peep at Naples, the Ionian Islands, and all that sort of thing; a fortnight's leave to have a turn at the cock in Albania; or even perhaps have a shy at a wild boar. I have often known men regret that their time there was up.'

'And you would have no regrets about leaving England for so long?' inquired Beatrice, in somewhat more serious tones than she had as yet spoken.

'Well, of course,' replied her cousin, 'I should be sorry not to see any of you for so long a time; but then, you know, when a man turns sailor he of course expects all that sort of thing. One might have been condemned to a brig upon "the Coast". Besides, I shall never be more than a few days distant from you, and can always make a dash home if any event of importance is about to take place in the family.'

'Such as my marriage, you know,' replied Beatrice demurely.

'Yes, you may be quite sure I shall be there whenever that takes place,' said Jack Phillimore, 'even if I am tried for desertion afterwards.'

'Oh, but you might not be asked, you know. I have such a thing as patriotism about me, and should never think of allowing my private affairs to interfere with the upholding of the "meteor flag of England, which shall yet terrific burn", et cetera.'

'Ah, well, Trixie, you know that I should be very unhappy if I thought your wedding could take place without my being present.'

'Give me a glass of wine, Jack Phillimore,' interposed Mrs Lyme Wregis, 'and don't put nonsense into the child's head. She is only just out of the schoolroom, and thinks of course that marriage means nothing more than orange flowers, a veil, and white satin.'

'How dare you say such things, Grandmamma? Why, you know that I am a grown-up young lady, and was eighteen last birthday, and have done with masters and all that sort of thing for months and months.'

'Well, now,' said the old lady, laughing at Beatrice's indignant protest, 'I shall leave you young people to have your talk out by yourselves while I take my usual nap before tea.'

'Then you have to leave almost at once, Jack?' said the girl in low tones, while her cousin closed the door behind Mrs Lyme Wregis.

'I leave Waterloo by the mail train tomorrow night,' he replied; 'and this is the last time that I shall see you, Trixie, till I don't know when. I have got so much to do tomorrow that it will be quite impossible for me to get out here; but I have counted on this evening. I have something to say to you before I leave England, something indeed that I could not leave England without saying. Cannot you guess what it is, Beatrice?'

The girl's lips syllabled a scarcely audible 'No', to which the blood that mantled her cheeks gave flat contradiction.

'Yes, I think you can, darling,' he continued. 'If I have never told you in actual words that I love you, it is because I have told you in so many other ways that it was needless. I have loved you for years. I loved you as a child, loved you as a school-girl, and now that you are a woman grown, I want you to tell me that you can love me in return. Can you not tell me that, darling? Can you not promise that, when I come back at the end of three years, you will be my wife?'

He took her two hands in his as he spoke, and bent his head to hear her answer, and it may be with some intention of sealing the compact with a kiss, should her reply be what he hoped for.

'No, Jack,' she replied softly, 'I cannot do that.'

'Have I been mistaken, Beatrice?' he exclaimed sadly, as he released her hands. 'Surely I cannot have been dolt, idiot enough to mistake mere cousinly love, the warm-hearted, affectionate love that a girl might innocently feel for a cousin she had known intimately from her childhood, for the more passionate love I hoped I had won. I shall carry a heavy heart away with me if this is so. Remember, Trixie, I am speaking to you now as men speak when their life's happiness rests upon a woman's answer. I ask you once more, can you not give me such love as I would fain have? Can you not regard me, no longer as a cousin, but as your betrothed husband.'

'You must not ask that question, Jack.'

'I cannot see that,' he rejoined in resolute tones. 'The minute I got my appointment I made up my mind to ask you that question before anything, and surely a man deserves a courteous reply, if it be to say him "nay". You may tell me, Beatrice, that I have already had it, and that it is unfair to press you further; but my whole life is at stake. I have looked forward for the last three years to the time when I should say this to you; and forgive me if I am loth to believe that it has been all a delusion on my part. I have even actually hugged to my heart the flattering belief that you cared for me to some extent in the way I hoped for. I utter no reproach. I am not the first fool that vanity has led astray about a woman's regard. I will trouble you no more, and only ask you to forgive me for thinking that you loved me well enough to be my wife. Good-bye, and God bless you.' And Jack Phillimore hastily pressed her hand, and then made for the door.

His steps were arrested ere his fingers had clasped the handle by a faint 'But, Jack.'

'But what?' he asked, as he turned again towards her.

'But I do love you,' she replied, with flushed cheeks.

'Well enough to be my wife, darling?' he whispered, as he stole his arm round her waist.

'Yes; and I was just about to tell you so, only you were so dreadfully impetuous. And Jack,' she continued, as she yielded to his embrace, 'when you began to tell me how you loved me it was so delightful that I could not interrupt you. I suppose I ought to have melted before,' she said half-shyly, half-saucily; 'but cannot you understand a girl being so proud of having won such a love that she could not bear to break in upon her lover's pleadings?'

'But, Beatrice, dearest, what made you so cruel to me at first? Why did you tell me you could not love me?'

'Oh, Jack, I did not. You asked me to promise to be your wife, and I told you I could not. Now that you have told me that you love me I can tell you all. Grandmamma, you see, is a very clever old woman. There is nothing goes on under her eyes but what she knows rather more about than the people concerned. I am ashamed to say that she discovered my secret. Horrible to confess, she had none of these doubts which so disturbed you. She seemed also to divine that you would ask this question before you left England, and she made me promise that I would not pledge myself to be your wife.'

'Well,' cried Jack, 'this is unaccountable. I declare I thought I was rather a favourite with Mrs Lyme Wregis, and never dreamt that she would have opposed me in this manner.'

'You are mistaken again,' said Beatrice. 'You have no stauncher friend than grandmamma; but she has a great objection to long engagements, and, as you know, she has stood in the light of a mother to me; so you see I was bound to promise what she wanted. And then again, you know, if I had refuséd to promise, and had not been asked, it would have been so very awkward, and made –'

But here Beatrice's speech was prematurely cut short, and her lips paid tribute for her sauciness.

'And now, Jack,' said the young lady, when she was at length released, 'I really must go upstairs and look after tea. If grandmamma has not by good luck taken a considerably longer doze than usual, she must be rather wondering what has become of us. Remember, though she very properly declined to allow her granddaughter to recklessly plight her faith to a sailor whose ship had the "blue Peter" at the fore (that is nautically put, I flatter myself), still, if perchance the said sailor should be in the same mind three years hence, she laid no –'

And once again Beatrice's speech was interrupted, as will happen to lovers in confidential intercourse.

Mrs Lyme Wregis had not only finished her doze, but was preternaturally wide awake, as the young couple entered the drawing-room. She eyed her niece keenly, and then exclaimed,

'Get me my tea, child; it has been drawing so long that it is doubtless as strong as the protestations Jack Phillimore has been making you downstairs. What has he promised to bring you home from foreign parts?' continued the old lady laughing.

'Shall I tell you, Mrs Lyme Wregis?' interrupted the young man eagerly.

'Yes; what is it to be this time? – cockatoos, humming-birds, Maltese filagree work, or what?'

'Something much more simple,' replied Jack; 'only a wedding-ring.'

'And, Beatrice,' interposed the old lady quickly, 'you have not promised to wear it, have you?'

'No, grandmamma, dear,' replied the girl; 'but I have not vowed to say "No" should he offer to put it on for me.'

'Ah,' replied the old lady, with a nod of satisfaction. 'Mind you put plenty of cream in my tea, Beatrice.'

## CHAPTER FIVE

## MISS CATERHAM HAS ANOTHER VISITOR

'There!' exclaimed Mary Chichester, as she sprang to her feet, after a half-hour passed by the side of a bed of scarlet geraniums bordered with 'golden chain'. 'I have snipped and snipped until I don't think I have left a bud in that border to break forth and destroy the harmony of our arrangements. I think I have done enough for this morning, and will go in and see what Auntie is about;' and as she slipped off her gardening-gloves, and concluded her soliloquy, she became conscious that a well-favoured, gentlemanly-looking man at the gate was watching her proceedings with apparent interest.

Finding himself discovered, the stranger raised his hat, and, opening the gate, came forward with a bow, and said,

'This is Miss Caterham's, I believe; and you, I presume, are Miss Chichester?'

'Certainly,' replied the girl, 'my aunt, Miss Caterham, lives here, and I am Mary Chichester; but you must excuse my saying that I cannot recollect that we have ever met before. Perhaps you wish to see my aunt on business?'

'Exactly,' replied the stranger; 'on *her* business, which I am about to make mine, I trust to Miss Caterham's benefit. You are quite right, neither you nor your aunt ever saw me before, Miss Chichester; but I have the authority of a very old friend of yours to excuse my intrusion – Mr Carbuckle.'

'Mr Carbuckle!' exclaimed Mary. 'Yes, he is a very old friend. You had better come in and see my aunt.'

It is very odd, thought the young girl, that Mr Carbuckle should send us another young man so quickly. Surely he cannot have come upon the same business as the other.

'You are very fond of your garden, Miss Chichester,' remarked the stranger, as he followed the young lady towards the cottage.

'Very. This time of year I spend a great deal of time in it. I am passionately fond of flowers, and we live a very quiet, retired life. Very hum-drum,' she continued, laughing, 'I suppose most girls would call it, but I have known no other, and do not find it so. Auntie, you see, is not strong, nor equal to going out much. However, we shall no doubt find her in here, and then – Well, I think I must leave you to present yourself!' and so saying, she opened the drawing-room door, and, advancing towards Miss Caterham, said briefly, 'This gentleman wishes to see you on business.'

The stranger bowed as he said, 'My name is Ringwood; you have doubtless received a note from Mr Carbuckle, introducing me, and saying how glad I should be if I could be of any assistance to you.'

'Any friend of Mr Carbuckle we shall always be delighted to see; but I certainly have received no note from him mentioning your name to me. Perhaps it miscarried; but I really don't know, Mr Ringwood, that I require assistance about anything.'

'It is very odd,' replied Mr Ringwood, 'that Carbuckle should have neglected to write; but as it is so I must ask you to take my own account of things. Carbuckle is, as you know, a very busy man, with more work to do than he knows how rightly to get through – what I hope to be myself in days to come, but young barristers at starting have always to complain that they have got no work to do. Carbuckle is a very old friend of my family, and he happened to tell me the other evening about the disappearance of Terence Finnigan. He told me *all* the facts, Miss Caterham,' and here Mr Ringwood threw a significant glance at Mary Chichester, which did not escape that young lady's notice. 'I ventured to doubt whether the search for Finnigan had been so thorough as it should have been, and he owned that perhaps it had not, adding that he could not possibly spare the time to supervise it himself. I was so interested in the whole story that I volunteered, if you would accord permission, to superintend a second search myself; and Carbuckle can vouch, Miss Caterham, that I, alas! have only too much spare time,' concluded the young man laughing.

But Mr Ringwood's laughter was of very short duration. Instead of thanking him for his volunteered assistance, or welcoming him as he had imagined a friend of Mr Carbuckle's might expect, Miss Caterham and her niece gazed at him with evident dismay and uncertainty. At length the elder lady seemed to recover her speech.

'I must trouble you to go away, sir. I don't know how you became mixed up in affairs of mine, or where you gained your knowledge; but I shall certainly require no assistance from you. Ring the bell, Mary, please.'

'Pray don't make yourself uneasy,' observed Mr Ringwood, rising, 'I will leave the house without further delay. I can see that you are labouring under some misapprehension about me. It was very careless of Carbuckle not to write, and it has placed me in a most unpleasant position. I beg to apologize for my intrusion, and will take care that you receive from Carbuckle testimony of the extenuating circumstances regarding it'; and, bowing low,

Mr Ringwood was about to retire, when the clear tones of Miss Chichester arrested his intention.

'One moment, Mr Ringwood; one moment, Auntie dear,' exclaimed the girl. 'Don't you think it is but justice to tell Mr Ringwood what he appears in our eyes. It is difficult to conceive what object any one can have in imposing upon us in this matter, and it certainly seems unlikely that Mr Carbuckle would have, almost simultaneously, sent two gentlemen to inquire into this business for us; but it might be so.'

Miss Chichester, remember, knew nothing about the 'Great Tontine'; consequently, whether Terence Finnigan was alive or dead was a thing that she conceived would probably interest nobody but herself and her aunt. That they should take an interest in what had become of their old servitor – one, too, who had laid her father in the grave – was natural; but of what importance could it be to any one else what had become of this battered, somewhat drunken waif? But with Miss Caterham it was different. She knew that the 'Great Tontine' was coming to a close. If she was not so accurately up in all the details concerning it as Mr Pegram, she yet knew enough to be aware that Terence Finnigan's death must be a matter of quite as much importance to two other people as his life was to herself. A vague feeling that foul play was intended him, if by chance he had not already met with it, shot through her mind; and she shivered at the thought that the courteous, gentlemanly man now addressing her might be anxious in the extreme to find Terence Finnigan, for the sole purpose of putting an end to him.

'Two gentlemen!' exclaimed Mr Ringwood. 'Do I understand you, Miss Chichester, that some one, claiming to have been sent by Mr Carbuckle, has called here to inquire about every detail you can remember concerning Terence Finnigan?'

'Certainly. A gentleman called upon my aunt two days ago, professing to be exactly what you represent yourself to be now, a friend of Mr Carbuckle's, come to make these very inquiries. My aunt answered all his questions, and he promised we should hear again from him shortly.'

'This is interesting,' said Mr Ringwood quickly. 'Of course, Miss Caterham, you look upon me as an impostor. I cannot blame you. There undoubtedly is an impostor in the field, and I can most thoroughly understand his object in the imposition.'

Mr Ringwood addressed this speech markedly to Miss Caterham. He thought she would understand it, whilst Mary would not. Mr Carbuckle had instructed him that Miss Chichester knew nothing about the 'Great Tontine', and that Miss Caterham specially desired that she should not. But the young lady was a shrewd observer, and noted as curious that Mr Ringwood should at once own that he could see an object in such an imposition.

'I did not see the other one to speak to,' exclaimed Miss Chichester; 'but I begin to think, Auntie, we are doing Mr Ringwood an injustice.'

'I do not know what to think,' replied Miss Caterham nervously. 'Mr Pegram said just the same thing. Mr Carbuckle would never send two gentlemen about this affair without letting one know. If he had only mentioned the name there could be no doubt about which is the impostor, and even Mr Ringwood admits that there is one. I don't know what to do; but I think Mr Ringwood had better go away.'

That Miss Caterham was strangely agitated was apparent to both her auditors – agitated to an extent that seemed unaccountable to both her niece and the young barrister. Stricken in years, living a secluded life, and suffering from very feeble action of the heart, the poor lady's nerves were easily upset. The terrible thought had flashed across her that the large stake so nearly within her grasp might lead one or other of her antagonists to desperate measures for the repression of a life so inimical to their interests as that of Terence Finnigan. She pictured herself already involved in schemes that might lead to a great criminal trial, and the termination of the 'Great Tontine' resulting in one of the famous murder cases of the age. Her terror that she should be involuntarily mixed up in any such tragedy, or that her use of Finnigan's name should bring destruction upon him, increased to such a degree that Mary crossed the room swiftly to her side and exclaimed, 'What is the matter, Aunt? you look almost as if you were going to faint.'

'I don't feel well. I don't know what is the matter with me,' faltered Miss Caterham, with a nervous twitching about the mouth. 'Take me upstairs, child. You will excuse me, sir.'

Although puzzled at the cause, Mary Chichester was not altogether surprised at her aunt's agitation; she knew what a very nervous person Miss Caterham was, and how easily she was frightened. As she led her aunt from the room the barrister opened the door for them, and in passing him the girl said, 'Wait a little, please, Mr Ringwood. I should like to see you again before you go.'

Left to himself the barrister did what most men similarly situated would have done in his place. He wandered aimlessly about the room, musing over the past conversation. His brain was of course busy as to what was to be made of the fact that some one else was interested in the discovery of Terence Finnigan. 'Pegram,' he muttered; 'a somewhat singular name. I am glad Miss Chichester told me to wait, as it is essential that I should get that name right. It conveys nothing to me, but it very likely would to Carbuckle. Pegram!' and here his eye fell on a card-basket. He turned two or three of the top ones carelessly over, and then suddenly exclaimed, 'Ah! here it is; Mr Robert Pegram. I *have* got the name right then; and now, what the deuce can

Pegram want with Terence Finnigan? Of course his interest in him must be in connection with the "Great Tontine". Pegram is either one of the last shareholders, or acting for one, and upon what manner of man Pegram or his principal may be, turns the use they will make of Finnigan's discovery. They may be merely interested in proving that Finnigan is dead, or, in the event of being first-class scoundrels, entertain a strong disposition to make him so. The stake is so large that it offers a terrible temptation; and, upon my word, when we read daily for what pitiful plunder murder is committed, I really should not be surprised, if they find Finnigan before we do, that we shall find him too late. The death of a friendless old man of that age could be compassed so easily, and would be so little likely to attract observation or inquiry.' Here his reflections were interrupted by the opening of the door, and Mary once more entered the room.

'I have to thank you,' said Ringwood, 'for your belief in me when appearances most decidedly looked against me, and also for giving me this further interview, as there are one or two questions that I wish to put to you.'

'It will be question for question, for I also am curious upon one or two points that I suspect you can clear up for me; but you shall begin.'

'Well, then, first: how do you imagine this Mr Pegram got at the fact that a friend of Carbuckle's was to call upon your aunt relative to this affair. You see, this is a fact known, I presume, only to Carbuckle, myself, and Miss Caterham.'

'Ah, that I own I can't tell you. You see I was not present at the interview, and only saw the gentleman as he was leaving the house.'

'And this name of "Pegram", I presume, is quite unknown to either yourself or Miss Caterham.'

'Quite; we never heard of him before. Have you any further questions to put?'

'No; there are several questions I should like to ask you about Terence Finnigan, but I do not think I am entitled to do so until you have heard from Mr Carbuckle that I am his *bona fide* representative.'

'Very well, then. Now, Mr Ringwood, it is my turn. First, what made you say so markedly to my aunt that you knew *all* the facts in connection with Terence Finnigan?'

'Simply that I understood Carbuckle had placed me in possession of the entire story,' replied the barrister jesuitically.

'I certainly thought that you meant more than that,' said the young lady; 'and now explain to me, please, the reason of the imposition. You said you could understand it, you know.'

'That, Miss Chichester, is exactly what I cannot do. My lips are sealed professionally. We lawyers are acquainted with a good deal that we are not at liberty to blurt out."

'I understood it was to be question for question, sir, and I really cannot understand why we are not to be acquainted with the reason of an imposture that has been perpetrated upon us, which surely concerns no one so much as ourselves.'

'I can only regret that my tongue is tied. I would tell you willingly if I might; but I must obey orders.'

Miss Chichester bit her lip. She was somewhat of a queen in her own very limited circle, and little accustomed to have her wishes or requests disregarded. What could it concern any one else to discover what had become of Terence Finnigan? The sole object of the imposition, as it suggested itself to her mind, was that the impostor might have hoped to obtain some small sum of money from her aunt, either as a reward for fictitious information, or for the purpose of prosecuting sham inquiry. It was absurd to make a mystery of this, and she came to the hasty conclusion that Mr Ringwood's refusal to answer that question was nothing more than the pomposity of a young man somewhat inflated with the dignity of his profession.

'Of course, if you decline to tell me there is no more to be said about it,' she observed at length; 'but if you intend to persist in such reticence, you must excuse my remarking that I do not think your professional assistance will be of much use to us. We are only poor women,' she continued with a smile, 'and, as such, cannot bear not to know what is going on. We like even to be told that there is nothing to tell.'

'I assure you, Miss Chichester,' he replied earnestly, 'that I can see no reason why the cause of this imposition should not be made known to you, but I am pledged to be silent about it. If I get permission to conduct this search for you, I trust to be allowed to inform you of all particulars concerning it, although,' he continued with a smile, 'I am afraid there will be a good deal, in the first instance, of reporting that I have nothing to tell; but now I will bid you good-bye. When I next call, Mr Carbuckle will justify your belief in me.'

'I like that girl,' muttered Ringwood to himself as he made his way down the walk. 'She has nice eyes and a superb figure, and of course she tickled my vanity by that delicate compliment of deciding that I was not the impostor. It is something to be written down a gentleman on the strength of one's personal appearance. I am afraid she must have thought me a bit of an ass making mountains of molehills. It must, of course, appear silly affectation to her my refusing to tell her the cause of that imposition. It is very curious that Miss Caterham should never have told her niece the story of the "Great Tontine". From what Carbuckle said, I should presume that Miss Chichester will chiefly benefit in the event of this missing Finnigan proving the last survivor. Well, the next thing is to see Carbuckle. The news that this Pegram is in the field will interest him, and decidedly make the chase more exciting.'

## CHAPTER SIX

# A CONSULTATION

Mr Carbuckle occupied a set of chambers in the Temple on the first floor of Plowden Buildings; one of those mysterious sets, consisting of half-a-dozen rooms all opening in and out of each other. The arrangement seems constructed for the express purpose of playing hide-and-seek, evading unwelcome visitors, or some similar object. As is usual in such sets, there were only two or three good rooms out of the half-dozen; and in Mr Carbuckle's case it happened to be three, which constituted, respectively, his bedroom, study, and sitting-room; and in this latter, on the evening after his visit to Miss Caterham, Mr Ringwood was seated, in company with his host. They had dined together for the express purpose of talking over Miss Caterham's business, and dinner being ended, the two men had drawn their chairs to the open window looking over the grass-plot towards the New Inn Library, to sip their claret and catch a whiff of the soft summer air from the river.

The twenty years since we last saw him have passed lightly over Mr Carbuckle's head. The dark hair is turned iron-grey. The well-knit figure of 1860 might be deemed to have become somewhat redundant in 1880. The rising junior has blossomed into a portly QC, and is making no one, but his clerk, knows how many thousands a-year. He is still constant as ever to the great hobbies of his younger days – the racecourse and the theatre; and somehow contrives, even when business is at its very hottest, to snatch a day at Ascot or Newmarket.

'I have no doubt whatever but you are right in your conjecture,' said Mr Carbuckle. 'Pegram is either a shareholder or the agent of a shareholder, but that is a thing you can easily ascertain. You have nothing to do but to get a line from Miss Caterham, accrediting you as her agent, and go down to the Board-room and look at the list of the subscribers. It is some time since I saw it, and then there were between forty and fifty names still left on. But I recollect, when I last talked to Miss Caterham about it, she told me there were only five or six left, and the probability is that one or two of those have been put out of it since. Then comes the question – what is Pegram's motive? I should imagine feverish curiosity to know whether the life of Miss Caterham's nominee has lapsed.'

'It strikes me,' replied Ringwood, 'that the first thing to ascertain is, how did this Pegram discover that I was to call on Miss Caterham on your behalf?'

'From Miss Caterham herself, no doubt,' replied Carbuckle. 'As I, in my hurry, had omitted to give your name, she would naturally think he came from me, and would tell him so; and of course, with the object he had in view, he would take very good care not to contradict her.'

'Ah! I dare say it was so. It is a pity that Miss Chichester was not present; I don't think she would have been so easily imposed upon.'

'Yes, you are bound to have great belief in Mary Chichester's detective powers,' replied Carbuckle, laughing. 'She recognized that you were not the impostor, proof, no doubt, of much intelligence.'

Ringwood was silent for some minutes, and ignoring his companion's last remark, observed quietly, 'I differ from you about Pegram's motive. My own idea is, that if they can find Terence Finnigan they intend to perpetrate a fraud. For instance, granting they find him, I should think a few hundred pounds would easily keep him out of the way till his death, which probably cannot be far off, or till the death of Pegram's nominee, when of course their interest in keeping Finnigan out of the way would cease. Recollect the stake is so big. It is a great temptation.'

'Yes,' said Mr Carbuckle, 'it might be so; I never thought of that. Now it would be a great point if we could discover Pegram. First of all, we should be able to get at what sort of a man he is, and to some extent judge whether he is likely to attempt a fraud of this nature; and in the second place, keeping a very sharp eye on Mr Pegram, it is quite possible we should find the missing Finnigan. We should be in fact hunting the hunter. But I am very much afraid Pegram will be hard to find; I should fancy he is only an agent. I don't think it likely the principal would intervene in a matter of this kind.'

'I know it is rather presumptuous to differ with one of your experience, but I think this probably is the principal, and I will tell you why. If my theory is right, the discovery of Terence Finnigan is merely the prelude to the perpetration of a great fraud. It must be obvious to the man who contemplates it, that the fewer accomplices he has the better. If he can do without any, better still. Now, again, I think it very likely that he would use his own name in this preliminary inquiry at Miss Caterham's. In the event of discovery he could easily pass it off as feverish curiosity, and if he appeared under an assumed name, he would certainly lay himself open to the grave suspicion of contemplating foul play of some description.'

'Yes, there is a good deal in what you say,' returned Mr Carbuckle; 'but a visit to the Board-room will settle the question in two minutes. By the way, when you are there see if Viscount Lakington is still left in the "Tontine". He was the last time I saw the list, and I can't help taking an interest in his share. It is curious enough, if it had not been for myself and Gerald Fitzpatrick he would never have gone into it at all.' And here the barrister related the story of that famous pool of *écarté* that was played the night of the Ascot Cup, at the little villa at Bracknell. 'Lakington and I,' he continued, 'are very old friends, although I don't see much of him now. He has never set foot upon a racecourse for years, and a very good thing for him too; the way he used to bet made one wink again. Of course, if your theory is right Pegram will be easy to get at, as his address will be opposite his name. If, on the contrary, I am right, Pegram will be as bad to find as Finnigan.'

'That is a point I will clear up the first day the Board-room is open. In the meantime, can you tell me why Miss Caterham is so jealous of Miss Chichester knowing that she is a shareholder in the "Tontine"?'

'Yes,' replied Mr Carbuckle; 'curious enough, Miss Caterham also took her share in the "Tontine" at my instigation. I was very much bitten by it, and rather given to persuade my friends to have a shy at it.'

'I presume you took a share yourself?' inquired Ringwood.

'Undoubtedly; but my nominee, poor fellow, lasted a very short time. Well, Miss Caterham is a little bit ashamed of this, the only bit of gambling she ever indulged in. She has always given her niece to understand that what little she has to leave will go to her. The best part of Miss Caterham's income consists, you must know, of an annuity, which of course dies with her. She has some good old-fashioned notions, that it would be unwise to dangle this possibility of wealth before a young girl's eyes, and has, consequently, always been very sedulous that the "Tontine" should be kept a profound secret from Mary.'

'She is a very charming young lady,' observed Ringwood. 'I suppose you have known her from a child?'

'Ever since she was five or six years old; her recognition that you were the gentleman, and not the swindler, seems to have much tickled your vanity. However, she is a very nice girl, and, though I honestly don't think that a knowledge of the "Great Tontine" would hurt her in the least, yet we must respect Miss Caterham's wishes on that point.'

'And Finnigan – does he know anything about it? Has he any idea what a valuable life his is?'

'Not in the least,' rejoined Mr Carbuckle. 'I fancy very few of the nominators confided to their nominees the fact that they *were* their nominees. At the stage the lottery has now arrived, it would be almost offering a premium on crime if the nominees were known; and in a case like

Finnigan's, for instance, if he knew it he would be certain to blurt it out in his drunken babble. He goes to be identified whenever he presents himself in town, and receives some few pounds which he supposes are from an annuity left him by his old master.'

'Well, our first move is clear enough,' said Ringwood: 'look Pegram up amongst the list of subscribers. If I find him amongst them, I am off, of course, at once for Pegram's "diggings" to find out all I can about him. In the meanwhile don't forget, please, to write to Miss Caterham and say Ringwood is the man, not Pegram. I can't go down again to Kew until they have heard from you, and there are some minor details about Finnigan I should like very much to get from Miss Chichester.'

'I tell you what it is, young man,' rejoined Mr Carbuckle, with a mock assumption of dignity. 'As your leader, I must remind you that you are importing a good deal too much of Miss Chichester into this case. Just remember, it is a suit of Caterham *versus* Pegram for conspiracy, and that Mary Chichester is not even a witness for the prosecution.'

'Don't talk nonsense,' replied Ringwood, laughing. 'The old proverb about cats and kings is usually held true; and I presume even a briefless barrister may be permitted to admire Miss Chichester.'

'Quite so,' replied Carbuckle, smiling. 'I will write you the note now, and you can either take it or post it at your own sweet will. There is only one thing: if you will take advice – which young men seldom do – you will stop at "admiration" until a few briefs come in, and I think you can have no fear but what they will in due course.'

Ringwood made no reply, but when his friend handed him the note, quietly observed, 'It is a necessity of the case, remember, that I see Miss Caterham at once to get authority from her to see the list of shareholders. And now, good night; when you see me next I shall either have a budget to unfold about Pegram, or be compelled to admit that I have discovered no trace whatever of him. As you say, we begin our search for Finnigan by looking for Pegram.'

Armed with Mr Carbuckle's missive, Ringwood lost no time in once more presenting himself at the cottage. The ladies, once convinced that he really was Mr Carbuckle's friend, welcomed him warmly, and expressed their gratitude for the trouble he was about to take for them. Miss Caterham was able now to regard him without fear or prejudice, and was fain to acknowledge the truth that Ronald Ringwood was a very pleasant, gentlemanly young man, with high spirits, and considerably more than average ability; but the poor lady was still unspeakably nervous on the subject of Mr Pegram, and was continually conjuring up to herself fantasies of crime more or less deeply tinted. Ringwood made no secret of how he intended to open the campaign, telling them that, in the opinion of himself and Mr Carbuckle, it was desirable, in the first place, to discover Mr Pegram, as it might very probably lead them without further trouble to the end of their goal in finding Terence Finnigan; and now Ringwood first realized, if he intended to call often at the cottage, what a delicate part he would have to play. It was quite evident that the idea of being even innocently connected with a great conspiracy had a sort of vague terror for Miss Caterham, all the more difficult to wrestle with because she compelled herself to confine her fears to her own breast. Her common-sense, of course, told her that there was nothing for which she could be held accountable; but her sensitive, nervous nature trembled at the idea of her name being in the papers, and she herself even dragged into the witness-box to give evidence at a great criminal trial. Ringwood could, of course, see her nervousness, and drew a tolerably correct deduction as to its cause. He wished now he had not been quite so communicative, and resolved to be much more guarded in the future, not foreseeing that Miss Caterham's very anxiety would make her more desirous of being kept accurately informed of the precise state of matters. In the next place, Mary Chichester took advantage of the opportunity she had made by offering to show him her garden to question him closely as to whether he could not explain what it was that occasioned her aunt's nervousness. She ridiculed the idea of seeking for this Mr Pegram; she could not be made to comprehend that the looking for one man was the way to find another. She had never heard Terence allude to Mr Pegram in her life, she said.

'I don't profess to understand it all, Mr Ringwood; but of one thing I feel certain, that I am only the recipient of a half-confidence. What your object can be in making a mystery to me I cannot tell; but while pretending that you are letting me know everything, you are in reality keeping back everything of importance I feel quite sure. I'll not believe two gentlemen of ability, like yourself and Mr Carbuckle, would deem it essential to find this Mr Pegram unless there were much stronger reasons for doing so than you choose to give me; and I'll not believe that my aunt could have been so wretchedly unnerved by such an imposition as was practised upon her unless she sees a great deal more in it than I can. The cause of that imposition you refused to tell me the other day, Mr Ringwood; do you do so now?'

Once more the young barrister pleaded that it was a secret he was pledged to maintain, and at the same time he recognized how impossible it would be to make Miss Chichester understand how their proceedings progressed as long as she was kept in ignorance of the 'Great Tontine'.

'Ah, well,' she replied, 'the last time it was mere curiosity that dictated the question; this time I ask earnestly to let me know what it is, on my aunt's account. She is in a state of nervous trepidation about something or other. If I knew what it was I could probably soothe her and be of use to her. Since her illness of five years ago she has been somewhat given to worry herself about trifles, to make mountains of molehills. Once let me know the bogey that is frightening her, and I can always coax and laugh her out of her fears; but this time I am powerless. She will not tell me, nor, it seems, will you, and for her sake I assure you I ought to know.'

'Miss Chichester,' he replied, 'it would be affectation to pretend that there is not a secret which I regret I am compelled to keep back from you. I tell you honestly I think you ought to know it. I would tell it you in one moment if I might; but it is of no use talking about it. My lips are sealed, and I cannot do it without permission.'

'Then I will wish you good-bye, Mr Ringwood,' replied the young lady, drawing herself up a little haughtily. 'I, of course, hope you will find poor Terence; but you must forgive me saying that, as I am only to be furnished with such meagre intelligence, I can take no further interest in the progress of your search;' and with a somewhat stately bend of her head Miss Chichester bade him adieu.

She was a high-minded girl, and held staunchly to the theory, no doubt, that men and women should abide by their promises and plighted words; but, for all that, she thought exception might be made in her own case, and felt somewhat indignant at Ronald Ringwood so steadfastly declining to tell her what this secret might be.

Ringwood duly attended at the Board day, and ascertained that Mr Pegram was a solicitor living in the town of Rydland, in North Wales.

'My theory right to start with, by Jove!' he muttered. 'What a bit of luck! I am off by the Irish mail tonight to see what I can make of Pegram. An intended fraud for a ducat.'

Duly installed at the 'Crown', Mr Ringwood commenced to prosecute his inquiries without delay. He had no difficulty in ascertaining that Mr Pegram was a well-to-do solicitor, who had lived in Rydland all his life; that he was not particularly popular amongst his brother townsmen; that his money was more derived from successful speculation in the new watering-place of Llanbarlym than his business as a solicitor; that he was now a widower, his wife having died some five or six years ago, and that about that time he had taken into partnership his eldest son, and the firm was now known as Pegram and Son. In reply to inquiries as to what age Mr Pegram might be, he was informed sixty or upwards, and that the son would probably number about half his father's years.

'So far so good,' said the young barrister to himself. 'It was no doubt the son who called upon Miss Caterham.'

But when he had learnt this much Mr Ringwood seemed to have come to the end of all information that it was possible to acquire about the Pegrams. Further than that the father was rather close-fisted, and the son somewhat given to play-acting, he could extract little further about the private life of the Pegrams. The old man always had kept very much to himself, and although Mr Robert, when he first came down from London and went into partnership with his father, had been very sociable, and joined freely in such little gaieties as were going on in the town, yet he had withdrawn from such social gatherings of late, and had become almost as great a recluse as his father.

'Odd, sir, very odd, sir,' observed the waiter, to whom a good deal of the above information was due. 'Mr Robert, he can sing a very good song; and when he acted in that piece, "Box and Cox", you know, sir, he made 'em all laugh fit to burst themselves. Such a cheerful gentleman, sir, it's a pity he don't go about more.'

Nothing to be made out of all this further than the facts that he had ascertained who the Pegrams were, and that, in all probability, Mr Robert was the gentleman who had called upon Miss Caterham. Ringwood was fain to admit that his inquiries had led to nothing. He had guardedly sounded several people, whom he thought might be likely to talk, as to whether Mr Pegram bore the credit of being an unscrupulous practitioner; but, further than that he was a sharp man of business, nobody had the slightest imputation to allege against him.

Well, there was nothing further to be done in Rydland at present, so he resolved to return to town by the night mail, and present his meagre budget of facts to Mr Carbuckle. In pursuance of this resolve he ordered an early dinner, and sat down to that meal in all the dignity conferred by finding himself sole tenant of the somewhat dingy coffee-room. He was meditating on the excessive weariness of 'taking your comfort at an inn', and thinking what an humourist Shenstone must have been, when the coffee-room door was suddenly opened, and a stoutish, florid, grizzle-haired man bustled in, bringing with him such a breeze of life and irrepressible activity that the whole place seemed at once peopled.

'Here you are, waiter; let some of them take these rugs and traps to my room. Now, what have you got to eat in the house? Don't be all day thinking about it, but pull yourself together at once, man. Hurry up, I tell you; I am as hungry as Dr Tanner when he arrived at that water-melon. Looks like setting in for a damp evening, sir.'

'The country wants rain,' replied Ringwood, 'and it is always better to have it at night than in the day time. Whether it is wet or no does not make much difference travelling in these days.'

'Off to town tonight, sir?' asked the stranger, interrogatively.

Ringwood nodded assent.

'There,' said the stranger, pointing to the bill of fare which the waiter had just placed in his hand, 'I know of course that you are out of everything good to eat, which, freely translated, means you never had it in your lives. Get me some of that, and that. Been here long, sir?'

Ringwood could not help smiling at his companion's curiosity as he replied, 'I came down here the day before yesterday.'

'Devilish rum place to take into your head to pay a visit to,' returned the stranger. 'This is about the most one-horse old town I ever came across. It hasn't moved a bit since I first knew it twenty years ago. If it wasn't that I had to see old lawyer Pegram occasionally on a bit of business I would never set foot in the old ramshackle place again. The old man did me a turn: he let me stand in with himself in the little "ring" of the early developers of Llanbarlym – a watering-place close by. I made a good bit of money out of it at the time, and have got some house property now there that is worth having. However, I did the old fox a bigger turn than he did me, little as it looked like it at the time. I persuaded him to take a share in a lottery that was a great craze in those days; not likely you ever heard of it. It was a thing that happened before you were breeched; but people went pretty mad about the "Great Tontine" at that time, I can tell you.'

Ringwood here intimated that he knew all about the 'Great Tontine', and always felt intense curiosity concerning it.

'Well, sir, by Jove, the "Great Tontine" is just about winding up. There are only two left in it, and I'm blessed if Pegram is not one. I believe, by the way, there is an old lady who can't find her nominee: that's probably because he is dead. As I said the other day, it's deuced lucky for the nominees that their names are kept dark, or else I should think they would have a sickly summer. Oh, I can tell you,' said the stranger, laughing, 'there's a fine melodrama here. Can't you fancy the two last nominators each trying to do away with his opponent's man in five acts?'

'Ah, well,' said Ringwood, 'I don't suppose Mr Pegram would dream of resorting to such extreme measures.'

'Well, murder is a strong order, no doubt; but I don't think old Pegram would be over scrupulous about smoothing his way to a hundred and sixty thousand pounds. So you have spent two days at Rydland, have you? Excuse me, but why did you do it?'

'Oh, like you,' replied Ringwood, laughing, 'perhaps I also am assisting in the development of Llanbarlym.'

'Guess you are rather late in the field, then,' replied the stranger. 'It really is curious what you could have found to do for two days in Rydland. Why, I could do the whole business of the place for the week in an hour.'

'It is time I was off,' said Ringwood, rising. 'I have a novel here which killed my time for me last night. If you will accept it perhaps it will do the same for you this evening.'

'Thank you,' replied the stranger. 'It's a good place to do it in,' he continued, with assumed gravity. 'But you are the first man I ever heard of who withdrew to this solitude to read his book. Good-bye; my name is Hemmingby, and I ''boss'' a show in town. I dare say you have heard of my name as manager of the ''Vivacity'' Theatre; and I'll have that ''Great Tontine'' dramatized as sure as you are alive; mind you come and see it. There is no telling what the British public will like. What they like one year they don't the next. There is only one thing certain: they are real positive in their dislikes, and when they won't have a piece you can't make them. Shouldn't wonder if there is a pot of money in this ''Great Tontine''. Once more, good-bye,' and exchanging a hearty hand grip, Ringwood left the manager to his reflections.

## CHAPTER SEVEN

## LAWYER PEGRAM'S VIEWS OF A COMPROMISE

Mr Hemmingby, sad to say, took very little advantage of the mental recreation with which Ringwood had provided him. An energetic man, he could always get through an evening very comfortably with his own thoughts and cigar, his busy brain planning, plotting, and devising schemes for the future, to be worked out as soon as he could spare the time and attention. The idea of producing a sensational drama out of the 'Great Tontine' had taken a strong hold of his imagination, and he passed his evening pretty well in what he called thinking it out.

'It's all very well,' he muttered, as he lit another cigar, and rang the bell for another bucket of cognac and seltzer, 'but I can't see where the heroine is to "chip" in; nobody ever heard of a play without a woman in it, and, as far as I know, this old maiden lady living at Kew is the only petticoat with a hand in the game. Can't make a heroine out of an old lady. The interest of the audience begins to flag when they are turned forty, and dies clean out ten years later. I don't see the last act yet quite. By Jove, what a fool I am! If I only wait I shall most likely see the last act played, and as for young women, there are probably three or four mixed up in the matter if I only knew it. In the meantime, I'll just put this big conception on one side till the game is played out; but as soon as it is I'll get one of those fellows in London to put it into dramatic shape for me and "run" it, or my name is not Sam Hemmingby. Well, tomorrow I must see what I can do for the Viscount, and sound old Pegram about a compromise. If I was only in it myself I'm blessed if I'd budge; I'd have all or nothing.'

If there was one thing for which the restless manager seemed to have utter contempt it was bed. His intimates in London had all sorts of jokes about him on this point, and declared that what sleep he did was accomplished in cabs and railway trains. Though one of the latest men at the latest haunts, where theatrical and literary men were wont to congregate, Mr Hemmingby might be seen at his theatre the next morning invariably before the hour at which rehearsal called the company together, looking as if he had retired to rest the evening previous at most orthodox hours.

He was up and breakfasted betimes the next morning, and then strolled leisurely up to the office of Pegram and Son. It was evidently only just open, but one of the clerks, to whom Mr Hemmingby was well known, informed him that Mr Pegram would be sure to be there in ten minutes, and asked him whether he would not sit down and wait.

'Oh, I suppose I am a little early,' said the manager. 'By the way, I don't see Mr Krabbe; I hope there is nothing wrong with the old gentleman. He has been that, by the way, ever since I first knew him. He must be a great age now.'

'Turned eighty, sir. He is quite broke down, and don't come to the office any more. He broke down rather suddenly about six months ago, just after your last visit, Mr Hemmingby. Mr Pegram was very kind to him – took him off to the seaside somewhere for change of air – but it was no good; he got a little better physically, but he is quite gone mentally, and grown very deaf. He was rather deaf, if you recollect, sir.'

'Dear me, I am very sorry to hear all this; and what has become of him? Do any of you ever see him now?'

'Well, he is living in a little cottage Mr Pegram took for him on the outside of the town, and a nurse they got from London takes care of him. I have seen him occasionally on a fine day sitting out in the little garden; but it's no use talking to him, I am told, he can hear very little of what you say, and even that he don't understand. He is just rotting away from old age – terribly changed in the last few months. Mr Pegram and Mr Robert go up and see him sometimes, but they say he hardly seems to know them. It will be a mercy, poor old fellow, when it's all over, as far as he is concerned. He is alive, and that is all, and his life can be no more good to him than if he were a cabbage. But here comes Mr Pegram,' and as he spoke the lawyer entered the room.

'Glad to see you, Hemmingby, glad to see you,' he exclaimed as he shook hands with the manager. 'Come along into my own room beyond here. Anything we can do for you? Your house property at Llanbarlym will turn money if you want to realize, and a man with many irons in the fire sometimes wants to lay his hands upon a few thousands; or I could get you a very fair mortgage, I dare say, if you like it better.'

'Yes, you are quite right, Pegram; men who have tried burning so many candles as you and I, know what it is to want ready money, and a good bit of it at times, if it is only to save losing a lot by putting up the shutters. However, that don't happen to be my case just now; and the Llanbarlym property is a paying investment that I mean to stick to, at all events, for the present. I thought I would just have a look at the houses, you know, and have a chat with you about how things are going. By the way, I am sorry to hear such a sad account of old Krabbe.'

'Ah, yes; a terrible break-down. He got an awkward illness, and at his time of life of course that is a serious business. We sent him away for change, and all that sort of thing; but it was of no use. The utter decay of the mental faculties, the doctors say, has temporarily strengthened the physical ones; but it is the dying flicker of the candle. I don't suppose the poor old fellow has many months' life left in him.'

'Do you think it would please him if I went to see him?' said Hemmingby. 'The old chap and I were always friendly.'

'Very kind indeed of you to think of it,' replied the lawyer; 'but I am afraid it would be quite useless; he does not always seem to know me, and as for Bob, he takes no notice of him whatever. He is well nursed and cared for, you may be sure, and that is all that can be done for him now.'

'By Jove! Pegram,' exclaimed the manager, 'it would be rather awkward for you if he had happened to be your nominee in the "Great Tontine";' and as he spoke Hemmingby shot a keen glance at his companion.

The lawyer smiled as he replied drily, 'Yes, he would not be a good life to depend upon just now.'

'You begin to look uncommonly like taking the whole pool. I wonder it doesn't occur to you lucky people who are still left in to compromise – eight thousand a-year will stand a little cutting up.'

'I have been thinking of that,' rejoined the lawyer eagerly. 'You – you know this Lord Lakington; tell me what sort of a man is he – indolent, accustomed to luxury, loves his ease I suppose?'

'Ahem, my friend, you seem to know him pretty well; I don't think you want me to tell you much about him.'

'It is so? Then what I have been told of Lord Lakington is true?' said Mr Pegram, interrogatively. 'He is selfish then, of course, as all such men must be.'

'Well, yes; I reckon he prefers going about in a brougham to riding in an omnibus; but what has all this got to do with it?'

'It might make Lord Lakington easier to deal with,' replied the lawyer, resuming his usual quiet manner.

'Ah, you think, then, a compromise would be judicious?' said Hemmingby.

'I think it might suit me if I could only see my way.'

'See your way!' exclaimed the manager. 'Good heavens! if you can't see your way in this you had better put up the shutters, say the old man is played out, and the business is to be disposed of. What on earth more do you want than to cry halves?'

'That arrangement might not quite suit me,' returned Pegram, as he scribbled idly on the sheet of paper in front of him.

'What! that's not good enough? What *do* you want? Do you expect to take up three-quarters? Yoy can't suppose Lakington will agree to that.'

'I don't know that I have quite thought it out yet,' returned the lawyer; 'but I have pretty nearly. I suppose Lord Lakington told you to speak to me on the subject?'

'Well, yes, in a way,' replied Hemmingby. 'Don't think I am authorized to make any proposals to you at all. I was merely asked to sound you as to whether you were disposed to compromise; nothing more, remember.'

'Very good. Then I think you may say I am, provided Lord Lakington accedes to my terms.'

'And they are – ?' inquired the manager.

'I shall do myself the honour of submitting them to Lord Lakington. It would be no good, you know, to put them before you; you are not empowered to treat,' said Pegram with a grin.

'No; you are right there,' replied Hemmingby; 'but don't you fall into the mistake of thinking that because Lakington did not know the value of money in his early days that he does not know it now. If your compromise means that you are to have fifteen shillings out of the sovereign, I don't think, my friend, that it will come off.'

'I have good hopes that Lord Lakington and myself will come to an amicable arrangement about the "Tontine".'

'Well, I hope so; though what maggot you have got in your head I am sure I can't guess. However, I am off now to look after one or two little things at Llanbarlym; but, as I go back to town by the night mail, I'll say good-bye.' And with that the manager took his departure.

The lawyer sat for some time after Mr Hemmingby left him immersed in thought. 'Yes,' he muttered to himself, 'luck seems to have left me of late in everything but this. It is destiny; I should be mad not to follow the road that fate so clearly indicates. What has been the one object of my life? For what have I toiled and striven all these years? Wealth. And why? As a means to an end. It has been my ambition that the grandson of the old cattle-jobber should take his place amongst the country gentlemen of England; and only be rich enough in these days, and the world speedily forgets what your grandfather was. If a man is not thin-skinned, and has perseverance, he may mingle with the best in the land. What a start in the road I want him to travel this will give Bob if I can only manage it for him. It is getting time he was married. I want to see my grandchildren growing up around me before I make an end of it. For my hopes it is essential that he should marry well. And where could he ever hope to get such a chance as this. A wife of high family, eight thousand a-year in prospective, and to come into half of it on the day of his marriage, is a tolerably pleasant prospect for a young fellow just turned thirty. It is the only possible wind-up to the affair. My own position in the "Tontine" is rather too delicate to prolong further than is absolutely necessary.' Here his meditations were interrupted by the abrupt entrance of Mr Robert Pegram, with a slightly dishevelled appearance, and other indications of a night passed in travelling.

'What! back again, Bob? Well, do you bring any news?'

'Yes; I have just arrived from Ireland,' said Robert Pegram, 'got a cup of coffee at the "Crown", and then came on here. No; I am sorry to say I have made nothing of the Irish quest. I have been to Mallow, Cork, and all round those parts, and, though I met lots of people who recollected the old fellow (he was a bit of a character, it seems, and popular down there), yet no one had seen anything of him for the last few years. You know we agreed beforehand that though we were bound to inquire about his native place we did not expect to get news of him there. Miss Caterham's people would have found him if he had been in that part of the country. We shall have to begin again, and I tell you what, dad, this fellow Finnigan will take a lot of finding.'

'But find him we must,' replied his father quickly, 'if it is only to be quite certain of keeping him out of the way for the remainder of his life.'

'We must do our best,' replied Robert Pegram; 'and now, have you thought out how we are to play our cards? Things are risky as they stand, you know. Surely we ought to come to a compromise with Lord Lakington.'

'Yes, my lad,' replied old Pegram, rubbing his hands; 'and Hemmingby was here only an hour ago to sound me on that very subject on the Viscount's behalf. Sit down, sit down, I have thought it all out; such a scheme! What do you say to a compromise, Bob, by which you get half and a charming wife to begin with, and the whole to wind up with?'

'What on earth do you mean, father?'

'I mean this: I have sent Lord Lakington word that I am good to compromise if he will agree to my terms. Now, Lord Lakington has got a grown-up daughter; I have no doubt she is pretty, although I don't know anything for certain on that point. I intend you to marry her.'

'Under which circumstances,' interposed Robert Pegram, 'I should have preferred your obtaining more precise information about her appearance.'

'Don't talk nonsense,' said the old gentleman testily; 'she has rank, station, everything you want. It is your duty to marry for these things. Well, there the whole thing lies in a nutshell. The Viscount and I both agree to settle our share of the "Great Tontine" on you and your wife, with this pull for him, that, while I hand you over my half on your marriage, the

Viscount will enjoy his for his lifetime. Now, Bob, what do you say to my scheme?'

It was soon apparent to his father that this projected matrimonial alliance did not meet with Mr Robert's approbation. He looked moodily into the empty grate, and was evidently turning the whole thing over in his mind with little feeling of elation.

'Why don't you speak?' asked his father at last. 'Don't you call the whole thing a master-piece? not a flaw in the plan, providing only that the man Finnigan never makes his existence known again.'

'There is another little hitch,' rejoined the son, 'which you don't seem to take into account. Lord Lakington will never give his consent. I know these swells better than you do; they don't marry their daughters to country solicitors, even if they are well off.'

'That is my business,' replied the old man. 'I fancy human nature is pretty much the same wherever you find it; and that a peer of the realm is quite as much alive to his own interests as anybody else.'

'This is all very well, father. We'll suppose you are right, and that Lord Lakington is willing to agree to your plans; still you will admit that I must have a little bit to say about it. Now, I don't want to be married at present; but when I commit that amiable indiscretion I don't want a stuck-up piece of goods like this Miss Phillimore for a wife. Why can't we come to a compromise without this marriage being in the bond?'

'Because, you fool,' replied his father sharply, 'there is no other possible means by which we can gain the whole stake, and I wish to win all. You know my great ambition is to see you take your place amongst the swells before I die. As for "stuck-up", don't you believe it. It's the under-bred ones put on those sort of airs.'

'Well, again, has it not ever occurred to you that Miss Phillimore would decline to have anything to say to me?'

'No, it hasn't,' exclaimed the old man, eagerly, 'because that is Lord Lakington's business; and when Lord Lakington sees how very much it is for his advantage this match will be, I fancy he will use all his influence in favour of it; and I think, from all I hear, Bob, that the young lady is likely to do as her father tells her.'

'Still, I tell you,' replied Robert Pegram, doggedly, 'I don't want this marriage. I have a feeling harm will come of it.'

'Don't be absurd,' replied his father. 'I have thought well over this thing; I intend to do all I can to bring it about. Everything looks favourable, and both Lord Lakington and myself have the best of all possible reasons for hurrying on the affair, viz., that any day might put either of us out of a position to compromise. After eighty a life becomes precarious.'

Robert Pegram responded to the latter part of his father's remark with a grim smile, but this matrimonial project disturbed him greatly. Fathers, as a rule, have a very imperfect knowledge of the weft of their son's lives. Although he did not dare to advance it, Robert Pegram was painfully aware of a very serious obstacle to his marrying any one. He was meshed, indeed, by an entanglement of his London days that might always have made such an arrangement liable to be the cause of some trouble; and circumstances had of late so strengthened the young lady's hand, that his marrying anybody without her permission would be fraught with very awkward consequences. Knowing that his father always expected him to materially improve his position by marriage, he had never ventured to hint at the chains that bound him. He was in an awkward fix, and could not for the life of him at present quite see his way out of it.

'Well,' continued Pegram senior, after a long pause, 'I shall be off the day after tomorrow to settle things with Lord Lakington; and when I come back, Bob, my boy,' he concluded with a grin, 'it will be, mark you, with orders to get your trousseau ready. In the mean time, I trust to you to spare neither time nor money to find Finnigan.'

'Stop a bit, father,' said the young man quickly; 'you may as well know it at once as later on. I can't go in for this marriage, so it is of no use talking about it. I have reasons – strong reasons – which I will tell you some day, but I cannot now. See Lord Lakington, arrange to go halves with him, and have done with it.'

'And if I do so,' replied the old man, wrathfully, 'neither a shilling of that nor any other property of mine shall ever descend to you.'

'Excuse me,' said the young man coolly, as he rose from his chair, and stood with his back against the mantelpiece, 'you seem to forget the "Tontine" is a game in which I am your partner. When partners quarrel at whist, remember the game generally goes against them.'

'I know it, I know it,' cried the old man, in almost beseeching tones. 'But, Bob, do remember that for over twenty years the sole aim of all my toiling and money-grubbing has been to make a real gentleman of you; to see you hand and glove with the best of them. Luck has gone against me of late, boy, as you know, and, though I have a goodish bit to leave behind me, it is nothing to what I once hoped for. For the last six months I have been brooding on this scheme. It is the sole way I see of obtaining all that I have aimed at; and even then you will not be the rich man I want you to be till after I am in my grave. Lord Lakington is far younger than me, and it is little likely I shall live to see you inherit his share of the "Great Tontine". Married to Miss Phillimore, you will be at once introduced to all these people I want to see you amongst; and though not near so much as I hoped, yet, don't be afraid, Bob, but what I'll find money enough. I can live upon very little down here, you know. Only do what your old father asks you, and say this marriage shall be, as far as it lies with you.'

Robert Pegram paused a few moments before he replied. He was not a bad-hearted young fellow, and really was fond of his father. He thought of his own complications. Well, they were beyond his control for the present; well, there would be a chapter of accidents to look to; something might turn up to render this marriage unnecessary. It is possible that the lady to whom his troth was pledged might release him. At all events, to accede to his father's request would be to temporize with the disagreeables, and that was a thing that Robert Pegram had all his life been much addicted to.

'I can't refuse you, father,' he said at length, 'although I shall have to contend with a difficulty of which you have no idea; but, as you wish it, so shall it be. I will marry Miss Phillimore if you can arrange so. There is my hand upon it,' and the two men clasped palms. 'There is only one thing more I must stipulate – that the whole affair is kept a profound secret until the day of the wedding.'

'Thank you, Bob, thank you. Secret, certainly. I'm not given to cackling, and don't want all the world to know that we are hatching a golden egg. I'll not open my mouth down here, nor in town either, except to Lord Lakington; and Bob, my lad, if money will tide over this little difficulty you have got to contend with, recollect I can find any moderate sum. I have seen gold overcome a good many.'

'Thanks; should I want any I will come to you,' replied the son sententiously.

CHAPTER EIGHT

# OLD MR KRABBE

Old lawyer Pegram on his way to town is little aware into what perplexities he has plunged his son. He is unaware, too, of another fact, viz. that his ambition is not that of Robert Pegram. The son likes wealth, because he thoroughly appreciates all that it can give; but as for using it as an end for improving his social status, that Robert Pegram cared very little about. His idea of life just now was a comfortable house in the West End of London, with – and this was a most important item in his scheme of existence – a theatre built on to it, to which his friends could be invited to witness perpetual performances wherein he should figure prominently. As for a wife, what he wanted was a jolly girl, with no nonsense about her, and similar theatrical tastes to himself. Being received at court would to him seem a small distinction as compared with admission into one of the leading amateur dramatic clubs of London. He was not only stage-struck, but stage-mad, and, even in ordinary life, perpetually acting. To become an 'Old Stager', or a Windsor 'Stroller', would have been to him Elysium, carrying with it that drop of *quassia* which lurks in every cup – the not being allowed to choose his own parts. The marrying of the Honourable Miss Phillimore might be regarded as a great step up the ladder by people generally for the son of a Welsh solicitor; but then Robert Pegram did not want to go up the social ladder. He was quite content with the rung upon which he rested. Histrionic honours alone could move him; and the recognition of half the peerage had small value in his eyes compared with the acquaintance of the leading London comedians. Still, he was quite alive to the charms of eight thousand a-year, and, provided only that Finnigan was dead, much struck with admiration of his father's scheme, to say nothing, too, of being far too dependent upon the old man not to submit to his dictation in this matter.

Robert Pegram having dutifully seen his father off by train, strolled back to the office. He found business rather slack. The old gentleman, for one thing, had been very sedulous in attendance there for the last week, and had consequently disposed of all that was pressing. Having answered two or three letters, Robert Pegram saw there was nothing more than what the clerks were quite competent to deal with. Putting on his hat, he passed through the clerks' room, informed Evans that he was going up to see old Mr Krabbe, and that if any one called he was to tell them that he, Mr Pegram junior, would be back in an hour. He strolled leisurely down the High Street of the little town, struck through its outskirts, and took his way up the Llanbarlym road. A little under a mile, and he came to a pretty little cottage standing somewhat off the road, passed through the garden gate, and proceeded to knock at the door. A woman's face appeared for a minute at the window, and then the door was immediately opened.

'It's you, is it?' said the woman, with a slight dash of acerbity in her tones as she stood back to let him enter. 'I am glad to see you back anyhow; but I tell you, I am getting real tired of this humdrum life. If I had known what it was I would never have undertaken it. Except your father, I have hardly seen a creature since you have been gone.'

'Well, it is not likely to last much longer,' replied Pegram. 'How is old Mr Krabbe this morning?'

'He is much as usual,' replied the woman. 'He has never been out of his room since you left, and people seem to have pretty well given up wanting to see him. Here and there passers-by come and ask after him, but, as I tell 'em, it's no use their seeing him. He is that deaf and foolish it's not likely he would know 'em, and strangers make him irritable.'

'Admirable, Mrs Clark, admirable; with his age and infirmities he is much better, no doubt, in his own room. Of course if he desires to sun himself in the garden any really warm day let him do so. I hope he does not give you much trouble.'

'You ought to be a tolerable judge of that,' retorted Mrs Clark with the slightest possible twinkle in her eye; 'you know quite as much about him as I do. It isn't so much that, but if I had known the insufferable dullness of this place I would never have taken the engagement, even though the reward is tempting.'

'Disagreeable and dull for you no doubt, Kitty; but, remember, it is only for a short time. You will never be asked to do it again.'

A tall, comely, fair woman this Mrs Clark, with her thick fair hair closely rolled away under a mob cap. She wore a plain print dress and a large white apron, and was apparently about five or six-and-thirty years of age; but there was one peculiarity about her that would have struck a close observer, to wit, that she was not so old a woman as she made herself appear. There was not a particle of coquetry in her attire, and she presented, on the whole, that extraordinary phenomenon of a woman who had no desire to appear either at her best or at her youngest.

'I cannot well replace you,' continued Pegram after a short pause; 'invalids always detest a change of their attendants. I will take care that you have books and everything else that will enliven your solitude, and you must cheer yourself up by thinking that you will not have to bear it long.'

'And I suppose you will be up here every day now you have come back?' said Mrs Clark in an interrogative manner.

'As often as I think prudent,' replied Pegram; 'but, like all country towns, this is a very scandalous little place, and, in spite of your age, Kitty, you are too good-looking a woman yet for rumour not to surmise that any over-anxiety about old Krabbe's health would be due to the attractions of his nurse. I have particular reasons, as you know, for not getting into a muddle with the governor now; he gets savage at the idea of anything of that sort. And now I must be off.'

That small communities should interest themselves in matters of very minor importance is only natural. Everybody knows everybody else more or less in a small country town, and usually, to some extent, every one takes some interest in his neighbour's doings. The illness of one so well known in Rydland as old Mr Krabbe was of course much talked about. For a good five-and-thirty years the townsfolk had been accustomed to see the old gentleman bend his way up to Pegram's office a few minutes before ten, and such was his unfailing punctuality, that his passage up the street was said to be accurate enough to set watches by. He had come to Rydland originally at the instigation of grandpapa Pegram, the old cattle-jobber, who had picked him up as a staid, middle-aged clerk, with much knowledge of the legal practice of the principality, who he thought might be a judicious right-hand man to his son, the present Pegram senior, then a young man just setting up as a solicitor; and the old gentleman had remained in the office ever since. Rydland naturally took great interest in Mr Krabbe's illness, and, although lawyer Pegram was by no means a popular man, yet upon this occasion Rydland was of opinion that he had behaved handsomely. His taking Mr Krabbe away to the seaside was behaving to an old and honourable servant as he should do, and his accompanying him himself showed a thoughtfulness for which, in spite of all the years he had lived amongst them, Rydland had never given him credit. People expressed some surprise that the invalid was not taken to Llanbarlym; but Pegram promptly explained that the air of that watering-place was too bracing. The patient required a softer and more balmy climate; and this statement the local medical man, under whose care Mr Krabbe had been, thoroughly endorsed. Then the news came to Rydland that the poor old gentleman was much worse; then that he had rallied again; finally, that the intellect was extinguished, and that, as is sometimes the case, the quenching of the fire of the mind had given more vitality to the fires of the body; that there was little or no chance of his recovery, although it was probable he would linger some months, perhaps even a year or more. Mr Pegram came home by himself in the first instance. He announced to the good people with whom Mr Krabbe had lodged for years that their old tenant was now so completely broken down, and so lamentably infirm, that it was impossible for him to return to them. He would require in future the care of a skilled nurse, and moreover, it was essential that his rooms should be upon the ground-floor. He paid up what slight arrears of rent there were, as he said Mr Krabbe was no longer able to transact his own affairs, and, after some little casting about, hired the cottage on the Llanbarlym road which his son has just visited. The cottage consisted of four rooms, and these Mr Pegram proceeded to furnish most comfortably, and then announced his intention of bringing home the invalid.

Two or three days later Mr Pegram returned, accompanied by Mr Krabbe and Mrs Clark, the London nurse, who had been engaged to take care of him. Not an ogress of the old school, as Mr Pegram observed to his friends.

'No, no; poor old Krabbe deserves better treatment than that from me and mine; we have spared no expense. My son has got hold of one of these new-fangled lady nurses, that can be thoroughly relied upon to treat their patient kindly.'

The few people present at the station when they arrived who knew Mr Krabbe remarked how feeble he was, and observed that he was so muffled up it was difficult to say much about his looks. He walked to the fly that was in readiness for him assisted by the lawyer and the nurse, and was then driven to the cottage. In the course of the next few days some of his old friends called to see him. In many cases the nurse declared firmly and authoritatively that her patient was too weakened by his journey to see them, and the privileged few who were admitted pronounced the old man much changed, and said further, that it was really no use going to see him, as he hardly appeared to know them, merely looked at them with a sort of dazed expression, and that they found it impossible to get an intelligible word out of him. He had been somewhat deaf before he fell ill, and it seemed now had almost lost the sense of hearing. Henceforth, as may be supposed, the old gentleman was troubled with few visitors, and even these the nurse rather discouraged, saying that the sight of them made her patient feverish and irritable. When the doctor, under whose care he had been previous to his going away, called to see his old patient, he found him a good deal wrapped up and dozing. He thought it a pity to rouse him, and the nurse told him – the doctor – that Mr Krabbe passed most of his time in that way. The doctor just ventured to place his finger on the sleeping man's pulse and came away astounded at its strength.

'Curious case, Mr Pegram, poor old Krabbe's,' said the doctor, as he met that gentleman the next day in the High Street. 'I saw him yesterday, and he has got a pulse as strong nearly as a man in good health – very different from the very faint and feeble beat before you took him away to the sea. The nurse tells me he sleeps most of his time. Is his appetite good?'

'Very fair,' replied the lawyer. 'He does nothing but sleep and eat.'

'Under those circumstances I should not be surprised if he lasted a long time yet. You see, when they get to that state they take nothing out of themselves. He has a wonderful lot of vitality left yet, and while his appetite lasts I don't see exactly what is to stop the machine. He will go very suddenly in the end, no doubt, but that may be a good many months off; however, a doctor is of no further use to him, and though of course I will call occasionally if you wish it, yet I tell you I can do nothing for him.'

'Just so, doctor,' replied old Pegram. 'No, it is quite unnecessary that you should trouble yourself any more. I will take care that he is provided with what little he requires, and that, poor old man, is all we can do for him now until it shall please Heaven to take him.'

As the summer wore on, old Krabbe might occasionally, on a very warm day, be seen sitting in the garden just outside the cottage door. He was usually much wrapped up, and the nurse told passers-by who stopped to inquire how he was that there seemed to be no keeping him warm enough. He showed a morbid dislike to being addressed by anybody, and would turn irritably away from any old acquaintance who ventured to ask after him with a grunt of displeasure. People speedily refrained from speaking to him, and the poor old octogenarian was left to make an end of it in the solitude he seemed to covet. All this had taken place a few months before this last visit of Robert Pegram to the cottage.

'Things are beginning to look deuced unpleasant all round,' muttered Robert Pegram, as he retraced his steps towards Rydland. 'The governor's scheme is all very well, very pretty indeed in theory; but I don't, somehow, think it will work out so smoothly. I did not quite like the way Kitty talked just now. She can make things unpleasant if she likes, and I am painfully aware, from former experience, that she undoubtedly knows how to produce that effect. However, my business at present is to find Terence Finnigan, and simply keep quiet about anything else. The dad wants no assistance in his own game at present from me, and, as it is quite possible nothing will come of it, that bother will settle itself. As far as Finnigan goes things look a little more hopeful, and the agent I left to make inquiries at Hampstead writes me word that he has struck the trail; that the old man told one or two of his intimates that he was going from there to Farnborough, and should take the opportunity of looking at his master's old regiment then quartered at Aldershot camp; and adds further that, after poking about Farnborough for two or three days, he has ascertained this to be true, although as yet he has failed to make out where he went when he left it; however, if we are really on the trace of him, it is only a matter of time working it out, and of course this early part of his wanderings will give us most trouble. Later on we shall probably come to places in which he has spent some time, and then people will remember him better. An aged Irishman, of rather convivial habits, and an old campaigner, ought to attract attention, if it was only by the stupendous lies he in all probability tells. I don't know, but I should guess that Finnigan would have some marvellous stories of his American experiences to narrate, and these alone would go far to identify the man we are in search of. Well, there is no use my going into Hampshire; this man from the Inquiry Office seems to be doing his work well, and for the present I may safely leave it in his hands. Later on, I think I must take it into my own. I should prefer to find Finnigan at last without assistance, or rather, to be quite certain that nobody else has found him.' And these reflections brought Mr Pegram once more to the office door.

Robert Pegram had got his barque in stormy waters, and was painfully aware of the fact, and he would have found nothing either comforting or reassuring in Mrs Clark's reflections on his departure could he but have known them. The nurse looked after him as he passed through the little garden, and said softly to herself,

'I don't quite understand what you are about, Robert, and it is curious your preferring me to a professional nurse. Though in a case like this, with all the experience I had with my old mother, I am as good as the best of them, and it may be better for your purposes; but, remember, I am pledged a guerdon for all this weary servitude, and if it be not paid, I will speak out, and then let them whom it concerns solve the riddle.'

Mrs Clark's thoughts certainly clothed themselves in more melodramatic form than is usual with nurses, lady or otherwise; but then Mrs Clark, as we shall see later on, had enjoyed a somewhat peculiar education.

## CHAPTER NINE

# THE LAWYER VISITS THE VISCOUNT

Mr Hemmingby upon his return to town duly apprised Lord Lakington that he had executed his commission.

'Old Pegram,' wrote the manager, 'says he is quite willing to compromise if you will accede to his terms, and what those terms are he prefers stating to you himself. I took the opportunity of remarking that your "sallet days" were over, and that you were not likely to pay fifty per cent for money now. Remember, you are dealing with a precious sharp – and not over-particular – attorney, who, no doubt, will look to have a pull of some kind in his bargain. I merely mention this because, if you are really anxious about this compromise, I think you will inevitably have to submit to getting a little the worst of it. There is a strong dash of the usurer in old Pegram, and in the pursuit of money he is callous of rebuff; still, I can hardly think that he would presume now to deal with your lordship as he might have done in those bygone days when you were on the turf. You will doubtless see or hear of him before long, most probably the former. Trusting you will find him not altogether impracticable, I remain,

'Yours very sincerely,
    'SAMUEL HEMMINGBY.'

The more Lord Lakington meditated on the possible issue of the 'Great Tontine' the more uncomfortable he became about it. He shrank from the recollection of that grinding poverty – for such it had really been to him – of some years ago. The idea of walking about town perfectly well dressed, but never with a shilling in his pockets, filled him with dismay. He thought of the petty ignominies and perpetual discomforts of that time with a shudder, and ruefully reflected that his present very comfortable existence hung upon the frail life of a very old lady. He grew nervous about his mother-in-law's health, and was feverishly anxious that this compromise with Pegram should be accomplished. Even then he knew there was an extremely unpleasant contingency to be faced. This missing nominee of the maiden lady might turn up, and, although Hemmingby professed to feel certain that he was dead and would never be heard of again, still the Viscount felt it would be much more satisfactory to see that fact recorded on his tombstone. The manager's note set him speculating again. What advantage was it this confounded attorney would seek to gain over him, and on what grounds could he urge that he was entitled to more than half? At one time he had nearly made up his mind to slip down to the 'Vivacity' Theatre and see Sam Hemmingby; but then he reflected that there could be no use in that, as the manager had evidently no idea as to what Pegram's proposals might be. There was nothing for it but to wait till he heard from that gentleman, and the lawyer did not keep him long in suspense. Forty-eight hours after he received the manager's note came another from Mr Pegram, requesting to know when it would be convenient for him to wait upon his lordship upon a matter of business; to which the Viscount replied, he should be at home the next day at twelve.

Lord Lakington had a sanctum of his own on the ground-floor at the back of the house, a pleasant little room, with a bay-window looking out upon the garden, which, though it surrounded the whole house, ran mainly at the back. Here the Viscount was accustomed to retire after breakfast to smoke his cigar, read the papers, write his letters, and generally give himself the idea of transacting a deal of business; and here, calming his nerves with a 'cabana', he sat the next morning awaiting the arrival of the old lawyer. Punctual to the moment came Mr Pegram's knock at the door, and in another moment he was ushered into the Viscount's snuggery. Lord Lakington looked his visitor sharply over as he motioned him to a chair. A little wizened old man, with spiky hair of iron-grey, and small, keen, restless eyes – eyes that, though they never seemed fairly to look at you, yet you felt were continually taking stock of you at unexpected moments. 'A more unpromising person to do business with,' thought his lordship, 'I think I have seldom come across.'

'I have ventured to request you to see me on a matter of business, Lord Lakington, in consequence of some conversation I had with our mutual friend, Mr Hemmingby, last week. We are both, it seems, concerned in the impending decision of this great lottery. In all human probability, the eight thousand per annum it represents must fall to either you or I in the course of the next year or two. It is a very big property, my lord, and would bear dividing. Many people, for instance, would think it more judicious to make a certainty of half than, by seeing their luck out, lose all. I do not know whether I am right, but I rather understood Mr Hemmingby that you were somewhat of this way of thinking.'

'I have gambled, Mr Pegram, as high as most men of my time, but I have done with all that now, and I honestly own I should be quite content to make a certainty of four thousand a-year.'

'And yet it seems a pity not to leave such a fine property intact. I own, my lord, myself, I hate to see a fine income split up and divided amongst a large family; I am a great advocate for the law of primogeniture. I have always been thankful that I have but one child myself – a son, my lord.'

'You know best, perhaps, Mr Pegram,' replied Lord Lakington, with a languid smile; 'but do you – excuse me – but do you really think that your family affairs have any bearing upon the matter in hand?'

'I think they have,' replied the lawyer drily.

The Viscount bowed his head in courteous assent to Mr Pegram's reply, and awaited with assumed nonchalance for that gentleman to unfold his scheme.

'You see,' continued the lawyer, 'that the very comfortable income we are each of us enjoying from the "Great Tontine" may terminate at any moment. Our shares this year will amount to two thousand six hundred apiece, and I have no doubt should be four if we could only discover the death of the nominee of that troublesome old woman at Kew (a most uncalled-for assertion on Mr Pegram's part, Miss Caterham never having troubled him in any respect); curtailment of income, my lord, always comes unpleasant to us. It means, for the most part, giving up luxuries to which we have accustomed ourselves: putting down our carriage; the drinking of wines, the cheapness of which makes them no nicer; in fact, a good deal of discomfort altogether. If I, a plain country lawyer, feel all this, it must surely come very much harder to a fashionable man of the world like your lordship.'

'It would be devilish hard and devilish disagreeable,' interposed the Viscount. 'As I told you at starting, I am as willing to guard against the chance of it as you can be.'

'Rumour, my lord, has it that your own fortune has been sadly impaired –'

'I tell you what it is, Mr Pegram,' interrupted the Viscount, sharply, 'I don't see what my private affairs have got to do with the question; and besides, sir, I consider it taking a great liberty on your part to suggest their discussion without invitation on my part.'

'I beg your lordship's pardon,' replied the lawyer, with a low bow; 'but it is absolutely necessary that I should touch upon them in some degree. Believe me, I will transgress no further than is absolutely necessary in that respect, but you will see in a few minutes that it is impossible to avoid alluding to them. Assuming rumour to be right,' continued Mr Pegram, 'the loss of this income would be a serious inconvenience to your lordship.'

The Viscount vouchsafed no reply.

'Four thousand a year – I will say four – is a very nice income for a single man, especially when, as in this case, there are no drawbacks: such as a house to keep up, improvements to be made, tenants wanting something done for them, and all that sort of thing.'

'If you think, Mr Pegram,' remarked the Viscount, with a slightly contemptuous smile on his lips, 'there is any necessity of pointing out to me the advantages of a net four thousand a year, you are labouring under a considerable mistake.'

'And yet, my lord, you don't seem inclined to even listen patiently to the only man who could show you how to make it a certainty for your lifetime.'

'I am quite prepared to listen to all you have got to say,' returned the Viscount. 'I only object to my private affairs being dragged into the discussion.'

'Suppose,' said the lawyer, slowly, 'I could show you a scheme by which this four thousand a year should be insured to you for life, while the other half of the "Tontine" would at once become the income of your daughter, the whole eight thousand per annum becoming her property at your death.'

To say that Lord Lakington was amazed at Mr Pegram's proposition would hardly convey the truth. He was literally astounded. Here was a man, who Hemmingby had warned him that he would find hard to deal with, who would probably drive with him a bitter bargain, who might be regarded as certain to insist upon having more or less the best of their agreement, actually offering, in the most disinterested way, to efface himself, and to divide the 'Tontine' between him – Lord Lakington – and his daughter. What could possibly be the man's motive? And for a minute or two the Viscount sat silently racking his brains as to what his companion's real aims could possibly be.

Mr Pegram, too, was in no hurry to continue the conversation. He wanted to let the pleasing picture he had just drawn sink well into the Viscount's mind before he spoke again, and also he had strong misgivings that his next proposition might be wrathfully received. Dogged, pertinacious, and per-severing, no nervous apprehensions ever turned Mr Pegram from the pur-suit of his own ends. He knew nothing of the great world; still he did know that the falcon does not mate with the jackdaw, and thought nothing more likely than that Lord Lakington would reject the alliance he was about to proffer with contemptuous indignation. But, he argued, he will get used to the idea after a bit, and then I think his self-interest will lead him to adopt it. In the meantime, this thing had got to be said, and the more shortly it was said the better, thought Mr Pegram.

'I told you, my lord,' he resumed at length, 'that I had one son; you, I understand, have also an only daughter. If you will consent to their making a match of it, I will settle my half of the "Tontine" on your daughter at her marriage. Your half would, of course, remain as it is, with the sole condition that it went to your daughter at your death.'

Lord Lakington rose slowly from his chair with a set look upon his face that even the old lawyer could see boded danger. 'Do you know, sir,' said the Viscount, in low, measured tones, 'that if you were a few years younger I should probably throw you out of the window?'

'I beg pardon, my lord,' said the lawyer in the most deprecatory tones, 'but it is so obviously the way to keep the property together. Of course I know Bob is no match for the Honourable Miss Phillimore, but I thought that, under the circumstances, I might venture to suggest it to your lordship; and again, I had not time to mention it before, but I shall have something pretty comfortable to leave behind me when my time comes, and that of course would go to my son.'

'You may spare yourself any further enumeration of the advantages of the connection,' replied the Viscount, contemptuously; 'your total ignorance of the conventionalities of society may be pleaded in extenuation of your having presumed to make me such a proposal; but you will understand distinctly that it is declined, and with considerable astonishment that you should ever have had the audacity to make it.'

'I do not understand these things myself,' rejoined the old lawyer, interlacing his fingers nervously, but making no attempt whatever to rise from his chair; 'but surely this sort of thing is done every day. It is a fair bargain – an exchange of wealth for rank. I thought our great nobles always repaired their fortunes in that way – married the daughters of wealthy manufacturers, merchants, or speculators.'

The Viscount's own marriage had been in this wise, and he cast a quick look at Mr Pegram to see if the conclusion of his speech had been intentional; but the lawyer looked serenely unconscious, although every word he uttered had been spoken with intent.

'That may be, sir,' replied Lord Lakington loftily; 'but we don't give our daughters as wives to country solicitors.'

'But we can make that all right, your lordship,' interrupted the old man eagerly. 'Only say the word, and Bob shall give up practice at once. He shall never set foot in the office again, I give you my word. As for me, I would never trouble the young couple. Nobody would ever know anything about the old lawyer down in Wales. Nobody will either see or hear anything of him. That Bob was ever a solicitor would speedily be forgotten, if, indeed, it need ever be known in London.'

He poured forth all this with a nervous impetuosity which somewhat astonished the Viscount.

'I tell you once for all, Mr Pegram, that your proposition is ridiculous, I may say impertinent. I was in hopes you had some reasonable compromise to offer me. When you have, I shall be happy to see you again. In the meanwhile I have the honour to wish you good morning,' and as he finished, Lord Lakington laid his hand on the bell.

'Good morning, my lord, good morning. If you could only be brought to see it in a business point of view, it is the most perfect arrangement that could possibly be made. Bob will be sorely disappointed when he hears your lordship will not consent.'

'Damn Bob,' said the Viscount, giving a furious jerk at the bell.

'And four thousand a-year, with no drawbacks. Such a snug income to run the risk of losing at any moment. If your lordship should change your mind in any way, I shall be staying for the week at the Tavistock Hotel, Covent Garden. Good day, my lord, good day,' and old Pegram made his way to the door.

Well, thought the old man, when he found himself in the Victoria Road, that is about as much as I expected to do this morning. It was not likely he would come to terms to start with. Rather too great a shock to his pride the idea of becoming connected with a Welsh solicitor. To talk about throwing a solicitor out of window, he little knows what an expensive amusement he would have found that. The way he damned Bob, too, to wind up with, certainly was not encouraging. But when he comes to reflect on losing that four thousand a-year a little longer, I should not be surprised if he became of my way of thinking, and that we arranged things pretty comfortably.

Lord Lakington paced up and down his little room in a perfect storm of indignation for a good half-hour after Mr Pegram left him. It was a damned, levelling, atheistical age he knew – an age that spoke openly of the disestablishment of the Church, and even ventured to hint that the House of Peers was a most unnecessary cog-wheel in the machinery of the State. All this was bad enough; but that a Welsh solicitor should deem his bumpkin, bullet-headed son fit mate for the Honourable Beatrice Phillimore was the most astounding instance of the democratic tendencies of the age that he had as yet encountered! The idea of a man with such a name as 'Pegram' ever presuming to think of marrying a Phillimore was an impertinence. To give an expression to such a thought was to insult him, and he began to regret seriously that he had not given orders for Mr Pegram to be put out of the house, instead of permitting him to leave like any ordinary visitor. Gradually the whirlwind of his wrath died away, though he fumed and fidgeted, and muttered occasional anathemas on the lawyer's impudence until summoned to luncheon. There the sight of his daughter's pretty bright face once more brought vividly before him the audacity of the old lawyer's proposal. The idea of his Beatrice being married to a Pegram! But a satisfactory cutlet, and a glass of peculiar brown sherry which he affected, and which, in its turn, sometimes affected him, gradually soothed his feelings, and brought him into a more tranquil frame of mind; and as he strolled up towards his club in the afternoon, Lord Lakington was reflecting more how annoying it was that he had not come to a satisfactory arrangement with Mr Pegram than upon the indignity put upon the house of Phillimore. The next day it was the same. He dwelt more and more upon how hard it would be to lose this very satisfactory income now. What small income remained to him out of his own fortune paid his tailor, bootmaker, and provided him with the necessaries of life; but, from past experience, he knew that it was about all that it would do. He was a man who loved his luxuries. He was a connoisseur in tobacco, and held it was hopeless to get a smokeable cigar in these days under a shilling. He delighted also in little dinners, to try inspirations or new discoveries in the art of cooking, and

> To taste of the best,
> Of the sweet, of the dry, and the still.

He was fond of the opera, and liked to give his daughter a box there occasionally; in fact, had all the luxurious tastes that a man who had begun life as he had done might be supposed to possess. And he had known for some years what it was to be deprived of all these things, and the idea that it might be so again worried the noble Viscount not a little.

Gradually he found himself reverting to the old lawyer's idea. What a confounded pity, he thought, the fellow is not a gentleman! If he had only been that the arrangement would have been so very perfect. I should have been comfortable for life. Trixie, poor girl, would have had a very nice income to start with, with the knowledge that there was lots more to come. It really is most provoking; and then Lord Lakington began to wonder what Pegram junior was like, whether he was more presentable than his father. I must say, he thought, old Pegram behaved handsomely on one point. I hardly gave him credit for it at the time, but he certainly promised to keep himself altogether in the background if we would consent to this marriage. Of course, when an objectionable relative volunteers a pledge of that kind it certainly smooths matters a bit; and if Pegram junior really is a presentable young fellow – Pooh! what nonsense I am talking. Hang it, he can't be. An obscure country solicitor! it is impossible. Still, day after day, as the Viscount turned the whole thing over in his mind, did the prospect of losing his income look more unpleasant, and what he denominated the old Welsh solicitor's outrageous proposal seem less preposterous. The man's selfish, sybarite nature was slowly, but surely, getting the better of his pride of birth, and it was so easy to make it out an excellent match for his daughter, who, though pretty, was portionless. She would be married to a man comfortably off to start with, and would eventually be in possession of some ten or twelve thousand a-year. Every point that the old lawyer had so artfully instilled into his mind recalled itself. Yes, the solicitor can be dropped; the old father promised to keep in the background; and yes, by Jove! Pegram must be made to change his name. If Pegram junior is only presentable, really it might be worth considering; and then he remembered – supreme piece of hypocrisy! – that he really had no business to decide. This thing concerned Beatrice as much as it did him, and it was not right that she should have no voice in the matter. At the end of the week a note reached Mr Pegram at the 'Tavistock', to the effect that, considering what a large sum of money was involved, Lord Lakington thought it would be advisable to see Mr Pegram again, to discuss if the compromise of the 'Tontine' was possible between them, and requesting the lawyer to call upon him the next day.

'It works, it works,' chuckled Mr Pegram. 'All the world is alive to self-interest, more especially your gay spendthrift dogs who have been throwing their own and other people's money out of window with both hands half their days. We may not settle it tomorrow, though I think we shall; but I will bet a guinea he don't damn Bob this time any way.'

CHAPTER TEN

# ROBERT PEGRAM DINES IN THE VICTORIA ROAD

When Lord Lakington's self-interest had so far mastered his pride as to induce him to write that note to Mr Pegram, desiring another interview, the result was nearly a foregone conclusion. For a week the Viscount had been arguing this matter with himself, setting it forth day by day in more and more plausible terms. He had finally worked himself round to the conclusion that his duty to his daughter required him to talk this thing over dispassionately with Pegram, in the first instance; and that he would be probably further bound to submit this proposal of marriage to Beatrice in the second, duly placing all its advantages before her eyes. Mr Pegram, on the other hand, met the Viscount with the greatest deference and humility. He vowed that nothing but his lordship's being in embarrassed circumstances having come to his ears in somewhat roundabout fashion would have emboldened him to propose such a scheme to a man of his lordship's rank and family. He dwelt quite plaintively upon the hardship of having to give up a handsome income to which one had got accustomed, artfully whining over his own loss in this respect in such a manner that the Viscount could not fail to see the application to his own case. To every stipulation of Lord Lakington's he gave ready assent. He was an old man, with no taste for London and gay people. He would go back to his own home in Wales, and they would rarely see him. If Bob would run down to Rydland for a few days now and again, that would be all he would ask. He would like to be present at the wedding; but even then he would not obtrude upon the bridal party. He could get into a quiet corner of the church, and look on from there. Nobody would know that he was more than an ordinary spectator; but he could not bear the idea of so much money going away, not so much from him – though that would be bad enough now he had got used to it – but also from his son afterwards.

Lord Lakington, now that he has admitted to himself that such a marriage is possible, is extremely gratified to find that he is allowed to dictate all the minor details of the projected alliance. The crafty old lawyer listens deferentially to the Viscount's proposals, and yields to them without demur, except

107

in the one instance, namely, that it would be advisable that Mr Robert Pegram should change his name. At that the old gentleman somewhat hesitates. It may be that he thinks it as well to appear to be giving up something on his side to show that the sacrifices are not all of Lord Lakington's making; or, it may be, that he had got used to his name after wearing it sixty odd years, and holds it in higher esteem than his neighbours'. A man's name may not be very euphonious, but it is, after all, a part of his identity, and he may well be indisposed to change it at the summary bidding of another. This point Mr Pegram insisted should be left in abeyance. He promised to take into consideration what his lordship had said, and declared that, personally, he was not violently prejudiced in favour of the name of Pegram, but that there would be many inconveniences attendant on changing it. Moreover, as he said, it was not him, but his son, that would have to change his name, and it was only reasonable to learn what Robert Pegram's views might be upon that subject. It was further agreed between them that Mr Pegram should now return to Wales, and that Mr Robert should forthwith repair to London, his lordship having by this time so effectually humbugged himself as to finish up the conversation with a burst of parental solicitude and tenderness that would have done honour to the stock comedy father, saying that he must, at all events, see the man to whom he proposed to entrust his sweet Beatrice before presenting him to her as a suitor.

Mr Pegram chuckled grimly as he packed his portmanteau that afternoon at the 'Tavistock' preparatory to taking the evening train for Rydland.

'I think I may count that as good as done,' he muttered. 'Not a bad week's work. Give him only another week to think about it, and my lord will be quite as anxious for that marriage as I am. As for the girl, I don't suppose there will be any bother with her; I always read in the papers, when I come across the matrimonial engagements of any of the aristocracy, that a "marriage has been arranged", &c., which is, of course, the proper and sensible way to make marriages. I don't suppose they allow any taking fancies to one another, as a rule. They thoroughly recognize the fact that income comes before affection, and that marriage on insufficient means should be made a criminal offence. Well, it is now for Bob to do his part. He seems to get on well enough with the young women in Rydland; but these London misses are perhaps a bit different.'

Although Mr Pegram might return to Rydland in the highest spirits at the satisfactory progress of his scheme, yet his son by no means partook of the elation. Robert Pegram was by no means shy, and could make the agreeable to the young ladies in his own class of life well enough; but he had been some few years in London, and did know that the fashionable ladies of the London world were very different from these. He was far from being one of those unabashed young gentlemen who, thrown into society higher than they are accustomed to, seek to cover their want of ease by vulgar swagger and somewhat boisterous self-assertion. Robert Pegram was not an innate snob, although he certainly lacked the polish of good society. He had had no opportunity of ever mixing with such people, nor, to do him justice, had he the slightest desire for it. He had an undefined idea that he should be rather awkward and uncomfortable, and probably commit some slight solecisms, both of speech and manner. As he would have tersely expressed it, 'These swells have ways of their own, which I ain't up to'; but, although this was by no means his ideal of marriage, and although he was entangled with another lady, and had a dread suspicion that this other lady would make considerable unpleasantness should she get the slightest hint of what he contemplated, yet Robert Pegram, like most mortals, was not insensible to the titillation of his vanity. How his old London associates would stare at seeing him with an honourable for his wife! What a splash he should cut in all the papers! He pictured to himself the announcement, 'On the – instant, at St George's, Hanover Square, Robert Pegram, Esq., to the Honourable Beatrice Phillimore, only daughter of Herbert, Viscount Lakington'; and then, again, four thousand a-year was a very pretty income to start with, to say nothing of lots more to tumble in after a while. Upon the whole, as he sped to town, Robert Pegram was tolerably well satisfied with his prospects. He was, however, much too shrewd a young man to suppose it was all quite such plain sailing as his father did. He knew that he was about to sail his barque in what were to him unknown waters; and he by no means held his father's comfortable creed, that human nature was pretty much the same wherever you found it. That was all very well in the abstract, but practically he considered human nature took, at all events, another aspect when you came to the aristocracy. However, this marriage must be brought off if he could compass it, and he resolved not to throw a chance away. The 'Tavistock' might do very well for his father, but that was no hostelry for a candidate for the hand of the Honourable Beatrice Phillimore to put up at. He determined to establish himself at the 'Grand', and, in the first instance, to call upon Lord Lakington at his club.

The Viscount punctiliously returned his card, and left a note inviting him to lunch at the institution in question. He thought it would be as well to have a look at his proposed son-in-law before presenting him in the Victoria Road, and he was agreeably surprised. As the old lawyer had predicted, the Viscount was now much enamoured of the scheme. He had dreaded finding a rather noisy, vulgar young man; but he found Robert Pegram, on the contrary, quiet and, if anything, rather diffident in manner. He certainly was not a particularly good-looking young fellow. The Viscount felt that to be a slight drawback. It was of no great consequence; but then he knew that women valued such things. That they fell in love over and over again with ugly men he knew also, but then they were seldom attracted towards them in the first instance; and it was important that Beatrice should fall in love, or, at all events, fancy this young man sufficiently to engage herself to him as speedily as possible. However, he broke the ice offhand with Robert Pegram, told him that he had talked this matter over with his father, and that, though of course he would never coerce his daughter, yet that he wished him all possible success in his wooing. Finally, he shook hands with him, and invited him to dine the next day in Victoria Road, and be presented to Miss Beatrice and her grandmamma.

There was no little curiosity in Victoria Road when the Viscount announced that he had asked the young gentleman to dine with them *en famille* the next night. It was not very often that he asked any one to dine there in this fashion, and when he did so it was either a relation or some old friend that they knew well, at least by name.

'Mr Pegram!' exclaimed Beatrice; 'what a singular name. Is there anything peculiar about the owner of this singular patronymic, papa?'

'Pegram!' echoed Mrs Lyme Wregis; ''tis an odd name. What is he? Where did you come across Mr Pegram, Lakington? I never heard you mention him before.'

'No, no,' replied the Viscount, somewhat nervously. 'Excellent people, whose acquaintance I have only lately made. The father is a man of large property down in North Wales; did me rather a good turn not long ago; I am anxious to be a little civil to the son. He is – a very rare thing for a young man in these days – actually, I think, a little shy.'

'Well, Trixie,' rejoined the old lady, laughing, 'I do call this very good of your papa. Having found such a curiosity as a shy young man, named Pegram, to bring him out here is kind of him. We must put on our best clothes tomorrow night to do him honour.'

'Is he nice, papa? Is he amusing?'

'My dear, I can tell you little more about him than I have already done. He is a quiet, gentleman-like young fellow, and that is all I can say about him. Amusing! Well, I don't know; he did not somehow strike me in that light.'

Mr Robert Pegram duly made his appearance the next evening in Victoria Road. The Viscount welcomed him warmly, and then presented him to his daughter and mother-in-law. Robert Pegram quite bore out the character the Viscount had given him. He was very quiet at first, and rather diffident. His anxiety to commit no solecisms of breeding made him of course ill at ease, and he thus appealed unwittingly to the good nature of both ladies. A shy man cannot help appearing somewhat of a fool; but, as one of our shrewdest observers has pointed out, that one of the easiest methods of making your way with English young ladies is this: 'If Providence has not made you a fool, pretend to be one. It is then that the timidest and most bashful of English girls will show her kind heart; she will try to lead you on, she will strive to find out your strong point.' And this is precisely what happened to Robert Pegram. In their anxiety to put him at his ease, the ladies were more than usually courteous to him; and Miss Trixie, in particular, strove very hard to make him feel at home amongst them. But there was one thing patent to both ladies, and it was just one of those slight points which well-bred women see intuitively, and about which they rarely make a mistake. It was clear to Mrs Lyme Wregis, as it was to Miss Trixie, that Robert Pegram had not been accustomed to move in good society. It was not that he committed himself in any way, his shyness would account for his want of ease; but he lacked an undefinable something, that final polish which is only acquired by mixing freely with the world.

But in vain did Lord Lakington prose for his guest's edification, and that nobleman was wont to be very didactic in his conversation. In vain did Mrs Lyme Wregis ask him good-humoured questions about his own part of the country. In vain did Miss Beatrice try topic after topic. There was, apparently, no getting on with Robert Pegram. Not only was he ill at ease at finding himself in society to which he was unaccustomed, but, to add to his embarrassment, he was lost in hopeless admiration of Beatrice Phillimore. Not only was she a very handsome girl, but it was beauty of a type that Robert Pegram hitherto had only viewed from afar. She was so unmistakably of high lineage, and showed the blue blood in her every pose and gesture. She looked thorough-bred to the tips of her delicate fingers. Although Robert Pegram would have probably said that Beatrice's dusky tresses, lustrous dark eyes, and lithe, slender figure were not exactly in his style, yet, for all that, he would honestly own that the Honourable Beatrice Phillimore was the handsomest girl he had ever come across. But, mingled with this admiration, came the uncomfortable reflection that it was absolutely necessary, in the course of a few days, that he should ask this young lady to be his wife; and, as he watched the quick play of her mobile features, he could not refrain from speculating as to what expression they might wear when he should have screwed up his courage to blurt forth that proposition. In spite of all the efforts of his entertainers, the guest bid fair to almost drop out of the conversation. Courteously as they endeavoured to include him in it, there was no making him talk.

It has, however, been said, and I believe there is much truth in the remark, that every man has one topic. Many of us, no doubt, can recall instances that make belief in this axiom come rather difficult, but the chances are we never struck the key-note. We never happened to turn the conversation on that one subject upon which the people chanced to be well informed.

Accident at last led Mrs Lyme Wregis to make a remark upon a piece then playing at the Haymarket Theatre, and the key-note was struck. If Mr Robert Pegram could talk about nothing else, he could talk 'theatricals'. Indeed, he never tired talking of the play and players. He had been in every theatre in London, and had seen every actor and actress of any note at all over and over again. His memory, indeed, was like a file of ten years' play bills. He could remember the production of almost every new piece, and who had played in it; could chronicle the successes and the failures, and gave his opinion freely upon the dramatists, the plays, and their representatives. In short, Mr Robert Pegram had found his tongue, and got fairly astride of his hobby. He told them story after story having reference to the footlights, finally winding up by a very good imitation of a popular comedian; and then, becoming suddenly conscious of the very prominent part he was assuming in the conversation, suddenly pulled up, coloured, wondered whether he had committed himself, and looked exquisitely uncomfortable. However, the good-humoured laughter of his audience somewhat reassured him, and he got on very well until the ladies withdrew, although his conversation to the last still savoured of 'the floats'.

'Fill your glass, Mr Pegram,' said the Viscount, as he pushed the claret-jug across; 'I had no idea you were such an enthusiast about the drama.'

Considering Lord Lakington had encountered his proposed son-in-law the first time the day before, and first heard of him only about a month ago, it would have been somewhat singular if he had known anything of his hobbies or pursuits.

'I was very fond of the theatre myself,' continued the Viscount, 'as a young man, but I have rather dropped out of theatrical circles of late years, and lost sight of my old friends in that way. Sam Hemmingby, the manager of the "Vivacity" Theatre, is the only one of the craft I ever come across now; you know him very likely.'

'Very well indeed, my lord; I have known him from a child. My father and he have been mixed up in business relations more or less for years.'

'Ah! fine fellow Hemmingby. He has done a good deal for the elevation of the stage since he took command of the "Vivacity".'

'I don't know about that,' replied Robert Pegram, drily; 'I don't think Sam Hemmingby troubles his head much about the elevation of the drama. He puts up what will draw, and if he gives the public a good entertainment I fancy it is because he finds they won't come to see a bad one.'

'Ah! perhaps you are right,' rejoined the Viscount, suddenly becoming conscious that on this particular subject Robert Pegram was an awkward customer to argue with; 'but we have a more important matter to talk over than the stage, and I trust, ha! ha!' – and here the Viscount gave a little affected laugh – 'a pleasanter one. Now you have been introduced to my daughter and Mrs Lyme Wregis, you will of course enjoy every facility for urging your suit. I think I may safely assume that Beatrice meets with your approbation. I fancy she may fairly claim to hold her own with any girl in London.'

'Nobody can be blind for one moment to Miss Phillimore's beauty; but,' said Mr Pegram, toying nervously with his napkin, 'I don't quite see, my lord. I don't think I could venture –'

'You don't see, sir! you can't venture! What am I to understand by this, Mr Pegram?' inquired the Viscount in his stateliest manner.

'Don't misunderstand me, pray don't misunderstand me, my lord,' continued the luckless Robert, making a positive ball of his napkin; 'but the fact is, I could not dare, I should never screw my courage up to ask Miss Phillimore to be my – my wife, unless your lordship would undertake to break the ice for me in some shape.'

The noble Viscount's brow cleared. That the ignoble race of Pegram should feel overwhelmed at the idea of allying itself with the blue blood of the Phillimores was all very right and proper, and just as it should be. If, for state purposes, that is, pecuniary consideration, such an alliance was necessary to the house of Lakington, it was well that their condescension should be thoroughly appreciated and acknowledged.

'Of course, my dear Pegram,' rejoined the Viscount with a bland smile, 'I shall arrange all the preliminaries for you. I am the last man in the world to brag on the score of family; but it would be affectation to pretend that it is not a great piece of condescension on my *part* to admit the pretensions of a new man like yourself to my daughter's hand. Your father has probably informed you that, if it were not for certain fortuitous pecuniary considerations, I should probably have declined such a proposal; but as it is so obviously to the interest of my daughter, whose happiness must ever be, of course, my first object in life, I will speak to Beatrice, and though of course I can put no constraint upon her inclinations, yet she is a good girl, who, I feel sure, will listen to her father's advice. She is a good and affectionate daughter, Pegram, and I feel satisfied that she will do her duty to – to her father. And now, unless you will have any more wine, we will join the ladies.'

Meanwhile upstairs in the drawing-room Mrs Lyme Wregis and Beatrice were duly discussing Mr Pegram.

'Well, Trixie, I pulled the string of the shower-bath with a vengeance when I alluded to the theatre before Mr Pegram,' said the old lady laughing; 'but I really was very thankful I did. It fidgeted me to death to see the poor man sitting there looking so exquisitely uncomfortable, and taking no part in the conversation. I, at all events, set his tongue going, and that was something. I declare, if your father had not told us he was the son of a gentleman of large property in Wales I should have put him down as a member of the theatrical profession.'

'I thought he was rather good fun, grandmamma; and I declare his imitation of Toole was very good, which we cannot usually say of gentlemen reproducing histrionic stars for our edification. It was a very lucky cast of yours, for I had quite exhausted my small stock of intelligence in trying to hit off a subject that he had something to say about. However, it did all very well as it was, though I fancy we should get a little too much of the footlights if we saw much of him, which is not likely.'

'It is very odd, my dear, how your father picked him up. I never heard him mention the name of Pegram amongst his friends, and Lakington was never the least reticent about talking about his friends and acquaintances. It is a somewhat remarkable name, one that I should hardly have forgot if I had ever heard it. Curious, too, his asking him to dinner.'

'Oh, I don't know, grandmamma,' replied Beatrice. 'Papa said, you know, that Mr Pegram's father had done him a service of some sort or other, and so I suppose he wanted to be civil to Mr Pegram; but I don't think papa quite hit it off, do you? If he had given him some dinner at his club, and then taken him to a theatre, I think Mr Pegram would have enjoyed himself; but taking him into society is, I fancy, rather a doubtful kindness.'

'Yes, poor man,' observed Mrs Lyme Wregis. 'He has evidently seen but little of the world, more especially our world. He was so very palpably on his best behaviour; so evidently afraid of saying or doing the wrong thing. Well, he ought by this to be convinced that we are not so very alarming.'

Here their conversation was interrupted by the entrance of the subject of it, followed by the Viscount. But Mr Robert Pegram was no bit reassured by his *tête-à-tête* with Lord Lakington, and seemed once more to be frozen up. He felt that he could not descant on theatrical topics the whole evening, and he literally could think of nothing else. The upsetting of a cup of tea over his legs tended still further to the confusion of his ideas. In spite of the efforts of his entertainers the conversation somewhat languished, as, when you can extract nothing but incoherent and monosyllabic replies, it is apt to do. However, no sooner had the clock marked ten than Mr Pegram pulled himself together and mustered sufficient courage to say 'Good night' in somewhat awkward fashion.

'A very nice, unassuming young man,' observed the Viscount patronizingly, as the door closed behind their guest. 'Heir to a very considerable property in Wales. Shy? yes; decidedly shy, and – ahem! – yes, wanting in polish. Still, the first is a fault on the right side, and the latter will improve.'

'Yes, papa, there is no doubt about his being decidedly shy,' laughed Beatrice. 'I declare if you called it "scared" I don't think you would have been far wrong. He looked, poor man, after he had upset that cup of tea, as if he thought grandmamma and I would beat him.'

Mr Robert Pegram, meanwhile, having lit a cigar, is indulging in reflections on the family he has just left as he makes his way up the Victoria Road. Relieved from the constraint of his high-bred hosts, his thoughts take shape in his own vernacular. 'As for the girl,' he muttered, 'by Jove! she is a screamer! I never saw such eyes and eyelashes; and as for her hand, why, she could never get her gloves small enough, I should think. But, unless her pompous old bloke of a father can tell me he has squared it for me, I shall never dare ask her to marry me.'

## CHAPTER ELEVEN

# THE VISCOUNT SPEAKS TO TRIXIE

Some four or five days had elapsed since Robert Pegram had made his first appearance in Victoria Road, and still Lord Lakington had not broken the intention of his being there to his daughter. It was not that the Viscount faltered the least in his purpose. He had reasoned himself quite comfortably into the idea that he was promoting his daughter's happiness by furthering this marriage, and still more clearly did he see that such an arrangement would ensure his own comfort for his lifetime; but yet, with all this, he felt a lurking suspicion that this marriage would be highly distasteful to Beatrice. He knew very well, although there were young ladies of tolerably level temperament who were quite content to leave all matrimonial arrangements in the hands of their friends, that Beatrice was not one of these. He was fond – yes, very fond – of his daughter; loved her, indeed, as much as was possible for a man of his selfish disposition to love anybody. Self-indulgent from his birth, yielding invariably to the whim or fancy of the hour from the day that he had become 'lord of himself, that heritage of woe', he had been assiduously cultivating the worship of self for now close upon fifty summers. Of all humanity's vices there are none to which we are so prone, and none which thrive so freely when fostered. Self-adoration of various kinds we are all given to. We pride ourselves on our appearance, on our talents, on our possessions, and in our selfishness feel unmitigated jealousy of being eclipsed on any one of these points. In the Viscount's case it took a more material form: Lord Lakington simply desired that neither his position nor his personal comforts should be interfered with; and that our personal comforts depend upon a tolerably well-filled pocket is, in the main, a fact past dispute. The more he thought over the situation the more convinced was Lord Lakington that it was positively essential to his position that this marriage should take place; and yet, plausibly as he might argue to himself that it would be a most advantageous match for Beatrice, he still had an uneasy sensation that Beatrice would not take that view of it. He knew that this thing had to be done; but he had an uncomfortable feeling that, for the first time in their lives, there was destined to be an unpleasantness between them. That the girl would dispute his dictum he had no fear. A few tears, girlish regrets, etc., were quite possible; young ladies will let their imaginations run riot, and picture ideal lovers as destined eventually to marry them; but that Beatrice would not eventually succumb dutifully to his decision he never doubted. Still it might be a disagreeable conversation. His lordship disliked rancorous dispute or argument, even with his friends. It was a ruffling of the rose-leaves, by no means in accord with his sybarite nature. Much more did he shrink from bringing tears to the eyes of his pretty Beatrice; but then his 'position' required it. Lord Lakington with positively empty pockets had been such a terrible anomaly in the London world, and more especially so to Lord Lakington himself. And yet nothing could be more natural to a man of his disposition than to put off such announcement to his daughter from day to day.

Mr Robert Pegram, in the mean while, had astonished the ladies not a little by calling twice. Once, of course, after dining at the house was easily understood; but a second visit a day or two after did puzzle them considerably. He had varied little from that first evening: had been awkward upon entering the room; had been evidently ill-at-ease until he had brought the conversation round to the playhouses, and then no 'theatrical weekly' could have been more fluent or more critical. Every now and then he would diverge into 'the stunning doings' at some music-hall, suddenly recollect he was talking to what he called 'real ladies, regular tip-toppers', and pull up abruptly, with evident signs of discomfort. But Beatrice, who had been infinitely amused with him, had drawn him out, and so smoothed over such little slips for him, that Mr Pegram had manifested open and unbounded admiration for that young lady; so much so, indeed, upon the second occasion, that after his departure Mrs Lyme Wregis had rallied her grand-daughter no little upon her conquest, to which Trixie had responded in a similar laughing fashion; and as they made no disguise of the subject before the Viscount, that nobleman felt still more inclined to postpone his inevitable disclosure.

Mr Pegram, in the mean while, felt delighted with the progress he conceived he was making. 'Why, she's a girl after my own heart, after all, bless'd if she isn't. She takes as much interest in theatricals as I do, and, if the old lady wasn't there, would appreciate a verse or two of "More or Less" as much as anybody else.'

But if Mr Robert was satisfied with the progress of things, his father was not. The old gentleman had an object in bringing things to a crisis as speedily as might be. He had no belief whatever in Bob's winning his bride quite so out of hand as suited his purpose. He did not doubt his son's powers of

117

fascination for a moment, only give him time. He honestly thought that most young ladies would yield to Bob's attentions in the end; but he argued, 'A girl likes to be courted, and it isn't to be expected a well-bred lass like this is going to knock under the minute a young fellow makes sheep-eyes at her, without she's made to understand it's a lot to her advantage to cut the sweethearting short. I wish this thing settled sharp, and I must give his lordship a jog about turning the family screw on. Why, I had to do it a trifle myself to Bob; and, now he's getting on so well with the young woman, it only wants that to settle it.'

The result of which reasoning was that the Viscount received a letter from the old lawyer to the effect that such an arrangement as this admitted of no delay, pointing out drily that people of great age rarely gave much notice of their departure; that, as a rule, they are ailing for two or three days, and then flickered peacefully out.

'I don't suppose, my lord, either your nominee or mine will differ from the ordinary run of such cases, and therefore, I say, let our agreement be either ratified at once, or else I shall cry off, and make the most of my chance of the "Great Tontine" as I best can elsewhere. I presume you have only to speak to your daughter to arrange the matter at once, as far as the engagement goes, and, believe me, the more speedily the wedding follows the better for both of us.'

The Viscount felt that this settled it; that the talk with Trixie was no longer to be delayed. Still, his manner betokened some slight embarrassment as, after reading that letter, he told Beatrice that he wished to see her in his study as he had something to say to her. He might wrap the thing up as he would; he might argue to himself that it was necessary that his position as Lord Lakington should be kept up; that Beatrice could hardly hope to make, in a pecuniary view, a better match; but, at the bottom of his heart, gloze it over as he might, he knew that he was about to sell his daughter for an annuity of four thousand a-year.

Though our specious sophistries fail to stifle the truth, we are rarely deterred from the course we have made up our minds to, but somewhat resemble the 'gourmet' who cannot refrain from a favourite dish, although he knows it will disagree with him.

'Well, papa,' exclaimed Trixie, laughing, as she seated herself in a low chair in the Viscount's study, 'what *have* I been doing? I do not think I have been what I used to call "sent for" since I was a little girl. Don't you remember that, when my offending got past endurance, and my poor governess could stand it no longer, I used to be informed that you wanted to see me in the study, and when it came to that, even I became afraid of the consequences? It was odd,' she continued, merrily, 'the effect that threat always had on my young imagination. On the few occasions it did occur it resulted in nothing but a grave lecture, but always left an impression on my mind that I had narrowly escaped unknown pains and penalties of the severest description, the only occasions upon which I ever recollect of being afraid of you, papa.'

The Viscount could not withstand a slight twinge as he listened to the girl's idle chatter. He had an undefined feeling that Beatrice was probably on the verge of the worst quarter of an hour she had ever yet passed in that room.

'What do you think of Mr Pegram?' he inquired.

'Mr Pegram!' she replied. 'He is a good-natured, funny little man, dreadfully afraid of grandmamma and me, whatever he may be of other ladies, and more theatrically insane than anybody I ever came across.'

'Yes, a very common hobby of young men. I had it to some slight extent myself in my early days. No great harm in it though, unless the disease gets to the height of taking a theatre, and that in the hands of an amateur generally means ruin; but he seems an amiable, good-natured sort of young fellow, and after a little polish will, I have no doubt, hold his own with most of the young ones about town.'

'I dare say,' replied Trixie vaguely, and marvelling much what in the world her father could mean by calling her into his study to discuss Mr Pegram.

'It is my duty, Beatrice, to lay before you a proposition on the part of Mr Pegram of the very greatest importance, not only to yourself, but to your whole family (the whole family being the Viscount Lakington). I must first call your attention to a subject which will doubtless seem absurd to a girl brought up as you have been, namely, to the fact that we live in a deplorably levelling age. That, as the butcher waxes fat – and butchers always do well, by the way – so does the baronet seem to waste. The land that the peer once looked upon as indubitably his own, the peasant, who ten years ago touched his hat to him, begins to conceive is his according to the law of Genesis; that is to say, whoever has possession of anything keeps it, with very little regard to what his title may be.

> "Those may take who have the power,
> And those may keep who can."

Primitive reasoning, my dear, but it strikes me we are fast lapsing back to first principles – community, socialism, and the rest; absurd as these so called civilizations have been shown from times immemorial. Well, we must go with the age, my dear, and the age points unmistakably to fusion. An empoverished aristocracy must be strengthened by alliance with the pluto-cracy, the Aryan must blend with the Semite; and, in short, there must be a general mixing, a sort of social salad, you understand, if society is still to continue.'

Trixie's face during this harangue was a study. She comprehended it not an iota further than a vague feeling that a proposition of some kind in connection with herself had been made to her father by Mr Pegram; but of what that was she had no conception, and, if truth must be told, rather fancied all this exordium bore reference to a box or tickets for some music-hall, which her father wished her to accept, although conscious it was not quite what the Honourable Beatrice Phillimore should be present at.

'Well, Beatrice,' continued the Viscount, 'it is needless to tell you that the Lakington coronet wants regilding. The moth is in our ermine, girl, and we have had to sell the precious stones in the circlet and replace them with paste. It rests with you to restore the family prestige. How? By marriage. The Scotch peerage are the shrewdest branch of our hierarchy, and invariably recuperate by judicious city connection. Mr Pegram, Beatrice, solicits the honour of your hand, and Mr Pegram, my dear –'

'Mr Pegram wants to marry me!' cried the girl, starting to her feet. 'Papa, you are joking, or else I would say at once, declined with thanks.'

'I am doing nothing of the sort, Beatrice,' replied the Viscount, huskily. 'I tell you, Mr Pegram places himself and fortune at your feet, and, in the interest of the house of Phillimore, it would be well if you could say yes.'

'You, papa, counsel me, Beatrice Phillimore, to wed a Mr Pegram, who is what? He can surely from his manner not be of the county families?'

'Perhaps not, my dear; but he represents something that ranks higher in this d—d democratic age – wealth!'

'But, papa, I do not look upon wealth as everything, and most especially when it comes to – to – to choosing a husband,' and here the girl blushed, and rather faltered in her speech. 'You would not wish me to marry a man I cannot love, simply because he is rich, surely.'

'My dear child, now please get all that fiddle-faddle about love in a cottage out of your head at once and for ever. I don't for one moment wish to force your inclinations, but, remember, people of position don't plunge into matrimony with the recklessness of the lower classes. We arrange such things, and expect there to be a sufficiency of income in the first place. The usual result of marriage is children. People of our class do not consider that they are entitled to leave their offspring to the care of Providence, or the parish.'

'But, papa, dear –'

'Excuse me, Trixie, I must request you to wait till you have heard all I have to say. I married your mother on this principle, and, I assure you during our brief wedded life we were quite as sincerely an attached couple as if our union had been the result of a love match. Had it been possible, as you may suppose, the son-in-law I would most gladly have welcomed would have been your cousin, who will wear the coronet after me.'

Poor Beatrice gazed at her father with speechless despair. Why was her marriage with Jack impossible?

'I should have been pleased to think that you would have been Lady Lakington in due course; but of course Jack must marry "money", and you, my dear, must do the same. Jack, poor fellow, is no more free to follow his fancy than I was, than you are. If, Trixie, our order has its privileges, it also has its duties.'

How was the girl to combat such a tissue of sophistry as this? She knew intuitively that her sire's whole argument was untrue, and yet she knew, false and worldly as such reasoning might be, that it was accepted as a necessity by a large proportion of those of her station. Still she was very earnest in her love for her cousin, and by no means to be persuaded to give him up in favour of Mr Pegram in such off-hand fashion as this.

'It may be as you say, papa,' she replied at length; 'and I can only say, if it is so, that those who do not boast of gentle blood are much to be envied by those who do; that the Smiths of this world are better off than the Phillimores, insomuch as they can wed those they love. But there is surely no necessity for my marrying at all; should I ever do so, it will be, you may rely upon it, with your approval; and in the meantime, I must ask you to tell Mr Pegram that I thank him for the honour he has done me, but must beg to decline.'

It was time to unmask the grand battery. The Viscount had judiciously crushed, as he thought, any *penchant* the girl might have for her cousin by demonstrating that Jack must marry 'money'. He had posed successfully as having sacrificed himself in like fashion for the propping up of the peerage to which he was born. No one had ever told Beatrice that her precious sire had run through every shilling of the Lakington lands in the days of his hot youth. Mrs Lyme Wregis had been loyal to her scapegrace son-in-law, and no word of his early iniquities had ever reached his daughter's ears. She believed implicitly that, as a needy nobleman, he married a great fortune, but that, in the vicissitudes of business, her mother's fortune was lost. She had also regarded her father as a man with whom the world had gone hard; who, by a judicious marriage, had retrieved the fallen fortunes of his house; and who, just as a great political career lay before him, had been ruined by the commercial disaster that had overwhelmed and killed her grandfather. She was passionately attached to him. Of a warm, impulsive nature, the loving some one was a necessity to her, and that, of course, meant loving them in her ardent, tempestuous fashion. Relatives on her mother's side she had none, and those of her father held rather aloof from the ruined gambler, who, in good sooth, had neglected them in the days of his opulence and splendour. So Beatrice concentrated all her affections on her father and grandmother, and latterly had admitted Jack Phillimore into that inner sanctuary, where, as has been the case from time immemorial, he speedily eclipsed the earlier gods. The other deities of the Pantheon are of small account when Cupid's winged shaft is fairly home in our heart.

'Beatrice,' replied the Viscount, after a short pause, 'it has become necessary that I should make you clearly understand the very painful situation in which I am placed. Fifteen, or even ten, years ago I was that most abject thing on earth – a pauper peer, shrinking from my fellows because I had not the wherewithal to associate with them. Nobody expected dinners from the ruined Lord Lakington, but they did expect that he should be decently gloved, and wear a hat that cast no shame upon those to whom it was lifted. I have known, Beatrice, what it was to scheme for my gloves, to reflect that trinkets were not a necessity, and might be profitably converted into boots or umbrellas; to walk, because I could not afford cabs, and was ashamed to be seen getting in or out of an omnibus. I declare I would sooner die than go through that grinding poverty again; and it rests with you to save me.'

'With me, papa!' faltered the girl, and her cheeks blanched as the words fell from her lips.

That her marriage with her cousin should be deemed impracticable was to be borne. It was an affair that of the future, but any engagement with Mr Pegram was not only distasteful, but imminently a thing of the present.

'Yes, Trixie. Listen to me: you and your grandmother think my improved circumstances of late are owing to my estates having what is termed come round; to mortgages having been paid off; to creditors having been appeased, &c. It is not so. I am as hopelessly ruined as I was when Thormanby won the Derby seventeen years ago, and your grandfather failed for over a million. What has kept me going has been simply the large interest I now derive from a lottery called the "Great Tontine". My dividend in that amounts at present to something like three thousand a-year;' and hereupon the Viscount proceeded to explain to his daughter the history of that quaint coquetry with fortune in which he had embarked in 1860. It took Beatrice some time before she understood the whole thing; but, as it gradually became clear to her, she positively sickened on recognizing how her father's future income depended upon her saying 'Yes' to Robert Pegram's suit. And he too was seeking her hand, not because he loved or admired her, but as a mere matter of expediency; because he would be, like her father, made certain of a moiety of this income during the Viscount's life, and would come into the whole of the property at his death.

'Let me think, papa, let me think!' she exclaimed, as she pushed back the dusky masses of hair from her temples. 'I must of course be a true daughter to you – anything rather than you should go through such humiliations again as you have told me of. My cheeks tingle even now at the bare recital of them; but oh, father dearest, I had dreamed of something so very different if ever I left you.'

'The illusions of our youth are rarely carried out, Trixie, and, believe me, it is best so. Young people invest the objects of their first fancy with all sorts of high-flown attributes that neither of them possess. He thinks her an angel, when she is only a rather pretty, frivolous, and not particularly good-tempered girl. She makes a hero of a rather stupid, commonplace young fellow who happens to dance well and talk nonsense fluently. Happiness in marriage is based, my dear, upon easy circumstances. Ample means soften the friction. In a well-appointed *ménage* diversity of taste and opinion are of little consequence; either can indulge their whims without annoying the other. But when the man must either smoke in the street or his wife's drawing-room, there being nowhere else; when her piano can be heard from garret to basement, and the dinner pervades the house from midday to midnight, believe me, love is wont to wear threadbare quicker than you think for.'

'For shame, papa,' cried Beatrice, springing to her feet. 'I'll not believe marriages are usually made in such sordid fashion, whatever my own lot may be. But I must have time; at present I am hardly able to realize what it is to give my hand to a man I don't love. Does grandmamma know of this?'

'No; nor must she. You know I love her dearly, that she's been the best of step-mothers, and that she and I have always been the best of friends; but, remember she is my nominee, Trixie; people do not like their near relatives speculating on their lives, and though it is her life, not her death, that I am interested in, I would not have her know of this for the world. Twenty years ago when I embarked in it I was thoughtless, and, though there is no harm in it, still you must promise me to preserve strict silence on the subject.'

'It shall be as you will, papa; but it would have comforted and strengthened me to talk the thing over with her, and she is so clever, and then she knows about me and –'

'You don't mean to tell me there is any nonsense between you and your cousin?' broke in the Viscount sharply. 'If he has entrapped a child like you into an engagement he has behaved infamously. He knows nothing can come of it; that he is as much bound to barter his prospective coronet for money as I was.'

'No, papa,' replied the girl sadly, 'there is no engagement between me and Jack; but I will leave you now. My head aches, and I must have a few hours to get used to the idea, if nothing more. I will let you know tomorrow whether I can marry Mr Pegram,' and so saying, Beatrice went out and fled to her room, that she might look this thing straight in the face. The first great calamity that had as yet darkened her young life, and one that she as yet could hardly realize.

## CHAPTER TWELVE

# THE SCENT GROWS COLD

'And you cannot carry it past Guildford?' said Mr Carbuckle, after a *tête-à-tête* dinner in his chambers with Ringwood. 'There the trail ends, and from that point Terence Finnigan disappears from mortal ken.'

'That is the state of the case,' replied his guest, somewhat gloomily, 'and where or how to make a fresh cast beats me. I told Greenway, our detective, to look in tonight; but he said in his last letter he could make nothing out of Guildford, though he had spent a week there, and meant giving it up in another day or so as mere waste of time and money.'

'Well, there is nothing for it but patience, though I begin to be sadly afraid Mr Finnigan has breathed his last just about the time when his life becomes extremely valuable.'

'Yes. I don't know what to think now; it may be so. Miss Chichester, as well as her aunt, seems desperately disappointed. They reckoned too much, I fear, on the new hand at the bellows, as I begin to think he did himself. At all events he feels pretty well beat now.'

'My dear Ringwood, you may rely upon the word of an old stager, all these sort of inquiries are very much like hunting on a bad-scenting day. Your hard-riding sportsmen vote it slow, and throw it up; but those enthusiasts who stick to the hounds are sometimes rewarded with a kill. Not particularly lively work no doubt, but interesting very to the inductive hound or inductive reasoner.'

'Neither Miss Mary nor Miss Caterham seem to appreciate the beauties of the chase,' rejoined Ringwood, laughing. 'The latter especially seems very anxious about it. Do you know, I think she is worrying herself a good deal about this business, and the old lady strikes me as not quite strong enough to stand such anxieties.'

'Oh, she has been delicate for some time. I must run down and take a look at my old friend. She has always worried a good deal about Mary's future, and I can fancy her getting into a state of feverish impatience over this business. She is passionately attached to the girl, who has always been to her as her own daughter, and whether she leaves her an heiress, or slenderly provided for, would naturally excite her a good deal, and excitement is not good for a rickety heart.'

'Miss Chichester deserves to be an heiress,' replied Ringwood emphatically, as he tossed off his claret. 'Here's her health, any way, though it is against my interest she should come into the "Great Tontine".'

'Holloa, treason in the camp; interest of plaintiff's counsel to lose her cause! What the devil do you mean?' inquired Mr Carbuckle. 'How can the girl's coming into a fortune hurt you?'

'In this way,' replied Ringwood: 'Mary Chichester is just the nicest girl I ever met. I could go very near falling in love with that girl; in fact, I wouldn't take my oath I've not already done so.'

'Well, my young friend, as at your time of life you're sure to fall in love with somebody, you ought to be devoutly thankful that you have committed that indiscretion in a quarter where it will possibly cease to be such. You cannot marry without money, and therefore are restricted in your affections to monied young ladies. Years hence we'll trust you will be able to do as you like on that point.'

'Pooh! you don't see it, Carbuckle. Of course, if she turned out an heiress I couldn't ask her to marry me till I had a fair practice, and in the mean while she would have married some other fellow.'

'I deny both assertions. I have known Mary Chichester from a child, and she will marry to please herself, whether she's rich or poor. She's as fearless, self-reliant a young lady as ever I came across. Grit to the backbone, but a woman to her heart's core. If you can win her she'll prove worth having, and help you up the ladder in such fashion as you little dream of, whether she come to you with gold galore, or only her bonnie face for her fortune. But, good lord, who ever heard of a Queen's Counsel fostering a love affair! and d—n it, sir, what do you, as an ambitious barrister, mean by dreaming of such rubbish? Let us have either a good dive into Blackstone, or – or – a cigar,' concluded Mr Carbuckle, as his eyes twinkled with laughter. 'The case can stand over to the next term I fancy. I don't know, though, it seems rather a bad case.'

Here a knock at the door cut the thread of their conversation, and, in answer to Carbuckle's mandate to come in, a little wizened, rat-like man insinuated (there is no other word for it) himself into the room. He did not walk in, step in, or come in; he seemed to wriggle in, as if deprecating objection at every step; he seemed to acknowledge that he had arrived under protest, and not in accordance with the fitness of things. He had a shy, nervous manner, that indicated doubt in his mind as to his right to be anywhere. The last man in the world you would have picked out for a

THE GREAT TONTINE

detective, and yet he was reputed clever in the Private Inquiry Office, to which he belonged; and it was to these somewhat amateur and unscrupulous halls of inquisition that both Ringwood and the Pegrams were driven, Scotland Yard not recognizing interference unless for the unmasking of accredited crime. Lost heirs, relations, and property would cost the State a considerable annual outlay if they took such researches upon themselves, to say nothing of the amount of fabulous inquiry they might find themselves committed to.

'Well, Greenway, anything fresh? Mr Carbuckle, our host,' – and here Ringwood duly designated the QC, – 'will, I am sure, permit you to take a chair.'

'No, sir; nothing,' remarked Mr Greenway, as he seated himself on the extreme edge of a chair near the door, deposited his hat underneath, and, in the words of the famous Mr Lamps of Mugby Junction, 'took a rounder'. 'Leastways, sir, nothing that bears upon Terence Finnigan more than I have told you; but I have found out not only another man who is on the same business, but a couple.'

'Indeed!' exclaimed Carbuckle. 'This grows interesting; tell us all about it.'

'Well, gentlemen, Guildford ain't a very big place, and it wasn't long before I discovered that there had been a chap before me making inquiries after this Terence Finnigan. It was only natural it should be so. You may be sure I wasn't very long before I managed to get sight of him. Easy for me, you see, because I of course represented him as my pal, and was directed straight where to find him in consequence. Once I had one good look at him, I took train for Aldershot; returning next day in a new name, a new make up, and putting up at a new public. I could make nothing myself out of Finnigan, but it struck me as well worth while to watch those who were employed on my own errand. If they found him, so should I. At all events you had told me, Mr Ringwood, there was another lot in the hunt, and that a look at their hand was worth having. Well, sir, of course for looking round the sort of publics and lodging-houses where one was likely to pick up news of a man like Finnigan, one personates rustic life a bit. I began as a pedlar. You see a pedlar gets in anywhere, and can hook in any amount of questions without attracting attention. T'other fellow was got up as a navvy in search of work, but of course, as I had heard about him, so would he probably hear about me; so, as I said, I nips back to Aldershot, and come back as an organ-grinder – a good character, sir, in our profession. You see you've "no English" when questions are inconvenient, and can always put 'em when it's safe, and servant girls are death upon gossiping with organs. Blessed if I don't think they have a hazy idea it's like being hand-and-glove with some of the real

127

opera swells. To pick up my friend the swarthy navigator, and see what he was about, didn't take much doing. He's rather mistaken his profession, and likely to cost his employers a good bit more than he's worth.' (Mr Greenway had all the jealousy essential to the artistic character.) 'Well, he wasn't doing much, and hardly worth while keeping an eye on. I was about to give him up when, hang me, if he wasn't joined one evening by a pal – no mistake about it from their greeting – a red-headed waggoner apparently, and it took me little time to twig he was also on the same lay. He was good, devilish good; not a flaw in his make up, nor manner, and he had sense enough to be sparing of his talk; but the fool forgot all about his hands. They'd never done farm work since he was born, no, nor any other work. This interested me, and I watched the pair close. In my assumed character, I had of course no difficulty in getting near 'em, and as, of course, they didn't believe I understood English, they were somewhat unguarded in their talk. Now, Mr Ringwood, this is for you to cypher out; the red-headed waggoner is unmistakably the master, the employer of the navigator, and he came down to look after things a bit himself.'

'Bob Pegram, by heaven!' exclaimed Ringwood.

'Well, sir, he is uncommon good for an amatoor,' rejoined Greenway; 'and d—mme, I believe he's worth two of the mutton-headed fellow he's employing. I stay'd there as long as he did, and meant to follow him wherever he went, but he slipped me next day. I believe he went back to town. Now, Mr Ringwood, may I ask who Mr Pegram is?'

'No harm in telling him, eh, Carbuckle?' inquired the young barrister.

'None whatever,' responded the QC. 'I dare say you could do with a glass of port after that long and exhaustive report of yours, Mr Greenway?'

As Mr Greenway not only replied he could, but demonstrated the truth of his assertion with wonderful facility, Mr Carbuckle silently replenished his glass, and Mr Greenway developed further capacity for dealing with that noble wine without its having any perceptible effect on his mental qualities.

'Mr Pegram and his son are the people who, like ourselves, are interested in finding Terence Finnigan. Solicitors by profession, it's their interest to find him *dead*, ours to find him alive; but we have a like interest in knowing what has become of him. I rather fancy it was young Mr Pegram – Mr Robert – you saw. He's theatrically inclined, I have heard, and has a taste for doing the detective I know. You remember his audacious imposition at Kew, Carbuckle?'

'Perfectly,' replied his host; 'and what is more, if Mr Robert Pegram is about to indulge in a series of these impersonations, I am not sure he wouldn't be better worth tracking than Finnigan.'

'Quite so, quite so,' exclaimed Ringwood, excitedly.

'If he finds Finnigan, we find him too; and,' he continued, lowering his voice so that Mr Greenway might not catch what he said, 'if my conjecture that they mean foul play prove right, we shall be behind the scenes to some extent.'

'Yes,' replied Carbuckle, musingly; 'and though I do not think they would risk a fraud, still I have seen too much unsuspected crime divulged in my time to ignore it being quite possible. From what you learnt of the Pegrams in Wales, I should fancy they would be rather slippery cards to lay hold of in that case. A sharp attorney knows just what he may risk without rendering himself liable to be called on to account for his misdeeds. By the way, have you ever seen Mr Hemmingby again? That man interested me from what you told me of him, and, moreover, from his knowledge of these Pegrams and their doings, it is likely he might sooner or later prove a most invaluable person to consult.'

'Yes, I have seen him two or three times. No, not concerning the concoction of a play, as I see you are about to suggest,' added Ringwood laughing; 'and yet, oddly enough, I was of use to him and a Mr Barrington about one. It was a point of law on which a piece was to turn, and they appealed to me. They had got into a jumble about it, and I put them straight, and, they were kind enough to say, improved the situation immensely. Bless you, sir, Hemmingby appointed me solicitor-general of the "Vivacity" Theatre, and asked me to dinner.'

'It's all over with him,' said Carbuckle in an abstracted manner. 'He's developing what are termed dramatic instincts. An inclination to love in a cottage, to look at his cases from a sensational point of view, and to become a lawyer of the play-houses. You don't suppose if you commit yourself by writing a farce, that any attorney will ever entrust you with a brief afterwards, even if the farce is d—d, do you?'

'Never fear, I'm not going to take to play-writing as a trade,' replied Ringwood laughing; 'but about our friend here. What instructions shall we give him? I'd say, watch young Pegram, and never mind the other fellow.'

'Except that watching the other fellow strikes me as the best way of keeping an eye on Pegram. I think Mr Greenway had best return to Guildford, and not let Mr Pegram slip him next time. Remember, we don't expect you to lose sight of him on his next appearance.'

'He'll not give me the slip next time, gentlemen. He wouldn't this, if I hadn't made sure he was settled down for two or three days. Good night, sir. I'll go back to Guildford the first thing tomorrow morning,' and with that the detective took his departure.

'And, now Monsieur le Monchard has taken his departure, if you won't think it an impertinence from an old friend, may I ask if you have any reason to think Mary Chichester likely to lend a favourable ear to your wooing?'

'None whatever,' rejoined Ringwood quickly. 'Miss Chichester and I are good friends, nothing more. I am dreadfully conscious of only wishing we were more; but I have no grounds for supposing that she views me in any other light than a gentleman bearing a good character from yourself, and who, having at present no employment, is anxious to kill his spare time by undertaking the discovery of Terence Finnigan. Miss Caterham thinks better of me than I deserve, and I will tell you why. She did me injustice to start with in taking me for an impostor; she naturally wants to make it up to me. Women usually do; it's a species of injustice they are much more sensitive to than men. A man will misunderstand you for half a lifetime, and vote it all due to your own confounded conceit, or shyness, or what not, and feel, if anything, a little indignant with you about it all. It is true the woman's good opinion is likely to be evanescent, while the man's will probably last; however, such is the case.'

'Yes; and, my dear Ronald, recollect when young gentlemen like you begin moralizing on human nature men of my time of life vote the conversation somewhat flat and uninteresting. Smoke and liquor as long as you like, but I am going to tackle those fifteen or twenty sheets of parchment there, upon which I have to display much intelligence at Westminster tomorrow.'

'Goth, barbarian, unfeeling monster; and I was about to unburden my lacerated heart to your unsympathetic ears.'

'You'll do,' replied Mr Carbuckle, drily. 'A man who can neglect a fair opportunity such as I gave you to pour forth his love tale, and then make a jest of his hopes and fears, has not scorched his wings much. Only one thing, Ronald, remember this, if you try to make a fool of Mary Chichester you'll probably find yourself the bigger sufferer in the first place, and I will never forgive you, in the second. Money or no money, that girl's worth any man's winning.'

'My dear Carbuckle, for God's sake do not misunderstand me! I know it, recognize it as thoroughly as yourself. I am half in love with her now. I only want the slightest encouragement on her part to be as far gone as a man can be, and have cruel misgivings it will never be accorded me. Pray don't think I wish to make a jest of my devotion to Miss Chichester; there's very little inclination on my part to jest about it, I assure you, although I did not want to bore you with the old old story.'

'All right, Ronald; I'm very glad I was mistaken, and admit I ought to have known you better. Now, either smoke silently or run away; I really must tackle my friend here,' and Carbuckle seated himself at his table.

'Good night,' replied Ringwood; 'I'll leave you to your own devices, or to worrying that bundle of sheets, and can only wish I had a similar job waiting me at home.'

## CHAPTER THIRTEEN

## RINGWOOD REPORTS PROGRESS AT KEW

Ronald Ringwood felt it imperative that he should run down to Kew and report progress to Miss Caterham. It was astonishing how punctilious he was about this, and the two ladies invariably welcomed him cordially, albeit they admitted after, his budget being duly unfolded, he had taken his departure, that the search for Terence Finnigan did not seem to make more progress than before. Still it is comforting to talk our affairs over with those who may be acting for us without reference to waste of time. Managers of theatres, publishers, and lawyers, as a rule, have bitter experience of this phase of humanity; aspiring dramatists, would-be authors, and anxious clients are ever keen to discuss their play, book, or case with those in charge of the same, and cannot understand that this all-important business to them is but a small item in the life of the manager, publisher, or solicitor.

A busy man like Mr Carbuckle could not possibly afford time for idle discussion. His visits at the cottage were rare nowadays, and usually made upon a Sunday. His avocations mercifully excused him from the cruel tax of idle calls, and when he came it was either to see his old friend, Miss Caterham, or because he had some news to tell. With Ringwood the case was different: he had plenty of leisure, and the ladies derived much satisfaction from talking over even the *non*-progress of the search for Terence Finnigan. They liked the young man for his own sake, and he gave them always, so to speak, glimpses of that great world which they lived so near, but of which they saw so little. Miss Caterham had mixed freely in it in her time, and it amused her to hear of its gay doings even yet.

Ronald Ringwood, of course, saw much of Mary Chichester under these circumstances, and the more he saw the more smitten did he become. He told the honest truth to Carbuckle when he said that he only wanted a little bit of encouragement from Miss Mary to be over head and ears in love with her; but he could not delude himself with the idea that she had ever given him reason to suppose she favoured him in that light. She treated him always in that free, frank fashion that the veriest neophyte can never mistake for love.

Unfeignedly glad to see him when he came, and unmistakably anxious to make his visit pleasant to him; but the firm clasp of the hand that gave him good-bye, and the smiling, unflinching glance of the clear, honest, brown eyes testified to the girl's heart not being as yet in accord with his coming or going.

A girl worth winning, too, is Mary Chichester, but, like most prizes of this world, by no means to be gathered at the first rude snatch. A tall, shapely maiden, with a superb, though by no means fragile figure. I must admit that neither hand nor foot could be called small, but they might have served as models for a sculptor in spite of their being of no Lilliputian proportions. If not exactly a beauty, she had a wonderfully winning face, which her wealth of brown hair and big, serious, brown eyes could not but render attractive. Critics might call the mouth a trifle large, but the ripe red lips and level white teeth more than covered this defect when she smiled, and that charm was enhanced by some little rarity. Miss Chichester was by no means one of those young ladies who abandon themselves to hysterical laughter on the slightest provocation, or who are wreathed in smiles at the remark that it is a fine day.

Mary, at all events, looks very handsome in Ronald Ringwood's eyes as she holds out her hand to him among the flower-beds as he enters the little garden that fronts Miss Caterham's cottage.

'Well,' she says gaily, 'to ask if you have found Terence would be too much, but I trust you bring substantial hopes of doing so. I cannot understand it: aunt has taken to worrying so over the business of late that I really do hope you have tidings of some sort with which to soothe her. She is making herself quite ill; she, who always took things so quietly, to be so disturbed about the fate of that poor "ne'er-do-weel", it puzzles me, Mr Ringwood.'

'I have news this time, Miss Chichester,' replied Ronald, as he shook hands. 'Not such news as I fear your aunt craves for, but still an incident in the chase which must certainly interest her and, I think, you. It may mean much, or it may mean little. The sequel will show; but it might be the clue to the man we seek.'

'What is it, Mr Ringwood? you have never yet had so much to tell us.'

'Had we not better go inside and see Miss Caterham? I must tell the story to her, and it would be too cruel to bore you with the whole thing over again.'

'Prettily put, sir,' rejoined Mary, laughing. 'Here you are in dread that your ignorance of floriculture may be exposed, while there you know your liking for tea and thin bread and butter will be appeased. But come inside, and I will minister myself to the harbinger of good news. It is quite tea-time, so please don't apologize,' and with that Miss Mary led the way to the house.

'I don't know about good news,' said Ringwood. 'It can hardly be called that; still, it is likely to help us in our search, and is, at all events, a curious discovery.'

'Mr Ringwood, Auntie, with a budget of intelligence for you which I am dying to hear; but he will divulge it to no one but yourself, though I *am* to be allowed to listen.'

Miss Caterham rose to receive her visitor, but her cheeks slightly flushed, and she was evidently somewhat fluttered at the idea that Finnigan was either discovered or in a fair way to be so.

Ringwood saw the eager look upon her face, and replied to it as he shook hands.

'News I have certainly for you, but Miss Chichester rather exaggerates its importance; it is singular, but may lead to nothing. Mr Pegram is taking a very active part in this search for Finnigan.'

And then Ringwood went on to narrate Greenway's story, and told of the disguised waggoner, whose hands betrayed him. But there was one thing he had not sufficiently borne in mind, namely, that this was just the kind of intelligence to arouse all Miss Caterham's morbid terror of finding herself involved in a great criminal trial. The good lady, indeed, showed her agitation so visibly that Mary Chichester signed to him to curtail his narrative as much as possible, and, in obedience to the hint, the barrister somewhat abruptly made an end of his story.

'Pray don't look so scared, Auntie,' exclaimed the young lady as she moved to a low chair by Miss Caterham's side, and possessed herself of one of her hands. 'There is surely nothing to be frightened about because this Mr Pegram, for some mysterious reason, seems as anxious to find poor Terence as we are.'

'You can't understand. You do not see what this may lead to,' exclaimed Miss Caterham nervously.

'What can it lead to? Surely nothing can come of it further than Mr Pegram finding Terence, in which case we shall probably find him too: at least, you think so, Mr Ringwood, do you not?' and the question was put with such evident intention that he should follow her lead that the barrister replied quickly,

'That is my belief, Miss Chichester, or, at the worst, discover he will never be found more in this world.'

'It is too terrible. I shall never be able to face it if my fears are realized. I wish I had never embarked in the thing, I am sure,' quavered Miss Caterham.

'There is really no foundation for your apprehensions at present,' interposed the barrister. 'I can assure you, my dear madam, I am not misleading you. I know of course what you fear; but, so far, at all events, your fears are groundless.'

'But do you believe they will continue groundless should the wretches find poor Terence?' exclaimed Miss Caterham in a voice raised to an unnatural pitch. 'You know the temptation, and it is I, miserable that I am, who am responsible for it. But for me the sleuth-hounds would not be on the unhappy man's track. Heaven grant they may never discover him.'

Ringwood could of course understand the workings of Miss Caterham's mind, although, had he any idea that her morbid fears had taken such entire possession of her, he would have been much more reticent concerning Mr Pegram's movements.

But to Mary Chichester this was all incomprehensible. She understood only that her aunt was getting on the verge of hysterics and the dread of some unknown catastrophe taking place, and waxing somewhat melodramatic in her language. People under strong excitement drop conventional dialogue, and express themselves with rather great coarseness, or in rather elevated words, according to their gifts.

'I don't think I can talk any more on this subject today; it makes me so dreadfully nervous,' said Miss Caterham, at length. 'I think I will go and lie down for a little while, and leave Mary to entertain you, Mr Ringwood,' and so saying the old lady walked towards the door.

'It would have been better, perhaps, had I not mentioned Mr Pegram's masquerade; but I thought, Miss Caterham, it would only amuse you; and then I know you like to be informed of how our search progresses,' said Ringwood.

'Yes; you must continue to inform me of everything; and remember, I trust to you that Mr Pegram is closely watched. It may be possible to prevent —' and here the good lady stopped abruptly in her speech, and bade him good-bye.

'Now, Mr Ringwood, am I to be made acquainted with this mystery or not? You see how it is with my aunt. As I told you before, she is fretting herself at some nameless terror. I am sure you were wrong to tell her as much as you did today.'

'I am afraid I was,' rejoined the barrister. 'I never thought it would agitate her in such fashion; but, Miss Chichester, as I said before, I am pledged to silence on the subject.'

'But surely there are circumstances that warrant the breaking of such a pledge. You must see for yourself that it is not good for my aunt to brood over this mystery; at all events, it is very plain to me. I care nothing about this secret as a secret, but I do care very much about Auntie's health; and if I could but talk this hobgoblin mystery over with her, I have little doubt of considerably dwarfing its proportions. It can be nothing very dreadful, I am sure, and it is only Aunt's nervousness makes her take the morbid view she doubtless does of it.'

'You are quite right; Miss Caterham is taking a very exaggerated view of things as far as I can guess; for, remember, I am, to some extent, in the dark about her thoughts.'

'And the terrible secret is –' interposed the young lady softly.

'Still to be a secret,' rejoined Ringwood, half-laughing.

Mary Chichester rose rather angrily from her chair. She was in little mood to forgive that half-laugh. She knew that her main motive for wishing to be made acquainted with this mystery was not mere womanly curiosity, but anxiety on account of her aunt's health. She was quite aware of Ringwood's devotion, and she had counted upon his telling her everything in reply to such an appeal as she had just made. Her aunt never had kept anything from her before, but, on the contrary, was wont to be open as day about all her own affairs, and had latterly taken counsel with Mary about divers little pecuniary arrangements, such as the investment of superfluous income, etc.

'Both you and Mr Carbuckle should have more discretion,' she replied, somewhat haughtily. 'If you had promised not to interfere between two people that had quarrelled, you would, I suppose, think yourselves bound to look on and see murder done.'

'That's putting rather a strong construction on the case,' rejoined Ringwood. 'You can hardly say Miss Caterham's life is endangered because she worries herself without cause. As for "the mystery", as you term it, I honestly think it would be better you should know it.'

'Then why don't you explain it to me?' retorted the young lady sharply.

'Miss Chichester, I am sure you would not think well of a man who broke his plighted word, and I should wish to stand well in your estimation. Allow me to put an extreme case in my turn. Suppose I was pledged to marry a girl, what should you think of me if I broke my troth?'

'Mr Ringwood, that is a very different thing. Oh, these lawyers, these lawyers, they are not to be argued with,' she continued, laughing. 'I'll have no more to say to *you*, but tell Mr Carbuckle I want to see him, and he'll find I have a good deal to say when I do see him.'

'But I may come down and tell you how things progress,' said Ringwood, who had risen from his seat and was handling his hat in somewhat irresolute manner, rather hoping to be asked to sit down again, or to look at the flowers, in short, invited to prolong his visit in some shape.

'No, Mr Ringwood, I'll have no half-confidences; henceforth make your reports to my aunt. I decline to hear anything more about the matter.'

'But surely you will give me the benefit of your advice about whether it will be judicious to impart such news as I may have to Miss Caterham.'

'I must decline to offer advice about a subject I do not in the least understand. Whenever you and Mr Carbuckle should think me fit to be trusted with this momentous secret, for my aunt's sake I will hear what you have to say. In the meantime I must go and look after her, so you will excuse me if I say good-bye.'

'Confound the "Great Tontine", Terence Finnigan, and the whole concern,' muttered Ringwood, as he made his way back to the railway station. 'I wish to heavens I had never taken the thing up. No, I don't; for it's a most interesting case, and I should never have known the nicest girl in England if I had not embarked in it. However, I am in a devil of a mess now; she's evidently real angry at not being taken into our confidence, and very naturally so. Still, what can I do? Of course the gipsy knows I'm in love with her, and deems that quite sufficient reason for breaking my word, committing perjury, or any other crime she may bid me perpetrate. It is odd women are keenly alive to such iniquity committed for another, but done to serve themselves they see no harm in it.'

CHAPTER FOURTEEN

# THE ANNOUNCEMENT OF TRIXIE'S MARRIAGE

Although the Viscount has wrung Trixie's consent to this marriage, he does not feel at all comfortable on the subject. Gloss over the thing speciously as he may, magnify its advantages to the very limit of his imagination, there is no getting over the fact that, at his bidding, his sweet Beatrice is going to marry a man socially far beneath her. Lord Lakington feels an unpleasant twinge every now and then, when the thought suggests itself of what he would have said to a country attorney who had presumed to aspire to the hand of the Honourable Beatrice Phillimore a few years back. What, indeed, had he said in the present case when Pegram senior had first ventured to broach the scheme to him? But the prospect of lapsing again into that state of grinding poverty from which the 'Great Tontine' had rescued him was too terrible to allow him to hesitate about gulping down all scruples that might remain to him on the subject of caste, and the Viscount was, in reality, of a most Brahminical way of thinking on that point.

Another thing, too, that he did not quite relish the idea of was the breaking the news of Beatrice's engagement to Mrs Lyme Wregis. That lady must, of course, be told at once, and though the Viscount and his mother-in-law were on the best of terms, yet he felt they would differ on this subject. He might give as plausible an account as he pleased of the bridegroom, represent him as the son of a gentleman of large property in Wales, etc.; but he knew that he should never blind Mrs Lyme Wregis to the fact that, whatever money Robert Pegram might have, he had never lived in good society. He had a strong suspicion, too, that the old lady had her own views about Trixie, and was disposed – and the Viscount always experienced a little irritation when he thought of it – to foster some nonsense between the girl and her cousin, Jack Phillimore.

'Rubbish!' he would mutter; 'as if they could ever muster up a sufficient income to marry on.' He forgot that his daughter had been brought up very differently from himself; that Trixie could remember none of the Lyme Wregis splendour, nor had she ever set eyes on Laketon, the seat of the

Phillimores, and from which, indeed, they took their title. Beatrice had only known the comfortable but modest home which her grandmother could give her – salvage from the wreck of the great financial argosy which its captain had so suddenly abandoned – so that the girl was moderate in her requirements and ideas of essentials.

As Lord Lakington leisurely ascended the stairs to the drawing-room the day after Trixie had yielded her assent to this marriage, he was conscious of a feeling of embarrassment that he had never experienced when making confession of his iniquities to his mother-in-law, and there had been a time when he had to plead guilty to a very labyrinth of pecuniary entanglements; but he had a conviction that Mrs Lyme Wregis would regard this in a much less lenient light than all the extravagances and money-scrapes of by-gone years. Plausible as the story was that he had to tell, yet he knew it would hardly impose upon Mrs Lyme Wregis; and his own selfish interest in the arrangement he did not dare confide to the straight-forward old lady. However, it had to be done, and he had told Trixie that if she would keep out of the way for the half-hour before lunch he would do it then.

'I am glad to find you alone, madam,' said the Viscount, 'as I have something rather particular to say to you.'

'What has gone wrong now?' inquired Mrs Lyme Wregis quickly. 'Surely, Lakington, you have not been doing anything foolish after all your bitter experience?'

'No,' replied the Viscount; 'I burnt my fingers rather too sharply in my day to venture near fire again. No; this concerns Beatrice.'

'Ah! she has told you about her invitation. I knew you would be pleased. It will be such a nice change for her.'

'You are quite right; I am pleased, and trust it will be a nice as well as a great change for her. It is, at all events, one young ladies are usually not averse to try sooner or later.'

'I don't understand you, Lakington.'

'I dare say not,' he rejoined, quietly. 'I don't think we are talking about quite the same invitation. Do you think you have quite shaken your cold off?'

'Stuff and nonsense! I never had a cold. It was all your imagination. You always do so fidget about my health.'

'Of course I do; so I do about my own and Trixie's. It's a most invaluable blessing, and not to be lightly tampered with.'

'Well, spare me a sanitary lecture now, and tell me all about Trixie's invitation; for, of course, you don't mean the Meynards'.'

'No; but you must be prepared to be a little astonished, although I don't know, you women see these things so much before we do that it may be no news to you, but only what you expected.'

'Lakington,' said the old lady, laughing, 'I declare if you don't stop wandering in your speech, for all the world as if you belonged to the Lower House, I'll have a fit.'

'That's where it is,' interposed the Viscount; 'can't you be surprised without being agitated?'

'I don't know about that,' rejoined Mrs Lyme Wregis; 'but I'll tell you what, my Lord, I can't get angry without being strongly moved.'

The Viscount knew this was true, and that the old lady would be tempestuous when put out.

'The invitation I am alluding to,' he said, speaking slowly, as a man dubious of what reception his speech might meet, 'is a proposal of marriage.'

'What?' cried his mother-in-law; 'so soon? She is winsome enough, goodness knows, though

"She's less o' a bride than a bairn."

I thought of her still as the bride in the old ballad. But who is it wants to marry the child?'

'That Mr Pegram, whom we have been entertaining of late. He's heir to a rattling good property, you know, down in Wales,' continued the Viscount rather hurriedly.

'That may be; but you don't mean to tell me that he's of good family, in fact, that he's fit to wed a Phillimore. You don't mean to say that you are pleased with this, Lakington?'

'I consider it a very good match for a portionless girl,' retorted the Viscount. 'They will have four thousand a-year to begin with, and nearly double that to come to them eventually. Neither good looks nor the blood of all the Phillimores are of much account without money. No one ought to be a better judge of that than myself,' and the naïveté with which it was said completely did away with any conceit there might be in the remark.

Mrs Lyme Wregis was quite willing to admit that she was a nobody herself, but she was keenly alive to her connection with 'blue blood'. The proudest Phillimore that ever stepped was not so jealous on the score of their race as she; and the idea of a mésalliance for her granddaughter, however gilded, was extremely repugnant to her. Till now she had looked upon it that the Viscount thoroughly agreed with her upon this point. Now she hardly knew what to think.

'And Beatrice, have you told her of the honour that has been vouchsafed her?' inquired the old lady, bitterly.

'Yes; I have put it before her, and thought it right to point out all the advantages of the proposal to her.'

Mrs Lyme Wregis did not speak, but a half-smile, half-sneer wreathed her lips for a moment, which expressed the word 'humbug' pretty plainly. Lord Lakington saw it, and put the right interpretation upon it.

'It's a big match for her,' he continued. 'The fusion of classes goes on pretty rapidly in these days. Just look, by Jove! at the sort of fellows they get in Parliament now. Wealth marries rank, and *vice versa*. Trixie is a sensible girl, and quite willing to be guided by her father in this matter.'

'Why, you don't mean to say that Beatrice has consented to marry him?' cried Mrs Lyme Wregis in a half-scream.

'Certainly; I came here to tell you the news and receive your congratulations. So very nice for her, you know; four thousand a-year to start with, and most satisfactory prospects, I assure you,' replied the Viscount in his jauntiest manner.

'I can't congratulate you; I can't believe it. I know girls sell themselves for an establishment, of course, I have seen it scores of times; but not Trixie. I couldn't think it of her. Let me speak to her, Lakington, before she ties herself to life-long misery. You hardly guess her warm, passionate nature. Married to a man she neither loves nor respects, I should tremble for her future. As my poor husband used to say, you may buy money too dear, and, heaven knows, that was his own case.'

'Hush, my dear madam! you are agitating yourself in a manner that I am afraid you will suffer for later on. The idea of parting with Beatrice has upset you. We will talk of this again; in the meantime, no doubt, you will be glad of a quarter of an hour's quiet before luncheon.'

Mrs Lyme Wregis was indeed very much put out by the announcement of her granddaughter's engagement. It not only annoyed, but puzzled her not a little. She had thought she understood the Viscount's character pretty well, and his advocating this marriage was in distinct opposition to all his opinions and prejudices. She had helped to pet and pamper him ever since she gave him her daughter. She had always pleaded on his behalf during Mr Lyme Wregis's lifetime, when even that free-handed speculator had been inclined to expostulate at the Viscount's unconscionable tugs at his purse-strings. She had sedulously watched over his comfort in the modest home she had afforded him and Beatrice, and even brought the girl up to consider that his wish and welfare was the first thing to be thought of. She was not blind to the indolent selfishness of his nature, and was aware that he could be very indifferent as to who paid the piper for his pleasure. At the bottom of her heart she knew that, but for her own firmness, this petted son-in-law would have spent what was left to her on his prodigal self.

Mrs Lyme Wregis was a woman of scarce any kith or kin; at all events, none that she cared about. When the crash came the Viscount, who both liked and respected his mother-in-law, was very tender and attentive to her; that she should cling to him in her sorrow was but natural. Poor lady! she had so few to cling to just then. Of the many who had sat at her table, and lounged in her drawing-room, there were few who sought out the widow of the bankrupt suicide.

In these days of civilization and refinement we sigh over our ruined friends with the soup, grow pathetic over their misfortunes with the *entrées*, are full of hopeful schemes for their re-establishment with the roast, determine to find them out with the second course, and have forgot all about them by the time coffee makes its appearance.

But if there was one thing Mrs Lyme Wregis deemed she could count upon, it was the Viscount's pride of race and reverence for his order. That a Phillimore should condescend to take a bride from the plutocracy was fitting, he raised her to his station; but that a female scion of the house should wed beneath her was not to be compensated for by any amount of ingots. Failing to marry in their class, they were bound in honour to remain spinsters, or seek such equivalent for the cloister as their country afforded them. Yet here was Lakington actually advocating his daughter's marriage to the plebeian Pegram for money. What could it mean? Beatrice, too, a strikingly pretty girl, and only just eighteen! What was it possessed him? Why this hurry to get the child married before she was well out? That Beatrice would have consented to such a marriage except under great pressure the old lady knew was impossible; and yet what possible arguments could the Viscount have to advance that had so quickly overborne all remembrance of Jack? Two things were clear to Mrs Lyme Wregis – that she must have a confidential talk with her granddaughter as soon as might be; and that this marriage must be delayed to the extent of her ability.

There was no flavour of wedding bells about that luncheon party. Trixie, pale and silent, scarce raised her eyes from her plate, and ate next to nothing. She knew that her grandmother was watching her, and mentally upbraiding her for her treason to Jack. She had no heart to take refuge in the sophistry that she was not engaged to him. Not in words, perhaps, but she was virtually. And what would Jack think of her when he heard how, a few weeks after he sailed, she had accepted the first man with money-bags she came across? What did her grandmother think of her? Well, her lips were sealed, they must think what they would; and, after all, if she must wed this man what did it matter?

Mrs Lyme Wregis saw clearly that Beatrice was very far from elated at her conquest. She might look somewhat pale; but there was a set expression about her mouth such as her grandmother had not seen there since the turbulent times of her childhood.

'Miss Trixie's bent on having her own way when she gets that look on her,' her old nurse used to say; and Mrs Lyme Wregis remembered that expression had ever been the herald of a fit of obstinacy, or rather, perhaps, resolute struggle for her own way. Little need for Trixie to struggle for that of late years, as both her grandmother and father indulged her to the top of her bent. She was, too, in the main, as reasonable as a young lady of eighteen can be expected.

Lord Lakington was quite conscious during the meal that the domestic circle was not in accord. He made conversation with a praiseworthy attempt to lighten things, and solaced himself for failure with an extra libation of brown sherry. He rather winced at his daughter's face, and wished this marriage could be averted; but when the remembrance of those days of impecuniosity came across him he shuddered, and felt that it behoved his daughter to sacrifice herself, and faltered no more in his purpose than Agamemnon.

'Now, Trixie, tell me all about it,' exclaimed Mrs Lyme Wregis, as soon as they found themselves in the drawing-room.

'I don't think I have anything to tell. Papa has no doubt told you that I am going to marry Mr Pegram.'

'Yes, child; but I want to hear your story. I have always pictured to myself your whispering the tale of your love into my ear, as your poor mother did before you. Surely you cannot pretend that you love this Mr Pegram?'

The tear-drops glittered for a moment in Beatrice's eyes; but she dashed them impatiently away, as with a forced laugh she replied –

'Love! No; as papa says, in our class that is the privilege of the wealthy. I shall have money, a great thing in these times, you know, grandmamma; a good deal in days to come, papa says. I must do as other girls do, marry some one who can keep me properly. I feel already that life is unendurable without a victoria and pair.'

'Trixie, darling, don't talk to me in that way. Come here, child, and tell me how it all came about.'

For a second the girl's face softened, and then the hard, resolute expression overspread it again.

'Oh, it was all very simple. It came off after the usual manner of such things, I imagine. Mr Pegram confided the state of his affections and annual income to papa, papa confided them to me, and expatiated considerably upon the latter. I was so struck with the latter that I felt a faint glow of inclination towards the proprietor, at all events, quite as much glow as was necessary under the circumstances, and murmured assent.'

'Don't talk in that unnatural way to me, child; please don't,' urged Mrs Lyme Wregis, softly. 'Let me see you your old self, Trixie, to the last, even if I am never to know how it all came about.'

'There it is, grandmamma; how should you understand it? You call me child; I am one no longer, but a fashionable young lady on the look-out for an establishment. We don't mind the prince being somewhat ugly and not particularly refined as long as his chariot-wheels are gilded, and the horses are up to the mark. Dowerless princesses, who haven't fairy godmothers, mustn't be particular, you know.'

'Oh, Trixie, darling, I am so very sorry for you,' said Mrs Lyme Wregis, sadly.

'Sorry, grandmamma! why you ought to be delighted to think that your troublesome charge has done so well for herself. Now I must run away and write to Lizzie Lester and Dot Newton, my two great school-friends, you know, and tell them all about it.'

Mrs Lyme Wregis made no answer; but her face was clouded with sorrow as she listened to Beatrice's miserable affectation of high spirits. She knew every inflexion of the girl's voice too well to be for a moment imposed upon.

Beatrice walked rapidly towards the door, then paused for a moment. Suddenly she turned round, dashed at her grandmother, threw her arms round her neck, and kissed her passionately; then quickly disengaging herself from the embrace in which the old lady strove to hold her, rushed from the room; and as the door closed behind her, Mrs Lyme Wregis felt hot tears on her cheek, which she knew were none of her shedding.

CHAPTER FIFTEEN

# MRS LYME WREGIS SUMMONS
# JACK PHILLIMORE TO THE FIELD

Mrs Lyme Wregis was indeed terribly put out at the intelligence of the proposed wedding. Since the catastrophe which had left her a widow, no such grave misfortune had befallen her. She had had little to trouble her in all these intermediate years. Her son-in-law had got into no fresh scrapes since that hopeless crash. Indeed, if he but abstain from felonious practices, it is not easy for the poor gentleman to get into such scrapes; while her granddaughter had been to her as the very apple of her eye. She was so fond, so proud of Beatrice – and she was a girl that those nearest and dearest to her might well be proud of. Bright, clever, and fairly accomplished, possessed of unusual personal attractions, and blessed with one of those sunny dispositions that go far to lighten a household, she was calculated to inspire warm affection in those around her. The attachment between Beatrice and her grandmother was strong, and the old lady, as we know, had indulged in a 'castle in the air' concerning her, which she believed based upon surer foundation than is usually vouchsafed to such shadowy edifices. The Viscount's announcement had ruthlessly shattered her pet scheme; and what had he proposed to substitute for it? Money! money! And who should know better what happiness wealth conferred than herself? Had she not been High-Priestess of Mammon, officiated at the altar of the golden calf? Money! Had she not seen men scheme, cringe, grovel for its possession? Who knew better than her how transitory was at times the possession of commercial wealth? and who knew better than her that, the golden dream once dissipated, those who but yesterday had fawned at your footstool held you in scant reverence? Who? What were these Pegrams? Fortunate traders, who, though now exulting over their honey, would probably find in the end that they had amassed their store for the benefit of others.

But the blue blood, that could never disappear. No one of the plutocracy that ever lived could more thoroughly have identified herself with the family with whom she had become connected than Mrs Lyme Wregis. She was more a Phillimore than any Phillimore of the race. And looking back with a somewhat good-natured cynicism upon the time when she had ruled as a queen of fashion, in virtue of her wealth, she mocked at such fleeting sceptre, and had changed her creed for belief in purity of blood, associated, if possible, with broad acres. But far above this whimsy on the old lady's part came her strong affection for her grandchild; and, whatever the girl might say, Mrs Lyme Wregis felt assured that this marriage would not be for her happiness. It was in vain she tried to talk it over with Beatrice. That young lady adhered rigidly to the *rôle* she had originally taken up: she declared herself to be of the world, worldly, and that the first thing a girl required in these days was an establishment, and that for a portionless miss to say 'No' to a man who offered her a house, carriages, and an opera-box, would be simply preposterous. But that such talk as this did not contain the girl's real sentiments Mrs Lyme Wregis was as convinced as she was of her own existence. Pierce the crust of cynicism in which it had pleased Beatrice to enshroud herself she could not, but that the girl was acting a part she was convinced. Again and again Trixie, after talking in her most bitterly worldly fashion, would suddenly clasp her grandmother round the neck, kiss her passionately, and dash from the room to give vent to, as her grandmother shrewdly guessed, a shower of tears.

With her father, of course, Beatrice had no reticence. She was very quiet, but very determined; and, indeed, rather astonished the Viscount by her plain-speaking.

'I will do this thing, papa,' she said, 'because I think it is right; because I think it my duty to prevent, if possible, your ever going through again the sordid troubles you before experienced. I don't wish for one moment to pass as a martyr, and of course I am not in the least insensible to the comforts of money and a good establishment; but, papa dear, I had planned a very different future for myself. No matter what; we will not touch upon it just now. I am changing all that – to some extent at all events – for your sake; and on my part I claim to be allowed to manage things in my own way. I must not see too much of Mr Pegram before this marriage. It will all come easier to me so, and I look to you to consult my wishes in that respect.'

'Certainly, my dear,' replied the Viscount; 'nothing will be easier. Pegram told me only yesterday that it was absolutely necessary that he should go down to Wales on business, which he said he was afraid would detain him some days. But you are aware, Beatrice, that there are strong reasons why there should be no unnecessary delay about your marriage; in fact, the Pegrams are very urgent on that point, and I have promised young Pegram that the week, if not the precise day, should be at all events fixed before he leaves town.'

'I will give you a definite answer tomorrow morning,' she replied.

'Thanks, darling; and yet, Beatrice, if this marriage is really repugnant to your feelings, never mind me, break it off at once. I seek only your happiness. I have known what it is to be miserably poor, and can endure it once more, though as one gets older it becomes doubtless harder to bear; but do not think of me. Of course there are girls who would jump at your prospects, and worldly people would say that I was mad not to use all my influence in Pegram's favour; but still, if you —'

'Hush, hush, papa,' she exclaimed, quickly interrupting him, for his speech was torture to her. 'All that is already settled; we will speak of this matter no more than is absolutely necessary. When I have settled the day there will surely be nothing else that need be discussed between us.'

She could no longer blind herself to the ingrained selfishness of her father's character. The sophistry with which he sought to gloss over the fact that she was sacrificing herself for his sake was too transparent. It wounded her deeply. That the father she had so adored all her life, and had looked upon as the incarnation of a gallant, high-bred gentleman, should be, after all, such a pitiful creature! She strove hard, even yet, to remain blind to his real character, but it was impossible to cheat herself into the belief of a few days back – to wit, that her father would make any sacrifice for her sake. She knew that was not so now, and knew, moreover, that he had small scruple about sacrificing her for himself. She never dreamt of blenching from this marriage. That she could assure her father's comfort for the remainder of his life by these means, and no other, seemed quite sufficient warrant that she should accept Pegram; but that the father of her imagination should be so far removed from the father of reality was sore grief to her. Poor Trixie, moreover, was doomed to confine her troubles to her own breast. It would have been so much easier, she thought, if she could have a good cry upon her grandmother's neck, and explain to her the reasons of her conduct; but it was impossible to do that without betraying the story of the 'Great Tontine', and that she had promised her father not to do.

Mrs Lyme Wregis, meanwhile, was more worried about this affair than about anything that had happened to her for many years. In spite of her age, her wits were as keen as ever they were, and the old lady felt sure that nothing but misery could come of this marriage. She knew that Beatrice would be marrying one man while in love with another – a dangerous experiment at all times – and she felt instinctively that there was some hidden motive which prompted, what she haughtily termed, this 'unnatural alliance'. To penetrate this secret she made now the object of her life; but, in spite of more than one cleverly-laid trap, both for the Viscount and her granddaughter, the days ran by, and she discovered nothing.

Lord Lakington and Beatrice adhered rigidly to their original argument, that the penniless daughter of a broken peer, in common prudence, was bound to accept the hand of the first gentleman who offered her such a home as her birth entitled her to. In vain did Mrs Lyme Wregis ejaculate 'gentleman' in tones of sarcastic interrogatory. The Viscount answered a little sharply, that if Mr Pegram lacked the polish of a man habituated to the world, that was simply the drawback of his provincial career; while Beatrice checked her with a grave, 'You forget, grandmamma, that I have promised to marry this man.'

Still, Mrs Lyme Wregis returned to the charge with all a woman's pertinacity; but when her trump card failed her, Mrs Lyme Wregis was fain to admit that she had lost the game.

It was in this wise. She found Beatrice one afternoon in that softer mood, now so rare with the girl. This was the opportunity for which the old lady had long waited. In a low voice she began to talk of Jack Phillimore, to wonder how he was getting on, to expatiate on his good qualities, on his good looks, and what a thorough, honest, straightforward young fellow he was, and how fortunate the girl might consider herself who acquired him for a husband. Beatrice, seated on a low stool at her grandmother's feet, leaning her arm lightly on the old lady's knee, a pet attitude of hers, listened with slightly flushed cheeks to the eulogium; and presently Mrs Lyme Wregis, who was scrutinizing the girl keenly through her spectacles, saw that her eyelashes were wet. It was the opportunity for which she had waited. Suddenly changing her tone, she exclaimed, with a light mocking laugh,

'And, poor fool, he thought you loved him.'

'He is no fool,' cried the girl sharply, throwing back her head, while her cheeks flushed and her eyes sparkled. 'I did love him, I do love him; but I am not going to marry him, for all that.'

'Do you think it was fair, Trixie,' changing her tones once more to those of gentle remonstrance, 'to lead him to love you, having those intentions?'

'Why not?' she replied. '"They loved and parted" is, I suppose, the epitaph of many a flirtation. There was no engagement between us, grand-mamma, as nobody should know better than yourself. But for you it is quite possible there might have been.'

'And I am most heartily sorry that I interfered to prevent it. If I had not made that mistake things might have been different now, eh, Trixie?'

'Oh, I don't know,' replied Beatrice, rising; 'I don't pretend to be better than other girls of my time. I am afraid that the penniless lover that is over the sea stands a poor chance against the wealthy suitor near at hand with most of us.'

Mrs Lyme Wregis knew that her chance was lost now, that her grand-daughter had resumed the mask of worldly cynicism which it had pleased her to put on with the announcement of her marriage. There was no likelihood of surprising her confidence. She made no further attempt to continue the conversation, but sat silently turning over in her own mind how she might best, at all events, retard, if not prevent, Beatrice's union with Mr Pegram. She would have been still further confirmed in her intention could she have seen her granddaughter when she entered her own bedroom shortly afterwards. The girl walked across to the toilet-table, and contemplated herself for some two or three minutes in the looking-glass.

'I wonder,' she muttered at length, 'it is not written in your face, "You mean, pitiful little liar!" To dare to say that there was no engagement between you and Jack! Not in words, perhaps, but I know perfectly well that he believed himself engaged to me, just as I believed myself engaged to him. What will he think of me when he hears; what a mean, contemptible, mercenary little wretch I shall seem in his eyes, marrying for gold, with his "farewell" still sounding in my ears! It is hard, and yet I cannot help myself. I could not endure the thought of poor papa brought down to shabby gentility. If Jack could but know, if grandmamma could but know why I do this thing; but it must not be. They must think their worst of me, and I cannot justify myself. I wonder whether there is a more miserable girl in all London;' and Beatrice threw herself upon her bed and indulged in a good cry.

Utterly disbelieving the stories both of the Viscount and her granddaughter, but feeling quite sure that there was some urgent reason for this marriage, which the two were determined to conceal from her, Mrs Lyme Wregis determined to oppose the arrangement by every means in her power. She had already succeeded in obtaining a much later date for its solemnization than that originally contemplated by her son-in-law; and she now, after considerable thought, made up her mind to write to Jack Phillimore, and tell him, that if he valued his intended bride he would present himself in England without delay. Mrs Lyme Wregis was not only a shrewd, but a very practical old lady. She knew perfectly well that naval officers on the Mediterranean station cannot run home at their own sweet will; she knew also that captains, admirals, and those in authority over them do not always coincide with the applicants as to the urgency of those reasons which necessitate their absenting themselves from their duties. In the days of her splendour she had known people in high places of all sorts, and she succeeded in obtaining from a high admiralty official a private letter to the captain of Jack's ship, recommending that Lieutenant Phillimore should have three months' leave, if the exigencies of the service permitted.

Jack Phillimore was seated at an open port, in the wardroom of Her Majesty's ship *Cassiope*, which lay at her moorings at the Grand Harbour of

Valetta. He was listening to his great chum Tom Ringwood's doleful and somewhat prosy account of a love affair gone askew.

'You never saw such a cantankerous old curmudgeon,' continued Tom; 'how he ever could have become the father of such a sweet girl as Bessie, – the sweetest girl in England,' added Tom emphatically, 'I cannot imagine. Said he objected to sailors on principle, that when they were afloat they could not take care of their wives, and that when they were on shore, it meant being on half-pay, and then they had not money enough to keep them. When I insinuated that he was a rich man, and we had thought that he would help us with some modest allowance, he replied most offensively, that now he had made his fortune he had no intention of spending it in supporting impecunious sons-in-law. In short, he made such a regular old beast of himself that I lost my temper, and it ended in my being forbidden the house, and all correspondence, etc., between us being strictly prohibited.'

'Poor old Tom,' replied Phillimore. 'If the girl only sticks to you, depend upon it, things will be sure to come right in the end. It seems almost a shame to contrast my good luck with your bad. I am engaged, like you, to the sweetest girl in England, that is to say, not exactly engaged, but I can trust my cousin Trixie to wait for me; only, when I get home I shall have the luck to start on my wooing with a fair wind, and need expect no opposition from her father and the powers that be.'

'Yes,' observed Tom Ringwood sententiously; 'some fellows have luck, and some have not. I am one of the latter, and that is what is the trouble with me. It was just like me to fall in love with the daughter of the most irritable old brute that I ever saw out of a lunatic asylum, or a badly-found ship stationed on "the Coast".'

At this juncture an orderly came up to them, and briefly remarking, 'Mail in from England, gentlemen,' handed them their respective letters. Jack Phillimore's face fell as he glanced over the addresses of the three letters placed in his hand, and failed to recognize Beatrice's handwriting. Two were soon dismissed, but the precise and somewhat formal handwriting of the third was unknown to him. He tore it open, a half-stifled exclamation escaped him; and when Tom Ringwood glanced at him in consequence, he saw that Jack had received bad news of some kind. Mrs Lyme Wregis's note was short, but very much to the purpose.

'Dear Jack,' she commenced, 'I made a great mistake when I prevented Trixie formally engaging herself to you before you left England. I confess it, and at my time of life people don't relish confessing themselves in the wrong; but there have been, I fear, worse mistakes made than mine – mistakes that in a few weeks it will be too late to set straight, and that, in my opinion, will be followed, in one case, by a lifetime of repentance. If you really love Beatrice, as I believe you do, come home on receipt of this without delay. *You* may save her; otherwise I fear she will be drawn into a marriage which she will regret to her dying day. I cannot explain things, for I am not behind the scenes, and can make no guess, therefore, as to what has induced Beatrice to yield her assent to a marriage which has nothing but a moderate amount of wealth to recommend it. I don't believe either your cousin or uncle are acting altogether of their own free will; but, whatever their motive, they have most scrupulously concealed it from me. I have no more to say than that nobody can save Beatrice from this ill-omened union but yourself; and, if ever you cared for her, be no laggard in coming to her help now. She needs help sorely, I am convinced. She is either too proud, or she is forbidden to ask counsel from me. I think I may safely say that you have had no letter from her these last two mails, nor, unless you hasten to England, are you ever likely to hear of her again as Beatrice Phillimore.

'I enclose a letter which may facilitate the obtaining of the requisite leave, and remain, my dear Jack, your sincere friend, and well-wisher, ARABELLA LYME WREGIS.'

'I am afraid you have heard bad news of some sort,' exclaimed Tom Ringwood.

'Could not be much worse, old fellow,' replied Phillimore. 'I must be off to England just as soon as ever I can get my leave arranged. My God! I was bragging of my luck just now; read that, old man, and tell me what it all means.'

Tom Ringwood ran his eye rapidly over Mrs Lyme Wregis's letter.

'You might pore over this for a week,' he said as he finished it, 'and be no wiser. Follow your correspondent's advice, and be off like a shot if you can get leave. I suppose that note she encloses is from some official swell, and therefore you will doubtless manage it. The homeward mail will be in tomorrow afternoon, or next morning at latest; you have just time to get everything comfortably settled, and go by it.'

Thanks to the missive with which Mrs Lyme Regis had furnished him, Jack Phillimore found no difficulty in obtaining a couple of months' leave; and the next afternoon saw him, his portmanteau packed, sitting with his crony, Tom Ringwood, awaiting the mail for England to be signalled.

'By the way, Jack,' said his chum, 'I got a letter yesterday as well as you, and, strange to say, there are one or two questions about you in it. It is from my brother Ronald. He is a barrister, you know; but stop, I had better read you what he says. I'll not bore you with family news and details, but come at once to what concerns you. "Have you not a great friend, hight one Jack Phillimore? and is he not with you now on board the *Cassiope*? He belongs I presume to Lord Lakington's family; and, if he is the right Jack Phillimore, he is, according to the 'peerage', the most noble Viscount's heir. Curious to say, I'm engaged in a case which may indirectly affect your friend's future prospects not a little. You may have heard, or much more probably may not, of the 'Great Tontine'. I fancy I hear your 'Why, what the devil is that?' Never mind, Tom, it would take some sheets of paper to explain clearly, and, as a rising barrister, I cannot devote that time to the occasion. Suffice it for you, that it is a very big lottery. If you can suppose sixteen hundred people have been drawing lots for some years for a hundred and sixty thousand pounds, and that there are now only three people left in it – of whom Lord Lakington is one – that will represent the case pretty clearly to your mind. I am watching the case for one of the other parties – but it is a pretty big windfall for whoever gets it – and the Viscount's chance, as far as I can judge, is certainly as good as any one's. Do you happen to know anything about him? He made the town talk and the turf world open their eyes years ago, I believe, but I fancy went a deuce of a smash to wind up with; anyway, he lives very quietly now, I imagine, as no one ever hears of him either in club, drawing-room, or journal." There, that is all, Master Jack; but it strikes me there is an off chance of a bit of real good luck coming your way in the end. It is on the cards, you see, that the coronet, when you come into it, may not be quite such a barren heritage as you have always painted it. I should think your uncle might be trusted now not to make "ducks and drakes" of a hundred and sixty thousand pounds if he got hold of it.'

'Yes; I think he might be depended upon to stick to it. What a *coup* it would be! It would pretty well clear the old place, I should think. What is it, Morrison?' he continued, as the door opened, and a bronze-looking sailor looked into the cabin. 'Mail steamer coming in, eh? Very well; take my traps on board, man a boat, and stand by till we come.'

'Aye, aye, sir,' said the seaman, and he vanished to obey the lieutenant's behest.

'Well, good-bye, Jack,' said Ringwood, as he shook hands with his friend at the gangway. 'We are pretty much in the same fix. But recollect this, a sweetheart that is not staunch to you is not worth breaking your heart about; but ours are, I bet my life. I would as soon doubt Bessie as Greenwich time.'

'Yes, old fellow,' replied Jack sadly; 'but nobody, so far, has been kind enough to inform you that Bessie is going to marry somebody else.'

'Should not believe them if they did,' rejoined Tom stoutly; 'but, on the other hand, you have not got a perfect wild beast of a father-in-law to contend with. Egad! how mad he would be if he could hear me this minute;' and so tickled was Tom Ringwood at the idea that he burst into a fit of uncontrolled laughter. 'One thing I thought of last night. It struck me that this "Great Tontine" may have something to do with the hitch in your matrimonial affairs. If you think so when you get home call upon my brother, Ronald Ringwood, at the Temple, and I am sure he will tell you all he can. He knows you by name perfectly, and is quite aware that you are an old shipmate and chum of mine. Once more good-bye.'

Jack made no reply, but pressed his friend's hands warmly, and ran lightly down the ladder. A few hours more and he was rapidly steaming westward, though hardly fast enough to keep pace with his anxieties.

## CHAPTER SIXTEEN

# MR PEGRAM ANNOUNCES HIS MARRIAGE

It had all along rather annoyed Mr Robert Pegram during his intercourse with Mrs Lyme Wregis, the Viscount, and Beatrice, that he should be, what he called in his phraseology, so 'dashed by the swells'. He might tell himself that it was all nonsense, that money made the man now-a-days, that he had a right to hold up his head with all the Lakington people, that he would behave like a shame-faced schoolboy no more; but it always resulted in the same thing, that, when he found himself in the presence of Mrs Lyme Wregis and the Honourable Beatrice Phillimore, he was pretty well as much over-awed as on the first occasion.

'Of course it will be all right when I am engaged,' he argued; but, very much to Bob Pegram's dismay, he found the ladies much more inaccessible than before. It was very natural. They had borne with him good-naturedly in the first instance, but his proposal had engendered positive dislike. Beatrice had determined that her duty to her father condemned her to marry Robert Pegram. She would do her duty by him as a wife, that is, if he did not ask too much of her; but love him? – never. Respect and esteem him? – well, that seemed well-nigh impossible. He had but once ventured to call her by her Christian name, and then the word had so stuck in his throat that it is doubtful whether she heard it. He would have as soon thought of embracing Mrs Lyme Wregis as attempting to kiss her hand even; and when he once ventured to hint that he should like to take his *fiancée* out for a walk, that he never had an opportunity of being alone with her, and that the young lady probably looked for some attention, the Viscount assured him with an easy smile,

'Such things are never done in our world, my dear Pegram, as you will see as soon as you become one of us.'

But if Mr Robert Pegram was subdued and tongue-tied in Victoria Road, that was by no means the case elsewhere. Vanity was a very strong point in his character, and it had more than once led him into indiscretions. It imbued him with a tendency to brag about successfully-planned *coups* before they were accomplished. He could not resist showing his associates what a shrewd, keen-witted fellow he was. One of those men, in short, given to counting their chickens before they are hatched, spending their winnings before the horses have passed the winning-post. He was as scheming and crafty an intriguer by nature as his sire, but he possessed none of that secret tenacity which made the latter hold to his aim with all the grim obstinacy of a bull-dog.

Mr Pegram junior's departure from London was fixed, circumstances urgently requiring his presence in Wales; but, now that his marriage was definitely settled, he could not, before he left town, resist the temptation of personally announcing it to Mr Hemmingby.

Accustomed to regard the manager as the dashing and successful conductor of a fashionable theatre with considerable reverence, Mr Pegram panted to appear before him in his new *rôle*. So far he had been rather grateful for Hemmingby's notice, but he intended henceforth to pose as a patron of the drama. He looked forward to seeing his name as amongst the recognized patrons of all dramatic benefits, &c. He had seen, and often envied those gorgeous young bloods of the West End who were upon such familiar terms with the manager, and were treated with such respect by all the satellites of the theatre. Now he intended to become one of them himself, and there was even a slight air of patronage in the way he entered the 'Vivacity' Theatre, and desired the janitor at the stage-door to take his card up to Mr Hemmingby. The manager was disengaged, and would see him with pleasure; and in a few seconds Mr Pegram found himself in Sam Hemmingby's sanctum.

'Well, Bob,' exclaimed the manager, as he rose from the table strewn with letters, drawings, newspaper cuttings, &c., all apparently in the wildest confusion, 'how are you? Do you want anything for tonight? or are you about to wend your way back to the Principality?'

'Yes, I am off to the Principality again tomorrow; but, you see, Hemmingby, you are one of my oldest friends, I suppose I ought to say one of my father's oldest friends. I have known you ever since I was quite a little chap, and I thought I should like to be the first to tell you myself.'

'Why what on earth has happened to you? you look as frolicsome as a lamb in spring-time. I reckon you have "struck 'ile" in some form.'

'Yes, you are about right; I am going to be married, and I flatter myself I have done about as well as any fellow with my chances could do. When you can combine beauty, rank, and four thousand a-year to start upon, with at least double, or more probably treble to come, I don't think a fellow in my position can be said to have done badly.'

'No, indeed; I congratulate you with all my heart; but who is the lady?'

'The Honourable Beatrice Phillimore, Lord Lakington's daughter; you know him, I think?'

'Lakington's daughter!' ejaculated the manager. 'By Jove, you fly high, Master Bob; but she cannot have any money.'

'She has what I tell you,' replied Pegram. 'She is one of the prettiest girls I ever saw. Did you ever see her?'

'Certainly I have; I have seen her many a time. Her father's an old friend of mine, and I have often given him a box expressly for her. From what you say, I may conclude that the marriage is definitely arranged. Excuse me, but how did Lord Lakington take the idea of it at first?'

'Well, between you and me, Hemmingby, I should say he was most obtusely blind to my merits and the advantages of the connection.'

'Well, Master Bob,' replied the manager, 'I have always given you credit for a pretty fair amount of cheek; but how the devil you mustered brass enough to ask Lord Lakington to give you his daughter beats me altogether, and that you should muster up courage to return to the charge is one of the most astounding pieces of audacity in all my experience.'

'Well, I fancy he had a baddish time of it to start with; but you know what a cunning, tenacious old file the governor is. It is difficult to turn him from anything he has set his heart upon.'

'Your father? Ah! it was your father then that had the idea of this marriage,' exclaimed Hemmingby. 'By Jove! I see it all now. By this artful manœuvre he contrives to make a certainty for you of —'

And here the manager stopped abruptly, and throwing himself back into the chair indulged in a fit of silent laughter.

He had stopped in his speech abruptly because he did not know whether Bob was in his father's confidence with regard to the 'Tontine', but the whole thing was all clear to him now. He knew the characters of old Pegram and the Viscount so well that he could picture to himself all that had passed between them as vividly as if he had been present. He could see the cunning, untiring old lawyer working insidiously on Lakington's selfishness, indolence, and love of ease, heedless of rebuff or insult, but doggedly and persistently pointing out to the Viscount the narrow circumstances, nay genteel penury, that the loss of the 'Tontine' must involve him in; and how that this marriage would insure him a comfortable income for his lifetime, and that the whole thing would centre in his daughter afterwards. Bob Pegram's conversation had revealed to him the exact terms agreed to by the contracting parties; but shrewd man of the world as Sam Hemmingby was, if, when Lord Lakington had asked him to sound Pegram about a compromise, the old lawyer had ventured to propose such conditions he, Hemmingby, would have pronounced it useless to suppose that Lord Lakington would accede to them.

'Well, Bob,' he said at length, 'I must once more congratulate you; but you must come and eat one more bachelor dinner with me. When will you be up in town again?'

'Well, in about a fortnight.'

'Very good. Now look here: this is a Tuesday, what do you say to Thursday fortnight? I will make up a pleasant party to meet you, drink your health afterwards, and hear you bid adieu to the vanities and wickedness of bachelorhood in a neat speech of reply; may I book it?'

'All right,' replied Bob; 'I shall be most happy.'

'Then that is satisfactorily settled; and now, my boy, I must turn you out, as I have got lots to do, and half-a-dozen people to see,' and with a hearty shake of the hand Mr Hemmingby dismissed his visitor.

'Egad! this will be a bit of news for my barrister friend,' exclaimed Sam Hemmingby, as he threw himself back into his chair. 'He seemed interested in the story of the "Great Tontine" that night I first met him down at Rydland. Here is the third act of the drama all ready for him now. I will ask him to meet Pegram, and – ah, yes – I will ask the Viscount also to be of the party. He will have all the leading characters under his own eye then,' continued the manager, laughing, 'and can draw them from the life. He will have nothing to do but to get that piece ready for the "Vivacity" as soon as possible. He is a 'cute man, lawyer Pegram. It was a bold conception on his part to settle up the "Tontine" after this fashion. I wonder how he got the Viscount's length, because, if I know anything about it, I feel sure Lakington's first impulse upon hearing his proposition must have been to throw him out of the window. But he reckoned him up well, and has carried his point in the end. He is about as hard-headed and unscrupulous a practitioner as ever I came across, is old Pegram. I am out of the whole business, and therefore it is nothing to me; but if I had been left in I should have wanted to see old Pegram's hand before I drew stakes. I wonder who the deuce his "life" is; by the way, it is just possible that it might be that old clerk that he takes such care of. I recollect that night at Llanbarlym, when I first told him of the "Tontine", he seemed to be a good deal struck with my idea of putting in a life you could watch over and take care of. It's just upon the cards that he put in old Krabbe. I don't think it's quite in Pegram's nature to take quite so much care of an old servant as he does of him, unless he has some special reason for doing so. It would be more in Pegram's line, I fancy, to pension off a dependent who is played out on a by no means extravagant scale, and not to trouble himself about him afterwards. However, it's all no business of mine. We'll have the dinner, and I'll do the play, that is, if Ringwood will write it. By Jove! if one could only get the newly-married couple to be present in a stage-box on a first night, what a draw it would be!

What a line for the posters – "The 'Great Tontine', under the patronage of the winners thereof." "The newly-married couple have kindly consented to be present on the first occasion." "For particulars, see handbills." And of course there would be a flaming account of the wedding in them. Bob Pegram, too, is just the very man who would do it. He would be delighted to see the house all staring at him, make him feel himself a star-actor down to the very heels of his boots; but I am afraid it would take all one's time to make the Honourable Beatrice see it, and I don't fancy my friend Bob is likely to be altogether master of that household. From all accounts the Phillimores are a pretty self-willed race. It is a wonderful instance of how pride knocks under to poverty, that the Viscount should ever have given his consent to such a match.'

The fortnight preceding the manager's dinner slipped away without making any perceptible difference to any of the characters in our story.

Mrs Lyme Wregis could still obtain no clue to the hidden motive of this marriage. Beatrice unmistakably avoided being alone with her more than she could help, and passed a good deal of her time in her own room under pretext of wedding preparations. She still affected the same worldly satisfaction with her prospects that she had assumed from the commencement, but the girl looked somewhat jaded, and her grandmother once or twice fancied that she could detect the traces of tears on cheeks somewhat paler than they were wont to be. At times Beatrice affected high spirits, which almost bordered on the hysterical, and exhibited an extravagance in taste as regards her trousseau such as had been hitherto utterly foreign to her nature. 'I always admired the story,' she muttered, 'of that dandy soldier who was wont to draw on new kid gloves before he went into action. I am about to undergo the death of all my happiness in this world; it is only fit that I should be bravely decked for the occasion. When one weds for gold, it is but right one should be attired in all the gorgeousness that gold can purchase.'

And her father encouraged her in all this. Although he would not acknowledge it to himself even, still he knew that she was sacrificing herself for his sake. It was but just, he thought, that she should be allowed to lavish what money she liked on her trousseau. He had seen, in the course of hard upon thirty years, so many broken hearts healed by the lavish administration of silks, laces, and jewellery, that he was actually blasphemer enough to believe that his daughter had joined the advanced sect of Belgravia, from the latter commandment of whose creed the word 'not' seems to be erased. And, in good sooth, Beatrice at this time gave fair grounds for supposing that she was one of the extremely 'chic' young ladies of the present day who pink themselves upon talking in a manner that would have made their grandmothers blush, but would have been quite in accord with the manners in vogue in the early days of the House of Hanover.

In fact, the girl hated to think. Let her go shopping to spend money, throw herself into any society that might be offered, but let her never be left alone with her own thoughts. Such was Beatrice's present feeling; and never before had she been so exacting to her father on the subject of tickets for the theatres and other places of amusement.

The Viscount responded nobly to all such calls made upon him. When his daughter was so bravely exerting herself to overcome her childish fancy, was it not his duty to give her every assistance? Engaged young ladies were always entitled to such little indulgences for the few weeks preceding their marriage, and Lord Lakington was quite aware that it was imperative that this marriage should be made as easy as possible for Beatrice.

Mrs Lyme Wregis, finding that she can make nothing of the problem that she had set herself to elucidate, is now incessantly calculating the earliest period at which Jack Phillimore can be in England. She both hopes and believes that Beatrice will break down when she sees Jack, and that she will drop this *rôle* which she is so evidently playing. She had so nearly melted that afternoon when Mrs Lyme Wregis spoke to her of her lover that the old lady was justified in thinking that when Jack was there to plead his own cause she would, at all events, exonerate herself, and deign to tell them why she did this thing.

Ronald Ringwood in the Temple is hammering away from another point of view at the identical same problem as Mrs Lyme Wregis, a lady of whose very existence he, at the present moment, is in total ignorance. He is as much befogged as she. Beyond Guildford they can discover no trace of Terence Finnigan, and the closest *espionage* of Mr Pegram's agents points to the conclusion that they are as much at fault as Mr Ringwood himself. His visits to Kew, too, have latterly been far less pleasant than formerly. Miss Caterham shows such nervous solicitude for intelligence, that it becomes painful; and she herself would find it almost difficult to say whether she would be best pleased to hear that there is no news of Terence Finnigan or to be told that he was found. She is anxious, of course, that Mary should, to say the least of it, have her chance of succeeding to the great prize; but, on the other hand, she has taken it firmly into her head that the discovery of Terence Finnigan will also be the discovery of a terrible crime, and she is haunted with the terror of finding herself mixed up in a *cause célèbre*. Ever since Ringwood had imprudently told her that the Pegrams were also searching for Finnigan, she has been firmly impressed that they were searching for him solely with a view to his destruction; and that the man's life hangs, in short, on whether he is first discovered by Ringwood or the Pegrams. It is a curious thing, that what most people, from his long absence and from his extreme age, would have thought the natural solution of Terence Finnigan's fate – to wit, that he was dead – never occurred to Miss Caterham; and there was no doubt that the poor lady suffered from excitement. Ringwood, too, was decidedly in the black books of Mary Chichester. For the sake of her aunt's health she judged, and judged rightly, that she ought to be taken into this secret. It was foolish of Miss Caterham not to allow the whole affair to be confided to Mary. If she could have talked the whole thing over with her niece, the girl's strong, clear, common-sense would have dissipated all these hysterical ideas which so perturbed the poor lady's mind. She would have pointed out that the Pegrams' object was much more likely to verify a death than to cause one; and the mere having some one to talk the thing over with would have done much to tranquillize her. It was in vain that Ringwood pleaded with Mr Carbuckle for permission to disregard Miss Caterham's injunctions upon this point. That gentleman replied that he could not help it, that it was very likely that he, Ringwood, was right; but that, although Miss Caterham was certainly weak and nervous, her mind was still perfectly clear, and there was no pretext whatever for disregarding her commands.

But Mary Chichester could not be brought to admit that Ringwood was not free to speak if he chose. She regarded his being pledged to secrecy as a mere piece of professional pedantry, and still adhered strongly to that very feminine dictum, that no young man who professed undisguised admiration for a girl had any business to withhold a secret from her; so that, upon the whole, she rather snubbed Ronald when he turned up at the cottage at Kew – would leave the room in the most pointed manner, to enable him, as she said, 'to talk over the great mystery' with her aunt; would pout a little, and at times would hardly be propitiated. She was a good, frank, unaffected girl, and had certainly taken rather a liking for Ronald; but she was not faultless, and had her whims and caprices. She liked to have her way: and to be thwarted about such a small matter as this was, as she told the barrister, humiliating.

## CHAPTER SEVENTEEN

# A DINNER AT THE 'WYCHERLEY'

Mr Robert Pegram having, it was to be hoped, got satisfactorily through the business that called him into Wales, is putting on his white cravat in his bedroom at the 'Grand' with much solicitude. Tonight he is to hold high revel with Sam Hemmingby, and the manager has written to tell him that he has secured the private dining-room at the 'Wycherley', and got half-a-dozen extremely pleasant men, including his proposed father-in-law, to meet him. To a man of Bob Pegram's proclivities, a dinner at the 'Wycherley' had a peculiar charm. It was not that the '*chef*' was such a great artist, albeit there were not many in London better; but the sheer swagger of being able to say he had dined there had in itself a subtle attraction.

The 'Wycherley' was a leading Dramatic and Literary Club, and on a somewhat bigger scale than most of those institutions. A large sprinkling of the leading men of both professions, as well as a considerable number of their brethren of the brush, belonged to it; while the remainder of its ranks were filled up principally from the bar, and that indefinite but incomprehensible body, yclept the 'men about town'. It was a club that affected Bohemianism; but it was Bohemianism in white ties, Bohemianism critical as to its side dishes, and fastidious about the exact dryness of its champagne. But it was a club remarkable for good fellowship and its sociability; a club wanting in the more punctilious manners of more stately establishments, wherein members showed an utter contempt for introductions, and addressed each other in a free and easy manner that would most likely have been pronounced vulgar and obtrusive in Pall Mall.

Mr Pegram was looking forward to his dinner with considerable glee and satisfaction, although the announcement that Lord Lakington had been asked to meet him had by no means added to his anticipation of enjoyment. 'His lordship,' as Mr Pegram remarked to himself, 'is all very well; but there is devilish little fun about him. He is stiff, and uncommon high. He takes exceeding good care that you shall never forget that he *is* Lord Lakington.' This was not altogether the case. The Viscount was an easy-going nobleman enough to all he considered his social equals; but, unfortunately, he had not as yet brought himself to regard his son-in-law in that category.

'How are you, Pegram?' exclaimed the manager, shaking hands with him, as Bob was duly ushered into the lobby of the 'Wycherley'. 'Lord Lakington, of course there is no occasion to name him; but I must introduce you to Serjeant Boteler, well known in his own profession, but better known at the "Wycherley" as the best judge of a horse or a ballet-girl in our conventual establishment; Mr Ringwood, of the same profession, but whose age precludes his possessing the same deep learning on those points; Mr John Shout, at whom I dare say you have at times had the presumption to laugh; Mr Dodsley, whom you of course have seen on the amateur stage; and, ha! here comes our last man, Colonel Ramsey, of the Brigade.' And having shaken hands with the new-comer, Hemmingby turned and rang the bell.

Dinner was speedily announced; the party trooped downstairs, and were quickly seated round an oval table. Mr Pegram is delighted. Serjeant Boteler of course he recognizes as one of the most terrible cross-examiners at the criminal bar, and with the reputation for investing the most part of his heavy retainers on the vicissitudes of Newmarket, Epsom, Ascot, &c.; whilst Mr John Shout, although from his meek demeanour you might have put him down as a steady-going curate, was, as Robert Pegram well knew, one of the greatest humourists of the London stage. The dinner was good. It was not often that any one had to complain of a dinner at the 'Wycherley'; albeit in the coffee-room men found fault, as men will who, having ordered fish and the joint, apparently expect it to expand into an elaborate French dinner. Dry 'Pommery' circulated freely. The conversation flowed as freely and pleasantly as the wine. Those coruscations of crackers, those fusillades of *bon mots*, and showers of epigrams which the gathering of two or three well-known *causeurs* are supposed to evoke, are, I fancy, somewhat problematical, or else we no longer have the men. Pleasant dinner-parties are doubtless as numerous as of yore, but the *Noctes Ambrosianæ* are among the legends of the past. It may be that, whereas wits and humourists of the day are but a very limited number in all ages, now that London society has got so big they have no chance to come together as they did at the beginning of the century. Anyway, although both Serjeant Boteler and Mr Shout told one or two good stories, and although there was plenty of lively talk generally, still there was not much a man might carry away beyond the recollection of a pleasant dinner-party.

Ringwood had been almost surprised out of his self-possession when Hemmingby introduced him to Mr Pegram. He had dropped him no hint of such a thing, for he had no idea that Ringwood was actively interesting himself in the winding up of the 'Great Tontine'; but the barrister had no doubt whatever that this was the son of the Rydland lawyer, that this was Pegram junior, who had played the amateur detective at Guildford, and who had paid that audacious visit to Miss Caterham. He studied this man carefully. He could not have said why, but it seemed to him that it had advanced him some steps in his search thus acquiring the personality of his opponent. A commonplace man enough to look at, he thought, and the good-natured countenance somewhat indicative of stupidity but for one thing: there was a cunning look about the quick, light blue eyes, which rather belied his first estimate. Still Ringwood was too shrewd a judge to trust altogether to appearance. He knew that the husk was a very small indication of what might be contained therein in studying the human race. In the Homeric days the great chiefs were, no doubt, men of thews and sinews; but that is certainly changed in the present century, the mighty 'braves' of which, from Napoleon to the present day, have, with one or two exceptions, been below the average height. Similarly, it would be hard to gather from the faces of some of our greatest thinkers the men they are. The conversation, so far, had been too general for Ringwood to have much chance of drawing Mr Pegram out, and therefore he had no opportunity of judging his mental calibre.

But at this juncture it occurred to Sam Hemmingby that he must propose a toast. Hemmingby had been a good deal in America, and had imbibed from our kinsfolk rather a habit of improving the occasion. It was a joke amongst his intimates, that at public dinners there was always great difficulty in keeping Sam Hemmingby down, even when he was not in the 'caste', that is to say, not entrusted with a toast; but in anything of a private nature they always declared it was hopeless. Tapping the table with his knife, the manager rose, and ruthlessly cutting short an animated discussion between Colonel Ramsay and Serjeant Boteler, who were eagerly discussing the past Ledger, said he must call upon them to drink the health of his young friend, Robert Pegram, upon the present auspicious occasion.

'I have known him from a boy, and this dinner, as most of you are, I think, aware, is to wish him God speed in launching on the sea of matrimony. He is about to marry the daughter of another very old friend of mine, if Lord Lakington will allow me to call him so' (a sonorous 'certainly' from the Viscount), 'and I want you all to fill a glass to the "long life, health, and happiness of Robert Pegram and the Honourable Beatrice Phillimore",' and here, to the immense astonishment of Mr Shout and Serjeant Boteler, the manager sat down.

As the comedian said afterwards, something must have disagreed with Sam Hemmingby, or he never could have thrown away such a chance of giving them fifteen minutes.

Upon Ringwood again this all came like a revelation. He had thought it rather a singular coincidence that both Lord Lakington and Robert Pegram should simultaneously be the manager's guests; but still, as Hemmingby had dropped no word concerning it, he looked upon it as a coincidence, and nothing more. Now, of course, the whole scheme was as clear to him as noonday. He saw that both the Viscount and the Pegrams regarded Miss Caterham's nominee as dead, and that by this marriage the whole 'Tontine' would be secured to their united families. Of course, they had come to an understanding about the division, and as soon as this marriage had taken place, would doubtless take steps for the winding up of the whole business. This would account for the anxiety of the Pegrams to ascertain the fate of Finnigan, as it would be apparently impossible to bring the thing to an end until his death could be placed beyond doubt; but further specula- tion on Ringwood's part was put a stop to by Mr Pegram rising to return thanks.

Mr Pegram had imbibed quite his share of dry champagne. I do not mean to say that Mr Pegram was at all drunk, but Mr Pegram had taken wine enough to induce that confidence in himself which, while it very often exhibits the shy man at his best, is apt to make the bore become more garrulous and the liar stupendous; and in the case of an under-bred man, to bring into prominence all those little vulgarisms which, as long as he was self-contained, were not visible. Mr Pegram, unluckily, felt that he ought to rise to the situation. He had borne the reputation of singing a good song, possessing great dramatic powers, and being altogether a funny dog amongst his chums during his London career; and it occurred to him that he ought to soar to the level of the company in which he found himself, and show that he also was a wit. He accordingly led off with all the stock jokes about his impending execution, affected to weep in a pathetic way over the renunci- ation of all his bachelor privileges of clubs (he did not belong to one), latch keys, and late hours, winding up with an impassioned declaration, that so charming was the lady to whom he was about to confide his destinies, that, far from dreading being turned off in the regular manner, he should only be too happy to be lynched on the spot.

Lord Lakington's face was a study during his future son-in-law's oration; and this, together with the absurd grimaces of the comedian, who affected to be moved by every variation in Pegram's speech, sent Serjeant Boteler and Colonel Ramsay into convulsions of laughter, which, believing to be due to his own humour, encouraged Bob Pegram to still higher flights. Suddenly dropping into a falsetto, he affected to be making the acknowledgements of his *fiancée*, the Honourable Beatrice Phillimore. The effect of this upon Lord Lakington was too palpable to every one but the luckless orator, and the 'devilish bad taste' which he muttered between his teeth did not escape the quick ear of Sam Hemmingby. The manager tried vainly to make some diversion, but Bob Pegram was not to be denied. It was only the cessation of the laughter of Boteler and Ramsay, consequent upon their perceiving how things stood, that at last brought that gentleman's speech to a conclusion.

We have all seen the explosion of the shell that suddenly breaks up a party of this description; and so it was upon this occasion. Mr Pegram had not resumed his seat above two or three minutes before the Viscount rose, and bade his host a courteous goodnight, and took his departure. It was in vain that Sam Hemmingby tried to pull his party together. The harmony of the evening had evidently all gone away. The guardsman and Serjeant Boteler speedily followed Lord Lakington's example. Ringwood lingered a little behind the rest, and then, in pursuance of the resolution he had just come to, said to his host before slipping on his great coat –

'Whether by accident or design, you have got all the remaining representatives of the "Great Tontine" here tonight. I am Miss Caterham's representative. She is the nominator, you must know, of the missing nominee.'

'By Jove! You don't say so? Oh d—n the coat! the gentleman won't want it yet for half an hour. Come back and have another cigar and a drink over this.'

'I have been puzzling all the evening,' said Ringwood, as he followed the manager back into the dining-room, 'whether this was mere accident, or whether you purposely asked me to meet these people.'

'Certainly not accident,' rejoined the manager. 'You see I had to give Bob Pegram a dinner; and then I thought I would ask the Viscount to meet him; and, as you seemed always rather interested on the subject of the "Tontine", and I have a hazy idea that if I keep you straight about the stage-craft of it you will make a big drama out of the subject some of these days, I thought it would be a good opportunity for you to see two of the leading characters.'

'Then you regard my client, Miss Caterham, as quite out of it?'

'Yes. Having now nothing to do with the affair myself, I should think her nominee was dead, or he would have been found before this. If I were still left in the "Tontine" I should regard your client as either a very troublesome old woman, for not seeing that an eye was kept on her nominee, or else I should suspect her of projecting a great fraud—'

'You think that possible, then?'

'Think it possible!' exclaimed the manager. 'Airth and skies, man, you can hardly expect everybody to play fair when there is a hundred and sixty thousand pounds on the *coup*. It ain't in human nature all round. I am not one who thinks that we are all born rogues; but there is a black side to human nature as well as a bright, and it is no use pretending there is not. Why, you see men risking penal servitude for life – ay, and get it – every week for a mere fraction of the money. No, Ringwood, I am not a suspicious fellow. I come across sharp customers at times; but I don't find, as a rule, that every one wants to get the best of me. Still, if I was left in this "Tontine" with Lord Lakington and Pegram, although the latter is a friend of twenty years' standing, and the former of even more, yet I should feel it my business to look closely after both of them. Miss Caterham being still in it, according to your idea, I can only recommend you to do for her what I should do were I in her place.'

'But you surely don't suppose,' exclaimed Ringwood, 'that either Lord Lakington or Mr Pegram would have resort to any foul play in the affair?'

'Now, my dear fellow,' rejoined the manager suavely, 'please remember that I am out of the "Tontine", and that it is no business of mine. Secondly, bear in mind that I insinuate nothing whatever against either of these gentlemen. Still, here is a fact for you to ponder over. Lakington has been a reckless gambler, and has run through every shilling he has. Still he is supposed never to have done a mean thing, and bears the character of a highly honourable gentleman; and yet, when it comes to seizing such a pool as this big "Tontine", he has made no scruple to stand in with Pegram and give away that beautiful girl, his daughter, to an "under-bred 'un" such as you saw tonight.'

Ringwood was lost in thought for a minute or two. That Lord Lakington should consent to give a daughter of his to Mr Bob Pegram was certainly a strong point in confirmation of Sam Hemmingby's theory; and it is a little difficult to say what men will not do when the temptation is so great.

'And what about Pegram?'

'I have got no more to tell you than I told you that night at Rydland, that he is cunning as a fox, and an uncommon sharp hand in all matters of business. Have another drink?'

'No, thank you; I must be going. You have told me quite as much as I could reasonably expect, and I thank you for it. And now, good night.'

'Good night. I would like to do you a turn, Ringwood, if I could; but, you see, these are both old friends of mine, and I can't interfere – quite possible, there is nothing to interfere about; and, at all events, I have no pretence for inquiring into things, and should of course succeed in quarrelling with them if it came to their ears, though nothing else came of it. It would be worth running a little risk, though, to prevent that handsome daughter of Lakington's throwing herself away on Bob Pegram; I have a "second chambermaid'' would do for him much better. However the odds are, Miss Beatrice would not thank me for interfering, and so you will have to puzzle out the thing your own way. Once more, good night.'

## CHAPTER EIGHTEEN

# JACK PHILLIMORE RETURNS FROM MALTA

Jack Phillimore, speeding homeward in the 'P. & O.' boat, has ample leisure to reflect upon the heavy clouds that have gathered over his love-affair. Naturally one of the gayest and lightest-hearted officers in Her Majesty's fleet, two or three acquaintances he had on board could not at all understand him in his present sombre mood. But Jack was terribly earnest in his love for his cousin. It had grown with her growth. He had petted her as a mere child in his midshipman's day, and as she grew older he was never so happy as when taking care of his cousin Beatrice. As she blossomed into womanhood Jack woke to the fact that he was in love, and from that hour, as his love deepened and strengthened, so the more did he cherish it. No word about love had actually passed between the pair until that evening prior to his embarkation; but there is very little necessity for words sometimes on these occasions. Looks and tones tell the old, old story more effectually than the most eloquent language. In fact, I do not believe, as a rule, that there is much said at the grand climacteric. We are always wondering what Mr Dash and Miss Blank can have to say to each other that takes so long in the telling; but, except in the early stages, I should say those stricken of the disorder were sparing of speech. For the last two years or more Jack had regarded his cousin as his future wife, and he had every reason to suppose that she was perfectly willing to tread her path through life hand in hand with him. Neither her father nor her grandmother ever attempted to interfere with the intimacy between the cousins, and Jack was not such a fool as to suppose they could be blind as to where that intimacy was tending; he drew the very natural deduction, that neither Lord Lakington nor Mrs Lyme Wregis saw any objection to the arrangement. True, Beatrice had refused to engage herself to him that evening, but then, had she not told him that her refusal was only in compliance with her grandmamma's wishes? while he knew that Mrs Lyme Wregis had objected to nothing more than the long engagement; and in the letter which summoned him to England, she showed that she not only repented having extracted that promise from Beatrice, but that he might still count upon her approval and advocacy. Then he thought over that passage in Bob Ringwood's letter, and wondered whether it could have anything to do with his cousin's projected marriage; but he could make nothing out of that. Even if his uncle was to come into this large sum of money, surely he would prefer the inheritor of his title to a stranger as a son-in-law, more especially when that heir had not only been always rather a favourite with him, but wanted to marry his daughter to boot. Again and again did Jack smoke far into the night a-pondering over all these points; but the more he thought over it the more inscrutable did the mystery become. That Beatrice had thrown him over for mere wealth he could not and would not believe, and Mrs Lyme Wregis's letter supported him in his incredulity. However, one thing was quite clear – the first thing he had to do on establishing himself in London was to go straight to the Victoria Road.

Jack Phillimore had no cause to complain of the malignity of the elements, for, tedious as he found it, the steamer achieved a very fair passage; and rather inside nine days on quitting Malta Jack found himself duly installed at the British Hotel in Jermyn Street. It was, he thought, too late that night; but an hour before luncheon-time next day he presented himself in the Victoria Road.

'Lord Lakington is not at home, but the ladies are in the drawing-room,' said the man-servant in response to his knock. 'Glad to see you back, Mr Phillimore,' continued Jackson, as he preceded the visitor up the stairs, for the young naval officer was very popular with all the domestics, and the idea that 'this Pegram' should carry off their young mistress from what they regarded as her rightful lover had moved them to much indignation.

Jackson had been perfectly correct in his statement that the ladies were in the drawing-room. Beatrice's attention had been of course aroused by the knock at the door, and she caught the tones of her cousin's voice upon the stairs as he replied courteously to Jackson's welcome. The consequence was, that, to the dismay of Mrs Lyme Wregis, as Jack Phillimore entered the door of the front drawing-room Beatrice disappeared by the door of the back.

Mrs Lyme Wregis was ensconced in her favourite seat in the window. She had seen the arrival of the mail steamer in the morning papers, and had been expecting Jack for the last hour. She welcomed him cordially, of course said nothing about Beatrice's abrupt disappearance, and, upon second thoughts, came to the conclusion that perhaps it was for the best. It would give her a few minutes in which to tell her story, while the girl might well require a little time to prepare herself for a meeting with her old lover.

Jack Phillimore was soon in possession of all that Mrs Lyme Wregis had to tell him, which, after all, was very little more than she had already made him acquainted with by letter. He certainly learnt that not only was the marriage most definitely settled, but that the very day for it was fixed. He was further informed that his successful rival was a Mr Robert Pegram, the son of a gentleman of considerable property in Wales; that the young couple were to commence life upon an income of four thousand a year; that Lord Lakington and Beatrice were both most lavish regarding the trousseau; and lastly, that she, Mrs Lyme Wregis, felt perfectly sure – and in spite of what her granddaughter might say to the contrary – that Beatrice was going to the altar under some sort of compulsion, and that her feeling for her betrothed was rather that of repugnance than mere indifference.

Having told her story, which, as Jack Phillimore remarked, contained not the slightest allusion to the Viscount's wealthy prospects, Jack came to the conclusion that as yet he was a very long way from unravelling the tangled skein of his love.

'But where is Trixie? Surely she will see me? She must feel bound to; if it is only,' he concluded, with a somewhat bitter smile, 'to receive my congratulations on her wedding.'

'Of course she will see you,' replied the old lady. 'Ring the bell, and I will send for her. Jackson,' continued the old lady, as that servant made his appearance in answer to the summons, 'tell one of the maids to let Miss Beatrice know that Mr Phillimore is here, and anxious to see her.'

A few minutes' delay, and then a smart lady's-maid entered the room.

'Miss Beatrice's love, sir, and she is very glad that you are back again; but she is so much engaged just now that it is impossible for her to come down.'

'It is useless, you see,' said Jack Phillimore, as the girl left the room; 'she won't even see me. She has made up her mind not to do so; no doubt, until after the wedding. I am as little likely to get at the real story of this marriage as you. I suppose,' he continued, with a faint smile, 'people will call me a great puppy not to be satisfied with a plain hint. I suppose I ought to be satisfied now that I am forgotten, and that she marries somebody else just because she regards him as able to give her luxuries which I could not; and yet,' he continued sadly, 'I thought Beatrice so very different.'

As for Mrs Lyme Wregis, she was perfectly dumbfounded by the failure of her ingenious scheme. She thought that if she could only bring the lovers together before this wedding was accomplished that everything would be cleared up, and Mr Pegram sent about his business; but it had never occurred to her that Beatrice would decline to see her cousin. And the old lady recognized, as thoroughly as Phillimore did, that Beatrice's excuse did not apply to this occasion only, but was a resolute intimation that she declined to see Jack until after the wedding.

'I have got the leave,' said Jack Phillimore, 'thanks to your influence, Mrs Lyme Wregis, which will about tide me over the wedding; and though I cannot possibly see how I can interfere, still nobody shall say that I gave up Beatrice without a struggle. I shall stay on in town up to the day, make every attempt I can to see her, and at all events, I shall have it out with my uncle, though I don't suppose much good will come of that. Good-bye. I can never be sufficiently grateful to you for all that you have done. It is a great comfort to know that one still retains a staunch friend in the garrison.'

He had hardly got down the stairs, the sound of his feet had scarce died away in the hall, when the drawing-room door was dashed open, and in rushed Beatrice, flushed and almost breathless with excitement.

'What did he say, grandmamma? Did he call me all sorts of bad names? – fickle, inconstant, and a mercenary wretch? Did he swear that he would never speak to me again? I do not suppose he ever will. He must look upon me as the meanest and most despicable girl he not only ever met, but ever heard of. It was unkind of you, grandmamma, to bring him home – for, of course, it was your doing – till all was over. But what did he say?'

'Like other people, he wants an explanation of your mysterious engagement, and declares he will see you before the wedding day.'

'That he shall never do,' replied the girl; and even as she spoke the door of the drawing-room quietly opened, and her cousin stood before her.

Jack Phillimore owed his noiseless appearance to a little bit of romance on the part of a woman. I have before said that the sympathies of the domestics of the house were all in Jack Phillimore's favour, and they were as indignant in their way as Mrs Lyme Wregis at Beatrice's breach of faith. So sympathetic was the lady's-maid, that she volunteered to let Jack Phillimore out, and having done so, stood at the open door watching him as he walked slowly away, when putting his hands in his pockets for his gloves, Phillimore discovered that they were missing. He was quite sure he had them when he called, so it was evident he must have left them in Mrs Lyme Wregis's drawing-room. He turned and went back for them, and as the girl was still standing at the open door, there was of course no necessity for knocking, so his re-entrance was noiseless.

'Beatrice!' he exclaimed.

Her eyes flashed, and an angry flush crossed her face as she exclaimed,

'If this is a little comedy of yours and grandmamma's, allow me to observe that I consider it in very bad taste. To persist on seeing me against my will is ungenerous, unmanly.'

Jack Phillimore was, in the main, by no means a hot-tempered fellow, but this was rather more than he *could* stand. He conceived, as I think most men in his situation would have done, that an explanation, under the circumstances, was most certainly due to him, and that he certainly did not merit being overwhelmed with reproaches for what was the veriest accident.

'I have simply come back for this pair of gloves on the table,' he rejoined, in a hard, constrained voice, 'and had no intention of forcing an interview upon you. I most certainly hold that you owe me some explanation of the sudden change in your feelings. When you throw over the man that you were virtually engaged to three months ago, I think you should, at all events, explain to him why you do it. The most heartless flirts let their adorers down easier than you. We are not a family noted for any great virtues, but a Phillimore's word has been generally thought to be relied on.'

'I never pledged myself to you,' she replied, faintly.

'Not actually in words, I grant you; but you know very well that we both looked upon ourselves as betrothed. There are promises of implication, just as binding as promises of words.'

'Spare me, Jack, spare me,' she murmured faintly; 'indeed, I cannot help myself.'

But his blood was up, and he was in no humour to receive the proffered olive branch.

'I will relieve you of my presence, and with congratulations upon your approaching marriage, bid you good-bye.'

The softer mood was all out of her now, her eyes flashed through her tears, and her cheeks flamed with anger, as she made two or three rapid steps towards him.

'Coward!' she hissed between her teeth. 'How dare you insult me thus?' and she swept from the room in right regal fashion.

As Jack Phillimore makes his way home through the park he is fain to admit that he has not made the most of the interview with which fortune had favoured him. If his confounded temper had not got the better of him he might, he thinks, on looking back upon it, have really done something with Beatrice. He is not the first, by a good many, who has thrown away a chance through loss of temper. After what has passed between them it is not likely that Beatrice will see him again. He will see his uncle; but he is not at all sanguine that he will get much satisfaction out of the Viscount. Then he wonders whether it is likely to be of the slightest use in seeing Ronald Ringwood. Hardly, he thinks. Lord Lakington's chance of winning a lottery can surely not have anything to say to Beatrice's marriage; still, it is well to know what chance there is of such a plum falling into the family. This shall be his programme for the morrow. He will catch the Viscount at his club, for he knows that, if it is at all decent weather, it is his uncle's custom, after his turn in the park, to take his lunch there; and in the afternoon he will make his way to Ronald Ringwood's chambers.

Jack had estimated his interview with his uncle very accurately. Lord Lakington welcomed him cordially back to England, but when Jack touched upon his passion for his cousin the Viscount was excessively polite, but equally unsatisfactory. He was very sorry for Jack; some boy-and-girl flirtation he knew there had been between him and Beatrice, but he had never regarded it as serious. He was very sorry, but things had gone much too far now; and even if they had not, he could hardly counsel his daughter to give up the brilliant prospects before her for the sake of a mere love-match.

'My dear Jack,' he said, 'just consider. You have got no money, at least what amounts to no money, to start housekeeping upon. It is only the lower classes who commit the turpitude of marriage without first building and furnishing a nest. Personally, I would sooner give you Beatrice than any man I know; but it never could be. It would be years, you know, before you were in any position to keep her. I am sorry for you, but have no doubt you will soon get over it. Remember that, as far as you are concerned, marriage with Beatrice is impossible;' and as Phillimore walked away he conscientiously repeated Charles Lamb's old joke – 'He did not know Pegram, but he damned him at hazard.'

In accordance with his resolve of the previous day, Jack Phillimore had no sooner finished his interview with his uncle than he set his face east, and made the best of his way to Ronald Ringwood's chambers in the Temple. He found that light of the law at home, in active discussion of a short pipe, and one of those sheaves of paper usually conspicuous in all legal proceedings. Jack's name, of course, was quite sufficient an introduction. Ringwood shook him heartily by the hand, put him into an easy-chair, proffered him tobacco in all shapes, and then said,

'Now you shall tell me what there is to tell about dear old Bob; by the time you have done that I hope you will feel that I am no longer a stranger.'

Jack Phillimore heartily responded to his host's cordial welcome. He lit one of the proffered cigars, and briefly told the little there was to tell about Bob Ringwood.

'By the way,' he continued, 'that was a very curious bit of news that you sent me in your last letter to him. I never heard my uncle make the slightest allusion to being engaged in any such big lottery as you mentioned. Of course I understand that it is only a chance, but if it did come off it would be a tremendous windfall for him. I should think it would enable him to clear Laketon.'

'That, of course, I cannot say, having no conception of the extent of his liabilities; but since I wrote Lord Lakington has taken steps to ensure that a big slice of that hundred and sixty thousand pounds falls to himself. I was talking over the whole thing with Mr Carbuckle, one of the great "guns" of our profession, and an old friend of the Viscount's, and he said it was quite one of the smartest moves he had ever heard of.'

'What the deuce do you mean?' said Phillimore.

'Why, surely you have heard that your cousin, the Honourable Miss Beatrice, is about to be married.'

'Yes; to a brute called Pegram, I am told. And why on earth she is going to marry him we can none of us understand, unless it is that the beast has lots of money.'

'I can make that clear to you in a very few words. Pegram senior is one of the three nominators left in the "Great Tontine". His son is to marry Lord Lakington's daughter, so that the Viscount and Pegram senior may share the whole hundred and sixty thousand pounds between them as soon as they can prove the death of the nominee of Miss Caterham, the third nominator left in. He was an old man of wandering habits, and, as he has not been heard of for some time, the probability is that the result of the inquiries the Pegrams are instituting will result in the discovery of his decease.'

'What a rascally plot,' exclaimed Jack Phillimore passionately. 'I begin to see it all now. Beatrice is sacrificing herself and me for the sake of her father. Do you know that I looked upon myself as engaged to my cousin when I left England some few months ago.'

'No, I cannot say I did; nor did I know of this projected marriage till about three nights ago. I certainly did know that Lord Lakington had a daughter, because, as Miss Caterham's representative of the "Great Tontine", I made it my duty to inquire about the other competitors. I, like the Pegrams, am diligently searching for Miss Caterham's missing nominee, although, of course, in diametrically opposite interest to theirs: my object being to find the old man alive, and theirs to find him dead. Now, you will not feel offended if I ask you one question?'

Jack shook his head in the negative.

'Do you love your cousin Beatrice in genuine earnest?'

'Do I love her? What nonsense you are talking; she is the only woman I ever cared a rush about in the course of my life. Have I not come home to claim her as my bride, and prevent this disgraceful marriage, if possible?'

'Then you will excuse my asking you one more delicate question. Have you been at all successful?'

'No; my uncle won't listen to me. He says the marriage is all arranged, and must take place; while Beatrice refuses to see me. I *did* see her by accident yesterday, and, to make matters worse, lost my confounded temper, and quarrelled with her.'

'Well, Mr Phillimore, you cannot be said to have done much for yourself as yet. What do you say to entering into partnership with me? If some vague suspicions I have formed should happen to be justified, there will be an end to this marriage at once.'

'I will do anything to save Beatrice from her imprudence. She may never be mine; but I am convinced that she is marrying this man very much against her own inclinations, and is likely to be a very miserable wife in consequence.'

'Just wait a bit, while I think it over,' replied Ringwood, and he began to walk up and down the room. Two or three minutes' thought, and he came to a stop; and, leaning his back against the mantel-piece, said, 'Now listen to me, and don't interrupt me till I have finished. You can easily understand, that to gain such a sum as this an unscrupulous person would not be likely to stick at any fraud which he fancied might escape detection. A very clever man, upon hearing that I was acting for Miss Caterham, remarked "I can only say, that, in your case, I should scrutinize the other competitors pretty closely." That is how I come to know so much about your uncle and the Pegrams as I do. Now, although noblemen at times have shown themselves by no means exempt from the frailties of their baser-born brethren, still I am not for a moment insinuating that Lord Lakington would condescend to foul play of any description; but, about these Pegrams, strictly between you and me, I don't feel implicit confidence. They are lawyers, and the old man especially has the reputation of being a hard, crafty man, very unscrupulous in driving a bargain, and dabbling a good deal in speculation and money-lending. I intend to investigate the proceedings of the Pegrams during the last few months pretty closely, and, if possible, find out who is their nominee. Now this ought to suit you as well as me. If Pegram has committed a fraud, this marriage will, of course, fall through; or we may succeed in finding such strong presumption that he has done so as to justify a postponement of the marriage. That would suit you; while, on my side, I should get rid of one of Miss Caterham's adversaries perhaps.'

'By Jove! that is a splendid idea. I will go in with you heart and soul.'

'Wait a bit. I must point out that there is one drawback to which you are liable. Should we fail, and—as is very probable—our *espionage* be discovered, it may lead you into a quarrel with your uncle and cousin.'

'I don't care what it leads to; I will do everything in my power to stop this marriage.'

'Very good; then the first thing we have got to do is to ascertain, if possible, who is likely to be old Pegram's nominee. I have a friend who, I think, will give us a valuable hint on that point if he can only be convinced that this marriage is against Miss Phillimore's inclination.'

'But when he hears all that I have to tell him surely that will be sufficient,' replied Phillimore, hastily.

'Well, she refused to see you; and when you achieved an interview by accident, according to your own account, a quarrel was the immediate result;

no, my dear Phillimore, that is hardly good enough to go to a jury on. Is there not any friend of the family who takes your part?'

'Yes; Mrs Lyme Wregis, Beatrice's grandmother. It was she who sent me word of this projected marriage, and called me home from Malta. Beatrice has lived with her all her life.'

'What! the widow of the famous financier who slew himself some sixteen or eighteen years ago? That is the very thing. It is very possible my friend Hemmingby, the manager of the "Vivacity", knows something of her – he does of most people – and if they are given to dramatic entertainment is sure to. You get a note from her, strongly backing up your case, and I think then Hemmingby will help us. He knows these Pegrams well, and almost hinted the other night that he could make a pretty shrewd guess in what direction to begin his inquiries.'

'All right,' said Phillimore, rising. 'I will get that letter from Mrs Lyme Wregis tomorrow, and we will expose these Pegram bandits before the week is out.'

'Hardly as soon as that, I fear,' replied Ringwood, as he shook hands. 'If we succeed in doing it before the marriage we shall do well.'

## CHAPTER NINETEEN

# THE YOUNG DETECTIVES

Jack Phillimore was as energetic a young gentleman of eight-and-twenty as needs be. Of a restless and active disposition, he was not at all the man to sit with his arms crossed under any circumstances. Never was there any one more utterly blind to the passive delights of indolence; never any one who more thoroughly failed to comprehend the languid delights of the *dolce far niente*. Jack, to use his own expression, was always 'taking it out of himself'. On the hottest day in summer he would contrive for himself active occupation of some sort. In fact, as his uncle once told him, on such an occasion it was enough to make people hot merely to look at him. That he should engage in this campaign against the Pegrams with all his characteristic energy was only natural. It was a fight for the hand of the girl he loved, mixed with that wholesome animosity towards a rival that can always be depended upon in the glamour of a first passion. He was in the Victoria Road soon after twelve; and, asking for Mrs Lyme Wregis, found that lady, as he anticipated, in the drawing-room alone. Beatrice, he felt pretty sure, would not see him; nor did he think it likely, as things stood, that his uncle would very much care to meet him. Jack was quite aware that he had a tolerably substantial grievance against him as well as his daughter; the Viscount, in spite of his plausible explanations, having undoubtedly given tacit acquiescence to his suit.

'I am afraid I did not play my cards well yesterday,' said Jack, the first greetings passed. 'I a little lost my temper. I was tried rather hardly.'

'Yes,' replied Mrs Lyme Wregis; 'you had a chance and failed to take advantage of it. There was a moment when she was in a melting mood; and if you had only been tender with her then, I think the chances are that she would have confessed everything, and we should at least have known the "why" of this strange marriage.'

Jack Phillimore did not think it necessary to tell Mrs Lyme Wregis that this was no longer a mystery, as far as he was concerned. He merely replied –

'I must do my best to remedy the mistake. In the meantime, strictly between ourselves, you will promise me, Mrs Lyme Wregis, not even to hint, not to breathe a word of what I am going to tell you?'

'You may rely upon my silence,' said the old lady, curtly.

'It has been suggested to me that there is something not quite right about these Pegrams, and surely that is a point that ought to be cleared up. I am given to understand that the man who holds possession of the clue quite declines to open his mouth on the matter unless he is first firmly convinced that Beatrice is in reality averse to this proposed marriage.'

'Well, why do you not tell him that she is so?'

'Ah, you see that, as a rejected lover, he would hardly credit my evidence on that point. There is only one person that I can think of whom he is likely to accept as an authority, and that is yourself.'

'Me! But who on earth, pray, is this mysterious unknown? And when, where, and how does he expect me to testify?'

'You know Mr Hemmingby, manager of the Vivacity Theatre, I think?'

'Yes, very slightly; Lakington has brought him up into our box once or twice. I am quite willing, if it pleases you, to admit that he seemed a pleasant, gentlemanly man enough; but you don't, surely, expect me to write and call him to the family counsels?'

'And yet if you do not, I don't know how we are to get this clue that I require.'

'But, my dear Jack, it is impossible. I cannot write to a man I only just know about such an extremely delicate subject as this. You must see that yourself.'

'Yes, I will admit it is very awkward; but I do not know what else to suggest. You would do a good deal to break off this Pegram marriage, would you not?'

'Most decidedly, although I should be running in direct opposition to your uncle. Still, I am convinced that Beatrice's heart is not in it, and that nothing but unhappiness can come of it; but I do not see it is possible for me to write to Mr Hemmingby.'

'Stop. I think I have it. You cannot write to Mr Hemmingby; but there is no reason why you should not write a letter to me, which I can show to him and which will doubtless have the same effect.'

'I do not mind doing that, Jack,' replied the old lady; 'only, remember, I must not be supposed to know that it is going to be shown to anybody, nor do I want to know anything about what you are doing for the present. It will be quite sufficient for me to hear all about it whenever you have that to tell to Mr Pegram's disadvantage which shall make this marriage impossible. It is a madness on the part of Beatrice and her father. Their attempting to keep me hood-winked about the real reasons of this match is simply a gross piece of disrespect on both their parts. No; I have argued my best against this marriage with each of them, and now I trust I am about to do something more.'

And so saying, the old lady rose, and going to a davenport which stood close at hand, proceeded to write rapidly for two or three minutes. She folded up her note, placed it in an envelope, directed it, and then, to Jack Phillimore's astonishment, proceeded to fasten it and stamp it.

'There,' she said, as she handed it him, 'you will find that all you want; but I prefer that it should go through the post, so that there may be no suspicion of its having been written for Mr Hemmingby's perusal. Drop it into the pillar-box as you go out. It will be at the British Hotel in the course of two or three hours.'

'Thank you very much,' said Jack, as he took the missive. 'It shall be posted as you wish. Armed with this, if I have any luck, I shall beat that beast Pegram yet; and now I will say good-bye. Do not expect to see me more than occasionally for some little time;' and with that Phillimore took his departure.

He had not been gone many minutes before Beatrice made her appearance. She very soon led up to the subject of her cousin's visit, of which, of course, she had been duly advertised. But Mrs Lyme Wregis was in no humour to indulge her granddaughter upon this occasion. She could not be got to talk over her late visitor at all, and her replies even to direct questions were of the briefest. Of course, what Jack Phillimore had to say could, and should, be nothing to Miss Beatrice now; but, for all that, the girl seemed curious to arrive at what had passed between him and her grandmother. But the most persistent cross-examination elicited nothing from Mrs Lyme Wregis; and when, at length, in reply to the direct question, 'Did Jack ask after me?' the old lady answered with no little asperity, 'No, indeed; not very likely, after the way you treated him yesterday,' Beatrice gave the thing up, and retreated to her room to cry over this cast-off lover of hers in a manner most highly inconsistent.

These poor rejected ones have many a salt tear to their memory before all is forgotten, an they but knew it.

Jack Phillimore dawdled over his lunch at the British Hotel, awaiting the arrival of that note of Mrs Lyme Wregis's which he had himself posted, and feeling a little disposed to anathematize that lady's over-caution. No sooner did it arrive than Jack sped to the Temple, and, placing it in Ringwood's hands, suggested the sooner they saw Mr Hemmingby the better. The two accordingly proceeded to the 'Vivacity', and were fortunate enough to find that Mr Hemmingby had not left the theatre. They were soon ushered into the manager's presence, and then, having introduced his companion, Ringwood went straight to the point. He had seen a good bit of Sam Hemmingby by this time, and knew that few things made that gentleman more impatient than what is termed 'beating about the bush'. Time is money, the manager was wont to observe. You have no business to waste mine because you have not made up your mind to speak out.

Sam Hemmingby had shaken hands courteously with Phillimore, and listened attentively to what Ringwood had to say.

'I gave you a hint,' he interposed at length, 'about what I should do if I were in your place, and I told you then that I had nothing now to do with it, and as they were both friends of mine, had excellent reasons for not meddling with what does not concern me.'

'Yes,' replied Ringwood, who had evidently got up his brief with great care; 'but you would not see the young lady sacrificed fraudulently to a Pegram when it is within your power to prevent it.'

'I tell you what it is, my legal friend,' observed the manager, with an amused smile, 'your language is florid, and I should think a little libellous. Allow me to remark that I know nothing about any fraud; and as for the lady, she is going to marry Bob Pegram of her own free will, and it is most obviously no business of mine even if she is only marrying him to please her relations.'

'But, my dear Hemmingby, I assure you you are all wrong. She is being entrapped into this marriage under false pretences, very much against her real inclinations. Will you just read this letter? It is from a lady you know, Mrs Lyme Wregis, and see what she says.'

'What the devil is it to me,' said the manager, testily, 'whom Miss Phillimore marries? I am neither guardian nor relation to her, and, of course, have nothing to do with it.'

But, for all that, he took the letter that Ringwood proffered. He read it carefully, and as he concluded, said,

'Well, the writer speaks her mind pretty plainly. She is the young lady's grandmother, is she not?'

Ringwood nodded assent.

'Well, it does seem rather throwing herself away,' continued the manager, 'a beautiful girl like Miss Phillimore marrying such a one-horse looking concern as Bob Pegram. Still, though they won't match, Bob is a good-tempered fellow; they will have plenty of gold dust, and I have no doubt will run together pretty comfortably.'

'But still,' burst in hot-headed Jack Phillimore, 'you are an old friend of Lord Lakington's; you would surely not see his daughter made miserable for life by being married to a man she cannot care about – a man like Pegram, whose account of himself, after all, is extremely doubtful.'

'Excuse me, Mr Phillimore,' replied the manager. 'That Bob Pegram is what he represents himself to be, I can vouch for; but you are a relation, and so have a claim to interfere; to say nothing,' he concluded slowly, and with a slight twinkle of his eye, 'of a rather *personal* interest in the matter *if* I mistake not.'

'Be quiet, Phillimore,' suddenly exclaimed Ringwood. 'Look here, Hemmingby, you know just as well as we do that this marriage is simply the amalgamation of the two last shareholders, as they suppose themselves, in the "Great Tontine". I declare I think, under the circumstances, that somebody ought to see that old Pegram's claim is all right. If Lord Lakington is too indolent to take the trouble, then I really think that Jack Phillimore, as Miss Beatrice's next nearest relation, is justified in seeing that Miss Beatrice's wedding settlements, which, in good truth, are involved in the "Tontine", are all right and genuine.'

'Quite so,' replied the manager. 'Still, as I said before, what have I to do with all this?'

'Everything and nothing,' replied Ringwood. 'We will investigate the Pegrams; but what we want you to do for us, is just to give us a hint where to begin.'

'I do not call this quite a fair question, Ringwood,' rejoined Sam Hemmingby. 'I went so far the other night as to tell you confidentially that I should look the Pegrams up pretty closely *if* I had a share in the "Tontine", and that should be enough for you.'

'Then, unfortunately, you see it is not. We will never mention your name, but you must give us a hint as to where to begin our investigations.'

'Well, I know it will be downright foolish of me to tell you. I have all the inward qualms that a man always has when he knows he is going to make a downright fool of himself; but before I do so you must answer me one question, Mr Phillimore. Am I right in thinking that you have a *personal* interest in this affair?'

'If you mean, am I in love with my cousin, Mr Hemmingby,' replied Jack, 'Yes. If you mean, did I consider myself engaged to her before this Robert Pegram made his appearance, Yes. If you mean, do I intend to marry her in spite of Pegram or anybody else, again, Yes.'

'Ahem!' rejoined the manager, laughing; 'I begin to think my dinner to Bob Pegram was a little premature. Taking all things together, I should not wonder if this marriage was a good bit further off than he anticipates.'

'And now,' exclaimed Ringwood, breathlessly, 'what is to be our first move?'

'I think,' replied Hemmingby, slowly, 'that the history of the illness of Mr Krabbe, from the time he broke down in Pegram's office, and had to give up work, down to the state of his health in his retirement at the present day, would very likely pay for looking into.'

'Crabb – Crabb; I never heard the name before,' observed Ringwood. 'How do you spell it – C-r-a-b-b?'

'No; it is rather singularly spelt – K-r-a-b-b-e – Krabbe. He was, till lately, old Pegram's confidential clerk, and that is where I should begin, no matter why.'

'Well, Phillimore,' exclaimed Ringwood, rising, 'we must be very grateful for what has been vouchsafed to us. Good-bye, Hemmingby; I do not suppose we shall get any more out of you.'

'No,' rejoined the manager, laughing. 'The oracle has spoken. When you have worked out the clue I have given you let me know the result, and I will tell you what I think of you as detectives.'

The two young men once more adjourned to Ringwood's rooms with a view to talking over matters, and settling the plan of the campaign without delay. One thing was perfectly clear to both of them, that, having with considerable difficulty obtained Hemmingby's advice, they were bound to act upon it without delay. To do this it was of course necessary that they should either go or send some one down to Rydland, and the *pros* and *cons* as to who should go were discussed at some length. But it was at last resolved that it should be undertaken by one of themselves; and then it became obvious that it must fall to Phillimore's lot.

If it had been an advantage to Ringwood to be brought face to face with Bob Pegram, and by so doing get an accurate knowledge of his antagonist's personality, yet it cut the other way now. Of course, if he went down to Rydland he would be very liable to meet Bob Pegram, and that gentleman would naturally wonder what could have brought him down to a place like that, and, to say nothing of the difficulty of explaining his presence in a little country town like Rydland, his investigations would be pretty certain to attract Bob Pegram's notice.

Now, none of these objections applied to Phillimore. He could go down there and peer about in any guise he liked. His would be a perfectly unknown face to the Pegrams, even if he did come across them; and therefore it was at last resolved that Jack Phillimore should proceed next day to Rydland. And by the time they had settled this important question, their appetites reminded them that it was quite time to see about dinner; and as there was still a good deal to be talked over between them, they agreed to dine together at the British Hotel, and continue the discussion.

Now, anybody less calculated for a delicate mission of this nature than Jack Phillimore could not possibly be imagined. The quick, impetuous, reckless sailor, taking any hearsay for fact, and jumping from thence to the most unjustifiable conclusions, was just about the last man in the world to conduct a delicate investigation. Jack Phillimore had admirable qualities for his profession – quick, cool, self-reliant, and decided, he was a born leader of men; but he had neither a logical nor inductive mind. Even Ronald Ringwood, as they sat over their wine after dinner, had doubts about his companion's fitness for the task he had undertaken, but, without mortally offending his companion, he saw no way now in which it could be entrusted to other hands.

Bitten by Ringwood's account as to young Pegram's masquerading at Guildford, Jack determined that he also must start upon his mission disguised. It was in vain that Ringwood urged there could be no necessity for so doing, that unless you were thoroughly accustomed to it, playing a part is difficult, and very liable to detection. A man is not always on the *qui vive*. He forgets his assumed character for the moment, and betrays himself to the lookers-on in that short interval of forgetfulness. But Jack, in reply, said that he only proposed to assume the garb of a sailor, and argued that that was a *rôle* in which it was impossible he could come to grief. Ringwood cited the case of Bob Pegram's hands as an instance how want of attention to a minor detail betrayed a man under such circumstances, and again hinted that perhaps they should be better to leave the affair to a detective. But no; Phillimore had made up his mind to undertake this matter himself, and there was consequently no more to be said; and when they separated, it was thoroughly understood that Phillimore, under the guise of a common sailor, should make his way to Rydland on the morrow, and pick up all the information concerning old Krabbe that he could manage.

## CHAPTER TWENTY

# JACK PHILLIMORE AT RYDLAND

If we have seen nothing of old lawyer Pegram of late, it must not be supposed that crafty practitioner was not keeping a watchful eye upon the web he had spun with so much care. He stayed down in Wales, exactly as he told Lord Lakington he should do when the marriage had been satisfactorily accomplished. He knew that the connection had been rather a difficult pill for Lord Lakington to swallow, and he had no wish to make it more difficult to him by ostentatiously parading himself as the bridegroom's father. So long as he attained his ends, the old lawyer was quite content to remain in the background. He thoroughly understood that neither tailors nor bootmakers could metamorphose him into a man accustomed to society; he therefore wisely adhered to his usual somewhat full-skirted black riding-coat and rather low-crowned hat, in which he might have passed for either a well-to-do farmer, prosperous corn-factor, or, indeed, for the thriving country solicitor he was.

His son, on the contrary, had recourse to the London tradesmen, and certainly, to some extent, benefited thereby. They had toned him down in his attire, and suppressed a tendency to flashiness for which Bob had an unmistakable weakness. Turned out by a London artist, Mr Bob Pegram was a plain but a tolerably gentlemanly-looking young man.

Although, in a business point of view, it suits Mr Bob Pegram, yet his vanity is rather wounded at the disinclination his *fiancée* unmistakably manifests for his society.

It is in vain that his father points out to him that he ought to consider himself fortunate that such is the case. Mr Bob Pegram, in his previous *amours*, had been wont to find his coming and going the occasion of much demonstration. He certainly cannot flatter himself on that point now, as anybody more serenely indifferent to his presence, since he has become engaged to her, than the Honourable Beatrice, Mr Bob Pegram is fain to confess that he has yet never encountered.

'Tut, boy!' his father would say, upon hearing him grumble on this point;

'it is the way of these swells. They do not think it in good style to be much in earnest about anything. You cannot well be away from here just now; and just think how inconvenient it would have been if this Miss Phillimore had wanted to keep you dangling at her apron-strings all the time! Once you are married, remember, you can see as much as you like of her; but, mark me, Bob, you must agree to no further putting off of this wedding. The Viscount has fixed it at a pretty long date, considering the circumstances, and I shall not feel comfortable until the knot is tied; no further postponement, remember.'

'No; quite right, father; I am tired myself of this ceremonious sweethearting. Courting is not courting when there is never a kiss nor a squeeze in it.'

The scene of the above conversation was the inner room of old Pegram's offices, what, indeed, was his own room; but since Bob had come into partnership with him he also had a writing-table there. At this juncture their talk was interrupted by the opening of the door, and the entrance of one of the clerks with some papers for his master's signature.

'Nothing new in the town, I suppose, Evans,' said Bob Pegram, looking up from his newspaper, the perusal of which the conversation of his father had interrupted. 'I suppose Tom Davis has not thrashed Slater, the butcher, for sticking him with that old bay horse. He was talking very big about it last market day.'

'No, Mr Robert; Tom Davis is always a bigger man in his cups than he is out of them. If he had thrashed half the men that he has threatened to after the "ordinary", there would be a sight of sore bones in Rydland. No; the only bit of news about this morning – if it is to be called a bit of news – is, that there is a sailor-chap in the town inquiring after poor old Mr Krabbe. I never recollect anybody asking after him before.'

'Well, no, Evans; he has not a relation in the world that we know of. However, I dare say we shall have the sailor here in course of time?'

'No doubt, sir,' replied Evans. 'Anybody inquiring after Mr Krabbe is certain to call at Pegram and Son's before he has done.' And so saying, Evans closed the door behind him.

'I say, governor,' exclaimed Mr Robert Pegram, 'that's deuced odd. Who can be inquiring after old Krabbe after all these years?'

'Well,' replied his father, 'nothing is more likely than that he should have some distant relatives who, hearing that he has retired, and is getting pretty nearly to the end of his tether, have thought it worth while to come and see if there is any pickings for a next-of-kin.'

Jack Phillimore, most artistically attired as a smart young sailor, with hands carefully stained, etc., had made his appearance in Rydland the previous night, and, putting up at a second class inn, had deferred his inquiries till the following day. And now Jack, unwittingly, began to experience the difficulties of the task he had undertaken. To begin upon, he attracted considerable attention in the quiet little country town. Rydland had nothing to do with ships and the shipping interest: it was a purely agricultural market town; and a thorough Jack tar such as Phillimore was a sight it rarely witnessed. The inhabitants, like most towns of its class, had plenty of spare time on their hands except on market-day. The consequence was, that Rydland came pretty generally to its shop-doors to look at the handsome sailor who was loafing about its streets inquiring for Mr Krabbe. The women especially were enthusiastic about the handsome seaman; and invented facts and anecdotes about Mr Krabbe with the most audacious effrontery for the gratification of talking to him. The men took to him for his frank, free, out-spoken manner; in fact, in four-and-twenty hours Jack Fluter, as it pleased him to call himself, was in a fair way of becoming the most popular man in Rydland. But Jack would have been disgusted if he had known that there was neither man nor woman that he had spoken to who, in spite of the nautical jargon that he affected, had not fathomed the fact that he was, at all events, born in a superior station to that which his present garb indicated him as holding.

As he smoked his evening pipe in the sanded parlour of the 'Greyhound', Jack Phillimore comforted himself with the reflection that he had done a rattling good day's work. He had ascertained that old Mr Krabbe had been a clerk in Pegram's office for something like five-and-thirty years. Everybody in Rydland knew him, a quiet, pleasant, kindly old gentleman; a man of middle age when he first came to Rydland, but a very old man now. He used to have Mrs Moody's first floor – she keeps the Berlin wool-shop in the market-place – until his illness; then Mr Pegram took a cottage for him out-side the town, and pensioned him off, and he lives there now, with a nurse to take care of him. Rather a mystery to Rydland that nurse. It was odd a good-looking woman at her age – and she could not be above six or seven-and-thirty, if she was that – could be induced to take such a place. However, they supposed Mr Pegram made it worth her while, and she knew it could not last long; though about this latter Rydland differed, and had much to say. Old people in Mr Krabbe's state, as some people pointed out, sometimes lingered on for years. He was slightly paralysed, and somewhat daft; 'just dazed like', as one of Jack Phillimore's informants explained to him. A goodly budget of information, thought Jack; all this to have acquired in one day.

On one point had he failed, and that was in seeing Mr Krabbe. He had been out to the cottage, seen the nurse, and quite agreed with Rydland that she was not at all the sort of woman that he should have expected to find holding such a post; but he had not succeeded in seeing Mr Krabbe. The nurse was very civil, and would have apparently made no difficulty about his seeing her patient, only that he was asleep. He slept, she said, a great deal, and it was a mercy that he did so. Disturbing him made him very irritable, and it seemed a pity to do so when it was very doubtful whether he would recognize his visitor when he saw him. Of course, as Jack said, in his case that could not be expected. He was a distant connection whom, in all probability, Mr Krabbe had never seen; still he should like to see the old man. The nurse told him if he called about noon the next day, the probability is that he would find Mr Krabbe awake, and that he could then see him.

Excessively well satisfied with his day's work, and the manner in which he had played his part, Jack laid out his plans for the next day. He conceived that he had nothing much to do now beyond seeing Mr Krabbe; but, as the train did not go till the afternoon, Jack determined further to call upon lawyer Pegram, and see what he could make out of him. The idea of thus venturing as a spy into the very heart of the enemy's camp tickled Jack Phillimore amazingly; he hugged himself upon the audacity of his invention, and called for another glass of brandy-and-water upon the strength of it. That and his pipe finished, Jack tripped off to bed as light-hearted as if he had already succeeded in exploding all Bob Pegram's matrimonial schemes, and was himself to take his pretty cousin to church in the morning.

Ten o'clock the next day saw Jack in Mr Pegram's offices, and respectfully inquiring of the clerks if he could see that gentleman. Evans went through the form of asking him his business, although, of course, he knew the moment he saw him that this was the sailor who had been inquiring about Mr Krabbe all over Rydland the previous day. Jack told Evans the same story that he had told the nurse at the cottage, to wit, that he was a distant connection of the old man; and further added, that he would like to ask Mr Pegram a few questions about the old gentleman's last illness, and thank him for the kindness he had shown him. Evans, of course, requested him to take a chair while he let Mr Pegram know that he, Jack Fluter, wished to see him. A few minutes more, and the clerk, requesting him 'to step this way', ushered him into the presence of the Pegrams, father and son.

'Well, my man, you want to see me; what is it? That is my son and partner, Mr Robert Pegram,' he continued, seeing Jack's eye wander towards that gentleman; 'you can speak out before him just as you would speak to me. Now what is it?'

'Well, damn that ugly beggar's audacity,' muttered Jack to himself. 'The idea of his having the presumption to think of Beatrice!' 'Well, your honour,' he replied to Mr Pegram's question, 'I ain't much of a hand at a yarn, but, you see, my father, he married a niece of old Mr Krabbe's; and so, as I was cruising in these parts, I thought I'd just have a look at the old gentleman, 'cause my mother she thought a deal of him, she did; and as I hear he lived with you a many years, I thought, may be, your honour would tell me something about him if I called.' And here Jack used his pocket-handkerchief, considerably more after the manner of the quarter-deck than the forecastle.

'Very good,' rejoined old Pegram. 'I shall be happy to supply you with all the information you require about Mr Krabbe; but, in the first place, let us know who you are exactly.'

'Jack Fluter, boatswain's mate on board Her Majesty's ship *Cassiope*.'

Neither old Pegram nor his son had the slightest previous knowledge of the name *Cassiope*, and yet they both felt intuitively that a common sailor would not have so pronounced the name of a ship.

'And the name of your captain is —' inquired the old lawyer.

'Fletcher, your honour; and a real smart officer he is. If he is hardish on the skulkers, he is a good skipper to the chaps as does their duty. They were telling me in the town, sir, that my great uncle served his biggest spell under your honour's command.'

'Mr Krabbe was over thirty years in our office, and when he broke down last year we pensioned him off as an old and valued servant. We found a nice little cottage for him about three quarters of a mile from the town, and got a practised nurse down from London to take care of him. You must know he has broken down both mentally and bodily; however, you will be glad to hear that he is well taken care of, and everything that can be done for a man in his position is, we trust, done for him.'

'Yes, I am told everywhere that your honour has been very kind to the poor old gentleman. I went out to his cottage yesterday to see him, but he was asleep, the nurse said, and she did not like to disturb him. I was thinking if your honour saw no harm in it, I'd just run out and try and have a look at him today.'

'Harm!' rejoined Pegram, as he once more eyed the sailor keenly through his spectacles; 'of course not. His old friends, relatives, or indeed anybody else, are quite welcome to see Mr Krabbe whenever they think fit. As I have no doubt his nurse told you, he sleeps a great deal, is very irritable, and apt at times to be very much put out by seeing those who are virtually strangers to him, that is, old acquaintances he can no longer recollect; of course, if, as is very likely, your presence annoys him you will cut your visit short.'

'Aye, aye, sir; the old gentleman ain't likely to know me, as he never saw me before; but my people will be main pleased to hear I have seen him, and we'll all feel grateful to your honour for the care you have taken of him. There's a many owners don't care what becomes of their "hands" when they are worn out; but your honour is one of the right sort, and finds snug harbourage for those as is past sea-going. Good-bye, and thank your honour kindly for all the care you have taken of my great-uncle;' and, with a regular sailor's scrape, Jack Phillimore took his departure:

'That fellow is no more a common sailor than I am,' remarked Mr Pegram, as the door closed behind their late visitor.

'No,' replied his son, whom business had often taken to Liverpool, and one or two other large seaport towns. 'He did not use his handkerchief much like a foremast hand.'

'No,' replied the old lawyer; 'that fellow is sailing under false colours, to use his own jargon. Who he is agent for, and what they are aiming at, is not so easy to guess. His present object, no doubt, is to see old Krabbe *in propriâ personâ*. Well, they won't make much of that, save that they will perhaps consider him rather a promising life to look at from their point of view. He don't look as if he would last much longer, Bob, eh?' and here old Pegram went off into a low chuckle, in which his son most heartily joined. 'It is odd,' he continued, 'too, who that fellow's employer can be. It is not likely to be Lord Lakington. He is too big a swell to think of anything of that kind; besides, damme, he don't even know there is such a person as old Krabbe.'

'No,' replied Bob Pegram, as he rose from his table and buried his hands in his pockets. 'This is a deuced rum business; that fellow can't be a spy of Miss Caterham's for the same reason. It is extremely improbable that either she or her lawyers know of old Krabbe's existence.'

'No,' muttered his father. 'This is queer, Bob, very queer. The sooner this marriage is over, my boy, the better. We have somebody pulling the strings against us who knows a good deal more of our game than I like. Whoever he is, he somehow or other has got more than an inkling that old Krabbe is "our life" – my nominee – in the "Great Tontine". It bodes us no good, Bob, to have so keen-witted a knave prying into our affairs.'

'No; in the meantime I must just slip down to the cottage and tell Mrs Clark that, irritable or not irritable, the old man *must* show this morning.'

'Yes; and perhaps the more waspish he is the better. But one moment, Bob; just send little Blinks in here – he is a sharp lad that, and I am just going to tell him to follow the sailor wherever he goes. I shall furnish him with money, because I expect that sailor means leaving Rydland tonight, and I am rather curious to know where he goes to.'

'Quite right, father; it is just as well that we should know who is poking his nose into our affairs, and young Blinks ought to have little difficulty in tracking our nautical friend to his lair;' and with that Mr Bob Pegram picked up his hat and left the room.

After giving young Blinks his instructions, and furnishing him with a small sum of money, old Pegram remained some two or three minutes immersed in thought. At last he rose from his chair, crossed the room to a strong safe, which was fixed against the wall in one corner, and opening it with a somewhat complicated key, took from it a voluminous parchment deed. He glanced over it for a few minutes, and then restored it to its place. 'I don't like it,' he muttered; 'it looks bad, very. I have a crafty antagonist spying into my game, who evidently has a strong suspicion of the weak point in it. Still, as long as he employs such bunglers to do his work as he has done this time, it will take him months before he becomes much wiser, even if he does then, and all I ask is a few weeks. Only let that deed be signed, and this marriage knot tied, and I will not only snap my fingers at him, but will perhaps a little astonish him besides.'

Jack Phillimore, after leaving Pegram and Son's office, continued to lounge about Rydland gossiping with everybody he came across, and still under the delusion that he was admirably personating the British seaman, and considerably increasing his stock of information as regarded old Krabbe. It was true such points as that Mr Krabbe had been much liked and respected as a man of very regular habits, though excessively partial to strong ale – in moderation, be it understood – and that he invariably covered his bald pate with what is usually determined a 'brown scratch' wig, might be certainly facts concerning that venerable old gentleman; but it was hard to see what use he and Ringwood were to make of such knowledge now they had acquired it. However, at the end of that time Jack Phillimore thought he had best proceed to the cottage, and, if possible, see Mr Krabbe in the flesh. After following the high road to Llanbarlym for about three quarters of a mile, he turned down a narrow lane to his right, and came, in about a couple of hundred yards, to a quiet, clean little cottage standing in a pretty garden. Passing through the garden, he tapped lightly at the door, which, after some slight delay, was opened by the same woman whom he had seen on the preceding day. She welcomed him with a smile, and said,

'Of course you have come out again to see the old man; if you will just step into the parlour and sit down he will be in in a few minutes. I am afraid you won't make much of him, for he is very queer and crotchety this morning; but then he is always that, more or less, and when it is an amiable day with him it is generally because he is rather drowsy. If you will take a chair,' she continued, opening the door of the parlour, 'I will bring him to you directly almost. No, not that one, please,' she exclaimed, laughing, as Jack was about to throw himself into a big leather arm-chair by the fire. 'That is Mr Krabbe's, and to find anybody in his own particular seat would put the old man out dreadfully.'

Complying with the nurse's instructions, Jack hastily stowed himself upon a more ordinary chair, and then awaited with no little curiosity the appearance of the old man, of whom he had heard so much during the last four-and-twenty hours. He had not long to wait. The door opened, and supported by the buxom nurse on the one side, and assisted by a stout stick, upon which he leaned a good deal, on the other, there appeared a sad specimen of senile old age. The old man in his prime had probably been below the middle height, but was now so bowed by age and infirmity as to be considerably shorter than his attendant, although she was no out of the way tall woman. The pale, wrinkled cheeks, heavy shaggy white eyebrows, and the tottering gait, all betokened a man of great age. He was habited in an old-fashioned double-breasted tailcoat with flap pockets, a buff waistcoat, black trousers cut in the mode of our grandfathers, from the fob of which projected a black silk ribbon with a massive gold seal, shoes and grey stockings; while his skull was surmounted with the 'brown scratch', of which Jack had heard so much, and which formed a rather ghastly contrast to his white cheeks and eyebrows; a heavy shawl handkerchief was loosely knotted round his throat, while the nurse also carried a rug and some other wraps on her arm. Of course Jack knew that he was a very old man, but he could not help thinking, that if he had been told he was a centenarian he should have felt no surprise. In one respect alone had he escaped the ruthless ravages of time – the eye was still comparatively bright, and, as the nurse told Jack in a stage whisper, 'his sight is wonderfully good, considering; but you must not expect him to hear or understand much.'

The old man dropped his shuffle and came to a dead stop when he saw Jack.

'What,' he piped out, in a shrill treble tone approaching to a falsetto, 'is he doing here?'

'He is come to call upon you,' shouted the nurse into his ear, 'and inquire how you are.'

'Much he knows about it,' piped the old man; 'I call it a very cold day.'

'You are quite right,' bawled Jack. 'It is cold, very cold, sir.'

'Cold! yes, I said "cold",' muttered the old man, in his childish treble. 'What did he want to say it was not cold for? People are always so contradictory and stupid;' and having thus relieved his mind, he shuffled towards the arm-chair by the fire, in which, with the nurse's assistance, he was speedily installed.

But a good deal more had to be done before things were entirely to his liking: the rug had to be placed over his legs, then an old-fashioned cloak had to be fetched from the other room and put round his shoulders; in fact, he was not content until he had been enveloped in a perfect cloud of wraps, from the midst of which his wizened old face peered out, while from his lips poured a string of querulous complaints against the cold, and the stupidity of people who did not recognize that it *was* cold.

'I don't think you will be able to make much of him,' said the nurse, quietly to Phillimore; 'and if you really have anything you wish to ask him, I am afraid you have little chance of getting an answer.'

Jack Phillimore had already recognized the impossibility of making anything out of Mr Krabbe. He *had* seen him, and felt that if he sat there and stared at him for an hour he should make nothing more of him. He rose, and was about to take his leave, when he was suddenly arrested by a very personal inquiry on the part of Mr Krabbe.

Since he had stopped maundering about the cold, the old gentleman had eyed Jack very intently, and now, as he had got up, suddenly piped out,

'Where is his pig-tail? Why does he not have a pig-tail? I recollect when I was a boy that all sailors had pig-tails. I don't believe that he is a real sailor; all sailors have pig-tails.'

'You are quite right,' said Jack, turning to the nurse. 'It is hopeless to make anything of him; still, my people at home will be glad to think that I have seen the old man. You must have weary work with him; but he is surely not likely to last very long now?'

The woman's manner to Jack suddenly changed. She had hitherto spoken in a good-natured way to him, but it was somewhat sullenly that she rejoined,

'It doesn't matter to me; if not him, it's another. But old people like this are very uncertain: they sometimes linger on for months, and sometimes flicker out very suddenly.'

'Well, good-bye; but I cannot think your present patient will trouble you long;' and slipping a small gratuity into the nurse's hand, for which she dropped him a somewhat pert curtsey, Phillimore took his departure, and made the best of his way back to Rydland.

Having paid his modest bill at the 'Greyhound', and packed up his bundle, Jack made his way to the railway station and took a ticket to London. He had some little time to wait, and paid very little attention to his few fellow-loungers on the platform. Certain it is, that when the train came up, and he jumped into a second-class carriage, he took no notice of a sleepy-looking youth, about sixteen, who got into the same compartment, coiled himself up in a corner, and apparently slumbered the whole way to town.

## CHAPTER TWENTY-ONE

# DEATH OF MISS CATERHAM

Ronald Ringwood has held rather aloof from the little cottage at Kew of late; for one thing, he really had nothing to communicate. All trace of the missing Finnigan seemed lost, and both the detective employed by Ringwood and Pegram's emissary had given up all hope of tracing the missing man from Guildford, and returned to town with a view to a fresh departure. And, in the second place, Ringwood was fain to confess that he had not got on quite so well with Mary Chichester of late. That young lady resented being kept in the dark as regards what she termed the great mystery. She argued, as we know, and with considerable reason, that it would be very much to her aunt's benefit if there was confidence between them on this point, and Miss Caterham consequently enabled to discuss the thing freely with her, Mary Chichester. But poor Miss Caterham had worked herself up into such a state of nervous apprehension of foul play on the part of her competitors for the great stake, as to be really not quite rational on that point. She could have put her fears in no very definite shape had she even tried to tell them to any one. She would have certainly expressed a strong opinion that the Pegrams, in seeking Terence Finnigan, were seeking him with murderous purpose. She had a hazy idea that even her own life might be aimed at; oblivious of the fact that she had disposed by will of her chance in the 'Great Tontine', as well as all her property, in favour of her niece, and that consequently her death would merely put Mary Chichester into her place as a shareholder in the 'Tontine', the decease of a nominee being the only thing that virtually extinguished the share. She would further have told you, although she had no knowledge on the subject, that she thought it quite possible Lord Lakington also had his emissaries working on his behalf. But just in proportion as she grew nervous and disturbed about the matter was her obstinate determination to keep the terrible secret from Mary; so much so, indeed, that she almost angrily refused the girl's pleading to share the obvious anxiety under which she was suffering, and once more most peremptorily forbade Ringwood to breathe a syllable concerning the 'Great

Tontine' to Miss Chichester. So distressed, indeed, was Mary about her aunt's state that she insisted upon her seeing her doctor. That gentleman prescribed anodynes and various composing draughts, but frankly told Miss Chichester that Miss Caterham's sleepless nights and low nervous state were caused by mental anxiety of some kind, and that his prescriptions could do but little for her. But the old lady remained obstinately silent as to her trouble, and, unfortunately, Mr Carbuckle, the only person who could have taken it upon himself to have informed Mary Chichester of what it was now obvious she ought to be acquainted with, was away on his holidays.

Ringwood was sitting in his chambers the morning after Jack Phillimore's departure for Rydland pondering over the 'Great Tontine' generally, and wondering especially what information regarding old Krabbe his new colleague would bring back. The more Ronald turned the thing over in his mind the more puzzled he was as to why Hemmingby had suggested this inquiry. He could not at all see the drift of the manager's proceeding. If old Krabbe was Pegram's nominee, however infirm he might be, he must be to the fore, although Phillimore might not succeed in seeing him. Still he would doubtless have little difficulty in gathering testimony to the fact of old Krabbe's being alive. Then his thoughts wandered off to Mary Chichester, and I am afraid that he anathematized poor Miss Caterham as an obstinate old woman for making such a mystery of the 'Tontine', and so occasioning heavy clouds to lour o'er the sunlit course of his love. Then he wondered whether Terence Finnigan really was in the land of the living, and what steps it was now possible to take that might give a chance of his discovery. And here his reflections were cut short by a sharp knock at his door.

In reply to his short 'come in', the door opened, and his clerk appeared: 'Mr Carbuckle has just sent over, sir. His compliments, and will you come across to his chambers at once.'

'All right,' replied Ringwood; and taking up his hat, he proceeded at once to comply with Mr Carbuckle's request.

Upon arriving at that gentleman's chambers, he found him pacing his study in a somewhat disturbed fashion.

'This is a very sad business, Ringwood,' he exclaimed, as he shook hands. 'Of course, poor old lady, at her time of life it is not a thing to be surprised at; but I cannot help blaming myself for not having been out to see her since I got back. I have not seen her since the beginning of the long vacation; but, after all, I have only been back four days. Still, from what Mary Chichester says in her letter, I am afraid, poor dear old lady, that the "Great Tontine" has killed her.'

'You are speaking, of course, of Miss Caterham; you do not surely mean to say that she is dead, poor thing.'

'Yes, I am sorry to say such is the case. I have just received a note from Mary Chichester informing me of the fact. She says the medical man says there is no doubt about its being "heart", brought on by the great mental anxieties she has suffered of late; and, from what you have now and again told me, I am afraid that, instead of getting over the little fright into which she was thrown by Mr Pegram's audacious attempt, as I thought she would, she has gone on hugging her fears to her own breast till they assumed gigantic proportions. I regret now I did not give you permission to speak out when you first told me that Mary Chichester was afraid her aunt was fidgeting and fretting over some mystery with which it were best that she, Mary, should be at once acquainted; but, dear me, I thought, poor lady, she would forget all about Mr Pegram in three or four weeks, and she always made such a point of her niece being kept in total ignorance of the big lottery.'

'Yes, it was so obvious even to myself, the low nervous state into which Miss Caterham had fallen, that I was only waiting your return to speak to you on the subject. I did not know you were back until I got your message just now. However, I suppose Miss Chichester will be let into the mystery of the whole secret now.'

'Well, yes; of course the will must put her in possession of the whole story. Miss Caterham, I know, has left her what little she has to leave, which, beyond that visionary share in the "Tontine", I am afraid won't come to much. But what I want you to do is this: as ill-luck would have it, I have a very pressing engagement that will take me out of town for the next day or two. It is an old-standing promise to my invalid sister, and it is so seldom, poor thing, that I can give her a day or two, that I really have not the heart to disappoint her. I want you to run down to Kew to tell Mary the whole state of the case; say that I shall come out to see her as soon as I return; and that I shall, of course, be present at the funeral. Any little thing that she wants assistance and advice about, in the meanwhile, I am sure you will undertake for her. Do this for me, like a good fellow, or else I shall have to telegraph to my sister that I can't come until tomorrow, which will be a great disappointment to her.'

'Of course I will,' replied Ringwood. 'I will drive out there almost at once. After the terms I have been on with poor Miss Caterham, and knowing them as I do, through you, there will be nothing much in my taking your place in your unavoidable absence. By the way, of course, if Miss Chichester asks me what was this secret which so troubled her aunt, there is now, I suppose, no objection to my telling her?'

'Ahem! – No; better not, perhaps,' replied the more cautious senior. 'You can tell her that Miss Caterham's will must explain everything.'

As Ringwood made his way down to Kew a little later, he pondered a good deal as to how he stood in Mary Chichester's estimation. He could not tell. At times they got on pleasantly enough together, but she undoubtedly always got angry when the mystery of the 'Tontine' came between them, and showed him her displeasure right royally at such times, treating him even with studied neglect, or scant courtesy, as the spirit of the moment might dictate. Still, when she smiled sweetly upon him, and was as bewitchingly agreeable as a good-looking young woman can be, he puzzled himself to know whether he really had obtained any hold on her affections. Young ladies are not wont to show the captives within their mesh that their hearts are softened towards them until they have declared themselves more explicitly than Ringwood had as yet done. It was not that his mind was not made up, but there were two things hampered him: in the first place, and it was probably, after all, the strongest of the two reasons that made him pause, he was not quite sure how such an avowal would be received; and secondly, he really had scruples about asking her to marry him while she was still in complete ignorance of the possibility of her becoming a large heiress. He argued with himself: if this marriage came about she might say, 'He knew this, and I did not; and married me on the chance of its coming off.' However, that was all now going to be cleared up, and Ringwood determined that, as soon as he decently could after Miss Caterham's funeral, he would declare his love to Mary Chichester.

He opened the gate of the little garden, from which all the summer splendour had departed. The beds he remembered all aglow with brilliant flowers now looked ragged and forlorn; indeed, from some of them the plants had already been taken up, preparatory to being housed for the winter. He made his way up the gravel walk, and knocked at the door.

'Yes, Miss Chichester would see him,' replied the maid, after disappearing for a few moments, and he was duly ushered into the drawing-room.

A little time, and Mary Chichester entered, and Ringwood could not help thinking that she had never looked better than she did now, as she swept towards him in her black draperies, and greeted him with extended hand. He had composed rather a neat little speech on his way down, with which to introduce himself, but it all vanished as he looked at Mary's pale, sad face, and all he said was,

'I am very, very sorry for you.'

'I knew you would be sorry to hear of the death of my poor aunt,' she replied. 'You have, of course, heard of it from Mr Carbuckle. I rather hope to see him in the course of the day.'

'I am here, Miss Chichester, as Mr Carbuckle's deputy; sincerely as I sympathize with you in your loss, I should hardly have ventured to intrude upon you until a few days later if it had not been for that. He has only just returned to town, and is compelled to leave it again for a couple of days, and begged me to run down here on his behalf. I need hardly say, if I can be of any use about anything, I am at your disposal.'

'Thank you; no. I shall want both advice and assistance later, but just at present Doctor Lomax, who was an old friend of my aunt's, and her regular medical attendant, has managed everything for me. I suppose I shall see Mr Carbuckle shortly?'

'He begged me say that he should come to you the minute he returned, and should, of course, attend the funeral.'

'Which I hope, Mr Ringwood, you will do also. You were a great favourite with my poor aunt; but on one point I sadly fear I was right, and that miserable secret which you allowed her to bear by herself really did hasten her death.'

'I sincerely trust, Miss Chichester, that on that point you are mistaken; as I told you before, I was powerless; my lips were sealed, as they are now. A few days more, and you will know everything.'

'Know everything!' she cried, passionately, and rising abruptly from her chair. 'What do I care about your mystery now? I wanted to know it before, that I might share the trouble with her who has been as a mother to me, that I might soothe and comfort her in her wretched nervous prostration. I wanted to know it, because I saw that bearing it alone was the cause of the weak, nervous state into which she had fretted herself. Had I shared the burden with her it might – who can say? – have kept her a little longer with me. I am blaming nobody,' continued Mary, as she paced the room with impatient steps; 'but it is so hard to think that a life we value might have been prolonged by more careful tending.'

'Poor Miss Caterham was so very resolute in her injunctions as to secrecy that we dared not disobey her. A few days more and then –'

'Too late, I tell you,' interrupted Mary; 'I have no desire now to know this miserable secret. It was no paltry curiosity that prompted me, but sheer anxiety for her whom I could see was not fit to bear its weight alone. I care not now if I never know it. Forgive me, Mr Ringwood, if in my grief I have said anything that might be deemed harsh; but the shock was very sudden, and – and – I think – I think – I had better say good-bye,' and putting her handkerchief to her eyes, Mary Chichester hurriedly left the room.

The day of the funeral arrived, and a little knot of mourners, which included Carbuckle and Ringwood, assembled at the cottage at Kew to follow poor Miss Caterham to her grave. The deceased lady had led so retired a life of late years that the mourners who gathered to pay their last tribute of respect were few in number; but if the gathering was small, the regrets of those who composed it were, at all events, sincere. Those who followed her to her last resting-place sorrowed honestly for the kind, amiable woman who, after a life of self-sacrifice, had now left them.

The deceased lady's solicitor was among those present, and intimated to Mr Carbuckle, and some two or three intimates, that he thought it would be most convenient, now all was over, that they should return to the cottage, and hear the will read. 'It is short and simple, and concerns you, Carbuckle, slightly.'

Mr Carbuckle at once assented; and he, Ringwood, Dr Lomax, and one or two more, accordingly returned to the cottage. Miss Chichester declined to be present; and the half-dozen men assembled in the little dining-room, where the 'baked meats' customary were duly set forth. After granting his companions a few minutes for their luncheon, the attorney produced the will, and clearing his throat with a preliminary glass of wine, said,

'The late Miss Caterham only made the will I hold in my hand a few weeks ago; I, when this was completed, destroying a previous will which differed from this only on one not very important point.'

He then proceeded, without further preamble, to read the will, which was very short, and, divested of legal verbiage, set forth that the testatrix, with the exception of two or three trifling legacies to servants, bequeathed what little she had to leave, including the furniture of the cottage, to Mary Chichester. This seemed all very natural and just as it should be to the half-dozen auditors, with the exception of Carbuckle and Ringwood. These two could not refrain from exchanging a glance of astonishment.

'What on earth has she done with her "Tontine" share?' thought Mr Carbuckle; 'she cannot surely have forgotten all about it. If so, and it should by any fluke happen to come off in her favour, there will be a pretty miscarriage of my poor old friend's intentions. She has I don't know how many nephews and nieces, while Mary Chichester is only her great-niece, and naturally all these others would come before her.'

Here his reflections were interrupted by the attorney, who handed him a packet.

'This, you will perceive, Mr Carbuckle, is addressed to yourself. I know the contents, having indeed written them out at the wish of my late client; but, as it is a matter placed by the deceased lady entirely in your hands, it is, of course, a private communication.'

'This packet,' said Carbuckle, as he and Ringwood returned together to town, 'I have no doubt refers to that "Tontine" share. I wonder why poor Miss Caterham has enclosed it to me in this mysterious manner; however, as soon as we get to my rooms we will see what she has done. You have been, and are, so deeply engaged in the affair, that I intend to take you into confidence at once.'

As soon as they were comfortably installed in Mr Carbuckle's chambers, that gentleman broke the seal, and drew two documents from the envelope. The first was a short legal document, by which the share, numbered 1477, of the 'Great Tontine', life nominee, Terence Finnigan, was bequeathed to Mary Chichester; the second was a letter, written at Miss Caterham's dictation, in which she told him that she placed this share in his hands in trust for Mary Chichester, with an earnest injunction that the girl was to know nothing about it unless the thing should be actually decided in her favour.

'If it is heaven's will,' Miss Caterham went on to say, 'that my darling Mary should become a great heiress, it will be quite time enough for her to know it when it is an actual fact; and on the other hand, I am desirous of sparing her the terrible fears and anxieties that have oppressed me during the last few weeks, and which, I feel, remain my lot until the "Great Tontine" is determined, or the death of Terence Finnigan ascertained.'

'Poor lady,' said Carbuckle, 'I wonder whether she ever thought that the grave might lay her fears at rest. I am sadly afraid, in her state, that the "Great Tontine" is answerable for her decease.'

'And what is more,' said Ringwood, somewhat disconsolately, as he took up his hat, 'the "Tontine" still remains a mystery as inscrutable as ever to Mary Chichester.'

'I am afraid so,' rejoined Carbuckle; 'but I shall undoubtedly comply with my old friend's instructions. As Mary *does* know nothing about it, she had better remain in her ignorance, unless the thing comes off in her favour.'

The upshot of all this was, that Ronald Ringwood came to a fresh determination with regard to Miss Chichester. Man has a natural desire to console a pretty woman in her affliction, and Ringwood felt that he could not see Mary in her sorrow without offering consolation; and that, over head and ears in love as he was, that must, of necessity, be of a somewhat impassioned kind, such as would be certain to result in a downright avowal of his love. The objections that stood in his way before Miss Caterham's death were there still; and it seemed to him that it would be now a downright mean thing to do to ask Mary to marry him while in ignorance of her possibly brilliant prospects. He resolved to hold aloof from her till the 'Great Tontine' was decided. He would rather she said him 'nay' as possessor of eight thousand a-year than she should unwittingly come into it as his wife.

Had he consulted his friend Mr Hemmingby on this point, I think that gentleman would have informed him emphatically, 'My dear sir, that sort of high-flown chivalry won't wash in these days.'

## CHAPTER TWENTY-TWO

# SAM HEMMINGBY PUZZLED

Ronald Ringwood was pacing up and down his rooms, pipe in mouth, and just meditating whether he should have a glass of grog at home and then 'turn in', or whether he should go down to a rather lively night-club, to which he was affiliated, and see what was doing. This momentous matter was decided for him by a pretty sharp rat-tat on his oak, the opening of which gave admission to Jack Phillimore.

'Only arrived in town about a couple of hours ago; drove straight to my hotel to doff my nautical "togs", and get into the more ordinary garb of London life; had something to eat, and as soon as I had appeased, what you will be delighted to hear was an extremely healthy appetite, came on here to see you. Of course I could not "wire" from Rydland for fear of some one "twigging" it, you know; one could not be too cautious against such foxy beggars as Pegram and Son. Now then, give me a chair and a pipe, and – well, yes, a little something to drink with it would not be amiss – and then lend me your ears; I have got a very ship-load of information to pour into them; I have done splendidly. I have collected all the facts possible about poor old Krabbe, even down to his wearing a wig; and I have wound up by seeing him. What do you think of that?'

'Bravo!' cried Ronald. 'Get into that big chair on the right-hand side; there is the brandy and cold water; the tobacco is in that jar, and that is the best pipe in the rack. Now, blaze away, and I will promise not to interrupt you until you have done.'

Thus adjured, Jack Phillimore proceeded to narrate, with the greatest complacency, all the biographical details that he had succeeded in gathering about old Mr Krabbe. He gave a spirited account of his interview with the Pegrams, father and son; then he described his expedition to the cottage; dwelt upon the charms of the buxom nurse, and jested at the idea of such a dried-up old mummy as Krabbe having such a comely care-taker, and wound up by saying, with a peal of laughter – 'And old Krabbe, Ringwood, was the only one of them who would have it that I was not a sailor – and why? Why do you think that he said I was no sailor? because I had no pig-tail. The old duffer, you see, had got back amongst his boyish days, and couldn't stand a sailor without a pig-tail.'

Ringwood had listened very attentively, and continued to smoke silently for some minutes after the other had finished.

'Well,' interrupted Jack Phillimore, 'what do you make of it all? You did not expect me to pick up such a budget of facts about old Krabbe in the time, did you?'

'No,' replied the barrister, slowly, 'you certainly picked up a good deal about the old man, and, as you say, you have seen him; but bar that latter point, the devil of it is, I cannot see what use we are to make of all this information now we have got it. Now, though Hemmingby did not exactly tell us so, I take it that when he told us to look up the latter days of Mr Krabbe, it was under the idea that the old man was Pegram's nominee. Well now, supposing he is, all we can make out of this is, that Pegram's nominee is a very, very shaky life. But then, if it comes to that, so no doubt is Miss Caterham's nominee, if I could find him, and Lord Lakington's also.'

'By Jove, though, this is a deuce of a go. You are quite right; our great object, of course, is to convict Pegram of fraud of some sort; but there is not a symptom of that in all the information I have picked up. What on earth could have made Hemmingby send us on such a fool's errand?'

'Well, I can only suppose,' cried Ringwood, 'that Hemmingby thought it doubtful whether Mr Krabbe really was still to the fore; but not only have you actually seen him, but nobody in Rydland previously expressed to you the slightest doubt about his living in that cottage.'

'Not a soul,' said Jack, 'and two or three I talked to about the old man spoke of occasionally seeing him; others, too, saw him come back from that change of air old Pegram took him for a few months back.'

'Yes,' interposed Ringwood; 'the evidence as to identity is very complete, and I am terribly afraid that our astute friend, the manager, has made a wrong cast altogether this time. However, we must talk matters over with him tomorrow, and see if he has anything further to suggest. It is of no use, Phillimore, our hammering any more at this now; let us talk about something else.'

Lovers are, we know, apt to do it; and to these stricken ones a *tête-à-tête* with a friend over a pipe about midnight offers irresistible temptation. Still, I think it was hardly fair of Ronald Ringwood to prelude the story of his love with that insidious 'let us talk about something else'. However, in this case it was the biter bit; for no sooner had Ringwood not finished, but come to a pause, in the tale of his passion for Mary Chichester, than his companion promptly poured forth the story of his undying affection for his cousin

Beatrice; his fixed determination that she should never be the bride of a beast like Pegram, nor, indeed, it seemed, as the hours stole on, of any other beast. It is true that Jack had already told the history of his ill-starred love to Ringwood; but who of us spares his friends the twice-told tale. When it comes to that old romance in which we play the Romeo, there are few of our male intimates who escape hearing of every sigh and thought that rends our manly bosom. But two young fellows, with a jar of tobacco and a good fire, and a love-story a-piece, as may be easily supposed, talked far into the night, and three had chimed from the neighbouring steeple before, with a hearty hand-grip, the pair separated.

The next afternoon saw the two detectives at the door of the 'Vivacity' Theatre, anxious to unfold the results of their inquiries to Mr Hemmingby, and still more anxious to hear what comment that astute gentleman might have to make upon them. Mr Hemmingby listened to the account of Jack Phillimore's proceedings with an amused smile, and for the first time Jack conceived doubts as to whether he had been such a success as a detective as so far he had thought himself.

'Sailor!' said the manager, 'what on airth put masquerading into your head? why the deuce you didn't go down as yourself I can't conceive. Oh! I know what you are going to say about the sailor – and I make no doubt but what you can play it – that you were the real article, and not a T. P. Cooke one; but, my dear sir, a sailor in Rydland would be something like a white elephant in the Strand – all heads would be turned to look at him; and then, when there was no necessity for it , you must needs go and see the Pegrams. Now, Mr Phillimore, I'll hold you anything you like from five to fifty that old Pegram knows by this, not only that you are not an ordinary sailor, but that you are John Phillimore, nephew of Viscount Lakington.'

'Absurd,' replied Jack, 'impossible; how could he possibly know?'

'Ah! that I really can't tell you; but I will certainly make you any reasonable bet that he does; and now, if you will excuse my saying so, you will never make a detective, Mr Phillimore.'

'Well,' said Jack, though with considerably less confidence than he had displayed before Mr Hemmingby had so derided his disguise, 'I am sure I followed your instructions pretty closely; that we can make nothing out of the particulars I have obtained is hardly my fault.'

'Now that is just where it is,' replied the manager. 'Listen to me for a moment. You went down there to obtain the particulars of Mr Krabbe's last illness. Now, if there is one thing pretty certain to be tried in a serious illness of that kind, it is change of air; now, did anybody tell you that Mr Krabbe went away for change of air?'

'Of course,' replied Jack; 'did I not tell you?'

'I am not quite sure; but one thing I know you didn't tell us, was where he went to.'

'Certainly I did not, because I never heard; nobody seemed to know exactly; but as he came back again, I should think it does not much matter where he went.'

'Ah,' replied Hemmingby; 'now that is precisely the point upon which I differ with you. I want to know where he went, at what hotel he stayed, and, in short, to follow him step by step back to his very cottage.'

'But,' interposed Ringwood, 'I still cannot see your object. Old Krabbe returned, and was seen and recognized by several people at the railway station and in the town. He has been recognized by several people since he has lived at the cottage.'

'Why, you don't mean to tell me,' exclaimed Jack Phillimore, 'that I did not see the real Mr Krabbe the other day?'

'Certainly not,' rejoined the manager; 'only bear in mind, as you had never seen him before, it is quite impossible for you to judge.'

'I am very willing to admit that,' replied Jack; 'but that does not apply to other people.'

'No. However, I have a whim to trace Mr Krabbe from the time he left Rydland to the time he returned to it; nothing in it, very likely, still that is my fancy; and as I don't think much of you fellows as detectives, I shall just take this in hand myself.'

'And what disguise do you mean to adopt?' inquired Jack.

'Disguise!' ejaculated Hemmingby, 'what do I want with a disguise. They know me by sight pretty well in Rydland, and are quite used to my coming down there. I shall even do as you did – go and see old Pegram; but then I shall go because he would think it odd if I didn't. I have some property at Llanbarlym, and occasionally take a run down to look after it. No; I have only one thing to be careful about, and that is how I make my inquiries concerning where Mr Krabbe went to for a change. I have a notion old Pegram will cock his ears if he hears anybody is manifesting curiosity on that point. I shall be off tonight, and come back by the night-mail tomorrow. I will go out myself and have a look at old Krabbe if I have time.'

The two young men were extremely delighted at Hemmingby taking up this search himself. What on earth he expected to elicit, supposing that he succeeded in tracing Mr Krabbe's wanderings in search of health, they could not conceive; but they both had an entire belief, that if the shrewd energetic manager took the thing in hand the Pegrams would be exploded in some fashion. He, at all events, would be able to identify Mr Krabbe, and in the meantime they had nothing to do but to wait and see what became of the manager's raid into the Welsh country.

Mr Hemmingby's proceedings in a great measure resembled those of Jack Phillimore. They were not quite so theatrical, nor were his inquiries made with the frankness that characterized the sailor; and on one point he differed most essentially from his predecessor, for whereas Jack had been delighted with the fund of information he had acquired, Hemmingby, although apparently successful, was rather dissatisfied with his budget. He had discovered with no great difficulty that Mr Krabbe had gone to Slackpool Super-mare.

'That's right, no doubt,' muttered Hemmingby to himself. 'I shall find he didn't stop there long, I'll engage. Old Pegram would have taken deuced good care nobody knew that much, unless I am all wrong about Mr Krabbe's change of air. Of course I shall have to go over to Slackpool and make further inquiries.'

But the thing that bothered Sam Hemmingby most was an incident that came out of his calling at the cottage to see old Mr Krabbe. The door had been opened to him by the nurse, and it did not escape the quick-eyed manager, that the woman gave a slight start upon seeing him. Like Jack Phillimore, he was told that the old man was asleep, and that he could not see him; but whereas the nurse had been smiling and courteous to the young sailor, she was unmistakably sullen and morose in her manner towards Hemmingby. Her replies were of the briefest, and couched in the most sulky tones; and she kept her eyes doggedly cast down, so that the manager failed to get a thorough good look into her face, although he prolonged the interview as much as possible for that express purpose.

'Well,' he muttered as he walked away, 'I am regularly gravelled this time. Who the deuce is that woman, and where on earth did I ever see her before? Odd, I can't recollect for the life of me; and I have a sort of idea that the jade did not mean I should, for she never looked at me after the first glance. What a dunderheaded old fool I am not to remember who she is; however, the only thing I feel pretty clear about is, that wherever I did see her before, it wasn't in a hospital, nor was she doing nurse.'

In vain and in vain did the manager rummage his brain, not only in the train, but even the first thing on waking the next morning; fit a name to the buxom nurse he could not.

'And yet that woman is the clue to the whole enigma, I have no doubt,' thought Hemmingby.

There could be little doubt that both Ringwood and Phillimore would call in upon the manager the next day to learn the result of his investigations. The manager made no secret whatever of his proceedings, with the one exception, that he did not think it any use to tell the young men that he had a vivid impression of having met the nurse before under very different circumstances. He announced his intention of proceeding the next day to Slackpool Super-mare, and suggested this time that Ringwood should accompany him.

'I shall have to leave it in your hands sooner or later,' said the manager, 'as I could never spare the time to work the thing right out, and you can.'

But when Jack suggested that he should also join in the search, Sam Hemmingby refused his assistance in the most peremptory manner.

'No,' he observed; 'I have not the slightest doubt in my own mind that you are perfectly well known to the Pegrams as John Phillimore, heir to Viscount Lakington. I think it more than likely that some of old Pegram's emissaries will be upon the look-out at Slackpool to see if you make any further inquiries that way; Ringwood and myself will attract no attention; Pegram will argue that I have no interest whatever in the "Tontine", and am a restless beggar, who may always be expected to turn up anywhere; while even if Bob Pegram himself should be there and recognize Ringwood – well, he is nothing but a friend of mine.'

It was in vain that Phillimore argued that it was perfectly ridiculous to suppose that his identity had been discovered. The manager was inexorable.

'I am just as sure,' he said, 'that the Pegrams have made out all about you as if they had told me so when I called upon them the other day. The fact of their mentioning nothing about the visit of a sailor was convincing proof to me that they had solved the riddle. Old Pegram would have asked me a question or two had he been still in doubt on the off-chance that I might make a likely surmise. No, no, Mr Phillimore; you stay here for the present, and don't think I shall not find something for you to do later on.'

To a man of Jack Phillimore's temperament this was some solace; for the idea of waiting with his hands in his pockets, while others fought out the battle for the hand of his cousin Beatrice, was excessively repugnant to him; but still, now Sam Hemmingby had condescended to take the thing in hand himself, there was nothing for it but to submit.

Like his trip to Rydland, the manager's visit to Slackpool was hurried; he was very soon back in London, and told Phillimore that things so far had turned out pretty much as he had expected. They had found out the hotel with very little difficulty at which old Pegram and his invalid charge had stayed; but, as the manager had anticipated, they had only remained there two nights, and after a good deal of trouble he had traced them to lodgings on the outskirts of the town.

'And now,' said Hemmingby, 'the search becomes interesting. They left those lodgings, but where they went to next I have left Ringwood to discover, if he can. You see, Mr Phillimore, it is quite likely there will be another move or two again after that; and every time, I fancy, the move will get more difficult to follow.'

'But, good heavens!' cried Jack, 'what on earth can be old Pegram's object in hopping about in this mysterious way from lodging to lodging?'

'That is exactly what I think we shall find out if we perseveringly trace lawyer Pegram and his invalid charge till we find them back again in Rydland. One would hardly have thought that such constant change of lodging could have been good for poor old Krabbe; they do not seem to have stayed more than two or three days in a place, that is, so far as we have gone.'

'But what do you think yourself, Mr Hemmingby?'

'I think nothing further than that it will be a very interesting study, as I have said all along, and perhaps rather astonish us when it is worked out.'

'And when shall you have anything for me to do?'

'When Ringwood has got a little further in his investigations. And now I must ask you to run away, for I have got a lot of letters and other things to attend to; but mark what I tell you, it may take time, but we'll ''bust'' Pegram certain in the end.'

'Good-bye,' replied Jack, 'only remember, as far as I am concerned, Pegram must be ''bust'' in time to prevent this marriage.'

## CHAPTER TWENTY-THREE

## 'CLOUDS ON THE HORIZON'

Whatever appearance she might keep up before her grandmother and the world generally, no young lady had ever contemplated her approaching marriage with greater dismay than did the Honourable Beatrice Phillimore. She might brazen it out, and say that, like other girls, she was going to marry money; that the great end of life was a good house, carriages, an opera-box, and liberal pin-money; but in the silence of the night season Beatrice's eyes would become wet with tears, and, in her heart of hearts, she owned that she would sooner have stood at the altar in cotton with her cousin Jack than robed in satin as the bride of Pegram. There were times when she had doubts whether she could really carry this marriage through; and had it been but her own fortune that depended upon it, Mr Pegram would have speedily found his gorgeous wedding gifts returned, and have been briefly informed that the lady had changed her mind. The one thing that made her position endurable was, that she saw so very little of her affianced. The Viscount had taken care of that by persuading Robert Pegram that it was not customary in their class.

Lord Lakington, though he might humbug his neighbours and even himself, was tolerably wide-awake where his own interests were concerned; and he thoroughly understood, that if this marriage was not made very easy for Beatrice, there was considerable likelihood that it would never take place. He played his part, too, with great skill. He kept the girl incessantly occupied. He, who had rarely troubled his head about her amusements further than procuring tickets for balls, theatres, &c., was now ever on the alert to act as escort. If it was too much for Mrs Lyme Wregis – and the Viscount's anxiety that that estimable lady should not over-fatigue herself was touching to witness – then he was at his daughter's disposal. The Viscount was killing two birds with one stone, although, it must be confessed, at considerable sacrifice of his personal comfort. He detested society other than in the form of dinners; and now, for the sake of his daughter, he was willing to go to any entertainment that she desired. It enabled him at the same time to take what he thought more care of his stepmother. He was always urging that, as he was going, there was no necessity for Mrs Lyme Wregis playing *chaperon*.

'You are good as gold, and a very gem of *chaperons*, as I am sure Beatrice will own; but still we must remember that you are not so young as you were, and we must not allow you to be fagged to death.'

But the old lady was somewhat contumacious on this point. She really enjoyed society, provided that she was not kept up too late. She knew from past experience, that she could rely upon Beatrice in this respect, and therefore insisted upon mixing in this whirl of gaiety that the Viscount had created to a much greater extent than he approved, extorting from that harassed peer, upon more than one occasion, some such *sotto voce* observation as 'confound the old lady, if she did but know what her life was worth'. So successful had the Viscount been in humbugging his neighbours on the subject of marriage, that but for one thing he would have succeeded in fairly humbugging himself. He had thoroughly accustomed himself to the jargon of 'New people, certainly; but immensely wealthy, and these, you know, are the days of fusion. Of course I do not mean to say that a girl like Beatrice might not have done better; but it will do, sir, it will do.'

But upon the few occasions that he was alone with Beatrice – and, to do the girl justice, these were as rare as she could make them – the veil was pretty rudely torn on one side. There was no doubt about it then, and it was impossible to shut his eyes to the fact that Beatrice Phillimore was about to marry this man Pegram for her father's sake; and she either could not or cared not to conceal that this wedding was extremely distasteful to her. These interviews, however, were, as beforesaid, rare; and though the Viscount undoubtedly suffered a few severe twinges of remorse at the time, yet in a few hours he resumed his specious reasoning, and once more convinced himself that really Beatrice might make a much worse match of it than with Bob Pegram. She was a silly girl, with some foolish *tendresse* for her cousin Jack, which of course could never come to anything. Jack's bounden duty in life was to marry money to prop up the title. Young girls would have these nonsensical fancies, and was it not the duty of parents and guardians to prevent their doing anything so foolish as indulging them? After turning matters over in his mind for two or three hours, assisting his cogitation by a glass of that brown sherry which he so much affected, the Viscount always arrived at the conclusion that he was a model parent, and had done his duty by his daughter both carefully and astutely.

As for Beatrice, she did not falter in her purpose, although there were times when she almost doubted whether her courage would not fail her. It was well enough in the daytime: there was the excitement of buying her *trousseau*, of perpetual entertainments to which she went; for, though it was the off-season, there was plenty going on in the London world, though in a quieter way than in the warm summer days of July; but the nights were – oh, so long and dreary. Again and again did she think over how she had treated her cousin. Again and again did she picture to herself that last scene with him. 'Coward,' she had called him; and was he not so? to congratulate her on her marriage. He must know that nothing but the most extreme pressure could have induced her to behave in this way; and then again she remembered that was just what was so utterly unaccountable, both to Jack and to her grandmother. They could conceive no reason whatever that should have made her accept Robert Pegram, unless it was the temptation his wealth might afford. Of course they could see that her father approved and backed her up in this marriage; but it was impossible for them to guess the pressure her father had put upon her; but they must never know it. She was pledged to keep the secret of the 'Great Tontine', at all events, for the present; and once let this marriage be accomplished, what object would she then have in revealing it.

'Oh, why does not Jack save me?' wailed the girl at times in her agony, reckless of the fact that, even presuming Jack Phillimore was in possession of the whole story, he would not at all see his way to guarantee four thousand a-year to his uncle for life. It was but the helpless cry for assistance we are all wont to raise when young to whatever may seem to be the tower of strength in our little world. A woman turns naturally to her lover; she looks upon him as capable of confronting every emergency. She neither knows nor cares to ask how, but simply looks to him to guard her from whatever ills may be impending. So much did this idea gather strength with Beatrice that at times she almost made up her mind to write to her cousin; but then again came the old fatal objection, she must condemn her father to poverty. If she chose to do so, there was no reason why she should not save herself; but then Beatrice felt that she could not do that. No; she supposed it must go on, and Jack and her grandmother must think the worst of her for all time. She often wonders what has become of her cousin, for although she is resolute never to see him, she keeps a sharp look-out upon his comings and goings in the Victoria Road; but he has seldom been near the house of late, and never, as she well knows, has he asked for her. A few minutes' talk with Mrs Lyme Wregis, and then he is gone again.

Mrs Lyme Wregis is in a slight flutter of excitement, in a state that the Viscount would have greatly disapproved, as also the cause thereof, had he but known it. Jack Phillimore had dropped a hint that it was more than probable this Pegram marriage would never take place. The old lady had declined to know anything of such intrigues as Jack might engage in with this view, and she was now suffering from intense curiosity as to what his scheme could be, coupled with considerable anxiety for its successful accomplishment. That she did not know more was due simply to her own commands; but although you may violently protest against being made an accomplice to a conspiracy, you may at the same time feel a most insatiable curiosity concerning all its details. The old lady comforts herself with the idea that she cannot, at all events, be kept long in suspense. The marriage has been postponed already, and Mr Pegram is very urgent that there should be no further delay. Whatever Jack Phillimore's scheme may be, it behoves him to put it into execution pretty quickly. A bare three weeks, and Beatrice will be a bride; and Mrs Lyme Wregis thinks sadly what a very different bridal she had always pictured to herself for her bonnie Trixie. She wonders whether Jack Phillimore is to be depended upon, or whether these hints he throws out are but the idle vapourings of a love-lorn lover. But no; she thinks better of Jack than that. He is not of the kind that are wont to talk so loudly of what they mean to do. She knew Jack was most thoroughly in earnest regarding Trixie, and judged that he was, at all events, striving to do what he hinted at, and believing also that he had a very fair chance of succeeding.

Indeed, Jack Phillimore was in a state of intense excitement at the present moment. He had no doubt whatever that the Pegrams were guilty of an elaborate fraud of some sort. He had no doubt, again, that they would be exposed in the long run; but what was to him a source of the greatest anxiety, was whether they would be so exposed before the day fixed for the marriage. Mr Hemmingby proved right in his conjecture; lawyer Pegram and his invalid charge had changed their lodgings a good many times; indeed, they seemed never to have stayed above a couple of nights in one place; and the worst was, that they seemed to move from house to house in such stealthy fashion. Ringwood, and even Phillimore himself (for Mr Hemmingby, having discovered no emissaries of the Pegrams on their footsteps, had allowed Jack to take part in the search), although never long losing the clue, yet at times had hard work to puzzle it out. It was this which made Jack so anxious. The days to the wedding were numbered, while the following the old lawyer through his rapid shifts of lodgings grew slower and more difficult with every change.

'It is pretty much as I expected,' said Sam Hemmingby. 'The more I see of it the more convinced I am that I started you on the right track. What do all these sudden shifts of lodgings mean? Clearly that old lawyer Pegram did not wish that any one should know where he took his poor old clerk to for change of air. Now what could have been his object in all this?'

'Well, I confess I cannot see,' exclaimed Phillimore.

'It goes a good way to prove that I am right in supposing old Krabbe to have been Pegram's nominee. In that case, he would naturally be very much alarmed about the old man's life; still, wherever he took him for change of air, there would be no necessity to make a mystery of it. But just suppose that Pegram had made up his mind that under no circumstances should Krabbe die.'

'I don't understand you,' exclaimed Jack. 'How the deuce was he to prevent it?'

'Ah! we shall see when we come to that last lodging, that he did prevent it in some way, I fancy. I have a strong suspicion that poor old Krabbe died at that last lodging.'

'But hang it, man! you appear to forget that I saw him, spoke to him, the time I was down at Rydland.'

'That is what I say,' replied the manager. 'Old Pegram would not allow him to die. He can give nature a good many points in a hundred, you bet your bottom dollar; but nature made a little mistake, which he, lawyer Pegram, was there to rectify; and, as you saw yourself, there was old Krabbe, not much to brag about, certainly, but still to the fore.'

'What! you mean to say that the old man I saw was an impostor?' exclaimed Jack Phillimore, for the first time really understanding what the manager's motive was in persistently tracking Mr Krabbe and his search for health. 'Why, this Pegram is a first-class scoundrel, and is perpetrating one of the most impudent frauds ever attempted.'

'I think,' replied the manager, laughing, 'I would be more moderate in my language, if I were you, until you had worked the Krabbe problem thoroughly out. However, you know now what I am driving at, and it looks to me just now very much as if I was right.'

Sanguine Jack Phillimore had no doubt about it whatever, and there now came to him the anxious question, Should they be able to prove it in time? Ringwood was down at Slackpool still patiently following up the track of lawyer Pegram this last spring; but he was for the present at fault, and the welcome telegram to announce the discovery of the trail had not as yet arrived, might not arrive, indeed – as Jack knew from his previous experience – for some days. Then it was hard to say how many more shifts of lodgings they would have to follow up; and so dubious did it seem to Jack Phillimore that Bob Pegram could be duly exploded before the day fixed for the wedding, that he began seriously to consider what was to be done in such case. Surely his uncle would be reasonable when he heard his story, and postpone this marriage; but then, as Ringwood had pointed out to him already, up to this it was all conjecture, they could prove nothing; and to bring such an allegation against a man without being able to substantiate it in any way was unheard-of, and likely to lead to the invocation of the law on the part of the accused. It was in vain that Jack tried to flatter himself that old Pegram was the sort of man to collapse from being threatened with such a charge. Hemmingby had laughed at the idea.

The manager had said, point blank –

'I am not so certain about Robert Pegram; but the old man is as cunning as a fox, and will die as hard. You will never frighten him out of anything. He is quite capable of fighting the case when we have got it up; but surely if you speak to the Viscount, and tell him what you suspect, a few days before the wedding, he will put it off. You may, I think, count upon that. No man likes being done, more especially on a large scale; and Lord Lakington can easily insist that each party to the contract shall disclose and produce his nominee. It is true,' concluded Hemmingby, meditatively, 'that I should not be in the least surprised if the Viscount had the dust thrown in his eyes even then.'

It was a singular thing about this somewhat ill-omened marriage, that while there were several people, including the two principals, who were very much averse to it, there were but two who were anxious to see it accomplished, viz., Lord Lakington and old Pegram. The former was getting excessively tired of all the social obligations that he had of late taken upon himself. He was fully convinced that they were absolutely necessary, that Beatrice must be kept in a whirl of gaiety which would not allow her to think; but, nevertheless, it bored him terribly. It had to be done, and therefore it was of no use attempting to shirk it; but he should be very glad indeed when it was all over, and he had settled down into his sure and tranquil enjoyment of four thousand per annum. That old Pegram should be anxious to bring to a conclusion such an excellent bargain as he had made was, under any circumstances, only to be expected; that a man, whose lifetime had been dedicated to the accumulation of money, should be keenly alive to the acquirement of such a plum as the 'Great Tontine' was only natural; while, if the conjectures of Ringwood and Phillimore were correct, the sooner this marriage was accomplished the sooner did the chance of any fraud on his part being discovered cease.

I have included the two principals amongst those who were averse to the wedding. What Beatrice's feelings are we already know; but Mr Bob Pegram's might have been supposed in favour of the match. They were, to some extent. He was keenly alive to the *éclat* of marrying the Honourable Beatrice Phillimore, daughter of Herbert Viscount Lakington; he was quite awake to the capital independent income he should at once be put in possession of, and, as we have before seen, he thirsted for the unrestrained theatrical delights which would be at his disposal; while as for resigning the desk in his father's office, nobody could have displayed less compunction. But there is a drop of bitterness in all our cups – unalloyed happiness is not given to humanity, – and, despite all the charms of birth, beauty, and wealth accompanying it, Robert Pegram viewed his forthcoming marriage with no little dismay. He stood, no doubt, in considerable awe of his future wife and father-in-law; but it was not that. There was another lady in the case – a lady with strong claims, and who, if the slightest hint of this proposed marriage reached her ears, would be likely to speak her mind; and when Bob Pegram thought of that he literally shuddered. It was not that the lady was either a shrew or a termagant, but she had a spirit of her own. She would be infamously treated; and then she knew – well, a great deal too much of Mr Robert Pegram's past life to make him feel comfortable as to what revelations might fall from her lips in the first burst of her hot wrath.

Mr Robert Pegram, in fact, had plighted his troth to this lady before his sire had broken to him his project for winding up the 'Great Tontine' in their favour. It may be remembered that Bob had slightly demurred when the alliance of himself with the Honourable Beatrice Phillimore was first suggested to him; but he was made of much weaker stuff than his grim old progenitor, and stood in wholesome awe of directly opposing his will. That his father was most sincerely attached to him Bob Pegram knew well, but a more arbitrary, despotic old man never existed. He had spent his life struggling to amass a handsome fortune, with the sole view of making his son a gentleman. He intended that all his accumulations, whatever they might be, should go to Bob at his death; but during his lifetime he exacted implicit obedience. He was not one of those fathers who worried his son by continually interposing about trivial matters. Old Pegram rarely interfered with Bob's whims and wishes; but when he did, the son knew it was hopeless to struggle against the stronger will. The old man would wax almost pathetic in his appeal that Bob would be guided by the light of his counsel, but at the same time he always contrived to let it be seen that he would be perfectly relentless in the event of disobedience. It was only in the case of his having contemplated going upon the stage that his father had ever threatened him with disinheritance; but he had done it upon that occasion, and with a curtness that Bob Pegram felt carried a most unpleasant flavour of reality about it. He had not dared to refuse compliance with his father's schemes; still less had he dared to tell him why he demurred; that would have been a confession of folly to his hard-headed, intriguing sire calculated to anger him to the highest pitch; so that, upon the whole, Bob Pegram was not much more happy about his forthcoming marriage than was his bride-elect. Bob felt, indeed, that the ground was mined under his feet. Still, if he could but tide over the next three weeks in safety, his marriage with the Honourable Beatrice would be a thing accomplished, and whatever the other lady might say in her wrath would be of comparatively little moment.

## CHAPTER TWENTY-FOUR

# BOB PEGRAM'S PERPLEXITIES

Pegram and Son were considerably astonished upon the return of young Blinks with his information. The boy had tracked Jack Phillimore to his hotel, and contrived to get hold of his name from some of the under-servants, and the knowledge that Jack Phillimore in person had been playing the spy down in Rydland set them thinking, to say the least of it. Of course they knew perfectly well who Jack Phillimore was. Pegram senior had made it his business long ago to know everything connected with Lord Lakington's family that was to be got at, either through the medium of the 'Peerage' or by diligent inquiry. But what could have been Jack Phillimore's object in seeking information about old Krabbe, and, further, in going to see him?

'There is only one possible solution to the question,' argued the old lawyer. 'Mr Phillimore could have no object in doing this on his account; he must be simply acting as the agent of Lord Lakington. Now what on earth is his Lordship's motive? and what could have made him think of wanting to know all about Krabbe? Somebody must have got hold of the Viscount, and been whispering stories to our disparagement. I suspect that is about what it is.'

But lawyer Pegram, as Hemmingby said, was not the man to be frightened out of his game lightly.

'We must be unrelaxing in our vigilance during the next three weeks,' he remarked to his son, 'and we must strenuously oppose any attempt to postpone the marriage. In the meantime, I will just slip over to Slackpool Super-mare. It is just possible that inquiring young people like Mr Phillimore may take it into their head to follow old Krabbe all through that little tour of ours. I should be sorry, Bob, if they did not get every possible information; should not you? I will just make matters smooth for them,' and the old gentleman chuckled slyly as he thought of an unsophisticated tracker like Phillimore seeking to follow a trail that he had been at some trouble to blind.

But although his father might face coming danger with unmoved front, yet Bob Pegram was not gifted with his sire's iron nerve. He was most seriously disconcerted at the idea of Lord Lakington making inquiries, and even hinted that it might be advisable to abandon this marriage altogether. I have said hinted, for that was quite as far as Bob Pegram dared to go, his father's louring brow being too significant to permit of his being more outspoken. But a further shock was in store for luckless Bob. No sooner had his sire departed on his mission to Slackpool, than Mr Hemmingby appeared in Rydland. Now, there was nothing in that; Mr Hemmingby often did appear in Rydland. But then, what made him go out to see old Krabbe? Of course he had known the old man before his illness, and had often talked about going to see him; but what made him do it just now? Was he, too, an agent of Lord Lakington's? And then he remembered that the Viscount had been present at that dinner which Hemmingby had given him at the 'Wycherley' on the strength of his approaching marriage. Bob was experiencing the uncomfortable feeling a reckless schemer has who becomes at last aware that he is being counter-mined in every direction. If Hemmingby was really prompting and instigating Lord Lakington to inquire about old Krabbe, then, in Bob Pegram's eyes, the game was pretty well up, as far as he was concerned. Even his father, he remembered, had expressed great satisfaction when Hemmingby was out of the 'Tontine', saying that there was, at all events, a dangerous antagonist disposed of; and Bob Pegram considered that Sam Hemmingby would be quite as dangerous an antagonist acting on behalf of somebody else as if he were working for himself. When you are playing with cogged dice it is awkward to have a veteran hazard player joining in the game; and the more he turned the manager's visit to Krabbe over in his mind, the more convinced Bob Pegram became that that was the position he stood in. It had been all so very easy up to this. There had been literally no difficulty in carrying on their mystification; but if Hemmingby had come down here with the firm conviction that old Krabbe was their 'life', and with a determination to look into things, Bob Pegram felt convinced that the manager would get to the rights of the story sooner or later.

Bob Pegram, of course, went out to the cottage to hear all about Hemmingby's visit, and he found Mrs Clark in no slight state of perturbation.

'It's what I have always dreaded, ever since you first told me that he had talked of coming out to see the old man. He took me so much aback that I declare to goodness I very nearly called him by his name straight out. I had no time to change my cap for one of a deeper border, to bring my hair more down, nor anything. I never dreamt of its being him, and opened the door as I might have done to any one. I did my best. After the first glance I kept my eyes well down, and no man ever got shorter answers to his questions; I gave him as little chance to hear my voice as might be. But mark, Robert; for all that, he knew me.'

'Do you mean to say,' exclaimed Bob Pegram, 'that he recognized you?'

'He did, in a way. He could not quite put a name to me, but I know he felt certain that I was some one he had seen before.'

'Good heavens!' exclaimed Bob Pegram, 'what is to be done?'

'Ah! that is just what I want you to tell me. I thought you would be here, or I should have sent a note up to say that I wanted to see you. Mr Hemmingby certainly did not recollect me precisely when he went away. He might call me to mind afterwards, though I don't think he would; but if he sees me once or twice more he is sure to recollect me. Now, you know what my orders have been, always to let anybody see Mr Krabbe when Mr Krabbe is ready to receive; but we can't help his being asleep or irritable, can we, poor dear?' and Mrs Clark indulged in a low peal of rippling laughter.

'You have managed admirably, Kitty, so far; but this is awkward, deuced awkward;' and Bob Pegram buried his hands in his pockets and began to pace up and down the little parlour. 'The governor is from home, too, to make matters worse. The advice of a long-headed file like him is worth anything in a fix.'

'I say, Bob dear, do you think he has the slightest suspicion who I am?'

'No, Kitty; he takes you simply for what you represent yourself to be – takes you simply for what all Rydland does, as a nurse that I picked up in London to take care of old Mr Krabbe.'

'And, upon my word, if I had thought it was intended that that old gentleman was to live so long I'd have thought twice before I would have taken the situation.'

'Come, come, Kitty; don't be cross. I know it is wearisome work for you, my dear; but remember, the thing is drawing to a finish now, and then comes your reward.'

'Time it did, indeed,' replied Kitty Clark a little sharply. 'I am sure no woman ever worked so hard for a husband. Think of my feelings too; just think what it is for a woman to make a regular guy of herself for months; to make herself look about ten years older than she really is; and all to oblige your lordship; and ah! hardest times of all, Bob, to know whenever she sees the man she loves she is looking a regular fright.'

'No, Kitty, my dear, that is just what you can't do; you are very clever, and the make-up is uncommonly good, no doubt. I quite admit that you have made the girl into the matron, but she is a very good-looking matron, all the same.'

'I don't believe you'll know me when you see me as my proper self again,' retorted Kitty coquettishly. 'Oh, Bob, do wait here whilst I run into the next room and slip on my own clothes; you have not seen me as my real self for months.'

'Oh, nonsense; don't be foolish. You know you promised to be most guarded about everything you said and did. Just suppose anybody should come.'

'Well, they would simply have to knock at the door until I was ready to open it. I am a nurse, not a hall porter, and nurses are allowed to change their dress occasionally. I will do it; I insist upon it. It is high time you saw me as I really am. I won't be ten minutes,' and Kitty Clark whisked out of the room in very unmatronly fashion.

'I thought she had left all her own things behind her,' muttered Bob Pegram; 'but I might have been certain that a woman's vanity would lead her to put just one dress at the bottom of the box. She would do it on the off-chance, I suppose, just as men throw a suit of dress-clothes into their portmanteau on the "spec" that they might be asked out to dinner while on their travels. Now, if any blundering fool should happen to blurt out the news of my approaching marriage to her, there will be a row with a vengeance. She don't see many people, and I don't think anybody in Rydland knows it; but these things leak out in a most extraordinary manner. The governor would be simply like a raving lunatic when he found out who she was; but she knows enough, and is 'cute enough, to rather bother the old man, I fancy. It strikes me I am likely to be married whichever way things go.'

And here his reflections were interrupted by the reappearance of Kitty Clark, no longer a matron, but a tall, dashing young lady about six-and-twenty, with a very neat figure, a profusion of fair hair and arrayed in very correct costume and high-heeled boots.

'There, Bob, that is more like it. Now do you feel ready to run away with me? How I wish you were going to! and that Mrs Clark had made her final exit, and that Mrs Robert Pegram and her husband, having been duly married, were "off to the Con-ti-nong" with papa Pegram's blessing ringing in their ears.'

'Well, Kitty, you may set your mind at rest on one point, you look prettier than ever. I declare, my dear, I really must have one –'

'Meaning, that you wish to impress a chaste salute, as the novelists say,' laughed the girl, yielding to her lover's embrace. 'Oh, Bob! it feels so awfully jolly to be one's self again. I am so tired and weary of masquerading as Mrs Clark, lady nurse of the Nursing Institute, Gower Street. When, when is it all to end, dearest? Of course I don't understand what it all means; but at times I feel afraid that I am engaged in an imposition which might get you into a terrible scrape.'

'Oh, nonsense, Kitty; it is necessary to keep up this mystification for a short time longer, but no harm can come of it. And now, my dear, I must run away; and as for ýou, you really must become Mrs Clark again without more delay. Just fancy if Rydland caught sight of you as you are now.'

'Good-bye, Bob,' replied the girl, as she put up her lips for him to kiss; 'you needn't be afraid but what I will very soon turn nurse again now. There is nobody left to look nice for, remember,' she added, laughing, and then stood well behind the door as Bob Pegram passed out so that no passer-by might catch a glimpse of her.

Mr Robert Pegram, as he made his way moodily back to Rydland, could not but feel that he was about to behave like a thorough blackguard to the soi-disant Mrs Clark. Although he had never hinted at what bargain he had made with her to his father, yet the girl had been perfectly right when she talked of herself as engaged to him. She was an old London flame of Bob Pegram's, and he had undoubtedly promised to marry her as soon as there was no further necessity for her enacting the rôle she was at present playing; but then this had been before his father had proposed the match with Lord Lakington's daughter to him. It may well be wondered how Bob Pegram came to select a young lady like Kitty as nurse for an old querulous invalid, but it was absolutely necessary that the nurse should be somebody upon whom the Pegrams could place implicit reliance. The finding of this confidential person had been left entirely to Bob, and it occurred to him that his old flame, Kitty Clyde of the Grecian Theatre, would be the very woman for their purpose. He had gone so far with her in the days when he contemplated adopting the stage as a profession as to become formally betrothed; but when old Mr Pegram issued his minatory mandate on the subject, Kitty, like a sensible young woman, saw that their marriage was hopeless, and they parted with bitter regrets on both sides, as well as a few tears on that of the lady. When Bob Pegram sought her out again, explained to the actress what he wanted her to do, begged her to help him in this thing as a matter of very great moment both to him and his father; and finally, when he made her understand that the result of the little mystification in which she was implored to assist would be to make him, Robert Pegram, a rich man and enable him to marry her in a few months, Kitty at once gave her consent. He was not very clear in his explanation of why he wanted Kitty to play his rôle, but hinted vaguely that it was to prevent the old man altering his will; and moreover, Kitty was not very curious on that point. She thought that it would be 'awfully jolly' to marry Bob Pegram and have lots of money, and was quite willing to do anything he asked her that led to that end. She had certainly never bargained that her servitude should be so long, and was getting extremely tired of the monotony of the existence to which she had condemned herself. Still, occasional interviews with Bob Pegram, such as this last, cheered her up and encouraged her to stick to her task; but even these were few and far between, and so afraid was Pegram of her detection, that he usually treated her as the nurse and resolutely abstained from playing the lover.

As for Bob Pegram, there was no doubt he would be very glad to keep his troth with Kitty if he could. When his father had told him to procure a suitable person from London to act as nurse for old Mr Krabbe, one who, sufficiently paid for it, might be depended on not to talk, that dramatic taste which was inherent in Bob's nature at once suggested to him that Kitty Clyde was the very woman for the part. She could make up old enough with a little trouble; and then where could he find any one he could rely on like Kitty, more especially if he promised to marry her at the expiration of her services? It never entered his mind that his father would propose to compromise the 'Tontine' after the manner he had, and he thought that when they had compounded with Lord Lakington for a division between them of the big lottery that all would be finished. He would have established a hold to some extent over his father by doing his bidding in this thing, and was foolish enough to fancy that he should by these means be able to induce him to consent to his marriage with Kitty Clyde. He really was fond of the girl. She was just his idea of what a wife ought to be, with tastes much in accordance with his own. But when the old lawyer broke to him his scheme for compromising the 'Great Tontine', Bob Pegram felt that it was all over; he gave up struggling with his destiny, and allowed himself to drift quietly where the Fates should will. He was not the sort of man to struggle much with destiny at any time, drifting, as a rule, pretty much where circumstances dictated; and when his father put his foot down in earnest, Bob Pegram never had the courage to resist his will. In the first instance, his vanity had been tickled. The idea of patronizing the play-houses with the Honourable Mrs Pegram on his arm was very soothing to his *amour propre*; the surprise and congratulations of his friends that he had done so well for himself, and had, to use the expression of some of his more immediate intimates, 'caught such a regular tip-topper for his wife', was also gratifying; but as he neared the goal, as the time drew near when the bells should ring out in jubilation of the alliance of the Phillimores and the Pegrams, and the termination of the 'Great Tontine', Bob Pegram got most uncomfortably nervous, and every day something was occurring to make him still more so. Now it was the sailor, now it was Hemmingby wanting to see Mr Krabbe; and Bob, walking into Rydland, repeated for the two hundredth time, 'What the devil did Hemmingby want to see Mr Krabbe for?' Bob Pegram, in fact, in these latter days, debated seriously with himself whether he should wait and play out his part of the little drama, or show a clean pair of heels to his father and all concerned.

Old Pegram returned the next day in high spirits.

'Ah! Bob, my boy,' he exclaimed, 'it is a wonderful thing what a little gold does, if you only apply it judiciously. If Mr Phillimore and his friends ever get at our last lodgings they'll be pretty clever. The landlady and her sister were sensible women, and quite agreeable to know nothing when I produced my arguments. While as for the servant, she is luckily a new one since we were there; so I think that is pretty fairly settled. I don't suppose that blundering young fellow that was down here ever would have made anything out of it, even if he ever had the "gumption" to try; but though I don't throw my money about, it was just as well to spend a little there to make sure.'

'I tell you what, father, something much more serious has taken place while you were away. Hemmingby has been down to see old Krabbe.'

'Ahem! that is curious. He did not see him, I suppose.'

'No,' replied Bob, with a grin. 'He was asleep, and could not be disturbed; but what is to be done if he comes down here again wanting to see him? I suppose we must let him do so.'

'No, Bob,' replied the old lawyer, quickly; 'I don't think that would do. Sam Hemmingby must be content to wait till after your marriage before he sees his old friend Mr Krabbe. You may be clever, Bob, but you are no match for Hemmingby. I can't think myself it was anything more than a mere freak his wanting to see the old man. He always did ask after him, you know, and has talked half-a-dozen times of going to see him. What earthly motive could Hemmingby have for interfering in any way? Why, he was out of the "Tontine" five months ago or more. Pooh! a mere whim, you may depend upon it. I don't suppose he will even think of asking to see him again.'

'He knows Lord Lakington, remember.'

'Of course he does,' replied the old lawyer; 'didn't he come here to try and compromise the "Tontine" on his Lordship's part in the first instance? It is hardly likely he would have done that if he had any evil suspicions about us.'

'But you must recollect this Phillimore, this sailor; he is a relation of Lord Lakington's.'

'Quite so; he is nephew and heir. I looked him out in the "Peerage" long ago; that is, I presume the young man who was here is the John Phillimore therein mentioned. But what of that? you never heard Hemmingby say anything about him. I doubt if Hemmingby even knows him.'

'Well,' rejoined Bob, doggedly, 'of course, we must do as you say; but I don't like Hemmingby's visit, and it is my opinion it would be less dangerous for him to see old Krabbe than not.'

'Stuff and nonsense! I will have nothing of the kind. I don't at all suppose that he will call again; but if he does, the old man must be asleep or unwell, or something or other.'

Bob Pegram did not dare tell his father what was really the most alarming sign in Hemmingby's visit, viz., his seeming recognition of Kitty Clyde. To do that would have been to confess who Kitty Clyde really was, and to admit that the manager's memory of her might at length go back to the times in which she played non-speaking parts in the Vivacity Theatre. So that, after all, his father's return brought but small comfort to the embarrassed Bob, who, as if the web of his father's scheme was not complicated enough, had thought fit to graft on to it another of his own.

## CHAPTER TWENTY-FIVE

# MEETING OF BEATRICE AND MARY

Two or three days after Miss Caterham's funeral Mr Carbuckle went down to Kew to see Mary Chichester. She welcomed him warmly. The sight of such an old friend as himself was a relief to her; for the girl had just begun to realize how alone in the world she stood.

'It is kind of you, Mr Carbuckle,' she said, as she shook hands, 'to steal an hour or two to come and see me, knowing, as I do, that all the bustle of your work has begun again.'

'It is only natural I should,' replied the barrister; 'I have known you, I am ashamed to say how long, and your poor aunt was, as you know, a much-valued friend of mine. But I must also tell you that Miss Caterham left a letter behind her, appointing me, in some sense, your guardian. I don't mean legally, of course; being of age, you are, in the eye of the law, mistress of your own actions. But my poor friend knew very well that a girl left so alone in the world as you are might probably want a male adviser of some sort. She has asked me to accept this trust; and if you are willing to put faith in an old fellow – well, not exactly an old fellow, although old enough to be your father – I shall very willingly accept the position.'

'It is very good of you,' replied Mary. 'I need your advice, even now. I do not think I could bear to go on living here all alone, even if I could afford to do so.'

'That latter is a question,' replied Mr Carbuckle, 'of which you can form a better opinion than me; but I presume your aunt's solicitor has told you exactly how you are situated. You are not a rich woman, but you have enough to live quietly upon. There are six thousand pounds in the three per cents which belong to you, besides all the personalty, meaning furniture, &c., which will amount to some hundreds more: so you may reckon your income as a trifle over two hundred a-year. This cottage, pretty as it is, is probably more than you want.'

These six thousand pounds represented the two thousand which Mary had inherited from her father, and the savings of Miss Caterham, which consisted principally of the interest accruing from the 'Great Tontine'; and that Terence Finnigan, if alive, should not have been forthcoming during the last two years had been a subject of great regret to Miss Caterham, her share of the interest during that time amounting to something considerable.

'Yes, the cottage is more than I want,' replied Mary; 'and will cost, besides, more than I consider prudent, even if I wished to live on here; but I do not. What I should like would be a home in some nice family; I, of course, paying whatever they deemed right for my board. Can you help me in this, Mr Carbuckle?'

'I don't know,' rejoined the barrister; 'but I must try. It is rather a queer notion this of yours, Mary. I may be all wrong, but I have an idea that families who receive young ladies upon those sort of terms are not very desirable people to make acquaintance with; however, all that I think in this case goes for nothing, as it is theory, not fact – not evidence, in short. I must make inquiries in all directions. If we could only hit off the right sort of people it would be an infinitely preferable and more healthy life for you than living in solitude. For the present, of course, you will stay on here; but the sooner you move the better.'

'I am going next week to spend a short time with the Lomaxes, who live about a mile from here. He was poor aunt's medical man, and I have known them for years.'

'Ah! that's right; a change, no doubt, will do you good. And now, Mary, I must say good-bye. You may rely upon my making inquiries in all directions for what you want; and I dare say we shall manage to hit it off before long.'

Mr Carbuckle certainly lost no time, not in making the inquiries himself – he was too busy for that – but in setting other people to make them. A few days, however, convinced him that what Mary Chichester wished was by no means easy to discover. That if he put an advertisement in the papers, he should find plenty of families ready to receive the young lady with open arms, he had no doubt; the said families being excessively anxious, at the same time, to know what the exact stipend was the young lady was prepared to pay for her board and lodging. But such a home as Mary Chichester wanted was only to be obtained by continual inquiry amongst friends and acquaintances. Whilst still perplexed with this problem, Mr Carbuckle one afternoon received a visit from Ronald Ringwood.

'Delighted to see you, Ringwood,' exclaimed the senior, as he greeted the young man. 'Do you bring me any intelligence of Terence Finnigan, or any other news connected with the "Great Tontine"? You have been digging and delving lately after the Pegram nominee, have you not? Acting under the impression that their nominee was a corpse, you have been hunting for his grave with the amiable purpose of disinterring him, though how on earth you found out who their nominee was is, I must say, beyond my comprehension.'

'Well, I dare say you will call that the weak point in our case. Our knowledge of Pegram's nominee is pure guess-work; but I feel pretty sure that we are on the right track, and have got the thread of a very pretty skein of fraud and deception if we can ever unravel the tangle. But the Pegrams are clever people, and, I am beginning to think, a little too much for amateur detectives; not, for the matter of that, the professionals seem to do any better with regard to Finnigan. The latest thing I have done in his case has been to offer a reward in some of the local journals near where he was last traced to – such as the "Hampshire Telegraph", the "Guildford Journal" – for any one who will give information which will lead to the discovery of Terence Finnigan; then follows a description of him, and of course an intimation as to where any one having knowledge of him after the 20th of July, 1878, is to apply.'

'That is a very good notion of yours,' rejoined Carbuckle. 'I wonder it never struck any of us before. You have advertised in all the daily journals; but the sort of people with whom a man like Finnigan would naturally consort seldom trouble their heads with the London papers but spell over the local "weekly" on Sundays. Finnigan has been missing so long now that I don't much think we are ever very likely to hear of him again. Still, I must say I think you are trying a very "likely fly" in advertising that reward in "the locals". You have hardly, I suppose, seen Miss Chichester since the funeral?'

'No,' rejoined Ringwood drily.

There was that in his manner which struck Mr Carbuckle. Aware, as he was, of the sentiments that Ringwood entertained for Mary, it suddenly occurred to him that something had gone wrong between the two. Was it, he wondered, that Ronald had hinted at his aspirations too soon, and found that they met with a chilling reception. The old maxim of 'take her with the tear in her e'e, man', may be all very well for widows, but it does not apply to maidens sorrowing for the loss of near relatives. He felt sorry for this if it was so; for looking upon Mary now as in some measure his ward, he thought that Ronald Ringwood was a young fellow calculated to make the girl a good husband, to say nothing of being a fair match for her in other respects. As for her chance of coming into the 'Great Tontine', that Mr Carbuckle considered as not worth consideration. He felt little doubt but what that aged and dissipated old Irishman, upon whom her hopes depended, was no more. However, it was without any allusion to the thought that flashed through his mind he continued,

'Mary was speaking to me the other day as to where she was to live in future: the cottage, she says, is more than she requires or can afford, and she rather dreads the idea of living in lodgings by herself. It must come rather hard upon a young woman. We know what life in chambers means, and then we have business to distract us, to say nothing of our clubs. What Mary wants is to find some family with whom she can make a home – paying, of course, something reasonable for her board, &c.'

Ringwood sat silent a few minutes and then said slowly –

'I don't know whether it would do, but you might, at all events, mention to Miss Chichester that if this marriage between Robert Pegram and Miss Phillimore really does come off, Mrs Lyme Wregis will want a young lady companion to take her granddaughter's place. Now, I quite understand that when Miss Chichester talks of seeking a home she does not at all entertain the idea of going out as a companion; but, remember, these are people we know something about, and what she wants is by no means easy to come across. As for Lord Lakington, you know all about him; while Mrs Lyme Wregis – I am assured by Jack Phillimore, from whom, by the way, I derive all this information – is a most charming old lady, and though very advanced in years, enjoying a complete immunity from the infirmities common to her time of life. What I mean is, that Miss Chichester will not be called upon to act as nurse to a rickety old woman, but simply be a companion to a bright, pleasant old lady. I think it might be worth mentioning to her, and introduced by you, there could never be any doubt about her station.'

'Ahem! I don't know; I don't think that is altogether the sort of thing that Mary means. I should fancy she looks forward to finding girls of her own age wherever she may make her home.'

'She will hardly want,' rejoined Ringwood, 'to go out much for the next few months; and though Mrs Lyme Wregis, no doubt, leads a quiet life, you must recollect Miss Caterham's was also of that description. What strikes me as its peculiar advantages are, that she could go there at once, as I understand Miss Phillimore is very anxious not only to see her successor, but to put her into the ways of the house. It is surely, at all events, worth submitting to Miss Chichester.'

'Quite so,' exclaimed Mr Carbuckle, laughing; 'and as I feel that nobody can place its advantages before her like yourself, I propose that you at once run down and see her on the subject.'

'No; that I must leave to you; I am too busy at present with the "Great Tontine" to spare the time.'

Mr Carbuckle could not help looking a little surprised. Ronald Ringwood had never hitherto seemed to find any difficulty in sparing two or three hours to run down to Kew.

'I am afraid my conjecture is right,' thought Mr Carbuckle, 'and that Mary has been foolish enough to let him see that his advances are unacceptable. Whether he has pressed his suit at the wrong time or not I don't know, but in this case it is the principals only that can set things right, and the interference of the bystander more apt to mar than make a match.'

'Very well, then,' he replied quietly, 'I shall myself mention the opportunity to Miss Chichester.' 'The idea,' he muttered to himself, 'of a barrister of his standing pretending he had not time for anything.'

The idea of finding somebody to take her place had for the last three or four weeks taken a strong hold on Beatrice's mind. The girl knew that her approaching marriage was, to say the least of it, most distasteful to her grandmother. She felt also that the poor lady would miss her sorely, though she was happily independent of that constant attention sometimes so necessary at her age. Still, Beatrice had been a constant companion to her since quite a child. That anybody could exactly fill her place she did not believe; but that her grandmother must have somebody with whom to exchange ideas, and who could occasionally read to her, was, Beatrice considered, imperative. Absolutely necessary, also, she held, was it that this somebody should be a lady, tolerably good-looking, and – to sum up all in that comprehensive woman's word – 'nice'. Beatrice was getting very anxious to discover this somebody as the wedding drew near. She was desirous that her grandmother should miss her as little as possible, and the girl's heart smote her when she thought how much she had avoided the old lady of late; but this coming marriage threw such a restraint over their intercourse that Beatrice could not bear it. She was sad enough about it herself, but the last drop of bitterness in her cup was that she was debarred from telling her grandmother and cousin the reason that made her consent to it. Her promise to her father forbade justifying herself in their eyes; and even if that promise had not been given, Beatrice felt that to confess her sacrifice would be to exhibit that beloved father in a very pitiful light to those nearest akin to him. There was, perhaps, no greater element in her misery – and Beatrice owned at times to herself that she was very miserable – than the thought that her noble progenitor was so very different from what she in her girlish adoration had pictured him. A few weeks back, and how indignantly she would have repudiated the notion that he could stoop to do this thing. The idea that her darling and indulgent father would sacrifice his daughter's happiness to ensure his own ease and comfort she would have rejected with scorn; and Beatrice heartily regretted that she had not been allowed to remain in that belief, instead of being so rudely enlightened as to the real selfishness and heartlessness of his nature. The Viscount's specious arguments had never for a moment deceived her. That shrewd, worldly, but fallacious reasoning, by which he had endeavoured to show that it was her interest and not his own that he was studying in assenting to this match, had never for one instant thrown dust in her eyes. She was far too quick-witted for that, and pondered bitterly at times as to whether she had been thus deceived in her estimate of others dear to her. Her cousin; had she not striven to part friends with him, and had he not rejected her overtures with insult? And then poor Beatrice burst into tears as she remembered that Jack had good cause for his wrath, if man is ever allowed to feel indignation at woman's falsity.

Beatrice communicated her feelings on the subject of a companion for her grandmother in the first place to her father, and the Viscount most thoroughly concurred, if only they could find a suitable person. The girl next sounded Mrs Lyme Wregis herself on the subject; and that lady, having taken the opportunity of once more recording her aversion to the marriage, observing 'that she still hoped and believed it would never take place', agreed with Beatrice that, if a young lady could be found who would consent to 'make herself agreeable to an old woman for a few hours in the course of the day, it would be pleasant'.

This was not exactly the sort of speech calculated to carry comfort to a betrothed maiden; but, improbable as the prediction seemed, Beatrice's heart gave a bound of satisfaction at the thought of 'grandmamma's being right after all'.

That Mrs Lyme Wregis should mention this contemplated arrangement to Jack Phillimore in one of his visits was but natural. The old lady, indeed, vaguely asked him if he knew of any young person likely to suit; and Jack, in his numerous confidential talks with Ronald Ringwood concerning the 'Great Tontine' in general, and the exploding of the Pegrams in particular, told it to Ringwood, as, for the matter of that, indeed, he did most things concerning himself and his love affair at this time. The latter, in his turn, had mentioned the thing to Mr Carbuckle, simply as the only thing of the kind he happened to know of, and also having a thorough understanding of the difficulty there would in all probability be in coming across such a home as Mary wanted; but advocate its advantages in person that he would not do. It was only after much deliberation that he had resolved to see Miss Chichester no more until after the decision of the 'Great Tontine', and he determined to adhere to that resolve. He did not want to explain all this to Mr Carbuckle, and that gentleman having, as we know, his own opinion on the subject, pressed him no further; but, as soon as Ringwood had taken his departure, he wrote to Lord Lakington, saying that, in consequence of his daughter's marriage, he understood Mrs Lyme Wregis was in want of a companion; that he ventured to write on behalf of a young lady who was a kind of ward of his own, and whose birth and breeding he would guarantee as perfectly unexceptionable.

'I can only further add, my dear Viscount,' he continued, 'that, having known her from a child, I can vouch for her being a good-humoured, unaffected, agreeable girl, and a very nice-looking one to boot. Recollect, it is a case in which salary is no object. My ward, owing to the recent death of her great-aunt, who brought her up, is in want of a home, and, from all I have heard of your respected step-mother, I have come to the conclusion they would suit one another. At all events, I think it is worth a trial on both sides. My information reached me in a rather round-about way, and I am told Mrs Lyme Wregis emphatically requires that her companion should be a lady. Mary Chichester is just as peremptory in her requirements on that point. She is very anxious that her future home should be with genuine gentlefolks, and not with *oroide* imitation. Though we have lost sight of each other of late years, our old friendship must be my excuse for addressing you on this point. If you have made no other arrangement, give this, at all events, a trial. What you want is, I fancy, as difficult to find as that which I am in search of; and, from experience, I can depose that *my want* is not easy to satisfy. Believe, my dear Lakington, yours sincerely, HENRY CARBUCKLE.'

And so it came about that, a few days later, Mr Carbuckle and his ward arrived, late in the afternoon, in the Victoria Road. Lord Lakington was at home to do the honours, and Mary was duly presented to Mrs Lyme Wregis and Beatrice. The two ladies were most favourably impressed with the tall, graceful, ladylike girl, who promised to more than satisfy even the somewhat fastidious requirements of the younger. Trixie, indeed, was greatly struck with the stranger, and showed much anxiety to smooth over all preliminaries, and to persuade Miss Chichester to take up her abode with them without delay.

'There is a very comfortable room all ready for you,' she urged, 'and I am so anxious to see grandmamma and yourself the friends I feel sure you will be before my – my – before I go, I mean.'

Mr Carbuckle, not heeding the signs of the times, ventured to congratulate Miss Beatrice on her approaching marriage; but Mary, upon whom the girl's hesitating speech had not been lost, did not fail to mark the slight angry flush that flashed across Beatrice's face, and the somewhat haughty manner in which she bowed her acknowledgements. The visit was a highly successful one. If the Victoria Road ladies were delighted with Mary, she, on her part, was much pleased with them, and at their earnest entreaty agreed to take up her abode with them in three days from that time.

'I think it will do very nicely,' said Miss Chichester, as they strolled up the road towards the South Kensington station; 'you have found what I want very quickly. Mrs Lyme Wregis appears to be a delightful old lady, and what a handsome girl Miss Phillimore is! By-the-bye, my guardian, did you notice how those splendid eyes of hers flashed when you congratulated her on her marriage? How comes it that she is going to marry this Mr Pegram? If I mistake not, there is very little love or esteem about it.'

'Well,' replied Mr Carbuckle, 'I don't think it is altogether a love-match; it is what the papers call a marriage that "has been arranged". You must remember that though she is the Honourable Beatrice Phillimore, yet she is a dowerless maiden, – I told you her noble father's history the other day, you know, – while Pegram represents wealth. I have an idea that you will know how that marriage came about before very long.'

'What *do* you mean?' inquired Mary, with some astonishment.

'Oh, nothing,' replied Mr Carbuckle, hastily; 'nothing more than I think that you and Miss Beatrice will become great friends in the few days that you will be together.'

'Yes,' replied Mary, slowly; 'I think I shall like her. I feel so sorry for her for one thing: I am sure her heart is not in this marriage, and, though I really have no right to say so, I declare she gave me the idea of looking forward to it almost with aversion. However, poor girl, I do not suppose I shall see much of her after she is married; but it was very clever of you to find what promises to be such a nice home for me so quickly.'

'I cannot lay claim to much credit about it,' replied Mr Carbuckle; 'I heard of it from Ronald Ringwood.'

'Mr Ringwood!' exclaimed the young lady; 'he has never been near me since the day after poor aunt's death, when he came down on your behalf. I do think, as a matter of common civility, he might have made the ordinary inquiries.'

Mr Carbuckle made no reply, but began to have his doubts as to whether that theory of his concerning Ringwood's premature avowal of affection was correct. The girl would hardly have expressed astonishment, he thought, at Ringwood's not coming to see her had that been the case. Mary, too, lapsed into silence, and no further conversation took place between them before the railway station was reached, whence Mary Chichester duly departed for the cottage at Kew.

## CHAPTER TWENTY-SIX

## JACK TACKLES THE LAWYER

The day fixed for the wedding draws very near, and it would be hard to say whether the Honourable Beatrice Phillimore or Robert Pegram regards it with most uneasiness. The more Beatrice thinks over this marriage, the more is she convinced that it is throwing away her life's happiness. She never half knew how dearly she loved her cousin till now, nor was she thoroughly alive to the wide difference between herself and her betrothed. They have not a sentiment in common. Their very habits of life are different, and she feels, without seeing them, that his friends could never be hers. As for Robert Pegram, he looks upon himself as a man sitting upon a mine, and that an explosion must come on his wedding-day, if it does not take place before. There is no avoiding it, and he thinks it will probably work him less harm under the former circumstances. Once safely married, he thinks that, backed by his father, Kitty Clyde's wrath upon hearing of his treachery will be easier to face than any other phase of what he terms the 'regular row' that is impending. But, besides the principals, there is another who contemplates the near approach of the ceremony with feelings of helpless indignation.

Jack Phillimore, sitting smoking in Ringwood's rooms, is as general in his condemnation of things as the curse of St Athanasius.

'What *are* we to do, Ronald?' he exclaimed, as he puffed savagely at a short clay pipe between his teeth. 'You say you have completely lost all trace of old Pegram and old Krabbe.'

'Yes,' replied Ringwood, moodily; 'I am dead beat at present. You see Slackpool Super-mare is a long, straggling place, ever extending along the water's edge, just as Brighton does. I have traced him from the principal inn at which he first put up to three successive lodgings, each time with greater difficulty. I have very little doubt that in a few days the researches of my agents down there will be successful; indeed, we thought they had been on Saturday, and that we had discovered where next they had moved to; but the two sisters who kept the house denied all knowledge of any lodgers answering to our description: so I suppose we must take it for granted we were mistaken; but it is a mere matter of time –'

'But confound it, man,' interrupted Jack Phillimore, 'that is exactly what we have not to spare. You forget this is Monday night, and that this accursed marriage is to take place next week. If that brute Pegram is not bowled out before then it will inevitably take place. My uncle is so infatuated with the idea of making a certainty of the "Great Tontine", that nothing but a thorough exposure of the "Pegram" fraud would induce him to back out of it; and once demonstrate to Beatrice that her quill-driving bridegroom will be in no position to write the big cheques she imagines, and I fancy she would follow suit. For faithless and fickle as she has been, I won't do her the injustice to suppose that she is marrying Robert Pegram for himself.'

'It is very doubtful whether we unravel the mystery of old Krabbe in time,' replied Ringwood, slowly. 'I tell you what; you must go straight to Lord Lakington, tell him what we suspect, and point out that it would be advisable to postpone the marriage for a month, or till such time as the thing is cleared up. He might even go so far as to tell Pegram, senior, what he had heard; and while professing no belief in the rumour, say that it would be as well that each should disclose to the other the name of his nominee, and afford facility for visiting them.'

'You don't know my uncle, Ronald,' rejoined Jack; 'he would not listen to me. He sees a big pile of money coming into the family through this marriage, and would be loath to believe it was not so. No; he would pooh-pooh me, politely hint that I was an interested witness against the Pegrams, and demand proofs. And then, what can I say? – nothing, but that Pegram and his invalid clerk changed their lodgings surprisingly often.'

'To which, of course, he might rejoin,' said Ringwood, laughing, 'rapacious landladies – bad cooking – vile tenants or bugs. I will own, Jack, I would infinitely prefer to thoroughly expose the Pegrams. I am pretty well convinced, in my own mind, that the old man they took away from Rydland is not the old man they brought back, the old man you saw; but we certainly cannot prove this as yet.'

There was a pause of some minutes, and each was apparently employed in devising some means by which the wedding might be postponed.

Suddenly Phillimore exclaimed, 'I have it! I'll go down to Rydland tomorrow, see old Pegram, and frighten him by disclosing how much we know; defy him to go on with this marriage under pain of exposure.'

Ringwood shook his head as he said, 'It is of no use, Jack. From all I have heard of him, you will not frighten old Pegram; and forgive my saying so, but I think you, or, for the matter of that, myself, would be a child in the hands of that crafty solicitor. It is madness, sheer madness, to think of that.'

'And what if it is madness?' replied the other hotly. 'I am prepared to perpetrate much greater madness sooner than this ceremony should take place; ah! even to breaking every bone in Robert Pegram's skin, and leaving him in such case that he would, at all events, not walk to the altar.'

'Do be reasonable, Jack; I assure you no good can come of this visit to Rydland. At all events, try my plan and see Lord Lakington first. Remember, we cannot resort to violent measures. Your threatening Pegram, depend upon it, will result in failure.'

'I differ from you *in toto*,' replied Phillimore, rising; 'and you must remember that my stake in this matter is a far heavier one than yours. The case is getting desperate, and you must forgive me if I play my game in my own way. Good night; I am off to Rydland tomorrow morning.'

'Ah! he will do no good,' muttered Ringwood, as the door closed behind his guest. 'From what Hemmingby tells me, and he knows him well, Pegram is just about the last man with whom to play the game of brag; but then, poor fellow, the fate of the girl he loves is hanging in the balance. I wonder if Mary was placed in like circumstances how I should bear it. I am afraid, like Jack, I should yearn to commit a murderous assault.'

That Jack Phillimore should be on his way to Rydland by an early train the next morning was not much to be wondered at. Between his passion for his cousin, and his firm belief that she was about to sacrifice herself to an impostor whom she despised, Jack was wound up to a pitch of nervous excitement which made it a relief to do anything. What he was to say, or how he was to open his case to the lawyer when he saw him, he had in no wise determined. Fierce denunciation of the Pegrams, father and son, was the only thing that seemed to clearly point itself out to him, and that he could deliver that with considerable energy and figurative embellishment he entertained no doubt. But even fiery, impetuous Jack Phillimore was constrained to admit that bluster was hardly the way to attain his end. Over and over again did he preach to himself that it behoved him, at all events, to be cool, solacing himself with the reflection that he might at the same time be cutting. Even as he walked up the street towards Pegram and Son's office, he muttered to himself, 'Be cool, Jack, my boy, be cool; cutting if you like, but be cool.'

He gave his card as he entered the office, and was speedily ushered into the presence of Mr Pegram. The old man was in the office alone, and bowing courteously to Jack, begged he would take a chair.

'Some relation, I presume, of Lord Lakington's, Mr Phillimore; and, under the present circumstances, I am only too delighted to see you. I trust you will dine with us tonight; and I need hardly add, that there is a bed at your service.'

Jack Phillimore was taken most thoroughly aback. He had fully expected to be received as an enemy endeavouring to pry into the secrets of Pegram and Son; instead of which, he was welcomed as one of the family, Mr Pegram evidently assuming that he not only knew all about the forthcoming marriage, but also concurred in it. How mistaken Hemmingby was! It was quite clear that the old lawyer had no idea that he had ever seen him before.

'Yes, I am a nephew of Lord Lakington's; I am afraid when you hear what I have to say that you will not feel disposed to be so friendly towards me. Has it never occurred to you, Mr Pegram, that the proposed marriage between your son and my cousin is hardly suitable?'

'May I ask,' replied the old lawyer, drily, 'if you are speaking on behalf of his Lordship?'

'Not exactly,' answered Jack; 'I am speaking as one of the family. As next heir to the title, I should imagine I have some right to express an opinion on the subject.'

Mr Pegram contented himself with a quiet bow of acquiescence.

'And I tell you,' continued Jack, in some danger of forgetting the coolness he had so laid down for himself, and not remembering the cutting, 'that no man of the world could have two opinions about it. I am not for one moment impugning the respectability of your family, Mr Pegram, but you must be aware that you are not exactly of the class with whom the Phillimores are wont to marry.'

The old lawyer twiddled a pen slowly between his fingers as he replied, in measured tones,

'Lord Lakington and Miss Beatrice appear to differ with you upon this point.'

'Don't mention my cousin's name,' exclaimed Jack, sharply; 'some undue influence has been brought to bear upon her, or else, I feel assured, she would never have given her assent to such a union.'

'Harsh language,' replied the lawyer; 'but you will allow me to point out that it is quite impossible that any unfair influence can have been used either by me or my son.'

'But I say it has, sir,' rejoined Jack, hotly. 'I know the whole story of the "Great Tontine", and how you have taken advantage of your share in it to make this infamous arrangement with my uncle. Beatrice is being sacrificed blindly that you may share this big lottery between you.'

'I must trouble you to listen to me, Mr Phillimore, quietly, if you please. I must premise, in the first place, that I am not in the least called upon to justify myself in your eyes; but I prefer to do so. That finding myself and your uncle the two last virtual shareholders in the "Tontine", the idea of a "divide" should come into my head was only natural. Upon finding he had an only daughter, as I had an only son, that I should think of marriage between the two, with a view to the whole thing falling at last into the hands of our mutual descendants, was also not peculiar. Such arrangements are made every day, and young men and young women married simply because their estates are adjoining. I wish to be perfectly candid with you, so don't hesitate to say that the respective shares in the "Tontine" of Lord Lakington and myself are settled on the engaged couple. His Lordship and Miss Beatrice, myself and my son, are surely the principals concerned in this affair, and we being all of one mind on the subject, you must forgive my discussing it no further with yourself, Mr Phillimore.'

To anybody who knew him Jack Phillimore would have been a study of considerable interest during the old lawyer's speech. He fidgeted on his chair; his lips twitched, and it would have been palpable to an observer that he was mastering his temper with considerable difficulty. Every word Mr Pegram uttered added fuel to the fire of his indignation. His explanation was so disgustingly reasonable and unanswerable, and his final declaration, that he would discuss the matter no further, completely overbalanced the sailor's judgement. It was in angry tones that he replied –

'And I tell you, sir, that your specious explanation is all a sham; that you have thrown dust in the eyes of my uncle and cousin, and bamboozled the Directors of this lottery, Heaven knows how; and I further tell you, that you have no more a share in the "Great Tontine" than I have; that your nominee is all a fraud, and that if you do not at once abandon all idea of this marriage, I shall expose you to my uncle, the managers of the concern, and the world generally.'

'Harsh words, as I observed before,' rejoined Pegram; 'I should not be over-stating it if I said violent language now. You will allow me to remark, in the first place, that you cannot possibly even know who my nominee is.'

'There you are wrong; it is your old clerk, Mr Krabbe.'

'I decline to admit for one moment that you are right,' rejoined Pegram; 'but admitting that Mr Krabbe is my nominee, may I ask you to point out where the fraud exists. Mr Krabbe, though very infirm, and not altogether in possession of his faculties, is alive to be seen at any time; as, if he can carry his memory back a little, Mr Phillimore can testify; you did him the honour of paying him a visit some three weeks ago.'

'I don't believe that old mummy I saw was Mr Krabbe a bit,' returned Jack, furiously.

'And I don't believe, for one moment, that you are Lieutenant Phillimore of the Royal Navy,' rejoined the old lawyer coolly; 'and am at this instant debating whether I shall send for a constable and give you in charge as a suspicious character.'

'By Heavens!' cried Jack, starting to his feet, 'you had better mind what you say, old gentleman, or you may chance to make me forget that your hair is white.'

'Not so fast, young man,' said the lawyer, also rising. 'Look here, Fluter Phillimore, or whatever your name is – though neither of those, I dare be sworn, – the other day you were wandering about Rydland in the garb of a common sailor; now you come down dressed as a gentleman, and pretend to be a nephew of Lord Lakington's, having doubtless picked up in your former visit that I am about to be connected with that family; you come here and accuse me of knavery and dishonesty upon no earthly grounds, and with what object it is difficult to conceive. Lawyers at all events, do not pay hush-money to mere blustering accusation. Now, mark me, my man, if you are to be found in Rydland tomorrow morning I'll give you in charge, as sure as you stand there; and you won't find it quite so easy to find bail down here, I am thinking.'

'Very well,' replied Jack, in a voice which shook with passion. 'It is war, then, without quarter, between us; you may rest assured, you damned insolent old pettifogger, that neither shall this marriage ever take place, nor another shilling of the "Tontine" find its way into your avaricious old fingers.' With which strong and personal, but hardly cool and cutting, climax, Phillimore took his departure.

He felt very sick at heart on his return to London, and far too dejected at his failure to go and confess it to Ringwood next day. It was a pity he had not done so, for he would have found a note there from his friend and calculated, at all events, to console him for his defeat, and that defeat it was Jack made no disguise to himself. It was all very well to swagger to old Pegram; but Jack knew that unless he could inoculate his uncle with his own and Ringwood's suspicions, he had no chance of breaking off this marriage. He was by no means sanguine about it, but thought it should, at all events, be tried, and the sooner the better; desirable, he thought, that interview should be got over before he again saw Ringwood. It would simplify his meeting with his friend, on the one hand, if he had to tell him that his scheme had proved equally futile as his own; on the other, should it by good luck be crowned with success, he felt that he should not in the least mind admitting his own failure. He knew his uncle's habits pretty well, and called therefore in the Victoria Road a few minutes after twelve the morning after his return from Rydland.

He caught the Viscount, as he expected, over his paper and 'after breakfast' cigar; and losing no time, plunged at once into his indictment against the Pegrams. But, bad as he had looked upon his chance previously, it had been made much worse that morning; for no sooner had Jack quitted Pegram and Son's office at Rydland, than the old lawyer sat down and wrote a most plausible account of the interview to Lord Lakington, which he took very good care should be 'mailed' by that night's post. Fresh from the perusal of this epistle, the Viscount was not only prepared for his nephew's visit and the object of it, but had been unwittingly supplied, thanks to Mr Pegram's foresight, with such rejoinders to his nephew's expostulations as would be difficult for Jack to confute.

'How do you do, Jack?' exclaimed the Viscount, extending his hand in his usual languid fashion towards his nephew. 'We see so little of you here that I really thought you had gone back to the Cass – Call – but I mean Malta; but I am very glad it is not so, and hope that, on consideration, you concur with me as to your marriage with Beatrice being an impossibility, and will do us the honour of being present at the ceremony; you ought, you know, as next Viscount; proper thing to do.'

'The very subject I have come to talk to you about,' replied Jack. 'Now, to begin with, we will put myself and my hopes altogether on one side.'

'Quite right, quite right; I am very pleased to see you take the sensible and reasonable view of the case.'

'I sincerely trust you will be of the same mind when you have heard me out. I have come here this morning, uncle, to implore you to postpone this wedding. I cannot as yet prove it, but I am quite convinced that these Pegrams are thorough impostors, as far as their share in the "Great Tontine" goes. Old Mr Pegram, no doubt, *was* in it, and his nominee was a clerk of his own, named Krabbe; but the real Krabbe died a little over a year ago, and they have substituted for him an old and infirm person, who, I presume, bears a considerable likeness to the dead man. You look surprised, as well you may, that I should be aware that the "Great Tontine" is the cause of what I cannot help calling this unnatural alliance. It is not worth while bothering you with how I learnt this; suffice it to say, that I heard before I left Malta that you were one of the last three left in this curious lottery. I have promised to keep my own feelings out of our conversation, and I will go further; I will promise to put my own prejudices on one side, although you can scarcely suppose that I covet this new connection. You are marrying Beatrice to this Robert Pegram so that the whole "Tontine" may eventually be theirs. I saw the old lawyer only yesterday, and he candidly admitted that was the settlement. He is settling, my dear uncle, what he has not got. His confounded knavery I have not as yet quite unravelled, but I do not hesitate to assert that he has no more to do with the "Tontine" than I have;' and here Jack paused, breathless with the impetuosity of his speech.

Had it not been for old Pegram's letter Lord Lakington would have been not a little astonished. He would have been much surprised at his nephew having any knowledge of the 'Tontine' at all; and he certainly would have been considerably staggered at hearing it positively asserted that Mr

Pegram's nominee was actually dead. He would at once have begun speculating as to whether he had not virtually come into the whole lottery, and no one could have been more keenly alive to the advantages eight thousand a-year possessed over four than himself.

'My dear Jack,' he rejoined, 'I detest the discussion of unpleasant subjects. I should not have touched upon the subject of your tearing down to Rydland with, not a bee, but a positive hive of bees, in your bonnet; or even remarked that I consider you behaved shamefully to my old friend Pegram. It is not quite the thing, you know, to use coarse language and denounce a man as a swindler without a shadow of proof.'

'The d—d, oily old hypocrite,' muttered Jack.

'Nor should I call it very good form if you came hanging about here disguised as a policeman, or a match-selling sailor, or anything of that sort, you know. Now, nothing can be more sensible than Pegram's letter. He says he can make every allowance for the irritation of a young man whose vanity had led him to believe that Beatrice was in love with him.'

Jack started from his chair with another smothered malediction, but recovered himself, and resumed his seat.

'As you are a near relation of mine,' continued the Viscount, 'he is willing for this once to pass over the scandalous accusation you thought fit to bring against him, but appeals to me to protect him from any repetition of such a charge; and he further adds, that – stop, I had better read to you the latter part of his letter:

' "I will candidly admit to your Lordship," he writes, "that Mr Krabbe is my nominee; that he is a very aged and infirm man, deaf, and not very bright in his intellect; but that he may linger on in his present condition for some little time is the opinion of his medical attendant. Plenty of people who knew him formerly have seen Mr Krabbe in his present state, as indeed also has your nephew. I most certainly am not desirous that such a scandal as this should be bruited abroad, and I can only say that anybody your Lordship chooses to send down to Rydland shall not only see Mr Krabbe, but have every facility afforded to make inquiries concerning him. Mr Phillimore even admitted, in the midst of his abuse, that he had no proof whatever to offer in support of his atrocious charge, and I think I may trust your Lordship to give no heed to what I can only really describe as the ravings of a disappointed and violent young man. I beg to remain, my dear Lord Lakington, yours very sincerely, PAUL PEGRAM." '

'But surely, uncle,' interposed Jack hotly, 'you will take my word in preference to this plausible old scoundrel. Only postpone this marriage a month, and I will pledge you my word to expose the most audacious fraud ever attempted.'

'You must excuse me, my dear Jack. The postponement of Beatrice's wedding will now create no end of gossip, and I can really see no reason whatever for it. Pegram's is the temperate letter of a quiet, sensible man, who seems to have behaved with much calmness under great provocation; while all the wild charges you bring against him are really what he calls sheer "ravings".'

'God grant you may find them so,' rejoined Jack sadly as he rose from his chair; 'but I am afraid you will find them all too true when too late. Good-bye, uncle; you will remember in the future that I did my best to save Beatrice.'

As he reached the door a thought suddenly struck him.

'Will you grant me one thing? Pegram invites you to send down any one you please to inquire into the truth of what I allege. Will you send some one you can depend upon?'

'Well, I have no one to send,' replied the Viscount. 'Of course I am quite convinced myself that you are utterly mistaken; but still, perhaps, in justice to Beatrice, it might be as well to make inquiries – a mere form, of course; but really, if I had anybody to send –'

'Will you leave this inquiry to a barrister, a friend of mine? He is already engaged in the affair of the "Great Tontine", on the part of the representative of Miss Caterham, whoever that may be, and has, consequently, quite as great an interest in looking after Mr Pegram's nominee as yourself.'

The Viscount hesitated for a few minutes, and then said, 'I will oblige you so far, Jack. If you will guarantee that this gentleman will neither insult nor make himself personally offensive to Mr Pegram, I will consent to his making such inquiries as may be made in one day.'

'I will pledge myself to Ronald Ringwood's keeping his temper,' replied Jack.

'One thing more,' exclaimed the Viscount. 'It is of course fully understood that you do not accompany him.'

'No,' said Jack; 'I should be very much the reverse of assistance to him. I willingly promise to intrude upon Pegram no more. Good-bye. It is the last chance,' he muttered, as he left the room; 'and though I fear it will lead to nothing, we must make the most of it. If I could only persuade him to postpone it for a month!'

## CHAPTER TWENTY-SEVEN

## KEEN HANDS AT A BARGAIN

Running off the main thoroughfare of Guildford is a quiet by-street, comprised principally of small, two-storied houses. It is not a street of shops, although various boards show that the tenants earn their living by the work of their hands. James Barnes, for instance, announces unostentatiously on the face of his edifice that 'Tailoring is done here', without indulging in a showy shop window. A few small retired tradesmen have taken up their abode there, no doubt, but the majority are still workers – people who have started as tailors, bootmakers, dressmakers, etc., without the capital necessary for display of showy shop-windows. In one window a simple card, describing 'Miss Meek' as a 'Milliner; Ladies own materials made up', is deemed quite sufficient announcement of the lady's business, without the exhibition of bonnets, mantles, &c.; and similarly, Mr Botcher, a little further on, thinks the pithy notice of 'Men's boots soled, heeled, and repaired here', quite sufficient designation of his occupation. Rather conspicuous amongst these tenements, as being a little larger than its fellows, and having a very well-to-do air about it, is a house bearing the terse announcement, 'Mrs Bulger, Laundress. Mangling done here'; and Mrs Bulger, the tenant, a hale, shrewd, bustling woman, verging on sixty, was reputed to be one of the most prosperous inhabitants of the street.

The first half of Mrs Bulger's life had been passed in domestic service, in which she had played several *rôles*, having begun in the laundry and ended in the kitchen, and wound up by winning the heart of a gourmandizing butler, who declared there was no resisting her pastry; and that when it came to pies, she had not her equal. The lamented Bulger had saved a bit of money, and being of a cheerful and sociable disposition, at once embarked in the 'Public' line. Whether an over-admiration of his wife's peculiar talent resulted in the too late discovery that 'pastry was pison', or whether he wished to emulate the North American Indians, who, in the words of Artemus Ward, 'drink with impunity, or with anybody who will ask them', it is impossible to say; but some twenty years previously, between his sociable disposition and his undue passion for pie, Bulger made an end of it. His widow carried on the business a little while; but, to use her own expression, 'it was not exactly to her liking, there was no end to it. Potmen and barmaids were all very well, but they were of no use unless you kept an eye on them'; and in a house that was doing a decent business, that meant the mistress never got to bed before midnight. Mrs Bulger looked sharply after her business, but, nevertheless, took very good care to let it be known that the good-will was for sale at a fair price; and as the house had always driven a thriving trade, she was not long before she found some one willing to take it off her hands. The widow reflected for a little as to what she should do next; for she had a tidy bit of capital with which to start in any calling that took her fancy, and had no idea of sitting still with her hands in her lap. After due reflection, she determined to revert to her first employment, and set up a laundry. To begin with, she had only one or two girls to assist her; but in this year of grace, eighty, she had four or five strapping wenches in her service; and the entire ground-floor of the little tenement was given up to the wash-tub, soap-sud, and mangle, as the back garden was to the clothes-line and the bleaching of linen. Mrs Bulger, in short, was mistress of a very prosperous business, and, far from trenching on her little capital, was steadily adding to it year by year. In fact, more than one of her sharp-sighted masculine neighbours had suggested their desire to step into the late lamented Bulger's shoes; but whether she had found the ex-butler trying (he was wont to become unbearably garrulous in his cups), or whether she appreciated her independence too keenly to surrender it, the widow elected to live alone.

Mrs Bulger's front room on the first floor, which formed her parlour, was swept and garnished this November night; and, from the rather elaborate preparations made for tea, it looked as if Mrs Bulger expected company. The good lady, indeed, was got up in what she gaily called her 'company clothes'. Her work-a-day garments had been exchanged for a handsome dark silk; while she further displayed a cap with rather bright ribbons, hardly compatible with her years. The good lady fidgeted about the apartment, now giving a slight poke to the fire, now moving the kettle a little, now pushing a pile of buttered toast a little further from the flame; in fact, generally betraying, by a score of restless motions, that company was not only expected, but was also a little behind time.

'The train is late, I suppose,' she muttered to herself, as for the ninth or tenth time she consulted a gold watch, which was suspended by a chain of similar metal, somewhat ostentatiously from her neck; 'but I suppose Polly can't be long now. It was real lucky her writing to propose coming here for a night or two just as I was about to write and ask her to do so. I wonder whether she has heard anything of late of her old flame, Terence Finnigan?

Old flame, indeed!' said the widow, with a slight giggle. 'Why, it is only some seven or eight years ago that he was mad to marry her; not but what Terence was a pleasant man enough if you could only keep the spirits from him. It must be nigh upon two years since he was in these parts; for he would never be near Guildford and not come and see Emma Bulger. Oh, dear!' continued Mrs Bulger, with a heavy sigh, 'it's so many years since we first met; five-and-thirty years ago, when I first went as still-room maid to old Mr Chichester of Leytonstone Hall, just before Terence went off soldiering with young Mr Fred. I am curious to know whether Polly Mattox has seen that advertisement in the "Guildford Journal". A hundred pound is a deal of money, and would bear dividing; but Polly was always a terrible one to take care of herself. She is a very nice woman, is Polly; we have known each other since we were girls, and I am sure I am very fond of her; but her best friend cannot deny that Polly Mattox is a little greedy-minded, a little grasping, when it comes to money. However, that must be her knock, I take it.' And so saying, Mrs Bulger bustled out of the room to admit her guest.

Mrs Mattox was a buxom, fresh-looking woman, some ten years younger than her hostess. She had unmistakable remains of good looks, which the smart flowers in her bonnet showed she had by no means resigned claim to. Like Mrs Bulger, she also had been left a widow; but not having her friend's energy or business capabilities, she determined to rely upon her personal charms, instead of her personal exertions, to furnish her with another home. This all happened some seven or eight years ago, and though Terence Finnigan had been excessively anxious to take the buxom Polly Gibson, as she was then, to his bosom, Polly had only laughed at her very elderly admirer, and thought it more prudent to accept the hand of Mr Mattox, a cousin by marriage of Mrs Bulger's. Mr Mattox had the advantage of being not only more than twenty years younger than Terence; but also, as the master of Portsmouth Workhouse, had, what the prudent Polly valued quite as highly, a comfortable home to offer.

'It's not my fault, Emma, the train was late, as the train always is on this dratted line; I am tired to death; just let me take off my bonnet, and I shall be only too glad of a cup of tea.'

'Never mind, Polly; I am real glad to see you, any way; just run into the next room, and get your bonnet off; you know where it is, and I will have the tea and toast on the table in a jiffy.'

Mrs Mattox nodded her head in reply, and having cast one rapid glance at her hostess's attire, retreated, with the prompt resolve that old Emma Bulger must be 'dressed up to'; for Polly had an insuperable objection to being out-shone in her raiment at any time; but to be out-dressed by a senior in her own class, and by one who, in her, Polly's, estimation, could never, at her very best, have held a candle to herself in point of good looks, was not to be thought of. Mrs Mattox was absent some little time, in spite of her thirst for a cup of tea; and her return showed that she had managed to unearth from her box a smart silken robe and cap to match, which her hostess, far from viewing with rancour, smiled on benignly, as a fitting tribute to her own gorgeous array.

'Well, Polly,' said Mrs Bulger, the tea being poured out, and her guest plentifully supplied with the buttered toast and other delicacies, 'I was just thinking of writing to you when I got your note. It is so long since I have seen you, that I was going to ask if you ever meant coming Guildford way again.'

'Yes; it's a good bit since I have been here,' replied Polly; 'but, you see, Portsmouth is lively, and Mattox and me we are popular; and Mattox, you see, he can't abear me out of his sight. He is always afraid,' continued Polly, giggling, 'that somebody will run away with me.'

'Well, my dear,' rejoined Mrs Bulger, 'he has no call to do that; you are not like a giddy young thing; you have come to an age as he might trust things to your own discretion.'

'That's what I tell Mattox,' observed Polly. 'When a man marries a good-looking wife, of course he must expect that she will have pretty things said to her; but she must know, better than him, when any one is going too far with them.'

'Well, I am sure, I never thought that Mattox would turn jealous,' replied Mrs Bulger, meditatively. 'If you had taken poor old Terence Finnigan I would not have been surprised at it.'

'Why, Emma, you surely never thought that I meant to take up with an old fellow like that in earnest! He was all very well to joke with, you know. One couldn't help being amused at the idea of his wanting a wife at his time of life; but, bless us, as you know, he could hardly keep himself, much less a wife. Remember, I have known him from a child, and if it amused the poor old chap to get up a flirtation with me, and I chose to humour him, what was the harm in it? But marry him, my dear Emma, how could you think I should ever make such a fool of myself!'

'Well, he certainly was a bit old for you; and money never did stick to his fingers since the days we first knew him at Mr Chichester's place; but women do such things at times. By the way, have you seen anything of him lately?'

'Yes, I see him at times; but he is very infirm, and very much changed from the Terence Finnigan you last saw. Men don't last for ever, you know, and I shouldn't think he will be above ground much longer.'

'What, then, he is still alive!' exclaimed Mrs Bulger.

'Oh, yes, he is alive, so far,' replied Mrs Mattox carelessly, and stealing a somewhat inquisitive gaze at her hostess.

Polly Mattox was a woman who had begun the world with good looks and an inordinate stock of vanity – two attributes that commonly bring their possessors to woe; but in her case they were so balanced by selfishness and low cunning, that, so far, Polly Mattox had gone through the world with considerable comfort to herself. The snares the former qualities had spread for her had been counteracted by the latter, and after two or three somewhat risky flirtations, she had married Gibson, a well-to-do tradesman, who had given her a comfortable home for many years; and if he had left her not so well-to-do a widow as she expected, why she had only her own extravagance to blame for it. The same prudence, as we know, characterized her second marriage. She had marked the somewhat eager way in which Mrs Bulger propounded her inquiry after Finnigan, and the cunning of her nature gave her instinctively a hazy idea that her friend had some further motive than mere curiosity concerning the octogenarian's fate.

'And where is he living now?' asked Mrs Bulger, with an assumption of indifference so transparent that her guest's suspicions as to her having some object in wishing to know Terence Finnigan's whereabouts were confirmed.

'Oh, I don't know exactly,' replied Polly, carelessly. 'Thank you, my dear, I will take another cup of tea.'

'But don't you think,' rejoined Mrs Bulger, as she handed the required refreshment, 'that you could find him if you tried?'

'Yes, I dare say I could lay my hand upon him if I wanted to.'

'Well, then, I wish you would, and the sooner the better. I have a particular reason for desiring to know where he is now living.'

'Why?' asked Polly laconically, as she slowly stirred her tea.

'Well,' replied Mrs Bulger, speaking with great deliberation, 'I have had a hint in a roundabout way, that some of those Chichester folks have been inquiring after him, and would take care of him for the remainder of his life if they could only find him.'

Mrs Bulger had spoken slowly, as one unaccustomed to the utterance of untruths. Especially did the lie not come trippingly upon her tongue on this occasion, as she was constructing it with a view to its fitting into the truth, which she half suspected Polly Mattox would eventually either wring or wheedle out of her. She knew that lady of old, and was quite aware that Mrs Mattox could hold her tongue with a most irritating persistency if she once had an idea that you were trying to get information out of her.

'They didn't write to you, did they?' inquired Polly.

'No; but you recollect when Mr Fred, as we used to call him, was killed out there in America, he left a daughter behind him; you have heard old Terence speak of her often.'

'Yes; but if she didn't write,' resumed the Portsmouth matron, 'how did you come to know that she was so anxious to discover Finnigan's whereabouts? Who gave you this hint?'

'Oh, never mind that; nobody you know,' returned Mrs Bulger, rendered a little irritable by Polly's persistent cross-examination. 'The question is, where is he living now?'

'Quite so,' replied Mrs Mattox, with the most provoking calmness; 'and as they have applied to you on the subject, and not to me, you had better give them all the information in your power.'

'But I tell you, you aggravating thing, I don't know where he is, and that I want you to tell me.'

'Look here, Emma Bulger,' replied the other quietly, 'it's no use your flying out in this way with me, you know that very well. If you want to know where Terence Finnigan is to be found, you had better tell me at once who it is are making inquiries for him, and all about the whole thing, then I'll help you; if not, I can hold my tongue as well as other people. The old man is tolerably comfortable now, and, for all I know, more happy than where, perhaps, these people would take him to. I always liked Terence, and am not given to let my tongue wag to his harm.'

'But it can be only to his good,' rejoined Mrs Bulger, in a much more piano tone, for she saw that Polly Mattox thoroughly meant what she said, and that, unless she was made a confidante of, she would persist in keeping her knowledge to herself; and yet Mrs Bulger rather demurred at striking her flag so early in the battle.

'I am not one that does things in the dark,' remarked Mrs Mattox. 'Before I bear witness about my friends I like to know what they are charged with. The Guardians down our way often tell the people that it would be more for their good to go into the workhouse than go on receiving out-of-door relief; but the ungrateful things don't see it as a rule, let alone being hard to satisfy when they are there.'

'But you don't suppose,' interrupted Mrs Bulger, 'that these people are advertising – I mean seeking – for Terence Finnigan only to put him in the workhouse, do you?'

'Oh! he has been advertised for, has he?' thought Mrs Mattox, who had not failed to note her hostess's slip. 'How should I know?' she replied. 'I haven't been given hints to on the subject.'

'You are enough to drive any one distracted, Polly, the way you go on nagging,' said Mrs Bulger, biting her lip, and reddening not a little between suppressed temper and the consciousness that the word 'advertising' had escaped her. 'Suppose, Polly, I had heard that there was a bit of money offered to any one who could give information concerning Terence Finnigan, what should you say?'

'That, knowing as you do I can give such information, you would at once say, "Polly Mattox, here is something to your advantage; I wish you luck, my dear."'

'I didn't ask you what you thought I might say; I asked what you would say,' said Mrs Bulger, in very meaning tones.

Mrs Mattox paused for a little before she replied. She was calculating the lowest possible terms that it was possible to offer. She was, of course, sure by this that Terence Finnigan was advertised for, and a reward offered concerning him. She had also a strong suspicion that her dear friend's hint amounted to no more than that she had stumbled across this advertisement. Of course she could read the papers quite as well as Emma Bulger. But then, again, some little time might elapse before she possessed herself of the requisite information; and she looked upon this as a case in which it might be dangerous to lose time, for fear of being forestalled by some one else. It might, perhaps, be safer to come to terms with Mrs Bulger at once. She accordingly answered at length,

'Well, Emma, you don't suppose that I should forget it was you who first put me up to it, if I do get the reward, do you?'

'Of course I don't, my dear; but still you might, you know. There is nothing like being business-like in these affairs. I hate haggling over things. I was always one to come to the point at once. I tell you this reward is worth sharing; but every day that goes by we run the chance of somebody else coming forward and getting it. You can't do without me any more than I can do without you; try it, and it's more than possible that in scheming for the whole cake you will only find an empty cupboard.'

Mrs Bulger could not have brought much stronger argument to bear. Polly's natural cunning had at once pointed out to her the danger of delay. It was very aggravating, but it was nevertheless clear to her that she must come at once to some sort of arrangement with her hostess.

'Shall I tell you what my terms are?' inquired Mrs Bulger.

Polly nodded assent.

'Halves,' replied the other, briefly.

'Well, upon my word, Emma Bulger,' exclaimed Polly, 'I do think you perfectly audacious in your demands. I am in possession of this information, and naturally entitled to the whole reward; but, in consideration of your being an old friend and putting me up to it, I was quite prepared to make you a handsome present – say a fourth.'

'Say a half,' replied the hostess, drily, 'and never mind taking the old friendship into consideration. Business is business; it's a pity to waste time.'

At first Mrs Mattox declared she had never heard of such a thing; that Mrs Bulger was at liberty to make the most of her knowledge; that a little study of the papers would, no doubt, bring the advertisement under her own eye; that, though she herself could lay her hand on Terence Finnigan, she did not think there was much danger of any one else making the discovery; and finally wound up by observing, that she was still willing to stretch a point on behalf of such a very dear friend as Mrs Bulger, and consent she should take one third.

But if Mrs Mattox was cunning, her hostess was obstinate. She felt pretty certain that Polly must come to her terms in the end; and once more exhorting Mrs Mattox to leave their old friendship out of the calculation, as most unbusiness-like, wound up by exclaiming, 'Halves she had said, and halves she meant having.'

After nearly an hour's wrangling between these two mercenary old women, Mrs Bulger's terms were at last acceded to, and her guest was then informed that the reward was for no less than a hundred pounds, the mention of which sum made Polly's eyes 'twinkle'. She had deemed that twenty or twenty-five at the outside would be the amount of it. It was further arranged between the two matrons, that they should go up to town by an early train the next morning and call upon Henry Carbuckle, QC, in Plowden's Buildings, to whom, according to the advertisement, the information was to be supplied.

'I wonder,' observed Polly, as for the twentieth time she read over the advertisement in the 'Guildford Journal', 'whether they would say it made any difference with regard to this,' and she laid her forefinger on the words, 'One hundred pounds.' 'I mean, you know,' she continued in explanation, 'he is not quite right in the head; and when I say that, my dear, I mean he is about as complete an idiot as ever you came across; and if they happen to want any information from him, I am sorry for them, because my impression is, they won't get it; but, anyway, they make no condition here as to what sort of state he is to be in.'

'What! the old man has quite lost his head?' exclaimed Mrs Bulger.

'Quite so; he got into a drunken bout some two years ago, down our way. You remember he was terrible fond of the spirits, and apt at times to be a bit quarrelsome in his drink; however, I can't speak too much about that. I don't know whether any one struck him, poor old fellow, or whether he simply fell because the liquor was too much for him, but he got a blow on the head that knocked the sense out of him, and well-nigh all the life; however, he got over it at last, and is alive still, but both his wits and memory have left him. Why, bless you, he don't even know me.'

'And where did you say he was?' inquired Mrs Bulger.

'I don't remember naming the place,' rejoined Polly, with a sly glance at her hostess; 'still never mind, Emma, you have driven a terrible hard bargain with me, but I always stick to what I say; halves you insisted it should be, and halves it shall be. As for poor old Terence, he is in Portsmouth Workhouse.'

## CHAPTER TWENTY-EIGHT

# NO ESCAPING ONE'S DESTINY

While Jack Phillimore was playing that very unsatisfactory game of brag, Ringwood was a little surprised by his clerk announcing that there were two women wanting to see him, who had been sent over from Mr Carbuckle's chambers. It had been arranged between the QC and Ringwood that the latter's name should not appear in any advertisement. Pegram and Son, they knew, were crafty people to deal with, and it was thought advisable that Ringwood should not be known as the principal manager in search of Terence Finnigan on the part of Miss Caterham.

'They say, sir, they have come over in consequence of the advertisement in the "Guildford Journal"; so I suppose you will see them.'

'All right, Sims; show them in; and Heaven grant they know rather more than those who have felt hitherto impelled to call in consequence of that notice.'

The two matrons, dressed for London, were something gorgeous to look upon. Mrs Mattox, who had not contemplated visiting the metropolis when leaving home, was, it is true, somewhat perturbed that she had not brought a certain bonnet lying in the recesses of a press at Portsmouth with her. She was tormented with the idea that, in the matter of head-dress, she was somewhat eclipsed by Emma Bulger; otherwise nothing had occurred to disturb the serenity of last night's compact. Ringwood's invitation to be seated was not complied with without considerable rustling of skirts and smoothing of draperies.

'We have come,' at length explained Mrs Bulger, 'in consequence of what we saw in the Guildford paper. It says there that a hundred pound will be given to any one who can give information about Terence Finnigan. Now, my friend here, Mrs Mattox, and myself want to know, in the first place, if that is right? My name, sir, is Bulger – Mrs Bulger, at your service.'

'Perfectly right, Mrs Bulger,' replied Ringwood, not a little amused. 'If you are giving this information jointly, fifty pounds will be paid to each of you as soon as, through your information, we have found Terence Finnigan or ascertained his decease. If we are indebted to you alone for what we want to know, of course the whole hundred will be paid to you.'

'Oh, sir, it is a joint affair,' interrupted Mrs Mattox. 'Emma there could not tell you much without me.'

'Quite right, Polly; it is a joint affair,' interposed Mrs Bulger, in all the serene consciousness of not only picking up fifty pounds from merely looking at a newspaper, but having also somewhat the best of it in that little matter of bonnets to boot. 'Now that the wages – I mean to say the terms – is found to be satisfactory, we'll proceed to business. We are both old friends of Terence Finnigan, fellow-servants in fact, sir; she was under-housemaid, and I was in the still-room at old Mr Chichester's, long ago. Maybe, you have heard that Terence was there as a groom before he went off to the soldiering with young Mr Fred?'

'That,' said Ringwood, 'from what Miss Chichester has told me, daughter of the young Mr Fred you are alluding to, must have been a considerable time ago. I trust, Mrs Bulger, you have seen him a good deal later than that.'

'Dear me! yes; he never was anywhere near Guildford – I live at Guildford, sir – but what he would come to see me; and Polly there, too, he was always regular sweet on Polly; it's not many years back that the old man was mad to marry her, wasn't he, Polly?'

'The old fool,' tittered Mrs Mattox, with a conscious toss of her head in recognition of the conquest – not much of a triumph, perhaps, but a scalp counts, even though it be that of Methuselah.

'Now, Mrs Bulger,' said Ringwood, who thought it high time to put a stop to the garrulity of the two ladies, 'you are a woman of business, I know; let's come to the point – when did you see Terence Finnigan last?'

'It might have been a year and a half, or, for the matter of that, I would not like to swear it was not two –'

'Beg pardon, sir,' interposed Mrs Mattox; 'but it don't so much matter when Emma saw Terence last, I should think, because I have seen him a good deal later than she has; I saw him three days ago.'

'No! did you?' ejaculated Ringwood, with unprofessional eagerness; 'and I suppose,' he continued, recovering himself, 'that there is no doubt of finding him again without difficulty.'

'Oh! he will be where I left him, never fear,' replied Mrs Mattox.

'And you have no objection, of course, to tell me where that is.'

'It will be all right about the hundred pound if I do?' inquired Polly, doubtfully, a remark which called forth a decided nod of approval from Mrs Bulger.

'Fifty pounds apiece will be paid you if I find Terence Finnigan at the place you are about to name.'

'Well then, sir, you will find him in Portsmouth Workhouse, of which institution I am the matron.'

'That makes matters very simple,' said Ringwood; 'may I ask where you ladies intend to stay in town?'

'We are going back by the afternoon train to my place at Guildford,' replied Mrs Bulger. 'Allow me to give you my card, and if ever you have a chance of recommending me to anybody in that neighbourhood, I know, sir, I can give satisfaction.'

'Well, Mrs Bulger, it will be necessary for me to go down to Portsmouth tomorrow; if you, or, at all events, Mrs Mattox, can meet me at Guildford and accompany me there, so much the better. Now, as I never saw Finnigan myself – although I have no doubt you are right about him – it will be needful that I should be accompanied by somebody who can identify him. Will it suit you to meet us at Guildford?'

'Perfectly,' chorussed both matrons; 'but you may depend, sir, we have known Terence Finnigan too long for there to be any mistake about its being him.'

'Then I shall consider that settled,' rejoined Ringwood, as he bowed his visitors out. 'By Jove!' he muttered, as the door closed, 'what a turn-up! Jack might have saved himself his journey into Wales, for I should think the discovery that Miss Chichester is still in the "Tontine" would completely knock this marriage on the head. It must, from all accounts, be so thorough a matter of expediency on both sides that such a complete flaw in the compact as this makes must infallibly lead to its being broken off. Well, I am sincerely glad, for Mary's sake; but I cannot help feeling very sorry for my own. If I am right in my view of the Pegrams, the "Tontine" now lies between Mary Chichester and Lord Lakington; and, good God! with his obvious taste for compromise, he can never overlook such an obvious wind-up as this will be. Of course he will endeavour to marry Mary; the Viscount is on the right side of fifty yet; is uncommon well-preserved, and does not look his age by six or seven years. The chance of marrying a coronet, with eight thousand a-year would commend itself to most young ladies. What a fool I am! I settled long ago that I would think no more of Mary unless the "Tontine" was decided against her; I am afraid I must now make up my mind to dismiss all such thoughts for good. Meanwhile, I must go over to Carbuckle and tell him all this.'

Mr Carbuckle was both astonished and delighted to hear of the discovery of Finnigan, and much pleased at Ringwood's prompt arrangements about proceeding to Portsmouth.

'Quite right,' he exclaimed; 'an old gentleman at his time of life, who has come to the workhouse, cannot be depended upon to live very long, although

I believe they often do attain great age in those unfortunately necessary institutions; but it is, of course, a point with us to prove this Finnigan alive as speedily as may be. Mary Chichester may, or may not, win the ''Great Tontine''; but remember, there are two years' arrears of interest for Miss Caterham's share, and these must amount to something like four thousand pounds, there being so few shareholders now left to divide. This she would be entitled to should Finnigan die an hour after we have established our point.'

'Yes, I quite see that; and you may depend upon my being off tomorrow. There is only one thing further to settle – who am I to take with me to prove his identity? because, I should not know him from Adam.'

'There cannot be a doubt about it,' replied Carbuckle; 'Mary Chichester herself, of course. Indeed, I do not know that we could lay our hands on any one at such short notice that could speak positively as to Finnigan. Miss Caterham's old servants might, no doubt; but they were discharged when Mary left the cottage, and it would probably take a few days to get hold of them.'

'You are quite right; it will be, no doubt, foolish to lose time about the matter, and I really cannot suggest any one else to identify Finnigan; but you will have to go yourself to Portsmouth. Never mind what they are, but I have strong reasons for not intruding myself upon Miss Chichester at present.'

'Stuff and nonsense!' replied the senior. 'I shouldn't know these women at Guildford, nor they me; and even if I should make them out, they would mistrust me, and think it all a trick to do them out of the reward. You and Mary *must* go. You are surely not such children that you want me to come down and take care of you?'

'I cannot help it; I really have very excellent reasons for declining to be Miss Chichester's convoy upon this occasion.'

'And I,' interrupted Carbuckle, 'have very excellent reasons to advance why you should not decline. You refused, I know, to see her the other day about finding a home in Lord Lakington's family. That was all very well; but *this* is a very different thing. You will, I am sure, not let any misunderstanding there may be between you, prevent your assisting Mary to what for her is a very considerable sum of money. No; do not interrupt, pray. Remember, this will nearly double her slender income; simply say you will go, and I will write a note to her in the Victoria Road at once, to say that Finnigan has been found, that you will call for her at ten tomorrow, and that she must be prepared to accompany you to Portsmouth to identify him. There! I have no time to say more; I am up to my neck in business. Call in here when you come back, and let me know all about it. I will not forget the note, never fear.'

And without giving him time for further remonstrance, Mr Carbuckle fairly hustled Ringwood out of the room.

'It is trying one pretty hard,' muttered Ronald Ringwood to himself, as he walked back towards his own chambers. 'I do not pretend to be better than my neighbours; but I want to run "straight", as far as I can, with regard to this girl. It would be a thundering mean thing to ask her to marry me now, knowing what I do; while, of course, she is in perfect ignorance of the difference Finnigan's discovery may make to her. It is not quite fair of Carbuckle. He knows I am over head and ears in love with her, and must see that the right thing for me to do is to stand aloof until this confounded "Tontine" is decided. I am quite willing to do everything in my power to assist her to this fortune, although, should she gain it, it will probably insure my own misery; but it is rather rough upon a fellow to keep throwing him into the society of the girl that stole his heart, when honour condemns him to talk commonplaces. That journey to Portsmouth will be pleasant. I only trust the train will rattle, so as to render conversation impossible. I wonder what Mary thinks of me? That I have carefully avoided her since her trouble will not count much in my favour. However, Carbuckle proved so ingeniously that it was absolutely necessary that I should go, there was no getting out of it. I wonder how Jack got on today in Wales? He, like myself, is having a weary time over this "Tontine". The confounded thing promises to rob us both of our sweethearts. I suppose I shall see him tonight, and hear all the details of his defeat. If he had waited till tomorrow he might have spared himself the journey.'

But, as we know, Jack Phillimore was in no humour to look in upon his chum and confess his disaster, and Ringwood therefore left a line for him at his chambers in case he should call, telling him that he might consider the Pegram alliance at an end; that there had been a fresh turn of the wheel in the affair of the 'Great Tontine', which was quite certain to cause the abandonment of that scheme by Lord Lakington; and begging him not to see the Viscount until he, Ringwood, should have returned from Portsmouth. At that other palpable solution of the big lottery which had flashed across his own brain, Ringwood did not venture to hint. It would be time enough to point out to Jack what he so dreaded when they should meet.

CHAPTER TWENTY-NINE

## TERENCE FINNIGAN

Ringwood presented himself in the Victoria Road the next morning in good time. Although there was no luggage to delay them, yet he, like most of us, was aware that a lady's bonnet is not put on in a minute. He was welcomed by Mary, who, having introduced him to Mrs Lyme Wregis and Beatrice, left the room in quest of her cloak and head-gear.

'You must pardon an old woman's curiosity; but this seems to us a most extraordinary errand that you are carrying Miss Chichester off upon. She has told us,' said Mrs Lyme Wregis, 'that this is an old servant of her family's, for whom they have been long in search; but now he *is* discovered, why does he not come to her, instead of her having to tear down to Portsmouth to see him?'

'It must, of course, seem odd to you; but this man Finnigan stands in a somewhat peculiar position to Miss Chichester. She has doubtless told you that he was by her father's side when he fell on the terrible field of Gettysburg, and that he has carried her many a time, when a child, in his arms. But what she could not tell you is, that Finnigan is so infirm in health, and has so failed in his mental powers, that his coming to her is impossible. Further, there is a necessity for proving the old man's identity, as there is a small sum of money coming to Miss Chichester that depends upon this Finnigan having been alive at a certain date. Neither myself nor Mr Carbuckle, who manages Miss Chichester's affairs, ever saw Finnigan, so it is positively necessary that Miss Chichester should run down and see that this is the right man. We have, for some time, offered a reward in the papers for his discovery; and though the people who have come forward to claim it are quite positive, we want to be sure of him.'

'I think you know a cousin of mine,' observed Beatrice demurely, – Mr Phillimore, a naval officer.'

'I have not known him very long,' replied Ringwood; 'but I happen to have seen a great deal of him during the short time we have been acquainted.'

And Ronald wondered in his own mind what this might portend. She refused to see Jack; yet here she was apparently seeking news of him. But if Ringwood was astonished, even Mrs Lyme Wregis opened her eyes at the *hardiesse* of Beatrice's next speech.

'We were what is conventionally termed "dear cousins" once,' continued Beatrice, in a slightly constrained voice. 'He disapproves the marriage I am about making; and I have seen but little of him lately. Will you give him my love, and say that I asked after him?' and the girl's lip twitched slightly as she finished the sentence. 'Will you do more for me, Mr Ringwood?' she added in defiant tones, as she caught the amazed expression of her grandmother's face. 'Will you ask him, from me, to grace my wedding with his presence?'

'Pray do not think, Miss Phillimore, do not think for one moment that I am presuming to discuss such a matter with you. I will do your bidding; but it is only fair to tell you that, from what I have heard your cousin say, I fancy this is a request he will hardly accede to.'

'And why not, sir?' exclaimed the girl, with a burst of ironical laughter. 'He would think it incumbent on him to attend my funeral, I suppose; why not my bridal? The two ceremonies bear a marvellous similitude at times.'

'My dear Beatrice!' exclaimed Mrs Lyme Wregis, in such unmistakable tones of consternation that, to Ringwood's infinite relief, the young lady was suddenly recalled to a sense of the fitness of things, and recognized the fact that a stranger was not exactly a confidant in whom to confide her distaste for her coming marriage.

The defiant expression died out of her face, and it was in the softly-modulated tones of every-day life that she said —

'Excuse me, Mr Ringwood, I am not quite myself. I have rather overdone it lately. My friends, wishing to honour me in my new character, have *fêted* me beyond my strength, and made me a little nervous and hysterical. Give Jack my love, and say I asked after him; and don't bore him with the other request. Weddings are apt to be dull affairs, except to the principals.'

'Now, Mr Ringwood, I am quite ready for you,' said Miss Chichester, as she entered the room. 'If the train goes at the time you say, we ought to be starting, I think.'

'Good luck go with you, Mary,' cried Beatrice, with a sudden assumption of gaiety that caused both her grandmother and Ringwood to wonder whether these varied transitions of mood would have an hysterical termination. 'You will find your trusty henchman broken in health, Mr Ringwood tells us, but alive; and you are about to come into money, Mary dear; and though I am younger than you, yet I know the value of that, and have learnt what some people will do for it, and others may have to do. I do not know how much it is; but only hope, my love, it is sufficient to place your future in your own control.'

'My dear Beatrice,' exclaimed Mrs Lyme Wregis sharply, 'you must excuse my remarking that you are talking a great deal of nonsense; and further, Miss Chichester, if you stay to listen to her rhapsodies you will undoubtedly miss your train. Good-bye, Mr Ringwood. We shall be only too happy to see you whenever you may find it convenient to look in upon us.'

Ringwood uttered a few words of acknowledgment in reply to Mrs Lyme Wregis's courteous invitation as he shook hands, and then rapidly escorted his fair charge to their cab, not a little relieved to find himself at last clear of a young woman in such an emotional state as the Honourable Beatrice Phillimore. He had all a man's horror of a scene, and felt that for the last few minutes he had been on the verge of one.

'My dear Beatrice,' said Mrs Lyme Wregis quietly, as the street-door closed behind the travellers, 'if your aversion to your marriage is so strong that you cannot even conceal it before strangers, for heaven's sake, child, tell your father before it is too late.'

'Ask me no questions, grandmamma,' cried the girl, with a strong suspicion of a sob. 'Aversion! dear me, no. Every one knows I am a very fortunate –' and, without finishing her speech, Beatrice Phillimore rushed hurriedly from the room.

The journey to Portsmouth Miss Chichester found somewhat monotonous. Her companion resolutely refused being anything but strictly the man of business. All the particulars of Finnigan's discovery he related to her; told her of the state of health in which she must be prepared to find the old man; how that they were to pick up two old servants of her grandfather's at Guildford – women who had known Finnigan well in former days, and quite recollected her father, but who had, of course, never seen her; and also did he explain to her, in purposely cloudy fashion, that she came into a small sum of money on reversion, the inheriting of which reversion had depended upon Terence Finnigan's out-living somebody else.

That Ringwood's explanation on this point was by no means clear troubled Miss Chichester very little; but she was not a little exasperated at finding that he carefully eschewed the discussion of anything but strictly business matters. On other topics he listened gravely to whatever she might have to say, but could not be induced to take his own part in the conversation. She knew that he could do this, – many a long talk had they had at Kew about books, pictures, events of the day, &c., – and Mary, not a little nettled at the impenetrable reserve of her old admirer, speedily relapsed into silence.

'Whatever he has taken offence at I am sure I cannot guess,' she muttered to herself; 'but he can hardly expect me to strive any longer to charm him out of the sulks.'

At Guildford they picked up Mrs Bulger and Mrs Mattox, both of whom were as profuse in curtseys and smiles at the sight of the granddaughter of their old master as the time would admit, signs of fealty which were renewed with still more demonstration on arrival at Portsmouth, and which should be valued more in proportion to their scarcity than as to their actual worth in these days.

Upon arrival at the famous seaport, Mrs Mattox at once took command of the party. That bustling matron felt that she was in her own domain, and that her knowledge of the streets and the tariff of the hack carriages was beyond dispute. Her instructions to the flyman, although by no means terse, were, at all events, sufficiently explicit, and in a very short time the party were deposited at the door of the workhouse in St Mary's Road – an expanse of staring red brick, unrelieved by decoration, calculated to cast a chill upon in-coming tenants, and throwing out scant sign of encouragement to the broken-down and needy compelled to throw themselves on its hospitality. Miss Chichester could not resist a shudder as she passed through its uninviting portals.

'It answers to my idea of a gaol,' she whispered to Ringwood. 'Poor Terence, I shall feel quite uncomfortable until he is out of this place. Indeed,' she added, 'I think the sooner we ourselves are out of it the better.'

They speedily found that their visit was by no means to be hurried through; that, before being permitted to see Finnigan, there was an important ceremony to be gone through, to decline which would evidently give dire displeasure to the matron of the institution. The famous Todgers' is not the only establishment that can do it when it pleases, and Mrs Mattox had written the preceding day to her husband, that a very extensive luncheon was to be provided for the gentle-folks about to honour them with a visit; and that gentleman, from past experience, knew that non-compliance with his wife's requests was wont to result in an unpleasantness of no brief duration; the fair Polly, indeed, possessing a power of nagging, mercifully but rarely vouchsafed her sex. They accordingly adjourned, in the first instance, to that lady's private apartments, where they were duly introduced, first to Mr Mattox, and then to a table so liberally spread that their hostess reflected, with much satisfaction, that even Emma Bulger could not find fault with it. Ringwood, as soon as he considered that they had made ample recognition of the entertainment provided for them, suggested that, as Miss Chichester and himself had to return to town by the afternoon train, it would be advisable that they should see Terence Finnigan without loss of time, and Mr Mattox at once rose to lead the way.

Traversing a long, narrow, whitewashed passage, the ghastliness of which served to heighten the resemblance of the place to a gaol, and glancing occasionally on their way through the half-open doors of wards, where little knots of wizened, decrepit old men cowered in their sad-coloured garments over the fire, they at last reached a door at which Mr Mattox paused.

'This is the ward, sir, in which we shall find Finnigan. Would Miss Chichester prefer to identify him herself, or shall my wife point him out to her?'

'Surely,' rejoined Mary, 'he can scarcely have changed so much in this brief time that I can have any difficulty in recognizing him.'

'Oh dear no!' interrupted Polly; 'anybody who has seen him of late years would know him in a moment. Best let Miss Chichester judge for herself, Thomas.'

Mr Mattox, thus adjured, threw open the door without further remark, and one glance round the room sufficed to show Mary her father's old servant, sitting very still in a wooden arm-chair by the side of the fire. A slight, wiry little man, whose face, considering his extreme age, was still wonderfully fresh and free from wrinkles; the grey hair was thin, no doubt, but the light blue eyes were still wondrous bright, although there was an absent look in them, as if for ever peering beyond the grave, upon which their owner was so rapidly verging. He took no notice whatever of their entrance, and continued to gaze, like the sphinx,

'With fixed, eternal stare,'

into the infinite.

'I suppose he talks at times,' inquired Ringwood, 'although he certainly does not look like it at present.'

'No sir; he rarely says anything, and sits all day just as you see him, except when roused up to take his food. Occasionally he will say, in a wandering way, that he must go to London to see Miss Mary; but who he meant by it we never understood until today.'

'And I presume,' added Ringwood, 'that, though you and Mrs Mattox knew him before, he takes no notice of you.'

'Not the slightest, sir. You see he had been a bit knocked about when he was brought in here, and, as far as his head goes, he never seems to have recovered it. He has never been able to give the slightest account of himself since he came, and if it had not been that Polly and I knew him well beforehand, we should not at this present moment have an idea who he was.'

'Will you speak to him, Miss Chichester,' said Ringwood; 'it is possible that your voice might in some sort recall his recollection.'

Mary crossed the room quickly, and laying her hand lightly on the old man's shoulder, said,

'How do you do, Terence? don't you remember Miss Mary?'

The old man turned his head towards her, and some slight signs of surprise at the fair apparition before him might have been discerned; but of recognition there was no symptom.

'Surely, Terence, you have not forgotten the child you used to carry in your arms – the "young misthress" as you used to call me! you must remember Miss Mary!'

The old man's face became slightly troubled; for the first time his lips moved, and he muttered 'Miss Mary' in a low, far-away voice; but it was evident that he in no-wise connected the name with the young lady who stood before him.

'It is of no use,' exclaimed Mrs Mattox, as she joined Mary; 'why, Miss, he was a sweetheart of mine some years ago, and he takes no more notice of me than if he had never seen me. When men come to forgetting the face of a woman they were once mad to marry, one cannot expect them to remember much else.'

Here Mrs Bulger bustled up, and also tried to attract the attention of her old fellow-servant; but it was all of no use. An expression of bewilderment spread over poor Terence's face at finding himself surrounded by such an unwonted number of visitors, but that he had previous acquaintance with any of them he exhibited no indication.

'Of course you have no doubt whatever, Miss Chichester, that this *is* Terence Finnigan?' said Ringwood. 'It is naturally sad for you to find an old servant in this state, but his physical health is apparently satisfactory. In a business point of view, his having forgotten the past is, as far as you are concerned, of no consequence. I think now, as soon as I have written a couple of cheques for these ladies in acknowledgement of their services, we must thank Mr and Mrs Mattox for their hospitality, and make the best of our way to the railway station.'

Terence Finnigan was heard to murmur 'Miss Mary' in a dazed sort of way to himself twice or thrice as they were leaving the ward. He seemed as if vainly striving to recall somebody in connection with that name, but clearly did not connect it with Miss Chichester.

'You tell me, Mr Ringwood,' said Mary, as she found herself once more in the train on her way to town, 'that I come into what for me is something considerable simply from the fact of that poor old man being alive. I trust it is enough to enable me to take care of Terence comfortably for the future.'

'Ample,' rejoined her companion. 'We really do not know exactly how much at present, but it is certainly more than sufficient for that purpose.'

'And now, Mr Ringwood, I wish you would answer me one other question; and that is, in what way, pray, have I offended you?'

That she had quite resolved not to charm this young man out of his sulks, we know; but then, you see, this was no reason why she should not, if possible, discover what he was sulking about.

'You offend me!' he replied. 'What can have put that into your head? Very far from having any cause of complaint, I have to thank you for some very pleasant afternoons in the old Kew days.'

'Then why do you not ever come and see me now?' inquired Mary curtly. 'I have not so many friends but what I can recollect those who have striven to comfort me in my trouble.'

'I do not think you can fairly accuse me of neglect on that point,' returned the barrister, with a vivid recollection of how nothing but a stern sense of honour had restrained him from flying to her side in her affliction; 'but first, one hesitated to intrude upon your grief; then you went to stay with the Lomaxes; and finally, you have taken refuge in the Victoria Road.'

'At Mr Ringwood's suggestion,' interposed Mary quietly; 'and I am very much obliged to you for discovering so comfortable a home for me.'

'I deserve no credit for that, Miss Chichester. Carbuckle mentioned your wish to me; I happened to know, through Jack Phillimore, of his cousin's contemplated marriage, and thought perhaps you would not mind passing a few months with Mrs Lyme Wregis, whom Jack declared to be the most charming old lady that ever breathed. Of course, I know it is not quite the thing you wanted; all I can say is, it was the only thing of the kind that either Carbuckle or I could hear of. I trust it will, at all events, do until we come across something more suitable. After a little, I have no doubt you will wish for a more lively home, where there are more young people, &c.'

'Pray do not trouble yourself on *that* point; Mrs Lyme Wregis and I get on very well together, and I am quite willing to endorse Mr Phillimore's opinion of her. By the way, he is a great friend of yours, is he not? Is it fair to ask you what manner of man he is?'

'Jack Phillimore is as good-hearted a fellow as ever stepped. He is a *man*, Miss Chichester, if you understand what I mean by that, and likely, I should say, to make his mark in his profession if he ever gets the chance. His cousin has dealt very hardly with him, and he is terribly cut up at the idea of the approaching marriage; and as I have also met the successful suitor, I may be allowed to say, that, except on the ground of wealth, how any girl could throw over Jack Phillimore for Pegram beats me: one is a gallant, handsome, high-bred gentleman; the other has no pretension to good looks, and I am sure will be pronounced, by men accustomed to good society, "a bit of a cad". Women do not use the term, but they thoroughly understand it, although I do not think they quite so quickly recognize one as we do.'

'I am sorry to hear this, for I have never met a girl that I took a greater fancy to than Beatrice Phillimore. I have known her, it is true, but a short time; still I cannot think she would be swayed solely by wealth in her choice of a husband. Even if she had given me her confidence – which she has not – I could not let you into the secret; but she certainly shrinks from any allusion to her wedding in a way that augurs ill for its being a happy one. But this is "Victoria", is it not?' and as she spoke the train glided into the station.

'Good-bye, Miss Chichester,' said Ringwood, as he shook hands after putting her into the cab. 'Should Miss Phillimore take you into her confidence, and you then find your present opinion confirmed, you can tell her that it is very improbable that her wedding with Mr Robert Pegram will ever take place.'

Having uttered which oracular prediction, Ringwood raised his hat and disappeared.

CHAPTER THIRTY

## BEATRICE REGAINS HER FREEDOM

It was in a very sombre mood that Jack Phillimore wended his way to the Temple the day after his interview with his uncle. It is true that Lord Lakington had accorded him this much, that his friend Ringwood might go down to Rydland as the Viscount's representative and see Mr Krabbe, whom Mr Pegram candidly avowed to be his nominee in the 'Great Tontine'.

'It is a wild chance,' thought Jack, 'and I suppose, as such, ought to be tried; but I am afraid it is little likely that Ronald will discover anything that may prevent this marriage. They will show him Mr Krabbe, just as they showed me Mr Krabbe, and he will know – which I didn't – that it is not the real man; but what is the use of that? We cannot prove it. He may make any amount of inquiries he likes in Rydland, and they will all tell him the same story – that Mr Krabbe lives in that cottage, and has done so ever since he broke down and became past work. Ringwood will feel sure, as he is now, that all these people have been bamboozled by the Pegrams. But there, again, neither my uncle nor anybody else – bar Hemmingby – will believe us. I declare, if Ringwood declines to go I shall really not be able to blame him. It seems as if nothing could possibly come of it; and yet I cannot bear the idea of leaving even the least likely stone unturned to prevent this marriage.'

'You never called here, and consequently never got my note,' said Ringwood, as he welcomed his visitor; 'I left a line for you. What did you do in Wales?'

'Worse than nothing. I doubt very much whether, under any circumstances, it was possible ever to have done anything. I am fain to confess old Pegram is not at all the sort of man one can brow-beat or frighten. However, I will own to making a thorough mess of the whole thing; I lost my temper, told old Pegram that he was an out-and-out scoundrel, that he was no more in the "Tontine" than I was, that his nominee was dead, and that the Mr Krabbe he showed me was not the real man; and wound up by swearing, that if he did not abandon this marriage I would expose him.'

'And you say he was not powerfully impressed with that,' said Ringwood, laughing.

'Well, I do not quite know,' replied Jack drily. 'He declared he would commit me as a rogue and a vagabond if I was found in the town next morning. Hemmingby was quite right; I did not impose upon him as the sailor one bit. And yesterday I followed your advice, and went and saw my uncle, and that was not a bit of use either; that confounded old Welsh villain had written up a most plausible account of our interview, owning, with affected candour, that his nominee *was* Mr Krabbe, begging my uncle to send anybody he liked to see and inquire into his identity. Further, he had the impertinence to add that he would look over my insulting accusation in consideration of my being such a near relative of his lordship's; that my words were the ravings of a vain, jealous, disappointed young man. Yes, upon my soul he did, Ronald; he had the impudence to say that of me. In short, I have played my last cards, and am utterly beaten. The marriage takes place next week, and I see no hope of exposing the Pegrams before that, unless you think you are likely to make anything out of your interview with old Krabbe.'

'My interview with old Krabbe! What do you mean?'

'I forgot to tell you. Clinging to what seems to be my last chance, I persuaded my uncle to take Pegram at his word, and send some one down to Rydland to see this "nominee" of his. He pleaded at first that he had no one to send, and I immediately mentioned your name as being already engaged in watching the wind-up of the "Great Tontine" on the late Miss Caterham's behalf. After a little he assented to this arrangement, upon the condition that I promised not to go with you. You must try, Ringwood; you are sharper than me, and may detect the fraud, cleverly as it has been contrived.'

'I doubt whether I should make more of it than you did; but I will own to feeling a curiosity to see the impersonator of a man whom we firmly believe to be dead, on insufficient grounds though it may be. Still, I have a bit of real good news for you; you will have to see Lord Lakington again, and I think I can promise you that you will find him then quite as keen to break off this marriage as you can wish.'

'You speak in riddles. You must furnish me with a new story to tell him, or else there will be very little use in my seeing my uncle again.'

'I will; Terence Finnigan is found.'

'What! Miss Caterham's missing nominee! No! are you quite sure it is the right man?'

'Quite. I went down to Portsmouth yesterday with Miss Chichester to see him. She identified him at once, as also did three other people, two of whom have known him for many years. He is an imbecile pauper in Portsmouth

Workhouse. He lost his senses in a drunken bout about two years ago, which accounts for his disappearance. This, I fancy, settles Pegram's little game effectually.'

'Hurrah! yes,' exclaimed Jack, springing from his chair, and pacing the room with rapid strides in his excitement. 'With a third person in it, their arrangement becomes impossible. It ensures the wedding being put off, at all events; and we shall learn the truth about Pegram's nominee before long, I have no doubt. By the way, I suppose you will hardly go down and see him now.'

'I do not know; you must remember that I am acting for Miss Caterham's heir, as well as endeavouring to help you, and of course her interest in the exposure of the Pegrams is considerable. I should like to consult Hemmingby about it.'

'Come along, then; let us run across and tell him the news.'

The two young men proceeded at once to the 'Vivacity', and after some little delay were shown into the manager's sanctum. Mr Hemmingby listened with great interest to Ringwood's story of the discovery of Finnigan. He roared with laughter at Jack's account of his interview with old Pegram, and laughingly told Phillimore that he was quite right to leave Rydland that evening, for that the lawyer was quite capable of keeping his word.

'Gad, sir, if he once got you into prison down in his own country I am blessed if I think you would have found it quite so easy to get out again.'

Mr Hemmingby further expressed great admiration at Pegram's letter; the open avowal that old Krabbe was his nominee, and that Lord Lakington was quite at liberty to send down anybody he liked to see him, and make inquiries concerning him, he pronounced a very clever stroke indeed.

'I tell you what, Ringwood,' said the manager at length, 'I have an idea about this. I should like to take advantage of your going down as Lord Lakington's accredited agent to accompany you, and see Mr Krabbe myself. You see, I knew the old man for many years; and though I have a strong suspicion that whoever they have got in that cottage is not the real man, yet I am curious to see an imitation which is so good that it has undoubtedly deceived many people who knew him quite well. I have another reason, which I have never mentioned to you as yet. When I endeavoured to see him, I was very much struck with the nurse who takes care of him. No; not mere good looks, Mr Phillimore, though she is comely enough, for the matter of that; but I was struck with the idea that I had seen her before, and in a very different capacity. As you may remember, it was one of the old man's "not-at-home" days, and therefore I had not much chance of looking at her; and I thought she was determined that it should be as slight as she could make it. I further fancied that she recognized me; and while puzzling my brains to recollect her, came to the conclusion that that woman held the key of Pegram's mystery. Now, if I accompany you, Ringwood, whether or not I make anything out of Mr Krabbe, I think it more than possible that I shall recollect that woman.'

'It is, at all events, well worth trying, Hemmingby; we will leave together by the early train tomorrow morning.'

'No; I don't think that will exactly do,' returned the manager. 'I won't go down with you, but follow, and join you somewhere near the cottage. I intend to get into Rydland myself late at night, and not, if possible, let the Pegrams know that I am in the town until after we have paid our visit to old Krabbe. I may be wrong, but I have an impression that they will put considerable obstacles in the way of my seeing their nominee. You go down tomorrow, call upon them that afternoon, and arrange to pay your visit about midday; never trouble about me; I shall turn up as you knock at the cottage door, you bet your life. As for you, Mr Phillimore, you will, of course, inform the Viscount that the "Tontine" is not reduced to a match yet; and, consequently, the dividing of the stakes not at present practicable. And I think now we may consider Bob Pegram's marriage as knocked pretty well into a cocked hat. They are smart, very smart, these Pegrams; but I reckon we shall prove one too many for them this time. However,' concluded the manager, laughing, 'I have no cause to brag, for Bob Pegram has had a dinner out of me on the strength of his marriage, and that is something to the good, anyhow.'

Lord Lakington was not a little disturbed by the announcement the next morning that Mr Phillimore wanted to see him. The Viscount hated being disturbed over his after-breakfast cigar and newspaper. Moreover, he felt quite certain that this interview with his nephew was not likely to be a pleasant one.

'Confound the fellow,' he muttered; 'he was here only yesterday, and now I suppose has come again bothering about Beatrice's marriage. I shall have to give him clearly to understand that this is a subject about which his advice is not needed, that it is all settled, and further interference on his part I shall regard as unpardonable presumption.'

Indeed, for a few minutes his Lordship debated whether he would not decline to see Jack; but feeling that he could hardly shut the door in the face of his own nephew, finally determined to admit him. Resolved, however, to take the bull by the horns, no sooner did Jack Phillimore make his appearance than the Viscount hastened to exclaim –

'Pray sit down. Delighted to see you, of course; but I trust that you have not come to re-open yesterday's conversation. It is impossible you can have heard anything from Rydland as yet, nor likely indeed that you will find these wild suspicions of yours substantiated. Now, my dear Jack, the thing lies in a nutshell: if you like to come to Beatrice's wedding we shall be very pleased to see you; if, on the contrary, you think fit to feel aggrieved, very well, stay away; but once for all, be good enough to understand that I decline all further discussion on the subject.'

'As far as discussion goes, certainly not, unless you like,' replied Jack. 'I have only come down this morning to put you in possession of a fact, not a suspicion, mind, and to point out the difference that that fact makes in the arrangement between you and Mr Pegram. I am not going to say a word about the marriage one way or the other; that is for you to determine. What I have to tell you is this. The nominee of the late Miss Caterham, who has been so long missing, has been found, is alive, tolerably well, and in no immediate danger of dying. Miss Caterham, of course, willed her share away, and, by curious coincidence, the young lady to whom she left it at present forms one of your family. Miss Chichester is at present the third shareholder. You know that she went to Portsmouth the day before yesterday to identify an old servant; that was the missing nominee – one Terence Finnigan. You will see at once that you and Pegram at the present moment are arranging to divide, not only what you have not got, but what you may never have. My suspicions, you see, I am putting quite in the background. What I have just told you is a fact that can be testified by unimpeachable witnesses. Miss Chichester herself can tell you that she saw Finnigan alive forty-eight hours ago, and either Mr Ringwood or Mr Carbuckle could tell you that the result of his being alive is as I say.'

'Egad! this makes a devil of a difference,' exclaimed the Viscount; 'that fellow Pegram always assured me Miss Caterham's nominee was dead. It is not likely that Beatrice would marry into that sort of family if there was any doubt about the settlements being all right, not that I wish to influence her in any way (the noble Viscount clung close as ever to his old hypocritical assumption); but I should think it my duty to place this material change in her marriage prospects before her. One cannot tell, but I can hardly suppose that she is so infatuated about young Mr Pegram as to overlook the fact, that the one thing which entitled the son of a country solicitor to aspire to the hand of a Phillimore was his wealth. You know, Jack, we can only be guided by facts; but I think it quite possible that your suspicions are correct, and that these Pegrams are confounded scoundrels.'

'Then I suppose you will write by tonight's post to Rydland to inform them of this discovery, and that, in consequence, the engagement must be regarded as completely at an end.'

'Certainly; that is, if Beatrice consents. I must of course consult her, and be guided by her wishes.'

'Exactly,' rejoined Jack, falling into the humour of his noble kinsman, and assisting him in the belief that he was a model father, whose first care was his daughter's happiness. 'You no doubt wish to talk matters over with Trixie as soon as possible, so I will get out of the way. The sooner you have polished off the Pegrams the better pleased I shall be.'

As Jack Phillimore shook hands with his uncle, his intention undoubtedly was to leave the house forthwith; but he was so elated with the march of events, that no sooner did he find himself outside of the door, than it occurred to him to dash upstairs and whisper an inkling of the good news to Mrs Lyme Wregis. He bounced into the room unannounced, and at once found himself face to face with his cousin. Beatrice started for a moment, but recovering herself, extended her hand, and said –

'You were very rude to me, sir, the last time we met. I sent you a message of reconciliation the day before yesterday by Mr Ringwood; you have run up, I trust, to say that you mean to comply with my request?'

'You mean, to come to your wedding? yes, Beatrice, I have promised to be there; but I do not think it will take place quite so soon as you fancy.'

The girl's face flushed; there was an angry light in her eyes.

'I do not understand you. I do not want to quarrel with you; and if you are going to say unkind things about my marriage I will not stop to hear them.'

'I have nothing further to say,' retorted Jack, 'than that your father wishes to see you in his study.'

Beatrice looked sharply at her cousin for a moment, as the remembrance of the last time her father wished to see her in his sanctum flashed across her; but the bright, confident smile on Jack's face reassured her, and with a little nod she passed through the door he held open for her. His next proceedings astonished Mrs Lyme Wregis not a little: darting across the room, he kissed the old lady's hand, thanked her warmly for her letter to him at Malta, and wound up by exclaiming –

'It is all right, Madam; we will bowl out the Pegrams – stock, lock, and barrel. When Beatrice comes back she will tell you she is a disengaged young woman, and that little beast Pegram will have his *congé* despatched by tonight's post. I cannot say it has been all my doing, but I have done my share, and, undoubtedly, without me, my uncle would probably have heard what he now knows too late. She would have been married. Now she won't be, at all events, to a Pegram.'

And without vouchsafing further explanation, Jack dashed downstairs, and out into the street, feeling that in his present state of high spirits no house was large enough to contain him.

Lord Lakington remained for some time after his nephew left him immersed in thought. What was he to do now? This arrangement with the

Pegrams must of course be put an end to. The sole reason for the marriage had disappeared, and the Viscount was not a little put out about it. The terrible thing to him was, that he found himself once again in exactly the position from which his compromise with the Welsh lawyer had rescued him. The very comfortable income he was at present enjoying was liable to vanish at any moment. Even if Jack's supposition be true, that the Pegrams' nominee was, in reality, dead, and that they were palming off an impostor in lieu of him, still there could be no doubt about this man Finnigan; and if he should happen to outlive Mrs Lyme Wregis, the Viscount saw that he would be reduced to those straits of genteel poverty, the remembrance of which made him shudder. Already he was turning over in his own mind what it would be best for him to do under the present circumstances; and the more he thought the thing over, the more it struck him that it would be a good thing should his nephew turn out to be right. Only let the Pegrams be proved out of the 'Tontine', and it might be possible to come to a compromise with the only other person left in it besides himself; and then he suddenly recollected that this other shareholder was Miss Chichester. Well, that would clearly facilitate matters. The young lady was at present residing under the same roof, and Carbuckle, her nominal guardian, was an old friend; so that there would be no difficulty about breaking the ice on the subject. Only let the Pegrams be convicted of fraud; and here the Viscount remembered the errand upon which he had that day despatched Mr Ringwood – a mere farce, as he thought yesterday, to which he had consented to pacify his impetuous nephew; but which he now most sincerely hoped might turn out to be a successful exposure of fraud. Here his meditations were interrupted by the appearance of Beatrice, who simply observed, as she entered –

'I heard from Jack you wanted me, papa.'

'Yes; I have something unpleasant to explain to you; I know it is most unpleasant for a girl to get talked about, and I am afraid, my dear Beatrice, that is what will happen to you if ruled by my advice. Of course, when a girl breaks off her engagement there is always considerable gossip about it; she is either declared to have behaved abominably, or pitied for having been shamefully ill-used; and yet, my darling Beatrice, as your father, and so naturally having your best interests at heart, if you can but assure me that your feelings are not too deeply involved, I must counsel you to break your troth with Robert Pegram.'

'My dear father,' exclaimed Miss Phillimore, and barely able to conceal a shade of indignation in her tones, at the idea that he should affect to believe that she would ever have contemplated this marriage, except to relieve him of the possibility of poverty.

'Don't interrupt me, child,' interposed the Viscount, endeavouring to keep

VICTORIAN VILLAINIES

up the comedy to the last; 'if your heart is engaged in this match, I won't say that I will oppose your wishes, but it is my duty to point out that a third shareholder has appeared in the "Great Tontine", and that Mr Pegram is in no position to make the very handsome settlements he intended, and probably –'

'Not another word,' exclaimed Beatrice, eagerly; 'you know perfectly well that it was for your sake I consented to wed this man. If it is not to benefit you, for heaven's sake let him go his way. As for me, let all London say what they will of me, I only know that I feel like the prisoner whose fetters have been struck off; I shall go to bed tonight with a lighter heart than ever I have had since I learnt that Robert Pegram was my wooer.'

'Then I will write by this very post, Trixie, to Wales, and put an end to your engagement. I regret to say there are grave suspicions of unfair play on the part of the Pegrams in the matter of the "Tontine". But who do you think this third shareholder is, the nominee of whom has been so unexpectedly discovered, after being lost for the last two years? no other than Miss Chichester.'

'What! do you mean Mary? – Mary Chichester, who is living with us now?'

'Just so,' rejoined the Viscount.

'I am glad; she is such a dear girl; and now she will be an heiress, and have lots of money, will she not?'

'That is as may be,' replied her father; 'but if it so happens, she will in some wise be an heiress at your expense. Please bear in mind, that you must not whisper a hint of the "Tontine" to your grandmother; the idea that I have speculated on her life might make her uncomfortable. There is no reason for such a feeling, but many people have whims on these points.'

## CHAPTER THIRTY-ONE

## EXPOSURE OF THE PEGRAM FRAUD

Mr Pegram was slightly disconcerted at not receiving a letter from Lord Lakington by return of post, in answer to the one which he had written detailing the account of Jack Phillimore's visit to Rydland; but he was made still further uneasy by receiving a visit in the afternoon from Mr Ringwood, who explained that he came as Lord Lakington's accredited agent to see Mr Krabbe, and make a few inquiries concerning him.

'I am bound to mention, Mr Pegram,' said Ringwood, in the course of conversation, 'that Lord Lakington would never have dreamt of sending me down here on such an errand if you had not yourself proposed it; but although placing no faith in his nephew's statement, he thought it would be more satisfactory to you and Mr Robert Pegram that the thing should be in some fashion investigated. There are, of course, plenty of people in the town who can testify to the old man living at the cottage being Mr Krabbe; and having heard them speak to this point, I will, with your permission, just call upon Mr Krabbe tomorrow morning, and that will, I think, be quite sufficient.'

'Pray do not think you want permission from me,' rejoined the old lawyer. 'Anybody is welcome to call upon the old man whenever they please. Mr Krabbe, it is true, will not always receive visitors; nor does his nurse consider it judicious to disturb him at the caprice of any passer-by who once knew him. His old friends go when they like, though it is poor work, sir, looking upon the wreck of a man you once knew, especially when, as is often poor Krabbe's case, he does not even recognize you.'

So it was all settled as Ringwood proposed, although Mr Pegram was secretly dissatisfied that the Viscount should have taken him at his word. He had calculated on a chivalrous reply from Lord Lakington, to the effect that he could not insult him by thinking of such a thing as sending down an agent to make the inquiry he courted. However, he was not a whit dismayed at any result that was likely to attend Ringwood's investigation.

'He is rather too oily, Bob, this one; they are much less likely to be dangerous when they are all bluster, like Mr Phillimore; this chap can keep his tongue quiet, I'll be bound. Well, he is not likely to learn enough in Rydland to set it wagging when he gets back to town.'

'He takes the thing very quietly,' returned Bob Pegram, 'and in a way that looks as if he thought he was here on a fool's errand.'

'I don't blame him a bit; but it is not what I expected from the noble Viscount,' said old Pegram. 'As a matter of business, he is quite right to inquire into our solvency, so to speak, before making the deal; but still, although I proposed it in consequence of his nephew's visit, I never thought he would have taken me up. It don't altogether fit in with my estimate of his character. Surely nothing else could have occurred to render him suspicious.'

'I can't say for that,' rejoined Bob; 'but I tell you what it is, this game is getting a precious sight too risky to be pleasant; and I declare I think it would be wiser to give it up.'

'Give it up!' replied his sire fiercely; 'what! when less than a week ensures our success! This Mr Ringwood may be ever so clever a man; but let him make what inquiries he will in the town, there is nobody to throw a doubt about Krabbe living in that cottage. And as for seeing him, what can be the use of that; he cannot possibly say whether he sees him or not. His wishing to pay the old gentleman that visit, does not look as if he was a very shrewd hand at picking up evidence.'

It may easily be supposed that the Pegrams took care that a vigilant eye should be kept on Ringwood; but that gentleman conducted his questioning with great openness, and seemed easily satisfied. In fact, he made up his mind to affect to treat the whole thing as a mere form. He was quite convinced that of himself he could discover nothing at Rydland; that, do his utmost, he should be as completely hoodwinked as Jack Phillimore, and that his sole chance of making any discovery lay in the unexpected appearance of Hemmingby. That keen-eyed gentleman might see through the imposition, more especially if he came upon the scene unannounced. And Ringwood was so far successful, that the easy-going manner in which he set about his task lulled the half-awakened suspicions of the Pegrams; but unfortunately the morrow's post put them thoroughly on the *qui vive*, for by it arrived that letter from Lord Lakington, in which he declined the honour of their alliance, on the ground that the nominee of the third shareholder in the 'Tontine', long supposed to be missing, was found; and, consequently, such a division of the big lottery as they had contemplated had become impossible.

A half-muttered execration escaped the old lawyer's lips, at the information that Terence Finnigan was still in the land of the living. All search for him had been so long futile, that, like Lord Lakington, he had ceased to take this third shareholder into his calculations, and thought that nothing but the discovery of his own fraud before the completion of his son's marriage could possibly prevent the entire success of his subtle and patiently worked-out plot. Now, like the spider, whose web has been suddenly demolished, he felt that his meshes were all to spin again; knowing, moreover, that Mr Phillimore, influenced by his mad passion for his cousin, had somehow got a clue to the so-far successful imposition that he had perpetrated. In all the consciousness of the triumph of knavery, he had derided the idea that Mr Phillimore would succeed in exposing him in time to break off the fast-approaching marriage; but if that gentleman, aided by clever advisers, was to have weeks, nay, months, to work out the puzzle, of which he had somehow contrived to guess the key, it was not a danger by any means to be laughed at. He was sitting in his office, pondering over what was now to be done, when Robert Pegram entered; and without a word his sire placed Lord Lakington's letter in his hands. If the father seemed to think their next move difficult of decision, the son came to a conclusion the minute he had mastered the contents of the epistle.

'That settles it,' exclaimed Robert Pegram. 'The whole thing is up now, and the sooner we back out the better. I should recommend reporting the sudden and painless death of Mr Krabbe by today's post, and sending down to this fellow Ringwood to say it is impossible he can see the old man, for he is no longer in the land of the living.'

'I don't agree with you in the least, Bob; we have carried on the imposition so far, why not a little farther? The impersonation of old Krabbe has even deceived the doctor, who attended him as long as there was any use in his doing so. The doctor, indeed, has been so convinced of having seen his old patient, he has twice sent the half-yearly certificates of his being alive necessary for receiving the dividends. What you have done so long you can surely do a little longer. One or other of the nominees will probably drop in the course of the next twelvemonth, and then we must compromise again with either Lord Lakington or Miss Caterham's representative. To play for the whole stake would be too dangerous; and though, probably, we may never make such terms again as we did this time, yet the half is a stake worth going for.'

But Bob Pegram was fairly frightened. He had none of his father's dogged resolution; was not, indeed, composed of the stuff of which great criminals are manufactured.

'It is hopeless, useless,' he replied; 'I say, as I said before, the game is up, and the sooner we get out of the whole affair the safer for our own skins. People, you know, will hardly look upon our little mystification in the light of a practical joke should the story come out; and as for the law, my knowledge of that profession goes far enough to suggest what an ugly name they would give it.'

'You fool,' rejoined his father; 'when old Krabbe dies, the fact must not be made public till two or three days after it occurs. Suppose I send such a notice as you propose to Mr Ringwood; cannot you imagine his thinking it a singular coincidence that the old man should die just as he has come down to see him? cannot you imagine his suspicions being awakened; his talking about this singular coincidence with some of the leading people in the town? and cannot you imagine these people, in some sort, constituting themselves a coroner's inquest for the identification of Krabbe? You are clever, Bob; but I think it will puzzle you to produce the body.'

Mr Robert Pegram was, for the moment, completely silenced by his father's view of the case. It certainly was quite possible that Ringwood might take that line of conduct, urging, with exasperating politeness, that he was sure it would be more satisfactory to Mr Pegram.

'You must see this as well as I do,' continued the old lawyer; 'even if we wanted to abandon our scheme, it is impossible to do so just now. I wonder who Miss Caterham's representative is, by the way; we must have a look at the old lady's will, which will doubtless tell us. From what you have told me about the little cottage at Kew, I should fancy her relatives are not rich people; the needier a man is, Bob – if it is a man – the easier it will be to drive a hard bargain with him; and if it is a girl, we might arrange another marriage for you. All this is, of course, supposing that Terence Finnigan should outlive Lord Lakington's representative.'

'I tell you, father, it is sheer madness to go on. This Mr Phillimore has already a suspicion about old Krabbe, amounting evidently in his own mind to a certainty. He has not openly told you so, but shown how thoroughly he believes in what he says by his utterly unwarranted action in the matter. The imposture, no doubt, has been successfully sustained so far, might be possibly for some weeks longer; but you must see, as well as I do, that their getting to the bottom of the Krabbe mystery is a mere matter of time; they are certain to ascertain the fact of his being dead at last. It was a cleverly-conceived scheme on your part, and has gone very near to proving successful; but only look at it coolly, and you must see we are beaten now. If this confounded Finnigan had not turned up I should have married the girl next week, whatever Mr John Phillimore might say to the contrary, and we should have wound up the "Great Tontine" successfully by its eventually all coming into our own family. Whatever the Phillimores might have found out then would have been of little consequence; the Viscount could hardly have prosecuted his own son-in-law, and must have held his tongue for his daughter's sake. Now my engagement is, of course, utterly broken off. The mere rumour that there is something wrong about our nominee will make Lord Lakington shy of treating with us for the future, and probably induce Miss Caterham's representative to look as keenly into the matter as Mr John Phillimore, only with a good deal more ability. It is no question of going on with our scheme, but resolves itself merely as to how we may best back out of it.'

'I still don't agree with you, Bob. You get frightened simply because you picture to yourself that our adversaries know as much as we do; absurd! This Mr Phillimore, inspired by the madness of jealousy, has chanced to make a lucky guess; but, boldly as he announces what we know to be the truth, he is evidently at a loss how to prove his words. Lord Lakington has broken with us not in the least on account of what his nephew has told him, but simply because of the discovery of this man Finnigan, which naturally for the present puts the late contract out of his power or mine. No, Bob; it is worth going on with a little longer. Life, after eighty, is precarious, and until we ascertain what state of health Finnigan is in we had best put a bold face upon it.'

'You are infatuated with your own scheme, father, and are shutting your eyes to the obvious fact that, clever as I admit it to have been, it has now failed. There is another thing, too – I doubt Mrs Clark standing to us any longer. She is so sick of the weariness and isolation of her life, that nothing but the assurance that a few days more would release her from it has induced her to stick to us so far.'

'Pooh, pooh! – double her salary; say unforeseen circumstances have postponed the conclusion of our little mystery for another few weeks. Services such as hers are only a question of money; she is getting treble her ordinary salary as it is. As I said before, double it. Inordinate wages reconcile all servants to monotony.'

'It is all very well,' replied Bob sullenly; 'but you don't suppose that this woman is unaware she has us in her power.'

'You have never been so foolish as to tell her anything?'

'No, nothing more than I was positively obliged; but she is far too clever a woman not to know that the story she could tell would be easy of interpretation to some of the people round here, whatever mystery it may seem to herself.'

'Do the best you can with her,' rejoined the old lawyer; 'we will talk the whole thing over another time; but back out of it or go on with it, we must hoodwink this Mr Ringwood today. Remember, you and Mrs Clark are bound to have old Mr Krabbe ready for him by midday;' and in this estimate of the present situation Bob Pegram was reluctantly forced to concur.

Ringwood's inquiries had, as he expected, led to nothing. That old Mr

Krabbe lived as a pensioner of the Pegrams in a little cottage just off the Llanbarlym Road was evidently firmly believed by the good people of Rydland. That anybody should be personating the ex-clerk had never been hinted at in the town, and the townsfolk would have been as much astonished at the suggestion as puzzled to account for the object of such a personation. It was with no little curiosity, therefore, that Ringwood strolled out to pay his pre-arranged visit; and his curiosity was excited, not with the hope of making any discovery himself, but simply as to what might be the result of Hemmingby's appearance on the scene. That he should find a very old man he had no doubt, and that man would not be Mr Krabbe. But then he felt that he of himself could make no more of this than had Jack Phillimore. He had no difficulty in finding the cottage, and though he kept a sharp look-out in all directions, had seen no signs of the manager, and it was not till he was about to rap at the door that a quick step upon the gravel walk behind him made him pause, and he saw Sam Hemmingby by his side.

'I got into Rydland late last night, and I do not think a soul I knew saw me slink out here. I came across country most of the way, for fear of meeting any one, and have been skulking behind the hedge for the last hour. I saw Bob Pegram go in by the back way about half an hour ago; he is come, I suppose, to warn this old counterfeit to get ready for you, and to keep an eye upon him while he plays his part.'

At this moment the door was opened by Mrs Clark, who was, at first, most palpably disconcerted by the appearance of Hemmingby on the scene. Recovering her composure after a few seconds, she ushered them into the little parlour, and addressing herself to Ringwood somewhat pointedly, explained in a low voice that Mr Krabbe would have finished dressing in a few minutes, and see them if they would sit down and wait.

'Where the deuce have I seen that woman before?' muttered the manager, as Mrs Clark left the room. 'I am more convinced than ever that I have seen her before, and that she knows me. It is just the way she went on the last time I was here – would not look at me, nor speak to me more than she was positively compelled. You'll see she'll keep her back to the light, and display the most unfeminine silence all the time we are here.'

'You think she is afraid of your recognizing her then?'

'Just so; and it was the hope that I should do so prompted me chiefly to volunteer accompanying you in this visit. I do not expect to make much of the old man, without believing him to be really old Krabbe. I have no doubt the old mummy they have got is so like him that it will be devilish hard to tell "t'other from which".'

At this juncture the same decrepit wreck of humanity that Jack Phillimore had seen tottered into the room, supported by the nurse on one side and his stick on the other. Pausing as soon as he had advanced three or four steps, he pointed with his stick at his visitors, and turning to Mrs Clark, exclaimed, in a piping treble –

'Tell them to go away.'

Forced to reply in some fashion, the nurse raised her voice and shouted into the octogenarian's ear –

'These gentlemen have come all the way from London to ask after you; won't you say "How do you do" to them?'

But the old gentleman only replied by incoherent mutterings, in which objurgations, such as, 'a pack of prying fools', seemed mingled with querulous complaints as to the scarcity of sunlight in these days as compared with those of his youth.

Hemmingby eyed the old man narrowly while the nurse busied herself in adjusting his cushions, wraps, etc., and crossing the room rapidly, held out his hand, and exclaimed –

'How do you do, Mr Krabbe?'

The old gentleman looked at him for a few seconds, then muttering sulkily that Hemmingby had got between him and the fire, nestled sullenly down amongst his cushions.

'It is wonderfully like the real article,' said Hemmingby in a low voice, as he resumed his seat by Ringwood. 'In spite of my doubts, I would not venture as yet to swear that he is not the real man.'

Ringwood's hopes rather fell at this announcement. He had fully expected to hear the manager pronounce Mr Krabbe an impostor as soon as he had had a look at him; while Hemmingby's strong impression, that he should, after a little, recognize the nurse, he had taken slight heed of.

'I am afraid, gentlemen, you will get little out of him today. He is very deaf, as you may see, at the best of times; and when he is out of temper, as is the case just now, he simply won't hear, scream at him as you will.'

Hemmingby was right in the prediction about the nurse. She kept her face as much as possible turned away from him, and addressed herself to Ringwood in low, measured tones, which struck the manager as having been deliberately adopted. He was disappointed, for he had reckoned upon her voice to recall this woman to his memory. As yet it had told him nothing, and he felt pretty sure that she would allow him to hear as little of it as might be. Clearly, if possible, he must force her to talk.

'No,' observed the manager; 'the old crittur don't recollect me a bit; and yet, poor old chap, he and I have been friendly for the last twenty years; but I suppose, ma'am, there are many of his old friends he don't recognize?'

'He recognizes very few of them now, sir,' rejoined the nurse, in the same low, mechanical tones.

'He knows Mr Pegram, of course,' said Hemmingby carelessly. 'When they are in that way they often lose all memory about the events and acquaintances of the latter part of their life, it is true; but it is hard upon forty years ago that he and the old lawyer came together.'

'Who said anything about Mr Pegram?' piped the octogenarian, from the depth of his cushions. 'He never comes near me now; why should he? What does he want with a worn-out old fellow like me? But I'd like to see him, I'd like to see him.'

A gleam of surprise flashed for a moment across the manager's face; but, transient as it was, the woman, who from under her downcast lids was stealthily watching him, saw it, and fidgeted nervously with her apron in consequence.

'It strikes me,' continued Hemmingby, 'that my old friend there is not quite so deaf as you make him out to be, Mrs – Mrs – '

'Clark, sir,' she replied. 'Excuse me; I told you just now that, though he really is very deaf, he exaggerates his deafness a good deal when out of humour. The name of Pegram would, of course, attract his attention.'

'Pegram!' quavered the invalid again; 'I want to see him about that right of foreshore in front of Rydland Terrace. If he don't buy it somebody else will, and build on it, likely as not. It will send his rents down in the Terrace if he lets any one build between him and the sea.'

There was a twinkle in Hemmingby's eye, which did not escape Mrs Clark, as he replied –

'Why, your head is as clear for business, Mr Krabbe, as ever it was; if you would only take to an ear-trumpet, I believe, when you have got through the winter, you might resume your old place in the office. Don't you think, ma'am, he will come round with the spring a bit?'

The nurse shook her head, but made no further reply.

'Well, Ringwood,' said the manager, rising, 'you were sent down here to see Mr Krabbe, and so put an end to a foolish rumour; I suppose you are satisfied now, and quite ready to vouch that he is alive, and in tolerably good case, for his age. Why, he's ready to blow old lawyer Pegram up for not calling on him this minute. I should like to shake hands with him before I go; perhaps, ma'am, you wouldn't mind telling him so.'

The nurse screamed the request into the old man's ear; but his sole reply was a severe fit of coughing and choking.

'I don't think he means to hear me, for one thing,' said the nurse, in the low, studied tones she had preserved all along; 'and, as you see, his cough troubles him terribly besides.'

'The eccentricities, as well as the infirmities, of age must be respected,' rejoined the manager gravely. 'Good-bye, Mrs – ah! yes – Clark.'

And nodding to the nurse, he was, accompanied by Ringwood, about to leave the room, when, to the intense astonishment of the latter, he turned swiftly round, crossed to the deaf man's chair, put his hand lightly on his shoulder, and whispered into his ear. Ringwood saw the invalid start as if the manager had bit him; but before he could observe more, Hemmingby hurried him into the lane, and led the way rapidly back to Rydland.

'Well,' said Ringwood, as they turned into the high road, 'what do you make of it all? and what, in heaven's name, possessed you to whisper into a deaf man's ear?'

'I can't explain matters more briefly,' rejoined Hemmingby, laughing, 'than by telling you what I said. It was merely this – "A leetle overdone, Bob; but you can have twenty pound a week at the 'Vivacity' whenever you like to join the profession."'

'Why, you don't mean to say –' exclaimed Ringwood.

'Yes, I do,' interrupted the manager. 'Bob Pegram plays old Krabbe, and devilish well he does it. As for the nurse, I still can't put a name to her; but would back her also to be theatrical.'

## CHAPTER THIRTY-TWO

# MARY PENETRATES THE MYSTERY

As the footsteps of the visitors died away Bob Pegram sprang from his chair, and, throwing his rug and wrappers upon the ground, exhibited the comic picture of a young man partially made up to represent an old one.

'It's all up, Kitty,' he exclaimed. 'I told the governor it was madness to continue the deception; but he was as obstinate as a pig, and refused to admit that he was beaten. Of course, neither he nor I ever reckoned upon Hemmingby turning up in this way; I wish I had taken your advice. You said the minute you saw your old manager that it was best to say old Mr Krabbe was too ill to receive visitors, that if we once played our little comedy before him he was certain to detect one, if not both of us; but I had bamboozled so many, that I was ass enough to think I could deceive him. What do you think he whispered into my ear before leaving, Kitty?'

'I don't know,' she replied; 'but it does not much matter. I saw that he had recognized you some little before that; whether he made me out also I cannot say; but that, I suppose, is not of much consequence now.'

'Do you know what all this means, girl? do you know that this means penal servitude for me? Why Hemmingby should turn against us in this fashion I cannot imagine; he could not have come here with that barrister fellow by accident. At all events, it is too risky for me, and I mean to be out of Rydland tonight.'

'Yes, Bob dear, if that is the case we cannot fly too quickly. I don't know what they can do to me; but, at all events, we will meet our fate together.'

'I am not sure if you had not better stay,' replied Bob doubtfully.

'I shall do nothing of the kind,' rejoined Miss Clyde; 'wherever you go I am going with you; you got me into this scrape, and you are bound to see me through it.'

'Very well; I am sure I only spoke for your own sake; I shall be only too glad to have such a charming travelling companion. Only mind, Kitty, I intend a long journey. I mean going to America if I am not interfered with, as I don't think this climate will suit my constitution any longer.'

'Only swear you will make me your wife, Bob, and I will go anywhere.'

'I will marry you as soon as ever I get to New York, I promise. And now, my dear, if we are to decamp without beat of drum, the sooner we make our preparations the better. As soon as I have got into my own clothes I shall go back to Rydland, draw some money from the Bank, send a portmanteau quietly down to the station, and slip up to London by the evening train. You had better join me at the station, dressed in your customary attire; but you must leave everything here except what you can carry in a handbag; to send any one for your trunks will attract attention.'

'All right,' replied the girl, 'you may trust me implicitly to obey you, though I have not yet vowed to do so. Have you any further directions to give me?'

'Only these, Kitty: take your own ticket at the station, and don't speak to me until after the train has started; I will take care to get into the same carriage with you.'

'And now, Bob dear, to change our dress. You wretched old thing, how I hate you!' And as she spoke, Miss Clyde threw the slightly exaggerated nurse's cap she wore by the side of the *ci-devant* Krabbe's scratch-wig, and allowed her own redundant tresses to tumble about her shoulders. 'Whatever happens to me,' she continued, 'it cannot be so bad as this; no imprisonment can be duller than the life I have led in this abominable cottage; and as for hair,' pouted Kitty, with a sly glance at her own locks, 'you may as well have it cut off as not be allowed to show it. Ah, Bob, I have done for you what no man has ever induced an actress to do yet; I have played an old woman *before my time*.'

'Never mind, Kitty,' replied Bob Pegram, laughing; 'it makes you look younger than ever when one sees you as your own proper self. And now to get rid of my wrinkles, eyebrows, and these antiquated garments.'

Bob Pegram, as, having resumed his own clothes, he walked quickly back to Rydland, rapidly turned over in his mind all the details of his projected flight. He had no choice but to make Kitty Clyde his companion, even if he had not been sufficiently attached to the girl to desire carrying her off with him. It was quite evident that nothing would have induced her to remain at the cottage after he had made up his mind to fly Rydland, and even if it had not escaped his lips in the first terror of detection, she was far too shrewd not to know that the minute the secret of the fictitious Mr Krabbe was penetrated, that attempting to continue the deception was useless. There was but one difficulty that he saw in the way of his stealthy retreat, and that was his father. To draw a good big sum from the Bank, and slip quietly away from

Rydland, was easy enough; but the bidding good-bye to his father was a different matter. Influenced entirely by his own selfish fears, he determined to spare the old lawyer that ceremony.

'He will probably be death upon going on with this scheme of his, although it has palpably miscarried, and it is waste of time to argue with him on that point,' thought Bob. 'He will furiously oppose my making a bolt of it, and urge me to stop and brazen it out, declaring that Lord Lakington, in common delicacy, cannot expose us: I don't feel as if there was much brazen left about me. Of course, he will want to know how I got on with Ringwood; and when I tell him how Hemmingby found me out, declare that if he promises to drop the thing at once, Hemmingby will never expose him. I am not so clear about that. At all events, I do not fancy walking about the streets on sufferance. I am devilish sick of Rydland; and as for Miss Phillimore, she is an honourable and a crasher, I know, but she is just a little too stand-off for me. Kitty Clyde is worth a dozen of her. No; mum is the word; only let me get clear away to America with Kitty, and I'll take to the stage as a profession. Why, Hemmingby said I was worth twenty pounds a week;' for, even in the midst of his consternation at the manager's discovery, Bob Pegram's vanity had been tickled at the delicate manner in which it was announced.

Adhering to this resolve, he kept carefully out of his father's way; but, moved by some compunction, employed a part of his time at 'The Crown' in writing a short note to him, in which, after explaining his own flight and his reasons for it, he strongly recommended the old man to follow his example before the thing got blown. He further reminded him that he had already obtained two dividends from the 'Tontine', by the fraudulent representation that old Krabbe was alive, and, consequently, placed himself at the mercy of Lord Lakington, or anybody else who chose to denounce him, including even that Mr John Phillimore whom he had threatened to commit as a rogue and a vagabond. At last, seeing that his train was nearly due, he strolled out of the hotel, gave the boots a shilling to carry the letter up to his father, and made the best of his way to the station.

Hard as old Pegram was, he a little broke down under his son's note. It has been said that every human being must have something to love, that it is a necessity of our existence, and such love as lawyer Pegram was capable of giving he had centred on his son. The great end of all his scheming, toiling, and plotting had been to leave Bob in the position of a country gentleman. He knew that he had been an indulgent father, and on the only two occasions upon which he had despotically required submission to his will it was so palpably for the young man's good that it should have disarmed resentment. He had opposed his going on the stage; he had insisted on his marrying the Honourable Beatrice Phillimore. What father in his position would not have done the first? while as for the second, was it not bidding him to wed wealth, beauty, and high connection?

'I knew he had not my nerve,' he muttered; 'but I never thought he would run off and leave his old father in the lurch in this way. If he had only had the pluck to stand staunch to his guns, though the game may be up as far as the "Great Tontine" is concerned, no harm would have come to us. We have not much descent to boast of, we Pegrams, and we may not be much to look at, but damme! Bob is the first of the breed that ever turned cur.'

However, the old lawyer quickly recovered himself, and after the first half-hour, faced the situation as undauntedly as ever. He went down that very night to the cottage, and after some little groping about in the dusk, found the key in its accustomed place under the door. He had taken the precaution of bringing matches and a piece of candle with him; striking a light, he proceeded to inspect the premises. He found them, as he anticipated, deserted. In the bedroom, where the phantom Krabbe had been supposed to reside, there were scattered about all the accessories of the masquerade. The shawls and wraps, the quaint costume, the stick, the wig, crape hair, camel's hair brushes, lining wires, and a variety of theatrical pigments. The room formerly occupied by Mrs Clark he found similarly littered. The snowy aprons, large caps, and common serge dresses which she had worn while personating a nurse, Kitty Clyde had abandoned with more glee than ceremony. After carefully searching the cottage, Pegram felt satisfied that no one had been there since Mrs Clark had abandoned it. Having gathered all the garments, both masculine and feminine, together with all the other odds and ends necessary for the carrying out the imposture they had been playing, he crammed the whole into the big trunk which Kitty had perforce left behind, locked it, saw that the windows were securely fastened, and then having turned the key of the cottage door, thrust it into his pocket and wended his way slowly homewards. He inquired carelessly of the servants the next morning by what train Mr Robert went to town, as if he had been perfectly aware of his intention, though not exactly certain of the time of his departure. A few desultory inquiries at the station convinced him that if Mrs Clark had fled by rail she had, at all events, not been recognized. It was hardly probable that any of the officials there would know her, he thought, the chances being that they had never set eyes upon her since her first arrival in Rydland some months before.

In the course of the afternoon there was a rumour afloat in the town that old Krabbe was dead, and inquirers at Mr Pegram's office were told it was true that the old man had died very suddenly and unexpectedly.

'They often flicker out in that way, as Dr Roberts, who always attended him, will tell you: he suffered no pain and it was a happy release,' remarked Mr Pegram in answer to questioning by former cronies of the dead man.

The easy-going country doctor was easily persuaded to give a certificate of the death without troubling himself to walk out to the cottage. A day later, and Rydland knew that Mr Krabbe's friends were desirous of laying him with his own family. Three or four strange-looking men arrived in Rydland, habited in rusty black, proceeded to the cottage, and were supposed to have coffined and carried away the dead man by the night mail, though none of the railway servants seemed able exactly to remember having seen a coffin with them. But there was nobody to make any particular inquiries into the case, any more than there was the slightest suspicion that there was anything wrong about it. That Mr Krabbe was dead, and had been carried away from Rydland to be buried by his own people, were facts that were received without comment, and in two or three days more, all talk about the old clerk had come to an end in Rydland.

A week had elapsed, and the old lawyer began to feel pretty comfortable as regarded the consequences of his audacious fraud. He had duly reported the death of his nominee to the Directors of the 'Great Tontine', enclosing Dr Roberts' certificate of death, all of which had been duly acknowledged.

Neither threat nor accusation was fulminated against him from any quarter; and Mr Pegram argued that, had evil been intended him by the discoverers of his imposture, he would have received notice of it ere this. That discovery had been made, he supposed, by Mr Ringwood, agent of Lord Lakington, for Bob had made no mention of Hemmingby, and he reasoned very plausibly that, after the terms on which he had lately stood with Lord Lakington's family, the Viscount would probably not press the charge against him; and could he but have had a peep into Sam Hemmingby's sanctum at the 'Vivacity', he would have given a grim smile in acknowledgement of his own astuteness. He had played a bold game to secure to his son the entire 'Tontine', and lost; yet though he had placed himself within the grip of the law, he bid fair to come off scatheless.

'Yes,' remarked Sam Hemmingby; 'we have regularly "bust up" that fraud. I ran down again to Rydland, as I told you I should, yesterday; Bob Pegram and the nurse have bolted, and they told me in the town that old Mr Krabbe had died suddenly, and that his relations had taken him for burial elsewhere. Of course nobody seemed to know where; nor, as far as casual inquiries went, could I make out that anybody had ever seen a coffin leave Rydland station. We have not, so far, succeeded in working the whole thing out, but the story is now pretty clear. Finding the old man sinking, they took him away for the benefit of his health. If he recovered, well and good; but if he did not, concealment of his death would become easier in a strange place.

That is no doubt what happened; and then Bob Pegram, with his theatrical instinct, conceived the design of personating the dead man himself. It was a very clever idea. They would have been puzzled to pick up a counterfeit so like the original as Bob Pegram made himself up to be. I declare, Ringwood,' replied the manager, enthusiastically, 'it was one of the best bits of character-acting I ever saw. As for the nurse, I have no doubt she is an old theatrical flame of Bob's, upon whom he thought he could thoroughly rely; she was obviously a younger woman than she pretended to be.'

'But how the deuce did they manage when young Pegram was up in London?' inquired Jack Phillimore.

'Easily enough,' replied Hemmingby; 'whenever that was the case, visitors would of course be informed that Mr Krabbe was too unwell to see anybody. Inconvenient inquirers would always be told the same story; and I do not suppose that I should have been allowed inside the house if I had gone there openly. There can be no doubt old Pegram sees now that his scheme is hopeless, and is backing quietly out of it; and both Lord Lakington and Miss Chichester will probably receive a notification in a few days, to the effect that Mr Pegram is no longer a shareholder in the "Tontine", in consequence of the death of his nominee.'

'Miss Chichester's letter would be addressed to Carbuckle. Oddly enough, she has been kept in total ignorance of the "Tontine", and has no idea that she is a shareholder, or even aware that there is such a thing,' observed Ringwood.

'Well,' continued Hemmingby, 'I suspect there is very little doubt that Pegram has drawn his dividends since the actual death of Mr Krabbe; and under those circumstances he has obtained money under false pretences, at the expense of the Viscount and Miss Chichester. Of course, if either of them stir to recover this, the Directors will have to prosecute. I rather hope they will not, although the old fox richly deserves it; still, I should be loath to see him get penal servitude. As far as your uncle goes, Mr Phillimore, I think he can hardly take proceedings, considering the terms upon which he stood with the Pegrams a week ago. But Miss Chichester's case is very different, as the money might easily be recovered from Pegram.'

'I can say nothing about that,' said Ringwood. 'As far as Miss Chichester is concerned, the decision will probably rest with Carbuckle.'

'My uncle will naturally decide for himself,' chimed in Jack Phillimore; 'still I quite agree with Hemmingby, that, under the circumstances, he cannot well prosecute.'

'Well, I trust Carbuckle will take the same view of it,' rejoined the manager as the young men rose. 'Good-bye; and remember, Mr Phillimore, only give me due notice, and I shall be delighted to give you a farewell bachelor dinner at the "Wycherley".'

'I say, Ronald,' remarked Jack Phillimore a little gravely, when they found themselves in the street, 'I am awfully afraid I have put my foot in it. You never told me about the "Tontine" being kept a secret from Miss Chichester; and when I went down to tell my uncle of the discovery of Finnigan, I blurted her name out as the third shareholder, and it is probably all over the house by this time.'

'I rather wish you had not done so,' rejoined Ringwood, 'simply because Miss Caterham expressed a strong wish in her will that Mary should be kept in ignorance of it, unless the "Tontine" should be decided in her favour; but it cannot be helped, and it can be, after all, no great harm done.'

Jack Phillimore was perfectly right in his conjecture, that Lord Lakington would not confine the knowledge of Miss Chichester being the third shareholder of the 'Tontine', to his own breast. He had, as we know, confided it to Beatrice, and it was not long before that sprightly young lady congratulated Mary on her position as an heiress.

'Rival heiresses, my dear! only to think that you or papa – which means me naturally – must come into eight thousand a year; and don't think me mercenary, as I know you must have thought me for consenting to that odious marriage, if I do not congratulate you should you prove successful; but your success would involve the death of my dear old grandmother, which I venture to hope will not occur for some years yet.'

'What on earth are you talking about, Beatrice? what *can* you mean by calling me an heiress? I am sure I should be just as sorry if anything happened to Mrs Lyme Wregis as you would be.'

'Mary Chichester!' exclaimed Beatrice, placing a hand upon either of her friend's shoulders, 'is this affectation? or do you mean seriously to tell me that you never heard of the "Great Tontine"?'

'The "Great Tontine"! no. And what, pray, is a "Tontine"?'

'Well,' rejoined Beatrice, 'I do not know that it is so very curious after all, for till four or five months ago I am sure I had never heard of a "Tontine", nor did I know the meaning of the word; but sit down here by me on this sofa, and I will tell you all about it.'

And then Miss Phillimore proceeded to explain the whole mystery of the big lottery to her friend, and many things that had puzzled Mary no little became easy of understanding now. This, then, was the portentous secret that had so weighed down her aunt; and the girl reflected sadly that, had Miss Caterham only confided in her, she might have done much to combat the nervous depression which had embittered the last weeks of her aunt's existence.

'Poor Terence!' she said at length, 'I had little idea that his life was of such value to us; I declare I wish I had been still in ignorance of the whole affair. There is something a little revolting in speculating on the lives of those we know and are fond of.'

'You are right, it is not nice,' rejoined Miss Phillimore; 'but that is by no means the worst it leads to. A few months back, when you were still searching for Terence Finnigan, this prize was supposed to lie between the Pegrams and ourselves; and in a moment of infatuation I consented to marry Mr Pegram, and so make a certainty of sharing it. Not caring for him in the least – in fact, if anything, slightly despising him – I was weak enough to promise him my hand; and what is more, Mary, if it had not been for the fortunate discovery which rendered this arrangement impracticable, I should have been too great a coward to break my engagement, and should by this have stood at the altar as his bride. You need never fear any repining on my part should the "Great Tontine" fall to your lot, for you have rescued me, hard though I strove to shut my eyes to it at the time, from what I know now would have been life-long misery.'

'You blame yourself too severely, Beatrice. I feel sure you would never have given your consent to that marriage if you had not been over-persuaded by others whose eyes were dazzled by the prospect of wealth – your father, perhaps.'

'My father,' interrupted Miss Phillimore, quickly, 'set before me, as he was bound to do, the advantages, of the match; and I, weak, sordid little idiot that I was, threw over the man whom I loved with all my heart and soul for those golden prospects.'

The girl was loyal to her father to the last. But Mary was a shrewd observer, and had not resided this last fortnight under the same roof with the noble Viscount without arriving at a pretty fair estimate of his character; and now that she was acquainted with the history of the 'Tontine', had no difficulty in guessing how Beatrice's engagement had been brought about.

## CHAPTER THIRTY-THREE

# WEDDING BELLS

It was quite open to question whether Lord Lakington was not as much dismayed at the explosion of the great Pegram fraud as the old lawyer himself. He was grateful to his nephew, no doubt, for preventing his falling a prey to a most audacious imposition; still the fact remained, that he, Viscount Lakington, was left in just as precarious a position regarding income as ever.

'The selfishness of one's own flesh and blood,' he muttered, as he paced his study in serious reflection about what was best for him to do, 'is perfectly disgusting. There are Beatrice and my precious nephew continually purring away like a couple of kittens, and with just as much consideration for their future. I suppose Trixie thinks her having had a narrow escape from marrying an adventurer entitles her to marry a pauper; while my graceless nephew, in consideration of his late services, no doubt thinks himself entitled to claim his cousin's hand. They cannot plead ignorance, for they are in possession now of the whole story of the "Tontine", and yet they go on philandering as if their marriage could by any means be possible, and never thinking for one moment what is to become of ME. I shall really have to speak to Trixie on the subject. Lovers, I know, are proverbially deficient in sympathy for any one but themselves; still, it is deuced selfish of them not to remember what a confoundedly unpleasant position I am in.'

Although the Viscount might argue to himself that it was his nephew's bounden duty to marry money, wherewith to prop up the coronet that would eventually fall to him, yet he had an inward conviction that Jack Phillimore would please himself about choosing a bride; and though he might talk of speaking to his daughter concerning the palpable love-affair going on between herself and her cousin, yet he knew that he had tried Beatrice's obedience to its uttermost limit when she consented to marry Robert Pegram. He knew the powerful motive that had gone to produce that obedience, and could form a pretty shrewd guess as to what that promise had cost her. He had no such reason to urge now, and felt that Beatrice was scarce likely to show such subserviency as to the disposal of her hand in future. He might set his face against the girl wedding her cousin, but he was perfectly aware that Mrs Lyme Wregis encouraged it. He might delay that wedding, no doubt, as Beatrice would hardly venture to take such a step without his consent, but it would be a wedding for all that; and then the Viscount began to think it did not so very much matter if it was. What irritated him was that these young people seemed so utterly to forget his position. Now that they knew all about the 'Tontine', they ought, clearly, to think what was to be done for him. However, in default of being guided by their counsel, his Lordship was now thinking for himself; and now occurred to him that idea which had flashed across Ronald Ringwood on the discovery of Finnigan.

'By the Lord,' he exclaimed, 'why should I not marry Miss Chichester myself, and settle the "Great Tontine" that way? A famous idea! beats the Pegram arrangement hollow; most suitable from every point of view. She is a good-looking girl, and would make a very tidy Viscountess; as for me – egad! I am no age; and,' he continued, after a few minutes' examination in the glass, 'wear devilish well to boot. It will work capitally, and please everybody all round. A coronet and a certainty of a good income. What can Miss Chichester ask for more? Jack may not like it, as it will very possibly cut him out of the title; but then, on the other hand, if he and Beatrice like to make fools of themselves, that will remove all possible objection. I will do it, and with as little delay as possible. I had better, perhaps, take Beatrice into my confidence at once; it would be as well to have her on my side, and she can, if she chooses, aid me materially. Girls object at times to youthful step-mothers, but she and Miss Chichester appear to get on well together. Besides, if she means realizing her present love-dream, who the second Lady Lakington is can be of little consequence to her.'

Having arrived at which conclusion the Viscount rang the bell, and desired the servant to let Miss Phillimore know that he wished to see her.

Beatrice speedily responded to the summons, and entered the room with some little curiosity, but none of that trepidation with which a summons to her father's sanctum had been invested of late.

'My shameful engagement is broken,' she whispered to herself, 'and I have promised to be Jack's wife; and therefore, whatever papa may endeavour to induce me to do, I cannot possibly be led into such trouble as I have escaped from.'

'My dear Beatrice,' commenced the Viscount diplomatically, 'I want to have a few minutes' talk with you. To begin with, I trust you and Jack mean nothing serious.'

'I cannot see anything preposterous, papa, in a girl showing her love for a man when she has promised to marry him. I have promised Jack that, and I mean to keep my word. If you refuse me your consent, we can only wait, and hope that, when you see we are really in earnest, you will no longer withhold it.'

'My dear Beatrice,' rejoined the Viscount, 'you cannot suppose that I have any intention of playing the choleric, pig-headed father of the old comedies. My principal object, my dear child, is to see you happily settled in life. I have been ambitious for you; I am so still. I think you are throwing yourself away in choosing for your husband a mere lieutenant in the navy. No; don't misunderstand me – a most unexceptional lieutenant, I grant you; but it means genteel poverty all the same. Now, I certainly had hoped –'

'To see your daughter happily married, papa dear,' interposed Beatrice smiling; 'and you will. I may never keep my carriage, but we shall not starve; and in the meanwhile there is not a happier girl in the kingdom than I am.'

'It is my duty,' rejoined the Viscount, 'to put the disagreeables of poverty before you just as I before pointed out the advantages of wealth; but there I stop. I shall never oppose your union with the man you have deliberately chosen; still you must excuse my remarking, you seem to have forgotten that the "Great Tontine" is left in a most unsatisfactory state, and that you may any day see me once more walking about, that most miserable of created beings, a pauper peer.'

'I trust not,' replied Beatrice, gravely; 'heaven send that grandmamma be spared to us for some years yet; but, at all events, it no longer rests with me to assist you. I tried my best to do my duty, and can honestly say that, to save you, I would have married Mr Pegram, despise myself though I should have done to my dying day.'

'No, Beatrice,' rejoined the Viscount, 'it is not you, but I, who am called on to sacrifice myself in the interests of the family this time. The regilding of the coronet becomes my duty. To prop up the viscountcy I must marry – marry money; and in proof of my earnestness, I shall entrust the preliminaries to you.'

'To me! why on earth to me? what *can* I do?' inquired Beatrice, taken not a little aback at the idea of her father in the guise of a wooer.

'Pshaw!' replied Lord Lakington. 'If you and Jack had not got into that semi-imbecile state that invariably characterizes young people on the verge of a love match, you must have seen the obvious solution of the "Tontine" difficulty. I intend to make Miss Chichester Viscountess Lakington. One would call it a match designed by heaven, only that the "Tontine" savours somewhat of invention in the other place. Now, I look to you, Trixie, to sound Miss Chichester on this point; and if you find that, like a sensible girl, she sees, as I have no doubt she will do, on which side her bread is buttered, then you can break the ice for me.'

'But, papa dear, I do not know – but I do not think – I mean – that I believe Mary has no idea of marrying just at present.'

'Of course she has not,' rejoined the Viscount. 'It would be very unlady-like if she had. Miss Chichester is far too well-bred a young woman to think of such a thing till some one shows symptoms of asking her.'

'But Mary has romantic notions on this point.'

'Romantic notions! fiddle-dee-dee! God bless me! what more romance can a girl expect than being transformed from a companion into the mistress of a house like Laketon? why, it is Cinderella on a small scale!'

'I will do my best, papa; but, indeed, indeed, I have great doubts of succeeding.'

'I understand, Trixie; as your father, I no doubt seem a sort of Methuselah in your eyes, though other young ladies by no means regard me as so antiquated. Tastes differ, and the boys don't always have it their own way. Do as I bid you, and let me know the result.'

About two or three days afterwards the Viscount, rather to his amazement, was informed by his daughter that Miss Chichester. upon being sounded as to the possibility of winding up the 'Tontine' in the way Lord Lakington proposed, had expressed herself very prettily, but very decidedly, in the negative. She was grateful to him, and all of them, for their kindness; she thoroughly appreciated and thanked Lord Lakington for the honour he had done her, and she was willing to meet his views about the 'Tontine' in any way; but that arrangement could never be; and the Viscount consequently had to once more ponder in his study over that, to him, stupendous problem of 'What is to become of ME?'

It speedily occurred to him that the next thing to try was to effect a compromise. Miss Chichester had stated her readiness to meet his views in any way but matrimony, and he would therefore write to Carbuckle, and propose a division of the big lottery, stipulating further, as part of the arrangement, that there should be no prosecution of the Pegrams, as Miss Phillimore's name would be almost sure to be mixed up in such a trial. 'In short,' concluded the Viscount, 'I made a confounded mistake in ever knowing these people at all; a still greater blunder in nearly allowing Beatrice to marry into such a family. No one likes to be reminded of his folly, and I am particularly anxious that the world should forget my daughter's ill-fated engagement.'

Now this stipulation, luckily for the Viscount, gave rise to a very considerable hitch in the negotiation. Mr Carbuckle, honestly anxious to do the best he could for his ward, was perfectly willing to accede to the

Viscount's proposal of a division. Four thousand a-year would be considered quite sufficient fortune for any girl; and it was very much better that Mary Chichester should make a certainty of that than stand out for the chance of winning everything, depending, as it did, upon such a precarious life as Terence Finnigan's. But Mr Carbuckle, like many of his fellows, had a vindictive dislike to being 'done'; and upon such occasions as he had been imposed upon had always manifested much persistency in retaliation. Now these Pegrams had no doubt swindled Mary Chichester out of something like thirteen hundred pounds, and the barrister had no idea of their not being brought to account for it. Not only, he held, did these fraudulent solicitors richly deserve punishment for their misdeeds, but it was further his duty to recover this money for his ward if possible; and he was given to understand that Mr Pegram was a substantial man, who could be easily compelled to disgorge his plunder. Lord Lakington, if he chose, might forgive him; but he, Mr Carbuckle, had clearly no power to condone their offence. It was his business to recover Mary Chichester's money, and from that point they were unable to move him. The Viscount was in despair, and his first idea was to approach Mary upon the subject, either through his daughter or nephew; but they both declined positively to discuss the thing with her in any shape.

'I should say the division was a judicious thing both for you and her; and that, on coming into such an income, Miss Chichester could well afford to lose such a sum. Do the magnanimous, and let these miserable Pegrams go,' said Jack. 'But then, you know, most people would simply laugh at the idea of being so foolish as sitting still under the loss of thirteen hundred pounds, which might be easily recovered; and remember, it is us for whom this trial would be unpleasant, not Miss Chichester.'

However, after a few days Mr Carbuckle came to the conclusion that his ward ought to be consulted on the point. He put it very fairly before her, and that young lady settled the thing in a most off-hand manner.

'My dear guardian,' she exclaimed, 'I have got to know and love these people very dearly. I would certainly make considerable sacrifice to save any of them from annoyance; and as for Beatrice, would forego a much bigger sum than what you name sooner than that miserably mistaken engagement of hers should be flouted in her face before all the world. Remember that, as far as I am concerned, four thousand a-year represents fabulous wealth – more, a great deal, than I shall ever know how to spend.'

'I don't know,' rejoined Mr Carbuckle, drily; 'it is astonishing how rapidly people's ideas enlarge with their income.'

'We will not argue about that,' replied Mary laughing. 'I told Lord Lakington that I would meet his wishes as to the "Tontine" in any way I could when he threw out a hint that some arrangement might be desirable; and therefore, all I can say is, my dear guardian, pray let the necessary deed, agreement, or whatever it is, be drawn out as soon as possible. Do you ever see Mr Ringwood, by the way?'

'Well, I cannot say that I have lately. Perhaps he is busy – busy making out his bill of costs against you, Miss Mary. I am afraid there is an awful settlement staring you in the face.'

'That, of course, I shall look to you to manage; but pray remember, that I wish it done on a very liberal scale.'

'Pooh! nonsense, child; I am only joking. Ringwood worked hard on your behalf in the "Tontine", it is true; but, I feel sure, would be as deeply affronted as I should be at the idea of any recompense in money for his services.'

'But what other recompense can I make him?' exclaimed Mary.

'Oh! well, I am sure I don't know; I must leave him to tell you that himself; but he is an audacious young man, and there is no knowing what he may ask for. Good-bye.'

Miss Chichester had more than once meditated upon the persistency with which Ringwood had held aloof from her. Adhering steadily to his determination, he had never been near the house in the Victoria Road since their expedition to Portsmouth, and Mary began to think that she had somewhat over-estimated her power over him. A short time back, and she would have been quite justified in considering him an admirer, likely, on very slight encouragement, to turn into a lover; but she thought now that his feeling towards her must have been probably nothing more than a mere passing fancy, and Mary was not altogether pleased with this reflection. Without giving her heart away before it was asked for, she had, nevertheless, thought a good deal of Ronald Ringwood, and felt rather indignant that he should have so soon ceased to think about her. Perhaps he would come down with this agreement regarding the division of the 'Tontine'. She would like to see him again, just to convince herself how mistaken she had been in supposing he had ever cared about her; and in that respect she was destined to be speedily gratified.

Mr Carbuckle was startled one morning by Ringwood bursting into his room, bearing in his hand a piece of pink tissue-paper.

'By Jove! Carbuckle,' he exclaimed, 'I think this is the hardest luck I ever heard of. Here is a telegram from Mattox, the master of Portsmouth Workhouse, come to say that Terence Finnigan is dead – died about half-past eight o'clock this morning – full particulars by post; and there is that agreement between Lord Lakington and Miss Chichester still unsigned. After all our trouble, to think she should lose four thousand a-year by about forty-eight hours! It was to have been signed the day after tomorrow.'

'Yes, this is very hard upon Mary, though she will fret less about it than any girl I know. I have no doubt that telegram is true, and, as you say, the deed not being signed, Lakington lands the whole "Tontine". What a *coup* for the noble Viscount! There is one thing – I will have that thirteen hundred pounds out of old Pegram now. I reluctantly consented to the abandoning of that claim when Mary was an heiress, but I shall have to point out to her now, that poor people cannot and must not allow themselves to be swindled out of such sums. I shall have to go down to the Victoria Road and tell them all about this, although I am confoundedly busy. It is no use asking you, I suppose?'

'I will go for you if you like,' replied Ringwood, quietly.

Mr Carbuckle stared at him for a minute, and then said:

'Well, I wish you would; and I will engage that, when you tell Miss Chichester the news, you will find her what we used to call in my racing days "a good loser".'

However young ladies may blind their masculine relations as to the state of their affections, they find it hard to throw dust in the eyes of their sisters. Mary Chichester was a by no means gushing young woman – not at all of that kind who wear their heart upon their sleeve. She had never breathed a word of the half-developed feeling which undoubtedly possessed her in favour of Ronald Ringwood; but for all that, Beatrice had penetrated her friend's secret, and strongly conjectured that, whenever the young barrister chose to throw himself at her feet, he would not woo in vain, granted even that she was the winner of the 'Great Tontine', and possessor of eight thousand a-year.

When Johnson, accordingly, threw open the door and announced Mr Ringwood, there was no little flutter in the drawing-room in the Victoria Road. Mary felt that from that interview she should be able to decide as to whether Ringwood really cared for her or not; while Beatrice felt no slight curiosity to ascertain for herself how far she was right in her suspicions. She had, it must be borne in mind, barely seen the two together so far, and on that one occasion Mary was comparatively a new acquaintance, and not the intimate friend she had since become. The curiosity, not only of Beatrice, but even of Mrs Lyme Wregis, was, however, thoroughly roused, when his greetings once said, Ringwood observed quietly –

'I have come, Miss Chichester, I regret to say, to break bad news to you; and if Mrs Lyme Wregis will excuse us, I should prefer that you alone heard my evil tidings in the first place.'

'Certainly, Mr Ringwood,' replied the old lady. 'Take him into the dining-room, Mary, my dear; and do not forget that, whatever trouble he may have to tell, Trixie and I are waiting upstairs to comfort you.'

Mary thanked the old lady with an eloquent glance, and merely saying, 'This way, Mr Ringwood, if you please,' led the way below.

No sooner had the door closed behind them than, turning towards the barrister, she exclaimed –

'Nothing has happened to Mr Carbuckle?'

'He is perfectly well,' replied Ringwood. 'My bad news, Miss Chichester, is connected with the "Great Tontine". I have received a telegram from Mr Mattox, the master, as you may remember, of Portsmouth Workhouse, to say that Terence Finnigan is dead.'

'Poor Terence!' replied the girl, 'I am sorry for him; though when existence has become so merely mechanical as his was, one cannot but feel that death is deprived of all its terrors.'

'His end, you will be glad to hear,' continued Ringwood, 'was painless. But you do not seem to realize, that by his death your share in the "Tontine" becomes void; and I am sorry to inform you, – and it is this more especially that Mr Carbuckle wished me to point out to you, – that the agreement between you and Lord Lakington being still unsigned, it is not worth the paper it is written on.'

'I understand,' replied Mary, quietly. 'You mean to say that Lord Lakington takes the whole "Tontine", and that my prospect of being an heiress has melted into thin air.'

'That, I regret to say, is the exact state of the case; and very, very hard luck for you it is.'

'Well, Mr Ringwood, I am not going to pretend to you that I am wholly indifferent to the loss of four thousand a year; but after all, remember, I only stand in the same position that I did three or four weeks ago; and never having had the spending of such an income, I very partially realize the loss of it. I shall always feel that I can never be sufficiently grateful to you for all the time and trouble you have wasted, first on my aunt's behalf, and then on my own.'

'Not altogether wasted,' replied Ringwood. 'As Carbuckle observed when he heard the news, now that you have lost a fortune you cannot afford to neglect small pickings. The finding of Terence Finnigan will still entitle you to recover from Mr Pegram your share of the money he so fraudulently acquired.'

'Pray tell my guardian that nothing will induce me to consent to any such proceedings being taken. It would be next to impossible to take them without dragging the whole story of the "Tontine" and the names of Lord Lakington and Beatrice before the public; and knowing as I do how Beatrice dreads the bare idea of such a thing, I would not have it happen to recover double the money; and now I presume there is no more to be said. Had I become the rich woman I expected, I should have consulted Mr Carbuckle whether it were in any way possible to repay your devotion to the cause of my aunt and myself. As a well-nigh penniless maiden, Mr Ringwood, I am afraid sincere thanks is all I have to offer,' and with this Mary moved towards the door.

'Stay a moment, Miss Chichester,' exclaimed Ringwood eagerly; 'I have something more to say to you – of little moment, it may be, to you, but a very grave matter to me. I have loved you sincerely, and hoped to make you my wife, almost from the beginning of our acquaintance. If I have never ventured to tell you so before, the "Tontine" must be my excuse. I was always in possession of the facts of the case, while you were not; and I dreaded not so much what the world might say as what you might think, when, supposing I had the good fortune to win you, you should discover that I had known of the possibility of your being an heiress all along. I could not face that; and I swore to keep aloof from you until this lottery was decided one way or the other. I could have even dared to put my fate to the test had you won the whole and become a great heiress. There would, at all events, have been nothing underhand about my wooing then. Whatever answer you may give me now, you must, at all events, acquit me of mercenary motives, and feel sure that I love you for yourself. I love you very dearly, Mary; do you think you could love me well enough to be my wife?'

'You have taken me so by surprise that I hardly know,' faltered the girl; 'but, believe me, no one can more thoroughly appreciate the delicacy of your conduct than I do, and it is that which makes me now hesitate. Your wife, Mr Ringwood, ought to be a woman who not only loves you dearly, but can enter fully into the career which I am sure is before you; and unless I feel certain I could be all this to you, I would say you "nay", whatever my own feelings might be. Will you give me a little time to think over it? Come and see me tomorrow, and I will honestly answer your question.'

'It is more than I dared to hope for,' replied Ringwood, as he raised her hand to his lips; 'please make my adieu upstairs, and till tomorrow, good-bye.'

That the finishing of the 'Great Tontine' resulted in a double wedding it is almost superfluous to add; but that Lord Lakington, under the strenuous pressure of his nephew and daughter, was induced to settle ten thousand pounds upon Mary Chichester as a wedding gift is a fact that deserves to be recorded, the Viscount, after the somewhile manner of those who have been spendthrifts in their youth, developing a laudable ambition for the accumulation of riches in his mature age.

# THE ROME EXPRESS

## MAJOR ARTHUR GRIFFITHS

## CHAPTER ONE

The Rome Express, the *direttissimo*, or most direct, was approaching Paris one morning in March, when it became known to the occupants of the *wagon-lit* that there was something amiss, very much amiss, in the car.

The train was travelling the last stage, between Laroche and Paris, a run of a hundred miles without a stop. It had halted at Laroche for early *café au lait*, and many, if not all the passengers, had turned out for breakfast. Of those in the sleeping-car, seven in number, six had been seen in the restaurant, or about the platform; the seventh, a lady, had not stirred. All had re-entered their berths to sleep or doze when the train went on, but several were on the move as it neared Paris, taking their turn at the lavatory, calling for water, towels, making the usual stir of preparation as the end of a journey was at hand.

There were many calls for the conductor, yet no conductor appeared. At last the attendant was found – lazy villain! – asleep, snoring loudly, stertorously, in his little bunk at the end of the car. He was roused with difficulty, and set about his work in a dull, unwilling, lethargic way, which promised badly for his *pourboires* from those he was supposed to serve.

By degrees all the passengers got dressed; all but two – the lady in 9 and 10, who had made no sign as yet; and the man who occupied alone a double berth next to her, numbered 7 and 8.

As it was the conductor's duty to call everyone, and as he was anxious, like the rest of his class, to get rid of his travellers as soon as possible after arrival, he rapped at each of the two closed doors behind which people presumably still slept.

The lady cried '*Très bien*', but there was no answer from No. 7 and 8.

Again and again the conductor knocked and called loudly. Still meeting with no response, he opened the door of the compartment and went in.

It was now broad daylight. No blind was down; indeed, the one narrow window was open, wide; and the whole of the interior of the compartment was plainly visible, all and everything in it.

The occupant lay on his bed motionless. Sound asleep? No, not merely asleep – the twisted unnatural lie of the limbs, the contorted legs, the one arm drooping listlessly but stiffly over the side of the berth, told of a deeper, more eternal sleep.

The man was dead. Dead – and not from natural causes.

One glance at the blood-stained bedclothes, one look at the gaping wound in the breast, at the battered, mangled face, told the terrible story.

It was murder! Murder most foul! The victim had been stabbed to the heart.

With a wild, affrighted cry the conductor rushed out of the compartment, and to the eager questioning of all who crowded round him, he could only mutter in confused and trembling accents –

'There! There! In there!'

Thus the fact of the murder became known to everyone by personal inspection, for everyone (even the lady had shown for just a moment) had looked in where the body lay. The compartment was filled for some ten minutes or more by an excited, gesticulating, polyglot mob of half a dozen, all talking at once in French, English, and Italian.

The first attempt to restore order was made by a tall man, middle-aged, but erect in his bearing, with bright eyes and alert manner, who took the conductor aside, and said sharply in good French, but with a strong English accent –

'Here! It's your business to do something. No one has any right to be in that compartment now. There may be reasons – traces – things to remove; never mind what. But get them all out. Be sharp about it; and lock the door. Remember you will be held responsible to justice.'

The conductor shuddered, so did many of the passengers who had overheard the Englishman's last words.

Justice! It is not to be trifled with anywhere, least of all in France, where the uncomfortable superstition prevails that everyone who can be reasonably suspected of a crime is held to be guilty of that crime until his innocence is clearly proved.

All those six passengers and the conductor were now brought within the category of the accused. They were all open to suspicion; they, and they alone, for the murdered man had been seen alive at Laroche, and the fell deed must have been done since then, while the train was in transit, that is to say, going at express speed, when no one could leave it except at peril of his life.

'Deuced awkward for us!' said the tall English general, Sir Charles Collingham by name, to his brother the parson, when he had re-entered their compartment and shut the door.

'I can't see it. As how?' asked the Reverend Silas Collingham, a typical

English cleric, with a rubicund face and square-cut white whiskers, dressed in a suit of black serge, and wearing the professional white tie.

'Why, we shall be detained, of course; arrested, probably – certainly detained. Examined, cross-examined, bully-ragged – I know something of the French police and their ways.'

'If they stop us, I shall write to *The Times*,' cried his brother, by profession a man of peace, but with a choleric eye that told of an angry temperament.

'By all means, my dear Silas, when you get the chance. That won't be just yet, for I tell you we're in a tight place, and may expect a good deal of worry.' With that he took out his cigarette-case, with his matchbox and tinder, lighted his cigarette, and calmly watched the smoke rising with all the *sangfroid* of an old campaigner accustomed to encounter and face the ups and downs of life. 'I only hope to goodness they'll run straight on to Paris,' he added in a fervent tone, not unmixed with apprehension. 'No! By jingo, we're slackening speed –'

'Why shouldn't we? It's right the guard, or chief of the train, or whatever you call him, should know what has happened.'

'Why, man, can't you see? While the train is travelling express, everyone must stay on board it; if it slows, it is possible to leave it.'

'Who would want to leave it?'

'Oh, I don't know,' said the General rather testily. 'Anyway, the thing's done now.'

The train had pulled up in obedience to the signal of alarm given by someone in the sleeping-car, but by whom it was impossible to say. Not by the conductor, for he seemed greatly surprised as the *chef de train* came up to him.

'How did you know?' he asked.

'Know! Know what? You stopped me.'

'I didn't.'

'Who rang the bell, then?'

'I did not. But I'm glad you've come. There has been a *sinistre* – the *assassinat*.'

'*Grand Dieu!*' cried the *chef*, jumping up on to the car, and entering into the situation at once. His business was only to verify the fact, and take all necessary precautions. He was a burly, brusque, peremptory person, the despotic, self-important French official, who knew what to do – as he thought – and did it without hesitation or apology.

'No one must leave the *wagon-lit*,' he said in a tone not to be misunderstood. 'Neither now, nor on arrival at the Gare.'

There was a shout of protest and dismay, which he quickly cut short.

'You will have to arrange it with the authorities in Paris; they can alone decide. My duty is plain: to detain you, place you under surveillance till then. Afterwards, we will see. Enough, Messieurs et Madame –'

He bowed with the instinctive gallantry of his nation to the female figure which now appeared at the door of her compartment. She stood for a moment listening, seemingly greatly agitated, and then, without a word, disappeared, retreating hastily into her own private room, where she shut herself in.

Almost immediately, at a signal from the guard, the train resumed its journey. The distance remaining to be traversed was short; half an hour more, and the Gare de Lyons was reached, where the bulk of the passengers – all, indeed, but the occupants of the *wagon-lit* – descended and passed through the barriers. The latter were again desired to keep their places, while a posse of officials came and mounted guard. Presently they were told to leave the car one by one, but to take nothing with them. All their handbags, rugs, and belongings were to remain in the berths, just as they lay. One by one they were marched under escort to a large and bare waiting-room, which had, no doubt, been prepared for their reception.

Here they took their seats on chairs placed at wide intervals apart, and were peremptorily forbidden to hold any communication with each other, by word or gesture. This order was enforced by a fierce-looking Garde de Paris in blue and red uniform, who stood facing them with his arms folded, gnawing his moustache and frowning severely.

Last of all, the conductor was brought in and treated like the passengers, but more distinctly as a prisoner. He had a Garde de Paris all to himself; and it seemed as though he was the object of peculiar suspicion. It had no great effect upon him, for, while the rest of the party were very plainly sad, and a prey to lively apprehension, the conductor sat dull and unmoved, with the stolid, sluggish, unconcerned aspect of a man just roused from sound sleep and relapsing into slumber, who takes little notice of what is passing around.

Meanwhile, the sleeping-car, with its contents, especially the corpse of the victim, was shunted into a siding, and sentries were placed on it at both ends. Seals had been affixed upon the entrance doors, so that the interior might be kept inviolate until it could be visited and examined by the Chef de la Sûreté, or head of the detective police.

Everyone and everything awaited the arrival of this all-important functionary.

CHAPTER TWO

M. Floçon, the Chef de la Sûreté, was an early man, and he paid a first visit to his bureau about 7 a.m.

He lived just round the corner in the Rue des Arcs, and had not far to go to the Prefecture. But even now, soon after daylight, he was correctly dressed, as became a responsible ministerial officer. He wore a tight frock-coat and an immaculate white tie; under his arm he carried the regulation portfolio, or *serviette d'avocat*, stuffed full of reports, *procès verbaux*, and documents dealing with cases in hand. He was altogether a very precise and natty little personage, quiet and unpretending in demeanour, with a mild, thoughtful face in which two small ferrety eyes blinked and twinkled behind gold-rimmed glasses. But when things went wrong, when he had to deal with fools, or when scent was keen, or the enemy near, he would become as fierce and eager as any terrier.

He had just taken his place at his table and begun to arrange his papers, which, being a man of method, he kept carefully sorted by lots each in an old copy of the *Figaro*, when he was called to the telephone. His services were greatly needed, as we know, at the Gare de Lyons, and the summons was to the following effect: *Sinistre train 45. Assassinat, homme, wagon lit. Tous voyageurs détenus. Prière venir sans aucun délai. Grande urgence* . . .

A fiacre was called instantly, and M. Floçon, accompanied by Galipaud and Block, the two first inspectors for duty, was driven with all possible speed across Paris.

He was met outside the station, just under the wide verandah, by the officials, who gave him a brief outline of the facts, so far as they were known, and as they have already been put before the reader.

'The passengers have been detained?' asked M. Floçon at once.

'Those in the sleeping-car only –'

'Tut, tut! They should have been all kept – at least until you had taken their names and addresses. Who knows what they might not have been able to tell?'

It was suggested that as the crime was committed presumably while the train was in motion, only those in the car could be implicated.

'We should never jump to conclusions,' said the Chef snappishly. 'Well, show me the *feuille de route* – the list of the travellers in the *wagon-lit*.'

'It cannot be found, M. le Chef.'

'Impossible! Why, it is the conductor's business to produce it at the end of the journey to his superiors, and *à qui de droit* – to us. Where is the conductor? In custody?'

'Surely, M. le Chef, but there is something wrong with him.'

'So I should think! Nothing of this kind could well occur without his knowledge. If he was doing his duty – unless, of course, he – but let us avoid hasty conjectures.'

'He has also lost the passengers' tickets, which you know he retains till the end of the journey. After the catastrophe, however, he was unable to lay his hand upon his pocket-book. It contained all his papers.'

'Worse and worse. There is something behind all this. Take me to him. Stay, can I have a private room close to the other – where the prisoners, the *détenus*, are? It will be necessary to hold investigations, draw up *procès verbaux*. M. le Juge will be here directly.'

M. Floçon was soon installed in a room actually communicating with the waiting-room, and as a preliminary of the first importance, taking precedence even of the examination of the sleeping-car, he ordered the conductor to be brought in to answer certain questions.

The man, Ludwig Groote, as he presently gave his name, thirty-two years of age, born at Amsterdam, looked such a sluggish, slouching, blear-eyed creature that M. Floçon began by a sharp rebuke.

'Now. *Alerte!* Are you always like this?' cried the Chef.

The conductor still stared straight before him with lacklustre eyes, and made no immediate reply.

'Are you drunk? Are you – Can it be possible?' he said, and in vague reply to a sudden strong suspicion, he went on –

'What were you doing between Laroche and Paris? Sleeping?'

The man roused himself a little. 'I think I slept. I must have slept. I was very drowsy. I had been up two nights; but so it is always, and I am not like this generally. I do not understand.'

'Hah!' The Chef thought he understood. 'Did you feel this drowsiness before leaving Laroche?'

'No, monsieur, I did not. Certainly not. I was fresh till then – quite fresh.'

'Hum; exactly; I see'; and the little Chef de Sûreté jumped to his feet and ran round to where the conductor stood sheepishly, and sniffed and smelt at him.

'Yes, yes.' Sniff, sniff, sniff, the little man danced round and round him, then took hold of the conductor's head with one hand, and with the other turned down his lower eyelid so as to expose the eyeball, sniffed a little more, and then resumed his seat.

'*Parfaitement.* And now, where is your *feuille de route?*'

'Pardon, monsieur, I cannot find it.'

'That is absurd. Where do you keep it? Look again – search – I must have it.'

The conductor shook his head hopelessly.

'It is gone, monsieur, and my pocket-book.'

'But your papers, the tickets –'

'Everything was in it, monsieur. I must have dropped it.'

Strange, very strange. However – the fact was to be recorded, for the moment. He could of course return to it.

'You can give me the names of the passengers?'

'No, monsieur. Not exactly. I cannot remember, not enough to distinguish between them.'

'*Fichtre!* But this is most devilishly irritating. To think that I have to do with a man so *bête* – such an idiot, such an ass!'

'At least you know how the berths were occupied, how many in each, and which persons? Yes? You can tell me that? Well, go on. By and by we will have the passengers in, and you can fix their places, after I have ascertained their names. Now, please! For how many was the *wagon?*'

'Sixteen. There were two compartments of four berths each, and four of two berths each.'

'Stay, let us make a plan. I will draw it; Here, now, is that right?' and the Chef held up the rough diagram, here shown –

| 4 Berths 1, 2, 3, 4 | 2 Berths 5, 6 | 2 7, 8 | 2 9, 10 | 2 11, 12 | 4 Berths 13, 14, 15, 16 | |
|---|---|---|---|---|---|---|
| a | b | c | d | e | f | |

| Entrance door | Corridor | Conductor's seat |
|---|---|---|

Entrance door

'Here we have the six compartments. Now take *a*, with berths 1, 2, 3, and 4. Were they all occupied?'

'No; only two, by Englishmen. I know that they talked English, which I understand a little. One was a *militaire*; the other, I think, a clergyman, or *pasteur.*'

'Good! we can verify that directly. Now, *b*, with berths 5 and 6. Who was there?'

'One gentleman. I don't remember his name. But I shall know him by appearance.'

'Go on. In *c*, two berths, 7 and 8?'

'Also one gentleman. It was he who – I mean, that is where the *sinistre* occurred.'

'Ah, indeed, in 7 and 8? Very well. And the next, 9 and 10?'

'A lady. Our only lady. She came from Rome.'

'One moment. Where did the rest come from? did any embark *en route*?'

'No, monsieur; all the passengers travelled through from Rome.'

'The dead man included? Was he Roman?'

'That I cannot say, but he came on board at Rome.'

'Very well. This lady – she was alone?'

'In the compartment, yes. But not altogether.'

'I do not understand?'

'She had her servant with her.'

'In the car?'

'No, not in the car. As a passenger by second class. But she came to her mistress sometimes, in the car.'

'For her service, I presume?'

'Well, yes, monsieur, when I would permit it. But she came a little too often, and I was compelled to protest, to speak to Madame la Comtesse –'

'She was a countess, then?'

'The maid addressed her by that title. That is all I know. I heard her.'

'When did you see the lady's maid last?'

'Last night. I think at Amberieux, about 8 p.m.'

'Not this morning?'

'No, sir, I am quite sure of that.'

'Not at Laroche? She did not come on board to stay, for the last stage, when her mistress would be getting up, dressing, and likely to require her?'

'No; I should not have permitted it.'

'And where is the maid now, d'you suppose?'

The conductor looked at him with an air of complete imbecility.

'She is surely somewhere near, in or about the station. She would hardly desert her mistress now,' he said stupidly, at last.

'At any rate we can soon settle that.' The Chef turned to one of his assistants, both of whom had been standing behind him all the time, and said –

'Step out, Galipaud, and see. No, wait. I am nearly as *bête* as this simpleton. Describe this maid.'

'Tall and slight, dark-eyed, very black hair. Dressed all in black, plain black bonnet. I cannot remember more.'

'Find her, Galipaud – keep your eye on her. We may want her – why, I cannot say, as she seems disconnected with the event, but still she ought to be at hand.' Then, turning to the conductor, he went on. 'Finish, please. You said 9 and 10 was the lady's. Well, 11 and 12?'

'It was vacant all through the run.'

'And the last compartment, for four?'

'There were two berths, occupied both by Frenchmen, at least so I judged them. They talked French to each other and to me.'

'Then now we have them all. Stand aside, please, and I will make the passengers come in. We will then determine their places and affix their names from their own admissions. Call them in, Block, one by one.'.

## CHAPTER THREE

The questions put by M. Floçon were much the same in every case, and were
limited in this early stage of the inquiry to the one point of identity.

The first who entered was a Frenchman. He was a jovial, fat-faced, portly
man, who answered to the name of Anatole Lafolay, and who described
himself as a traveller in precious stones. The berth he had occupied was No.
13 in compartment *f*. His companion in the berth was a younger man,
smaller, slighter, but of much the same stamp. His name was Jules Devaux,
and he was a commission agent. His berth had been No. 15 in the same
compartment, *f*. Both these Frenchmen gave their addresses with the names
of many people to whom they were well known, and established at once a
reputation for respectability which was greatly in their favour.

The third to appear was the tall, grey-headed Englishman, who had taken
a certain lead at the first discovery of the crime. He called himself General
Sir Charles Collingham, an officer of Her Majesty's Army; and the clergyman who shared the compartment was his brother, the Reverend Silas
Collingham, rector of Theakstone-Lammas, in the county of Norfolk. Their
berths were numbered 1 and 4 in *a*.

Before the English General was dismissed, he asked whether he was likely
to be detained.

'For the present, yes,' replied M. Floçon briefly. He did not care to be asked
questions. That, under the circumstances, was his business.

'Because I should like to communicate with the British Embassy.'

'You are known there?' asked the Chef, not choosing to believe the story at
first. It might be a ruse of some sort.

'I know Lord Dufferin personally; I was with him in India. Also Colonel
Papillon, the military attaché; we were in the same regiment. If I sent to the
Embassy, the latter would, no doubt, come himself.'

'How do you propose to send?'

'That is for you to decide. All I wish is that it should be known that my
brother and I are detained under suspicion, and incriminated.'

'Hardly that, Monsieur le Général. But it shall be as you wish. We will telephone from here to the post nearest the Embassy to inform His Excellency –'

'Certainly, Lord Dufferin, and my friend, Colonel Papillon.'

'Of what has occurred. And now, if you will permit me to proceed?'

So the single occupant of the compartment *b*, that adjoining the Englishmen, was called in. He was an Italian, by name Natale Ripaldi; a dark-skinned man, with very black hair and a bristling black moustache. He wore a long dark cloak of the Inverness order, and, with the slouch hat he carried in his hand, and his downcast, secretive look, he had the rather conventional aspect of a conspirator.

'If monsieur permits,' he volunteered to say after the formal questioning was over, 'I can throw some light on this catastrophe.'

'And how so, pray? Did you assist? Were you present? If so, why wait to speak till now?' said the Chef, receiving the advance rather coldly. It behoved him to be very much on his guard.

'I have had no opportunity till now of addressing anyone in authority. You are in authority, I presume?'

'I am the Chef de la Sûreté.'

'Then, monsieur, remember, please, that I can give some useful information when called upon. Now, indeed, if you will receive it.'

M. Floçon was so anxious to approach the inquiry without prejudice that he put up his hand.

'We will wait, if you please. When M. le Juge arrives, then, perhaps; at any rate, at a later stage. That will do now, thank you.'

The Italian's lip curled with a slight indication of contempt at the French detective's methods, but he bowed without speaking, and went out.

Last of all the lady appeared, in a long sealskin travelling cloak, and closely veiled. She answered M. Floçon's questions in a low, tremulous voice, as though greatly perturbed.

She was the Contessa di Castagneto, she said, an Englishwoman by birth; but her husband had been an Italian, as the name implied, and they resided in Rome. He was dead – she had been a widow for two or three years, and was on her way now to London.

'That will do, madame, thank you,' said the Chef politely, 'for the present at least.'

'Why, are we likely to be detained? I trust not.' Her voice became appealing, almost piteous. Her hands, restlessly moving, showed how much she was distressed.

'Indeed, Madame la Comtesse, it must be so. I regret it infinitely; but until we have gone further into this, have elicited some facts, arrived at some conclusions – But there, madame, I need not, must not say more.'

'Oh, monsieur, I was so anxious to continue my journey. Friends are awaiting me in London. I do hope – I most earnestly beg and entreat you to spare me. I am not very strong; my health is indifferent. Do, sir, be so good as to release me from –'

As she spoke, she raised her veil, and showed what no woman wishes to hide, least of all when seeking the goodwill of one of the opposite sex. She had a handsome face – strikingly so. Not even the long journey, the fatigue, the worries and anxieties which had supervened, could rob her of her marvellous beauty.

She was a brilliant brunette, dark-skinned; but her complexion was of a clear, pale olive, and as soft, as lustrous as pure ivory. Her great eyes, of a deep velvety brown, were saddened by near tears. She had rich red lips, the only colour in her face, and these, habitually slightly apart, showed pearly-white glistening teeth.

It was difficult to look at this charming woman without being affected by her beauty. M. Floçon was a Frenchman, gallant and impressionable; yet he steeled his heart. A detective must beware of sentiment, and he seemed to see something insidious in this appeal, which he resented.

'Madame, it is useless,' he answered gruffly. 'I do not make the law; I have only to support it. Every good citizen is bound to that.'

'I trust I am a good citizen,' said the Countess, with a wan smile, but very wearily. 'Still, I should wish to be let off now. I have suffered greatly, terribly, by this horrible catastrophe. My nerves are quite shattered. It is too cruel. However, I can say no more, except to ask that you will let my maid come to me.'

M. Floçon, still obdurate, would not even consent to that.

'I fear, madame, that for the present at least you cannot be allowed to communicate with anyone, not even with your maid.'

'But she is not implicated; she was not in the car. I have not seen her since –'

'Since?' repeated M. Floçon, after a pause.

'Since last night, at Amberieux, about eight o'clock. She helped me to undress, and saw me to bed. I sent her away then, and said I should not need her till we reached Paris. But I want her now, indeed I do.'

'She did not come to you at Laroche?'

'No. Have I not said so? The conductor,' – here she pointed to the man, who stood staring at her from the other side of the table – 'he made difficulties about her being in the car, saying that she came too often, stayed too long, that I must pay for her berth, and so on. I did not see why I should do that; so she stayed away.'

'Except from time to time?'

'Precisely.'

'And the last time was at Amberieux?'

'As I have told you, and the conductor will tell you the same.'

'Thank you, madame, that will do.' The Chef rose from his chair, plainly intimating that the interview was at an end.

## CHAPTER FOUR

He had other work to do, and was eager to get at it. So he left Block to show the Countess back to the waiting-room, and, motioning to the conductor that he might also go, the Chef hastened to the sleeping car, the examination of which, too long delayed, claimed his urgent attention.

It is the first duty of a good detective to visit the actual theatre of a crime and overhaul it inch by inch, – seeking, searching, investigating, looking for any, even the most insignificant, traces of the murderer's hands.

The sleeping-car, as I have said, had been shunted, its doors were sealed, and it was under strict watch and ward. But everything, of course, gave way before the Chef de la Sûreté, and, breaking through the seals, he walked in, making straight for the little room or compartment where the body of the victim still lay untended and absolutely untouched.

It was a ghastly sight, although not new in M. Floçon's experience. There lay the corpse in the narrow berth, just as it had been stricken. It was partially undressed, wearing only shirt and drawers. The former lay open at the chest, and showed the gaping wound that had, no doubt, caused death, probably instantaneous death. But other blows had been struck; there must have been a struggle, fierce and embittered, as for dear life. The savage truculence of the murderer had triumphed, but not until he had battered in the face, destroying features and rendering recognition almost impossible.

A knife had given the mortal wound; that was at once apparent from the shape of the wound. It was the knife, too, which had gashed and stabbed the face, almost wantonly; for some of these wounds had not bled, and the plain inference was that they had been inflicted after life had sped.

M. Floçon examined the body closely, but without disturbing it. The police medical officer would wish to see it as it was found. The exact position, as well as the nature of the wounds, might afford evidence as to the manner of death.

But the Chef looked long, and with absorbed, concentrated interest, at the murdered man, noting all he actually saw, and conjecturing a good deal more.

The features of the mutilated face were all but unrecognizable, but the hair, which was abundant, was long, black, and inclined to curl; the black moustache was thick and drooping. The shirt was of fine linen, the drawers silk. On one finger were two good rings, the hands were clean, the nails well kept, and there was every evidence that the man did not live by manual labour. He was of the easy, cultured class, as distinct from the workman or operative.

This conclusion was borne out by his light baggage, which still lay about the berth – hat-box, rugs, umbrella, brown morocco hand-bag. All were the property of someone well to do, or at least possessed of decent belongings. One or two pieces bore a monogram, 'F.Q.', the same as on the shirt and underlinen; but on the bag was a luggage label, with the name 'Francis Quadling, passenger to Paris', in full. Its owner had apparently no reason to conceal his name. More strangely, those who had done him to death had been at no pains to remove all traces of his identity.

M. Floçon opened the hand-bag, seeking for further evidence; but found nothing of importance – only loose collars, cuffs, a sponge and slippers, two Italian newspapers of an earlier date. No money, valuables, or papers. All these had been removed probably, and presumably, by the perpetrator of the crime.

Having settled the first preliminary but essential points, the Chef next surveyed the whole compartment critically. Now, for the first time, he was struck with the fact that the window was open to its full height.

Since when was this? It was a question to be put presently to the conductor and any others who had entered the car, but the discovery drew him to examine the window more closely, and with good results.

At the ledge, caught on a projecting point on the far side, partly in, partly out of the car, was a morsel of white lace, a scrap of feminine apparel; although what part, or how it had come there, was not at once obvious to M. Floçon. A long and minute inspection of this bit of lace, which he was careful not to detach as yet from the place in which he found it, showed that it was ragged and frayed, and fast caught where it hung. It could not have been blown there by any chance air; it must have been torn from the article to which it belonged, whatever that might be – headdress, *bonnet de nuit*, nightdress, or neckerchief. The lace was of a kind to serve any of these purposes.

Inspecting further, M. Floçon made a second discovery. On the small table under the window was a short length of black jet beading, part of the trimming or ornamentation of a lady's dress.

These two objects of feminine origin – one partly outside the car, the other near it, but quite inside – gave rise to many conjectures. It led, however, to the inevitable conclusion that a woman had been at some time or other in the berth. M. Floçon could not but connect these two *trouvailles* with the fact of the open window. The latter might, of course, have been the work of the murdered man himself at an earlier hour. Yet it is unusual, as the detective imagined, for a passenger, and especially an Italian, to lie under an open window in a sleeping-berth when travelling by express train before daylight in March.

Who opened that window, then, and why? Perhaps some further facts might be found on the outside of the car. With this idea, M. Floçon left it, and passed on to the line or permanent way.

Here he found himself a good deal below the level of the car. These *wagons-lits* have no footboards like ordinary carriages; access to them is gained from a platform by the steps at each end. The Chef was short of stature, and he could only approach the window outside by calling one of the Gardes de Paris and ordering him to make the small ladder (*faire la petite échelle*). This meant stooping and giving a back, on which little M. Floçon climbed nimbly, and so was raised to the necessary height.

A close scrutiny revealed nothing unusual. The exterior of the car was encrusted with the mud and dust gathered in the journey, none of which appeared to have been disturbed.

M. Floçon re-entered the carriage neither disappointed nor pleased; his mind was in an open state, ready to receive any impressions, and as yet only one that was at all clear and distinct was borne in on him.

This was the presence of the lace and the jet beads in the theatre of the crime. The inference was fair and simple. He came logically and surely to this:

1.  That some woman had entered the compartment.

2.  That whether or not she had come in before the crime, she was there after the window had been opened, which was not done by the murdered man.

3.  That she had leaned out, or partly passed out, of the window at some time or other, as the scrap of lace testified.

4.  Why had she leaned out? To seek some means of exit or escape, of course.

But escape from whom? from what? The murderer? Then she must know him, and unless an accomplice (if so, why run from him?), she would give up her knowledge on compulsion, if not voluntarily, as seemed doubtful, seeing she (his suspicions were consolidating) had not done so already.

But there might be another even stronger reason to attempt escape at such imminent risk as leaving an express train at full speed. To escape from her

312

own act and the consequences it must entail – escape from horror first, from detection next, and then from arrest and punishment.

All this would imperiously impel even a weak woman to face the worst peril, to look out, lean out, even try the terrible but impossible feat of climbing out of the car.

So M. Floçon, by fair process of reasoning, reached a point which incriminated one woman, the only woman possible, and that was the titled, high-bred lady who called herself the Contessa di Castagneto.

This conclusion gave a definite direction to further search. Consulting the rough plan which he had constructed to take the place of the missing *feuille de route*, he entered the compartment which the Contessa had occupied, and which was actually next door.

It was in the tumbled, untidy condition of a sleeping-place but just vacated. The sex and quality of its recent occupant were plainly apparent in the goods and chattels lying about, the property and possessions of a delicate, well-bred woman of the world, things still left as she had used them last – rugs still unrolled, a pair of easy-slippers on the floor, the sponge in its waterproof bag on the bed, brushes, bottles, buttonhook, hand-glass, many things belonging to the dressing-bag, not yet returned to that receptacle. The maid was no doubt to have attended to all these, but as she had not come, they remained unpacked and strewn about in some disorder.

M. Floçon pounced down upon the contents of the berth, and commenced an immediate search for a lace scarf, or any wrap or cover with lace.

He found nothing, and was hardly disappointed. It told more against the Contessa, who, if innocent, would have no reason to conceal or make away with a possibly incriminating possession, the need for which she could not of course understand.

Next, he handled the dressing-bag, and with deft fingers replaced everything.

Everything was forthcoming but one glass bottle, a small one, the absence of which he noted, but thought of little consequence, till, by and by, he came upon it under peculiar circumstances.

Before leaving the car, and after walking through the other compartments, M. Floçon made an especially strict search of the corner where the conductor had his own small chair, his only resting-place, indeed, throughout the journey. The Chef had not forgotten the attendant's condition when first examined, and he had even then been nearly satisfied that the man had been hocussed, narcotized, drugged.

Any doubts were entirely removed by his picking up near the conductor's seat a small silver-topped bottle and a handkerchief, both marked with coronet and monogram, the last of which, although the letters were much interlaced and involved, were decipherable as S.L.L.C.

It was that of the Contessa, and corresponded with the marks on her other belongings.

He put it to his nostril and recognized at once by its smell that it had contained tincture of laudanum, or some preparation of that drug.

CHAPTER FIVE

M. Floçon was an experienced detective, and he knew so well that he ought to be on his guard against the most plausible suggestions, that he did not like to make too much of these discoveries. Still, he was distinctly satisfied, if not exactly exultant, and he went back towards the station with a strong predisposition against the Contessa di Castagneto.

Just outside the waiting-room, however, his assistant, Galipaud, met him with news which rather dashed his hopes, and gave a new direction to his thoughts.

The lady's-maid was not to be found.

'Impossible!' cried the Chef, and then at once suspicion followed surprise.

'I have looked, monsieur, inquired everywhere; the maid has not been seen. She certainly is not here.'

'Did she go through the barrier with the other passengers?'

'No one knows; no one remembers her; not even the *chef de train*. But she has gone. That is positive.'

'Yet it was her duty to be here; to attend to her service. Her mistress would certainly want her – has asked for her! Why should she run away?'

This question presented itself as one of infinite importance, to be pondered over seriously before he went further into the inquiry.

Did the Contessa know of this disappearance?

She had asked imploringly for her maid. True, but might that not be a blind? Women are born actresses, and at need can assume any part, convey any impression. Might not the Contessa have wished to be dissociated from the maid, and therefore have affected complete ignorance of her flight?

'I will try her further,' said M. Floçon to himself.

But then, supposing that the maid had taken herself off of her own accord? Why was it? Why had she done so? Because – because she was afraid of something. If so, of what? No direct accusation could be brought against her on the face of it. She had not been in the sleeping-car at the time of the murder, while the Contessa as certainly was; and, according to strong

315

presumption, in the very compartment where the deed was done. If the maid was afraid, why was she afraid?

Only on one possible hypothesis. That she was either in collusion with the Contessa, or possessed of some guilty knowledge tending to incriminate the Contessa and probably herself. She had run away to avoid any inconvenient questioning tending to get her mistress into trouble, which would react probably on herself.

'We must press the Contessa on this point closely; I will put it plainly to M. le Juge,' said the Chef, as he entered the private room set apart for the police authorities, where he found M. Beaumont le Hardi, the instructing judge, and the Commissary of the Quartier (arrondissement).

A lengthy conference followed among the officials. M. Floçon told all he knew, all he had discovered, gave his views with all the force and fluency of a public prosecutor, and was congratulated warmly on the progress he had made.

'I agree with you, M. le Chef,' said the instructing judge: 'we must have in the Contessa first, and pursue the line indicated as regards the missing maid.'

'I will fetch her, then. Stay, what can be going on in there?' cried M. Floçon, rising from his seat and running into the outer waiting-room, which, to his surprise and indignation, he found in great confusion.

The Garde de Paris who was on sentry was struggling, in personal conflict almost, with the English General. There was a great hubbub of voices, and the Contessa was lying back half fainting in her chair.

'What's all this? How dare you, sir?' This to the General, who now had the Garde by the throat with one hand and with the other was preventing him from drawing his sword. 'Desist – forbear! You are opposing legal authority; desist, or I will call in assistance and will have you secured and removed.'

The little Chef's blood was up; he spoke warmly, with all the force and dignity of an official who sees the law outraged.

'It is entirely the fault of this ruffian of yours; he has behaved most brutally,' replied Sir Charles, still holding him tight.

'Let him go, monsieur; your behaviour is inexcusable. What! you, a military officer of the highest rank, to assault a sentinel! For shame! *Fi! C'est inoui!*'

'He deserves to be scragged, the beast!' went on the General, as with one sharp turn of the wrist he threw the Garde off, and sent him flying nearly across the room, where, being free at last, the Frenchman drew his sword and brandished it threateningly – from a distance.

But M. Floçon interposed with uplifted hand and insisted upon an explanation.

'It is just this,' replied Sir Charles, speaking fast and with much fierceness:

'that lady there – poor thing, she is ill, you can see that for yourself, suffering, over-wrought; she asked for a glass of water, and this brute, triple brute, as you say in French, refused to bring it.'

'I could not leave the room,' protested the Garde. 'My orders were precise.'

'So I was going to fetch the water,' went on the General angrily, eyeing the Garde as though he would like to make another grab at him, 'and this fellow interfered.'

'Very properly,' added M. Floçon.

'Then why didn't he go himself, or call someone? Upon my word, monsieur, you are not to be complimented upon your people, nor your methods. I used to think that a Frenchman was gallant, courteous, especially to ladies.'

The Chef looked a little disconcerted, but remembering what he knew against this particular lady, he stiffened and said severely, 'I am responsible for my conduct to my superiors, and not to you. Besides, you appear to forget your position. You are here, detained – all of you' – he spoke to the whole room – 'under suspicion. A ghastly crime has been perpetrated – by someone among you –'

'Do not be too sure of that,' interposed the irrepressible General.

'Who else could be concerned? The train never stopped after leaving Laroche,' said the Chef, allowing himself to be betrayed into argument.

'Yes, it did,' corrected Sir Charles, with a contemptuous laugh; 'shows how much you know.'

Again the Chef looked unhappy. He was on dangerous ground, face to face with a new fact affecting all his theories – if fact it was, not mere assertion, and that he must speedily verify. But nothing was to be gained – much, indeed, might be lost – by prolonging this discussion in the presence of the whole party. It was entirely opposed to the French practice of investigation, which works secretly, taking witnesses separately, one by one, and strictly preventing all intercommunication or collusion among them.

'What I know or do not know is my affair,' he said, with an indifference he did not feel. 'I shall call upon you, M. le Général, for your statement in due course, and that of the others.' He bowed stiffly to the whole room. 'Everyone must be interrogated. M. le Juge is now here, and he proposes to begin, madame, with you.'

The Contessa gave a little start, shivered, and turned very pale.

'Can't you see she is not equal to it?' cried the General hotly. 'She has not yet recovered. In the name of – I do not say chivalry, for that would be useless – but of common humanity, spare madame, at least for the present.'

'That is impossible, quite impossible. There are reasons why Madame la

Comtesse should be examined first. I trust, therefore, she will make an effort.'

'I will try, if you wish it.' She rose from her chair and walked a few steps rather feebly, then stopped.

'No, no, Contessa, do not go,' said Sir Charles hastily, in English, as he moved across to where she stood and gave her his hand. 'This is sheer cruelty, sir, and cannot be permitted.'

'Stand aside!' shouted M. Floçon; 'I forbid you to approach that lady, to address her, or communicate with her. Garde, advance, do your duty.'

But the Garde de Paris, although his sword was still out of its sheath, showed great reluctance to move. He had no desire to try conclusions again with this very masterful person, who was, moreover, a general; as the Garde had served, he had a deep respect for generals, even of foreign growth.

Meanwhile the General held his ground and continued his conversation with the Countess, speaking still in English, thus exasperating M. Floçon, who did not understand the language, almost to madness.

'This is not to be borne!' he cried. 'Here, Galipaud, Block'; and when his two trusty assistants came rushing in, he pointed furiously to the General. 'Seize him, remove him by force if necessary. He shall go to the *violon* – to the nearest lock-up.'

The noise attracted also the Judge and the Commissary, and there were now six officials in all, including the Garde de Paris, all surrounding the General, a sufficiently imposing force to overawe even the most recalcitrant fire-eater.

But now the General seemed to see only the comic side of the situation, and he burst out laughing.

'What, all of you? How many more? Why not bring up cavalry and artillery, horse, foot, and guns?' he asked derisively. 'All to prevent one old man from offering his services to one weak woman! Messieurs, *mes compliments!*'

'Really, Charles, I fear you are going too far,' said his brother the clergyman, who, however, had been manifestly enjoying the whole scene.

'Indeed, yes. It is not necessary, I assure you,' added the Contessa, with tears of gratitude in her big brown eyes. 'I am most touched, most thankful. You are a true soldier, a true English gentleman, and I shall never forget your kindness.' Then she put her hand in his with a pretty, winning gesture that was reward enough for any man.

Meanwhile, the Judge, the senior official present, had learned exactly what had happened, and he now addressed the General with a calm but stern rebuke.

'Monsieur will not, I trust, oblige us to put in force the full power of the law. I might, if I chose, and as I am fully entitled, commit you at once to Mazas, to keep you *au secret* in a solitary cell. Your conduct has been deplorable, well calculated to traverse and impede justice. But I am willing to believe that you were led away, not unnaturally, *en galant homme* – it is the characteristic of your nation, of your cloth – and that on more mature consideration you will acknowledge and not repeat your error.'

M. Beaumont le Hardi was a grave, florid, soft-voiced person, with a bald head and a comfortably-lined white waistcoat; one who sought his ends by persuasion, not force, but who had the instincts of a gentleman, and little sympathy with the peremptory methods of his more inflammable colleague.

'Oh, with all my heart, monsieur,' said Sir Charles cordially. 'You saw, or at least know, how this has occurred. I did not begin it, nor was I the most to blame. But I was in the wrong, I admit. What do you wish me to do now?'

'Give me your promise to abide by our rules – they may be irksome, but we think them necessary – and hold no further converse with your companions.'

'Certainly, certainly, monsieur – at least after I have said one word more to Madame la Comtesse.'

'No, no, I cannot permit even that –'

But Sir Charles, in spite of the warning finger held up by the Judge, insisted upon crying out to her, as she was being led into the other room –

'Courage, dear lady, courage. Don't let them bully you. You have nothing to fear.'

Any further defiance of authority was now prevented by her almost forcible removal from the room.

## CHAPTER SIX

The stormy episode just ended had rather a disturbing effect on M. Floçon, who could scarcely give his full attention to all the points, old and new, that had now arisen in the investigation. But he would have time to go over them at his leisure, while the work of interrogation was undertaken by the Judge.

The latter had taken his seat at a small table, and just opposite was his *greffier*, or clerk, who was to write down question and answer, *verbatim*. A little to one side, with the light full on the face, the witness was seated, bearing the scrutiny of three pairs of eyes – the Judge first, and behind him, those of the Chef de la Sûreté and the Commissary of Police.

'I trust, madame, that you are equal to answering a few questions?' began M. le Hardi blandly.

'Oh yes, I hope so. Indeed, I have no choice,' replied the Contessa, bravely resigned.

'They will refer principally to your maid.'

'Ah!' said the Contessa quickly and in a troubled voice, yet she bore the gaze of the three officials without flinching.

'I want to know a little more about her, if you please.'

'Of course. Anything I know I will tell you.' She spoke now with perfect self-possession. 'But if I might ask – why this interest?'

'I will tell you frankly. You asked for her, we sent for her, and –'

'Yes?'

'She cannot be found. She is not in the Gare.'

The Contessa all but jumped from her chair in her surprise – surprise that seemed too spontaneous to be feigned.

'Impossible! it cannot be. She would not dare to leave me here like this, all alone.'

'Parbleu! she has dared. Most certainly she is not here.'

'But what can have become of her?'

'Ah, madame, what indeed? Can you form any idea? We hoped you might have been able to enlighten us.'

'I cannot, monsieur, not in the least.'

'Perchance you sent her on to your hotel to warn your friends that you were detained? To fetch them, perhaps, to you in your trouble?'

The trap was neatly contrived, but she was not deceived.

'How could I? I knew of no trouble when I saw her last.'

'Oh, indeed? and when was that?'

'Last night, at Amberieux, as I have already told that gentleman.' She pointed to M. Floçon, who was obliged to nod his head.

'Well, she has gone away somewhere. It does not much matter, still it is odd, and for your sake, we should like to help you to find her, if you do wish to find her?'

Another little trap which failed.

'Indeed I hardly think she is worth keeping after this barefaced desertion.'

'No indeed. And she must be held to strict account for it, must justify it, give her reasons. So we must find her for you —'

'I am not at all anxious, really,' the Contessa said quickly, and the remark told against her.

'Well, now, Madame la Comtesse, as to her description. Will you tell us what was her height, figure, colour of eyes, hair, general appearance?'

'She was tall, above the middle height, at least; slight, good figure, black hair and eyes.'

'Pretty?'

'*Comme çi, comme ça*. Some people might think so, in her own class.'

'How was she dressed?'

'In plain dark serge, bonnet of black straw and brown ribbons. I do not allow my maid to wear colours.'

'*Parfaitement*. And her name, age, place of birth?'

'Hortense Petitpré, thirty-two, born, I believe, in Paris.'

The Judge, when these particulars had been given, looked over his shoulder towards the Chef, but said nothing. It was quite unnecessary, for M. Floçon, who had been writing in his note-book, now rose and left the room. He called Galipaud to him, saying sharply —

'Here is the more detailed description of the *femme de chambre*, and in writing. Have it copied and circulate it at once. Give it to the stationmaster, and to the agents of police round about here. I have an idea — only an idea — that this woman has not gone far. It may be worth nothing, still there is the chance. People who are wanted often hang about the very place they would *not* stay in if they were wise. Anyhow, set a watch for her and come back here.'

Meanwhile, the Judge had continued his questioning.

'And where, madame, did you obtain your maid?'

'In Rome. She was there, out of place. I heard of her at an agency and registry office, when I was looking for a maid a month or two ago.'

'Then she has not been long in your service?'

'No; as I tell you, she came to me in December last.'

'Well recommended?'

'Strongly. She had lived with good families, French and English.'

'And with you, what was her character?'

'Irreproachable.'

'Well, so much for Hortense Petitpré. She is not far off, I daresay. When we want her we shall be able to lay hands on her, I do not doubt, madame may rest assured.'

'Pray take no trouble in the matter. I certainly should not keep her.'

'Very well, very well. And now, another small matter. I see,' he referred to the rough plan of the *wagon-lit* prepared by M. Floçon – 'I see that you occupied the compartment *d*, with berths Nos. 9 and 10?'

'I think 9 was the number of my berth.'

'It was. You may be certain of that. Now next door to your compartment – do you know who was next door? I mean in 7 and 8?'

The Contessa's lip quivered, and she was a prey to sudden emotion as she answered in a low voice –

'It was where – where –'

'*Bien*, madame,' said the Judge, reassuring her as he would a little child. 'You need not say. It is no doubt very distressing to you. *Enfin*, you know?'

She bent her head slowly, but uttered no word.

'Now this man, this poor man, had you noticed him at all? No – no – not afterwards, of course. It would not be likely. But during the journey. Did you speak to him, or he to you?'

'No, no – distinctly no.'

'Nor see him?'

'Yes, I saw him, I believe, at Modane with the rest when we dined.'

'Ah! exactly so. He dined at Modane. Was that the only occasion on which you saw him? You had never met him previously in Rome, where you resided?'

'Whom do you mean? The murdered man?'

'Who else?'

'No, not that I am aware of. At least I did not recognize him as a friend.'

'I presume, if he was among your friends –'

'Pardon me, that he certainly was not,' interrupted the Contessa.

'Well, among your acquaintances – he would probably have made himself known to you?'

'I suppose so.'

'And he did not do so? He never spoke to you, nor you to him?'

'I never saw him, the occupant of that compartment, except on that one occasion. I kept a good deal in my compartment during the journey.'

'Alone? It must have been very dull for you,' said the judge pleasantly.

'I was not always alone,' said the Contessa hesitatingly, and with a slight flush. 'I had friends in the car.'

'Oh – oh –' the exclamation was long-drawn and rather significant. 'Who were they? You may as well tell us, madame, we should certainly find out.'

'I have no wish to withhold the information,' she replied, not turning pale, possibly at the imputation conveyed. 'Why should I?'

'And these friends were –?'

'Sir Charles Collingham and his brother. They came and sat with me occasionally; sometimes one, sometimes the other.'

'During the day?'

'Of course, during the day.' Her eyes flashed, as though the question was another offence.

'Have you known them long?'

'The General I met in Roman society last winter. It was he who introduced his brother.'

'Very good, so far. The General knew you, took an interest in you. That explains his strange, unjustifiable conduct just now –'

'I do not think it was either strange or unjustifiable,' interrupted the Contessa hotly. '*He* is a gentleman.'

'Quite a *preux cavalier*, of course. But we will pass on. You are not a good sleeper, I believe, madame?'

'Indeed no, I sleep badly, as a rule.'

'Then you would be easily disturbed. Now, last night, did you hear anything strange in the car, more particularly in the adjoining compartment?'

'Nothing.'

'No sound of voices raised high, no noise of a conflict, a struggle?'

'No, monsieur.'

'That is odd. I cannot understand it. We know, beyond all question, from the appearance of the body – the corpse – that there was a fight, an encounter. Yet you, a wretched sleeper, with only a thin plank of wood between you and the affray, hear nothing, absolutely nothing. It is *most* extraordinary.'

'I was asleep. I must have been asleep.'

'A light sleeper would certainly be awakened. How can you explain – how can you reconcile that?' The question was blandly put, but the Judge's incredulity verged upon actual insolence.

'Easily: I had taken a soporific. I always do, on a journey. I am obliged to keep something, sulphonal or chloral, by me, on purpose.'

'Then this, madame, is yours?' And the Judge, with an air of undisguised triumph, produced the small glass vial which M. Floçon had picked up in the sleeping-car near the conductor's seat.

The Countess, with a quick gesture, put out her hand to take it.

'No, I cannot give it up. Look as near as you like, and say is it yours?'

'Of course it is mine. Where did you get it? Not in my berth?'

'No, madame, not in your berth.'

'But where?'

'Pardon me, we shall not tell you – not just now.'

'I missed it last night,' went on the Countess, slightly confused.

'After you had taken your dose of chloral?'

'No, before.'

'And why did you want this? It is laudanum.'

'For my nerves. I have a toothache. I – I – really, sir, I need not tell you all my ailments.'

'And the maid had removed it?'

'So I presume; she must have taken it out of the bag in the first instance.'

'And then kept it?'

'That is what I can only suppose.'

'Ah!'

CHAPTER SEVEN

When the Judge had brought down the interrogation of the Countess to the production of the small glass bottle, he paused, and with a long drawn 'Ah!' of satisfaction, looked round at his colleagues.

Both M. Floçon and the Commissary nodded their heads approvingly, plainly sharing his triumph.

Then they all put their heads together in close, whispered conference.

'Admirable, M. le Juge!' said the Chef. 'You have been most adroit. It is a clear case.'

'No doubt,' said the Commissary, who was a blunt, rather coarse person, believing that to take anybody and everybody into custody is always the safest and simplest course. 'It looks black against her. I think she ought to be arrested at once.'

'We might, indeed we ought to have more evidence, more definite evidence, perhaps?' The Judge was musing over the facts as he knew them. 'I should like, before going further, to look at the car,' he said, suddenly coming to a conclusion.

The Chef de la Sûreté readily agreed. 'We will go together,' he said, adding, 'Madame will remain here, please, until we return. It may not be for long.'

'And afterwards?' asked the Contessa, whose nervousness had if anything increased during the whispered colloquy of the officials.

'Ah, afterwards! Who knows?' was the reply, with a shrug of the shoulders, all most enigmatic and unsatisfactory.

'What have we against her?' said the Judge, as soon as they had gained the absolute privacy of the sleeping-car.

'The bottle of laudanum and the conductor's condition. He was undoubtedly drugged,' answered the Chef; and the discussion which followed took the form of a dialogue between them, for the Commissary took no part in it.

'Yes; but why by the Countess? How do we know that positively?'

'It is her bottle,' said M. Floçon.

'Her story may be true – that she missed it, that the maid took it.'

'We have nothing whatever against the maid. We know nothing about her.'

'No. Except that she has disappeared. But that tells more against her mistress. It is all very vague. I do not see my way quite, as yet.'

'But the fragment of lace, the broken bead? Surely, M. le Juge, they are a woman's, and only one woman was in the car –'

'So far as we know.'

'But if these could be proved to be hers?'

'Ah! if you could prove that!'

'Easy enough. Have her searched, here at once, in the Gare. There is a female searcher attached to the Douane.'

'It is a strong measure. She is a lady.'

'Ladies who commit crimes must not expect to be handled with kid gloves.'

'She is an Englishwoman, or with English connections; titled, too. I hesitate, upon my word. Suppose we are wrong? It may lead to unpleasantness. M. le Préfet is anxious to avoid complications possibly international.'

As he spoke, he bent over, and, taking a magnifier from his pocket, examined the lace, which still fluttered where it was caught.

'It is fine lace, I think. What say you, M. Floçon? You may be more experienced in such matters.'

'The finest, or nearly so; I believe it is Valenciennes – the trimming of some underclothing, I should think. That surely is sufficient, M. le Juge?'

M. Beaumont le Hardi gave a reluctant consent, and the Chef went back himself to see that the searching was undertaken without loss of time.

The Contessa protested, but vainly, against this new indignity. What could she do? A prisoner, practically friendless – for the General was not within reach – to resist was out of the question. Indeed, she was plainly told that force would be employed unless she submitted with a good grace. There was nothing for it but to obey.

Mère Tontaine, as the female searcher called herself, was an evil-visaged, corpulent old creature, with a sickly, soft, insinuating voice, and a greasy, familiar manner that was most offensive. They had given her the scrap of torn lace and the débris of the jet as a guide, with very particular directions to see if they corresponded with any part of the lady's apparel.

She soon showed her quality.

'Aha! Oho! What is this, my pretty princess? How comes so great a lady into the hands of Mère Tontaine? But I will not harm you, my beauty, *ma chérie, ma mie*. Oh no, no, I will not trouble you, dearie. No, trust to me'; and she held out one skinny claw, and looked the other way.

The Contessa did not or would not understand.

'Madame has money?' went on the old hag in a half-threatening, half-coaxing whisper, as she came up quite close, and fastened on her victim like a bird of prey.

'If you mean that I am to bribe you –'

'Fie, the nasty word! But just a small present, a pretty *pourboire*, one or two yellow bits, twenty, thirty, forty francs – you'd better.' She shook the soft arm she held roughly, and anything seemed preferable than to be touched by this horrible woman.

'Wait, wait!' cried the Contessa, shivering all over, and, feeling hastily for her purse, she took out several napoleons.

'Aha! Oho! One, two, three,' said the searcher in a fat, wheedling voice. 'Four, yes, four, five'; and she clinked the coins together in her palm, while a covetous light came into her faded eyes at the joyous sound. 'Five – make it five at once, d'ye hear me? – or I'll call them in and tell them. That will go against you, my princess. What, try and bribe a poor old woman, la Mère Tontaine, honest and incorruptible Tontaine? Five, then, five!'

With trembling haste the Contessa emptied the whole contents of her purse in the old hag's hand.

'*Bonne aubaine*. Nice pickings. It is a misery what they pay me here. I am, oh, so poor, and I have children, many babies. You will not tell them – La Rousse – you dare not. No, no, no.'

Thus muttering to herself, she shambled across the room to a corner, where she stowed the money safely away. Then she came back, showed the bit of lace, and pressed it into the Contessa's hands.

'Do you know this, *ma mie*? Where it comes from, where there is much more? I was told to look for it, to search for it on you'; and with a quick gesture she lifted the edge of the Contessa's skirt, dropping it next moment with a low, chuckling laugh.

'Oho! Aha! You were right, my pretty, to pay me, my pretty – right. And some day, today, tomorrow, whenever I ask you, you will remember la Mère Tontaine.'

The Contessa listened with dismay. What had she done? Put herself into the power of this greedy and unscrupulous old beldame?

'And this, my princess? What have we here, aha?'

Mère Tontaine held up next the broken bit of jet ornament for inspection, and as the Contessa leaned forward to examine it more closely, gave it into her hand.

'You recognize it, of course. But be careful, *ma mie! Gare!* If anyone were looking, it would ruin you. I could not save you then. Sh! Say nothing, only look, and quick, give it me back. I must have it to show.'

All this time the Contessa was turning the jet over and over in her open palm, with a perplexed, disturbed, but hardly a terrified air.

Yes, she knew it, or thought she knew it. It had been – But how had it come here, into the possession of this base myrmidon of the French police?

'Give it me, quick!' There was a loud knock at the door. 'They are coming. Remember!' Mère Tontaine put her long finger to her lip. 'Not a word! I have found nothing, of course. Nothing, I can swear to that, and you will not forget Mère Tontaine?'

Now M. Floçon stood at the open door awaiting the searcher's report. He looked much disconcerted when the old woman took him on one side and briefly explained that the search had been altogether fruitless.

There was nothing to justify suspicion, nothing, so far as she could find.

The Chef looked from one to the other – from the hag he had employed in this unpleasant quest, to the lady on whom it had been tried. The Contessa, to his surprise, did not complain. He had expected further and strong upbraidings. Strange to say, she took it very quietly. There was no indignation in her face. She was still pale, and her hands trembled, but she said nothing, made no reference, at least, to what she had just gone through.

Again he took counsel with his colleague, while the Contessa was kept apart.

'What next, M. Floçon?' asked the Judge. 'What shall we do with her?'

'Let her go,' answered the Chef briefly.

'What! do you suggest this, M. le Chef,' said the Judge slyly, 'after your strong and well-grounded suspicions?'

'They are as strong as ever, stronger; and I feel sure I shall yet justify them. But what I wish now is to let her go at large, under surveillance.'

'Ah! you would shadow her?'

'Precisely. By a good agent. Galipaud, for instance. He speaks English, and he can, if necessary, follow her anywhere, even to England.'

'She can be extradited,' said the Commissary, with his one prominent idea of arrest.

'Do you agree, M. le Juge? Then, if you will permit me, I will give the necessary orders, and perhaps you will inform the lady that she is free to leave the station?'

The Contessa now had reason to change her opinion of the French officials. Great politeness now replaced the first severity that had been so cruel. She was told, with many bows and apologies, that her regretted but unavoidable detention was at an end. Not only was she freely allowed to depart, but she was escorted by both M. Floçon and the Commissary outside, to where an omnibus was in waiting, and all her baggage piled on top, even to the dressing-bag, which had been neatly repacked for her.

But the little silver-topped vial had not been restored to her, nor the handkerchief.

In her joy at her deliverance, either she had not given these a second thought, or she did not wish to appear anxious to recover them.

Nor did she notice that, as the bus passed through the gates at the bottom of the large slope that leads from the Lyons Gare, it was followed at a discreet distance by a modest fiacre, which pulled up, eventually, outside the Hôtel Madagascar. Its occupant, M. Galipaud, kept the Contessa in sight, and, entering the hotel at her heels, waited till she had left the bureau, when he held a long conference with the proprietor.

## CHAPTER EIGHT

A first stage in the inquiry had now been reached, with results that seemed promising, and were yet contradictory.

No doubt the watch to be set on the Contessa might lead to something yet – something to bring first plausible suspicion to a triumphant issue; but the examination of the other occupants of the car should not be allowed to slacken on that account. The Contessa might have some confederate among them – this pestilent English General, perhaps, who had made himself so conspicuous in her defence; or someone of them might throw light upon her movements, upon her conduct during the journey.

Then, with a spasm of self-reproach, M. Floçon remembered that two distinct suggestions had been made to him by two of the travellers, and that, so far, he had neglected them. One was the significant hint from the Italian that he could materially help the inquiry. The other was the General's sneering assertion that the train had not continued its journey uninterruptedly between Laroche and Paris.

Consulting the Judge, and laying these facts before him, it was agreed that the Italian's offer seemed the most important, and he was accordingly called in next.

'Who and what are you?' asked the Judge carelessly, but the answer roused him at once to intense interest, and he could not quite resist a glance of reproach at M. Floçon.

'My name I have given you – Natale Ripaldi. I am a detective officer belonging to the Roman police.'

'*Tiens!*' cried M. Floçon, colouring deeply. 'This is unheard of. Why in the name of all the devils have you withheld this most astonishing statement until now?'

'Monsieur surely remembers. I told him half an hour ago I had something important to communicate –'

'Yes, yes, of course. But why were you so reticent? *Grand Dieu!*'

'Monsieur was not so encouraging that I felt disposed to force on him what I knew he would have to hear in due course.'

'It is monstrous – quite abominable, and shall not end here. Your superiors shall hear of your conduct,' went on the Chef hotly.

'They will also hear, and, I think, listen to my version of the story – that I offered you fairly, and at the first opportunity, all the information I had, and that you refused to accept it.'

'You should have persisted. It was your manifest duty. You are an officer of the law, or you say you are.'

'Pray telegraph at once, if you think fit, to Rome, to the police authorities, and you will find that Natale Ripaldi – your humble servant – travelled by the *direttissimo* with their knowledge and authority. And here are my credentials, my official card, some official letters –'

'And what, in a word, have you to tell us?'

'I can tell you who the murdered man was.'

'We know that already.'

'Possibly; but only his name, I apprehend. I know his profession, his business, his object in travelling, for I was appointed to watch and follow him. That is why I am here.'

'Was he a suspicious character, then? A criminal?'

'At any rate he was absconding from Rome, with valuables.'

'A thief, in fact?'

The Italian put out the palms of his hands with a gesture of doubt and deprecation.

'Thief is a hard, ugly word. That which he was removing was, or had been, his own property.'

'Tut, tut! do be more explicit and get on,' interrupted the little Chef testily.

'I ask nothing better; but if questions are put to me –'

M. le Juge interposed.

'Give us your story. We can interrogate you afterwards.'

'The murdered man is Francis A. Quadling, of the firm of Correse & Quadling, bankers, in the Via Condotti, Rome. It was an old house, once of good, of the highest repute, but of late years it had fallen into difficulties. Its financial soundness was doubted in certain circles, and the Government was warned that a great scandal was imminent. So the matter was handed over to the police, and I was directed to make inquiries, and to keep my eye on this Quadling' – he jerked his thumb towards the platform, where the body might be supposed to be.

'This Quadling was the only surviving partner. He was well known and liked in Rome, indeed, many who heard the adverse reports disbelieved them, I myself among the number. But my duty was plain –'

'Naturally,' echoed the fiery little Chef.

'I made it my business to place the banker under surveillance, to learn his habits, his ways of life, see who were his friends, the houses he visited. I soon knew much that I wanted to know, although not all. But one fact I discovered, and think it right to inform you of it at once. He was on intimate terms with La Castagneto – at least, he frequently called upon her.'

'La Castagneto! Do you mean the Contessa of that name, who was a passenger in the *wagon-lit*?'

'*Altro!* it is she I mean.' The officials looked at each other eagerly, and M. Beaumont le Hardi quickly turned over the sheets on which the Contessa's evidence was recorded.

She had denied acquaintance with this murdered man, Quadling, and here was positive evidence that they were on intimate terms!

'He was at her house on the very day we all left Rome – in the evening, towards dusk. The Contessa had an apartment in the Via Margutta, and when he left her he returned to his own place in the Condotti, entered the bank, stayed half an hour, then came out with one hand-bag and rug, called a *botta*, and was driven straight to the railway station.'

'And you followed?'

'Of course. When I saw him walk straight to the *wagon-lit*, and ask the conductor for 7 and 8, I knew that his plans had been laid, and that he was on the point of leaving Rome secretly. When, presently, La Castagneto also arrived, I concluded that she was in his confidence, and that possibly they were eloping together.'

'Why did you not arrest him?'

'I had no authority, even if I had had the time. Although I was ordered to watch the Signor Quadling, I had no warrant for his arrest. But I decided on the spur of the moment what course I should take. It seemed to be the only one, and that was to embark in the same train and stick close to my man.'

'You informed your superiors, I suppose?'

'Pardon me, monsieur,' said the Italian blandly to the Chef, who asked the question, 'but have you any right to inquire into my conduct towards my superiors? In all that affects the murder I am at your orders, but in this other matter it is between me and them.'

'Ta, ta, ta! They will tell us if you will not. And you had better be careful, lest you obstruct justice. Speak out, sir, and beware. What did you intend to do?'

'To act according to circumstances. If my suspicions were confirmed –'

'What suspicions?'

'Why – that this banker was carrying off any large sum in cash, notes, securities, as in effect he was.'

'Ah! You know that? How?'

'By my own eyes. I looked into his compartment once and saw him in the act of counting them over, a great quantity, in fact –'

Again the officials looked at each other significantly. They had got at last to a motive for the crime.

'And that, of course, would have justified his arrest?'

'Exactly. I proposed, directly we arrived in Paris, to claim the assistance of your police and take him into custody. But his fate interposed.'

There was a pause, a long pause, for another important point had been reached in the inquiry: the motive for the murder had been made clear, and with it the presumption against the Contessa gained terrible strength.

But there was more, perhaps, to be got out of this dark-visaged Italian detective, who had already proved so useful an ally.

'One or two words more,' said the Judge to Ripaldi. 'During the journey, now, did you have any conversation with this Quadling?'

'None. He kept very much to himself.'

'You saw him, I suppose, at the restaurants?'

'Yes, at Modane and Laroche.'

'But did not speak to him?'

'Not a word.'

'Had he any suspicion, do you think, as to who you were?'

'Why should he? He did not know me. I had taken pains he should never see me.'

'Did he speak to any other passenger?'

'Very little. To the Contessa. Yes, once or twice, I think, to her maid.'

'Ah! that maid. Did you notice her at all? She has not been seen. It is strange. She seems to have disappeared.'

'To have run away, in fact?' suggested Ripaldi, with a queer smile.

'Well, at least she is not here with her mistress. Can you offer any explanation of that?'

'She was perhaps afraid. The Contessa and she were very good friends, I think. On better, more familiar terms, than is usual between mistress and maid.'

'The maid knew something?'

'Ah, monsieur, it is only an idea. But I give it you for what it is worth.'

'Well, well, this maid – what was she like?'

'Tall, dark, *belle fille*, not too reserved. She made other friends – the conductor and the English Colonel. I saw the last speaking to her. I spoke to her myself.'

333

'What can have become of her?' said the Judge.

'Would M. le Juge like me to go in search of her? That is, if you have no more questions to ask, no wish to detain me further?'

'We will consider that, and let you know in a moment, if you will wait outside.'

And then, when alone, the officials deliberated.

It was a good offer, the man knew her appearance, he was in possession of all the facts, he could be trusted —

'Ah, but can he, though?' queried the Chef. 'How do we know he has told us truth? What guarantee have we of his loyalty, his good faith? — What if he is also concerned in the crime — has some guilty knowledge? What if he killed Quadling himself, or was an accomplice before or after the fact?'

'All these are possibilities, of course, but — pardon me, dear colleague — a little far-fetched, eh?' said the Judge. 'Why not utilize this man? If he betrays us — serves us ill — if we had reason to lay hands on him again, he could hardly escape us.'

'Let him go, and send someone with him,' said the Commissary, the first practical suggestion he had yet made.

'Excellent!' cried M. le Juge. 'You have another man here, Chef; let him go with this Italian.'

They called in Ripaldi and told him, 'We will accept your services, monsieur, and you can begin your search at once. In what direction do you propose to begin?'

'Where has her mistress gone?'

'How do you know she has gone?'

'At least, she is no longer with us out there. Have you arrested her — or what?'

'No, she is still at large, but we have our eye upon her. She has gone to her hotel — the Madagascar, off the Grands Boulevards.'

'Then it is there that I shall look for the maid. No doubt she preceded her mistress to the hotel, or she will join her there very shortly.'

'You would not make yourself known, of course? They might give you the slip. You have no authority to detain them, not in France.'

'I should take my precautions, and I can always appeal to the police.'

'Exactly. That would be your proper course. But you might lose valuable time, a great opportunity, and we wish to guard against that, so we shall associate one of our own people with you in your proceedings.'

'*Altro!* if you wish. It will, no doubt, be best.' The Italian readily assented, but a shrewd listener might have guessed from the tone of his voice that the proposal was not exactly pleasing to him.

'I will call in Block,' said the Chef; and the second detective inspector appeared to take his instructions.

He was a stout, stumpy little man, with a barrel-like figure, greatly emphasized by the short frock-coat he wore; he had smallish pig's eyes buried deep in a fat face, and his round, chubby cheeks hung low over his turned-down collar.

'This gentleman,' went on the Chef, indicating Ripaldi, 'is a member of the Roman police, and has been so obliging as to offer us his services. You will accompany him, in the first instance, to the Hôtel Madagascar. Put yourself in communication with Galipaud, who is there on duty.'

'Would it not be sufficient if I made myself known to M. Galipaud?' suggested the Italian. 'I have seen him here, I should recognize him –'

'That is not so certain; he may have changed his appearance. Besides, he does not know the latest developments, and might not be very cordial.'

'You might write me a few lines to take to him.'

'I think not. We prefer to send Block,' replied the Chef briefly and decidedly. He did not like this pertinacity, and looked at his colleagues as though he sought their concurrence in altering the arrangements for the Italian's mission. It might be wiser to detain him still.

'It was only to save trouble that I made the suggestion,' hastily put in Ripaldi. 'Naturally I am in your hands. And if I do not meet with the maid at the hotel, I may have to look further, in which case Monsieur – Block? thank you – would no doubt render valuable assistance.'

This speech restored confidence, and a few minutes later the two detectives, already excellent friends from the freemasonry of a common craft, left the station in a closed cab.

CHAPTER NINE

'What next?' asked the Judge.

'That pestilent English officer, if you please, M. le Juge,' said the Chef. 'That fire-eating, swashbuckling soldier, with his blustering barrack-room ways. I long to come to close quarters with him. He ridiculed me, taunted me, said I knew nothing – we will see, we will see.'

'In fact, you wish to interrogate him yourself. Very well. Let us have him in.'

When Sir Charles Collingham entered, he included the three officials in one cold, stiff bow, waited a moment, and then, finding he was not offered a chair, said with studied politeness –

'I presume I may sit down?'

'Pardon. Of course; pray be seated,' said the Judge hastily, and evidently a little ashamed of himself.

'Ah! thanks. Do you object?' went on the General, taking out a silver cigarette-case. 'May I offer one?' He handed round the box affably.

'We do not smoke on duty,' answered the Chef rudely. 'Nor is smoking permitted in a court of justice.'

'Come, come, I wish to show no disrespect. But I cannot recognize this as a court of justice, and I think, if you will forgive me, that I shall take three whiffs. It may help me keep my temper.'

He was evidently making game of them. There was no symptom remaining of the recent effervescence when he was acting as the Contessa's champion, and he was perfectly – nay, insolently calm and self-possessed.

'You call yourself General Collingham?' went on the Chef.

'I do not call myself. I am General Sir Charles Collingham, of the British Army.'

'Retired? *En retraite?*'

'No, I am still on the active list.'

'These points will have to be verified.'

'With all my heart. You have already sent to the British Embassy?'

'Yes, but no one has come,' answered the Chef contemptuously.

'If you disbelieve me, why do you question me?'

'It is our duty to question you, and yours to answer. If not, we have means to make you. You are suspected, inculpated in a terrible crime, and your whole attitude is – is – objectionable – unworthy – disgr –'

'*Doucement, très doucement,* my dear colleague,' interposed the Judge. 'If you will permit me, I will take up this. And you, M. le Général, I am sure you cannot wish to impede or obstruct us; we represent the law of this country.'

'Have I done so, M. le Juge?' answered the General, with the utmost courtesy, as he threw away his half-burned cigarette.

'No, no. I do not imply that in the least. I only entreat you, as a good and gallant gentleman, to meet us in a proper spirit and give us your best help.'

'Indeed, I am quite ready. If there has been any unpleasantness, it has surely not been of my making, but rather of that little man there.' The General pointed to M. Floçon rather contemptuously, and nearly started a fresh disturbance.

'Well, well, let us say no more of that, and proceed to business. I understand,' said the Judge, after fingering a few pages of the dispositions in front of him, 'that you are a friend of the Contessa di Castagneto? Indeed, she has told us so herself.'

'It was very good of her to call me her friend. I am proud to hear she so considers me.'

'How long have you known her?'

'Four or five months. Since the beginning of the last winter season in Rome.'

'Did you frequent her house?'

'If you mean, was I permitted to call on her on friendly terms, yes.'

'Did you know all her friends?'

'How can I answer that? I know whom I met there from time to time.'

'Exactly. Did you often meet among them a Signor – Quadling?'

'Quadling – Quadling? I cannot say that I have. The name is familiar somehow, but I cannot recall the man.'

'Have you never heard of the Roman bankers, Correse & Quadling?'

'Ah, of course. Although I have had no dealing with them. Certainly I have never met Mr Quadling.'

'Not at the Contessa's?'

'Never – of that I am quite sure.'

'And yet we have had positive evidence that he was a constant visitor there.'

'It is perfectly incomprehensible to me. Not only have I never met him, but I have never heard the Contessa mention his name.'

'It will surprise you, then, to be told that he called at her apartment in the Via Margutta on the very evening of her departure from Rome. Called, was admitted, was closeted with her for more than an hour.'

'I am surprised, astounded. I called there myself about 4 p.m. to offer my services for the journey, and I too stayed till after five. I can hardly believe it.'

'I have more surprises for you, General. What will you think when I tell you that this very Quadling – this friend, acquaintance, call him what you please, but at least intimate enough to pay her a visit on the eve of a long journey – was the man found murdered in the *wagon lit*?'

'Can it be possible? Are you sure?' cried Sir Charles, almost starting from his chair. 'And what do you deduce from all this? What do you imply? An accusation against that lady? Absurd!'

'I respect your chivalrous desire to stand up for a lady who calls you her friend, but we are officials first, and sentiment cannot be permitted to influence us. We have good reasons for suspecting that lady. I tell you that frankly, and trust to you as a soldier and man of honour not to abuse the confidence reposed in you.'

'May I not know those reasons?'

'Because she was in the car – the only woman, you understand – between Laroche and Paris.'

'Do you suspect a female hand, then?' asked the General, evidently much interested and impressed.

'That is so, although I am exceeding my duty in revealing this.'

'And you are satisfied that this lady, a refined, delicate person in the best society, of the highest character – believe me, I know that to be the case – whom you yet suspect of an atrocious crime, was the only female in the car?'

'Obviously. Who else? What other woman could possibly have been in the car? No one got in at Laroche; the train never stopped till it reached Paris.'

'On that last point at least you are quite mistaken, I assure you. Why not upon the other also?'

'The train stopped?' interjected the Chef. 'Why has no one told us that?'

'Possibly because you never asked. But it is nevertheless the fact. Verify it. Everyone will tell you the same.'

The Chef himself hurried to the door and called in the conductor. He was within his rights, of course, but the action showed distrust, at which the General only smiled, but he laughed outright when the still stupid and half-dazed conductor, of course, corroborated the statement at once.

'At whose instance was the train pulled up?' asked the Chef, and the Judge nodded his head approvingly.

To know that would fix fresh suspicion.

But the conductor could not answer the question.

Someone had rung the alarm-bell – so at least the guard had declared; otherwise they should not have stopped. Yet he, the conductor, had not done so, nor did any passenger come forward to admit giving the signal. But there had been a halt. Yes, assuredly.

'This is a new light,' the Judge confessed. 'Do you draw any conclusion from it?' he went on to ask the General.

'That is surely your business. I have only elicited the fact to disprove your theory. But if you wish, I will tell you how it strikes me.'

The Judge bowed assent.

'The bare fact that the train was halted would mean little. That would be the natural act of a timid or excitable person involved indirectly in such a catastrophe. But to disavow the act starts suspicion. The fair inference is that there was some reason, an unavowable reason, for halting the train.'

'And that reason would be –'

'You must see it without my assistance, surely! Why, what else but to afford someone an opportunity to leave the car.'

'But how could that be? You would have seen that person, some of you, especially at such a critical time. The corridor would be full of people, both exits were thus practically overlooked.'

'My idea is – it is only an idea, understand – that the person had already left the car – that is to say, the interior of the car.'

'Escaped how? Where? What do you mean?'

'Escaped through the open window of the compartment where you found the murdered man.'

'You noticed the open window, then?' quickly asked the Chef. 'When was that?'

'Directly I entered the compartment at the first alarm. It occurred to me at once that someone might have gone through it.'

'But no woman could have done it. To climb out of an express train going at top speed would be an impossible feat for a woman,' said the Chef doggedly.

'Why, in God's name, do you still harp upon the woman? Why should it be a woman more than a man?'

'Because' – it was the Judge who spoke, but he paused a moment in deference to a gesture of protest from M. Floçon. The little Chef was much concerned at the utter want of reticence displayed by his colleague.

'Because,' went on the Judge with decision – 'because this was found in the compartment'; and he held out the piece of lace and the scrap of passementerie for the General's inspection, adding quickly, 'You have seen these, or one of them, or something like them before. I am sure of it; I call upon you; I demand – no, I appeal to your sense of honour, Sir Collingham. Tell me, please, exactly what you know.'

## CHAPTER TEN

The General sat for a time staring hard at the bit of torn lace and the broken beads. Then he spoke out firmly –

'It is my duty to withhold nothing. It is not the lace. That I could not swear to; for me – and probably for most men – two pieces of lace are very much the same. But I think I have seen these beads, or something exactly like them, before.'

'Where? When?'

'They formed part of the trimming of a mantle worn by the Contessa di Castagneto.'

'Ah!' it was the same interjection uttered simultaneously by the three Frenchmen, but each had a very different note; in the Judge it was deep interest, in the Chef triumph, in the Commissary indignation, as when he caught a criminal red-handed.

'Did she wear it on the journey?' continued the Judge.

'As to that I cannot say.'

'Come, come, General, you were with her constantly; you must be able to tell us. We insist on being told.' This fiercely, from the now jubilant M. Floçon.

'I repeat that I cannot say. To the best of my recollection, the Contessa wore a long travelling cloak – an ulster, as we call them. The jacket with those bead ornaments may have been underneath. But if I have seen them – as I believe I have – it was not during this journey.'

Here the Judge whispered to M. Floçon, 'The searcher did not discover any second mantle.'

'How do we know the woman examined thoroughly?' he replied. 'Here, at least, is direct evidence as to the beads. At last the net is drawing round this fine Countess.'

'Well, at any rate,' said the Chef aloud, returning to the General, 'these beads were found in the compartment of the murdered man. I should like that explained, please.'

341

'By me? How can I explain it? And the fact does not bear upon what we were considering, as to whether anyone had left the car.'

'Why not?'

'The Contessa, as we know, never left the car. As to her entering this particular compartment – at any previous time – it is highly improbable. Indeed, it is rather insulting her to suggest it.'

'She and this Quadling were close friends.'

'So you say. On what evidence I do not know, but I dispute it.'

'Then how could the beads get there? They were her property, worn by her.'

'Once, I admit, but not necessarily on this journey. Suppose she had given the mantle away – to her maid, for instance; I believe ladies often pass on their things to their maids.'

'It is all pure presumption, a mere theory. This maid – she has not as yet been imported into the discussion.'

'Then I would suggest that you do so without delay. She is to my mind a – well, rather a curious person.'

'You know her – spoke to her?'

'I know her, in a way. I had seen her in the Via Margutta, and I nodded to her when she came first into the car.'

'And on the journey – you spoke to her frequently?'

'I? Oh dear no, not at all. I noticed her, certainly; I could not help it, and perhaps I ought to tell her mistress. She seemed to make friends a little too readily with people.'

'As for instance –?'

'With the conductor to begin with. I saw them together at Laroche, in the buffet at the bar; and that Italian, the man who was in here before me; indeed, with the murdered man. She seemed to know them all.'

'Do you imply that the maid might be of use in this inquiry?'

'Most assuredly I do. As I tell you, she was constantly in and out of the car, and more or less intimate with several of the passengers.'

'Including her mistress, the Contessa,' put in M. Floçon.

The General laughed pleasantly.

'Most ladies are, I presume, on intimate terms with their maids. They say no man is a hero to his valet. It is the same, I suppose, with the other sex.'

'So intimate,' went on the little Chef, with much malicious emphasis, 'that now the maid has disappeared lest she might be asked inconvenient questions about her mistress.'

'Disappeared? You are sure?'

'She cannot be found, that is all we know.'

'It is as I thought, then. She it was who left the car!' cried Sir Charles, with so much vehemence that the officials were startled out of their dignified reserve, and shouted back almost in a breath –

'Explain yourself. Quick, quick. What in God's name do you mean?'

'I had my suspicions from the first, and I will tell you why. At Laroche the car emptied, as you may have heard; everyone except the Contessa, at least, went over to the restaurant for early coffee; I with the rest. I was one of the first to finish, and I strolled back to the platform to get a few whiffs of a cigarette. At that moment I saw, or thought I saw, the end of a skirt disappearing into the *wagon-lit*. I concluded it was this maid, Hortense, who was taking her mistress a cup of coffee. Then my brother came up, we exchanged a few words, and entered the car together.'

'By the same door as that through which you had seen the skirt pass?'

'No, by the other. My brother went back to his berth, but I paused in the corridor to finish my cigarette after the train had gone on. By this time everyone but myself had returned to his berth, and I was on the point of lying down again for half an hour, when I distinctly heard the handle turned of the compartment I knew to be vacant all through the run.'

'That was the one with berths 11 and 12?'

'Probably. It was next to the Contessa. Not only was the handle turned, but the door partly opened –'

'It was not the conductor?'

'Oh no, he was in his seat – you know it, at the end of the car – sound asleep, snoring; I could hear him.'

'Did anyone come out of the vacant compartment?'

'No; but I was almost certain, I believe I could swear that I saw the same skirt, just the hem of it, a black skirt, sway forward beyond the door, just for a second. Then all at once the door was closed again fast.'

'What did you conclude from this? Or did you think nothing of it?'

'I thought very little. I supposed it was that the maid wished to be near her mistress as we were approaching Paris, and I had heard from the Contessa that the conductor had made many difficulties. But you see, after what has happened, that there was a reason for stopping the train.'

'Quite so,' M. Floçon readily admitted, with a scarcely concealed sneer.

He had quite made up his mind now that it was the Contessa who had rung the alarm-bell, in order to allow of the escape of the maid, her confederate and accomplice.

'And you still have an impression that someone – presumably this woman – got off the car, somehow, during the stoppage?' he asked.

'I suggest it, certainly. Whether it was or could be so, I must leave to your superior judgement.'

'What! A woman climb out like that? Bah! *à d'autres.*' (Tell that to the marines.)

'You have, of course, examined the exterior of the car, dear colleague?' now said the Judge.

'Assuredly, once, but I will do it again. Still, the outside is quite smooth, there is no footboard. Only an acrobat could succeed in thus escaping, and then only at the peril of his life. But a woman – oh no! it is too absurd.'

'With help she might, I think, get up on to the roof,' quickly remarked Sir Charles. 'I have looked out of the window of my compartment. It would be nothing for a man, nor much for a woman if assisted.'

'That we will see for ourselves,' said the Chef ungraciously.

'The sooner the better,' added the Judge, and the whole party rose from their chairs, intending to go straight to the car, when the Garde de Paris appeared at the door, followed close by an English military officer in uniform, whom he was trying to keep back, but with no great success. It was Colonel Papillon of the Embassy.

'Halloa, Jack! you *are* a good chap,' cried the General, quickly going forward to shake hands. 'I was sure you would come.'

'Come, sir! Of course I came. I was just going to an official function, as you see, but His Ex. insisted, my horse was at the door, and here I am.'

All this was in English, but the attaché turned now to the officials, and with many apologies for his intrusion, suggested that they should allow his friend, the General, to return with him to the Embassy when they had done with him.

'Of course we will answer for him. He shall remain at your disposal, and will appear whenever called upon.' He turned to Sir Charles, asking, 'You will promise that, sir?'

'Oh, willingly. I had always meant to stay on a bit in Paris. And really I should like to see the end of this. But my brother? He must get home for next Sunday's duty. He has nothing to tell, but he would come back to Paris at any time if his evidence was wanted.'

The French Judge very obligingly agreed to all these proposals, and two more of the detained passengers, making four in all, now left the Gare.

Then the officials proceeded to the car, which still remained as the Chef had left it.

Here they soon found how just were the General's previsions.

### CHAPTER ELEVEN

The three officials went straight to where the still open window showed the particular spot to be examined. The exterior of the car was a little smirched and stained with the dust of the journey, lying thick in parts, and in others there were a few great splotches of mud plastered on.

The Chef paused for a moment to get a general view, looking with the light of the General's suggestion, for either hand or foot marks, anything like a trace of the passage of a feminine skirt, across the dusty surface.

But nothing was to be seen, nothing definite or conclusive at least. Only here and there a few lines and scratches that might be encouraging, but proved little.

Then the Commissary, drawing nearer, called attention to some suspicious spots sprinkled about the window, but above it towards the roof.

'What is it?' asked the Chef, as his colleague with the point of his long forefinger nail picked at the thin crust on the top of one of these spots, disclosing a dark, viscous core.

'I could not swear to it, but I believe it is blood.'

'Blood! *Mon Dieu!*' cried the Chef, as he dragged his powerful magnifying glass out of his pocket and applied it to the spot. 'Look, M. le Juge,' he added, after a long and minute examination. 'What say you?'

'It has that appearance. Only medical evidence can positively decide, but I believe it is blood.'

'Now we are on the right track, I feel convinced. Someone fetch a ladder.'

One of these curious French ladders, narrow at the top, splayed out at the base, was quickly leant against the car, and the Chef ran up, using his magnifier as he climbed.

'There is more here, much more, and something like – yes, beyond question it is – the print of two hands upon the roof. It was here she climbed.'

'No doubt. I can see it now exactly. She would sit on the window ledge, the lower limbs inside the car here and held there. Then with her hands she would draw herself up to the roof,' said the Judge.

'But what nerve! what strength of arm!'

'It was life and death. Within the car was more terrible danger. Fear will do much in such a case. We all know that. *Eh bien!* what more?'

By this time the Chef had stepped on to the roof of the car.

'More, more, much more! Footprints, as plain as a picture. A woman's feet. Wait, let me follow them to the end,' said the Chef, cautiously creeping forward to the end of the car.

A minute or two more, and he rejoined his colleagues on the ground level, and, rubbing his hands, declared joyously that it was all perfectly clear.

'Dangerous or not, difficult or not, she did it. I have traced her; have seen where she must have lain crouching ever so long, followed her all along the top of the car, to the end where she got down above the little platform exit. Beyond doubt she left the car when it stopped, and by arrangement with her confederate.'

'The Contessa?'

'Who else?'

'And at a point near Paris. The English General said the halt was within twenty minutes' run of the Gare.'

'Then it is from that point we must commence our search for her. The Italian has gone on the wrong scent.'

'Not necessarily. The maid, we may be sure, will try to communicate with her mistress.'

'Still, it would be well to secure her before she can do that,' said the Judge.

'With all we know now, a sharp interrogation might extract some very damaging admissions from her,' went on the Chef eagerly. 'Who is to go? I have sent away both my assistants. Of course I can telephone for another man, or I might go myself.'

'No, no, dear colleague, we cannot spare you just yet. Telephone by all means. I presume you would wish to be present at the rest of the interrogatories?'

'Certainly, you are right. We may elicit more about this maid. Let us call in the conductor now. He is said to have had relations with her. Something more may be got out of him.'

The more did not amount to much. Groote, the conductor, came in, cringing and wretched, in the abject state of a man who has lately been drugged and is now slowly recovering. Although sharply questioned, he had nothing to add to his first story.

'Speak out,' said the Judge harshly. 'Tell us everything plainly and promptly, or I shall send you straight to gaol. The order is already made out'; and as he spoke, he waved a flimsy bit of paper before him.

'I know nothing,' the conductor protested piteously.

'That is false. We are fully informed, and no fools. We are certain that no such catastrophe could have occurred without your knowledge or connivance.'

'Indeed, gentlemen, indeed —'

'You were drinking with this maid at the buffet at Laroche. You had more drink with her, or from her hands, afterwards in the car.'

'No, gentlemen, that is not so. I could not – she was not in the car.'

'We know better. You cannot deceive us. You were her accomplice, and her mistress, also, I have no doubt.'

'I declare solemnly that I am quite innocent of all this. I hardly remember what happened at Laroche or after. I do not deny the drink at the buffet. It was very nasty, I thought, and could not tell why, nor why I could not hold my head up when I got back to the car.'

'You went off to sleep at once? Is that what you pretend?'

'It must have been so. Yes. Then I knew nothing more, not till I was aroused.'

And beyond this, a tale to which the conductor stuck with undeviating persistence, they could elicit nothing.

'He is either too clever for us or an absolute *crétin* and fool,' said the Judge wearily, at last, when Groote had gone out. 'We had better commit him to Mazas and hold him there *au secret* under our hands. After a day or two of that he may be less difficult.'

'It is quite clear he was drugged, that the maid put opium or laudanum into his drink at Laroche.'

'And enough of it apparently, for he says he went off to sleep directly he returned to the car,' the Judge remarked.

'He says so. But he must have had a second dose, or why was the vial found on the ground by his seat?' asked the Chef thoughtfully, as much of himself as of the others.

'I cannot believe in a second dose. How was it administered – by whom? It was laudanum, and could only be given in a drink. He says he had no second drink. And by whom? The maid? He says he did not see the maid again.'

'Pardon me, M. le Juge, but do you not give too much credibility to the conductor? For me, his evidence is tainted, and I hardly believe a word of it. Did he not tell me at first he had not seen this maid after Amberieux at 8 p.m. Now he admits that he was drinking with her at the buffet at Laroche. It is all a tissue of lies, his losing the pocket-book and his papers too. There is something to conceal. Even his sleepiness, his stupidity, are likely to have been assumed.'

'I do not think he is acting; he has not the ability to deceive us like that.'

'Well, then, what if the Contessa took him the second drink?'

'Oh! oh! That is the purest conjecture. There is nothing whatever to suggest or support that.'

'Then how explain the finding of the vial near the conductor's seat?'

'May it not have been dropped there on purpose?' put in the Commissary, with another flash of intelligence.

'On purpose?' queried the Chef crossly, foreseeing an answer that would not please him.

'On purpose to bring suspicion on the lady?'

'I don't see it in that light. That would imply that she was not in the plot, and plot there certainly was; everything points to it. The drugging, the open window, the maid's escape.'

'A plot, no doubt, but organized by whom? These two women only? Could either of them have struck the fatal blow? Hardly. Women have the wit to conceive, but neither courage nor brute force to execute. There was a man in this, rest assured.'

'Granted. But who? That fire-eating Sir Collingham?' quickly asked the Chef, giving rein once more to his hatred.

'That is not a solution that commends itself to me, I must confess,' declared the Judge. 'The General's conduct has been blameworthy and injudicious, but he is not of the stuff that makes criminals.'

'Who, then? The conductor? No? The *pasteur*? No? The French gentlemen? – well, we have not examined them yet; but from what I saw at the first cursory glance, I am not disposed to suspect them.'

'What of that Italian?' asked the Commissary. 'Are you sure of him? His looks did not please me greatly, and he was very eager to get away from here. What if he takes to his heels?'

'Block is with him,' the Chef put in hastily, with the evident desire to stifle an unpleasant misgiving. 'We have touch of him if we want him, as we may.'

How much they might want him they only realized when they got further in their inquiry!

## CHAPTER TWELVE

Only the two Frenchmen remained for examination. They had been left to the last by pure accident. The exigencies of the inquiry had led to the preference of others, but these two well-broken and submissive gentlemen made no visible protest. However much they may have chafed inwardly at the delay, they knew better than to object; any outburst of discontent would, they knew, recoil on themselves. Not only were they perfectly patient now when summoned before the officers of justice, they were most eager to give every assistance to the law, to go beyond the mere letter, and, if needs be, volunteer information.

The first called in was the elder, M. Anatole Lafolay, a true Parisian *bourgeois*, fat and comfortable, unctuous in speech, and exceedingly deferential.

The story he told was in its main outlines that which we already know, but he was further questioned, by the light of the latest facts and ideas as now elicited.

The line adroitly taken by the Judge was to get some evidence of collusion and combination among the passengers, especially with reference to two of them, the two women of the party. On this important point M. Lafolay had something to say.

Asked if he had seen or noticed the lady's maid on the journey, he answered 'yes' very decisively and with a smack of the lips, as though the sight of this pretty and attractive person had given him considerable satisfaction.

'Did you speak to her?'

'Oh no. I had no opportunity. Besides, she had her own friends – great friends, I fancy. I caught her more than once whispering in the corner of the car with one of them.'

'And that was –?'

'I think the Italian gentleman; I am almost sure I recognized his clothes. I did not see his face, it was turned from me – towards hers, and very close, I may be permitted to say.'

'And they were *au mieux?*'

'*Au mieux mieux*, I should say. Very intimate indeed. I should not have been surprised if – when I turned away *bien entendu* – if he did not touch, just touch, her red lips. It would have been excusable – forgive me, messieurs.'

'Aha! They were so intimate as that? Indeed! And did she reserve her favours exclusively for him? Did no one else address her, pay her court *conter fleurettes* – you understand?'

'I saw her with the conductor, I believe, at Laroche, but only then. No, the Italian was her chief companion.'

'Did anyone else notice the flirtation, do you think?'

'Possibly. There was no secrecy. It was very marked. We could all see.'

'And her mistress too?'

'That I will not say. The lady I saw but little during the journey.'

A few more questions, mainly personal, as to his address, business, probable presence in Paris for the next few weeks, and M. Lafolay was permitted to depart.

The examination of the younger Frenchman, a smart, alert young man, of pleasant, insinuating address, with a quick, inquisitive eye, followed the same lines, and was distinctly corroborative on all the points to which M. Lafolay spoke. But M. Jules Devaux had something startling to impart concerning the Contessa.

When asked if he had seen her or spoken to her, he shook his head.

'No; she kept very much to herself,' he said. 'I saw her but little, hardly at all, except at Modane. She kept her own berth.'

'Where she received her own friends?'

'Oh, beyond doubt. The Englishmen both visited her there, but not the Italian.'

'The Italian? Are we to infer that she knew the Italian?'

'That is what I wish to convey. Not on the journey, though. Between Rome and Paris she did not seem to know him. It was afterwards; this morning, in fact, that I came to the conclusion that there was some secret understanding between them.'

'Why do you say that, M. Devaux?' cried the Chef excitedly. 'Let me urge you and implore you to speak out, and fully. This is of the utmost, of the very first importance.'

'Well, gentlemen, I will tell you. As you are well aware, on arrival at this Gare we were all ordered to leave the car, and marched to the waiting-room, out there. As a matter of course, the lady entered first, and she was seated when I went in. There was a strong light on her face.'

'Was her veil down?'

'Not then. I saw her lower it later, and, as I think, for reasons I will presently put before you. Madame has a beautiful face, and I gazed at it with sympathy, grieving for her, in fact, in such a trying situation; when suddenly I saw a great and remarkable change come over it.'

'Of what character?'

'It was a look of horror, disgust, surprise – a little perhaps of all three; I could not quite say which, it faded so quickly and was followed by a cold, deathlike pallor. Then almost immediately she lowered her veil.'

'Could you form any explanation for what you saw in her face? What caused it?'

'Something unexpected, I believe, some shock, or the sight of something shocking. That was how it struck me, and so forcibly that I turned to look over my shoulder, expecting to find the reason there. And it was.'

'That reason –?'

'Was the entrance of the Italian, who came just behind me. I am certain of this; he almost told me so himself, not in words, but the unmistakable leer he gave her in reply. It was wicked, sardonic, devilish, and proved beyond doubt that there was some secret, some guilty secret perhaps, between them.'

'And was that all?' cried both the Judge and M. Floçon in a breath, leaning forward in their eagerness to hear more.

'For the moment, yes. But I was so interested, so *intrigué* by this, that I watched the Italian closely, awaiting, expecting further developments. They were long in coming; indeed, I am only at the end now.'

'Explain, pray, as quickly as possible, and in your own words.'

'It was like this, monsieur. When we were all seated, I looked round, and did not at first see our Italian. At last I discovered he had taken a back seat, through modesty perhaps, or to be out of observation – how was I to know? He sat in the shadow by a door, that, in fact, which leads into this room. He was thus in the background, rather out of the way, but I could see his eyes glittering in that far-off corner, and they were turned in our direction, always fixed upon the lady, you understand. She was next me, the whole time.

'Then, as you will remember, monsieur, you called us in one by one, and I, with M. Lafolay, were the first to appear before you. When I returned to the outer room, the Italian was still staring, but not so fixedly or continuously, at the lady. From time to time his eyes wandered towards a table near which he sat, and which was just in the gangway or passage by which people must pass into your presence.

'There was some reason for this, I felt sure, although I did not understand it immediately.

'Presently I got at the hidden meaning. There was a small piece of paper, rolled up or crumpled up into a ball, lying upon this table, and the Italian wished, nay was desperately anxious, to call the lady's attention to it. If I had had any doubt of this, it was quite removed after the man had gone into the inner room. As he left us, he turned his head over his shoulder significantly and nodded very slightly, but still perceptibly, at the ball of paper.

'Well, gentlemen, I was now satisfied in my own mind that this was some artful attempt of his to communicate with the lady, and had she fallen in with it, I should have immediately informed you, the proper authorities. But whether from stupidity, dread, disinclination, a direct, definite refusal to have any dealings with this man, the lady would not – at any rate did not – pick up the ball, as she might have done easily when she in her turn passed the table on her way to your presence.

'I have no doubt it was thrown there for her, and probably you will agree with me. But it takes two to make a game of this sort, and the lady would not join. Neither on leaving the room nor on returning would she take up the missive.'

'And what became of it, then?' asked the Chef in breathless excitement.

'I have it here.' M. Devaux opened the palm of his hand and displayed the scrap of paper in the hollow rolled up into a small tight ball.

'When and how did you become possessed of it?'

'I got it only just now, when I was called in here. Before that I could not move. I was tied to my chair, practically, and ordered strictly not to move.'

'Perfectly. Monsieur's conduct has been admirable. And now tell us – what does it contain? Have you looked at it?'

'By no means. It is just as I picked it up. Will you gentlemen take it, and if you think fit, tell me what is there? Some writing – a message of some sort, or I am greatly mistaken.'

'Yes, here are words written in pencil,' said the Chef, unrolling the paper, which he handed on to the Judge, who read the contents aloud –

'*Sois discrète. Silence absolute. Si tu me trahis tu seras aussi perdu.*'

A long silence followed, broken first by the Judge, who said at last solemnly to Devaux –

'Monsieur, in the name of justice I beg to thank you most warmly. You have acted with admirable tact and judgement, and have rendered us invaluable assistance. Have you anything further to tell us?'

'No, gentlemen. That is all. And you – you have no more questions to ask? Then I presume I may withdraw?'

Beyond doubt it had been reserved for the last witness to produce facts that constituted the very essence of the inquiry.

## CHAPTER THIRTEEN

The examination was now over, and, the *procès verbaux* having been drawn up and signed, the investigating officials remained for some time in conference.

'It lies with those three, of course – the two women and the Italian. They are jointly, conjointly concerned, although the exact degrees of guilt cannot quite be apportioned,' said the Chef de la Sûreté.

'And all three are at large!' added the Judge.

'If you will issue warrants for arrest, M. le Juge, we can take them – two of them at any rate – when we choose.'

'That should be at once,' remarked the Commissary, eager, as usual, for decisive action.

'Very well. Let us proceed in that way. Prepare the warrants,' said the Judge, turning to his clerk. 'And you,' he went on, addressing M. Floçon, 'dear colleague, will you see to their execution? Madame is at the Hôtel Madagascar; that will be easy. The Italian Ripaldi we shall hear of through your inspector Block. As for the maid, Hortense Petitpré, we must search for her. That too, M. le Chef, you will of course undertake?'

'I will charge myself with it, certainly. My man should be here by now, and I will instruct him at once. Ask for him,' said M. Floçon to the Garde de Paris whom he called in.

'M. l'Inspecteur is there,' said the Garde, pointing to the outer room. 'He has just returned.'

'Returned? You mean arrived.'

'No, monsieur, returned. It is Block, who left an hour or more ago.'

'Block? Then something has happened – he has some special information, some great news! Shall we see him, M. le Juge?'

When Block appeared, it was evident that something had gone wrong with him. His face wore a look of hot, flurried excitement, and his manner was one of abject, cringing self-abasement.

353

'What is it?' asked the little Chef sharply. 'You are alone. Where is your man?'

'Alas, monsieur! how shall I tell you? He has gone – disappeared! I have lost him!'

'Impossible! You cannot mean it! Gone, now, just when we most want him? Never!'

'It is so, unhappily.'

'Idiot! *Triple bête!* You shall be dismissed, discharged from this hour. You are a disgrace to the service of the Sûreté.'

M. Floçon raved furiously at his abashed subordinate, blaming him a little too harshly and unfairly, forgetting that until quite recently there had been no strong suspicion against the Italian. We are apt at times to expect others to be intuitively possessed of knowledge that has only come to us at a much later date.

'How was it? Explain. Of course you have been drinking. It is that, or your great gluttony. You were seduced into some eating-house.'

'Monsieur, you shall hear the exact truth. When we started more than an hour ago, our fiacre took the usual route, by the Quais and along the riverside. My gentleman made himself most pleasant –'

'No doubt,' growled the Chef.

'Offered me an excellent cigar, and talked – not about the affair, you understand – but of Paris, the theatres, the races, Longchamps, Auteuil, the grand restaurants. He knew everything, all Paris, like his pocket. I was much surprised, but he told me his business often brought him here. He had been employed to follow up several great Italian criminals, and had made a number of important arrests in Paris.'

'Get on, get on! come to the essential.'

'Well, in the middle of the journey, when we were about the Pont Henri Quatre, he said, "Figure to yourself, my friend, that it is now near noon, that nothing has passed my lips since before daylight at Laroche. What say you? Could you eat a mouthful, just a scrap on the thumb-nail? Could you?"'

'And you – greedy, gourmandizing beast! – you agreed?'

'*Ma foi*, monsieur, I too was hungry. It was my regular hour. *Enfin* – anyhow, for my sins I accepted. We entered the first restaurant, that of the "Reunited Friends", you know it, perhaps, monsieur? A good house, especially noted for *tripes à la mode de Caen*.' In spite of his anguish, Block smacked his fat lips at the thought of this most succulent but very greasy dish.

'How often must I tell you to get on?'

'Forgive me, monsieur, but it is all part of my story. We had oysters, two dozen Marennes, and a glass or two of Chablis *mouton*; then a good portion of *tripes*, and with them a bottle, only one, monsieur, of Pontet Canet; after that a *biftek aux pommes* and a little Burgundy, then an *omelette au rhum*.'

'Great heavens! you should be the fat man in a fair, not an agent of the Sûreté.'

'It was all this that helped me to my destruction. He ate, this *satané* Italian, like three, and I too, I was so hungry – forgive me, sir – I did my share. But by the time we reached the cheese, a fine, ripe Camembert, had our coffee, and one thimbleful of green Chartreuse, I was *plein jusqu'au bec*, gorged up to the beak.'

'And what of your duty, your service, pray?'

'I did think of it, monsieur, but then, he, the Italian, was just the same as myself. He was a colleague. I had no fear of him, not till the very last, when he played me this evil turn. I suspected nothing when he brought out his pocket-book – it was stuffed full, monsieur; I saw that and my confidence increased – called for the reckoning, and paid with an Italian bank-note. The waiter looked doubtful at the foreign money, and went out to consult the *patron* (master). A minute after, my man got up, saying –

'"There may be some trouble about changing that bank-note. Excuse me one moment, pray." He went out, monsieur, and piff-paff, he was no more to be seen.'

'Ah, *nigaud* (ass), you are too foolish to live! Why did you not follow him? Why let him out of your sight?'

'But, monsieur, I was not to know, was I? I was to accompany him, not to watch him. I have done wrong, I confess. But then, who was to tell he meant to run away?'

The Chef could not deny the justice of this defence. It was only now, at the eleventh hour, that the Italian had become inculpated, and the question of his possible anxiety to escape had never been considered.

'He was so artful,' went on Block in further extenuation of his offence. 'He left everything behind. His overcoat, stick, this book – his own private memorandum-book seemingly –'

'Book? Hand it me,' said the Chef, and when it came into his hands he began to turn over the leaves hurriedly.

It was a small brass-bound notebook or diary, and was full of close writing in pencil.

'I do not understand, not more than a word here and there. It is no doubt Italian. Do you know that language, M. le Juge?'

'Not perfectly, but I can read it. Allow me.'

He also turned over the pages, pausing to read a passage here and there, and nodding his head from time to time, evidently struck with the importance of the matter recorded.

Meanwhile, M. Floçon continued an angry conversation with his offending subordinate.

'You will have to find him, Block, and that speedily, within twenty-four hours – today, indeed – or I will break you like a stick, and send you into the gutter. Of course, such a consummate ass as you have proved yourself would not think of searching the restaurant or the immediate neighbourhood, or of making inquiries as to whether he had been seen, or as to which way he had gone?'

'Pardon me, monsieur is too hard on me. I have been unfortunate, a victim to circumstances, still I believe I know my duty. Yes, I made inquiries, and, what is more, I heard of him.'

'Where? how?' asked the Chef gruffly, but obviously much interested.

'He never spoke to the *patron*, but walked out and let the change go. It was a note for a hundred *lire*, a hundred francs, and the restaurant bill was no more than seventeen francs.'

'Hah! that is greatly against him indeed.'

'He was much pressed, in a great hurry. Directly he crossed the threshold he called the first cab and was driving away, but he was stopped –'

'The devil! Why did they not keep him, then?'

'Stopped, but only for a moment, and accosted by a woman.'

'A woman?'

'Yes, monsieur. They exchanged but three words. He wished to pass on, to leave her, she would not consent, then they both got into the cab and were driven away together.'

The officials were now listening with all ears.

'Tell me,' said the Chef, 'quick, this woman – what was she like? Did you get her description?'

'Tall, slight, well formed, dressed all in black. Her face – it was a *sergent de ville* who saw her, and he said she was *belle fille*, dark, brunette, black hair.'

'It is the maid herself!' cried the little Chef, springing up and slapping his thigh in exuberant glee. 'The maid! the missing maid!'

CHAPTER FOURTEEN

The joy of Chef de la Sûreté at having thus come, as he supposed, upon the track of the missing maid, Hortense Petitpré, was somewhat dashed by the doubts freely expressed by the Judge as to the result of any search. Since Block's return, M. Beaumont le Hardi had developed strong symptoms of discontent and disapproval at his colleague's proceedings.

'But if it was this Hortense Petitpré how did she get there, by the bridge Henri Quatre, when we thought to find her somewhere down the line? It cannot be the same woman.'

'I beg your pardon, gentlemen,' interposed Block. 'May I say one word? I believe I can supply some interesting information about Hortense Petitpré. I understand that someone like her was seen here in the station not more than an hour ago.'

'Peste! Why were we not told this sooner?' cried the Chef impetuously. 'Who saw her? Did he speak to her? Call him in; let us see how much he knows.'

The man was summoned, one of the subordinate railway officials, who made a specific report.

Yes, he had seen a tall, slight, neat-looking woman, dressed entirely in black, who, according to her account, had arrived at 10.30 by the slow omnibus train from Dijon.

'Fichtre!' said the Chef angrily; 'and this is the first we have heard of it.'

'Monsieur was much occupied at the time, and, indeed, then we had not heard of your inquiry.'

'I sent to the Chef de Gare quite early, two or three hours since, about 9 a.m. This is most exasperating!'

'Instructions to look out for this woman have only just reached us, monsieur. There were certain formalities, I suppose.'

For once the Chef de la Sûreté cursed in his heart the red-tape, roundabout ways of French officialism.

'Well, well! Tell me about her,' he said, with a resignation he did not feel. 'Who saw her?'

'I, monsieur. I spoke to her myself. She was on the outside of the station, alone, unprotected, in a state of agitation and alarm. I went up and offered my services. Then she told me she had come from Dijon, that friends who were to have met her had not appeared. I suggested that I should put her into a cab and send her to her destination. But she was afraid of losing her friends, and preferred to wait.'

'A fine story! Did she appear to know what had happened? Had she heard of the murder?'

'Something, monsieur.'

'Who could have told her? Did you?'

'No, not I. But she knew.'

'Was not that in itself suspicious? The fact has not yet been made public.'

'It was in the air, monsieur. There was a general impression that something had happened. That was to be seen on every face, in the whispered talk, the movement to and fro of the police and the Gardes de Paris.'

'Did she speak of it, or refer to it?'

'Only to ask if the murderer was known; whether the passengers had been detained; whether there was any inquiry in progress; and then –'

'What then?'

'This gentleman,' pointing to Block, 'came out, accompanied by another. They passed pretty close to us, and I noticed that the lady slipped quickly on one side.'

'She recognized her confederate, of course, but did not wish to be seen just then. Did he, the person with Block here, see her?'

'Hardly, I think; it was all so quick, and they were gone, in a minute, to the cab-stand.'

'What did your woman do?'

'She seemed to have changed her mind all at once, and declared she would not wait for her friends. Now she was in quite a hurry to go.'

'Of course! and left you like a fool planted there. I suppose she took a cab and followed the others, Block here and his companion.'

'I believe she did. I saw her cab close behind theirs.'

'It is too late to lament this now,' said the Chef, after a short pause, looking at his colleagues. 'At least, it confirms our ideas, and brings us to certain definite conclusions. We must lay hands on these two. Their guilt is all but established. Their own acts condemn them. They must be arrested without a moment's delay.'

'If you can find them!' suggested the Judge, with a very perceptible sneer.

'That we shall certainly do. Trust to Block, who is very nearly concerned. His future depends on his success. You quite understand that, *mon brave?*'

Block made a gesture half-deprecating, half-confident.

'I do not despair, gentlemen; and if I might make so bold, M. le Chef, I will ask you to assist? If you would give orders direct from the Prefecture to make the round of the cab-stands, to ask of all the agents in charge the information we need? Before night we shall have heard from the *cocher* who drove them what became of this couple, and so get our birds themselves, or a point of fresh departure.'

'And you, Block, where shall you go?'

'Where I left him, or rather where he left me,' replied the detective inspector, with an attempt at wit, which fell quite flat, being extinguished by a frigid look from the Judge.

'Go,' said M. Floçon briefly and severely to his subordinate; 'and remember that you have now to justify your retention in the Police de la Sûreté.'

Then, turning to M. Beaumont le Hardi, the Chef went on pleasantly –

'Well, M. le Juge, it promises, I think; it is all fairly satisfactory, eh?'

'I am sorry I cannot agree with you,' replied the Judge harshly. 'On the contrary, I consider that we – or more exactly you, for neither I nor M. Garraud accept any share in it – you have so far failed, and miserably.'

'*De grâce*, M. le Juge, you are too severe,' protested M. Floçon quite humbly.

'Well! Look at it from all points of view. What have we got? What have we gained? Nothing, or, if anything, it is of the smallest, and it is already jeopardized, if not absolutely lost.'

'We have at least gained the positive assurance of the guilt of certain individuals.'

'Whom you have allowed to slip through your fingers.'

'Ah, not so, M. le Juge! We have one under surveillance. My man Galipaud is there at the hotel watching the Contessa.'

'Do not talk to me of your men, M. Floçon,' angrily interposed the Judge. 'One of them has given us a touch of his quality. Why should not the other be equally foolish? I quite expect to hear that the Contessa also has gone, that would be the climax.'

'It shall not happen. I will take the warrant and arrest her now, at once, myself,' cried M. Floçon.

'Well, that will be something, yet not much. Yes, she is only one, and not to my mind, the most criminal. We do not know as yet the exact responsibility of each, the exact measure of their guilt; but I do not myself believe that the Contessa was a prime mover, or, indeed, more than an accessory. She was drawn into it, perhaps involved, how or why we cannot know, but possibly by fortuitous circumstances that put an unavoidable pressure upon her; a consenting party, but under protest. That is my view of the lady.'

M. Floçon shook his head. Prepossessions with him were tenacious, and he had made up his mind about the Contessa's guilt.

'When you again interrogate her, M. le Juge, by the light of your present knowledge, I believe you will think otherwise. She will confess – you will make her, your skill is unrivalled – and you will then admit, M. le Juge, that I was right in my suspicions.'

'Ah, well, produce her! We shall see,' said the Judge, somewhat mollified by M. Floçon's fulsome flattery.

'I will bring her to your chamber of instruction within an hour, M. le Juge,' said the Chef very confidently.

But he was doomed to disappointment in this as he was in other respects.

## CHAPTER FIFTEEN

Let us go back a little in point of time, and follow the movements of Sir Charles Collingham.

It was barely 11 a.m. when he left the Gare de Lyons with his brother, the Reverend Silas, and the military attaché, Colonel Papillon. They paused for a moment outside the station while the baggage was being got together.

'See, Silas,' said the General, pointing to the clock, 'you will have plenty of time for the 11.50 train to Calais for London, but you must hurry up and drive straight across Paris to the Nord. I suppose he can go, Jack?'

'Certainly, as he has promised to return if called upon.'

And Mr Collingham promptly took advantage of the permission.

'But you, General, what are your plans?' went on the attaché.

'I shall go to the club first, get a room, dress, and all that. Then call at the Hôtel Madagascar. There is a lady there – one of our party, in fact – and I should like to ask after her. She may be glad of my services.'

'English? Is there anything we can do for her?'

'Yes, she is an Englishwoman, but the widow of an Italian – the Contessa di Castagneto.'

'Oh, but I know her!' said Papillon. 'I remember her in Rome two or three years ago. A deuced pretty woman, very much admired, but she was in deep mourning then, and went out very little. I wished she had gone out more. There were lots of men ready to fall at her feet.'

'You were in Rome, then, some time back? Did you ever come across a man there, Quadling, the banker?'

'Of course I did. Constantly. He was a good deal about – a rather free-living, self-indulgent sort of chap. And now you mention his name, I recollect they said he was much smitten by this particular lady, the Contessa di Castagneto.'

'And did she encourage him?'

'Lord! how can I tell? Who shall say how a woman's fancy falls? It might have suited her too. They said she was not in very good circumstances, and he was thought to be a rich man. Of course we know better than that now.'

'Why *now*?'

'Haven't you heard? It was in the *Figaro* yesterday, and in all the Paris papers. Quadling's bank has gone smash; he has bolted with all the ready he could lay hands upon.'

'He didn't get far, then!' cried Sir Charles. 'You look surprised, Jack. Didn't they tell you? This Quadling was the man murdered in the *wagon-lit*. It was no doubt for the money he carried with him.'

'Was it Quadling? My word! what a terrible Nemesis. Well, *nil nisi bonum*, but I never thought much of the chap, and your friend the Contessa has had an escape. But now, sir, I must be moving. My function is for twelve noon. If you want me, mind you send – 207 Rue Miromesnil, or to the Embassy; but let us arrange to meet this evening, eh? Dinner and a theatre – what do you say?'

Then Colonel Papillon rode off, and the General was driven to the Boulevard des Capucines, having much to occupy his thoughts by the way.

It did not greatly please him to have this story of the Contessa's relations with Quadling, as first hinted at by the police, endorsed now by his friend Papillon. Clearly she had kept up her acquaintance, her intimacy to the very last: why otherwise should she have received him, alone, been closeted with him for an hour or more on the very eve of his flight? It was a clandestine acquaintance too, or seemed so, for Sir Charles, although a frequent visitor at her house, had never met Quadling there.

What did it all mean? And yet, what, after all, did it matter to him?

A good deal really more than he chose to admit to himself, even now, when closely questioning his secret heart. The fact was, the Contessa had made a very strong impression on him from the first. He had admired her greatly during the past winter at Rome, but then it was only a passing fancy, as he thought – the pleasant platonic flirtation of a middle-aged man, who never expected to inspire or feel a *grande passion*. Only now, when he had shared a serious trouble with her, had passed through common difficulties and dangers, he was finding what accident may do – how it may fan a first liking into a stronger flame. It was absurd, of course. He was fifty-one, he had weathered many trifling *affaires de cœur*, and here he was, bowled over at last, and by a woman he was not certain was entitled to his respect.

What was he to do?

The answer came at once and unhesitatingly, as it would to any other honest, chivalrous gentleman.

'By George, I'll stick to her through thick and thin! I'll trust her whatever happens or has happened, come what may. Such a woman as that is above suspicion. She *must* be straight. I should be a beast and a blackguard double distilled to think anything else. I am sure she can put all right with a word, can explain everything when she chooses. I will wait till she does.'

Thus fortified and decided, Sir Charles took his way to the Hôtel Mâdagascar about noon. At the porter's lodge he inquired for the Contessa, and begged that his card might be sent up to her. The man looked at it, then at the visitor, as he stood there waiting rather impatiently, then again at the card. At last he walked out and across the inner courtyard of the hotel to the bureau. Presently the manager came back, bowing low, and, holding the card in his hand, began a desultory conversation.

'Yes, yes,' cried the General, angrily cutting short all references to the weather and the number of English visitors in Paris. 'But be so good as to let Madame la Comtesse know that I have called.'

'Ah, to be sure! I came to tell Monsieur le Général that madame will hardly be able to see him. She is indisposed, I believe. At any rate, she does not receive today.'

'As to that, we shall see. I will take no answer except direct from her. Take or send up my card without further delay. I insist! Do you hear?' said the General, so fiercely that the manager turned tail and fled upstairs.

Perhaps he yielded his ground the more readily that he saw over the General's shoulder the figure of Galipaud the detective looming in the archway. It had been arranged that, as it was not advisable to have the inspector hanging about the courtyard of the hotel, the *concierge* or the manager should keep watch over the Contessa and detain any visitors who might call upon her. Galipaud had taken post at a *marchand de vin* over the way, and was to be summoned whenever his presence was thought necessary.

There he was now, standing just behind the General, and for the present unseen by him.

But then a telegraph messenger came in and up to the lodge. He held the usual blue envelope in his hand, and called out the name on the address –

'Castagneto. Contessa Castagneto.'

At sound of which the General turned sharply, to find Galipaud advancing and stretching out his hand to take the message.

'Pardon me,' cried Sir Charles, promptly interposing and understanding the situation at a glance. 'I am just going up to see that lady. Give me the telegram.'

Galipaud would have disputed the point, when the General, who had already recognized him, said quietly –

'No, no, M. l'Inspecteur, you have no earthly right to it. I guess why you are here, but you are not entitled to interfere with private correspondence. Stand back'; and seeing the detective hesitate, he added peremptorily –

'*Assez. Je vous ordonne. Retirez vous, et plus vite que ça!*'

The manager now returned, and admitted that Madame la Comtesse would receive her visitor. A few seconds more, and the General was admitted into her presence.

'How truly kind of you to call!' she said at once, coming up to him with both hands outstretched and frank gladness in her eyes.

Yes, she was very attractive in her plain, dark travelling dress draping her tall, graceful figure; her beautiful, pale face was enhanced by the rich tones of her dark brown, wavy hair, while just a narrow band of white muslin at her wrists and neck set off the dazzling clearness of her skin.

'Of course I came. I thought you might want me, or might like to know the latest news,' he answered, as he held her hands in his for a few seconds longer than was perhaps absolutely necessary.

'Oh, do tell me! Is there anything fresh?' There was a flash of crimson colour in her cheek, which faded almost instantly.

'This much. They have found out who the man was.'

'Really? Positively? Whom do they say now?'

'Perhaps I had better not tell you. It may surprise you, shock you to hear. I think you knew him –'

'Nothing can well shock me now. I have had too many shocks already. Whom do they think it is?'

'A Mr Quadling, a banker, who is supposed to have absconded from Rome.'

She received the news so impassively, with such strange self-possession, that for a moment he was disappointed in her. But then, quick to excuse, he suggested –

'You may have already heard?'

'Yes; the police people at the railway station told me they thought it was Mr Quadling.'

'But you knew him?'

'Certainly. They were my bankers, much to my sorrow. I shall lose heavily by their failure.'

'That also has reached you, then?' interrupted the General hastily and somewhat uneasily.

'To be sure. The man told me of it himself. Indeed, he came to me the very day I was leaving Rome, and made me an offer – a most obliging offer.'

'To share his fallen fortunes?'

'Sir Charles Collingham! How can you? That creature!' The contempt in her tone was immeasurable.

'I had heard – well, some one said that –'

'Speak out, General; I shall not be offended. I know what you mean. It is perfectly true that the man once presumed to pester me with his attentions. But I would as soon have looked at a courier or a cook. And now –'

There was a pause. The General felt on delicate ground. He could ask no questions – anything more must come from the Contessa herself.

'But let me tell you what his offer was. I don't know why I listened to it. I ought to have at once informed the police. I wish I had.'

'It might have saved him from his fate.'

'Every villain gets his deserts in the long-run,' she said, with bitter sententiousness. 'And this Mr Quadling is – But wait, you shall know him better. He came to me to propose – what do you think? – that he – his bank, I mean – should secretly repay me the amount of my deposit, all the money I had in it. To join me in his fraud, in fact –'

'The scoundrel! Upon my word, he has been well served. And that was the last you saw of him?'

'I saw him on the journey, at Turin, at Modane, at – Oh, Sir Charles, do not ask me any more about him!' she cried, with a sudden outburst, half grief, half dread. 'I cannot tell you – I am obliged to – I – I –'

'Then do not say another word,' he said promptly.

'There are other things. But my lips are sealed – at least for the present. You do not – will not think any worse of me?'

She laid her hand gently on his arm, and his closed over it with such evident goodwill that a blush crimsoned her cheek. It still hung there, and deepened when he said warmly –

'As if anything could make me do that! Don't you know – you may not, but let me assure you, Contessa – that nothing could happen to shake me in the high opinion I have of you. Come what may, I shall trust you, believe in you, think well of you – always.'

'How sweet of you to say that! and now, of all times,' she murmured quite softly, and looking up for the first time, shyly, to meet his eyes.

Her hand was still on his arm, covered by his, and she nestled so close to him that it was easy, natural, indeed, for him to slip his other arm around her waist and draw her to him.

'And now – of all times – may I say one word more?' he whispered in her ear. 'Will you give me the right to shelter and protect you, to stand by you, share your troubles, or keep them from you –?'

'No, no, no indeed, not now!' She looked up appealingly, the tears brimming up in her bright eyes. 'I cannot, will not accept this sacrifice. You are only speaking out of your true-hearted chivalry. You must not join yourself to me, you must not involve yourself –'

He stopped her protests by the oldest and most effectual method known in such cases. That first sweet kiss sealed the compact so quickly entered into between them.

And after that she surrendered at discretion. There was no more hesitation or reluctance; she accepted his love as he had offered it, freely, with whole heart and soul, crept up under his sheltering wing like a storm-beaten dove re-entering the nest, and there, cooing softly, 'My knight – my own true knight and lord,' yielded herself willingly and unquestioningly to his tender caresses.

Such moments snatched from the heart of pressing anxieties are made doubly sweet by their sharp contrast with a background of trouble.

## CHAPTER SIXTEEN

They sat there, these two, hand locked in hand, saying little, satisfied now to be with each other and their new-found love. The time flew by far too fast, till at last Sir Charles, with a half laugh, suggested –

'Do you know, dearest Contessa –'

She corrected him in a soft, low voice.

'My name is Sabine – Charles.'

'Sabine, darling. It is very prosaic of me, perhaps, but do you know that I am nearly starved? I came on here at once. I have had no breakfast.'

'Nor have I,' she answered, smiling. 'I was thinking of it when – when you appeared like a whirlwind, and since then, events have moved so fast.'

'Are you sorry, Sabine? Would you rather go back to – to – before?' She made a pretty gesture of closing his traitor lips with her small hand.

'Not for worlds. But you soldiers – you are terrible men! Who can resist you?'

'Bah! It is you who are irresistible. But there, why not put on your jacket and let us go out to lunch somewhere – Durand's, Voisin's, the Café de la Paix? Which do you prefer?'

'I suppose they will not try to stop us?'

'Who should try?' he asked.

'The people of the hotel – the police – I cannot exactly say whom; but I dread something of the sort. I don't quite understand that manager. He has been up to see me several times, and he spoke rather oddly, rather rudely.'

'Then he shall answer for it,' snorted Sir Charles hotly. 'It is the fault of that brute of a detective, I suppose. Still they would hardly dare –'

'A detective? What? Here? Are you sure?'

'Perfectly sure. It is one of those from the Gare de Lyons. I knew him again directly, and he was inclined to be interfering. Why, I caught him trying – but that reminds me – I rescued this telegram from his clutches.'

He took the little blue envelope from his breast pocket and handed it to her kissing the tips of her fingers as she took it from him.

'Ah!'

A sudden ejaculation of dismay escaped her, when, after rather carelessly tearing the message open, she had glanced at it.

'What is the matter?' he asked in eager solicitude. 'May I not know?'

She made no offer to give him the telegram, and said in a faltering voice, and with much hesitation of manner, 'I do not know. I hardly think – of course I do not like to withhold anything, not now. And yet, this is a business which concerns me only, I am afraid. I ought not to drag you into it.'

'What concerns you is very much my business too. I do not wish to force your confidence, still –'

She gave him the telegram quite obediently, with a little sigh of relief, glad to realize now, for the first time after many years, that there was someone to give her orders and take the burden of trouble off her shoulders.

He read it, but did not understand it in the least. It ran: 'I must see you immediately, and beg you will come. You will find Hortense here. She is giving trouble. You only can deal with her. Do not delay. Come at once, or we must go to you – Ripaldi, Hôtel Ivoire, Rue Bellechasse.'

'What does this mean? Who sends it? Who is Ripaldi?' asked Sir Charles rather brusquely.

'He – he – oh, Charles, I shall have to go. Anything would be better than his coming here.'

'Ripaldi? Haven't I heard the name? He was one of those in the *wagon-lit*, I think? The police chief called it out once or twice. Am I not right? Please tell me – am I not right?'

'Yes, yes; this man was there with the rest of us. A dark man, who sat near the door –'

'Ah, to be sure. But what – what in Heaven's name has he to do with you? How does he dare to send you such an impudent message as this? Surely, Sabine, you will tell me? You will admit that I have a right to ask?'

'Yes, of course. I will tell you, Charles, everything; but not here – not now. It must be on the way. I have been very wrong, very foolish – but oh, come, come, do let us be going. I am so afraid he might –'

'Then I may go with you? You do not object to that?'

'I much prefer it – much. Do let us make haste!'

She snatched up her sealskin jacket, and held it to him prettily, that he might help her into it, which he did neatly and cleverly, smoothing her great puffed-out sleeves under each shoulder of the coat, still talking eagerly and taking no toll for his trouble as she stood patiently, passively before him.

'And this Hortense? It is your maid, is it not – the woman who had taken herself off? How comes it that she is with that Italian fellow? Upon my soul, I don't understand – not a little bit.'

'I cannot explain that either. It is most strange, most incomprehensible, but we shall soon know. Please, Charles, please do not get impatient.'

They passed together down into the hotel courtyard and across it, under the archway which led past the *concierge*'s lodge into the street.

On seeing them, he came out hastily and placed himself in front, quite plainly barring their egress.

'Oh, madame, one moment,' he said in a tone that was by no means conciliatory. 'The manager wants to speak to you; he told me to tell you, and stop you if you went out.'

'The manager can speak to madame when she returns,' interposed the General angrily, answering for the Contessa.

'I have had my orders, and I cannot allow her —'

'Stand aside, you scoundrel!' cried the General, blazing up; 'or upon my soul I shall give you such a lesson, you will be sorry you were ever born.'

At this moment the manager himself appeared in reinforcement and the *concierge* turned to him for protection and support.

'I was merely giving madame your message, M. Auguste, when this gentleman interposed, threatened me, maltreated me —'

'Oh, surely not; it is some mistake'; the manager spoke most suavely. 'But certainly I did wish to speak to madame. I wished to ask her whether she was satisfied with her *appartement*. I find that the rooms she has generally occupied have fallen vacant, *justement à propos*. Perhaps madame would like to look at them, and move?'

'Thank you, M. Auguste, you are very good; but at another time. I am very much pressed just now. When I return in an hour or two, not now.'

The manager was profuse in his apologies, and made no further difficulty.

'Oh, as you please, madame. Perfectly. By and by, later, when you choose.'

The fact was, the desired result had been obtained. For now, on the far side from where he had been watching, Galipaud appeared, no doubt in reply to some secret signal, and the detective with a short nod in acknowledgement had evidently removed his embargo.

A cab was called, and Sir Charles, having put the Contessa in, was turning to give the driver his instructions, when a fresh complication arose.

Some one coming round the corner had caught a glimpse of the lady disappearing into the fiacre, and cried out from afar.

'Stay! Stop! I want to speak to that lady; detain her.' It was the sharp voice of little M. Floçon, whom most of those present, certainly the Contessa and Sir Charles, immediately recognized.

'No, no, no – don't let them keep me – I cannot wait now,' she whispered in earnest, urgent appeal. It was not lost on her loyal and devoted friend.

'*Allez!*' he shouted to the cabman, with all the peremptory insistance of one trained to give words of command. '*En route. Au galop. Joli pourboire.* Tell him where to go, Sabine. I'll follow – in less than no time.'

The fiacre rattled off at top speed, and the General turned to confront M. Floçon.

The little Chef de la Sûreté was white to the lips with rage and disappointment; but he also was a man of promptitude, and before falling foul of this pestilent Englishman, who had again marred his plans, he shouted to Galipaud –

'Quick! After them! Follow her wherever she goes. Take this,' – he thrust a paper into his subordinate's hand. 'It is a *mandat d'amener*. Arrest her wherever you find her, and bring her to the Quai l'Horloge,' the euphemistic title of the headquarters of the French police.

The pursuit was started at once, and then the Chef turned upon Sir Charles.

'Now *à nous deux*,' he said fiercely. 'You must account to me for what you have done.'

'Must I?' answered the General mockingly and with a little laugh. 'It is perfectly easy. Madame was in a hurry, so I helped her to get away. *Voilà tout.*'

'You have traversed and opposed the action of the law. You have impeded me, the Chef de la Sûreté, in the execution of my duty. It is not the first time, but now you must answer for it.'

'Dear me!' said the General in the same flippant, irritating tone.

'You will have to accompany me now to the Prefecture.'

'And if it does not suit me to go?'

'I will have you carried there, *ligoté*, tied hand and foot, by the *sergents de ville*, like any common rapscallion taken in *flagrant délit* who resists the authority of the police.'

'Oho, you talk very big, M. le Chef. Perhaps you will be so obliging as to tell me what I have done.'

'You have connived at the escape of a criminal from justice –'

'That lady? Psha!'

'She is charged with a heinous crime – that in which you yourself were implicated – the murder of that man in the *wagon*.'

'Bah! You must be a stupid goose, *bête comme une oie*, to hint at such a thing! A lady of birth, breeding, the highest respectability – impossible!'

'All that has not prevented her from allying herself with base, common wretches. I do not say she struck the blow, but I believe she inspired, concerted, approved it, leaving her confederates to do the actual deed.'

'Confederates?'

'The man Ripaldi, your Italian fellow-traveller; her maid Hortense Petitpré, who was missing this morning.'

The General was fairly staggered at this unexpected blow. Half an hour ago he would have scouted the very thought, indignantly repelled the spoken words that even hinted a suspicion of Sabine Castagneto. But that telegram, signed Ripaldi, the introduction of the maid's name, and the suggestion that she was troublesome, the threat that if the Contessa did not go, they would come to her, and her marked uneasiness thereat – all this implied plainly the existence of collusion, of some secret relations, some secret understanding between her and the others.

He could not entirely conceal the trouble that now overcame him; it certainly did not escape so shrewd an observer as M. Floçon, who promptly tried to turn it to good account.

'Come, M. le Général,' he said, with much assumed *bonhomie*. 'I can see how it is with you, and you have my sincere sympathy. We are all of us liable to be carried away, and there is much excuse for you in this. But now – believe me, I am justified in saying it – now I tell you that our case is strong against her, that it is not mere speculation, but supported by facts. Now surely you will come over to our side?'

'As how?'

'Tell us frankly all you know – where that lady has gone, help us to lay our hands on her.'

'Your own people will do that. I heard you order that man to follow her.'

'Probably; still I would rather have the information from you. It would satisfy me of your goodwill. I need not then proceed to extremities –'

'I certainly shall not give it you,' said the General hotly. 'Anything I know about or have heard from the Contessa Castagneto is sacred; besides, I still believe in her – thoroughly. Nothing you have said can shake me.'

'Then I must ask you to accompany me to the Prefecture. You will come, I trust, on my *invitation*.' The Chef spoke quietly, but with considerable dignity, and he laid a slight stress upon the last word.

'Meaning that if I do not, you will have resort to something stronger?'

'That will be quite unnecessary, I am sure – at least I hope so. Still –'

'I will go where you like, only I will tell you nothing more, not a single word; and before I start, I must let my friends at the Embassy know where to find me.'

'Oh, with all my heart,' said the little Chef, shrugging his shoulders. 'We will call there on our way, and you can tell the *concierge*. They will know where to find us.'

## CHAPTER SEVENTEEN

Sir Charles Collingham and his escort, M. Floçon, entered a cab together and were driven first to the Faubourg St Honoré. The General tried hard to maintain his nonchalance, but he was yet a little crestfallen at the turn things had taken, and M. Floçon, who, on the other hand, was elated and triumphant, saw it. But no words passed between them until they arrived at the portals of the British Embassy, and the General handed out his card to the magnificent porter who received them.

'Kindly let Colonel Papillon have that without delay.' The General had written a few words: 'I have got into fresh trouble. Come on to me at the Police Prefecture if you can spare the time.'

'The Colonel is now in the Chancery: will not monsieur wait?' asked the porter, with superb civility.

But the Chef would not suffer this, and interposed, answering abruptly for Sir Charles —

'No. It is impossible. We are going to the Quai l'Horloge. It is an urgent matter.'

The porter knew what the Quai l'Horloge meant, and he guessed intuitively who was speaking. Every Frenchman can recognize a police officer, and has, as a rule, no great opinion of him.

'*Bien!*' now said the porter curtly, as he banged the wicket-gate on the retreating cab, and he did not hurry himself in giving the card to Colonel Papillon.

'Does this mean that I am a prisoner?' asked Sir Charles, his gorge rising, as it did easily.

'It means, monsieur, that you are in the hands of justice until your recent conduct has been fully explained,' said the Chef, with the air of a despot.

'But I protest —'

'I wish to hear no further observations, monsieur. You may reserve them till you can give them to the right person (*à qui de droit*).'

The General's temper was sorely ruffled. He did not like it at all; yet what

372

could he do? Prudence gained the day, and after a struggle he decided to submit, lest worse might befall him.

There was, in truth, worse to be encountered. It was very irksome to be in the power of this now domineering little man on his own ground, and eager to show his power. It was with a very bad grace that Sir Charles obeyed the curt orders he received, to leave the cab, to enter at a side door of the Prefecture, to follow his pompous conductor along the long vaulted passages of this rambling building, up many flights of stone stairs, to halt obediently at the command of the Chef when at length they reached a closed door on an upper storey.

'It is here!' said M. Floçon, as he turned the handle unceremoniously without knocking. 'Enter.'

A man was seated at a small desk in the centre of a big bare room, who rose at once at the sight of M. Floçon, and bowed deferentially without speaking.

'Baume,' said the Chef shortly, 'I wish to leave this gentleman with you. Make him at home' – the words were spoken in manifest irony – 'and when I call, you bring him at once to my cabinet. You, monsieur, you will oblige me by staying here.'

Sir Charles nodded carelessly, took the first chair that offered, and sat down by the fire.

He was to all intents and purposes in custody, and he examined his gaoler at first wrathfully, then curiously, struck with his rather strange figure and appearance. Baume, as the Chef had called him, was a short, thick-set man with a great shock head sunk in low between a pair of enormous shoulders, betokening great physical strength; he stood on very thin but greatly twisted bow legs, and the quaintness of his figure was emphasized by the short black blouse or smockfrock he wore over his other clothes like a French artisan.

He was a man of few words, and those not the most polite in tone, for when the General began with a banal remark about the weather, M. Baume replied shortly –

'I wish to have no talk'; and when Sir Charles pulled out his cigarette-case, as he did almost automatically from time to time when in any situation of annoyance or perplexity, Baume raised his hand warningly and grunted –

'*Défendu.*'

'Then I'll be hanged if I don't smoke in spite of every man jack of you!' cried the General hotly, rising from his seat and speaking unconsciously in English.

'*Plait-il?*' asked Baume gruffly. He was one of the detective staff, and was only doing his duty according to his lights, and he said so with such an injured air that the General was pacified, laughed, and relapsed into silence without lighting his cigarette.

The time ran on, from minutes into nearly an hour, a very trying wait for Sir Charles. There is always something irritating in doing antechamber, in kicking one's heels in the waiting-room of any functionary or official, high or low, and the General found it hard to possess himself in patience, when he thought he was being thus ignominiously treated by a man like M. Floçon. All the time, too, he was worrying himself about the Contessa, wondering first how she had fared; next, where she was just then; last of all, and longest, whether it was possible for her to be mixed up in anything compromising or criminal.

Suddenly an electric bell struck in the room. There was a table telephone at Baume's elbow; he took up the handle, put the tube to his mouth and ear, got his message answered, and then, rising, said abruptly to Sir Charles –

'Come.'

When the General was at last ushered into the presence of the Chef de la Sûreté, he found to his satisfaction that Colonel Papillon was also there, and at M. Floçon's side sat the instructing judge, M. Beaumont le Hardi, who, after waiting politely until the two Englishmen had exchanged greetings, was the first to speak, and in apology.

'You will, I trust, pardon us, M. le Général, for having detained you here and so long. But there were, as we thought, good and sufficient reasons. If those have now lost some of their cogency, we still stand by our action as having been justifiable in the execution of our duty. We are now willing to let you go free, because – because –'

'We have caught the person, the lady you helped to escape,' blurted out the Chef, unable to resist making the point.

'The Contessa? Is she here, in custody? Never!'

'Undoubtedly she is in custody, and in very close custody too,' went on M. Floçon gleefully. '*Au secret*, if you know what that means – in a cell separate and apart, where no one is permitted to see or speak to her.'

'Surely not that? Jack – Papillon – this must not be. I beg of you, implore, insist, that you will get his lordship to interpose.'

'But, sir, how can I? You must not ask impossibilities. The Contessa Castagneto is really an Italian subject now.'

'She is English by birth, and whether or no, she is a woman, a high-bred lady; and it is abominable, unheard of, to subject her to such monstrous treatment,' said the General.

'But these gentlemen declare that they are fully warranted that she has put herself in the wrong – greatly, culpably in the wrong.'

'I don't believe it!' cried the General indignantly. 'Not from these chaps, a pack of idiots, always on the wrong tack! I don't believe a word, not if they swear.'

'But they have documentary evidence – papers of the most damaging kind against her.'

'Where? How?'

'He – M. le Juge – has been showing me a notebook'; and the General's eyes, following Jack Papillon's, were directed to a small *carnet*, or memorandum-book, which the Judge, interpreting the glance, was tapping significantly with his finger.

Then the Judge said blandly, 'It is easy to perceive that you protest, M. le Général, against that lady's arrest. Is it so? Well, we are not called upon to justify it to you, not in the very least. But we are dealing with a *galant homme*, an officer of high rank and consideration, and you shall know things that we are not bound to tell, to you or to anyone.'

'First,' he continued, holding up the notebook, 'do you know what this is? Have you ever seen it before?'

'I am dimly conscious of the fact, and yet I cannot say when or where.'

'It is the property of one of your fellow-travellers – an Italian called Ripaldi.'

'Ripaldi?' said the General, remembering with some uneasiness that he had seen the name at the bottom of the Contessa's telegram. 'Ah! now I understand.'

'You had heard of it, then? In what connection?' asked the Judge a little carelessly, but it was a suddenly planned pitfall.

'I now understand,' replied the General, perfectly on his guard, 'why the notebook was familiar to me. I had seen it in that man's hands in the waiting-room. He was writing in it.'

'Indeed? A favourite occupation evidently. He was fond of confiding in that notebook, and committed to it much that he never expected would see the light – his movements, intentions, ideas, even his inmost thoughts. The book – which he no doubt lost inadvertently – is very incriminating to himself and his friends.'

'What do you imply?' hastily inquired Sir Charles.

'Simply that it is on that which is written here that we base one part, perhaps the strongest, of our case against the Contessa. It is strangely but convincingly corroborative of our suspicions against her.'

'May I look at it for myself?' went on the General in a tone of contemptuous disbelief.

'It is in Italian. Perhaps you can read that language? If not, I have translated the most important passages,' said the Judge, offering some other papers.

'Thank you; if you will permit me, I should prefer to look at the original'; and the General, without more ado, stretched out his hand and took the notebook.

What he read there, as he quickly scanned its pages, shall be told in the next chapter. It will be seen that there were things written that looked very damaging to his dear friend, Sabine Castagneto.

Ripaldi's diary – its ownership plainly shown by the record of his name in full, Natale Ripaldi, inside the cover – was a commonplace notebook bound in shabby drab cloth, its edges and corners strengthened with some sort of white metal. The pages were of coarse paper, lined blue and red, and they were dog-eared and smirched as though they had been constantly turned over and used.

The earlier entries were little more than a record of work to do or done.

'Jan. 11. To call at Café di Roma, 12.30. Beppo will meet me.

'Jan. 13. Traced M.L. Last employed as a model at S.'s studio, Palazzo B.

'Jan. 15. There is trouble brewing at the Circulo Bonafede; Louvain, Malatesta, and the Englishman Sprot, have joined it. All are noted Anarchists.

'Jan. 20. Mem., pay Trattore. The Bestia will not wait. X. is also pressing, and Mariuccia. Situation tightens.

'Jan. 23. Ordered to watch Q. Could I work him? No. Strong doubts of his solvency.

'Feb. 10, 11, 12. After Q. No grounds yet.

'Feb. 27. Q. keeps up good appearance. Any mistake? Shall I try him? Sorely pressed. X. threatens me with Prefettura.

'March 1. Q. in difficulties. Out late every night. Is playing high; poor luck.

'March 3. Q. means mischief. Preparing for a start?

'March 10. Saw Q. about, here, there, everywhere.'

Then followed a brief account of Quadling's movements on the day before his departure from Rome, very much as they have been described in a previous chapter. These were made mostly in the form of reflections, conjectures, hopes, and fears; hurry-scurry of pursuit had no doubt broken the immediate record of events, and these had been entered next day in the train.

'March 17 (the day previous). He has not shown up. I thought to see him at

377

the buffet at Genoa. The conductor took him his coffee to the car. I hoped to have begun an acquaintance.

'12.30. Breakfasted at Turin. Q. did not come to table. Found him hanging about outside restaurant. Spoke; got short reply. Wishes to avoid observation, I suppose.

'But he speaks to others. He has claimed acquaintance with madame's lady's maid, and he wants to speak to the mistress. "Tell her I must speak to her," I heard him say, as I passed close to them. Then they separated hurriedly.

'At Modane he came to the Douane, and afterwards into the restaurant. He bowed across the table to the lady. She hardly recognized him, which is odd. Of course she must know him; then why –? There is something between them, and the maid is in it.

'What shall I do? I could spoil any game of theirs if I stepped in. What are they after? His money, no doubt.

'So am I; I have the best right to it, for I can do most for him. He is absolutely in my power, and he'll see that – he's no fool – directly he knows who I am, and why I'm here. It will be worth his while to buy me off, if I'm ready to sell myself, and my duty, and the Prefettura – and why shouldn't I? What better can I do? Shall I ever have such a chance again? Twenty, thirty, forty thousand lire, more, even, at one stroke; why, it's a fortune! I could go to the Republic, to America, North or South, send for Mariuccia – no, cospetto! I will continue free! I will spend the money on myself, as I alone will have earned it, and at such risk.

'I have worked it out thus:

'I will go to him at the very last, just before we are reaching Paris. Tell him, threaten him with arrest, then give him his chance of escape. No fear that he won't accept it; he must, whatever he may have settled with the others. Altro! I snap my fingers at them. He has most to fear from me.'

The next entries were made after some interval, a long interval – no doubt, after the terrible deed had been done – and the words were traced with trembling fingers, so that the writing was most irregular and scarcely legible.

'Ugh! I am still trembling with horror and fear. I cannot get it out of my mind; I never shall. Why, what tempted me? How could I bring myself to do it?

'But for these two women – they are fiends, furies – it would never have been necessary. Now one of them has escaped, and the other – she is here, so cold-blooded, so self-possessed and quiet – who would have thought it of her? That she, a lady of rank and high breeding, gentle, delicate, tender-hearted. Tender? the fiend! Oh, shall I ever forget her?

'And now she has me in her power! But have I not her also? We are in the same boat – we must sink or swim together. We are equally bound, I to her, she to me. What are we to do? How shall we meet inquiry? *Santissima Donna!* why did I not risk it, and climb out like the maid? It was terrible for the moment, but the worst would have been over, and now –'

There was yet more, scribbled in the same faltering, agitated handwriting, and from the context the entries had been made in the waiting-room of the Gare.

'I must attract her attention. She will not look my way. I want her to understand that I have something special to say to her, and that, as we are forbidden to speak, I am writing it herein – that she must contrive to take the book from me and read unobserved.

'*Cospetto!* she is stupid! Has fear dazed her entirely? No matter, I will set it all down.'

Now followed what the police deemed such damaging evidence.

'Contessa. Remember. Silence – absolute silence. Not a word as to who I am, or what is common knowledge to us both. It is done. That cannot be undone. Be brave, resolute; admit nothing. Stick to it that you know nothing, heard nothing. Deny that you knew *him*, or me. Swear you slept soundly the night through, make some excuse, say you were drugged, anything, only be on your guard, and say nothing about me. I warn you. Leave me alone. Or – but your interests are my interests; we must stand or fall together. Afterwards I will meet you – I *must* meet you somewhere. If we miss at the station front, write to me Poste Restante, Grand Hôtel, and give me an address. This is imperative. Once more, silence and discretion.'

This ended the writing in the notebook, and the whole perusal occupied Sir Charles from fifteen to twenty minutes, during which the French officials watched his face closely, and his friend Colonel Papillon anxiously.

But the General's mask was impenetrable, and at the end of his reading he turned back to read and re-read many pages, holding the book to the light, and seeming to examine the contents very curiously.

'Well?' said the Judge at last, when he met the General's eye.

'Do you lay great store by this evidence?' asked the General in a calm, dispassionate voice.

'Is it not natural that we should? Is it not strongly, conclusively incriminating?'

'It would be so, of course, if it were to be depended upon. But as to that I have my doubts, and grave doubts.'

'Bah!' interposed the Chef; 'that is mere conjecture, mere assertion. Why should not the book be believed? It is perfectly genuine –'

'Wait, M. le Chef,' said the General, raising his hand. 'Have you not noticed – surely it cannot have escaped so astute a police functionary – that the entries are not all in the same handwriting?'

'What! Oh, that is too absurd!' cried both the officials in a breath.

They saw at once that if this discovery were admitted to be an absolute fact, the whole drift of their conclusions must be changed.

'Examine the book for yourselves. To my mind it is perfectly clear and beyond all question,' insisted Sir Charles. 'I am quite positive that the last pages were written by a different hand from the first.'

## CHAPTER NINETEEN

For several minutes both the Judge and the Chef de la Sûreté pored over the notebook, examining page after page, shaking their heads, and declining to accept the evidence of their eyes.

'I cannot see it,' said the Judge at last; adding reluctantly, 'No doubt there is a difference, but it is to be explained.'

'Quite so,' put in M. Floçon. 'When he wrote the early part, he was calm and collected; the last entries, so straggling, so ragged, and so badly written, were made when he was fresh from the crime, excited, upset, little master of himself. Naturally he would use a different hand.'

'Or he would wish to disguise it. It was likely he would so wish,' further remarked the Judge.

'You admit, then, that there is a difference?' argued the General shrewdly. 'But there is more than a disguise. The best disguise leaves certain unchangeable features. Some letters, capital G's, h's, and others, will betray themselves through the best disguise. I know what I am saying. I have studied the subject of handwriting; it interests me. These are the work of two different hands. Call in an expert; you will find I am right.'

'Well, well,' said the Judge, after a pause, 'let us grant your position for the moment. What do you deduce? What do you infer therefrom?'

'Surely you can see what follows – what this leads us to?' said Sir Charles rather disdainfully.

'I have formed an opinion – yes, but I should like to see if it coincides with yours. You think –'

'I *know*,' corrected the General. 'I know that, as two persons wrote in that book, either it is not Ripaldi's book, or the last of them was not Ripaldi. I saw the last writer at his work, saw him with my own eyes. Yet he did not write with Ripaldi's hand – this is incontestable, I am sure of it, I will swear it – *ergo*, he is not Ripaldi.'

'But you should have known this at the time,' interjected M. Floçon fiercely. 'Why did you not discover the change of identity? You should have seen that this was not Ripaldi.'

'Pardon me. I did not know the man. I had not noticed him particularly on the journey. There was no reason why I should. I had no communication, no dealings, with any of my fellow-passengers except my brother and the Contessa.'

'But some of the others would surely have remarked the change?' went on the Judge, greatly puzzled. 'That alone seems enough to condemn your theory, M. le Général.'

'I take my stand on fact, not theory,' stoutly maintained Sir Charles, 'and I am satisfied I am right.'

'But if that was not Ripaldi, who was it? Who would wish to masquerade in his dress and character, to make entries of that sort, as if under his hand?'

'Someone determined to divert suspicion from himself to others –'

'But stay – does he not plainly confess his own guilt?'

'What matter if he is not Ripaldi? Directly the inquiry was over, he could steal away and resume his own personality – that of a man supposed to be dead, and therefore safe from all interference and future pursuit.'

'You mean – Upon my word, I compliment you, M. le Général. It is really ingenious! remarkable, indeed! superb!' cried the Judge, and only professional jealousy prevented M. Floçon from conceding the same praise.

'But how – what – I do not understand,' asked Colonel Papillon in amazement. His wits did not travel quite so fast as those of his companions.

'Simply this, my dear Jack,' explained the General: 'Ripaldi must have tried to blackmail Quadling, as he proposed, and Quadling turned the tables on him. They fought, no doubt, and Quadling killed him, possibly in self-defence. He would have said so, but in his peculiar position as an absconding defaulter he did not dare. That is how I read it, and I believe that now these gentlemen are disposed to agree with me.'

'In theory, certainly,' said the Judge heartily. 'But oh! for some more positive proof of this change of character! If we could only identify the corpse, prove clearly that it is not Quadling. And still more, if we had not let this so-called Ripaldi slip through our fingers! You will never find him, M. Floçon, never.'

The Chef hung his head in guilty admission of this reproach.

'We may help you in both these difficulties, gentlemen,' said Sir Charles pleasantly. 'My friend here, Colonel Papillon, can speak as to the man Quadling. He knew him well in Rome, a year or two ago.'

'Please wait one moment only'; the Chef de la Sûreté touched a bell, and briefly ordered two fiacres to the door at once.

'That is right, M. Floçon,' said the Judge. 'We will all go to the Morgue. The body is there by now. You will not refuse your assistance, monsieur?'

'One moment. As to the other matter, M. le Général?' went on M. Floçon. 'Can you help us to find this miscreant, whoever he may be?'

'Yes. The man who calls himself Ripaldi is to be found – or, at least, you would have found him an hour or so ago – at the Hôtel Ivoire, Rue Bellechasse. But time has been lost, I fear.'

'Nevertheless, we will send there.'

'The woman Hortense was also with him when last I heard of them.'

'How do you know?' began the Chef suspiciously.

'Psha!' interrupted the Judge; 'that will keep. This is the time for action, and we owe too much to the General to distrust him now.'

'Thank you; I am pleased to hear you say that,' went on Sir Charles. 'But if I have been of some service to you, perhaps you owe me a little in return. That poor lady! Think what she is suffering. Surely, to oblige me, you will now set her free?'

'Indeed, monsieur, I fear – I do not see how, consistently with my duty' – protested the Judge.

'At least allow her to return to her hotel. She can remain there at your disposal. I will promise you that.'

'How can you answer for her?'

'She will do what I ask, I think, if I may send her just two or three lines.'

The Judge yielded, smiling at the General's urgency, and shrewdly guessing what it implied.

Then the three departures from the Prefecture took place within a short time of each other.

A posse of police went to arrest Ripaldi; the Contessa returned to the Hôtel Madagascar; and the Judge's party started for the Morgue – only a short journey – where they were presently received with every mark of respect and consideration.

The *préposé*, or officer in charge, was summoned, and came out bareheaded to the fiacre, bowing low before his distinguished visitors.

'*Bon jour*, Père la Pêche,' said M. Floçon in a sharp voice. 'We have come for an identification. The body from the Gare de Lyons – he of the murder in the *wagon-lit* – is it yet arrived?'

'But surely, *à votre service*, M. le Chef,' replied the old man obsequiously. 'If messieurs will give themselves the trouble to enter the office, I will lead them behind, direct into the mortuary chamber. There are many people in yonder.'

It was the usual crowd of sightseers passing slowly before the plate glass of this, the most terrible shop-front in the world, where the goods exposed, *la marchandise*, are hideous corpses laid out in rows upon the marble slabs, the battered, tattered remnants of outraged humanity, insulted by the most terrible indignities in death.

Who make up this curious throng, and what strange morbid motives drag them there? Those fat, comfortable-looking *bonnes*, with their baskets on their arms; the decent *ouvriers* in dusty blouses, idling between the hours of work; the *voyous*, male or female, in various stages of wretchedness and degradation? A few, no doubt, are impelled by motives we cannot challenge – they are torn and tortured by suspense, trembling lest they may recognize missing dear ones among the exposed; others stare carelessly at the day's 'take', wondering, perhaps, if they may come to the same fate; one or two are idle *flâneurs*, not always French, for the Morgue is a favourite haunt with the irrepressible tourist doing Paris. Strangest of all, the murderer himself, the doer of the fell deed, comes here, to the very spot where his victim lies stark and reproachful, and stares at it spellbound, fascinated, filled more with remorse, perchance, than fear at the risk he runs. So common is this trait, that in mysterious murder cases the police of Paris keep a disguised officer among the crowd at the Morgue, and have thereby made many memorable arrests.

'This way, messieurs, this way'; and Père la Pêche led the party through one or two rooms into the inner and back recesses of the buildings. It was behind the scenes at the Morgue, and they were made free of its most gruesome secrets as they passed along.

The temperature had suddenly fallen far below freezing-point, and the icy cold chilled to the very marrow. Still worse was an all-pervading, acrid odour of artificially suspended animal decay. The cold-air process, that latest of scientific contrivances to arrest the waste of tissue, has now been applied at the Morgue to preserve and keep the bodies fresh, and allow them to be for a longer time exposed than when running water was the only aid. There are, moreover, many specially-contrived refrigerating chests, in which those still unrecognized corpses are laid by for months, to be dragged out, if needs be, like carcases of meat.

'What a loathsome place!' cried Sir Charles. 'Hurry up, Jack! let us get out of this, in Heaven's name!'

'Where's my man?' quickly asked Colonel Papillon in response to this appeal.

'There, the third from the left,' whispered M. Floçon. 'We hoped you would recognize the corpse at once.'

'That? Impossible! You do not expect it, surely? Why, the face is too much mangled for anyone to say who it is.'

'Are there no indications, no marks or signs, to say whether it is Quadling or not?' asked the Judge in a greatly disappointed tone.

'Absolutely nothing. And yet I am quite satisfied it is not him. For the simple reason that –'

'Yes, yes, go on.'

'That Quadling in person is standing out there among the crowd.'

M. Floçon was the first to realize the full meaning of Colonel Papillon's surprising statement.

'Run, run, Père la Pêche! Have the outer doors closed; let no one leave the place.'

'Draw back, gentlemen!' he went on, and he hustled his companions with frantic haste out at the back of the mortuary chamber. 'Pray Heaven he has not seen us! He would know us, even if we do not him.'

Then with no less haste he seized Colonel Papillon by the arm and hurried him by the back passages through the *greffe* into the outer, public chamber, where the astonished crowd stood, silent and perturbed, awaiting explanation of their detention.

'Quick, monsieur!' whispered the Chef; 'point him out to me.'

The request was not unnecessary, for when Colonel Papillon went forward, and, putting his hand on a man's shoulder, saying, 'Mr Quadling, I think,' the police officer was scarcely able to restrain his surprise.

The person thus challenged was very unlike anyone he had seen before that day, Ripaldi most of all. The moustache was gone, the clothes were entirely changed; a pair of dark green spectacles helped the disguise. It was strange indeed that Papillon had known him; but at the moment of recognition Quadling had removed his glasses, no doubt that he might the better examine the object of his visit to the Morgue, that gruesome record of his own fell handiwork.

Naturally he drew back with well-feigned indignation, muttering half-unintelligible words in French, denying stoutly both in voice and gesture all acquaintance with the person who thus abruptly addressed him.

'This is not to be borne,' he cried. 'Who are you that dares –'

'Ta! ta!' quietly put in M. Floçon; 'we will discuss that fully, but not here. Come into the *greffe*; come, I say, or must we use force?'

There was no escaping now, and with a poor attempt at bravado the stranger was led away.

'Now, Colonel Papillon, look at him well. Do you know him? Are you satisfied it is –'

'Mr Quadling, late banker, of Rome. I have not the slightest doubt of it. I recognize him beyond all question.'

'That will do. Silence, sir!' This to Quadling. 'No observations. I too can recognize you now as the person who called himself Ripaldi an hour or two ago. Denial is useless. Let him be searched; thoroughly, you understand, Père la Pêche? Call in your other men; he may resist.'

They gave the wretched man but scant consideration, and in less than three minutes had visited every pocket, examined every secret receptacle, and practically turned him inside out.

After this there could no longer be any doubt of his identity, still less of his complicity in the crime.

First among the many damning evidences of his guilt was the missing pocket-book of the conductor of the *wagon-lit*. Within was the *feuille de route* and the passengers' tickets, all the papers which the man Groote had lost so unaccountably. They had, of course, been stolen from his person with the obvious intention of impeding the inquiry into the murder. Next, in another inner pocket was Quadling's own wallet, with his own visiting cards, several letters addressed to him by name; above all, a thick sheaf of bank-notes of all nationalities – English, French, Italian, and amounting in total value to several thousands of pounds.

'Well, do you still deny? Bah! it is childish, useless, mere waste of breath. At last we have penetrated the mystery. You may as well confess. Whether or no, we have enough to convict you by independent testimony,' said the Judge severely. 'Come, what have you to say?'

But Quadling, with pale, averted face, stood obstinately mute. He was in the toils, the net had closed round him, they should have no assistance from him.

'Come, speak out; it will be best. Remember, we have means to make you –'

'Will you interrogate him further, M. Beaumont le Hardi? Here, at once?'

'No, let him be removed to the Dépôt of the Prefecture; it will be more convenient; to my cabinet.'

Without more ado a fiacre was called, and the prisoner was taken off under escort, M. Floçon seated by his side, one *sergent de ville* in front, another on the box, and lodged in a secret cell at the Quai l'Horloge.

'And you, gentlemen?' said the Judge to Sir Charles and Colonel Papillon. 'I do not wish to detain you further, although there may be points you might help us to elucidate if I might venture to still trespass on your time?'

Sir Charles was eager to return to the Hôtel Madagascar, and yet he felt that he should best serve his dear Contessa by seeing this to the end. So he readily assented to accompany the Judge, and Colonel Papillon, who was no less curious, agreed to go too.

'I sincerely trust,' said the Judge *en route*, 'that our people have laid hands on that woman Petitpré. I believe that she holds the key to the situation, that when we hear her story we shall have a clear case against Quadling; and – who knows? – she may completely exonerate Madame la Comtesse.'

During the events just recorded, which occupied a good hour, the police agents had time to go and come from the Rue Bellechasse. They did not return empty-handed, although at first it seemed as if they had made a fruitless journey. The Hôtel Ivoire was a very second-class place, a *garni*, or hotel with furnished rooms let out by the week to lodgers with whom the proprietor had no very close acquaintance. His *concierge* did all the business, and this functionary produced the register, as he is bound by law, for the inspection of the police officers, but afforded little information as to the day's arrivals.

'Yes, a man calling himself Dufour had taken rooms about mid-day, one for himself, one for madame who was with him, also named Dufour – his sister, he said'; and he went on at the request of the police officers to describe them.

'Our birds,' said the senior agent briefly. 'They are wanted. We belong to the Sûreté police.'

'*Très bien.*' Such visits were not new to the *concierge*.

'But you will not find monsieur; he is out; there hangs his key. Madame? No, she is within. Yes, that is certain, for not long since she rang her bell. There, it goes again.'

He looked up at the furiously oscillating bell, but made no move.

'Bah! they do not pay for service; let her come and say what she needs.'

'Exactly; and we will bring her,' said the officer, making for the stairs and the room indicated.

But on reaching the door, they found it locked. From within? Hardly, for as they stood there in doubt, a voice inside cried vehemently –

'Let me out! *Au secours!* Help! Send for the police. I have much to tell them. *Vite!* Let me out.'

'We are here, *ma belle*, just as you require us. But wait; step down, Gaston, and see if the *concierge* has a second key. If not, call in a locksmith – the nearest. A little patience only, my beauty. Do not fear.'

The key was quickly produced, and an entrance effected.

A woman stood there in a defiant attitude, with arms akimbo; she, no doubt, of whom they were in search. A tall, rather masculine-looking creature, with a dark, handsome face, bold black eyes just now flashing fiercely, rage in every feature.

'Madame Dufour?' began the police officer.

'Dufour! *Flûte!* My name is Hortense Petitpré; who are you? *La Rousse?*' (Police.)

'At your service. Have you anything to say to us? We have come on purpose to take you to the Prefecture quietly, if you will let us; or –'

'I will go quietly. I ask nothing better. I have to lay information against a miscreant – a murderer – the vile assassin who would have made me his accomplice – the banker, Quadling, of Rome!'

In the fiacre Hortense Petitpré talked on with such incessant abuse, virulent and violent, of Quadling, that her charges were neither precise nor intelligible.

It was not until she appeared before M. Beaumont le Hardi, and was handled with great dexterity by that practised examiner, that her story took definite form.

What she had to say will be best told in the clear, formal language of the official *procès verbal.*

The *prévenue,* or witness inculpated, stated:–

'She was named Aglaé Hortense Petitpré, thirty-four years of age, a French-woman, born in Paris, Rue de Vincennes No. 374. Was engaged by the Contessa Castagneto, November 19, 189—, in Rome, as lady's maid, and there, at her mistress's domicile, became acquainted with the Sieur Francis Quadling, a banker of the Via Condotti, Rome.

'Quadling had pretensions to the hand of the Contessa, and sought, by bribes and entreaties, to interest witness in his suit. Witness often spoke of him in complimentary terms to her mistress, who was not very favourably disposed towards him.

'One afternoon (two days before the murder) Quadling paid a lengthened visit to the Contessa. Witness did not hear what occurred, but Quadling came out much distressed, and again urged her to speak to the Contessa. He had heard of the approaching departure of the lady from Rome, but said nothing of his own intentions.

'Witness was much surprised to find him in the *wagon-lit,* but had no talk to him till the following morning, when he asked her to obtain an interview for him with the Contessa, and promised a large *gratification.* In making this offer he produced a wallet and exhibited a very large number of notes.

'Witness was unable to persuade the Contessa, although she returned to the subject frequently. Witness so informed Quadling, who then spoke to the lady, but was coldly received.

'During the journey witness thought much over the situation. Admitted that the sight of Quadling's money had greatly disturbed her, but, although pressed, would not say when the first idea of robbing him took possession of her. (Note by Judge – That she had resolved to do so is, however, perfectly clear, and the conclusion is borne out by her acts. It was she who secured the Contessa's medicine bottle; she, beyond doubt, who drugged the conductor's drink at Laroche. In no other way can her presence in the *wagon-lit* between Laroche and Paris be accounted for – presence which she does not deny.)

'Witness at last reluctantly confessed that she entered the compartment where the murder was committed, and at a critical moment. An affray was actually in progress between the Italian Ripaldi and the incriminated man Quadling, but the witness arrived as the last fatal blow was struck by the latter.

'She saw it struck, and saw the victim fall lifeless on the floor.

'Witness declared she was so terrified she could at first utter no cry, nor call for help, and before she could recover herself the murderer threatened her with the ensanguined knife. She threw herself on her knees, imploring pity, but the man Quadling told her that she was an eye-witness, and could take him to the guillotine, – she also must die.

'Witness at last prevailed on him to spare her life, but only on condition that she would leave the car. He indicated the window as the only way of escape; but on this for a long time she refused to venture, declaring that it was only to exchange one form of death for another. Then, as Quadling again threatened to stab her, she was compelled to accept this last chance, never hoping to win out alive.

'With Quadling's assistance, however, she succeeded in climbing out through the window and in gaining the roof. He had told her to wait for the first occasion when the train slackened speed to leave it and shift for herself. With this intention he gave her a thousand francs, and bade her never show herself again.

'Witness descended from the train not far from the small station of Villeneuve on the line, and there took the omnibus train for Paris. Landed at the Gare de Lyons, she heard of the inquiry in progress, and then, waiting outside, saw Quadling disguised as the Italian leave in company with another man. She followed and marked Quadling down, meaning to denounce him on the first opportunity. Quadling, however, on issuing from the restaurant, had accosted her, and at once offered her a further sum of five thousand francs as the price of silence, and she had gone with him to the Hôtel Ivoire, where she was to receive the sum.

'Quadling had paid it, but on one condition, that she would remain at the Hôtel Ivoire until the following day. Apparently he had distrusted her, for he had contrived to lock her into her compartment. As she did not choose to be so imprisoned, she summoned assistance, and was at length released by the police.'

This was the substance of Hortense Petitpré's deposition, and it was corroborated in many small details.

When she appeared before the Judge, with whom Sir Charles Collingham and Colonel Papillon were seated, the former at once pointed out that she was wearing a dark mantle trimmed with the same sort of passementerie as that picked up in the *wagon-lit*.

## L'ENVOI

Quadling was in due course brought before the Court of Assize and tried for his life. There was no sort of doubt of his guilt, and the jury so found, but, having regard to certain extenuating circumstances, they recommended him to mercy. The chief of these was Quadling's positive assurance that he had been first attacked by Ripaldi; he declared that the Italian detective had in the first instance tried to come to terms with him, demanding 50,000 francs as his *pourboire* for allowing him to go at large; that when Quadling distinctly refused to be blackmailed, Ripaldi struck at him with a knife, but that the blow failed to take effect.

Then Quadling closed with him and took the knife from him. It was a fierce encounter, and might have ended either way, but the unexpected entrance of the woman Petitpré took off Ripaldi's attention, and then he, Quadling, maddened and reckless, stabbed him to the heart.

It was not until after the deed was done that Quadling realized the full measure of his crime and its inevitable consequences. Then, in a daring effort to extricate himself, he intimidated the woman Petitpré, and forced her to escape through the *wagon-lit* window.

It was he who had rung the signal bell to stop the train and give her a chance of leaving it. It was after the murder, too, that he conceived the idea of personating Ripaldi, and, having disfigured him beyond recognition, as he hoped, he had changed clothes and compartments.

On the strength of this confession Quadling escaped the guillotine, but he was transported to New Caledonia for life.

The money taken on him was forwarded to Rome, and was usefully employed in reducing his liabilities to the depositors in the bank.

One other word.

Some time in June the following announcement appeared in all the Paris papers:—

'Yesterday, at the British Embassy, General Sir Charles Collingham, KCB, was married to Sabine, Contessa di Castagneto, widow of the Italian Count of that name.'

# IN THE FOG

RICHARD HARDING DAVIS

CHAPTER ONE

The Grill is the club most difficult of access in the world. To be placed on its rolls distinguishes the new member as greatly as though he had received a vacant Garter or had been caricatured in *Vanity Fair*.

Men who belong to the Grill Club never mention that fact. If you were to ask one of them which clubs he frequents, he will name all save that particular one. He is afraid if he told you he belonged to the Grill, that it would sound like boasting.

The Grill Club dates back to the days when Shakespeare's Theatre stood on the present site of *The Times* office. It has a golden Grill which Charles the Second presented to the Club, and the original manuscript of *Tom and Jerry in London*, which was bequeathed to it by Pierce Egan himself. The members, when they write letters at the Club, still use sand to blot the ink.

The Grill enjoys the distinction of having blackballed, without political prejudice, a Prime Minister of each party. At the same sitting at which one of these fell, it elected, on account of his brogue and his bulls, Quiller, QC, who was then a penniless barrister.

When Paul Preval, the French artist who came to London by royal command to paint a portrait of the Prince of Wales, was made an honorary member – only foreigners may be honorary members – he said, as he signed his first wine card, 'I would rather see my name on that, than on a picture in the Louvre.'

At which Quiller remarked, 'That is a devil of a compliment, because the only men who can read their names in the Louvre today have been dead fifty years.'

On the night after the great fog of 1897 there were five members in the Club, four of them busy with supper and one reading in front of the fireplace. There is only one room to the Club, and one long table. At the far end of the room the fire of the grill glows red, and, when the fat falls, blazes into flame, and at the other there is a broad bow window of diamond panes, which looks down upon the street. The four men at the table were strangers to each other, but as they picked at the grilled bones, and sipped their scotch and soda, they conversed with such charming animation that a visitor to the Club, which does not tolerate visitors, would have counted them as friends of long acquaintance, certainly not as Englishmen who had met for the first time, and without the form of an introduction. But it is the etiquette and tradition of the Grill, that whoever enters it must speak with whomever he finds there. It is to enforce this rule that there is but one long table, and whether there are twenty men at it or two, the waiters, supporting the rule, will place them side by side.

For this reason the four strangers at supper were seated together, with the candles grouped about them, and the long length of the table cutting a white path through the outer gloom.

'I repeat,' said the gentleman with the black pearl stud, 'that the days for romantic adventure and deeds of foolish daring have passed, and that the fault lies with ourselves. Voyages to the Pole I do not catalogue as adventures. That African explorer, young Chetney, who turned up yesterday after he was supposed to have died in Uganda, did nothing adventurous. He made maps and explored the sources of rivers. He was in constant danger, but the presence of danger does not constitute adventure. Were that so, the chemist who studies high explosives, or who investigates deadly poisons, passes through adventures daily. No, "adventures are for the adventurous". But one no longer ventures. The spirit of it has died of inertia. We are grown too practical, too just, above all, too sensible. In this room, for instance, members of this Club have, at the sword's point, disputed the proper scanning of one of Pope's couplets. Over so weighty a matter as spilled Burgundy on a gentleman's cuff, ten men fought across this table, each with his rapier in one hand and a candle in the other. All ten were wounded. The question of the spilled Burgundy concerned but two of them. The eight others engaged because they were men of "spirit". They were, indeed, the first gentlemen of the day. Tonight, were you to spill Burgundy on my cuff, were you even to insult me grossly, these gentlemen would not consider it incumbent upon them to kill each other. They would separate us, and tomorrow morning appear as witnesses against us at Bow Street. We have here tonight, in the persons of Sir Andrew and myself, an illustration of how the ways have changed.'

The men around the table turned and glanced toward the gentleman in front of the fireplace. He was an elderly and somewhat portly person, with a kindly, wrinkled countenance, which wore continually a smile of almost childish confidence and good nature. It was a face which the illustrated prints had made intimately familiar. He held a book from him at arm's-length, as if to adjust his eyesight, and his brows were knit with interest.

'Now, were this the eighteenth century,' continued the gentleman with the black pearl, 'when Sir Andrew left the Club tonight I would have him bound and gagged and thrown into a sedan chair. The watch would not interfere, the passers-by would take to their heels, my hired bullies and ruffians would convey him to some lonely spot where we would guard him until morning. Nothing would come of it, except added reputation to myself as a gentleman of adventurous spirit, and possibly an essay in *The Tatler*, with stars for names, entitled, let us say, "The Budget and the Baronet".'

'But to what end, sir?' inquired the youngest of the members. 'And why Sir Andrew, of all persons – why should you select him for this adventure?'

The gentleman with the black pearl shrugged his shoulders.

'It would prevent him speaking in the House tonight. The Navy Increase Bill,' he added gloomily. 'It is a Government measure, and Sir Andrew speaks for it. And so great is his influence and so large his following that if he does' – the gentleman laughed ruefully – 'if he does, it will go through. Now, had I the spirit of our ancestors,' he exclaimed, 'I would bring chloroform from the nearest chemist's and drug him in that chair. I would tumble his unconscious form into a hansom cab, and hold him prisoner until daylight. If I did, I would save the British taxpayer the cost of five more battleships, many millions of pounds.'

The gentlemen again turned, and surveyed the baronet with freshened interest. The honorary member of the Grill, whose accent already had betrayed him as an American, laughed softly.

'To look at him now,' he said, 'one would not guess he was deeply concerned with the affairs of state.'

The others nodded silently.

'He has not lifted his eyes from that book since we first entered,' added the youngest member. 'He surely cannot mean to speak tonight.'

'Oh, yes, he will speak,' muttered the one with the black pearl moodily. 'During these last hours of the session the House sits late, but when the Navy bill comes up on its third reading he will be in his place – and he will pass it.'

The fourth member, a stout and florid gentleman of a somewhat sporting appearance, in a short smoking-jacket and black tie, sighed enviously.

'Fancy one of us being as cool as that, if he knew he had to stand up within an hour and rattle off a speech in Parliament. I'd be in a devil of a funk myself. And yet he is as keen over that book he's reading as though he had nothing before him until bedtime.'

'Yes, see how eager he is,' whispered the youngest member. 'He does not lift his eyes even now when he cuts the pages. It is probably an Admiralty Report, or some other weighty work of statistics which bears upon his speech.'

The gentleman with the black pearl laughed morosely.

'The weighty work in which the eminent statesman is so deeply engrossed,' he said, 'is called *The Great Rand Robbery*. It is a detective novel, for sale at all bookstalls.'

The American raised his eyebrows in disbelief.

'*The Great Rand Robbery?*' he repeated incredulously. 'What an odd taste!'

'It is not a taste, it is his vice,' returned the gentleman with the pearl stud. 'It is his one dissipation. He is noted for it. You, as a stranger, could hardly be expected to know of this idiosyncrasy. Mr Gladstone sought relaxation in the Greek poets, Sir Andrew finds his in Gaboriau. Since I have been a member of Parliament I have never seen him in the library without a shilling shocker in his hands. He brings them even into the sacred precincts of the House, and from the Government benches reads them concealed inside his hat. Once started on a tale of murder, robbery, and sudden death, nothing can tear him from it, not even the call of the division bell, nor of hunger, nor the prayers of the party Whip. He gave up his country house because when he journeyed to it in the train he would become so absorbed in his detective stories that he was invariably carried past his station.' The member of Parliament twisted his pearl stud nervously, and bit at the edge of his moustache. 'If it only were the first pages of *The Rand Robbery* that he were reading,' he murmured bitterly, 'instead of the last! With such another book as that, I swear I could hold him here until morning. There would be no need of chloroform to keep him from the House.'

The eyes of all were fastened upon Sir Andrew, and each saw with fascination that with his forefinger he was now separating the last two pages of the book. The member of Parliament struck the table softly with his open palm.

'I would give a hundred pounds,' he whispered, 'if I could place in his hands at this moment a new story of Sherlock Holmes – a thousand pounds,' he added wildly – 'five thousand pounds!'

The American observed the speaker sharply, as though the words bore to him some special application, and then at an idea which apparently had but just come to him, smiled in great embarrassment.

Sir Andrew ceased reading, but, as though still under the influence of the book, sat looking blankly into the open fire. For a brief space no one moved until the baronet withdrew his eyes and, with a sudden start of recollection, felt anxiously for his watch. He scanned its face eagerly, and scrambled to his feet.

The voice of the American instantly broke the silence in a high, nervous accent.

'And yet Sherlock Holmes himself,' he cried, 'could not decipher the mystery which tonight baffles the police of London.'

At these unexpected words, which carried in them something of the tone of a challenge, the gentlemen about the table started as suddenly as though the American had fired a pistol in the air, and Sir Andrew halted abruptly and stood observing him with grave surprise.

The gentleman with the black pearl was the first to recover.

'Yes, yes,' he said eagerly, throwing himself across the table. 'A mystery that baffles the police of London. I have heard nothing of it. Tell us at once, pray do – tell us at once.'

The American flushed uncomfortably, and picked uneasily at the table-cloth.

'No one but the police has heard of it,' he murmured, 'and they only through me. It is a remarkable crime, to which, unfortunately, I am the only person who can bear witness. Because I am the only witness, I am, in spite of my immunity as a diplomat, detained in London by the authorities of Scotland Yard. My name,' he said, inclining his head politely, 'is Sears, Lieutenant Ripley Sears of the United States Navy, at present Naval Attaché to the Court of Russia. Had I not been detained today by the police I would have started this morning for Petersburg.'

The gentleman with the black pearl interrupted with so pronounced an exclamation of excitement and delight that the American stammered and ceased speaking.

'Do you hear, Sir Andrew?' cried the member of Parliament jubilantly. 'An American diplomat halted by our police because he is the only witness of a most remarkable crime – the most remarkable crime, I believe you said, sir,' he added, bending eagerly toward the naval officer, 'which has occurred in London in many years.'

The American moved his head in assent and glanced at the two other members. They were looking doubtfully at him, and the face of each showed that he was greatly perplexed.

Sir Andrew advanced to within the light of the candles and drew a chair toward him.

'The crime must be exceptional indeed,' he said, 'to justify the police in interfering with a representative of a friendly power. If I were not forced to leave at once, I should take the liberty of asking you to tell us the details.'

The gentleman with the pearl pushed the chair toward Sir Andrew, and motioned him to be seated.

'You cannot leave us now,' he exclaimed. 'Mr Sears is just about to tell us of this remarkable crime.'

He nodded vigorously at the naval officer and the American, after first glancing doubtfully toward the servants at the far end of the room, leaned forward across the table. The others drew their chairs nearer and bent toward him. The baronet glanced irresolutely at his watch, and with an exclamation of annoyance snapped down the lid. 'They can wait,' he muttered. He seated himself quickly and nodded at Lieutenant Sears.

'If you will be so kind as to begin, sir,' he said impatiently.

'Of course,' said the American, 'you understand that I understand that I am speaking to gentlemen. The confidences of this Club are inviolate. Until the police give the facts to the public press, I must consider you my confederates. You have heard nothing, you know no one connected with this mystery. Even I must remain anonymous.'

The gentlemen seated around him nodded gravely.

'Of course,' the baronet assented with eagerness, 'of course.'

'We will refer to it,' said the gentleman with the black pearl, 'as "The Story of the Naval Attaché".'

'I arrived in London two days ago,' said the American, 'and I engaged a room at the Bath Hotel. I know very few people in London, and even the members of our embassy were strangers to me. But in Hong Kong I had become great pals with an officer in your navy, who has since retired, and who is now living in a small house in Rutland Gardens opposite the Knightsbridge barracks. I telegraphed him that I was in London, and yesterday morning I received a most hearty invitation to dine with him the same evening at his house. He is a bachelor, so we dined alone and talked over all our old days on the Asiatic Station, and of the changes which had come to us since we had last met there. As I was leaving the next morning for my post at Petersburg, and had many letters to write, I told him, about ten o'clock, that I must get back to the hotel, and he sent out his servant to call a hansom.

'For the next quarter of an hour, as we sat talking, we could hear the cab whistle sounding violently from the doorstep, but apparently with no result.

'"It cannot be that the cabmen are on strike," my friend said, as he rose and walked to the window.

'He pulled back the curtains and at once called to me.

'"You have never seen a London Fog, have you?" he asked. "Well, come here. This is one of the best, or, rather, one of the worst, of them." I joined him at the window, but I could see nothing. Had I not known that the house looked out upon the street I would have believed that I was facing a dead wall. I raised the sash and stretched out my head, but still I could see nothing. Even the light of the street lamps opposite, and in the upper windows of the barracks, had been smothered in the yellow mist. The lights of the room in which I stood penetrated the fog only to the distance of a few inches from my eyes.

'Below me the servant was still sounding his whistle, but I could afford to wait no longer, and told my friend that I would try and find the way to my hotel on foot. He objected, but the letters I had to write were for the Navy Department, and, besides, I had always heard that to be out in a London fog was the most wonderful experience, and I was curious to investigate one for myself.

'My friend went with me to his front door, and laid down a course for me to follow. I was first to walk straight across the street to the brick wall of the Knightsbridge Barracks. I was then to feel my way along the wall until I came to a row of houses set back from the sidewalk. They would bring me to a cross street. On the other side of this street was a row of shops which I was to follow until they joined the iron railings of Hyde Park. I was to keep to the railings until I reached the gates at Hyde Park Corner, where I was to lay a diagonal course across Piccadilly, and tack in toward the railings of Green Park. At the end of these railings, going east, I would find the Walsingham, and my own hotel.

'To a sailor the course did not seem difficult, so I bade my friend good night and walked forward until my feet touched the paving. I continued upon it until I reached the curbing of the sidewalk. A few steps further, and my hands struck the wall of the barracks. I turned in the direction from which I had just come, and saw a square of faint light cut in the yellow fog. I shouted "All right," and the voice of my friend answered, "Good luck to you." The light from his open door disappeared with a bang, and I was left alone in a dripping, yellow darkness. I have been in the Navy for ten years, but I have never known such a fog as that of last night, not even among the icebergs of Behring Sea. There one at least could see the light of the binnacle, but last night I could not even distinguish the hand by which I guided myself along the barrack wall. At sea a fog is a natural phenomenon. It is as familiar as the rainbow which follows a storm, it is as proper that a fog should spread upon the waters as that steam shall rise from a kettle. But a fog which springs from the paved streets, that rolls between solid house-fronts, that forces cabs to move at half speed, that drowns policemen and extinguishes the electric lights of the music hall, that to me is incomprehensible. It is as out of place as a tidal wave on Broadway.

'As I felt my way along the wall, I encountered other men who were coming from the opposite direction, and each time when we hailed each other I stepped away from the wall to make room for them to pass. But the third time I did this, when I reached out my hand, the wall had disappeared, and the further I moved to find it the further I seemed to be sinking into space. I had the unpleasant conviction that at any moment I might step over a precipice. Since I had set out I had heard no traffic in the street, and now, although I listened some minutes, I could only distinguish the occasional footfalls of pedestrians. Several times I called aloud, and once a jocular gentleman answered me, but only to ask me where I thought he was, and then even he was swallowed up in the silence. Just above me I could make out a jet of gas which I guessed came from a street lamp, and I moved over to that, and, while I tried to recover my bearings, kept my hand on the iron post. Except for this flicker of gas, no larger than the tip of my finger, I could distinguish nothing about me. For the rest, the mist hung between me and the world like a damp and heavy blanket.

'I could hear voices, but I could not tell from whence they came, and the scrape of a foot moving cautiously, or a muffled cry as some one stumbled, were the only sounds that reached me.

'I decided that until some one took me in tow I had best remain where I was, and it must have been for ten minutes that I waited by the lamp, straining my ears and hailing distant footfalls. In a house near me some people were dancing to the music of a Hungarian band. I even fancied I could hear the windows shake to the rhythm of their feet, but I could not make out from which part of the compass the sounds came. And sometimes, as the music rose, it seemed close at my hand, and again, to be floating high in the air above my head. Although I was surrounded by thousands of house-holders – 13 – I was as completely lost as though I had been set down by night in the Sahara Desert. There seemed to be no reason in waiting longer for an escort, so I again set out, and at once bumped against a low iron fence. At first I believed this to be an area railing, but on following it I found that it stretched for a long distance, and that it was pierced at regular intervals with gates. I was standing uncertainly with my hand on one of these when a square of light suddenly opened in the night, and in it I saw, as you see a picture thrown by a biograph in a darkened theatre, a young gentleman in evening dress, and back of him the lights of a hall. I guessed from its elevation and distance from the sidewalk that this light must come from the door of a house set back from the street, and I determined to approach it and ask the young man to tell me where I was. But in fumbling with the lock of the gate I instinctively bent my head, and when I raised it again the door had partly closed, leaving only a narrow shaft of light. Whether the young man had re-entered the house, or had left it I could not tell, but I hastened to open the gate, and as I stepped forward I found myself upon an asphalt walk. At the same instant there was the sound of quick steps upon the path, and some one rushed past me. I called to him, but he made no reply, and I heard the gate click and the footsteps hurrying away upon the sidewalk.

'Under other circumstances the young man's rudeness, and his reckless-ness in dashing so hurriedly through the mist, would have struck me as peculiar, but everything was so distorted by the fog that at the moment I did not consider it. The door was still as he had left it, partly open. I went up the path, and, after much fumbling, found the knob of the door-bell and gave it a sharp pull. The bell answered me from a great depth and distance, but no movement followed from inside the house, and although I pulled the bell again and again I could hear nothing save the dripping of the mist about me. I was anxious to be on my way, but unless I knew where I was going there was little chance of my making any speed, and I was determined that until I learned my bearings I would not venture back into the fog. So I pushed the door open and stepped into the house.

'I found myself in a long and narrow hall, upon which doors opened from either side. At the end of the hall was a staircase with a balustrade which ended in a sweeping curve. The balustrade was covered with heavy Persian rugs, and the walls of the hall were also hung with them. The door on my left was closed, but the one nearer me on the right was open, and as I stepped opposite to it I saw that it was a sort of reception or waiting-room, and that it was empty. The door below it was also open, and with the idea that I would surely find some one there, I walked on up the hall. I was in evening dress, and I felt I did not look like a burglar, so I had no great fear that, should I encounter one of the inmates of the house, he would shoot me on sight. The second door in the hall opened into a dining-room. This was also empty. One person had been dining at the table, but the cloth had not been cleared away, and a flickering candle showed half-filled wineglasses and the ashes of cigarettes. The greater part of the room was in complete darkness.

'By this time I had grown conscious of the fact that I was wandering about in a strange house, and that, apparently, I was alone in it. The silence of the place began to try my nerves, and in a sudden, unexplainable panic I started for the open street. But as I turned, I saw a man sitting on a bench, which the curve of the balustrade had hidden from me. His eyes were shut, and he was sleeping soundly.

'The moment before I had been bewildered because I could see no one, but at sight of this man I was much more bewildered.

'He was a very large man, a giant in height, with long yellow hair which hung below his shoulders. He was dressed in a red silk shirt that was belted at the waist and hung outside black velvet trousers which, in turn, were stuffed into high black boots. I recognized the costume at once as that of a Russian servant, but what a Russian servant in his native livery could be doing in a private house in Knightsbridge was incomprehensible.

'I advanced and touched the man on the shoulder, and after an effort he awoke, and, on seeing me, sprang to his feet and began bowing rapidly and making deprecatory gestures. I had picked up enough Russian in Petersburg to make out that the man was apologizing for having fallen asleep, and I also was able to explain to him that I desired to see his master.

'He nodded vigorously, and said, "Will the Excellency come this way? The Princess is here."

'I distinctly made out the word "princess", and I was a good deal embarrassed. I had thought it would be easy enough to explain my intrusion to a man, but how a woman would look at it was another matter, and as i followed him down the hall I was somewhat puzzled.

'As we advanced, he noticed that the front door was standing open, and with an exclamation of surprise, hastened toward it and closed it. Then he rapped twice on the door of what was apparently the drawing-room. There was no reply to his knock, and he tapped again, and then timidly, and cringing subserviently, opened the door and stepped inside. He withdrew himself at once and stared stupidly at me, shaking his head.

'"She is not there," he said. He stood for a moment gazing blankly through the open door, and then hastened toward the dining-room. The solitary candle which still burned there seemed to assure him that the room also was empty. He came back and bowed me toward the drawing-room. "She is above," he said; "I will inform the Princess of the Excellency's presence."

'Before I could stop him he had turned and was running up the staircase, leaving me alone at the open door of the drawing-room. I decided that the adventure had gone quite far enough, and if I had been able to explain to the Russian that I had lost my way in the fog, and only wanted to get back into the street again, I would have left the house on the instant.

'Of course, when I first rang the bell of the house I had no other expectation than that it would be answered by a parlour-maid who would direct me on my way. I certainly could not then foresee that I would disturb a Russian princess in her boudoir, or that I might be thrown out by her athletic bodyguard. Still, I thought I ought not now to leave the house without making some apology, and, if the worst should come, I could show my card. They could hardly believe that a member of an Embassy had any designs upon the hat-rack.

'The room in which I stood was dimly lighted, but I could see that, like the hall, it was hung with heavy Persian rugs. The corners were filled with palms, and there was the unmistakable odour in the air of Russian cigarettes, and strange, dry scents that carried me back to the bazaars of Vladivostock. Near the front windows was a grand piano, and at the other end of the room a heavily carved screen of some black wood, picked out with ivory. The screen was overhung with a canopy of silken draperies, and formed a sort of alcove. In front of the alcove was spread the white skin of a polar bear, and set on that was one of those low Turkish coffee tables. It held a lighted spirit-lamp and two gold coffee cups. I had heard no movement from above stairs, and it must have been fully three minutes that I stood waiting, noting these details of the room and wondering at the delay, and at the strange silence.

'And then, suddenly, as my eye grew more used to the half-light, I saw, projecting from behind the screen as though it were stretched along the back of a divan, the hand of a man and the lower part of his arm. I was as startled as though I had come across a footprint on a deserted island. Evidently the man had been sitting there since I had come into the room, even since I had entered the house, and he had heard the servant knocking upon the door. Why he had not declared himself I could not understand, but I supposed that possibly he was a guest, with no reason to interest himself in the Princess's other visitors, or perhaps, for some reason, he did not wish to be observed. I could see nothing of him except his hand, but I had an unpleasant feeling that he had been peering at me through the carving in the screen, and that he still was doing so. I moved my feet noisily on the floor and said tentatively, "I beg your pardon."

'There was no reply, and the hand did not stir. Apparently the man was bent upon ignoring me, but as all I wished was to apologize for my intrusion and to leave the house, I walked up to the alcove and peered around it. Inside the screen was a divan piled with cushions, and on the end of it nearer me the man was sitting. He was a young Englishman with light yellow hair and a deeply bronzed face. He was seated with his arms stretched out along the back of the divan, and with his head resting against a cushion. His attitude was one of complete ease. But his mouth had fallen open, and his eyes were set with an expression of utter horror. At the first glance I saw that he was quite dead.

'For a flash of time I was too startled to act, but in the same flash I was convinced that the man had met his death from no accident, that he had not died through any ordinary failure of the laws of nature. The expression on his face was much too terrible to be misinterpreted. It spoke as eloquently as words. It told me that before the end had come he had watched his death approach and threaten him.

'I was so sure he had been murdered that I instinctively looked on the floor for the weapon, and, at the same moment, out of concern for my own safety, quickly behind me; but the silence of the house continued unbroken.

'I have seen a great number of dead men; I was on the Asiatic Station during the Japanese–Chinese war. I was in Port Arthur after the massacre. So a dead man, for the single reason that he is dead, does not repel me, and, though I knew that there was no hope that this man was alive, still for decency's sake, I felt his pulse, and while I kept my ears alert for any sound from the floors above me, I pulled open his shirt and placed my hand upon his heart. My fingers instantly touched upon the opening of a wound, and as I withdrew them I found them wet with blood. He was in evening dress, and in the wide bosom of his shirt I found a narrow slit, so narrow that in the dim light it was scarcely discernible. The wound was no wider than the smallest blade of a pocket-knife, but when I stripped the shirt away from the chest and left it bare, I found that the weapon, narrow as it was, had been long enough to reach his heart. There is no need to tell you how I felt as I stood by the body of this boy, for he was hardly older than a boy, or of the thoughts that came into my head. I was bitterly sorry for this stranger, bitterly indignant at his murderer, and, at the same time, selfishly concerned for my own safety and for the notoriety which I saw was sure to follow. My instinct was to leave the body where it lay, and to hide myself in the fog, but I also felt that since a succession of accidents had made me the only witness to a crime, my duty was to make myself a good witness and to assist to establish the facts of this murder.

'That it might possibly be a suicide, and not a murder, did not disturb me for a moment. The fact that the weapon had disappeared, and the expression on the boy's face were enough to convince, at least me, that he had had no hand in his own death. I judged it, therefore, of the first importance to discover who was in the house, or, if they had escaped from it, who had been in the house before I entered it. I had seen one man leave it; but all I could tell of him was that he was a young man, that he was in evening dress, and that he had fled in such haste that he had not stopped to close the door behind him.

'The Russian servant I had found apparently asleep, and, unless he acted a part with supreme skill, he was a stupid and ignorant boor, and as innocent of the murder as myself. There was still the Russian princess whom he had expected to find, or had pretended to expect to find, in the same room with the murdered man. I judged that she must now be either upstairs with the servant, or that she had, without his knowledge, already fled from the house. When I recalled his apparently genuine surprise at not finding her in the drawing-room, this latter supposition seemed the more probable. Nevertheless, I decided that it was my duty to make a search, and after a second hurried look for the weapon among the cushions of the divan, and upon the floor, I cautiously crossed the hall and entered the dining-room.

'The single candle was still flickering in the draught, and showed only the white cloth. The rest of the room was draped in shadows. I picked up the candle, and, lifting it high above my head, moved around the corner of the table. Either my nerves were on such a stretch that no shock could strain them further, or my mind was inoculated to horrors, for I did not cry out at what I saw nor retreat from it. Immediately at my feet was the body of a beautiful woman, lying at full length upon the floor, her arms flung out on either side of her, and her white face and shoulders gleaming dully in the unsteady light of the candle. Around her throat was a great chain of diamonds, and the light played upon these and made them flash and blaze in tiny flames. But the woman who wore them was dead, and I was so certain as to how she had died that without an instant's hesitation I dropped on my knees beside her and placed my hands above her heart. My fingers again touched the thin slit of a wound. I had no doubt in my mind but that this was the Russian princess, and when I lowered the candle to her face I was assured that this was so. Her features showed the finest lines of both the Slav and the Jewess; the eyes were black, the hair blue-black and wonderfully heavy, and her skin, even in death, was rich in color. She was a surpassingly beautiful woman.

'I rose and tried to light another candle with the one I held, but I found that my hand was so unsteady that I could not keep the wicks together. It was my intention to again search for this strange dagger which had been used to kill both the English boy and the beautiful princess, but before I could light the second candle I heard footsteps descending the stairs, and the Russian servant appeared in the doorway.

'My face was in darkness, or I am sure that at the sight of it he would have taken alarm, for at that moment I was not sure but that this man himself was the murderer. His own face was plainly visible to me in the light from the hall, and I could see that it wore an expression of dull bewilderment. I stepped quickly toward him and took a firm hold upon his wrist.

'"She is not there," he said. "The Princess has gone. They have all gone."

'"Who have gone?" I demanded. "Who else has been here?"

'"The two Englishmen," he said.

'"What two Englishmen?" I demanded. "What are their names?"

'The man now saw by my manner that some question of great moment hung upon his answer, and he began to protest that he did not know the names of the visitors and that until that evening he had never seen them.

'I guessed that it was my tone which frightened him, so I took my hand off his wrist and spoke less eagerly.

'"How long have they been here?" I asked, "and when did they go?"

'He pointed behind him toward the drawing-room.

'"One sat there with the Princess," he said; "the other came after I had placed the coffee in the drawing-room. The two Englishmen talked together and the Princess returned here to the table. She sat there in that chair, and I brought her cognac and cigarettes. Then I sat outside upon the bench. It was a feast day, and I had been drinking. Pardon, Excellency, but I fell asleep.

When I woke, your Excellency was standing by me, but the Princess and the two Englishmen had gone. That is all I know."

'I believed that the man was telling me the truth. His fright had passed, and he was now apparently puzzled, but not alarmed.

'"You must remember the names of the Englishmen," I urged. "Try to think. When you announced them to the Princess what name did you give?"

'At this question he exclaimed with pleasure, and, beckoning to me, ran hurriedly down the hall and into the drawing-room. In the corner furthest from the screen was the piano, and on it was a silver tray. He picked this up and, smiling with pride at his own intelligence, pointed at two cards that lay upon it. I took them up and read the names engraved upon them.'

The American paused abruptly, and glanced at the faces about him. 'I read the names,' he repeated. He spoke with great reluctance.

'Continue!' cried the Baronet, sharply.

'I read the names,' said the American with evident distaste, 'and the family name of each was the same. They were the names of two brothers. One is well known to you. It is that of the African explorer of whom this gentleman was just speaking. I mean the Earl of Chetney. The other was the name of his brother, Lord Arthur Chetney.'

The men at the table fell back as though a trapdoor had fallen open at their feet.

'Lord Chetney?' they exclaimed in chorus. They glanced at each other and back to the American with every expression of concern and disbelief.

'It is impossible!' cried the Baronet. 'Why, my dear sir, young Chetney only arrived from Africa yesterday. It was so stated in the evening papers.'

The jaw of the American set in a resolute square, and he pressed his lips together.

'You are perfectly right, sir,' he said, 'Lord Chetney did arrive in London yesterday morning, and yesterday night I found his dead body.'

The youngest member present was the first to recover. He seemed much less concerned over the identity of the murdered man than at the interruption of the narrative.

'Oh, please let him go on!' he cried. 'What happened then? You say you found two visiting cards. How do you know which card was that of the murdered man?'

The American, before he answered, waited until the chorus of exclamations had ceased. Then he continued as though he had not been interrupted.

'The instant I read the names upon the cards,' he said, 'I ran to the screen and, kneeling beside the dead man, began a search through his pockets. My hand at once fell upon a card-case, and I found on all the cards it contained the title of the Earl of Chetney. His watch and cigarette-case also bore his name. These evidences, and the fact of his bronzed skin, and that his cheekbones were worn with fever, convinced me that the dead man was the African explorer, and the boy who had fled past me in the night was Arthur, his younger brother.

'I was so intent upon my search that I had forgotten the servant, and I was still on my knees when I heard a cry behind me. I turned, and saw the man gazing down at the body in abject horror.

'Before I could rise, he gave another cry of terror, and, flinging himself into the hall, raced toward the door to the street. I leaped after him, shouting to him to halt, but before I could reach the hall he had torn open the door, and I saw him spring out into the yellow fog. I cleared the steps in a jump and ran down the garden walk but just as the gate clicked in front of me. I had it open on the instant, and, following the sound of the man's footsteps, I raced after him across the open street. He, also, could hear me, and he instantly stopped running, and there was absolute silence. He was so near that I almost fancied I could hear him panting, and I held my own breath to listen. But I could distinguish nothing but the dripping of the mist about us, and from far off the music of the Hungarian band, which I had heard when I first lost myself.

'All I could see was the square of light from the door I had left open behind me, and a lamp in the hall beyond it flickering in the draught. But even as I watched it, the flame of the lamp was blown violently to and fro, and the door, caught in the same current of air, closed slowly. I knew if it shut I could not again enter the house, and I rushed madly toward it. I believe I even shouted out, as though it were something human which I could compel to obey me, and then I caught my foot against the curb and smashed into the sidewalk. When I rose to my feet I was dizzy and half stunned, and though I thought then that I was moving toward the door, I know now that I probably turned directly from it; for, as I groped about in the night, calling frantically for the police, my fingers touched nothing but the dripping fog, and the iron railings for which I sought seemed to have melted away. For many minutes I beat the mist with my arms like one at blind man's buff, turning sharply in circles, cursing aloud at my stupidity and crying continually for help. At last a voice answered me from the fog, and I found myself held in the circle of a policeman's lantern.

'That is the end of my adventure. What I have to tell you now is what I learned from the police.

'At the station-house to which the man guided me I related what you have just heard. I told them that the house they must at once find was one set back from the street within a radius of two hundred yards from the Knightsbridge Barracks, that within fifty yards of it some one was giving a dance to the music of a Hungarian band, and that the railings before it were as high as a man's waist and filed to a point. With that to work upon, twenty men were at once ordered out into the fog to search for the house, and Inspector Lyle himself was despatched to the home of Lord Edam, Chetney's father, with a warrant for Lord Arthur's arrest. I was thanked and dismissed on my own recognizance.

'This morning, Inspector Lyle called on me, and from him I learned the police theory of the scene I have just described.

'Apparently I had wandered very far in the fog, for up to noon today the house had not been found, nor had they been able to arrest Lord Arthur. He did not return to his father's house last night, and there is no trace of him; but from what the police knew of the past lives of the people I found in that lost house, they have evolved a theory, and their theory is that the murders were committed by Lord Arthur.

'The infatuation of his elder brother, Lord Chetney, for a Russian princess, so Inspector Lyle tells me, is well known to every one. About two years ago the Princess Zichy, as she calls herself, and he were constantly together, and Chetney informed his friends that they were about to be married. The woman was notorious in two continents, and when Lord Edam heard of his son's infatuation he appealed to the police for her record.

'It is through his having applied to them that they know so much concerning her and her relations with the Chetneys. From the police Lord Edam learned that Madame Zichy had once been a spy in the employ of the Russian Third Section, but that lately she had been repudiated by her own government and was living by her wits, by blackmail, and by her beauty. Lord Edam laid this record before his son, but Chetney either knew it already or the woman persuaded him not to believe in it, and the father and son parted in great anger. Two days later the marquis altered his will, leaving all of his money to the younger brother, Arthur.

'The title and some of the landed property he could not keep from Chetney, but he swore if his son saw the woman again that the will should stand as it was, and he would be left without a penny.

'This was about eighteen months ago, when apparently Chetney tired of the Princess, and suddenly went off to shoot and explore in Central Africa. No word came from him, except that twice he was reported as having died of fever in the jungle, and finally two traders reached the coast who said they had seen his body. This was accepted by all as conclusive, and young Arthur was recognized as the heir to the Edam millions. On the strength of this supposition he at once began to borrow enormous sums from the money-lenders. This is of great importance, as the police believe it was these debts which drove him to the murder of his brother. Yesterday, as you know, Lord

Chetney suddenly returned from the grave, and it was the fact that for two years he had been considered as dead which lent such importance to his return and which gave rise to those columns of detail concerning him which appeared in all the afternoon papers. But, obviously, during his absence he had not tired of the Princess Zichy, for we know that a few hours after he reached London he sought her out. His brother, who had also learned of his reappearance through the papers, probably suspected which would be the house he would first visit, and followed him there, arriving, so the Russian servant tells us, while the two were at coffee in the drawing-room. The Princess, then, we also learn from the servant, withdrew to the dining-room, leaving the brothers together. What happened one can only guess.

'Lord Arthur knew now that when it was discovered he was no longer the heir, the money-lenders would come down upon him. The police believe that he at once sought out his brother to beg for money to cover the post-obits, but that, considering the sum he needed was several hundreds of thousands of pounds, Chetney refused to give it him. No one knew that Arthur had gone to seek out his brother. They were alone. It is possible, then, that in a passion of disappointment, and crazed with the disgrace which he saw before him, young Arthur made himself the heir beyond further question. The death of his brother would have availed nothing if the woman remained alive. It is then possible that he crossed the hall, and with the same weapon which made him Lord Edam's heir destroyed the solitary witness to the murder. The only other person who could have seen it was sleeping in a drunken stupor, to which fact undoubtedly he owed his life. And yet,' concluded the Naval Attaché, leaning forward and marking each word with his finger, 'Lord Arthur blundered fatally. In his haste he left the door of the house open, so giving access to the first passer-by, and he forgot that when he entered it he had handed his card to the servant. That piece of paper may yet send him to the gallows. In the meantime he has disappeared completely, and somewhere, in one of the millions of streets of this great capital, in a locked and empty house, lies the body of his brother, and of the woman his brother loved, undiscovered, unburied, and with their murder unavenged.'

In the discussion which followed the conclusion of the story of the Naval Attaché the gentleman with the pearl took no part. Instead, he arose, and, beckoning a servant to a far corner of the room, whispered earnestly to him until a sudden movement on the part of Sir Andrew caused him to return hurriedly to the table.

'There are several points in Mr Sears's story I want explained,' he cried. 'Be seated, Sir Andrew,' he begged. 'Let us have the opinion of an expert. I do not care what the police think, I want to know what you think.'

But Sir Andrew rose reluctantly from his chair.

'I should like nothing better than to discuss this,' he said. 'But it is most important that I proceed to the House. I should have been there some time ago.' He turned toward the servant and directed him to call a hansom.

The gentleman with the pearl stud looked appealingly at the Naval Attaché. 'There are surely many details that you have not told us,' he urged. 'Some you have forgotten.'

The Baronet interrupted quickly.

'I trust not,' he said, 'for I could not possibly stop to hear them.'

'The story is finished,' declared the Naval Attaché; 'until Lord Arthur is arrested or the bodies are found there is nothing more to tell of either Chetney or the Princess Zichy.'

'Of Lord Chetney perhaps not,' interrupted the sporting-looking gentleman with the black tie, 'but there'll always be something to tell of the Princess Zichy. I know enough stories about her to fill a book. She was a most remarkable woman.' The speaker dropped the end of his cigar into his coffee cup and, taking his case from his pocket, selected a fresh one. As he did so he laughed and held up the case that the others might see it. It was an ordinary cigar-case of well-worn pig-skin, with a silver clasp.

'The only time I ever met her,' he said, 'she tried to rob me of this.'

The Baronet regarded him closely.

'She tried to rob you?' he repeated.

'Tried to rob me of this,' continued the gentleman in the black tie, 'and of the Czarina's diamonds.' His tone was one of mingled admiration and injury.

'The Czarina's diamonds!' exclaimed the Baronet. He glanced quickly and suspiciously at the speaker, and then at the others about the table. But their faces gave evidence of no other emotion than that of ordinary interest.

'Yes, the Czarina's diamonds,' repeated the man with the black tie. 'It was a necklace of diamonds. I was told to take them to the Russian Ambassador in Paris who was to deliver them at Moscow. I am a Queen's Messenger,' he added.

'Oh, I see,' exclaimed Sir Andrew in a tone of relief. 'And you say that this same Princess Zichy, one of the victims of this double murder, endeavoured to rob you of – of – that cigar-case.'

'And the Czarina's diamonds,' answered the Queen's Messenger imperturbably. 'It's not much of a story, but it gives you an idea of the woman's character. The robbery took place between Paris and Marseilles.'

The Baronet interrupted him with an abrupt movement. 'No, no,' he cried, shaking his head in protest. 'Do not tempt me. I really cannot listen. I must be at the House in ten minutes.'

'I am sorry,' said the Queen's Messenger. He turned to those seated about him. 'I wonder if the other gentlemen –' he inquired tentatively. There was a chorus of polite murmurs, and the Queen's Messenger, bowing his head in acknowledgment, took a preparatory sip from his glass. At the same moment the servant to whom the man with the black pearl had spoken, slipped a piece of paper into his hand. He glanced at it, frowned, and threw it under the table.

The servant bowed to the Baronet.

'Your hansom is waiting, Sir Andrew,' he said.

'The necklace was worth twenty thousand pounds,' began the Queen's Messenger. 'It was a present from the Queen of England to celebrate –' The Baronet gave an exclamation of angry annoyance.

'Upon my word, this is most provoking,' he interrupted. 'I really ought not to stay. But I certainly mean to hear this.' He turned irritably to the servant. 'Tell the hansom to wait,' he commanded, and, with an air of a boy who is playing truant, slipped guiltily into his chair.

The gentleman with the black pearl smiled blandly, and rapped upon the table.

'Order, gentlemen,' he said. 'Order for the story of the Queen's Messenger and the Czarina's diamonds.'

CHAPTER TWO

'The necklace was a present from the Queen of England to the Czarina of Russia,' began the Queen's Messenger. 'It was to celebrate the occasion of the Czar's coronation. Our Foreign Office knew that the Russian Ambassador in Paris was to proceed to Moscow for that ceremony, and I was directed to go to Paris and turn over the necklace to him. But when I reached Paris I found he had not expected me for a week later and was taking a few days' vacation at Nice. His people asked me to leave the necklace with them at the Embassy, but I had been charged to get a receipt for it from the Ambassador himself, so I started at once for Nice. The fact that Monte Carlo is not two thousand miles from Nice may have had something to do with making me carry out my instructions so carefully.

'Now, how the Princess Zichy came to find out about the necklace I don't know, but I can guess. As you have just heard, she was at one time a spy in the service of the Russian government. And after they dismissed her she kept up her acquaintance with many of the Russian agents in London. It is probable that through one of them she learned that the necklace was to be sent to Moscow, and which one of the Queen's Messengers had been detailed to take it there. Still, I doubt if even that knowledge would have helped her if she had not also known something which I supposed no one else in the world knew but myself and one other man. And, curiously enough, the other man was a Queen's Messenger too, and a friend of mine. You must know that up to the time of this robbery I had always concealed my despatches in a manner peculiarly my own. I got the idea from that play called *A Scrap of Paper*. In it a man wants to hide a certain compromising document. He knows that all his rooms will be secretly searched for it, so he puts it in a torn envelope and sticks it up where any one can see it on his mantel shelf. The result is that the woman who is ransacking the house to find it looks in all the unlikely places, but passes over the scrap of paper that is just under her nose. Sometimes the papers and packages they give us to carry about Europe are of very great value, and sometimes they are special makes of cigarettes, and orders to court dressmakers. Sometimes we know what we are carrying and sometimes we do not. If it is a large sum of money or a treaty, they generally tell us. But, as a rule, we have no knowledge of what the package contains; so, to be on the safe side, we naturally take just as great care of it as though we knew it held the terms of an ultimatum or the crown jewels. As a rule, my confrères carry the official packages in a despatch-box, which is just as obvious as a lady's jewel bag in the hands of her maid. Every one knows they are carrying something of value. They put a premium on dishonesty. Well, after I saw the *Scrap of Paper* play, I determined to put the government valuables in the most unlikely place that any one would look for them. So I used to hide the documents they gave me inside my riding-boots, and small articles, such as money or jewels, I carried in an old cigar-case. After I took to using my case for that purpose I bought a new one, exactly like it, for my cigars. But to avoid mistakes, I had my initials placed on both sides of the new one, and the moment I touched the case, even in the dark, I could tell which it was by the raised initials.

'No one knew of this except the Queen's Messenger of whom I spoke. We once left Paris together on the Orient Express. I was going to Constantinople and he was to stop off at Vienna. On the journey I told him of my peculiar way of hiding things and showed him my cigar-case. If I recollect rightly, on that trip it held the grand cross of St Michael and St George, which the Queen was sending to our Ambassador. The Messenger was very much entertained at my scheme, and some months later when he met the Princess he told her about it as an amusing story. Of course, he had no idea she was a Russian spy. He didn't know anything at all about her, except that she was a very attractive woman. It was indiscreet, but he could not possibly have guessed that she could ever make any use of what he told her.

'Later, after the robbery, I remembered that I had informed this young chap of my secret hiding-place, and when I saw him again I questioned him about it. He was greatly distressed, and said he had never seen the importance of the secret. He remembered he had told several people of it, and among others the Princess Zichy. In that way I found out that it was she who had robbed me, and I know that from the moment I left London she was following me and that she knew then that the diamonds were concealed in my cigar-case.

'My train for Nice left Paris at ten in the morning. When I travel at night I generally tell the *chef de gare* that I am a Queen's Messenger, and he gives me a compartment to myself, but in the daytime I take whatever offers. On this morning I had found an empty compartment, and I had tipped the guard to keep every one else out, not from any fear of losing the diamonds, but because I wanted to smoke. He had locked the door, and as the last bell had rung I supposed I was to travel alone, so I began to arrange my traps and make myself comfortable. The diamonds in the cigar-case were in the inside pocket of my waistcoat, and as they made a bulky package, I took them out, intending to put them in my hand bag. It is a small satchel like a bookmaker's, or those hand bags that couriers carry. I wear it slung from a strap across my shoulder, and, no matter whether I am sitting or walking, it never leaves me.

'I took the cigar-case which held the necklace from my inside pocket and the case which held the cigars out of the satchel, and while I was searching through it for a box of matches I laid the two cases beside me on the seat.

'At that moment the train started, but at the same instant there was a rattle at the lock of the compartment, and a couple of porters lifted and shoved a woman through the door, and hurled her rugs and umbrellas in after her.

'Instinctively I reached for the diamonds. I shoved them quickly into the satchel and, pushing them far down to the bottom of the bag, snapped the spring lock. Then I put the cigars in the pocket of my coat, but with the thought that now that I had a woman as a travelling companion I would probably not be allowed to enjoy them.

'One of her pieces of luggage had fallen at my feet, and a roll of rugs had landed at my side. I thought if I hid the fact that the lady was not welcome, and at once endeavoured to be civil, she might permit me to smoke. So I picked her hand bag off the floor and asked her where I might place it.

'As I spoke I looked at her for the first time, and saw that she was a most remarkably handsome woman.

'She smiled charmingly and begged me not to disturb myself. Then she arranged her own things about her, and, opening her dressing-bag, took out a gold cigarette case.

'"Do you object to smoke?" she asked.

'I laughed and assured her I had been in great terror lest she might object to it herself.

'"If you like cigarettes," she said, "will you try some of these? They are rolled especially for my husband in Russia, and they are supposed to be very good."

'I thanked her, and took one from her case, and I found it so much better than my own that I continued to smoke her cigarettes throughout the rest of the journey. I must say that we got on very well. I judged from the coronet on her cigarette-case, and from her manner, which was quite as well bred as that of any woman I ever met, that she was some one of importance, and though she seemed almost too good looking to be respectable, I determined that she was some *grande dame* who was so assured of her position that she could afford to be unconventional. At first she read her novel, and then she made some comment on the scenery, and finally we began to discuss the current politics of the Continent. She talked of all the cities in Europe, and seemed to know every one worth knowing. But she volunteered nothing about herself except that she frequently made use of the expression, "When my husband was stationed at Vienna," or "When my husband was promoted to Rome." Once she said to me, "I have often seen you at Monte Carlo. I saw you when you won the pigeon championship." I told her that I was not a pigeon shot, and she gave a little start of surprise. "Oh, I beg your pardon," she said; "I thought you were Morton Hamilton, the English champion." As a matter of fact, I do look like Hamilton, but I know now that her object was to make me think that she had no idea as to who I really was. She needn't have acted at all, for I certainly had no suspicions of her, and was only too pleased to have so charming a companion.

'The one thing that should have made me suspicious was the fact that at every station she made some trivial excuse to get me out of the compartment. She pretended that her maid was travelling back of us in one of the second-class carriages, and kept saying she could not imagine why the woman did not come to look after her, and if the maid did not turn up at the next stop, would I be so very kind as to get out and bring her whatever it was she pretended she wanted.

'I had taken my dressing-case from the rack to get out a novel, and had left it on the seat opposite to mine, and at the end of the compartment farthest from her. And once when I came back from buying her a cup of chocolate, or from some other fool errand, I found her standing at my end of the compartment with both hands on the dressing-bag. She looked at me without so much as winking an eye, and shoved the case carefully into a corner. "Your bag slipped off on the floor," she said. "If you've got any bottles in it, you had better look and see that they're not broken."

'And I give you my word, I was such an ass that I did open the case and looked all through it. She must have thought I *was* a Juggins. I get hot all over whenever I remember it. But in spite of my dulness, and her cleverness, she couldn't gain anything by sending me away, because what she wanted was in the hand bag and every time she sent me away the hand bag went with me.

'After the incident of the dressing-case her manner changed. Either in my absence she had had time to look through it, or, when I was examining it for broken bottles, she had seen everything it held.

'From that moment she must have been certain that the cigar case, in which she knew I carried the diamonds, was in the bag that was fastened to my body, and from that time on she probably was plotting how to get it from me.

'Her anxiety became most apparent. She dropped the great lady manner, and her charming condescension went with it. She ceased talking, and, when I spoke, answered me irritably, or at random. No doubt her mind was entirely occupied with her plan. The end of our journey was drawing rapidly nearer, and her time for action was being cut down with the speed of the express train. Even I, unsuspicious as I was, noticed that something was very wrong with her. I really believe that before we reached Marseilles if I had not, through my own stupidity, given her the chance she wanted, she might have stuck a knife in me and rolled me out on the rails. But as it was, I only thought that the long journey had tired her. I suggested that it was a very trying trip, and asked her if she would allow me to offer her some of my cognac.

'She thanked me and said, "No," and then suddenly her eyes lighted, and she exclaimed, "Yes, thank you, if you will be so kind."

'My flask was in the hand bag, and I placed it on my lap and with my thumb slipped back the catch. As I keep my tickets and railroad guide in the bag, I am so constantly opening it that I never bother to lock it, and the fact that it is strapped to me has always been sufficient protection. But I can appreciate now what a satisfaction, and what a torment too, it must have been to that woman when she saw that the bag opened without a key.

'While we were crossing the mountains I had felt rather chilly and had been wearing a light racing coat. But after the lamps were lighted the compartment became very hot and stuffy, and I found the coat uncomfortable. So I stood up, and, after first slipping the strap of the bag over my head, I placed the bag in the seat next me and pulled off the racing coat. I don't blame myself for being careless; the bag was still within reach of my hand, and nothing would have happened if at that exact moment the train had not stopped at Arles. It was the combination of my removing the bag and our entering the station at the same instant which gave the Princess Zichy the chance she wanted to rob me.

'I needn't say that she was clever enough to take it. The train ran into the station at full speed and came to a sudden stop. I had just thrown my coat into the rack, and had reached out my hand for the bag. In another instant I would have had the strap around my shoulder. But at that moment the Princess threw open the door of the compartment and beckoned wildly at the people on the platform. "Natalie!" she called, "Natalie! here I am. Come here! This way!" She turned upon me in the greatest excitement. "My maid!" she cried. "She is looking for me. She passed the window without seeing me. Go, please, and bring her back." She continued pointing out of the door and beckoning me with her other hand. There certainly was something about that woman's tone which made one jump. When she was giving orders you

IN THE FOG

had no chance to think of anything else. So I rushed out on my errand of mercy, and then rushed back again to ask what the maid looked like.

'"In black," she answered, rising and blocking the door of the compartment. "All in black, with a bonnet!"

'The train waited three minutes at Arles, and in that time I suppose I must have rushed up to over twenty women and asked, "Are you Natalie?" The only reason I wasn't punched with an umbrella or handed over to the police was that they probably thought I was crazy.

'When I jumped back into the compartment the Princess was seated where I had left her, but her eyes were burning with happiness. She placed her hand on my arm almost affectionately, and said in a hysterical way, "You are very kind to me. I am so sorry to have troubled you."

'I protested that every woman on the platform was dressed in black.

'"Indeed I am so sorry," she said, laughing; and she continued to laugh until she began to breathe so quickly that I thought she was going to faint.

'I can see now that the last part of that journey must have been a terrible half hour for her. She had the cigar-case safe enough, but she knew that she herself was not safe. She understood if I were to open my bag, even at the last minute, and miss the case, I would know positively that she had taken it. I had placed the diamonds in the bag at the very moment she entered the compartment, and no one but our two selves had occupied it since. She knew that when we reached Marseilles she would either be twenty thousand pounds richer than when she left Paris, or that she would go to jail. That was the situation as she must have read it, and I don't envy her her state of mind during that last half hour. It must have been hell.

'I saw that something was wrong, and in my innocence I even wondered if possibly my cognac had not been a little too strong. For she suddenly developed into a most brilliant conversationalist, and applauded and laughed at everything I said, and fired off questions at me like a machine gun, so that I had no time to think of anything but of what she was saying. Whenever I stirred she stopped her chattering and leaned toward me, and watched me like a cat over a mouse-hole. I wondered how I could have considered her an agreeable travelling companion. I thought I would have preferred to be locked in with a lunatic. I don't like to think how she would have acted if I had made a move to examine the bag, but as I had it safely strapped around me again, I did not open it, and I reached Marseilles alive. As we drew into the station she shook hands with me and grinned at me like a Cheshire cat.

'"I cannot tell you," she said, "how much I have to thank you for." What do you think of that for impudence?

'I offered to put her in a carriage, but she said she must find Natalie, and

419

that she hoped we would meet again at the hotel. So I drove off by myself, wondering who she was, and whether Natalie was not her keeper.

'I had to wait several hours for the train to Nice, and as I wanted to stroll around the city I thought I had better put the diamonds in the safe of the hotel. As soon as I reached my room I locked the door, placed the hand bag on the table and opened it. I felt among the things at the top of it, but failed to touch the cigar-case. I shoved my hand in deeper, and stirred the things about, but still I did not reach it. A cold wave swept down my spine, and a sort of emptiness came to the pit of my stomach. Then I turned red-hot, and the sweat sprung out all over me. I wet my lips with my tongue, and said to myself, "Don't be an ass. Pull yourself together, pull yourself together. Take the things out, one at a time. It's there, of course it's there. Don't be an ass."

'So I put a brake on my nerves and began very carefully to pick out the things one by one, but after another second I could not stand it, and I rushed across the room and threw out everything on the bed. But the diamonds were not among them. I pulled the things about and tore them open and shuffled and rearranged and sorted them, but it was no use. The cigar-case was gone. I threw everything in the dressing-case out on the floor, although I knew it was useless to look for it there. I knew that I had put it in the bag. I sat down and tried to think. I remembered I had put it in the satchel at Paris just as that woman had entered the compartment, and I had been alone with her ever since, so it was she who had robbed me. But how? It had never left my shoulder. And then I remembered that it had – that I had taken it off when I had changed my coat and for the few moments that I was searching for Natalie. I remembered that the woman had sent me on that goose chase, and that at every other station she had tried to get rid of me on some fool errand.

'I gave a roar like a mad bull, and I jumped down the stairs six steps at a time.

'I demanded at the office if a distinguished lady of title, possibly a Russian, had just entered the hotel.

'As I expected, she had not. I sprang into a cab and inquired at two other hotels, and then I saw the folly of trying to catch her without outside help, and I ordered the fellow to gallop to the office of the Chief of Police. I told my story, and the ass in charge asked me to calm myself, and wanted to take notes. I told him this was no time for taking notes, but for doing something. He got wrathy at that, and I demanded to be taken at once to his Chief. The Chief, he said, was very busy, and could not see me. So I showed him my silver greyhound. In eleven years I had never used it but once before. I stated in pretty vigorous language that I was a Queen's Messenger, and that if the Chief of Police did not see me instantly he would lose his official head. At that the fellow jumped off his high horse and ran with me to his Chief – a smart young chap, a colonel in the army, and a very intelligent man.

'I explained that I had been robbed in a French railway carriage of a diamond necklace belonging to the Queen of England, which her Majesty was sending as a present to the Czarina of Russia. I pointed out to him that if he succeeded in capturing the thief he would be made for life, and would receive the gratitude of three great powers.

'He wasn't the sort that thinks second thoughts are best. He saw Russian and French decorations sprouting all over his chest, and he hit a bell, and pressed buttons, and yelled out orders like the captain of a penny steamer in a fog. He sent her description to all the city gates, and ordered all cabmen and railway porters to search all trains leaving Marseilles. He ordered all passengers on outgoing vessels to be examined, and telegraphed the proprietors of every hotel and pension to send him a complete list of their guests within the hour. While I was standing there he must have given at least a hundred orders, and sent out enough commissaires, sergents de ville, gendarmes, bicycle police, and plain-clothes Johnnies to have captured the entire German army. When they had gone he assured me that the woman was as good as arrested already. Indeed, officially, she was arrested; for she had no more chance of escape from Marseilles than from the Château d'If.

'He told me to return to my hotel and possess my soul in peace. Within an hour he assured me he would acquaint me with her arrest.

'I thanked him, and complimented him on his energy, and left him. But I didn't share in his confidence. I felt that she was a very clever woman, and a match for any and all of us. It was all very well for him to be jubilant. He had not lost the diamonds, and had everything to gain if he found them; while I, even if he did recover the necklace, would only be where I was before I lost them, and if he did not recover it I was a ruined man. It was an awful facer for me. I had always prided myself on my record. In eleven years I had never mislaid an envelope, nor missed taking the first train. And now I had failed in the most important mission that had ever been intrusted to me. And it wasn't a thing that could be hushed up, either. It was too conspicuous, too spectacular. It was sure to invite the widest notoriety. I saw myself ridiculed all over the Continent, and perhaps dismissed, even suspected of having taken the thing myself.

'I was walking in front of a lighted café, and I felt so sick and miserable that I stopped for a pick-me-up. Then I considered that if I took one drink I would probably, in my present state of mind, not want to stop under twenty, and I decided I had better leave it alone. But my nerves were jumping like a frightened rabbit, and I felt I must have something to quiet them or I would go crazy. I reached for my cigarette-case, but a cigarette seemed hardly adequate, so I put it back again and took out this cigar-case, in which I keep only the strongest and blackest cigars. I opened it and stuck in my fingers, but instead of a cigar they touched on a thin leather envelope. My heart stood perfectly still. I did not dare to look, but I dug my finger nails into the leather and I felt layers of thin paper, then a layer of cotton, and then they scratched on the facets of the Czarina's diamonds!

'I stumbled as though I had been hit in the face, and fell back into one of the chairs on the sidewalk. I tore off the wrappings and spread out the diamonds on the café table; I could not believe they were real. I twisted the necklace between my fingers and crushed it between my palms and tossed it up in the air. I believe I almost kissed it. The women in the café stood up on the chairs to see better, and laughed and screamed, and the people crowded so close around me that the waiters had to form a bodyguard. The proprietor thought there was a fight, and called for the police. I was so happy I didn't care. I laughed, too, and gave the proprietor a five-pound note, and told him to stand every one a drink. Then I tumbled into a fiacre and galloped off to my friend the Chief of Police. I felt very sorry for him. He had been so happy at the chance I gave him, and he was sure to be disappointed when he learned I had sent him off on a false alarm.

'But now that I had found the necklace, I did not want him to find the woman. Indeed, I was most anxious that she should get clear away, for if she were caught the truth would come out, and I was likely to get a sharp reprimand, and sure to be laughed at.

'I could see now how it had happened. In my haste to hide the diamonds when the woman was hustled into the carriage, I had shoved the cigars into the satchel, and the diamonds into the pocket of my coat. Now that I had the diamonds safe again, it seemed a very natural mistake. But I doubted if the Foreign Office would think so. I was afraid it might not appreciate the beautiful simplicity of my secret hiding-place. So, when I reached the police station, and found that the woman was still at large, I was more than relieved.

'As I expected, the Chief was extremely chagrined when he learned of my mistake, and that there was nothing for him to do. But I was feeling so happy myself that I hated to have any one else miserable, so I suggested that this attempt to steal the Czarina's necklace might be only the first of a series of such attempts by an unscrupulous gang, and that I might still be in danger.

'I winked at the Chief and the Chief smiled at me, and we went to Nice together in a saloon car with a guard of twelve carabineers and twelve plain-clothes men, and the Chief and I drank champagne all the way. We marched together up to the hotel where the Russian Ambassador was stopping, closely surrounded by our escort of carabineers, and delivered the necklace with the most profound ceremony. The old Ambassador was immensely impressed, and when we hinted that already I had been made the object of an attack by robbers, he assured us that his Imperial Majesty would not prove ungrateful.

'I wrote a swinging personal letter about the invaluable services of the Chief to the French Minister of Foreign Affairs, and they gave him enough Russian and French medals to satisfy even a French soldier. So, though he never caught the woman, he received his just reward.'

The Queen's Messenger paused and surveyed the faces of those about him in some embarrassment.

'But the worst of it is,' he added, 'that the story must have got about; for, while the Princess obtained nothing from me but a cigar-case and five excellent cigars, a few weeks after the coronation the Czar sent me a gold cigar-case with his monogram in diamonds. And I don't know yet whether that was a coincidence, or whether the Czar wanted me to know that he knew that I had been carrying the Czarina's diamonds in my pigskin cigar-case. What do you fellows think?'

## CHAPTER THREE

Sir Andrew rose with disapproval written in every lineament.

'I thought your story would bear upon the murder,' he said. 'Had I imagined it would have nothing whatsoever to do with it I would not have remained.' He pushed back his chair and bowed stiffly. 'I wish you good night,' he said.

There was a chorus of remonstrance, and under cover of this and the Baronet's answering protests a servant for the second time slipped a piece of paper into the hand of the gentleman with the pearl stud. He read the lines written upon it and tore it into tiny fragments.

The youngest member, who had remained an interested but silent listener to the tale of the Queen's Messenger, raised his hand commandingly.

'Sir Andrew,' he cried, 'in justice to Lord Arthur Chetney I must ask you to be seated. He has been accused in our hearing of a most serious crime, and I insist that you remain until you have heard me clear his character.'

'You!' cried the Baronet.

'Yes,' answered the young man briskly. 'I would have spoken sooner,' he explained, 'but that I thought this gentleman' – he inclined his head toward the Queen's Messenger – 'was about to contribute some facts of which I was ignorant. He, however, has told us nothing, and so I will take up the tale at the point where Lieutenant Sears laid it down and give you those details of which Lieutenant Sears is ignorant. It seems strange to you that I should be able to add the sequel to this story. But the coincidence is easily explained. I am the junior member of the law firm of Chudleigh & Chudleigh. We have been solicitors for the Chetneys for the last two hundred years. Nothing, no matter how unimportant, which concerns Lord Edam and his two sons is unknown to us, and naturally we are acquainted with every detail of the terrible catastrophe of last night.'

The Baronet, bewildered but eager, sank back into his chair.

'Will you be long, sir?' he demanded.

'I shall endeavor to be brief,' said the young solicitor; 'and,' he added, in a tone which gave his words almost the weight of a threat,' I promise to be interesting.'

'There is no need to promise that,' said Sir Andrew, 'I find it much too interesting as it is.' He glanced ruefully at the clock and turned his eyes quickly from it.

'Tell the driver of that hansom,' he called to the servant, 'that I take him by the hour.'

'For the last three days,' began young Mr Chudleigh, 'as you have probably read in the daily papers, the Marquis of Edam has been at the point of death, and his physicians have never left his house. Every hour he seemed to grow weaker; but although his bodily strength is apparently leaving him forever, his mind has remained clear and active. Late yesterday evening word was received at our office that he wished my father to come at once to Chetney House and to bring with him certain papers. What these papers were is not essential; I mention them only to explain how it was that last night I happened to be at Lord Edam's bedside. I accompanied my father to Chetney House, but at the time we reached there Lord Edam was sleeping, and his physicians refused to have him awakened. My father urged that he should be allowed to receive Lord Edam's instructions concerning the documents, but the physicians would not disturb him, and we all gathered in the library to wait until he should awake of his own accord. It was about one o'clock in the morning, while we were still there, that Inspector Lyle and the officers from Scotland Yard came to arrest Lord Arthur on the charge of murdering his brother. You can imagine our dismay and distress. Like every one else, I had learned from the afternoon papers that Lord Chetney was not dead, but that he had returned to England, and on arriving at Chetney House I had been told that Lord Arthur had gone to the Bath Hotel to look for his brother and to inform him that if he wished to see their father alive he must come to him at once. Although it was now past one o'clock, Arthur had not returned. None of us knew where Madame Zichy lived, so we could not go to recover Lord Chetney's body. We spent a most miserable night, hastening to the window whenever a cab came into the square, in the hope that it was Arthur returning, and endeavouring to explain away the facts that pointed to him as the murderer. I am a friend of Arthur's, I was with him at Harrow and at Oxford, and I refused to believe for an instant that he was capable of such a crime; but as a lawyer I could not help but see that the circumstantial evidence was strongly against him.

'Toward early morning Lord Edam awoke, and in so much better a state of health that he refused to make the changes in the papers which he had intended, declaring that he was no nearer death than ourselves. Under other circumstances, this happy change in him would have relieved us greatly, but none of us could think of anything save the death of his elder son and of the charge which hung over Arthur.

'As long as Inspector Lyle remained in the house my father decided that I, as one of the legal advisers of the family, should also remain there. But there was little for either of us to do. Arthur did not return, and nothing occurred until late this morning, when Lyle received word that the Russian servant had been arrested. He at once drove to Scotland Yard to question him. He came back to us in an hour, and informed me that the servant had refused to tell anything of what had happened the night before, or of himself, or of the Princess Zichy. He would not even give them the address of her house.

'"He is in abject terror," Lyle said. "I assured him that he was not suspected of the crime, but he would tell me nothing."

'There were no other developments until two o'clock this afternoon, when word was brought to us that Arthur had been found, and that he was lying in the accident ward of St George's Hospital. Lyle and I drove there together, and found him propped up in bed with his head bound in a bandage. He had been brought to the hospital the night before by the driver of a hansom that had run over him in the fog. The cab-horse had kicked him on the head, and he had been carried in unconscious. There was nothing on him to tell who he was, and it was not until he came to his senses this afternoon that the hospital authorities had been able to send word to his people. Lyle at once informed him that he was under arrest, and with what he was charged, and though the inspector warned him to say nothing which might be used against him, I, as his solicitor, instructed him to speak freely and to tell us all he knew of the occurrences of last night. It was evident to any one that the fact of his brother's death was of much greater concern to him, than that he was accused of his murder.

'"That," Arthur said contemptuously, "that is damned nonsense. It is monstrous and cruel. We parted better friends than we have been in years. I will tell you all that happened – not to clear myself, but to help you to find out the truth." His story is as follows: Yesterday afternoon, owing to his constant attendance on his father, he did not look at the evening papers, and it was not until after dinner, when the butler brought him one and told him of its contents, that he learned that his brother was alive and at the Bath Hotel. He drove there at once, but was told that about eight o'clock his brother had gone out, but without giving any clew to his destination. As Chetney had not at once come to see his father, Arthur decided that he was still angry with him, and his mind, turning naturally to the cause of their quarrel, determined him to look for Chetney at the home of the Princess Zichy.

'Her house had been pointed out to him, and though he had never visited it, he had passed it many times and knew its exact location. He accordingly drove in that direction, as far as the fog would permit the hansom to go, and walked the rest of the way, reaching the house about nine o'clock. He rang, and was admitted by the Russian servant. The man took his card into the drawing-room, and at once his brother ran out and welcomed him. He was followed by the Princess Zichy, who also received Arthur most cordially.

'"You brothers will have much to talk about," she said. "I am going to the dining-room. When you have finished, let me know."

'As soon as she had left them, Arthur told his brother that their father was not expected to outlive the night, and that he must come to him at once.

'"This is not the moment to remember your quarrel," Arthur said to him; "you have come back from the dead only in time to make your peace with him before he dies."

'Arthur says that at this Chetney was greatly moved.

'"You entirely misunderstand me, Arthur," he returned. "I did not know the governor was ill, or I would have gone to him the instant I arrived. My only reason for not doing so was because I thought he was still angry with me. I shall return with you immediately, as soon as I have said good-by to the Princess. It is a final good-by. After tonight, I shall never see her again."

'"Do you mean that?" Arthur cried.

'"Yes," Chetney answered. "When I returned to London I had no intention of seeking her again, and I am here only through a mistake." He then told Arthur that he had separated from the Princess even before he went to Central Africa, and that, moreover, while at Cairo on his way south, he had learned certain facts concerning her life there during the previous season, which made it impossible for him to ever wish to see her again. Their separation was final and complete.

'"She deceived me cruelly," he said; "I cannot tell you how cruelly. During the two years when I was trying to obtain my father's consent to our marriage she was in love with a Russian diplomat. During all that time he was secretly visiting her here in London, and her trip to Cairo was only an excuse to meet him there.'

'"Yet you are here with her tonight," Arthur protested, "only a few hours after your return."

'"That is easily explained," Chetney answered. "As I finished dinner tonight at the hotel, I received a note from her from this address. In it she said she had but just learned of my arrival, and begged me to come to her at once. She wrote that she was in great and present trouble, dying of an incurable illness, and without friends or money. She begged me, for the sake of old times, to come to her assistance. During the last two years in the jungle all my former feeling for Zichy has utterly passed away, but no one could have dismissed the appeal she made in that letter. So I came here, and found her, as you have seen her, quite as beautiful as she ever was, in very good health, and, from the look of the house, in no need of money.

' "I asked her what she meant by writing me that she was dying in a garret, and she laughed, and said she had done so because she was afraid, unless I thought she needed help, I would not try to see her. That was where we were when you arrived. And now," Chetney added, "I will say good-by to her, and you had better return home. No, you can trust me, I shall follow you at once. She has no influence over me now, but I believe, in spite of the way she has used me, that she is, after her queer fashion, still fond of me, and when she learns that this good-by is final there may be a scene, and it is not fair to her that you should be here. So, go home at once, and tell the governor that I am following you in ten minutes."

' "That," said Arthur, "is the way we parted. I never left him on more friendly terms. I was happy to see him alive again, I was happy to think he had returned in time to make up his quarrel with my father, and I was happy that at last he was shut of that woman. I was never better pleased with him in my life." He turned to Inspector Lyle, who was sitting at the foot of the bed taking notes of all he told us.

' "Why in the name of common sense," he cried, "should I have chosen that moment of all others to send my brother back to the grave?" For a moment the Inspector did not answer him. I do not know if any of you gentlemen are acquainted with Inspector Lyle, but if you are not, I can assure you that he is a very remarkable man. Our firm often applies to him for aid, and he has never failed us; my father has the greatest possible respect for him. Where he has the advantage over the ordinary police official is in the fact that he possesses imagination. He imagines himself to be the criminal, imagines how he would act under the same circumstances, and he imagines to such purpose that he generally finds the man he wants. I have often told Lyle that if he had not been a detective he would have made a great success as a poet, or a playwright.

'When Arthur turned on him Lyle hesitated for a moment, and then told him exactly what was the case against him.

' "Ever since your brother was reported as having died in Africa," he said, "your Lordship has been collecting money on post-obits. Lord Chetney's arrival last night turned them into waste paper. You were suddenly in debt for thousands of pounds – for much more than you could ever possibly pay. No one knew that you and your brother had met at Madame Zichy's. But you knew that your father was not expected to outlive the night, and that if your brother were dead also, you would be saved from complete ruin, and that you would become the Marquis of Edam."

' "Oh, that is how you have worked it out, is it?" Arthur cried. "And for me to become Lord Edam was it necessary that the woman should die, too?''

'''They will say,'' Lyle answered, ''that she was a witness to the murder – that she would have told.''

'''Then why did I not kill the servant as well?'' Arthur said.

'''He was asleep, and saw nothing.''

'''And you believe *that*?'' Arthur demanded.

'''It is not a question of what I believe,'' Lyle said gravely. ''It is a question for your peers.''

'''The man is insolent!'' Arthur cried. ''The thing is monstrous! Horrible!''

'Before we could stop him he sprang out of his cot and began pulling on his clothes. When the nurses tried to hold him down, he fought with them.

'''Do you think you can keep me here,'' he shouted, ''when they are plotting to hang me? I am going with you to that house!'' he cried to Lyle. ''When you find those bodies I shall be beside you. It is my right. He is my brother. He has been murdered, and I can tell you who murdered him. That woman murdered him. She first ruined his life, and now she has killed him. For the last five years she has been plotting to make herself his wife, and last night, when he told her he had discovered the truth about the Russian, and that she would never see him again, she flew into a passion and stabbed him, and then, in terror of the gallows, killed herself. She murdered him, I tell you, and I promise you that we will find the knife she used near her – perhaps still in her hand. What will you say to that?''

'Lyle turned his head away and stared down at the floor. ''I might say,'' he answered, ''that you placed it there.''

'Arthur gave a cry of anger and sprang at him, and then pitched forward into his arms. The blood was running from the cut under the bandage, and he had fainted. Lyle carried him back to the bed again, and we left him with the police and the doctors, and drove at once to the address he had given us. We found the house not three minutes' walk from St George's Hospital. It stands in Trevor Terrace, that little row of houses set back from Knightsbridge, with one end in Hill Street.

'As we left the hospital Lyle had said to me, ''You must not blame me for treating him as I did. All is fair in this work, and if by angering that boy I could have made him commit himself I was right in trying to do so; though, I assure you, no one would be better pleased than myself if I could prove his theory to be correct. But we cannot tell. Everything depends upon what we see for ourselves within the next few minutes.''

'When we reached the house, Lyle broke open the fastenings of one of the windows on the ground floor, and, hidden by the trees in the garden, we scrambled in. We found ourselves in the reception-room, which was the first room on the right of the hall. The gas was still burning behind the colored glass and red silk shades, and when the daylight streamed in after us it gave the hall a hideously dissipated look, like the foyer of a theatre at a matinée, or the entrance to an all-day gambling hell. The house was oppressively silent, and because we knew why it was so silent we spoke in whispers. When Lyle turned the handle of the drawing-room door, I felt as though some one had put his hand upon my throat. But I followed close at his shoulder, and saw, in the subdued light of many-tinted lamps, the body of Chetney at the foot of the divan, just as Lieutenant Sears had described it. In the drawing-room we found the body of the Princess Zichy, her arms thrown out, and the blood from her heart frozen in a tiny line across her bare shoulder. But neither of us, although we searched the floor on our hands and knees, could find the weapon which had killed her.

' "For Arthur's sake," I said, "I would have given a thousand pounds if we had found the knife in her hand, as he said we would."

' "That we have not found it there," Lyle answered, "is to my mind the strongest proof that he is telling the truth, that he left the house before the murder took place. He is not a fool, and had he stabbed his brother and this woman, he would have seen that by placing the knife near her he could help to make it appear as if she had killed Chetney and then committed suicide. Besides, Lord Arthur insisted that the evidence in his behalf would be our finding the knife here. He would not have urged that if he knew we would *not* find it, if he knew he himself had carried it away. This is no suicide. A suicide does not rise and hide the weapon with which he kills himself, and then lie down again. No, this has been a double murder, and we must look outside of the house for the murderer."

'While he was speaking Lyle and I had been searching every corner, studying the details of each room. I was so afraid that, without telling me, he would make some deductions prejudicial to Arthur, that I never left his side. I was determined to see everything that he saw, and, if possible, to prevent his interpreting it in the wrong way. He finally finished his examination, and we sat down together in the drawing-room, and he took out his notebook and read aloud all that Mr Sears had told him of the murder and what we had just learned from Arthur. We compared the two accounts word for word, and weighed statement with statement, but I could not determine from anything Lyle said which of the two versions he had decided to believe.

' "We are trying to build a house of blocks," he exclaimed, "with half of the blocks missing. We have been considering two theories," he went on: "one that Lord Arthur is responsible for both murders, and the other that the dead woman in there is responsible for one of them, and has committed suicide; but, until the Russian servant is ready to talk, I shall refuse to believe in the guilt of either."

'"What can you prove by him?" I asked. "He was drunk and asleep. He saw nothing."

'Lyle hesitated, and then, as though he had made up his mind to be quite frank with me, spoke freely.

'"I do not know that he was either drunk or asleep," he answered. "Lieutenant Sears describes him as a stupid boor. I am not satisfied that he is not a clever actor. What was his position in this house? What was his real duty here? Suppose it was not to guard this woman, but to watch her. Let us imagine that it was not the woman he served, but a master, and see where that leads us. For this house has a master, a mysterious, absentee landlord, who lives in St Petersburg, the unknown Russian who came between Chetney and Zichy, and because of whom Chetney left her. He is the man who bought this house for Madame Zichy, who sent these rugs and curtains from St Petersburg to furnish it for her after his own tastes, and, I believe, it was he also who placed the Russian servant here, ostensibly to serve the Princess, but in reality to spy upon her. At Scotland Yard we do not know who this gentleman is; the Russian police confess to equal ignorance concerning him. When Lord Chetney went to Africa, Madame Zichy lived in St Petersburg; but there her receptions and dinners were so crowded with members of the nobility and of the army and diplomats, that among so many visitors the police could not learn which was the one for whom she most greatly cared."

'Lyle pointed at the modern French paintings and the heavy silk rugs which hung upon the walls.

'"The unknown is a man of taste and of some fortune," he said, "not the sort of man to send a stupid peasant to guard the woman he loves. So I am not content to believe, with Mr Sears, that the servant is a boor. I believe him instead to be a very clever ruffian. I believe him to be the protector of his master's honor, or, let us say, of his master's property, whether that property be silver plate or the woman his master loves. Last night, after Lord Arthur had gone away, the servant was left alone in this house with Lord Chetney and Madame Zichy. From where he sat in the hall he could hear Lord Chetney bidding her farewell; for, if my idea of him is correct, he understands English quite as well as you or I. Let us imagine that he heard her entreating Chetney not to leave her, reminding him of his former wish to marry her, and let us suppose that he hears Chetney denounce her, and tell her that at Cairo he has learned of this Russian admirer – the servant's master. He hears the woman declare that she has had no admirer but himself, that this unknown Russian was, and is, nothing to her, that there is no man she loves but him, and that she cannot live, knowing that he is alive, without his love. Suppose Chetney believed her, suppose his former infatuation for her returned, and that in a moment of weakness he forgave her and took her in his arms. That is the moment the Russian master has feared. It is to guard against it that he has placed his watchdog over the Princess, and how do we know but that, when the moment came, the watchdog served his master, as he saw his duty, and killed them both? What do you think?" Lyle demanded. "Would not that explain both murders?"

'I was only too willing to hear any theory which pointed to any one else as the criminal than Arthur, but Lyle's explanation was too utterly fantastic. I told him that he certainly showed imagination, but that he could not hang a man for what he imagined he had done.

' "No," Lyle answered, "but I can frighten him by telling him what I think he has done, and now when I again question the Russian servant I will make it quite clear to him that I believe he is the murderer. I think that will open his mouth. A man will at least talk to defend himself. Come," he said, "we must return at once to Scotland Yard and see him. There is nothing more to do here."

'He arose, and I followed him into the hall, and in another minute we would have been on our way to Scotland Yard. But just as he opened the street door a postman halted at the gate of the garden, and began fumbling with the latch.

'Lyle stopped, with an exclamation of chagrin.

' "How stupid of me!" he exclaimed. He turned quickly and pointed to a narrow slit cut in the brass plate of the front door. "The house has a private letter-box," he said, "and I had not thought to look in it! If we had gone out as we came in, by the window, I would never have seen it. The moment I entered the house I should have thought of securing the letters which came this morning. I have been grossly careless." He stepped back into the hall and pulled at the lid of the letter-box, which hung on the inside of the door, but it was tightly locked. At the same moment the postman came up the steps holding a letter. Without a word Lyle took it from his hand and began to examine it. It was addressed to the Princess Zichy, and on the back of the envelope was the name of a West End dressmaker.

' "That is of no use to me," Lyle said. He took out his card and showed it to the postman. "I am Inspector Lyle from Scotland Yard," he said. "The people in this house are under arrest. Everything it contains is now in my keeping. Did you deliver any other letters here this morning?"

'The man looked frightened, but answered promptly that he was now upon his third round. He had made one postal delivery at seven that morning and another at eleven.

'"How many letters did you leave here?" Lyle asked.

'"About six altogether," the man answered.

'"Did you put them through the door into the letter-box?"

'The postman said, "Yes, I always slip them into the box, and ring and go away. The servants collect them from the inside."

'"Have you noticed if any of the letters you leave here bear a Russian postage stamp?" Lyle asked.

'The man answered, "Oh, yes, sir, a great many."

'"From the same person, would you say?"

'"The writing seems to be the same," the man answered. "They come regularly about once a week – one of those I delivered this morning had a Russian postmark."

'"That will do," said Lyle eagerly. "Thank you, thank you very much."

'He ran back into the hall, and, pulling out his penknife, began to pick at the lock of the letter-box.

'"I have been supremely careless," he said in great excitement. "Twice before when people I wanted had flown from a house I have been able to follow them by putting a guard over their mail-box. These letters, which arrive regularly every week from Russia in the same handwriting, they can come but from one person. At least, we shall now know the name of the master of this house. Undoubtedly it is one of his letters that the man placed here this morning. We may make a most important discovery."

'As he was talking he was picking at the lock with his knife, but he was so impatient to reach the letters that he pressed too heavily on the blade and it broke in his hand. I took a step backward and drove my heel into the lock, and burst it open. The lid flew back, and we pressed forward, and each ran his hand down into the letter-box. For a moment we were both too startled to move. The box was empty.

'I do not know how long we stood staring stupidly at each other, but it was Lyle who was the first to recover. He seized me by the arm and pointed excitedly into the empty box.

'"Do you appreciate what that means?" he cried. "It means that some one has been here ahead of us. Some one has entered this house not three hours before we came, since eleven o'clock this morning."

'"It was the Russian servant!" I exclaimed.

'"The Russian servant has been under arrest at Scotland Yard," Lyle cried. "He could not have taken the letters. Lord Arthur has been in his cot at the hospital. That is his alibi. There is some one else, some one we do not suspect, and that some one is the murderer. He came back here either to obtain those letters because he knew they would convict him, or to remove something he had left here at the time of the murder, something incriminating – the weapon, perhaps, or some personal article; a cigarette-case, a handkerchief with his name upon it, or a pair of gloves. Whatever it was it must have been damning evidence against him to have made him take so desperate a chance."

' "How do we know," I whispered, "that he is not hidden here now?"

' "No, I'll swear he is not," Lyle answered. "I may have bungled in some things, but I have searched this house thoroughly. Nevertheless," he added, "we must go over it again, from the cellar to the roof. We have the real clew now, and we must forget the others and work only it." As he spoke he began again to search the drawing-room, turning over even the books on the tables, and the music on the piano.

' "Whoever the man is," he said over his shoulder, "we know that he has a key to the front door and a key to the letter-box. That shows us he is either an inmate of the house or that he comes here when he wishes. The Russian says that he was the only servant in the house. Certainly we have found no evidence to show that any other servant slept here. There could be but one other person who would possess a key to the house and the letter-box – and he lives in St Petersburg. At the time of the murder he was two thousand miles away." Lyle interrupted himself suddenly with a sharp cry and turned upon me with his eyes flashing. "But was he?" he cried. "Was he? How do we know that last night he was not in London, in this very house when Zichy and Chetney met?"

'He stood staring at me without seeing me, muttering, and arguing with himself.

' "Don't speak to me," he cried, as I ventured to interrupt him. "I can see it now. It is all plain. It was not the servant, but his master, the Russian himself, and it was he who came back for the letters! He came back for them because he knew they would convict him. We must find them. We must have those letters. If we find the one with the Russian postmark, we shall have found the murderer." He spoke like a madman, and as he spoke he ran around the room with one hand held out in front of him as you have seen a mind-reader at a theatre seeking for something hidden in the stalls. He pulled the old letters from the writing-desk, and ran them over as swiftly as a gambler deals out cards; he dropped on his knees before the fireplace and dragged out the dead coals with his bare fingers, and then with a low, worried cry, like a hound on a scent, he ran back to the waste-paper basket and, lifting the papers from it, shook them out upon the floor. Instantly he gave a shout of triumph, and, separating a number of torn pieces from the others, held them up before me.

' "Look!" he cried. "Do you see? Here are five letters, torn across in two places. The Russian did not stop to read them, for, as you see, he has left them

IN THE FOG

still sealed. I have been wrong. He did not return for the letters. He could not have known their value. He must have returned for some other reason, and, as he was leaving, saw the letter-box, and taking out the letters, held them together – so – and tore them twice across, and then, as the fire had gone out, tossed them into this basket. Look!'' he cried, ''here in the upper corner of this piece is a Russian stamp. This is his own letter – unopened!''

'We examined the Russian stamp and found it had been cancelled in St Petersburg four days ago. The back of the envelope bore the postmark of the branch station in upper Sloane Street, and was dated this morning. The envelope was of official blue paper and we had no difficulty in finding the two other parts of it. We drew the torn pieces of the letter from them and joined them together side by side. There were but two lines of writing, and this was the message: ''I leave Petersburg on the night train, and I shall see you at Trevor Terrace after dinner Monday evening.''

'''That was last night!'' Lyle cried. ''He arrived twelve hours ahead of his letter – but it came in time – it came in time to hang him!'''

The Baronet struck the table with his hand.

'The name!' he demanded. 'How was it signed? What was the man's name?'

The young solicitor rose to his feet and, leaning forward, stretched out his arm. 'There was no name,' he cried. 'The letter was signed with only two initials. But engraved at the top of the sheet was the man's address. That address was ''THE AMERICAN EMBASSY, ST PETERSBURG, BUREAU OF THE NAVAL ATTACHÉ'', and the initials,' he shouted, his voice rising into an exultant and bitter cry, 'were those of the gentleman who sits opposite who told us that he was the first to find the murdered bodies, the Naval Attaché to Russia, Lieutenant Sears!'

A strained and awful hush followed the Solicitor's words, which seemed to vibrate like a twanging bowstring that had just hurled its bolt. Sir Andrew, pale and staring, drew away with an exclamation of repulsion. His eyes were fastened upon the Naval Attaché with fascinated horror. But the American emitted a sigh of great content, and sank comfortably into the arms of his chair. He clapped his hands softly together.

'Capital!' he murmured. 'I give you my word I never guessed what you were driving at. You fooled *me*, I'll be hanged if you didn't – you certainly fooled me.'

The man with the pearl stud leaned forward with a nervous gesture. 'Hush! be careful!' he whispered. But at that instant, for the third time, a servant, hastening through the room, handed him a piece of paper which he scanned eagerly. The message on the paper read, 'The light over the Commons is out. The House has risen.'

The man with the black pearl gave a mighty shout, and tossed the paper from him upon the table.

'Hurrah!' he cried. 'The House is up! We've won!' He caught up his glass, and slapped the Naval Attaché violently upon the shoulder. He nodded joyously at him, at the solicitor, and at the Queen's Messenger. 'Gentlemen, to you!' he cried; 'my thanks and my congratulations!' He drank deep from the glass, and breathed forth a long sigh of satisfaction and relief.

'But I say,' protested the Queen's Messenger, shaking his finger violently at the solicitor, 'that story won't do. You didn't play fair – and – and you talked so fast I couldn't make out what it was all about. I'll bet you that evidence wouldn't hold in a court of law – you couldn't hang a cat on such evidence. Your story is condemned tommy-rot. Now my story might have happened, my story bore the mark –'

In the joy of creation the story-tellers had forgotten their audience, until a sudden exclamation from Sir Andrew caused them to turn guiltily toward him. His face was knit with lines of anger, doubt, and amazement.

'What does this mean?' he cried. 'Is this a jest, or are you mad? If you know this man is a murderer, why is he at large? Is this a game you have been playing? Explain yourselves at once. What does it mean?'

The American, with first a glance at the others, rose and bowed courteously.

'I am not a murderer, Sir Andrew, believe me,' he said; 'you need not be alarmed. As a matter of fact, at this moment I am much more afraid of you than you could possibly be of me. I beg you please to be indulgent. I assure you, we meant no disrespect. We have been matching stories, that is all, pretending that we are people we are not, endeavoring to entertain you with better detective tales than, for instance, the last one you read, *The Great Rand Robbery*.'

The Baronet brushed his hand nervously across his forehead.

'Do you mean to tell me,' he exclaimed, 'that none of this has happened? That Lord Chetney is not dead, that his solicitor did not find a letter of yours written from your post in Petersburg, and that just now, when he charged you with murder, he was in jest?'

'I am really very sorry,' said the American, 'but you see, sir, he could not have found a letter written by me in St Petersburg because I have never been in Petersburg. Until this week, I have never been outside of my own country. I am not a naval officer. I am a writer of short stories. And tonight, when this gentleman told me that you were fond of detective stories, I thought it would be amusing to tell you one of my own – one I had just mapped out this afternoon.'

'But Lord Chetney *is* a real person,' interrupted the Baronet, 'and he did go to Africa two years ago, and he was supposed to have died there, and his brother, Lord Arthur, has been the heir. And yesterday Chetney did return. I read it in the papers.'

'So did I,' assented the American soothingly; 'and it struck me as being a very good plot for a story. I mean his unexpected return from the dead, and the probable disappointment of the younger brother. So I decided that the younger brother had better murder the older one. The Princess Zichy I invented out of a clear sky. The fog I did not have to invent. Since last night I know all that there is to know about a London fog. I was lost in one for three hours.'

The Baronet turned grimly upon the Queen's Messenger.

'But this gentleman,' he protested, 'he is not a writer of short stories; he is a member of the Foreign Office. I have often seen him in Whitehall, and, according to him, the Princess Zichy is not an invention. He says she is very well known, that she tried to rob him.'

The servant of the Foreign Office looked unhappily at the Cabinet Minister, and puffed nervously on his cigar.

'It's true, Sir Andrew, that I am a Queen's Messenger,' he said appealingly, 'and a Russian woman once did try to rob a Queen's Messenger in a railway carriage – only it did not happen to me, but to a pal of mine. The only Russian princess I ever knew called herself Zabrisky. You may have seen her. She used to do a dive from the roof of the Aquarium.'

Sir Andrew, with a snort of indignation, fronted the young solicitor.

'And I suppose yours was a cock-and-bull story, too,' he said. 'Of course, it must have been, since Lord Chetney is not dead. But don't tell me,' he protested, 'that you are not Chudleigh's son either.'

'I'm sorry,' said the youngest member, smiling in some embarrassment, 'but my name is not Chudleigh. I assure you, though, that I know the family very well, and that I am on very good terms with them.'

'You should be!' exclaimed the Baronet; 'and, judging from the liberties you take with the Chetneys, you had better be on very good terms with them, too.'

The young man leaned back and glanced toward the servants at the far end of the room.

'It has been so long since I have been in the Club,' he said, 'that I doubt if even the waiters remember me. Perhaps Joseph may,' he added. 'Joseph!' he called, and at the word a servant stepped briskly forward.

The young man pointed to the stuffed head of a great lion which was suspended above the fireplace.

'Joseph,' he said, 'I want you to tell these gentlemen who shot that lion. Who presented it to the Grill?'

Joseph, unused to acting as master of ceremonies to members of the Club, shifted nervously from one foot to the other.

'Why, you – you did,' he stammered.

'Of course I did!' exclaimed the young man. 'I mean, what is the name of the man who shot it? Tell the gentlemen who I am. They wouldn't believe me.'

'Who you are, my lord?' said Joseph. 'You are Lord Edam's son, the Earl of Chetney.'

'You must admit,' said Lord Chetney, when the noise had died away, 'that I couldn't remain dead while my little brother was accused of murder. I had to do something. Family pride demanded it. Now, Arthur, as the younger brother, can't afford to be squeamish, but personally I should hate to have a brother of mine hanged for murder.'

'You certainly showed no scruples against hanging me,' said the American, 'but in the face of your evidence I admit my guilt, and I sentence myself to pay the full penalty of the law as we are made to pay it in my own country. The order of this court is,' he announced, 'that Joseph shall bring me a wine-card, and that I sign it for five bottles of the Club's best champagne.'

'Oh, no!' protested the man with the pearl stud, 'it is not for *you* to sign it. In my opinion it is Sir Andrew who should pay the costs. It is time you knew,' he said, turning to that gentleman, 'that unconsciously you have been the victim of what I may call a patriotic conspiracy. These stories have had a more serious purpose than merely to amuse. They have been told with the worthy object of detaining you from the House of Commons. I must explain to you, that all through this evening I have had a servant waiting in Trafalgar Square with instructions to bring me word as soon as the light over the House of Commons had ceased to burn. The light is now out, and the object for which we plotted is attained.'

The Baronet glanced keenly at the man with the black pearl, and then quickly at his watch. The smile disappeared from his lips, and his face was set in stern and forbidding lines.

'And may I know,' he asked icily, 'what was the object of your plot?'

'A most worthy one,' the other retorted. 'Our object was to keep you from advocating the expenditure of many millions of the people's money upon more battleships. In a word, we have been working together to prevent you from passing the Navy Increase Bill.'

Sir Andrew's face bloomed with brilliant colour. His body shook with suppressed emotion.

'My dear sir!' he cried, 'you should spend more time at the House and less at your Club. The Navy Bill was brought up on its third reading at eight o'clock this evening. I spoke for three hours in its favour. My only reason for wishing to return again to the House tonight, was to sup on the terrace with my old friend, Admiral Simons; for my work at the House was completed five hours ago, when the Navy Increase Bill was passed by an overwhelming majority.'

The Baronet rose and bowed. 'I have to thank you, sir,' he said, 'for a most interesting evening.'

The American shoved the wine-card which Joseph had given him toward the gentleman with the black pearl.

'You sign it,' he said.

# THE BEETLE

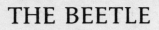

RICHARD MARSH

# BOOK I

# THE HOUSE WITH THE OPEN WINDOW

*The Surprising Narration of Robert Holt*

### CHAPTER ONE

## OUTSIDE

'No room! – Full up!'

He banged the door in my face.

That was the final blow.

To have tramped about all day looking for work; to have begged even for a job which would give me money enough to buy a little food; and to have tramped and to have begged in vain – that was bad. But, sick at heart, depressed in mind and in body, exhausted by hunger and fatigue, to have been compelled to pocket any little pride I might have left, and solicit, as the penniless, homeless tramp which indeed I was, a night's lodging in the casual ward – and to solicit it in vain! – that was worse. Much worse. About as bad as bad could be.

I stared, stupidly, at the door which had just been banged in my face. I could scarcely believe that the thing was possible. I had hardly expected to figure as a tramp; but, supposing it conceivable that I could become a tramp, that I should be refused admission to that abode of all ignominy, the tramps' ward, was to have attained a depth of misery of which never even in nightmares I had dreamed.

As I stood wondering what I should do, a man slouched towards me out of the shadow of the wall.

'Won't 'e let yer in?'

'He says it's full.'

'Says it's full, does 'e? That's the lay at Fulham, – they always says it's full. They wants to keep the number down.'

I looked at the man askance. His head hung forward; his hands were in his trouser pockets; his clothes were rags; his tone was husky.

'Do you mean that they say it's full when it isn't, – that they won't let me in although there's room?'

'That's it – bloke's a-kiddin' yer.'

'But, if there's room, aren't they bound to let me in?'

'Course they are – and, blimey, if I was you I'd make 'em. Blimey I would!'

He broke into a volley of execrations.

'But what am I to do?'

'Why, give 'em another rouser – let 'em know as you won't be kidded!'

I hesitated; then, acting on his suggestion, for the second time I rang the bell. The door was flung wide open, and the grizzled pauper, who had previously responded to my summons, stood in the open doorway. Had he been the Chairman of the Board of Guardians himself he could not have addressed me with greater scorn.

'What, here again! What's your little game? Think I've nothing better to do than to wait upon the likes of you?'

'I want to be admitted.'

'Then you won't be admitted!'

'I want to see someone in authority.'

'Ain't yer seein' someone in authority?'

'I want to see someone beside you – I want to see the master.'

'Then you won't see the master!'

He moved the door swiftly to; but, prepared for such a manoeuvre, I thrust my foot sufficiently inside to prevent his shutting it. I continued to address him.

'Are you sure that the ward is full?'

'Full two hours ago!'

'But what am I to do?'

'I don't know what you're to do!'

'Which is the next nearest workhouse?'

'Kensington.'

Suddenly opening the door, as he answered me, putting out his arm he thrust me backwards. Before I could recover the door was closed. The man in rags had continued a grim spectator of the scene. Now he spoke.

'Nice bloke, ain't he?'

'He's only one of the paupers – has he any right to act as one of the officials?'

'I tell yer some of them paupers is wuss than the orficers – a long sight wuss! They thinks they owns the 'ouses, blimey they do. Oh it's a—fine world, this is!'

He paused. I hesitated. For some time there had been a suspicion of rain in the air. Now it was commencing to fall in a fine but soaking drizzle. It only needed that to fill my cup to overflowing. My companion was regarding me with a sort of sullen curiosity.

'Ain't you got no money?'

'Not a farthing.'

'Done much of this sort of thing?'

'It's the first time I've been to a casual ward – and it doesn't seem as if I'm going to get in now.'

'I thought you looked as if you was a bit fresh – What are yer goin' to do?'

'How far is it to Kensington?'

'Work'us? – about three mile – but, if I was you, I'd try St George's.'

'Where's that?'

'In the Fulham Road. Kensington's only a small place, they do you well there, and it's always full as soon as the door's opened – you'd 'ave more chawnce at St George's.'

He was silent. I turned his words over in my mind, feeling as little disposed to try the one place as the other. Presently he began again.

'I've travelled from Reading this—day, I 'ave—tramped every—foot! – and all the way as I come along, I'll 'ave a shakedown at 'Ammersmith, I says – and now I'm as fur off from it as ever! This is a — fine country, this is – I wish every — soul in it was swept into the — sea, blimey, I do! But I ain't goin' to go no further – I'll 'ave a bed in 'Ammersmith or I'll know the reason why.'

'How are you going to manage it – have you got any money?'

'Got any money? – My crikey! – I look as though I 'ad – I sound as though I 'ad too! I ain't 'ad no brads, 'cept now and then a brown, this larst six months.'

'How are you going to get a bed then?'

' 'Ow am I going to? – why, like this way.' He picked up two stones, one in either hand. The one in his left he flung at the glass which was over the door of the casual ward. It crashed through it, and through the lamp beyond. 'That's 'ow I'm goin' to get a bed.'

The door was hastily opened. The grizzled pauper reappeared. He shouted, as he peered at us in the darkness.

'Who done that?'

'I done it, guvnor – and, if you like, you can see me do the other. It might do your eyesight good.'

Before the grizzled pauper could interfere, he had hurled the stone in his right hand through another pane. I felt that it was time for me to go. He was earning a night's rest at a price which, even in my extremity, I was not disposed to pay.

When I left two or three other persons had appeared upon the scene, and the man in rags was addressing them with a degree of frankness, which, in that direction, left little to be desired. I slunk away unnoticed. But had not gone far before I had almost decided that I might as well have thrown in my fortune with the bolder wretch, and smashed a window too. Indeed, more than once my feet faltered, as I all but returned to do the feat which I had left undone.

A more miserable night for an out-of-door excursion I could hardly have chosen. The rain was like a mist, and was not only drenching me to the skin, but it was rendering it difficult to see more than a little distance in any direction. The neighbourhood was badly lighted. It was one in which I was a stranger. I had come to Hammersmith as a last resource. It had seemed to me that I had tried to find some occupation which would enable me to keep body and soul together in every other part of London, and that now only Hammersmith was left. And, at Hammersmith, even the workhouse would have none of me!

Retreating from the inhospitable portal of the casual ward, I had taken the first turning to the left – and, at the moment, had been glad to take it. In the darkness and the rain, the locality which I was entering appeared unfinished. I seemed to be leaving civilization behind me. The path was unpaved; the road rough and uneven, as if it had never been properly made. Houses were few and far between. Those which I did encounter, seemed, in the imperfect light, amid the general desolation, to be cottages which were crumbling to decay.

Exactly where I was I could not tell. I had a faint notion that, if I only kept on long enough, I should strike some part of Walham Green. How long I should have to keep on I could only guess. Not a creature seemed to be about of whom I could make inquiries. It was as if I was in a land of desolation.

I suppose it was between eleven o'clock and midnight. I had not given up my quest for work till all the shops were closed – and in Hammersmith, that night, at any rate, they were not early closers. Then I had lounged about dispiritedly, wondering what was the next thing I could do. It was only because I feared that if I attempted to spend the night in the open air, without food, when the morning came I should be broken up, and fit for nothing, that I sought a night's free board and lodging. It was really hunger which drove me to the workhouse door. That was Wednesday. Since the Sunday night preceding nothing had passed my lips save water from the public fountains – with the exception of a crust of bread which a man had given me whom I had found crouching at the root of a tree in Holland Park. For three days I had been fasting – practically all the time upon my feet. It seemed to me that if I had to go hungry till the morning I should collapse – there would be an end. Yet, in that strange and inhospitable place, where was I to get food at that time of night, and how?

I do not know how far I went. Every yard I covered, my feet dragged more. I was dead beat, inside and out. I had neither strength nor courage left. And within there was that frightful craving, which was as though it shrieked aloud. I leant against some palings, dazed and giddy. If only death had come upon me quickly, painlessly, how true a friend I should have thought it! It was the agony of dying inch by inch which was so hard to bear.

It was some minutes before I could collect myself sufficiently to withdraw from the support of the railings, and to start afresh. I stumbled blindly over the uneven road. Once, like a drunken man, I lurched forward, and fell upon my knees. Such was my backboneless state that for some seconds I remained where I was, half disposed to let things slide, accept the good the gods had sent me, and make a night of it just there. A long night, I fancy, it would have been, stretching from time unto eternity.

Having regained my feet, I had gone perhaps another couple of hundred yards along the road – Heaven knows that it seemed to me just then a couple of miles! – when there came over me again that overpowering giddiness which, I take it, was born of my agony of hunger. I staggered, helplessly, against a low wall which, just there, was at the side of the path. Without it I should have fallen in a heap. The attack appeared to last for hours; I suppose it was only seconds; and, when I came to myself, it was as though I had been aroused from a swoon of sleep – aroused, to an extremity of pain. I exclaimed aloud,

'For a loaf of bread what wouldn't I do!'

I looked about me, in a kind of frenzy. As I did so I for the first time became conscious that behind me was a house. It was not a large one. It was one of those so-called villas which are springing up in multitudes all round London, and which are let at rentals of from twenty-five to forty pounds a year. It was detached. So far as I could see, in the imperfect light, there was not another building within twenty or thirty yards of either side of it. It was in two storeys. There were three windows in the upper storey. Behind each the blinds were closely drawn. The hall door was on my right. It was approached by a little wooden gate.

The house itself was so close to the public road that by leaning over the wall I could have touched either of the windows on the lower floor. There were two of them. One of them was a bow window. The bow window was open. The bottom centre sash was raised about six inches.

CHAPTER TWO

## INSIDE

I realized, and, so to speak, mentally photographed all the little details of the house in front of which I was standing with what almost amounted to a gleam of preternatural perception. An instant before, the world swam before my eyes. I saw nothing. Now I saw everything, with a clearness which, as it were, was shocking.

Above all, I saw the open window. I stared at it, conscious, as I did so, of a curious catching of the breath. It was so near to me; so very near. I had but to stretch out my hand to thrust it through the aperture. Once inside, my hand would at least be dry. How it rained out there! My scanty clothing was soaked; I was wet to the skin! I was shivering. And, each second, it seemed to rain still faster. My teeth were chattering. The damp was liquefying the very marrow in my bones.

And, inside that open window, it was, it must be, so warm, so dry!

There was not a soul in sight. Not a human being anywhere near. I listened; there was not a sound. I alone was at the mercy of the sodden night. Of all God's creatures the only one unsheltered from the fountains of Heaven which He had opened. There was not one to see what I might do; not one to care. I need fear no spy.

Perhaps the house was empty; nay, probably. It was my plain duty to knock at the door, rouse the inmates, and call attention to their oversight – the open window. The least they could do would be to reward me for my pains. But, suppose the place was empty, what would be the use of knocking? It would be to make a useless clatter. Possibly to disturb the neighbourhood, for nothing. And, even if the people were at home, I might go unrewarded. I had learned, in a hard school, the world's ingratitude. To have caused the window to be closed – the inviting window, the tempting window, the convenient window! – and then to be no better for it after all, but still to be penniless, hopeless, hungry, out in the cold and the rain – better anything than that. In such a situation, too late, I should say to myself that mine had been the conduct of a fool. And I should say it justly too. To be sure.

Leaning over the low wall I found that I could very easily put my hand inside the room. How warm it was in there! I could feel the difference of temperature in my finger-tips. Very quietly I stepped right over the wall. There was just room to stand in comfort between the window and the wall. The ground felt to the foot as if it were cemented. Stooping down, I peered through the opening. I could see nothing. It was black as pitch inside. The blind was drawn right up; it seemed incredible that anyone could be at home, and have gone to bed, leaving the blind up, and the window open. I placed my ear to the crevice. How still it was! Beyond doubt, the place was empty.

I decided to push the window up another inch or two, so as to enable me to reconnoitre. If anyone caught me in the act, then there would be an opportunity to describe the circumstances, and to explain how I was just on the point of giving the alarm. Only, I must go carefully. In such damp weather it was probable that the sash would creak.

Not a bit of it. It moved as readily and as noiselessly as if it had been oiled. This silence of the sash so emboldened me that I raised it more than I intended. In fact, as far as it would go. Not by a sound did it betray me. Bending over the sill I put my head and half my body into the room. But I was no forwarder. I could see nothing. Not a thing. For all I could tell the room might be unfurnished. Indeed, the likelihood of such an explanation began to occur to me. I might have chanced upon an empty house. In the darkness there was nothing to suggest the contrary. What was I to do?

Well, if the house was empty, in such a plight as mine I might be said to have a moral, if not a legal, right, to its bare shelter. Who, with a heart in his bosom, would deny it me? Hardly the most punctilious landlord. Raising myself by means of the sill I slipped my legs into the room.

The moment I did so I became conscious that, at any rate, the room was not entirely unfurnished. The floor was carpeted. I have had my feet on some good carpets in my time; I know what carpets are; but never did I stand upon a softer one than that. It reminded me, somehow, even then, of the turf in Richmond Park – it caressed my instep, and sprang beneath my tread. To my poor, travel-worn feet, it was luxury after the puddly, uneven road. Should I, now I had ascertained that the room was, at least, partially furnished, beat a retreat? Or should I push my researches further? It would have been rapture to have thrown off my clothes, and to have sunk down, on the carpet, then and there, to sleep. But – I was so hungry; so famine-goaded; what would I not have given to have lighted on something good to eat!

I moved a step or two forward, gingerly, reaching out with my hands, lest I struck, unawares, against some unseen thing. When I had taken three or four such steps, without encountering an obstacle, or, indeed, anything at all, I began, all at once, to wish I had not seen the house; that I had passed it by;

that I had not come through the window; that I were safely out of it again. I became, on a sudden, aware, that something was with me in the room. There was nothing, ostensible, to lead me to such a conviction; it may be that my faculties were unnaturally keen; but, all at once, I knew that there was something there. What was more, I had a horrible persuasion that, though unseeing, I was seen; that my every movement was being watched.

What it was that was with me I could not tell; I could not even guess. It was as though something in my mental organization had been stricken by a sudden paralysis. It may seem childish to use such language; but I was overwrought, played out; physically speaking, at my last counter; and, in an instant, without the slightest warning, I was conscious of a very curious sensation, the like of which I had never felt before, and the like of which I pray that I never may feel again – a sensation of panic fear. I remained rooted to the spot on which I stood, not daring to move, fearing to draw my breath. I felt that the presence with me in the room was something strange, something evil.

I do not know how long I stood there, spellbound, but certainly for some considerable space of time. By degrees, as nothing moved, nothing was seen, nothing was heard, and nothing happened, I made an effort to better play the man. I knew that, at the moment, I played the cur. And endeavoured to ask myself of what it was I was afraid. I was shivering at my own imaginings. What could be in the room, to have suffered me to open the window and to enter unopposed? Whatever it was, was surely to the full as great a coward as I was, or why permit, unchecked, my burglarious entry. Since I had been allowed to enter, the probability was that I should be at liberty to retreat – and I was sensible of a much keener desire to retreat than I had ever had to enter.

I had to put the greatest amount of pressure upon myself before I could summon up sufficient courage to enable me to even turn my head upon my shoulders – and the moment I did so I turned it back again. What constrained me, to save my soul I could not have said – but I was constrained. My heart was palpitating in my bosom; I could hear it beat. I was trembling so that I could scarcely stand. I was overwhelmed by a fresh flood of terror. I stared in front of me with eyes in which, had it been light, would have been seen the frenzy of unreasoning fear. My ears were strained so that I listened with an acuteness of tension which was painful.

Something moved. Slightly, with so slight a sound, that it would scarcely have been audible to other ears save mine. But I heard. I was looking in the direction from which the movement came, and, as I looked, I saw in front of me two specks of light. They had not been there a moment before, that I would swear. They were there now. They were eyes – I told myself they were eyes. I had heard how cats' eyes gleam in the dark, though I had never seen them, and I said to myself that these were cats' eyes; that the thing in front of me was nothing but a cat. But I knew I lied. I knew that these were eyes, and I knew they were not cats' eyes, but what eyes they were I did not know – nor dared to think.

They moved – towards me. The creature to which the eyes belonged was coming closer. So intense was my desire to fly that I would much rather have died than stood there still; yet I could not control a limb; my limbs were as if they were not mine. The eyes came on – noiselessly. At first they were between two and three feet from the ground; but, on a sudden, there was a squelching sound, as if some yielding body had been squashed upon the floor. The eyes vanished – to reappear, a moment afterwards, at what I judged to be a distance of some six inches from the floor. And they again came on.

So it seemed that the creature, whatever it was to which the eyes belonged, was, after all, but small. Why I did not obey the frantic longing which I had to flee from it, I cannot tell; I only know, I could not. I take it that the stress and privations which I had lately undergone, and which I was, even then, still undergoing, had much to do with my conduct at that moment, and with the part I played in all that followed. Ordinarily I believe that I have as high a spirit as the average man, and as solid a resolution; but when one has been dragged through the Valley of Humiliation, and plunged, again and again, into the Waters of Bitterness and Privation, a man can be constrained to a course of action of which, in his happier moments, he would have deemed himself incapable. I know this of my own knowledge.

Slowly the eyes came on, with a strange slowness, and as they came they moved from side to side as if their owner walked unevenly. Nothing could have exceeded the horror with which I awaited their approach – except my incapacity to escape them. Not for an instant did my glance pass from them – I could not have shut my eyes for all the gold the world contains! – so that as they came closer I had to look right down to what seemed to be almost the level of my feet. And at last, they reached my feet. They never paused. On a sudden I felt something on my boot, and, with a sense of shrinking, horror, nausea, rendering me momentarily more helpless, I realized that the creature was beginning to ascend my legs, to climb my body. Even then what it was I could not tell – it mounted me, apparently, with as much ease as if I had been horizontal instead of perpendicular. It was as though it were some gigantic spider – a spider of the nightmares; a monstrous conception of some dreadful vision. It pressed lightly against my clothing with what might, for all the world, have been spider's legs. There was an amazing host of them – I felt the pressure of each separate one. They embraced me softly, stickily, as if the creature glued and unglued them, each time it moved.

Higher and higher! It had gained my loins. It was moving towards the pit of my stomach. The helplessness with which I suffered its invasion was not the least part of my agony – it was that helplessness which we know in dreadful dreams. I understood, quite well, that if I did but give myself a hearty shake, the creature would fall off; but I had not a muscle at my command.

As the creature mounted its eyes began to play the part of two small lamps; they positively emitted rays of light. By their rays I began to perceive faint outlines of its body. It seemed larger than I had supposed. Either the body itself was slightly phosphorescent, or it was of a peculiar yellow hue. It gleamed in the darkness. What it was there was still nothing to positively show, but the impression grew upon me that it was some member of the spider family, some monstrous member, of the like of which I had never heard or read. It was heavy, so heavy indeed, that I wondered how, with so slight a pressure, it managed to retain its hold – that it did so by the aid of some adhesive substance at the end of its legs I was sure – I could feel it stick. Its weight increased as it ascended – and it smelt! I had been for some time aware that it emitted an unpleasant, foetid odour; as it neared my face it became so intense as to be unbearable.

It was at my chest. I became more and more conscious of an uncomfortable wobbling motion, as if each time it breathed its body heaved. Its forelegs touched the bare skin about the base of my neck; they stuck to it – shall I ever forget the feeling? I have it often in my dreams. While it hung on with those in front it seemed to draw its other legs up after it. It crawled up my neck, with hideous slowness, a quarter of an inch at a time, its weight compelling me to brace the muscles of my back. It reached my chin, it touched my lips – and I stood still and bore it all, while it enveloped my face with its huge, slimy, evil-smelling body, and embraced me with its myriad legs. The horror of it made me mad. I shook myself like one stricken by the shaking ague. I shook the creature off. It squashed upon the floor. Shrieking like some lost spirit, turning, I dashed towards the window. As I went, my foot, catching in some obstacle, I fell headlong to the floor.

Picking myself up as quickly as I could I resumed my flight – rain or no rain, oh to get out of that room! I already had my hand upon the sill, in another instant I should have been over it – then, despite my hunger, my fatigues, let anyone have stopped me if they could! – when someone behind me struck a light.

## CHAPTER THREE

# THE MAN IN THE BED

The illumination which instantly followed was unexpected. It startled me, causing a moment's check, from which I was just recovering when a voice said,

'Keep still!'

There was a quality in the voice which I cannot describe. Not only an accent of command, but a something malicious, a something saturnine. It was a little guttural, though whether it was a man speaking I could not have positively said; but I had no doubt it was a foreigner. It was the most disagreeable voice I had ever heard, and it had on me the most disagreeable effect; for when it said, 'Keep still!' I kept still. It was as though there was nothing else for me to do.

'Turn round!'

I turned round, mechanically, like an automaton. Such passivity was worse than undignified, it was galling; I knew that well. I resented it with secret rage. But in that room, in that presence, I was invertebrate.

When I turned I found myself confronting someone who was lying in bed. At the head of the bed was a shelf. On the shelf was a small lamp which gave the most brilliant light I had ever seen. It caught me full in the eyes, having on me such a blinding effect that for some seconds I could see nothing. Throughout the whole of that strange interview I cannot affirm that I saw clearly; the dazzling glare caused dancing specks to obscure my vision. Yet, after an interval of time, I did see something; and what I did see I had rather have left unseen.

I saw someone in front of me lying in a bed. I could not at once decide if it was a man or a woman. Indeed at first I doubted if it was anything human. But, afterwards, I knew it to be a man – for this reason, if for no other, that it was impossible such a creature could be feminine. The bedclothes were drawn up to his shoulders; only his head was visible. He lay on his left side, his head resting on his left hand; motionless, eyeing me as if he sought to read my inmost soul. And, in very truth, I believe he read it. His age I could not guess; such a look of age I had never imagined. Had he asserted that he had been living through the ages, I should have been forced to admit that, at least, he looked it. And yet I felt that it was quite within the range of possibility that he was no older than myself – there was a vitality in his eyes which was startling. It might have been that he had been afflicted by some terrible disease, and it was that which had made him so supernaturally ugly.

There was not a hair upon his face or head, but, to make up for it, the skin, which was a saffron yellow, was an amazing mass of wrinkles. The cranium, and, indeed, the whole skull, was so small as to be disagreeably suggestive of something animal. The nose, on the other hand, was abnormally large; so extravagant were its dimensions, and so peculiar its shape, it resembled the beak of some bird of prey. A characteristic of the face – and an uncomfortable one! – was that, practically, it stopped short at the mouth. The mouth, with its blubber lips, came immediately underneath the nose, and chin, to all intents and purposes, there was none. This deformity – for the absence of chin amounted to that – it was which gave to the face the appearance of something not human – that, and the eyes. For so marked a feature of the man were his eyes, that, ere long, it seemed to me that he was nothing but eyes.

His eyes ran, literally, across the whole of the upper portion of his face – remember, the face was unwontedly small, and the columna of the nose was razor-edged. They were long, and they looked out of narrow windows, and they seemed to be lighted by some internal radiance, for they shone out like lamps in a lighthouse tower. Escape them I could not, while, as I endeavoured to meet them, it was as if I shrivelled into nothingness. Never before had I realized what was meant by the power of the eye. They held me enchained, helpless, spell-bound. I felt that they could do with me as they would; and they did. Their gaze was unfaltering, having the bird-like trick of never blinking; this man could have glared at me for hours and never moved an eyelid.

It was he who broke the silence. I was speechless.

'Shut the window.' I did as he bade me. 'Pull down the blind.' I obeyed. 'Turn round again.' I was still obedient. 'What is your name?'

Then I spoke – to answer him. There was this odd thing about the words I uttered, that they came from me, not in response to my will power, but in response to his. It was not I who willed that I should speak; it was he. What he willed that I should say, I said. Just that, and nothing more. For the time I was no longer a man; my manhood was merged in his. I was, in the extremest sense, an example of passive obedience.

'Robert Holt.'

'What are you?'

'A clerk.'

'You look as if you were a clerk.' There was a flame of scorn in his voice which scorched me even then. 'What sort of a clerk are you?'

'I am out of a situation.'

'You look as if you were out of a situation.' Again the scorn. 'Are you the sort of clerk who is always out of a situation? You are a thief.'

'I am not a thief.'

'Do clerks come through the window?' I was still – he putting no constraint on me to speak. 'Why did you come through the window?'

'Because it was open.'

'So! – Do you always come through a window which is open?'

'No.'

'Then why through this?'

'Because I was wet – and cold – and hungry – and tired.'

The words came from me as if he had dragged them one by one – which, in fact, he did.

'Have you no home?'

'No.'

'Money?'

'No.'

'Friends?'

'No.'

'Then what sort of a clerk are you?'

I did not answer him – I did not know what it was he wished me to say. I was the victim of bad luck, nothing else – I swear it. Misfortune had followed hard upon misfortune. The firm by whom I had been employed for years suspended payment. I obtained a situation with one of their creditors, at a lower salary. They reduced their staff, which entailed my going. After an interval I obtained a temporary engagement; the occasion which required my services passed, and I with it. After another, and a longer interval, I again found temporary employment, the pay for which was but a pittance. When that was over I could find nothing. That was nine months ago, and since then I had not earned a penny. It is so easy to grow shabby, when you are on the everlasting tramp, and are living on your stock of clothes. I had trudged all over London in search of work – work of any kind would have been welcome, so long as it would have enabled me to keep body and soul together. And I had trudged in vain. Now I had been refused admittance as a casual – how easy is the descent! But I did not tell the man lying on the bed all this. He did not wish to hear – had he wished he would have made me tell him.

It may be that he read my story, unspoken though it was – it is conceivable.

His eyes had powers of penetration which were peculiarly their own – that I know.

'Undress!'

When he spoke again that was what he said, in those guttural tones of his in which there was a reminiscence of some foreign land. I obeyed, letting my sodden, shabby clothes fall anyhow upon the floor. A look came on his face, as I stood naked in front of him, which, if it was meant for a smile, was a satyr's smile, and which filled me with a sensation of shuddering repulsion.

'What a white skin you have – how white! What would I not give for a skin as white as that – ah yes!' He paused, devouring me with his glances; then continued. 'Go to the cupboard; you will find a cloak; put it on.'

I went to a cupboard which was in a corner of the room, his eyes following me as I moved. It was full of clothing – garments which might have formed the stock-in-trade of a costumier whose speciality was providing costumes for masquerades. A long dark cloak hung on a peg. My hand moved towards it, apparently of its own volition. I put it on, its ample folds falling to my feet.

'In the other cupboard you will find meat, and bread, and wine. Eat and drink.'

On the opposite side of the room, near the head of his bed, there was a second cupboard. In this, upon a shelf, I found what looked like pressed beef, several round cakes of what tasted like rye bread, and some thin, sour wine, in a straw-covered flask. But I was in no mood to criticize; I crammed myself, I believe, like some famished wolf, he watching me, in silence, all the time. When I had done, which was when I had eaten and drunk as much as I could hold, there returned to his face that satyr's grin.

'I would that I could eat and drink like that – ah yes! – Put back what is left.' I put it back – which seemed an unnecessary exertion, there was so little to put. 'Look me in the face.'

I looked him in the face – and immediately became conscious, as I did so, that something was going from me – the capacity, as it were, to be myself. His eyes grew larger and larger, till they seemed to fill all space – till I became lost in their immensity. He moved his hand, doing something to me, I know not what, as it passed through the air – cutting the solid ground from underneath my feet, so that I fell headlong to the ground. Where I fell, there I lay, like a log.

And the light went out.

CHAPTER FOUR

# A LONELY VIGIL

I knew that the light went out. For not the least singular, nor, indeed, the least distressing part of my condition was the fact that, to the best of my knowledge and belief, I never once lost consciousness during the long hours which followed. I was aware of the extinction of the lamp, and of the black darkness which ensued. I heard a rustling sound, as if the man in the bed was settling himself between the sheets. Then all was still. And throughout that interminable night I remained, my brain awake, my body dead, waiting, watching, for the day. What had happened to me I could not guess. That I probably wore some of the external evidences of death my instinct told me – I knew I did. Paradoxical though it may sound, I felt as a man might feel who had actually died – as, in moments of speculation, in the days gone by, I had imagined it as quite possible that he would feel. It is very far from certain that feeling necessarily expires with what we call life. I continually asked myself if I could be dead – the inquiry pressed itself on me with awful iteration. Does the body die, and the brain – the I, the ego – still live on? God only knows. But, then! The agony of the thought.

The hours passed. By slow degrees, the silence was eclipsed. Sounds of traffic, of hurrying footsteps – life! – were ushers of the morn. Outside the window sparrows twittered – a cat mewed, a dog barked – there was the clatter of a milk can. Shafts of light stole past the blind, increasing in intensity. It still rained, now and again it pattered against the pane. The wind must have shifted, because, for the first time, there came, on a sudden, the clang of a distant clock striking the hour – seven. Then, with the interval of a lifetime between each chiming, eight – nine – ten.

So far, in the room itself there had not been a sound. When the clock had struck ten, as it seemed to me, years ago, there came a rustling noise, from the direction of the bed. Feet stepped upon the floor – moving towards where I was lying. It was, of course, now broad day, and I, presently, perceived that a figure, clad in some queer coloured garment, was standing at my side, looking down at me. It stooped, then knelt. My only covering was unceremoniously thrown off me, so that I lay there in my nakedness. Fingers prodded me then and there, as if I had been some beast ready for the butcher's stall. A face looked into mine, and, in front of me, were those dreadful eyes. Then, whether I was dead or living, I said to myself that this could be nothing human – nothing fashioned in God's image could wear such a shape as that. Fingers were pressed into my cheeks, they were thrust into my mouth, they touched my staring eyes, shut my eyelids, then opened them again, and – horror of horrors! – the blubber lips were pressed to mine – the soul of something evil entered into me in the guise of a kiss.

Then this travesty of manhood reascended to his feet, and said, whether speaking to me or to himself I could not tell,

'Dead! – dead! – as good as dead! – and better! We'll have him buried.'

He moved away from me. I heard a door open and shut, and knew that he was gone.

And he continued gone throughout the day. I had no actual knowledge of his issuing out into the street, but he must have done so, because the house appeared deserted. What had become of the dreadful creature of the night before I could not guess. My first fear was that he had left it behind him in the room with me – it might be, as a sort of watchdog. But, as the minutes and the hours passed, and there was still no sign or sound of anything living, I concluded that, if the thing was there, it was, possibly, as helpless as myself, and that during its owner's absence, at any rate, I had nothing to fear from its too pressing attentions.

That, with the exception of myself, the house held nothing human, I had strong presumptive proof more than once in the course of the day. Several times, both in the morning and the afternoon, people without endeavoured to attract the attention of whoever was within. Vehicles – probably trades-men's carts – drew up in front, their stopping being followed by more or less assiduous assaults upon the knocker and the bell. But in every case their appeals remained unheeded. Whatever it was they wanted, they had to go unsatisfied away. Lying there, torpid, with nothing to do but listen, I was, possibly, struck by very little, but it did occur to me that one among the callers was more persistent than the rest.

The distant clock had just struck noon when I heard the gate open, and someone approached the front door. Since nothing but silence followed, I supposed that the occupant of the place had returned, and had chosen to do so as silently as he had gone. Presently, however, there came from the doorstep a slight but peculiar call, as if a rat was squeaking. It was repeated three times, and then there was the sound of footsteps quietly retreating, and the gate re-closing. Between one and two the caller came again; there was a repetition of the same signal – that it was a signal I did not doubt; followed by the same retreat. About three the mysterious visitant returned. The signal was repeated, and, when there was no response, fingers tapped softly against the panels of the front door. When there was still no answer, footsteps stole softly round the side of the house, and there came the signal from the rear – and then, again, tapping of fingers against what was, apparently, the back door. No notice being taken of these various proceedings, the footsteps returned the way they went, and, as before, the gate was closed.

Shortly after darkness had fallen this assiduous caller returned, to make a fourth and more resolute attempt to call attention to his presence. From the peculiar character of his manœuvres it seemed that he suspected that whoever was within had particular reasons for ignoring him without. He went through the familiar pantomime of the three squeaky calls both at the front door and the back – followed by the tapping of the fingers on the panels. This time, however, he also tried the window panes – I could hear, quite distinctly, the clear, yet distinct, noise of what seemed like knuckles rapping against the windows behind. Disappointed there, he renewed his efforts at the front. The curiously quiet footsteps came round the house, to pause before the window of the room in which I lay – and then something singular occurred.

While I waited for the tapping, there came, instead, the sound of someone or something, scrambling on to the window-sill – as if some creature, unable to reach the window from the ground, was endeavouring to gain the vantage of the sill. Some ungainly creature, unskilled in surmounting such an obstacle as a perpendicular brick wall. There was the noise of what seemed to be the scratching of claws, as if it experienced considerable difficulty in obtaining a hold on the unyielding surface. What kind of creature it was I could not think – I was astonished to find that it was a creature at all. I had taken it for granted that the persevering visitor was either a woman or a man. If, however, as now seemed likely, it was some sort of animal, the fact explained the squeaking sounds – though what, except a rat did squeak like that was more than I could say – and the absence of any knocking or ringing.

Whatever it was, it had gained the summit of its desires – the window-sill. It panted as if its efforts at climbing had made it short of breath. Then began the tapping. In the light of my new discovery, I perceived, clearly enough, that the tapping was hardly that which was likely to be the product of human fingers – it was sharp and definite, rather resembling the striking of the point of a nail against the glass. It was not loud, but in time – it continued with much persistency – it became plainly vicious. It was accompanied by what I can only describe as the most extraordinary noises. There were squeaks, growing angrier and shriller as the minutes passed; what seemed like gaspings for breath; and a peculiar buzzing sound like, yet unlike, the purring of a cat.

The creature's resentment at its want of success in attracting attention was unmistakable. The tapping became like the clattering of hailstones; it kept up a continuous noise with its cries and pantings; there was the sound as of some large body being rubbed against the glass, as if it were extending itself against the window, and endeavouring, by force of pressure, to gain an entrance through the pane. So violent did its contortions become that I momentarily anticipated the yielding of the glass, and the excited assailant coming crashing through. Considerably to my relief the window proved more impregnable than seemed at one time likely. The stolid resistance proved, in the end, to be too much either for its endurance or its patience. Just as I was looking for some fresh manifestation of fury, it seemed rather to tumble than to spring off the sill; then came, once more, the same sound of quietly retreating footsteps; and what, under the circumstances, seemed odder still, the same closing of the gate.

During the two or three hours which immediately ensued nothing happened at all out of the way – and then took place the most surprising incident of all. The clock had struck ten some time before. Since before the striking of the hour nothing and no one had passed along what was evidently the little frequented road in front of that uncanny house. On a sudden two sounds broke the stillness without – of someone running, and of cries. Judging from his hurrying steps someone seemed to be flying for his life – to the accompaniment of curious cries. It was only when the runner reached the front of the house that, in the cries, I recognized the squeaks of the persistent caller. I imagined that he had returned, as before, alone, to renew his attacks upon the window – until it was made plain, as it quickly was, that, with him, was some sort of a companion. Immediately there arose, from without, the noise of battle. Two creatures, whose cries were, to me, of so unusual a character, that I found it impossible to even guess at their identity, seemed to be waging war to the knife upon the doorstep. After a minute or two of furious contention, victory seemed to rest with one of the combatants, for the other fled, squeaking as with pain. While I listened, with strained attention, for the next episode in this queer drama, expecting that now would come another assault upon the window, to my unbounded surprise I heard a key thrust in the keyhole, the lock turned, and the front door thrown open with a furious bang. It was closed as loudly as it was opened. Then the door of the room in which I was, was dashed open, with the same display of excitement, and of clamour, footsteps came hurrying in, the door was slammed to with a force which shook the house to its foundations, there was a rustling as of bed-clothes, the brilliant illumination of the night before, and a voice, which I had only too good reason to remember said,

'Stand up.'

I stood up, automatically, at the word of command, facing towards the bed.

There, between the sheets, with his head resting on his hand, in the attitude in which I had seen him last, was the being I had made acquaintance with under circumstances which I was never likely to forget – the same, yet not the same.

CHAPTER FIVE

# AN INSTRUCTION TO COMMIT BURGLARY

That the man in the bed was the one whom, to my cost, I had suffered myself to stumble on the night before, there could, of course, not be the faintest doubt. And yet, directly I saw him, I recognized that some astonishing alteration had taken place in his appearance. To begin with, he seemed younger – the decrepitude of age had given place to something very like the fire of youth. His features had undergone some subtle change. His nose, for instance, was not by any means so grotesque; its beak-like quality was less conspicuous. The most part of his wrinkles had disappeared, as if by magic. And, though his skin was still as yellow as saffron, his contours had rounded – he had even come into possession of a modest allowance of chin. But the most astounding novelty was that about the face there was something which was essentially feminine; so feminine, indeed, that I wondered if I could by any possibility have blundered, and mistaken a woman for a man; some ghoulish example of her sex, who had so yielded to her depraved instincts as to have become nothing but a ghastly reminiscence of womanhood.

The effect of the changes which had come about in his appearance – for, after all, I told myself that it was impossible that I could have been such a simpleton as to have been mistaken on such a question as gender – was heightened by the self-evident fact that, very recently, he had been engaged in some pitched battle; some hand to hand, and, probably, discreditable encounter, from which he had borne away uncomfortable proofs of his opponent's prowess. His antagonist could hardly have been a chivalrous fighter, for his countenance was marked by a dozen different scratches which seemed to suggest that the weapons used had been someone's finger-nails. It was, perhaps, because the heat of the battle was still in his veins that he was in such a state of excitement. He seemed to be almost overwhelmed by the strength of his own feelings. His eyes seemed literally to flame with fire. The muscles of his face were working as if they were wholly beyond his own control. When he spoke his accent was markedly foreign; the words rushed from his lips in an inarticulate torrent; he kept repeating the same thing over and over again in a fashion which was not a little suggestive of insanity.

'So you're not dead! – you're not dead – you're alive! – you're alive! Well – how does it feel to be dead? I ask you! – Is it not good to be dead? To keep dead is better – it is the best of all! To have made an end of all things, to cease to strive and to cease to weep, to cease to want and to cease to have, to cease to annoy and to cease to long, to no more care – no! – not for anything, to put from you the curse of life – forever! – is that not the best? Oh yes! – I tell you! – do I not know? But for you such knowledge is not yet. For you there is the return to life, the coming out of death – you shall live on! – for me! – Live on!'

He made a movement with his hand, and, directly he did so, it happened as on the previous evening, that a metamorphosis took place in the very abysses of my being. I woke from my torpor, as he put it, I came out of death, and was alive again. I was far, yet, from being my own man; I realized that he exercised on me a degree of mesmeric force which I had never dreamed that one creature could exercise on another; but, at least, I was no longer in doubt as to whether I was or was not dead. I knew I was alive.

He lay, watching me, as if he was reading the thoughts which occupied my brain – and, for all I know, he was.

'Robert Holt, you are a thief.'

'I am not.'

My own voice, as I heard it, startled me – it was so long since it had sounded in my ears.

'You are a thief! Only thieves come through windows – did you not come through the window?' I was still – what would my contradiction have availed me? 'But it is well that you came through the window – well you are a thief – well for me! for me! It is you that I am wanting – at the happy moment you have dropped yourself into my hands – in the nick of time. For you are my slave – at my beck and call – my familiar spirit, to do with as I will – you know this – eh?'

I did know it, and the knowledge of my impotence was terrible. I felt that if I could only get away from him; only release myself from the bonds with which he had bound me about; only remove myself from the horrible glamour of his near neighbourhood; only get one or two square meals and have an opportunity of recovering from the enervating stress of mental and bodily fatigue – I felt that then I might be something like his match, and that, a second time, he would endeavour in vain to bring me within the compass of his magic. But, as it was, I was conscious that I was helpless, and the consciousness was agony. He persisted in reiterating his former falsehood.

'I say you are a thief! – a thief, Robert Holt, a thief! You came through a window for your own pleasure, now you will go through a window for mine – not this window, but another.' Where the jest lay I did not perceive; but it tickled him, for a grating sound came from his throat which was meant for laughter. 'This time it is as a thief that you will go – oh yes, be sure.'

He paused, as it seemed, to transfix me with his gaze. His unblinking eyes never for an instant quitted my face. With what a frightful fascination they constrained me – and how I loathed them!

When he spoke again there was a new intonation in his speech – something bitter, cruel, unrelenting.

'Do you know Paul Lessingham?'

He pronounced the name as if he hated it – and yet as if he loved to have it on his tongue.

'What Paul Lessingham?'

'There is only one Paul Lessingham! *The* Paul Lessingham – the *great* Paul Lessingham!'

He shrieked, rather than said this, with an outburst of rage so frenzied that I thought, for the moment, that he was going to spring on me and rend me. I shook all over. I do not doubt that, as I replied, my voice was sufficiently tremulous.

'All the world knows Paul Lessingham – the politician – the statesman.'

As he glared at me his eyes dilated. I still stood in expectation of a physical assault. But, for the present, he contented himself with words.

'Tonight you are going through his window like a thief!'

I had no inkling of his meaning – and, apparently, judging from his next words, I looked something of the bewilderment I felt.

'You do not understand? – no! – it is simple! – what could be simpler? I say that tonight – tonight! – you are going through his window like a thief. You came through my window – why not through the window of Paul Lessingham, the politician – the statesman.'

He repeated my words as if in mockery. I am – I make it my boast! – of that great multitude which regards Paul Lessingham as the greatest living force in practical politics; and which looks to him, with confidence, to carry through that great work of constitutional and social reform which he has set himself to do. I daresay that my tone, in speaking of him, savoured of laudation – which, plainly, the man in the bed resented. What he meant by his wild words about my going through Paul Lessingham's window like a thief, I still had not the faintest notion. They sounded like the ravings of a madman.

As I continued silent, and he yet stared, there came into his tone another note – a note of tenderness – a note of which I had not deemed him capable.

'He is good to look at, Paul Lessingham – is he not good to look at?'

I was aware that, physically, Mr Lessingham was a fine specimen of manhood, but I was not prepared for the assertion of the fact in such a quarter – nor for the manner in which the temporary master of my fate continued to harp and enlarge upon the theme.

'He is straight – straight as the mast of a ship – he is tall – his skin is white; he is strong – do I not know that he is strong – how strong! – oh yes! Is there a better thing than to be his wife? his well-beloved? the light of his eyes? Is there for a woman a happier chance? Oh no, not one! His wife! – Paul Lessingham!'

As, with soft cadences, he gave vent to these unlooked-for sentiments, the fashion of his countenance was changed. A look of longing came into his face – of savage, frantic longing – which, unalluring though it was, for the moment transfigured him. But the mood was transient.

'To be his wife – oh yes! – the wife of his scorn! the despised and rejected!'

The return to the venom of his former bitterness was rapid – I could not but feel that this was the natural man. Though why a creature such as he was should go out of his way to apostrophize, in such a manner, a publicist of Mr Lessingham's eminence, surpassed my comprehension. Yet he stuck to his subject like a leech – as if it had been one in which he had an engrossing personal interest.

'He is a devil – hard as the granite rock – cold as the snows of Ararat. In him there is none of life's warm blood – he is accursed! He is false – ay, false as the fables of those who lie for love of lies – he is all treachery. Her whom he has taken to his bosom he would put away from him as if she had never been – he would steal from her like a thief in the night – he would forget she ever was! But the avenger follows after, lurking in the shadows, hiding among the rocks, waiting, watching, till his time shall come. And it shall come! – the day of the avenger! – ay, the day!'

Raising himself to a sitting posture, he threw his arms above his head, and shrieked with a demoniac fury. Presently he became a trifle calmer. Reverting to his recumbent position, resting his head upon his hand, he eyed me steadily; then asked me a question which struck me as being, under the circumstances, more than a little singular.

'You know his house – the house of the great Paul Lessingham – the politician – the statesman?'

'I do not.'

'You lie! – you do!'

The words came from him with a sort of snarl – as if he would have lashed me across the face with them.

'I do not. Men in my position are not acquainted with the residences of men in his. I may, at some time, have seen his address in print; but, if so, I have forgotten it.'

He looked at me intently, for some moments, as if to learn if I spoke the truth; and apparently, at last, was satisfied that I did.

'You do not know it? – Well! I will show it you, – I will show the house of the great Paul Lessingham.'

What he meant I did not know; but I was soon to learn – an astounding revelation it proved to be. There was about his manner something hardly human; something which, for want of a better phrase, I would call vulpine. In his tone there was a mixture of mockery and bitterness, as if he wished his words to have the effect of corrosive sublimate, and to sear me as he uttered them.

'Listen with all your ears. Give me your whole attention. Hearken to my bidding, so that you may do as I bid you. Not that I fear your obedience – oh no!'

He paused – as if to enable me to fully realize the picture of my helplessness conjured up by his jibes.

'You came through my window, like a thief. You will go through my window, like a fool. You will go to the house of the great Paul Lessingham. You say you do not know it? Well, I will show it you. I will be your guide. Unseen, in the darkness and the night, I will stalk beside you, and will lead you to where I would have you go – You will go just as you are, with bare feet, and head uncovered, and with but a single garment to hide your nakedness. You will be cold, your feet will be cut and bleeding – but what better does a thief deserve? If any see you, at the least they will take you for a madman; there will be trouble. But have no fear; bear a bold heart. None shall see you while I stalk at your side. I will cover you with the cloak of invisibility – so that you may come in safety to the house of the great Paul Lessingham.'

He paused again. What he said, wild and wanton though it was, was beginning to fill me with a sense of the most extreme discomfort. His sentences, in some strange, indescribable way, seemed, as they came from his lips, to warp my limbs; to enwrap themselves about me; to confine me, tighter and tighter, within, as it were, swaddling clothes; to make me more and more helpless. I was already conscious that whatever mad freak he chose to set me on, I should have no option but to carry it through.

'When you come to the house, you will stand, and look, and seek for a window convenient for entry. It may be that you will find one open, as you did mine; if not, you will open one. How – that is your affair, not mine. You will practise the arts of a thief to steal into his house.'

The monstrosity of his suggestion fought against the spell which he again was casting upon me, and forced me into speech – endowed me with the power to show that there still was in me something of a man; though every second the strands of my manhood, as it seemed, were slipping faster through the fingers which were strained to clutch them.

'I will not.'

He was silent. He looked at me. The pupils of his eyes dilated – until they seemed all pupil.

'You will – Do you hear? – I say you will.'

'I am not a thief, I am an honest man – why should I do this thing?'

'Because I bid you.'

'Have mercy!'

'On whom – on you, or on Paul Lessingham? – Who, at any time, has shown mercy unto me, that I should show mercy unto any?'

He stopped, and then again went on – reiterating his former incredible suggestion with an emphasis which seemed to eat its way into my brain.

'You will practise the arts of a thief to steal into his house; and, being in, will listen. If all be still, you will make your way to the room he calls his study.'

'How shall I find it? I know nothing of his house.'

The question was wrung from me; I felt that the sweat was standing in great drops upon my brow.

'I will show it you.'

'Shall you go with me?'

'Ay – I shall go with you. All the time I shall be with you. You will not see me, but I shall be there. Be not afraid.'

His claim to supernatural powers, for what he said amounted to nothing less, was, on the face of it, preposterous, but, then, I was in no condition to even hint at its absurdity. He continued.

'When you have gained the study, you will go to a certain drawer, which is in a certain bureau, in a corner of the room – I see it now; when you are there you shall see it too – and you will open it.'

'Should it be locked?'

'You still will open it.'

'But how shall I open it if it is locked?'

'By those arts in which a thief is skilled. I say to you again that that is your affair, not mine.'

I made no attempt to answer him. Even supposing that he forced me, by the wicked, and unconscionable exercise of what, I presumed, were the hypnotic powers with which nature had to such a dangerous degree endowed him, to carry the adventure to a certain stage, since he could hardly, at an instant's notice, endow me with the knack of picking locks, should the drawer he alluded to be locked – which might Providence permit! – nothing serious might issue from it after all. He read my thoughts.

'You will open it – though it be doubly and trebly locked, I say that you will open it – In it you will find –' he hesitated, as if to reflect – 'some letters; it may be two or three – I know not just how many – they are bound about by a silken ribbon. You will take them out of the drawer, and, having taken them, you will make the best of your way out of the house, and bear them back to me.'

'And should anyone come upon me while engaged in these nefarious proceedings – for instance, should I encounter Mr Lessingham himself, what then?'

'Paul Lessingham? – You need have no fear if you encounter him.'

'I need have no fear! – If he finds me, in his own house, at dead of night, committing burglary!'

'You need have no fear of him.'

'On your account, or on my own? – At least he will have me haled to gaol.'

'I say you need have no fear of him. I say what I mean.'

'How, then, shall I escape his righteous vengeance? He is not the man to suffer a midnight robber to escape him scatheless – shall I have to kill him?'

'You will not touch him with a finger – nor will he touch you.'

'By what spell shall I prevent him?'

'By the spell of two words.'

'What words are they?'

'Should Paul Lessingham chance to come upon you, and find you in his house, a thief, and should seek to stay you from whatever it is you may be at, you will not flinch nor flee from him, but you will stand still, and you will say –'

Something in the crescendo accents of his voice, something weird and ominous, caused my heart to press against my ribs, so that when he stopped, in my eagerness I cried out,

'What?'

'THE BEETLE!'

As the words came from him in a kind of screech, the lamp went out, and the place was all in darkness, and I knew, so that the knowledge filled me with a sense of loathing, that with me, in the room, was the evil presence of the night before. Two bright specks gleamed in front of me; something flopped from off the bed on to the ground; the thing was coming towards me across the floor. It came slowly on, and on, and on. I stood still, speechless in the sickness of my horror. Until, on my bare feet, it touched me with slimy feelers, and my terror lest it should creep up my naked body lent me voice, and I fell shrieking like a soul in agony.

It may be that my shrieking drove it from me. At least, it went. I knew it went. And all was still. Until, on a sudden, the lamp flamed out again, and there, lying, as before, in bed, glaring at me with his baleful eyes, was the being whom, in my folly, or in my wisdom – whichever it was! – I was beginning to credit with the possession of unhallowed, unlawful powers.

'You will say that to him; those two words; they only; no more. And you will see what you will see. But Paul Lessingham is a man of resolution. Should he still persist in interference, or seek to hinder you, you will say those two words again. You need do no more. Twice will suffice, I promise you – Now go – Draw up the blind; open the window; climb through it. Hasten to do what I have bidden you. I wait here for your return – and all the way I shall be with you.'

## CHAPTER SIX

# A SINGULAR FELONY

I went to the window; I drew up the blind, unlatching the sash, I threw it open; and clad, or, rather, unclad as I was, I clambered through it into the open air. I was not only incapable of resistance, I was incapable of distinctly formulating the desire to offer resistance. Some compelling influence moved me hither and thither, with completest disregard of whether I would or would not.

And yet, when I found myself without, I was conscious of a sense of exultation at having escaped from the miasmic atmosphere of that room of unholy memories. And a faint hope began to dawn within my bosom that, as I increased the distance between myself and it, I might shake off something of the nightmare helplessness which numbed and tortured me. I lingered for a moment by the window; then stepped over the short dividing wall into the street; and then again I lingered.

My condition was one of dual personality – while, physically, I was bound, mentally, to a considerable extent, I was free. But this measure of freedom on my mental side made my plight no better. For, among other things, I realized what a ridiculous figure I must be cutting, barefooted and bareheaded, abroad, at such an hour of the night, in such a boisterous breeze – for I quickly discovered that the wind amounted to something like a gale. Apart from all other considerations, the notion of parading the streets in such a condition filled me with profound disgust. And I do believe that if my tyrannical oppressor had only permitted me to attire myself in my own garments, I should have started with a comparatively light heart on the felonious mission on which he apparently was sending me. I believe, too, that the consciousness of the incongruity of my attire increased my sense of helplessness, and that, had I been dressed as Englishmen are wont to be, who take their walks abroad, he would not have found in me, on that occasion, the facile instrument, which, in fact, he did.

There was a moment, in which the gravelled pathway first made itself known to my naked feet, and the cutting wind to my naked flesh, when I think it possible that, had I gritted my teeth, and strained my every nerve, I might have shaken myself free from the bonds which shackled me, and bade defiance to the ancient sinner who, for all I knew, was peeping at me through the window. But so depressed was I by the knowledge of the ridiculous appearance I presented that, before I could take advantage of it the moment passed – not to return again that night.

I did catch, as it were, at its fringe, as it was flying past me, making a hurried movement to one side – the first I had made, of my own initiative, for hours. But it was too late. My tormentor – as if, though unseen, he saw – tightened his grip, I was whirled round, and sped hastily onwards in a direction in which I certainly had no desire of travelling.

All the way I never met a soul. I have since wondered whether in that respect my experience was not a normal one; whether it might not have happened to any. If so, there are streets in London, long lines of streets, which, at a certain period of the night, in a certain sort of weather – probably the weather had something to do with it – are clean deserted; in which there is neither foot-passenger nor vehicle – not even a policeman. The greater part of the route along which I was driven – I know no juster word – was one with which I had some sort of acquaintance. It led, at first, through what, I take it, was some part of Walham Green; then along the Lillie Road, through Brompton, across the Fulham Road, through the network of streets leading to Sloane Street, across Sloane Street into Lowndes Square. Who goes that way goes some distance, and goes through some important thoroughfares; yet not a creature did I see, nor, I imagine, was there a creature who saw me. As I crossed Sloane Street, I fancied that I heard the distant rumbling of a vehicle along the Knightsbridge Road, but that was the only sound I heard.

It is painful even to recollect the plight in which I was when I was stopped – for stopped I was, as shortly and as sharply, as the beast of burden, with a bridle in its mouth, whose driver puts a period to his career. I was wet – intermittent gusts of rain were borne on the scurrying wind; in spite of the pace at which I had been brought, I was chilled to the bone; and – worst of all! – my mud-stained feet, all cut and bleeding, were so painful – for, unfortunately, I was still susceptible enough to pain – that it was agony to have them come into contact with the cold and the slime of the hard, unyielding pavement.

I had been stopped on the opposite side of the square – that nearest to the hospital; in front of a house which struck me as being somewhat smaller than the rest. It was a house with a portico; about the pillars of this portico was trelliswork, and on the trelliswork was trained some climbing plant. As I stood, shivering, wondering what would happen next, some strange impulse mastered me, and, immediately, to my own unbounded amazement, I found myself scrambling up the trellis towards the verandah above. I am no gymnast, either by nature or by education; I doubt whether, previously, I had ever attempted to climb anything more difficult than a step ladder. The result was, that, though the impulse might be given me, the skill could not, and I had only ascended a yard or so when, losing my footing, I came slithering down upon my back. Bruised and shaken though I was, I was not allowed to inquire into my injuries. In a moment I was on my feet again, and again I was impelled to climb – only, however, again to come to grief. This time the demon, or whatever it was, that had entered into me, seeming to appreciate the impossibility of getting me to the top of that verandah, directed me to try another way. I mounted the steps leading to the front door, got on to the low parapet which was at one side, thence on to the sill of the adjacent window – had I slipped then I should have fallen a sheer descent of at least twenty feet to the bottom of the deep area down below. But the sill was broad, and – if it is proper to use such language in connection with a transaction of the sort in which I was engaged – fortune favoured me. I did not fall. In my clenched fist I had a stone. With this I struck the pane of glass, as with a hammer. Through the hole which resulted, I could just insert my hand, and reach the latch within. In another minute the sash was raised, and I was in the house – I had committed burglary.

As I look back and reflect upon the audacity of the whole proceeding, even now I tremble. Hapless slave of another's will although in very truth I was, I cannot repeat too often that I realized to the full just what it was that I was being compelled to do – a fact which was very far from rendering my situation less distressful! – and every detail of my involuntary actions was projected upon my brain in a series of pictures, whose clear-cut outlines, so long as memory endures, will never fade. Certainly no professional burglar, nor, indeed, any creature in his senses, would have ventured to emulate my surprising rashness. The process of smashing the pane of glass – it was plate glass – was anything but a noiseless one. There was, first, the blow itself, then the shivering of the glass, then the clattering of fragments into the area beneath. One would have thought that the whole thing would have made din enough to have roused the Seven Sleepers. But, here, again the weather was on my side. About that time the wind was howling wildly – it came shrieking across the square. It is possible that the tumult which it made deadened all other sounds.

Anyhow, as I stood within the room which I had violated, listening for signs of someone being on the alert, I could hear nothing. Within the house there seemed to be the silence of the grave. I drew down the window, and made for the door.

It proved by no means easy to find. The windows were obscured by heavy curtains, so that the room inside was dark as pitch. It appeared to be unusually full of furniture – an appearance due, perhaps, to my being a stranger in the midst of such Cimmerian blackness. I had to feel my way, very gingerly indeed, among the various impedimenta. As it was I seemed to come into contact with most of the obstacles there were to come into contact with, stumbling more than once over footstools, and over what seemed to be dwarf chairs. It was a miracle that my movements still continued to be unheard – but I believe that the explanation was, that the house was well built; that the servants were the only persons in it at the time; that their bedrooms were on the top floor; that they were fast asleep; and that they were little likely to be disturbed by anything that might occur in the room which I had entered.

Reaching the door at last, I opened it – listening for any promise of being interrupted – and – to adapt a hackneyed phrase – directed by the power which shaped my end, I went across the hall and up the stairs. I passed up the first landing, and, on the second, moved to a door upon the right. I turned the handle, it yielded, the door opened, I entered, closing it behind me. I went to the wall just inside the door, found a handle, jerked it, and switched on the electric light – doing, I make no doubt, all these things, from a spectator's point of view, so naturally, that a judge and jury would have been with difficulty persuaded that they were not the product of my own volition.

In the brilliant glow of the electric light I took a leisurely survey of the contents of the room. It was, as the man in the bed had said it would be, a study – a fine, spacious apartment, evidently intended rather for work than for show. There were three separate writing-tables, one very large and two smaller ones, all covered with an orderly array of manuscripts and papers. A typewriter stood at the side of one. On the floor, under and about them, were piles of books, portfolios, and official-looking documents. Every available foot of wall space on three sides of the room was lined with shelves, full as they could hold with books. On the fourth side, facing the door, was a large lock-up oak bookcase, and, in the further corner, a quaint old bureau. So soon as I saw this bureau I went for it, straight as an arrow from a bow – indeed, it would be no abuse of metaphor to say that I was propelled towards it like an arrow from a bow.

It had drawers below, glass doors above, and between the drawers and the doors was a flap to let down. It was to this flap my attention was directed. I put out my hand to open it; it was locked at the top. I pulled at it with both hands; it refused to budge.

So this was the lock I was, if necessary, to practise the arts of a thief to open. I was no picklock; I had flattered myself that nothing, and no one, could make me such a thing. Yet now that I found myself confronted by that unyielding flap, I found that pressure, irresistible pressure, was being put upon me to gain, by any and every means, access to its interior. I had no option but to yield. I looked about me in search of some convenient tool with which to ply the felon's trade. I found it close beside me. Leaning against the wall, within a yard of where I stood, were examples of various kinds of weapons – among them, spear-heads. Taking one of these spear-heads, with much difficulty I forced the point between the flap and the bureau. Using the leverage thus obtained, I attempted to prise it open. The flap held fast; the spear-head snapped in two. I tried another, with the same result; a third, to fail again. There were no more. The most convenient thing remaining was a queer, heavy-headed sharp-edged hatchet. This I took, brought the sharp edge down with all my force upon the refractory flap. The hatchet went through – before I had done with it, it was open with a vengeance.

But I was destined on the occasion of my first – and, I trust, last – experience of the burglar's calling, to carry the part completely through. I had gained access to the flap itself only to find that at the back were several small drawers, on one of which my observation was brought to bear in a fashion which it was quite impossible to disregard. As a matter of course it was locked, and, once more, I had to search for something which would serve as a rough-and-ready substitute for the missing key.

There was nothing at all suitable among the weapons – I could hardly for such a purpose use the hatchet; the drawer in question was such a little one that to have done so would have been to shiver it to splinters. On the mantelshelf, in an open leather case, were a pair of revolvers. Statesmen, nowadays, sometimes stand in actual peril of their lives. It is possible that Mr Lessingham, conscious of continually threatened danger, carried them about with him as a necessary protection. They were serviceable weapons, large, and somewhat weighty – of the type which, I believe, upon occasion the police are armed. Not only were all the barrels loaded, but, in the case itself there was a supply of cartridges more than sufficient to charge them all again.

I was handling the weapons, wondering – if, in my condition, the word was applicable – what use I could make of them to enable me to gain admission to that drawer, when there came, on a sudden, from the street without, the sound of approaching wheels. There was a whirring within my brain, as if someone was endeavouring to explain to me to what service to apply the revolvers, and I, perforce, strained every nerve to grasp the meaning of my invisible mentor. While I did so, the wheels drew rapidly nearer, and, just as I was expecting them to go whirling by, stopped – in front of the house. My heart leapt in my bosom. In a convulsion of frantic terror, again, during the passage of one frenzied moment, I all but burst the bonds that held me, and

THE BEETLE

fled, haphazard, from the imminent peril. But the bonds were stronger than I – it was as if I had been rooted to the ground.

A key was inserted in the keyhole of the front door, the lock was turned, the door thrown open, firm footsteps entered the house. If I could I would not have stood upon the order of my going, but gone at once, anywhere, anyhow; but, at that moment, my comings and goings were not matters in which I was consulted. Panic fear raging within, outwardly I was calm as possible, and stood, turning the revolvers over and over, asking myself what it could be that I was intended to do with them. All at once it came to me in an illuminating flash – I was to fire at the lock of the drawer, and blow it open.

A madder scheme it would have been impossible to hit upon. The servants had slept through a good deal, but they would hardly sleep through the discharge of a revolver in a room below them – not to speak of the person who had just entered the premises, and whose footsteps were already audible as he came up the stairs. I struggled to make a dumb protest against the insensate folly which was hurrying me to infallible destruction, without success. For me there was only obedience. With a revolver in either hand I marched towards the bureau as unconcernedly as if I would not have given my life to have escaped the dénouement which I needed but a slight modicum of common sense to be aware was close at hand. I placed the muzzle of one of the revolvers against the keyhole of the drawer to which my unseen guide had previously directed me, and pulled the trigger. The lock was shattered, the contents of the drawer were at my mercy. I snatched up a bundle of letters, about which a pink ribbon was wrapped. Startled by a noise behind me, immediately following the report of the pistol, I glanced over my shoulder.

The room door was open, and Mr Lessingham was standing with the handle in his hand.

## CHAPTER SEVEN

# THE GREAT PAUL LESSINGHAM

He was in evening dress. He carried a small portfolio in his left hand. If the discovery of my presence startled him, as it could scarcely have failed to do, he allowed no sign of surprise to escape him. Paul Lessingham's impenetrability is proverbial. Whether on platforms addressing excited crowds, or in the midst of heated discussion in the House of Commons, all the world knows that his coolness remains unruffled. It is generally understood that he owes his success in the political arena in no slight measure to the adroitness which is born of his invulnerable presence of mind. He gave me a taste of its quality then. Standing in the attitude which has been familiarized to us by caricaturists, his feet apart, his broad shoulders well set back, his handsome head a little advanced, his keen blue eyes having in them something suggestive of a bird of prey considering just when, where, and how to pounce, he regarded me for some seconds in perfect silence – whether outwardly I flinched I cannot say; inwardly I know I did. When he spoke, it was without moving from where he stood, and in the calm, airy tones in which he might have addressed an acquaintance who had just dropped in.

'May I ask, sir, to what I am indebted for the pleasure of your company?'

He paused, as if waiting for my answer. When none came, he put his question in another form.

'Pray, sir, who are you, and on whose invitation do I find you here?'

As I still stood speechless, motionless, meeting his glance without a twitching of an eyebrow, nor a tremor of the hand, I imagine that he began to consider me with an even closer intentness than before. And that the – to say the least of it – peculiarity of my appearance, caused him to suspect that he was face to face with an adventure of a peculiar kind. Whether he took me for a lunatic I cannot certainly say; but, from his manner, I think it possible he did. He began to move towards me from across the room, addressing me with the utmost suavity and courtesy.

'Be so good as to give me the revolver, and the papers you are holding in your hand.'

As he came on, something entered into me, and forced itself from between my lips, so that I said, in a low, hissing voice, which I vow was never mine, 'THE BEETLE!'

Whether it was, or was not, owing, in some degree, to a trick of my imagination, I cannot determine, but, as the words were spoken, it seemed to me that the lights went low, so that the place was all in darkness, and I again was filled with the nauseous consciousness of the presence of something evil in the room. But if, in that matter, my abnormally strained imagination played me a trick, there could be no doubt whatever as to the effect which the words had on Mr Lessingham. When the mist of the blackness – real or supposititious – had passed from before my eyes, I found that he had retreated to the extremest limits of the room, and was crouching his back against the bookshelves, clutching at them, in the attitude of a man who has received a staggering blow, from which, as yet, he has had no opportunity of recovering. A most extraordinary change had taken place in the expression of his face; in his countenance amazement, fear, and horror seemed struggling for the mastery. I was filled with a most discomforting qualm as I gazed at the frightened figure in front of me, and realized that it was that of the great Paul Lessingham, the god of my political idolatry.

'Who are you? – In God's name, who are you?'

His very voice seemed changed; his frenzied, choking accents would hardly have been recognized by either friend or foe.

'Who are you? – Do you hear me ask, who are you? In the name of God, I bid you say!'

As he perceived that I was still, he began to show a species of excitement which it was unpleasant to witness, especially as he continued to crouch against the bookshelf, as if he was afraid to stand up straight. So far from exhibiting the impassivity for which he was renowned, all the muscles in his face and all the limbs in his body seemed to be in motion at once; he was like a man afflicted with the shivering ague – his very fingers were twitching aimlessly, as they were stretched out on either side of him, as if seeking for support from the shelves against which he leaned.

'Where have you come from? what do you want? who sent you here? what concern have you with me? is it necessary that you should come and play these childish tricks with me? why? why?'

The questions came from him with astonishing rapidity. When he saw that I continued silent, they came still faster, mingled with what sounded to me like a stream of inchoate abuse.

'Why do you stand there in that extraordinary garment – it's worse than nakedness, yes, worse than nakedness! For that alone I could have you punished, and I will! – and try to play the fool? Do you think I am a boy to be bamboozled by every bogey a blunderer may try to conjure up? If so, you're wrong, as whoever sent you might have had sense enough to let you know. If you tell me who you are, and who sent you here, and what it is you want, I will be merciful; if not, the police shall be sent for, and the law shall take its course – to the bitter end! – I warn you – Do you hear? You fool! tell me who you are?'

The last words came from him in what was very like a burst of childish fury. He himself seemed conscious, the moment after, that his passion was sadly lacking in dignity, and to be ashamed of it. He drew himself straight up. With a pocket-handkerchief which he took from an inner pocket of his coat, he wiped his lips. Then, clutching it tightly in his hand, he eyed me with a fixedness which, under any other circumstances, I should have found unbearable.

'Well, sir, is your continued silence part of the business of the rôle you have set yourself to play?'

His tone was firmer, and his bearing more in keeping with his character.

'If it be so, I presume that I at least have liberty to speak. When I find a gentleman, even one gifted with your eloquence of silence, playing the part of burglar, I think you will grant that a few words on my part cannot justly be considered to be out of place.'

Again he paused. I could not but feel that he was employing the vehicle of somewhat cumbrous sarcasm to gain time, and to give himself the opportunity of recovering, if the thing was possible, his pristine courage. That, for some cause wholly hidden from me, the mysterious utterance had shaken his nature to its deepest foundation, was made plainer by his endeavour to treat the whole business with a sort of cynical levity.

'To commence with, may I ask if you have come through London, or through any portion of it, in that costume – or rather, in that want of costume? It would seem out of place in a Cairene street, – would it not? – even in the Rue de Rabagas – was it not the Rue de Rabagas?'

He asked the question with an emphasis the meaning of which was wholly lost on me. What he referred to either then, or in what immediately followed, I, of course, knew no more than the man in the moon – though I should probably have found great difficulty in convincing him of my ignorance.

'I take it that you are a reminiscence of the Rue de Rabagas – that, of course – is it not of course? The little house with the blue-grey venetians, and the piano with the F sharp missing? Is there still the piano? With the tinny treble – indeed, the whole atmosphere, was it not tinny? – You agree with me? – I have not forgotten. I am not even afraid to remember – you perceive it?'

A new idea seemed to strike him – born, perhaps, of my continued silence.

'You look English – is it possible that you are not English? What are you then – French? We shall see!'

He addressed me in a tongue which I recognized as French, but with which I was not sufficiently acquainted to understand. Although, I flatter myself that – as the present narrative should show – I have not made an ill-use of the opportunities which I have had to improve my, originally, modest education, I regret that I have never had so much as a ghost of a chance to acquire an even rudimentary knowledge of any language except my own. Recognizing, I suppose, from my looks, that he was addressing me in a tongue to which I was a stranger, after a time he stopped, added something with a smile, and then began to talk to me in a lingo to which, in a manner of speaking, I was even stranger, for this time I had not the faintest notion what it was – it might have been gibberish for all that I could tell. Quickly perceiving that he had succeeded no better than before, he returned to English.

'You do not know French? – nor the *patois* of the Rue de Rabagas? Very good – then what is it that you do know? Are you under a vow of silence, or are you dumb – except upon occasion? Your face is English – what can be seen of it, and I will take it, therefore, that English spoken words convey some meaning to your brain. So listen, sir, to what I have to say – do me the favour to listen carefully.'

He was becoming more and more his former self. In his clear, modulated tones there was a ring of something like a threat – a something which went very far beyond his words.

'You know something of a period which I choose to have forgotten – that is plain; you come from a person who, probably, knows still more. Go back to that person and say that what I have forgotten I have forgotten; nothing will be gained by anyone by an endeavour to induce me to remember – be very sure upon that point, say that nothing will be gained by anyone. That time was one of mirage, of delusion, of disease. I was in a condition, mentally and bodily, in which pranks could have been played upon me by any trickster. Such pranks were played. I know that now quite well. I do not pretend to be proficient in the *modus operandi* of the hankey-pankey man, but I know that he has a method, all the same – one susceptible, too, of facile explanation. Go back to your friend, and tell him that I am not again likely to be made the butt of his old method – nor of his new one either. – You hear me, sir?'

I remained motionless and silent – an attitude which, plainly, he resented.

'Are you deaf and dumb? You certainly are not dumb, for you spoke to me just now. Be advised by me, and do not compel me to resort to measures which will be the cause to you of serious discomfort. – You hear me, sir?'

Still, from me, not a sign of comprehension – to his increased annoyance.

'So be it. Keep your own counsel, if you choose. Yours will be the

479

bitterness, not mine. You may play the lunatic, and play it excellently well, but that you do understand what is said to you is clear. – Come to business, sir. Give me that revolver, and the packet of letters which you have stolen from my desk.'

He had been speaking with the air of one who desired to convince himself as much as me – and about his last words there was almost a flavour of braggadocio. I remained unheeding.

'Are you going to do as I require, or are you insane enough to refuse? – in which case I shall summon assistance, and there will quickly be an end of it. Pray do not imagine that you can trick me into supposing that you do not grasp the situation. I know better. – Once more, are you going to give me that revolver and those letters?'

Yet no reply. His anger was growing momentarily greater – and his agitation too. On my first introduction to Paul Lessingham I was not destined to discover in him any one of those qualities of which the world held him to be the undisputed possessor. He showed himself to be as unlike the statesman I had conceived, and esteemed, as he easily could have done.

'Do you think I stand in awe of you? – you! – of such a thing as you! Do as I tell you, or I myself will make you – and, at the same time, teach you a much-needed lesson.'

He raised his voice. In his bearing there was a would-be defiance. He might not have been aware of it, but the repetitions of the threats were, in themselves, confessions of weakness. He came a step or two forward – then, stopping short, began to tremble. The perspiration broke out upon his brow; he made spasmodic little dabs at it with his crumpled-up handkerchief. His eyes wandered hither and thither, as if searching for something which they feared to see yet were constrained to seek. He began to talk to himself, out loud, in odd disconnected sentences – apparently ignoring me entirely.

'What was that? – It was nothing. – It was my imagination. – My nerves are out of order. – I have been working too hard. – I am not well. – *What's that?*'

This last inquiry came from him in a half-stifled shriek – as the door opened to admit the head and body of an elderly man in a state of considerable undress. He had the tousled appearance of one who had been unexpectedly roused out of slumber, and unwillingly dragged from bed. Mr Lessingham stared at him as if he had been a ghost, while he stared back at Mr Lessingham as if he found a difficulty in crediting the evidence of his own eyes. It was he who broke the silence – stutteringly.

'I am sure I beg your pardon, sir, but one of the maids thought that she heard the sound of a shot, and we came down to see if there was anything the matter – I had no idea, sir, that you were here.' His eyes travelled from Mr

Lessingham towards me – suddenly increasing, when they saw me, to about twice their previous size. 'God save us! – who is that?'

The man's self-evident cowardice possibly impressed Mr Lessingham with the conviction that he himself was not cutting the most dignified of figures. At any rate, he made a notable effort to, once more, assume a bearing of greater determination.

'You are quite right, Matthews, quite right. I am obliged by your watchfulness. At present you may leave the room – I propose to deal with this fellow myself – only remain with the other men upon the landing, so that, if I call, you may come to my assistance.'

Matthews did as he was told, he left the room – with, I fancy, more rapidity than he had entered it. Mr Lessingham returned to me, his manner distinctly more determined, as if he found his resolution reinforced by the near neighbourhood of his retainers.

'Now, my man, you see how the case stands, at a word from me you will be overpowered and doomed to undergo a long period of imprisonment. Yet I am still willing to listen to the dictates of mercy. Put down that revolver, give me those letters – you will not find me disposed to treat you hardly.'

For all the attention I paid him, I might have been a graven image. He misunderstood, or pretended to misunderstand, the cause of my silence.

'Come, I see that you suppose my intentions to be harsher than they really are – do not let us have a scandal, and a scene – be sensible! – give me those letters!'

Again he moved in my direction; again, after he had taken a step or two, to stumble and stop, and look about him with frightened eyes; again to begin to mumble to himself aloud.

'It's a conjurer's trick! – Of course! – Nothing more. – What else could it be? – I'm not to be fooled. – I'm older than I was. I've been overdoing it – that's all.'

Suddenly he broke into cries.

'Matthews! Matthews! – Help! help!'

Matthews entered the room, followed by three other men, younger than himself. Evidently all had slipped into the first articles of clothing they could lay their hands upon, and each carried a stick, or some similar rudimentary weapon.

Their master spurred them on.

'Strike the revolver out of his hand, Matthews! – knock him down! – take the letters from him! – don't be afraid! – I'm not afraid!'

In proof of it, he rushed at me, as it seemed half blindly. As he did so I was constrained to shout out, in tones which I should not have recognized as mine,

'THE BEETLE!'

And that moment the room was all in darkness, and there were screams as of someone in an agony of terror or of pain. I felt that something had come into the room, I knew not whence nor how – something of horror. And the next action of which I was conscious was, that under cover of the darkness, I was flying from the room, propelled by I knew not what.

CHAPTER EIGHT

# THE MAN IN THE STREET

Whether anyone pursued I cannot say. I have some dim recollection, as I came out of the room, of women being huddled against the wall upon the landing, and of their screaming as I went past. But whether any effort was made to arrest my progress I cannot tell. My own impression is that not the slightest attempt to impede my headlong flight was made by anyone.

In what direction I was going I did not know. I was like a man flying through the phantasmagoric happenings of a dream, knowing neither how nor whither. I tore along what I suppose was a broad passage, through a door at the end into what, I fancy, was a drawing-room. Across this room I dashed, helter-skelter, bringing down, in the gloom, unseen articles of furniture, with myself sometimes on top, and sometimes under them. In a trice, each time I fell, I was on my feet again – until I went crashing against a window which was concealed by curtains. It would not have been strange had I crashed through it – but I was spared that. Thrusting aside the curtains, I fumbled for the fastening of the window. It was a tall French casement, extending, so far as I could judge, from floor to ceiling. When I had it open I stepped through it on to the verandah without – to find that I was on the top of the portico which I had vainly essayed to ascend from below.

I tried the road down which I had tried up – proceeding with a breakneck recklessness of which now I shudder to think. It was, probably, some thirty feet above the pavement, yet I rushed at the descent with as much disregard for the safety of life and limb as if it had been only three. Over the edge of the parapet I went, obtaining, with my naked feet, a precarious foothold on the latticework – then down I commenced to scramble. I never did get a proper hold, and when I had descended, perhaps, rather more than half the distance – scraping, as it seemed to me, every scrap of skin off my body in the process – I lost what little hold I had. Down to the bottom I went tumbling, rolling right across the pavement into the muddy road. It was a miracle I was not seriously injured – but in that sense, certainly, that night the miracles were on my side. Hardly was I down, than I was up again – mud and all.

Just as I was getting on to my feet I felt a firm hand grip me by the shoulder. Turning I found myself confronted by a tall, slenderly built man, with a long, drooping moustache, and an overcoat buttoned up to the chin, who held me with a grasp of steel. He looked at me – and I looked back at him.

'After the ball – eh?'

Even then I was struck by something pleasant in his voice, and some quality as of sunshine in his handsome face.

Seeing that I said nothing he went on – with a curious, half mocking smile.

'Is that the way to come slithering down the Apostle's pillar? – Is it simple burglary, or simpler murder? – Tell me the glad tidings that you've killed St Paul, and I'll let you go.'

Whether he was mad or not I cannot say – there was some excuse for thinking so. He did not look mad, though his words and actions alike were strange.

'Although you have confined yourself to gentle felony, shall I not shower blessings on the head of him who has been robbing Paul? – Away with you!'

He removed his grip, giving me a gentle push as he did so – and I was away. I neither stayed nor paused.

I know little of records, but if anyone has made a better record than I did that night between Lowndes Square and Walham Green I should like to know just what it was – I should, too, like to have seen it done.

In an incredibly short space of time I was once more in front of the house with the open window – the packet of letters – which were like to have cost me so dear – gripped tightly in my hand.

CHAPTER NINE

# THE CONTENTS OF THE PACKET

I pulled up sharply – as if a brake had been suddenly, and even mercilessly, applied to bring me to a standstill. In front of the window I stood shivering. A shower had recently commenced – the falling rain was being blown before the breeze. I was in a terrible sweat – yet tremulous as with cold; covered with mud; bruised, and cut, and bleeding – as piteous an object as you would care to see. Every limb in my body ached; every muscle was exhausted; mentally and physically I was done; had I not been held up, willy nilly, by the spell which was upon me, I should have sunk down, then and there, in a hopeless, helpless, hapless heap.

But my tormentor was not yet at an end with me.

As I stood there, like some broken and beaten hack, waiting for the word of command, it came. It was as if some strong magnetic current had been switched on to me through the window to draw me into the room. Over the low wall I went, over the sill – once more I stood in that chamber of my humiliation and my shame. And once again I was conscious of that awful sense of the presence of an evil thing. How much of it was fact, and how much of it was the product of imagination I cannot say; but, looking back, it seems to me that it was as if I had been taken out of the corporeal body to be plunged into the inner chambers of all nameless sin. There was the sound of something flopping from off the bed on to the ground, and I knew that the thing was coming at me across the floor. My stomach quaked, my heart melted within me – the very anguish of my terror gave me strength to scream – and scream! Sometimes, even now, I seem to hear those screams of mine ringing through the night, and I bury my face in the pillow, and it is as though I was passing through the very Valley of the Shadow.

The thing went back – I could hear it slipping and sliding across the floor. There was silence. And, presently, the lamp was lit, and the room was all in brightness. There, on the bed, in the familiar attitude between the sheets, his head resting on his hand, his eyes blazing like living coals, was the dreadful cause of all my agonies. He looked at me with his unpitying, unblinking glance.

'So! – Through the window again! – like a thief! – Is it always through that door that you come into a house?'

He paused – as if to give me time to digest his gibe.

'You saw Paul Lessingham – well? – the great Paul Lessingham! – Was he, then, so great?'

His rasping voice, with its queer foreign twang, reminded me, in some uncomfortable way, of a rusty saw – the things he said, and the manner in which he said them, were alike intended to add to my discomfort. It was solely because the feat was barely possible that he only partially succeeded.

'Like a thief you went into his house – did I not tell you that you would? Like a thief he found you – were you not ashamed? Since, like a thief he found you, how comes it that you have escaped – by what robber's artifice have you saved yourself from gaol?'

His manner changed – so that, all at once, he seemed to snarl at me.

'Is he great? – well! – is he great – Paul Lessingham? You are small, but he is smaller – your great Paul Lessingham! – Was there ever a man so less than nothing?'

With the recollection fresh upon me of Mr Lessingham as I had so lately seen him I could not but feel that there might be a modicum of truth in what, with such an intensity of bitterness, the speaker suggested. The picture which, in my mental gallery, I had hung in the place of honour, seemed, to say the least, to have become a trifle smudged.

As usual, the man in the bed seemed to experience not the slightest difficulty in deciphering what was passing through my mind.

'That is so – you and he, you are a pair – the great Paul Lessingham is as great a thief as you – and greater – for, at least, than you he has more courage.'

For some moments he was still; then exclaimed, with sudden fierceness,

'Give me what you have stolen!'

I moved towards the bed – most unwillingly – and held out to him the packet of letters which I had abstracted from the little drawer. Perceiving my disinclination to his near neighbourhood, he set himself to play with it. Ignoring my outstretched hand, he stared me straight in the face.

'What ails you? Are you not well? Is it not sweet to stand close at my side? You, with your white skin, if I were a woman, would you not take me for a wife?'

There was something about the manner in which this was said which was so essentially feminine that once more I wondered if I could possibly be mistaken in the creature's sex. I would have given much to have been able to strike him across the face – or, better, to have taken him by the neck, and thrown him through the window, and rolled him in the mud.

He condescended to notice what I was holding out to him.

'So! – that is what you have stolen! That is what you have taken from the drawer in the bureau – the drawer which was locked – and which you used the arts in which a thief is skilled to enter. Give it to me – thief!'

He snatched the packet from me, scratching the back of my hand as he did so, as if his nails had been talons. He turned the packet over and over, glaring at it as he did so – it was strange what a relief it was to have his glance removed from off my face.

'You kept it in your inner drawer, Paul Lessingham, where none but you could see it – did you? You hid it as one hides treasure. There should be something here worth having, worth seeing, worth knowing – yes, worth knowing! – since you found it worth your while to hide it up so closely.'

As I have said, the packet was bound about by a string of pink ribbon – a fact on which he presently began to comment.

'With what a pretty string you have encircled it – and how neatly it is tied! Surely only a woman's hand could tie a knot like that – who would have guessed yours were such agile fingers? – So! An endorsement on the cover! What's this? – let's see what's written! – "The letters of my dear love, Marjorie Lindon".'

As he read these words, which, as he said, were endorsed upon the outer sheet of paper which served as a cover for the letters which were enclosed within, his face became transfigured. Never did I suppose that rage could have so possessed a human countenance. His jaw dropped open so that his yellow fangs gleamed through his parted lips – he held his breath so long that each moment I looked to see him fall down in a fit; the veins stood out all over his face and head like seams of blood. I know not how long he continued speechless. When his breath returned, it was with chokings and gaspings, in the midst of which he hissed out his words, as if their mere passage through his throat brought him near to strangulation.

'The letters of his dear love! – of his dear love! – his! – Paul Lessingham's! – So! – It is as I guessed – as I knew – as I saw! – Marjorie Lindon! – Sweet Marjorie! – His dear love! – Paul Lessingham's dear love! – She with the lily face, the corn-hued hair! – What is it his dear love has found in her fond heart to write Paul Lessingham?'

Sitting up in bed he tore the packet open. It contained, perhaps, eight or nine letters – some mere notes, some long epistles. But, short or long, he devoured them with equal appetite, each one over and over again, till I thought he never would have done re-reading them. They were on thick white paper, of a peculiar shade of whiteness, with untrimmed edges. On each sheet a crest and an address were stamped in gold, and all the sheets were of the same shape and size. I told myself that if anywhere, at any time, I saw writing paper like that again, I should not fail to know it. The caligraphy was, like the paper, unusual, bold, decided, and, I should have guessed, produced by a J pen.

All the time that he was reading he kept emitting sounds, more resembling yelps and snarls than anything more human – like some savage beast nursing its pent-up rage. When he had made an end of reading – for the season – he let his passion have full vent.

'So! – That is what his dear love has found it in her heart to write Paul Lessingham! – Paul Lessingham!'

Pen cannot describe the concentrated frenzy of hatred with which the speaker dwelt upon the name – it was demoniac.

'It is enough! – it is the end! – it is his doom! He shall be ground between the upper and the nether stones in the towers of anguish, and all that is left of him shall be cast on the accursed stream of the bitter waters, to stink under the blood-grimed sun! And for her – for Marjorie Lindon! – for his dear love! – it shall come to pass that she shall wish that she was never born – nor he! – and the gods of the shadows shall smell the sweet incense of her suffering! – It shall be! it shall be! It is I that say it – even I!'

In the madness of his rhapsodical frenzy I believe that he had actually forgotten I was there. But, on a sudden, glancing aside, he saw me, and remembered – and was prompt to take advantage of an opportunity to wreak his rage upon a tangible object.

'It is you! – you thief! – you still live! – to make a mock of one of the children of the gods!'

He leaped, shrieking, off the bed, and sprang at me, clasping my throat with his horrid hands, bearing me backwards on to the floor; I felt his breath mingle with mine . . . and then God, in His mercy, sent oblivion.

# BOOK II

## THE HAUNTED MAN

### *The Story according to Sydney Atherton, Esquire*

#### CHAPTER TEN

#### REJECTED

It was after our second waltz I did it. In the usual quiet corner – which, that time, was in the shadow of a palm in the hall. Before I had got into my stride she checked me – touching my sleeve with her fan, turning towards me with startled eyes.

'Stop, please!'

But I was not to be stopped. Cliff Challoner passed, with Gerty Cazell. I fancy that, as he passed, he nodded. I did not care. I was wound up to go, and I went it. No man knows how he can talk till he does talk – to the girl he wants to marry. It is my impression that I gave her recollections of the Restoration poets. She seemed surprised – not having previously detected in me the poetic strain, and insisted on cutting in.

'Mr Atherton, I am so sorry.'

Then I did let fly.

'Sorry that I love you! – why? Why should you be sorry that you have become the one thing needful in any man's eyes – even in mine? The one thing precious – the one thing to be altogether esteemed! Is it so common for a woman to come across a man who would be willing to lay down his life for her that she should be sorry when she finds him?'

'I did not know that you felt like this, though I confess that I have had my – my doubts.'

'Doubts! – I thank you.'

'You are quite aware, Mr Atherton, that I like you very much.'

'Like me! – Bah!'

'I cannot help liking you – though it may be "bah".'

'I don't want you to like me – I want you to love me.'

'Precisely – that is your mistake.'

'My mistake! – in wanting you to love me! – when I love you –'

'Then you shouldn't – though I can't help thinking that you are mistaken even there.'

'Mistaken! – in supposing that I love you! – when I assert and reassert it with the whole force of my being! What do you want me to do to prove I love you – take you in my arms and crush you to my bosom, and make a spectacle of you before every creature in the place?'

'I'd rather you wouldn't, and perhaps you wouldn't mind not talking quite so loud. Mr Challoner seems to be wondering what you're shouting about.'

'You shouldn't torture me.'

She opened and shut her fan – as she looked down at it I am disposed to suspect that she smiled.

'I am glad we have had this little explanation, because, of course, you are my friend.'

'I am not your friend.'

'Pardon me, you are.'

'I say I'm not – if I can't be something else, I'll be no friend.'

She went on – calmly ignoring me – playing with her fan.

'As it happens, I am, just now, in rather a delicate position, in which a friend is welcome.'

'What's the matter? Who's been worrying you – your father?'

'Well – he has not – as yet; but he may be soon.'

'What's in the wind?'

'Mr Lessingham.'

She dropped her voice – and her eyes. For the moment I did not catch her meaning.

'What?'

'Your friend, Mr Lessingham.'

'Excuse me, Miss Lindon, but I am by no means sure that anyone is entitled to call Mr Lessingham a friend of mine.'

'What! – Not when I am going to be his wife?'

That took me aback. I had had my suspicions that Paul Lessingham was more with Marjorie than he had any right to be, but I had never supposed that she could see anything desirable in a stick of a man like that. Not to speak of a hundred and one other considerations – Lessingham on one side of the House, and her father on the other; and old Lindon girding at him anywhere and everywhere – with his high-dried Tory notions of his family importance – to say nothing of his fortune.

I don't know if I looked what I felt – if I did, I looked uncommonly blank.

'You have chosen an appropriate moment, Miss Lindon, to make to me such a communication.'

She chose to disregard my irony.

'I am glad you think so, because now you will understand what a difficult position I am in.'

'I offer you my hearty congratulations.'

'And I thank you for them, Mr Atherton, in the spirit in which they are offered, because from you I know they mean so much.'

I bit my lip – for the life of me I could not tell how she wished me to read her words.

'Do I understand that this announcement has been made to me as one of the public?'

'You do not. It is made to you, in confidence, as my friend – as my greatest friend; because a husband is something more than friend.' My pulses tingled. 'You will be on my side?'

She had paused – and I stayed silent.

'On your side – or Mr Lessingham's?'

'His side is my side, and my side is his side; – you will be on our side?'

'I am not sure that I altogether follow you.'

'You are the first I have told. When papa hears it is possible that there will be trouble – as you know. He thinks so much of you and of your opinion; when that trouble comes I want you to be on our side – on my side.'

'Why should I? – what does it matter? You are stronger than your father – it is just possible that Lessingham is stronger than you; together, from your father's point of view, you will be invincible.'

'You are my friend – are you not my friend?'

'In effect, you offer me an Apple of Sodom.'

'Thank you – I did not think you so unkind.'

'And you – are you kind? I make you an avowal of my love, and, straightway, you ask me to act as chorus to the love of another.'

'How could I tell you loved me – as you say! I had no notion. You have known me all your life, yet you have not breathed a word of it till now.'

'If I had spoken before?'

I imagine that there was a slight movement of her shoulders – almost amounting to a shrug.

'I do not know that it would have made any difference – I do not pretend that it would. But I do know this, I believe that you yourself have only discovered the state of your own mind within the last half-hour.'

If she had slapped my face she could not have startled me more. I had no notion if her words were uttered at random, but they came so near the truth they held me breathless. It was a fact that only during the last few minutes had I really realized how things were with me – only since the end of that first waltz that the flame had burst out in my soul which was now consuming me. She had read me by what seemed so like a flash of inspiration that I hardly knew what to say to her. I tried to be stinging.

'You flatter me, Miss Lindon, you flatter me at every point. Had you only discovered to me the state of your mind a little sooner I should not have discovered to you the state of mine at all.'

'We will consider it *terra incognita*.'

'Since you wish it.' Her provoking calmness stung me – and the suspicion that she was laughing at me in her sleeve. I gave her a glimpse of the cloven hoof. 'But, at the same time, since you assert that you have so long been innocent, I beg that you will continue so no more. At least, your innocence shall be without excuse. For I wish you to understand that I love you, that I have loved you, that I shall love you. Any understanding you may have with Mr Lessingham will not make the slightest difference. I warn you, Miss Lindon, that, until death, you will have to write me down your lover.'

She looked at me, with wide open eyes – as if I almost frightened her. To be frank, that was what I wished to do.

'Mr Atherton!'

'Miss Lindon?'

'That is not like you at all.'

'We seem to be making each other's acquaintance for the first time.'

She continued to gaze at me with her big eyes – which, to be candid, I found it difficult to meet. On a sudden her face was lighted by a smile – which I resented.

'Not after all these years – not after all these years! I know you, and though I daresay you're not flawless, I fancy you'll be found to ring pretty true.'

Her manner was almost sisterly – elder-sisterly. I could have shaken her. Hartridge coming to claim his dance gave me an opportunity to escape with such remnants of dignity as I could gather about me. He dawdled up – his thumbs, as usual, in his waistcoat pockets.

'I believe, Miss Lindon, this is our dance.'

She acknowledged it with a bow, and rose to take his arm. I got up, and left her, without a word.

As I crossed the hall I chanced on Percy Woodville. He was in his familiar state of fluster, and was gaping about him as if he had mislaid the Koh-i-noor, and wondered where in the thunder it had got to. When he saw it was I he caught me by the arm.

'I say, Atherton, have you seen Miss Lindon?'

'I have.'

'No! – Have you? – By Jove! – Where? I've been looking for her all over the place, except in the cellars and the attics – and I was just going to commence on them. This is our dance.'

'In that case, she's shunted you.'

'No! – Impossible!' His mouth went like an O – and his eyes ditto, his

THE BEETLE

eyeglass clattering down on to his shirt front. 'I expect the mistake's mine.
Fact is, I've made a mess of my programme. It's either the last dance, or this
dance, or the next, that I've booked with her, but I'm hanged if I know which.
Just take a squint at it, there's a good chap, and tell me which one you think it
is.'

I 'took a squint' – since he held the thing within an inch of my nose I could
hardly help it; one 'squint', and that was enough – and more. Some men's
ball programmes are studies in impressionism, Percy's seemed to me to be a
study in madness. It was covered with hieroglyphics, but what they meant,
or what they did there anyhow, it was absurd to suppose that I could tell – I
never put them there! – Proverbially, the man's a champion hasher.

'I regret, my dear Percy, that I am not an expert in cuneiform writing. If
you have any doubt as to which dance is yours, you'd better ask the lady –
she'll feel flattered.'

Leaving him to do his own addling I went to find my coat – I panted to get
into the open air; as for dancing I felt that I loathed it. Just as I neared the
cloakroom someone stopped me. It was Dora Grayling.

'Have you forgotten that this is our dance?'

I had forgotten – clean. And I was not obliged by her remembering.
Though as I looked at her sweet, grey eyes, and at the soft contours of her
gentle face, I felt that I deserved well kicking. She is an angel – one of the
best! – but I was in no mood for angels. Not for a very great deal would I have
gone through that dance just then, nor, with Dora Grayling, of all women in
the world, would I have sat it out. – So I was a brute and blundered.

'You must forgive me, Miss Grayling, but – I am not feeling very well,
and – I don't think I'm up to any more dancing. – Good night.'

493

CHAPTER ELEVEN

# A MIDNIGHT EPISODE

The weather out of doors was in tune with my frame of mind – I was in a deuce of a temper, and it was a deuce of a night. A keen north-east wind, warranted to take the skin right off you, was playing catch-who-catch-can with intermittent gusts of blinding rain. Since it was not fit for a dog to walk, none of your cabs for me – nothing would serve but pedestrian exercise.

So I had it.

I went down Park Lane – and the wind and rain went with me – also, thoughts of Dora Grayling. What a bounder I had been – and was! If there is anything in worse taste than to book a lady for a dance, and then to leave her in the lurch, I should like to know what that thing is – when found it ought to be made a note of. If any man of my acquaintance allowed himself to be guilty of such a felony in the first degree, I should cut him. I wished someone would try to cut me – I should like to see him at it.

It was all Marjorie's fault – everything! past, present, and to come! I had known that girl when she was in long frocks – I had, at that period of our acquaintance, pretty recently got out of them; when she was advanced to short ones; and when, once more, she returned to long. And all that time – well, I was nearly persuaded that the whole of the time I had loved her. If I had not mentioned it, it was because I had suffered my affection, 'like the worm, to lie hidden in the bud' – or whatever it is the fellow says.

At any rate, I was perfectly positive that if I had had the faintest notion that she would ever seriously consider such a man as Lessingham I should have loved her long ago. Lessingham! Why, he was old enough to be her father – at least he was a good many years older than I was. And a wretched Radical! It is true that on certain points I, also, am what some people would call a Radical – but not a Radical of the kind he is. Thank Heaven, no! No doubt I have admired traits in his character, until I learnt this thing of him. I am even prepared to admit that he is a man of ability – in his way! which is, emphatically, not mine. But to think of him in connection with such a girl as Marjorie Lindon – preposterous! – Why, the man's as dry as a stick – drier!

494

And cold as an iceberg. Nothing but a politician, absolutely. He a lover! – how I could fancy such a stroke of humour setting all the benches in a roar. Both by education, and by nature, he was incapable of even playing such a part; as for being the thing – absurd! If you were to sink a shaft from the crown of his head to the soles of his feet, you would find inside him nothing but the dry bones of parties and of politics.

What my Marjorie – if everyone had his own, she is mine, and, in that sense, she always will be mine – what my Marjorie could see in such a dry-as-dust out of which even to construct the rudiments of a husband was beyond my fathoming.

Suchlike agreeable reflections were fit company for the wind and the wet, so they bore me company all down the lane. I crossed at the corner, going round the hospital towards the square. This brought me to the abiding-place of Paul the Apostle. Like the idiot I was, I went out into the middle of the street, and stood awhile in the mud to curse him and his house – on the whole, when one considers that that is the kind of man I can be, it is, perhaps, not surprising that Marjorie disdained me.

'May your following,' I cried – it is an absolute fact that the words were shouted! – 'both in the House and out of it, no longer regard you as a leader! May your party follow after other gods! May your political aspirations wither, and your speeches be listened to by empty benches! May the Speaker persistently and strenuously refuse to allow you to catch his eye, and, at the next election, may your constituency reject you! – Jehoram! – what's that?'

I might well ask. Until that moment I had appeared to be the only lunatic at large, either outside the house or in it, but, on a sudden, a second lunatic came on the scene, and that with a vengeance. A window was crashed open from within – the one over the front door, and someone came plunging through it on to the top of the portico. That it was a case of intended suicide I made sure – and I began to be in hopes that I was about to witness the suicide of Paul. But I was not so assured of the intention when the individual in question began to scramble down the pillar of the porch in the most extraordinary fashion I ever witnessed – I was not even convinced of a suicidal purpose when he came tumbling down, and lay sprawling in the mud at my feet.

I fancy, if I had performed that portion of the act I should have lain quiet for a second or two, to consider whereabouts I was, and which end of me was uppermost. But there was no nonsense of that sort about that singularly agile stranger – if he was not made of indiarubber he ought to have been. So to speak, before he was down he was up – it was all I could do to grab at him before he was off like a rocket.

Such a figure as he presented is seldom seen – at least, in the streets of London. What he had done with the rest of his apparel I am not in a position to say – all that was left of it was a long, dark cloak which he strove to wrap round him. Save for that – and mud! – he was bare as the palm of my hand. Yet it was his face that held me. In my time I have seen strange expressions on men's faces, but never before one such as I saw on his. He looked like a man might look who, after living a life of undiluted crime, at last finds himself face to face with the devil. It was not the look of a madman – far from it; it was something worse.

It was the expression on the man's countenance, as much as anything else, which made me behave as I did. I said something to him – some nonsense, I know not what. He regarded me with a silence which was supernatural. I spoke to him again – not a word issued from those rigid lips; there was not a tremor of those awful eyes – eyes which I was tolerably convinced saw something which I had never seen, or ever should. Then I took my hand from off his shoulder, and let him go. I know not why – I did.

He had remained as motionless as a statue while I held him – indeed, for any evidence of life he gave, he might have been a statue; but, when my grasp was loosed, how he ran! He had turned the corner and was out of sight before I could say, 'How do!'

It was only then – when he had gone, and I had realized the extra-double-express-flash-of-lightning rate at which he had taken his departure – that it occurred to me of what an extremely sensible act I had been guilty in letting him go at all. Here was an individual who had been committing burglary, or something very like it, in the house of a budding cabinet minister, and who had tumbled plump into my arms, so that all I had to do was to call a policeman and get him quodded – and all that I had done was something of a totally different kind.

'You're a nice type of an ideal citizen!' I was addressing myself. 'A first chop specimen of a low-down idiot – to connive at the escape of the robber who's been robbing Paul. Since you've let the villain go, the least you can do is to leave a card on the Apostle, and inquire how he's feeling.'

I went to Lessingham's front door and knocked – I knocked once, I knocked twice, I knocked thrice, and the third time, I give you my word, I made the echoes ring – but still there was not a soul that answered.

'If this is a case of a seven or seventy-fold murder, and the gentleman in the cloak had made a fair clearance of every living creature the house contains, perhaps it's just as well I've chanced upon the scene – still I do think that one of the corpses might get up to answer the door. If it is possible to make noise enough to waken the dead, you bet I'm on to it.'

And I was – I punished that knocker! until I warrant the pounding I gave it was audible on the other side of Green Park. And, at last, I woke the dead – or rather, I roused Matthews to a consciousness that something was going on.

Opening the door about six inches, through the interstice he protruded his ancient nose.

'Who's there?'

'Nothing, my dear sir, nothing and no one. It must have been your vigorous imagination which induced you to suppose that there was – you let it run away with you.'

Then he knew me – and opened the door about two feet.

'Oh, it's you, Mr Atherton. I beg your pardon, sir – I thought it might have been the police.'

'What then? Do you stand in terror of the minions of the law – at last?'

A most discreet servant, Matthews – just the fellow for a budding cabinet minister. He glanced over his shoulder – I had suspected the presence of a colleague at his back, now I was assured. He put his hand up to his mouth – and I thought how exceedingly discreet he looked, in his trousers and his stockinged feet, and with his hair all rumpled, and his braces dangling behind, and his nightshirt creased.

'Well, sir, I have received instructions not to admit the police.'

'The deuce you have! – From whom?'

Coughing behind his hand, leaning forward, he addressed me with an air which was flatteringly confidential.

'From Mr Lessingham, sir.'

'Possibly Mr Lessingham is not aware that a robbery has been committed on his premises, that the burglar has just come out of his drawing-room window with a hop, skip, and a jump, bounded out of the window like a tennis-ball, flashed round the corner like a rocket.'

Again Matthews glanced over his shoulder, as if not clear which way discretion lay, whether fore or aft.

'Thank you, sir. I believe that Mr Lessingham is aware of something of the kind.' He seemed to come to a sudden resolution, dropping his voice to a whisper. 'The fact is, sir, that I fancy Mr Lessingham's a good deal upset.'

'Upset?' I stared at him. There was something in his manner I did not understand. 'What do you mean by upset? Has the scoundrel attempted violence?'

'Who's there?'

The voice was Lessingham's, calling to Matthews from the staircase, though, for an instant, I hardly recognized it, it was so curiously petulant. Pushing past Matthews, I stepped into the hall. A young man, I suppose a footman, in the same undress as Matthews, was holding a candle – it seemed the only light about the place. By its glimmer I perceived Lessingham standing halfway up the stairs. He was in full war paint – as he is not the sort of man who dresses for the House, I took it that he had been mixing pleasure with business.

'It's I, Lessingham – Atherton. Do you know that a fellow has jumped out of your drawing-room window?'

It was a second or two before he answered. When he did, his voice had lost its petulance.

'Has he escaped?'

'Clean – he's a mile away by now.'

It seemed to me that in his tone, when he spoke again, there was a note of relief.

'I wondered if he had. Poor fellow! more sinned against than sinning! Take my advice, Atherton, and keep out of politics. They bring you into contact with all the lunatics at large. Good night! I am much obliged to you for knocking us up. Matthews, shut the door.'

Tolerably cool, on my honour – a man who brings news big with the fate of Rome does not expect to receive such treatment. He expects to be listened to with deference, and to hear all that there is to hear, and not to be sent to the rightabout before he has had a chance of really opening his lips. Before I knew it – almost! – the door was shut, and I was on the doorstep. Confound the Apostle's impudence! next time he might have his house burnt down – and him in it! – before I took the trouble to touch his dirty knocker.

What did he mean by his allusion to lunatics in politics – did he think to fool me? There was more in the business than met the eye – and a good deal more than he wished to meet mine – hence his insolence. The creature.

What Marjorie Lindon could see in such an opusculum surpassed my comprehension; especially when there was a man of my sort walking about who adored the very ground she trod upon.

## CHAPTER TWELVE

# A MORNING VISITOR

All through the night, waking and sleeping, and in my dreams, I wondered what Marjorie could see in him! In those same dreams I satisfied myself that she could, and did, see nothing in him, but everything in me – oh the comfort! The misfortune was that when I awoke I knew it was the other way round – so that it was a sad awakening. An awakening to thoughts of murder.

So, swallowing a mouthful and a peg, I went into my laboratory to plan murder – legalized murder – on the biggest scale it ever has been planned. I was on the track of a weapon which would make war not only an affair of a single campaign, but of a single half-hour. It would not want an army to work it either. Once let an individual, or two or three at most, in possession of my weapon-that-was-to-be, get within a mile or so of even the largest body of disciplined troops that ever yet a nation put into the field, and – pouf! – in about the time it takes you to say that they would be all dead men. If weapons of precision, which may be relied upon to slay, are preservers of the peace – and the man is a fool who says that they are not! – then I was within reach of the finest preserver of the peace imagination ever yet conceived.

What a sublime thought to think that in the hollow of your own hand lies the life and death of nations – and it was almost in mine.

I had in front of me some of the finest destructive agents you could wish to light upon – carbon-monoxide, chlorine-trioxide, mercuric-oxide, conine, potassamide, potassium-carboxide, cyanogen – when Edwards entered. I was wearing a mask of my own invention, a thing that covered ears and head and everything, something like a diver's helmet – I was dealing with gases a sniff of which meant death; only a few days before, unmasked, I had been doing some fool's trick with a couple of acids – sulphuric and cyanide of potassium – when, somehow, my hand slipped, and, before I knew it, minute portions of them combined. By the mercy of Providence I fell backwards instead of forwards – sequel, about an hour afterwards Edwards found me on the floor, and it took the remainder of that day, and most of the doctors in town, to bring me back to life again.

Edwards announced his presence by touching me on the shoulder – when I am wearing that mask it isn't always easy to make me hear.

'Someone wishes to see you, sir.'

'Then tell someone that I don't wish to see him.'

Well-trained servant, Edwards – he walked off with the message as decorously as you please. And then I thought there was an end – but there wasn't.

I was regulating the valve of a cylinder in which I was fusing some oxides when, once more, someone touched me on the shoulder. Without turning I took it for granted it was Edwards back again.

'I have only to give a tiny twist to this tap, my good fellow, and you will be in the land where the bogies bloom. Why will you come where you're not wanted?' Then I looked round. 'Who the devil are you?'

For it was not Edwards at all, but quite a different class of character.

I found myself confronting an individual who might almost have sat for one of the bogies I had just alluded to. His costume was reminiscent of the 'Algerians' whom one finds all over France, and who are the most persistent, insolent and amusing of pedlars. I remember one who used to haunt the *répétitions* at the Alcazar at Tours – but there! This individual was like the originals, yet unlike – he was less gaudy and a good deal dingier, than his Gallic prototypes are apt to be. Then he wore a burnoose – the yellow, grimy-looking article of the Arab of the Soudan, not the spick and span Arab of the boulevard. Chief difference of all his face was clean shaven – and whoever saw an Algerian of Paris whose chiefest glory was not his well-trimmed moustache and beard?

I expected that he would address me in the lingo which these gentlemen call French – but he didn't.

'You are Mr Atherton?'

'And you are Mr – Who? – how did you come here? Where's my servant?'

The fellow held up his hand. As he did so, as if in accordance with a pre-arranged signal, Edwards came into the room looking excessively startled. I turned to him.

'Is this the person who wished to see me?'

'Yes, sir.'

'Didn't I tell you to say that I didn't wish to see him?'

'Yes, sir.'

'Then why didn't you do as I told you?'

'I did, sir.'

'Then how comes he here?'

'Really, sir,' – Edwards put his hand up to his head as if he was half asleep – 'I don't quite know.'

'What do you mean by you don't know? Why didn't you stop him?'

'I think, sir, that I must have had a touch of sudden faintness, because I tried to put out my hand to stop him, and – I couldn't.'

'You're an idiot. – Go!' And he went. I turned to the stranger. 'Pray, sir, are you a magician?'

He replied to my question with another.

'You, Mr Atherton – are you also a magician?'

He was staring at my mask with an evident lack of comprehension.

'I wear this because, in this place, death lurks in so many subtle forms, that, without it, I dare not breathe.' He inclined his head – though I doubt if he understood. 'Be so good as to tell me, briefly, what it is you wish with me.'

He slipped his hand into the folds of his burnoose, and, taking out a slip of paper, laid it on the shelf by which we were standing. I glanced at it, expecting to find on it a petition, or a testimonial, or a true statement of his sad case; instead it contained two words only – 'Marjorie Lindon'. The unlooked-for sight of that well-loved name brought the blood into my cheeks.

'You come from Miss Lindon?'

He narrowed his shoulders, brought his finger-tips together, inclined his head, in a fashion which was peculiarly Oriental, but not particularly explanatory – so I repeated my question.

'Do you wish me to understand that you do come from Miss Lindon?'

Again he slipped his hand into his burnoose, again he produced a slip of paper, again he laid it on the shelf, again I glanced at it, again nothing was written on it but a name – 'Paul Lessingham'.

'Well? – I see – Paul Lessingham. What then?'

'She is good – he is bad – is it not so?'

He touched first one scrap of paper, then the other. I stared.

'Pray how do you happen to know?'

'He shall never have her – eh?'

'What on earth do you mean?'

'Ah! – what do I mean!'

'Precisely, what do you mean? And also, and at the same time, who the devil are you?'

'It is as a friend I come to you.'

'Then in that case you may go; I happen to be over-stocked in that line just now.'

'Not with the kind of friend I am!'

'The saints forfend!'

'You love her – you love Miss Lindon! Can you bear to think of him in her arms?'

I took off my mask – feeling that the occasion required it. As I did so he brushed aside the hanging folds of the hood of his burnoose, so that I saw more of his face. I was immediately conscious that in his eyes there was, in an especial degree, what, for want of a better term, one may call the mesmeric quality. That his was one of those morbid organizations which are oftener found, thank goodness, in the east than in the west, and which are apt to exercise an uncanny influence over the weak and the foolish folk with whom they come in contact – the kind of creature for whom it is always just as well to keep a seasoned rope close handy. I was, also, conscious that he was taking advantage of the removal of my mask to try his strength on me – than which he could not have found a tougher job. The sensitive something which is found in the hypnotic subject happens, in me, to be wholly absent.

'I see you are a mesmerist.'

He started.

'I am nothing – a shadow!'

'And I'm a scientist. I should like, with your permission – or without it! – to try an experiment or two on you.'

He moved further back. There came a gleam into his eyes which suggested that he possessed his hideous power to an unusual degree – that, in the estimation of his own people, he was qualified to take his standing as a regular devil-doctor.

'We will try experiments together, you and I – on Paul Lessingham.'

'Why on him?'

'You do not know?'

'I do not.'

'Why do you lie to me?'

'I don't lie to you – I haven't the faintest notion what is the nature of your interest in Mr Lessingham.'

'My interest? – that is another thing; it is your interest of which we are speaking.'

'Pardon me – it is yours.'

'Listen! you love her – and he! But at a word from you he shall not have her – never! It is I who say it – I!'

'And, once more, sir, who are you?'

'I am of the children of Isis!'

'Is that so? – It occurs to me that you have made a slight mistake – this is London, not a dog-hole in the desert.'

'Do I not know? – what does it matter? – you shall see! There will come a time when you will want me – you will find that you cannot bear to think of him in her arms – her whom you love! You will call to me, and I shall come, and of Paul Lessingham there shall be an end.'

While I was wondering whether he was really as mad as he sounded, or whether he was some impudent charlatan who had an axe of his own to grind, and thought that he had found in me a grindstone, he had vanished from the room. I moved after him.

'Hang it all! – stop!' I cried.

He must have made pretty good travelling, because, before I had a foot in the hall, I heard the front door slam, and, when I reached the street, intent on calling him back, neither to the right nor to the left was there a sign of him to be seen.

CHAPTER THIRTEEN

# THE PICTURE

'I wonder what that nice-looking beggar really means, and who he happens to be?' That was what I said to myself when I returned to the laboratory. 'If it is true that, now and again, Providence does write a man's character on his face, then there can't be the slightest shred of a doubt that a curious one's been written on his. I wonder what his connection has been with the Apostle – or if it's only part of his game of bluff.'

I strode up and down – for the moment my interest in the experiments I was conducting had waned.

'If it was all bluff I never saw a better piece of acting – and yet what sort of finger can such a precisian as St Paul have in such a pie? The fellow seemed to squirm at the mere mention of the rising-hope-of-the-Radical's name. Can the objection be political? Let me consider – what has Lessingham done which could offend the religious or patriotic susceptibilities of the most fanatical of Orientals? Politically, I can recall nothing. Foreign affairs, as a rule, he has carefully eschewed. If he has offended – and if he hasn't the seeming was uncommonly good! – the cause will have to be sought upon some other track. But, then, what track?'

The more I strove to puzzle it out, the greater the puzzlement grew.

'Absurd! – The rascal has had no more connection with St Paul than St Peter. The probability is that he's a crack-pot; and if he isn't, he has some little game on foot – in close association with the hunt of the oof-bird! – which he tried to work off on me, but couldn't. As for – for Marjorie – my Marjorie! – only she isn't mine, confound it! – if I had had my senses about me, I should have broken his head in several places for daring to allow her name to pass his lips – the unbaptized Mohammedan! – Now to return to the chase of splendid murder!'

I snatched up my mask – one of the most ingenious inventions, by the way, of recent years; if the armies of the future wear my mask they will defy my weapon! – and was about to re-adjust it in its place, when someone knocked at the door.

'Who's there? – Come in!'

It was Edwards. He looked round him as if surprised.

'I beg your pardon, sir – I thought you were engaged. I didn't know that – that gentleman had gone.'

'He went up the chimney, as all that kind of gentlemen do. – Why the deuce did you let him in when I told you not to?'

'Really, sir, I don't know. I gave him your message, and – he looked at me, and – that is all I remember till I found myself standing in this room.'

Had it not been Edwards I might have suspected him of having had his palm well greased – but, in his case, I knew better. It was as I thought – my visitor was a mesmerist of the first class; he had actually played some of his tricks, in broad daylight, on my servant, at my own front door – a man worth studying. Edwards continued:

'There is someone else, sir, who wishes to see you – Mr Lessingham.'

'Mr Lessingham!' At that moment the juxtaposition seemed odd, though I daresay it was so rather in appearance than in reality. 'Show him in.'

Presently in came Paul.

I am free to confess – I have owned it before! – that, in a sense, I admire that man – so long as he does not presume to thrust himself into a certain position. He possesses physical qualities which please my eye – speaking as a mere biologist. I like the suggestion conveyed by his every pose, his every movement, of a tenacious hold on life – of reserve force, of a repository of bone and gristle on which he can fall back at pleasure. The fellow's lithe and active; not hasty, yet agile; clean built, well hung – the sort of man who might be relied upon to make a good recovery. You might beat him in a sprint – mental or physical – though to do that you would have to be spry! – but in a staying race he would see you out. I do not know that he is exactly the kind of man whom I would trust – unless I knew that he was on the job – which knowledge, in his case, would be uncommonly hard to attain. He is too calm; too self-contained; with the knack of looking all round him even in moments of extremest peril – and for whatever he does he has a good excuse. He has the reputation, both in the House and out of it, of being a man of iron nerve – and with some reason; yet I am not so sure. Unless I read him wrongly his is one of those individualities which, confronted by certain eventualities, collapse – to rise, the moment of trial having passed, like Phoenix from her ashes. However it might be with his adherents, he would show no trace of his disaster.

And this was the man whom Marjorie loved. Well, she could show some cause. He was a man of position – destined, probably, to rise much higher; a man of parts – with capacity to make the most of them; not ill-looking; with agreeable manners – when he chose; and he came within the lady's definition of a gentleman, 'he always did the right thing, at the right time, in the right way.' And yet –! Well, I take it that we are all cads, and that we most of us are prigs; for mercy's sake do not let us all give ourselves away.

He was dressed as a gentleman should be dressed – black frock coat, black vest, dark grey trousers, stand-up collar, smartly-tied bow, gloves of the proper shade, neatly brushed hair, and a smile, which if it was not childlike, at any rate was bland.

'I am not disturbing you?'

'Not at all.'

'Sure? – I never enter a place like this, where a man is matching himself with nature, to wrest from her her secrets, without feeling that I am crossing the threshold of the unknown. The last time I was in this room was just after you had taken out the final patents for your System of Telegraphy at Sea, which the Admiralty purchased – wisely. – What is it, now?'

'Death.'

'No? – really? – what do you mean?'

'If you are a member of the next government, you will possibly learn; I may offer them the refusal of a new wrinkle in the art of murder.'

'I see – a new projectile. How long is this race to continue between attack and defence?'

'Until the sun grows cold.'

'And then?'

'There'll be no defence – nothing to defend.'

He looked at me with his calm, grave eyes.

'The theory of the Age of Ice towards which we are advancing is not a cheerful one.' He began to finger a glass retort which lay upon a table. 'By the way, it was very good of you to give me a look in last night. I am afraid you thought me peremptory – I have come to apologize.'

'I don't know that I thought you peremptory; I thought you – queer.'

'Yes.' He glanced at me with that expressionless look upon his face which he could summon at will, and which is at the bottom of the superstition about his iron nerve. 'I was worried, and not well. Besides, one doesn't care to be burgled, even by a maniac.'

'Was he a maniac?'

'Did you see him?'

'Very clearly.'

'Where?'

'In the street.'

'How close were you to him?'

'Closer than I am to you.'

'Indeed. I didn't know you were so close to him as that. Did you try to stop him?'

'Easier said than done – he was off at such a rate.'

'Did you see how he was dressed – or, rather, undressed?'

'I did.'

'In nothing but a cloak on such a night. Who but a lunatic would have attempted burglary in such a costume?'

'Did he take anything?'

'Absolutely nothing.'

'It seems to have been a curious episode.'

He moved his eyebrows – according to members of the House the only gesture in which he has been known to indulge.

'We become accustomed to curious episodes. Oblige me by not mentioning it to anyone – to anyone.' He repeated the last two words, as if to give them emphasis. I wondered if he was thinking of Marjorie. 'I am communicating with the police. Until they move I don't want it to get into the papers – or to be talked about. It's a worry – you understand?'

I nodded. He changed the theme.

'This that you're engaged upon – is it a projectile or a weapon?'

'If you are a member of the next government you will possibly know; if you aren't you possibly won't.'

'I suppose you have to keep this sort of thing secret?'

'I do. It seems that matters of much less moment you wish to keep secret.'

'You mean that business of last night? If a trifle of that sort gets into the papers, or gets talked about – which is the same thing! – you have no notion how we are pestered. It becomes an almost unbearable nuisance. Jones the Unknown can commit murder with less inconvenience to himself than Jones the Notorious can have his pocket picked – there is not so much exaggeration in that as there sounds. – Good-bye – thanks for your promise.' I had given him no promise, but that was by the way. He turned as to go – then stopped. 'There's another thing – I believe you're a specialist on questions of ancient superstitions and extinct religions.'

'I am interested in such subjects, but I am not a specialist.'

'Can you tell me what were the exact tenets of the worshippers of Isis?'

'Neither I nor any man – with scientific certainty. As you know, she had a brother; the cult of Osiris and Isis was one and the same. What, precisely, were its dogmas, or its practices, or anything about it, none, now, can tell. The Papyri, hieroglyphics, and so on, which remain are very far from being exhaustive, and our knowledge of those which do remain, is still less so.'

'I suppose that the marvels which are told of it are purely legendary?'

'To what marvels do you particularly refer?'

'Weren't supernatural powers attributed to the priests of Isis?'

'Broadly speaking, at that time, supernatural powers were attributed to all the priests of all the creeds.'

'I see.' Presently he continued. 'I presume that her cult is long since extinct – that none of the worshippers of Isis exist today.'

I hesitated – I was wondering why he had hit on such a subject; if he really had a reason, or if he was merely asking questions as a cover for something else – you see, I knew my Paul.

'That is not so sure.'

He looked at me with that passionless, yet searching glance of his.

'You think that she still is worshipped?'

'I think it possible, even probable, that, here and there, in Africa – Africa is a large order! – homage is paid to Isis, quite in the good old way.'

'Do you know that as a fact?'

'Excuse me, but do you know it as a fact? – Are you aware that you are treating me as if I was on the witness stand? – Have you any special purpose in making these inquiries?'

He smiled.

'In a kind of a way I have. I have recently come across rather a curious story; I am trying to get to the bottom of it.'

'What is the story?'

'I am afraid that at present I am not at liberty to tell it you; when I am I will. You will find it interesting – as an instance of a singular survival. – Didn't the followers of Isis believe in transmigration?'

'Some of them – no doubt.'

'What did they understand by transmigration?'

'Transmigration.'

'Yes – but of the soul or of the body?'

'How do you mean? – transmigration is transmigration. Are you driving at something in particular? If you'll tell me fairly and squarely what it is I'll do my best to give you the information you require; as it is, your questions are a bit perplexing.'

'Oh, it doesn't matter – as you say, "transmigration is transmigration."' I was eyeing him keenly; I seemed to detect in his manner an odd reluctance to enlarge on the subject he himself had started. He continued to trifle with the retort upon the table. 'Hadn't the followers of Isis a – what shall I say? – a sacred emblem?'

'How?'

'Hadn't they an especial regard for some sort of a – wasn't it some sort of a – beetle?'

'You mean *Scarabæus sacer* – according to Latreille, *Scarabæus Egyp-*

*tiorum*? Undoubtedly – the scarab was venerated throughout Egypt – indeed, speaking generally, most things that had life, for instance, cats, as you know, Orisis continued among men in the figure of Apis the bull.'

'Weren't the priests of Isis – or some of them – supposed to assume, after death, the form of a – scarabæus?'

'I never heard of it.'

'Are you sure? – think!'

'I shouldn't like to answer such a question positively, offhand, but I don't, on the spur of the moment, recall any supposition of the kind.'

'Don't laugh at me – I'm not a lunatic! – but I understand that recent researches have shown that even in some of the most astounding of the ancient legends there was a substratum of fact. Is it absolutely certain that there could be no shred of truth in such a belief?'

'In what belief?'

'In the belief that a priest of Isis – or anyone – assumed after death the form of a scarabæus?'

'It seems to me, Lessingham, that you have lately come across some uncommonly interesting data, of a kind, too, which it is your bounden duty to give to the world – or, at any rate, to that portion of the world which is represented by me. Come – tell us all about it! – what are you afraid of?'

'I am afraid of nothing – and some day you shall be told – but not now. At present, answer my question.'

'Then repeat your question – clearly.'

'Is it absolutely certain that there could be no foundation of truth in the belief that a priest of Isis – or anyone – assumed after death the form of a beetle?'

'I know no more than the man in the moon – how the dickens should I? Such a belief may have been symbolical. Christians believe that after death the body takes the shape of worms – and so, in a sense, it does – and, sometimes, eels.'

'That is not what I mean.'

'Then what do you mean?'

'Listen. If a person, of whose veracity there could not be a vestige of a doubt, assured you that he had seen such a transformation actually take place, could it conceivably be explained on natural grounds?'

'Seen a priest of Isis assume the form of a beetle?'

'Or a follower of Isis?'

'Before, or after death?'

He hesitated. I had seldom seen him wear such an appearance of interest – to be frank, I was keenly interested too! – but, on a sudden there came into his eyes a glint of something that was almost terror. When he spoke, it was with the most unwonted awkwardness.

'In – in the very act of dying.'

'In the very act of dying?'

'If – he had seen a follower of Isis in – the very act of dying, assume – the form of a – a beetle, on any conceivable grounds would such a transformation be susceptible of natural explanation?'

I stared – as who would not? Such an extraordinary question was rendered more extraordinary by coming from such a man – yet I was almost beginning to suspect that there was something behind it more extraordinary still.

'Look here, Lessingham, I can see you've a capital tale to tell – so tell it, man! Unless I'm mistaken, it's not the kind of tale in which ordinary scruples can have any part or parcel – anyhow, it's hardly fair of you to set my curiosity all agog, and then to leave it unappeased.'

He eyed me steadily, the appearance of interest fading more and more, until, presently, his face assumed its wonted expressionless mask – somehow I was conscious that what he had seen in my face was not altogether to his liking. His voice was once more bland and self-contained.

'I perceive you are of opinion that I have been told a tarradiddle. I suppose I have.'

'But what is the tarradiddle? – don't you see I'm burning?'

'Unfortunately, Atherton, I am on my honour. Until I have permission to unloose it, my tongue is tied.' He picked up his hat and umbrella from where he had placed them on the table. Holding them in his left hand, he advanced to me with his right outstretched. 'It is very good of you to suffer my continued interruption; I know, to my sorrow, what such interruptions mean – believe me, I am not ungrateful. What is this?'

On the shelf, within a foot or so of where I stood, was a sheet of paper – the size and shape of half a sheet of post note. At this he stooped to glance. As he did so, something surprising occurred. On the instant a look came on to his face which, literally, transfigured him. His hat and umbrella fell from his grasp on to the floor. He retreated, gibbering, his hands held out as if to ward something off from him, until he reached the wall on the other side of the room. A more amazing spectacle than he presented I never saw.

'Lessingham!' I exclaimed. 'What's wrong with you?'

My first impression was that he was struck by a fit of epilepsy – though anyone less like an epileptic subject it would be hard to find. In my bewilderment I looked round to see what could be the immediate cause. My eye fell upon the sheet of paper. I stared at it with considerable surprise. I had not noticed it there previously, I had not put it there – where had it come from? The curious thing was that, on it, produced apparently by some

process of photogravure, was an illustration of a species of beetle with which I
felt that I ought to be acquainted, and yet was not. It was of a dull golden
green; the colour was so well brought out – even to the extent of seeming to
scintillate, and the whole thing was so dexterously done that the creature
seemed alive. The semblance of reality was, indeed, so vivid that it needed a
second glance to be assured that it was a mere trick of the reproducer. Its
presence there was odd – after what we had been talking about it might seem
to need explanation; but it was absurd to suppose that that alone could have
had such an effect on a man like Lessingham.

With the thing in my hand, I crossed to where he was – pressing his back
against the wall, he had shrunk lower inch by inch till he was actually
crouching on his haunches.

'Lessingham! – come, man, what's wrong with you?'

Taking him by the shoulder, I shook him with some vigour. My touch had
on him the effect of seeming to wake him out of a dream, of restoring him to
consciousness as against the nightmare horrors with which he was struggling. He gazed up at me with that look of cunning on his face which one
associates with abject terror.

'Atherton? – Is it you? – It's all right – quite right – I'm well – very well.'

As he spoke, he slowly drew himself up, till he was standing erect.

'Then, in that case, all I can say is that you have a queer way of being very
well.'

He put his hand up to his mouth, as if to hide the trembling of his lips.

'It's the pressure of overwork – I've had one or two attacks like this – but
it's nothing, only – a local lesion.'

I observed him keenly; to my thinking there was something about him
which was very odd indeed.

'Only a local lesion! – If you take my strongly-urged advice you'll get a
medical opinion without delay – if you haven't been wise enough to have
done so already.'

'I'll go today – at once; but I know it's only mental overstrain.'

'You're sure it's nothing to do with this?'

I held out in front of him the photogravure of the beetle. As I did so he
backed away from me, shrieking, trembling as with palsy.

'Take it away! take it away!' he screamed.

I stared at him, for some seconds, astonished into speechlessness. Then I
found my tongue.

'Lessingham! – It's only a picture! – Are you stark mad?'

He persisted in his ejaculations.

'Take it away! take it away! – Tear it up! – Burn it!'

His agitation was so unnatural – from whatever cause it arose! – that, fearing the recurrence of the attack from which he had just recovered, I did as he bade me. I tore the sheet of paper into quarters, and, striking a match, set fire to each separate piece. He watched the process of incineration as if fascinated. When it was concluded, and nothing but ashes remained, he gave a gasp of relief.

'Lessingham,' I said, 'you're either mad already, or you're going mad – which is it?'

'I think it's neither. I believe I am as sane as you. It's – it's that story of which I was speaking; it – it seems curious, but I'll tell you all about it – some day. As I observed, I think you will find it an interesting instance of a singular survival.' He made an obvious effort to become more like his usual self. 'It is extremely unfortunate, Atherton, that I should have troubled you with such a display of weakness – especially as I am able to offer you so scant an explanation. One thing I would ask of you – to observe strict confidence. What has taken place has been between ourselves. I am in your hands, but you are my friend, I know I can rely on you not to speak of it to anyone – and, in particular, not to breathe a hint of it to Miss Lindon.'

'Why, in particular, not to Miss Lindon?'

'Can you not guess?'

I hunched my shoulder.

'If what I guess is what you mean, is not that a cause the more why silence would be unfair to her?'

'It is for me to speak, if for anyone. I shall not fail to do what should be done. – Give me your promise that you will not hint a word to her of what you have so unfortunately seen?'

I gave him the promise he required.

There was no more work for me that day. The Apostle, his divagations, his example of the coleoptera, his Arabian friend – these things were as microbes which, acting on a system already predisposed for their reception, produced high fever; I was in a fever – of unrest. Brain in a whirl! – Marjorie, Paul, Isis, beetle, mesmerism, in delirious jumble. Love's upsetting! – in itself a sufficiently severe disease; but when complications intervene, suggestive of mystery and novelties, so that you do not know if you are moving in an atmosphere of dreams or of frozen facts – if, then, your temperature does not rise, like that rocket of M. Verne's – which reached the moon, then you are a freak of an entirely genuine kind, and if the surgeons do not preserve you, and place you on view, in pickle, they ought to for the sake of historical doubters, for no one will believe that there ever was a man like you, unless you yourself are somewhere around to prove them Thomases.

Myself – I am not that kind of man. When I get warm I grow heated, and when I am heated there is likely to be a variety show of a gaudy kind. When Paul had gone I tried to think things out, and if I had kept on trying something would have happened – so I went on the river instead.

### CHAPTER FOURTEEN

## THE DUCHESS' BALL

That night was the Duchess of Datchet's ball – the first person I saw as I entered the dancing-room was Dora Grayling.

I went straight up to her.

'Miss Grayling, I behaved very badly to you last night. I have come to make to you my apologies – to sue for your forgiveness!'

'My forgiveness?' Her head went back – she has a pretty bird-like trick of cocking it a little on one side. 'You were not well. Are you better?'

'Quite. – You forgive me? Then grant me plenary absolution by giving me a dance for the one I lost last night.'

She rose. A man came up – a stranger to me; she's one of the best hunted women in England – there's a million with her.

'This is my dance, Miss Grayling.'

She looked at him.

'You must excuse me. I am afraid I have made a mistake. I had forgotten that I was already engaged.'

I had not thought her capable of it. She took my arm, and away we went, and left him staring.

'It's he who's the sufferer now,' I whispered, as we went round – she can waltz!

'You think so? It was I last night – I did not mean, if I could help it, to suffer again. To me a dance with you means something.' She went all red – adding, as an afterthought, 'Nowadays so few men really dance. I expect it's because you dance so well.'

'Thank you.'

We danced the waltz right through, then we went to an impromptu shelter which had been rigged up on a balcony. And we talked. There's something sympathetic about Miss Grayling which leads one to talk about one's self – before I was half aware of it I was telling her of all my plans and projects – actually telling her of my latest notion which, ultimately, was to result in the

THE BEETLE

destruction of whole armies as by a flash of lightning. She took an amount of interest in it which was surprising.

'What really stands in the way of things of this sort is not theory but practice – one can prove one's facts on paper, or on a small scale in a room; what is wanted is proof on a large scale, by actual experiment. If, for instance, I could take my plant to one of the forests of South America, where there is plenty of animal life but no human, I could demonstrate the soundness of my position then and there.'

'Why don't you?'

'Think of the money it would cost.'

'I thought I was a friend of yours.'

'I had hoped you were.'

'Then why don't you let me help you?'

'Help me? – How?'

'By letting you have the money for your South American experiment – it would be an investment on which I should expect to receive good interest.'

I fidgeted.

'It is very good of you, Miss Grayling, to talk like that.'

She became quite frigid.

'Please don't be absurd! – I perceive quite clearly that you are snubbing me, and that you are trying to do it as delicately as you know how.'

'Miss Grayling!'

'I understand that it was an impertinence on my part to volunteer assistance which was unasked; you have made that sufficiently plain.'

'I assure you –'

'Pray don't. Of course, if it had been Miss Lindon it would have been different; she would at least have received a civil answer. But we are not all Miss Lindon.'

I was aghast. The outburst was so uncalled for – I had not the faintest notion what I had said or done to cause it; she was in such a surprising passion – and it suited her! – I thought I had never seen her look prettier – I could do nothing else but stare. So she went on – with just as little reason.

'Here is someone coming to claim this dance – I can't throw all my partners over. Have I offended you so irremediably that it will be impossible for you to dance with me again?'

'Miss Grayling! – I shall be only too delighted.' She handed me her card. 'Which may I have?'

'For your own sake you had better place it as far off as you possibly can.'

'They all seem taken.'

'That doesn't matter; strike off any name you please, anywhere and put your own instead.'

515

It was giving me an almost embarrassingly free hand. I booked myself for the next waltz but two – who it was who would have to give way to me I did not trouble to inquire.

'Mr Atherton! – Is that you?'

It was – it was also she. It was Marjorie! And so soon as I saw her I knew that there was only one woman in the world for me – the mere sight of her sent the blood tingling through my veins. Turning to her attendant cavalier, she dismissed him with a bow.

'Is there an empty chair?'

She seated herself in the one Miss Grayling had just vacated. I sat down beside her. She glanced at me, laughter in her eyes.. I was all in a stupid tremblement.

'You remember that last night I told you that I might require your friendly services in diplomatic intervention?' I nodded – I felt that the allusion was unfair. 'Well, the occasion's come – or, at least, it's very near.' She was still – and I said nothing to help her. 'You know how unreasonable papa can be.'

I did – never a more pig-headed man in England than Geoffrey Lindon – or, in a sense, a duller. But, just then, I was not prepared to admit it to his child.

'You know what an absurd objection he has to – Paul.'

There was an appreciative hesitation before she uttered the fellow's Christian name – when it came it was with an accent of tenderness which stung me like a gadfly. To speak to me – of all men – of the fellow in such a tone was – like a woman.

'Has Mr Lindon no notion of how things stand between you?'

'Except what he suspects. That is just where you are to come in, papa thinks so much of you – I want you to sound Paul's praises in his ear – to prepare him for what must come.' Was ever rejected lover burdened with such a task? Its enormity kept me still. 'Sydney, you have always been my friend – my truest, dearest friend. When I was a little girl you used to come between papa and me, to shield me from his wrath. Now that I am a big girl I want you to be on my side once more, and to shield me still.'

Her voice softened. She laid her hand upon my arm. How, under her touch, I burned.

'But I don't understand what cause there has been for secrecy – why should there have been any secrecy from the first?'

'It was Paul's wish that papa should not be told.'

'Is Mr Lessingham ashamed of you?'

'Sydney!'

'Or does he fear your father?'

'You are unkind. You know perfectly well that papa has been prejudiced against him all along, you know that his political position is just now one of the greatest difficulty, that every nerve and muscle is kept on the continual strain, that it is in the highest degree essential that further complications of every and any sort should be avoided. He is quite aware that his suit will not be approved of by papa, and he simply wishes that nothing shall be said about it till the end of the session – that is all.'

'I see! Mr Lessingham is cautious even in love-making – politician first, and lover afterwards.'

'Well! – why not? – would you have him injure the cause he has at heart for want of a little patience?'

'It depends what cause it is he has at heart.'

'What is the matter with you? – why do you speak to me like that? – it is not like you at all.' She looked at me shrewdly, with flashing eyes. 'Is it possible that you are – jealous? – that you were in earnest in what you said last night? – I thought that was the sort of thing you said to every girl.'

I would have given a great deal to take her in my arms, and press her to my bosom then and there – to think that she should taunt me with having said to her the sort of thing I said to every girl.

'What do you know of Mr Lessingham?'

'What all the world knows – that history will be made by him.'

'There are kinds of history in the making of which one would not desire to be associated. What do you know of his private life – it was to that that I was referring.'

'Really – you go too far. I know that he is one of the best, just as he is one of the greatest, of men; for me, that is sufficient.'

'If you do know that, it is sufficient.'

'I do know it – all the world knows it. Everyone with whom he comes in contact is aware – must be aware, that he is incapable of a dishonourable thought or action.'

'Take my advice, don't appreciate any man too highly. In the book of every man's life there is a page which he would wish to keep turned down.'

'There is no such page in Paul's – there may be in yours; I think that probable.'

'Thank you. I fear it is more than probable. I fear that, in my case, the page may extend to several. There is nothing Apostolic about me – not even the name.'

'Sydney! – you are unendurable! – It is the more strange to hear you talk like this since Paul regards you as his friend.'

'He flatters me.'

'Are you not his friend?'

'Is it not sufficient to be yours?'

'No – who is against Paul is against me.'

'That is hard.'

'How is it hard? Who is against the husband can hardly be for the wife – when the husband and the wife are one.'

'But as yet you are not one. – Is my cause so hopeless?'

'What do you call your cause? – are you thinking of that nonsense you were talking about last night?'

'You call it nonsense. – You ask for sympathy, and give – so much!'

'I will give you all the sympathy you stand in need of – I promise it! My poor, dear Sydney! – don't be so absurd! Do you think that I don't know you? You're the best of friends, and the worst of lovers – as the one, so true; so fickle as the other. To my certain knowledge, with how many girls have you been in love – and out again. It is true that, to the best of my knowledge and belief, you have never been in love with me before – but that's the merest accident. Believe me, my dear, dear Sydney, you'll be in love with someone else tomorrow – if you're not half-way there tonight. I confess quite frankly, that, in that direction, all the experience I have had of you has in no wise strengthened my prophetic instinct. Cheer up! – one never knows! – Who is this that's coming?'

It was Dora Grayling who was coming – I went off with her without a word – we were half-way through the dance before she spoke to me.

'I am sorry that I was cross to you just now, and – disagreeable. Somehow I always seem destined to show to you my most unpleasant side.'

'The blame was mine – what sort of side do I show you? You are far kinder to me than I deserve – now, and always.'

'That is what you say.'

'Pardon me, it's true – else how comes it that, at this time of day, I'm without a friend in all the world?'

'You! – without a friend! – I never knew a man who had so many! – I never knew a person of whom so many men and women join in speaking well!'

'Miss Grayling!'

'As for never having done anything worth doing, think of what you have done. Think of your discoveries, think of your inventions, think of – but never mind! The world knows you have done great things, and it confidently looks to you to do still greater. You talk of being friendless, and yet when I ask, as a favour – as a great favour! – to be allowed to do something to show my friendship, you – well, you snub me.'

'I snub you!'

'You know you snubbed me.'

'Do you really mean that you take an interest in – in my work?'

'You know I mean it.'

She turned to me, her face all glowing – and I did know it.

'Will you come to my laboratory tomorrow morning?'

'Will I! – won't I!'

'With your aunt?'

'Yes, with my aunt.'

'I'll show you round, and tell you all there is to be told, and then if you still think there's anything in it, I'll accept your offer about that South American experiment – that is, if it still holds good.'

'Of course it still holds good.'

'And we'll be partners.'

'Partners? – Yes – we will be partners.'

'It will cost a terrific sum.'

'There are some things which never can cost too much.'

'That's not my experience.'

'I hope it will be mine.'

'It's a bargain?'

'On my side, I promise you that it's a bargain.'

When I got outside the room I found that Percy Woodville was at my side. His round face was, in a manner of speaking, as long as my arm. He took his glass out of his eye, and rubbed it with his handkerchief – and directly he put it back he took it out and rubbed it again. I believe that I never saw him in such a state of fluster – and, when one speaks of Woodville, that means something.

'Atherton, I am in a devil of a stew.' He looked it. 'All of a heap! – I've had a blow which I shall never get over!'

'Then get under.'

Woodville is one of those fellows who will insist on telling me their most private matters – even to what they owe their washerwoman for the ruination of their shirts. Why, goodness alone can tell – heaven knows I am not sympathetic.

'Don't be an idiot! – you don't know what I'm suffering! – I'm as nearly as possible stark mad.'

'That's all right, old chap – I've seen you that way more than once before.'

'Don't talk like that – you're not a perfect brute!'

'I bet you a shilling that I am.'

'Don't torture me – you're not. Atherton!' He seized me by the lapels of my coat, seeming half beside himself – fortunately he had drawn me into a recess, so that we were noticed by few observers. 'What do you think has happened?'

'My dear chap, how on earth am I to know?'

'She's refused me!'

'Has she! – Well I never! – Buck up – try some other address – there are quite as good fish in the sea as ever came out of it.'

'Atherton, you're a blackguard.'

He had crumpled his handkerchief into a ball, and was actually bobbing at his eyes with it – the idea of Percy Woodville being dissolved in tears was excruciatingly funny – but, just then, I could hardly tell him so.

'There's not a doubt of it – it's my way of being sympathetic. Don't be so down, man – try her again!'

'It's not the slightest use – I know it isn't – from the way she treated me.'

'Don't be so sure – women often say what they mean least. Who's the lady?'

'Who? – Is there more women in the world than one for me, or has there ever been? You ask me who! What does the word mean to me but Marjorie Lindon!'

'Marjorie Lindon?'

I fancy that my jaw dropped open – that, to use his own vernacular, I was 'all of a heap'. I felt like it.

I strode away – leaving him mazed – and all but ran into Marjorie's arms.

'I'm just leaving. Will you see me to the carriage, Mr Atherton?' I saw her to the carriage. 'Are you off? – can I give you a lift?'

'Thank you – I am not thinking of being off.'

'I'm going to the House of Commons – won't you come?'

'What are you going there for?'

Directly she spoke of it I knew why she was going – and she knew that I knew, as her words showed.

'You are quite well aware of what the magnet is. You are not so ignorant as not to know that the Agricultural Amendment Act is on tonight, and that Paul is to speak. I always try to be there when Paul is to speak, and I mean to always keep on trying.'

'He is a fortunate man.'

'Indeed – and again indeed. A man with such gifts as his is inadequately described as fortunate. – But I must be off. He expected to be up before, but I heard from him a few minutes ago that there has been a delay, but that he will be up within half-an-hour. – Till our next meeting.'

As I returned into the house, in the hall I met Percy Woodville. He had his hat on.

'Where are you off to?'

'I'm off to the House.'

'To hear Paul Lessingham?'

'Damn Paul Lessingham!'

'With all my heart!'

'There's a division expected – I've got to go.'

'Someone else has gone to hear Paul Lessingham – Marjorie Lindon.'

'No! – you don't say so! – by Jove! – I say, Atherton, I wish I could make a speech – I never can. When I'm electioneering I have to have my speeches written for me, and then I have to read 'em. But, by Jove, if I knew Miss Lindon was in the gallery, and if I knew anything about the thing, or could get someone to tell me something, hang me if I wouldn't speak – I'd show her I'm not the fool she thinks I am!'

'Speak, Percy, speak! – you'd knock 'em silly, sir! – I tell you what I'll do – I'll come with you! I'll to the House as well! – Paul Lessingham shall have an audience of three.'

CHAPTER FIFTEEN

# MR LESSINGHAM SPEAKS

The House was full. Percy and I went upstairs – to the gallery which is theoretically supposed to be reserved for what are called 'distinguished strangers' – those curious animals. Trumperton was up, hammering out those sentences which smell, not so much of the lamp as of the dunderhead. Nobody was listening – except the men in the Press Gallery; where is the brain of the House, and ninety per cent of its wisdom.

It was not till Trumperton had finished that I discovered Lessingham. The tedious ancient resumed his seat amidst a murmur of sounds which, I have no doubt, some of the pressmen interpreted next day as 'loud and continued applause'. There was movement in the House, possibly expressive of relief; a hum of voices; men came flocking in. Then, from the Opposition benches, there rose a sound which was applause, – and I perceived that, on a cross bench close to the gangway, Paul Lessingham was standing up bareheaded.

I eyed him critically – as a collector might eye a valuable specimen, or a pathologist a curious subject. During the last four and twenty hours my interest in him had grown apace. Just then, to me, he was the most interesting man the world contained.

When I remembered how I had seen him that same morning, a nerveless, terror-stricken wretch, grovelling, like some craven cur, upon the floor, frightened, to the verge of imbecility, by a shadow, and less than a shadow, I was confronted by two hypotheses. Either I had exaggerated his condition then, or I exaggerated his condition now. So far as appearance went, it was incredible that this man could be that one.

I confess that my feeling rapidly became one of admiration. I love the fighter. I quickly recognized that here we had him in perfection. There was no seeming about him then – the man was to the manner born. To his finger-tips a fighting man. I had never realized it so clearly before. He was coolness itself. He had all his faculties under complete command. While never, for a moment, really exposing himself, he would be swift in perceiving the slightest weakness in his opponents' defence, and, so soon as he saw it, like lightning, he would slip in a telling blow. Though defeated, he would hardly be disgraced; and one might easily believe that their very victories would be so expensive to his assailants, that, in the end, they would actually conduce to his own triumph.

'Hang me!' I told myself, 'if, after all, I am surprised if Marjorie does see something in him.' For I perceived how a clever and imaginative young woman, seeing him at his best, holding his own, like a gallant knight, against overwhelming odds, in the lists in which he was so much at home, might come to think of him as if he were always and only there, ignoring altogether the kind of man he was when the joust was finished.

It did me good to hear him, I do know that – and I could easily imagine the effect he had on one particular auditor who was in the Ladies' Cage. It was very far from being an 'oration!' in the American sense; it had little or nothing of the fire and fury of the French Tribune; it was marked neither by the ponderosity nor the sentiment of the eloquent German; yet it was as satisfying as are the efforts of either of the three, producing, without doubt, precisely the effect which the speaker intended. His voice was clear and calm, not exactly musical, yet distinctly pleasant, and it was so managed that each word he uttered was as audible to every person present as if it had been addressed particularly to him. His sentences were short and crisp; the words which he used were not big ones, but they came from him with an agreeable ease; and he spoke just fast enough to keep one's interest alert without involving a strain on the attention.

He commenced by making, in the quietest and most courteous manner, sarcastic comments on the speeches and methods of Trumperton and his friends which tickled the House amazingly. But he did not make the mistake of pushing his personalities too far. To a speaker of a certain sort nothing is easier than to sting to madness. If he likes, his every word is barbed. Wounds so given fester; they are not easily forgiven; – it is essential to a politician that he should have his firmest friends among the fools; or his climbing days will soon be over. Soon his sarcasms were at an end.

He began to exchange them for sweet-sounding phrases. He actually began to say pleasant things to his opponents; apparently to mean them. To put them in a good conceit with themselves. He pointed out how much truth there was in what they said; and then, as if by accident, with what ease and at how little cost, amendments might be made. He found their arguments, and took them for his own, and flattered them, whether they would or would not, by showing how firmly they were founded upon fact; and grafted other arguments upon them, which seemed their natural sequelæ; and transformed them, and drove them hither and thither; and brought them – their own arguments! – to a round, irrefragable conclusion, which was diametrically the reverse of that to which they themselves had brought them. And he did it all with an aptness, a readiness, a grace, which was incontestable. So that, when he sat down, he had performed that most difficult of all feats, he had delivered what, in a House of Commons' sense, was a practical, statesmanlike speech, and yet one which left his hearers in an excellent humour.

It was a great success – an immense success. A parliamentary triumph of almost the highest order. Paul Lessingham had been coming on by leaps and bounds. When he resumed his seat, amidst applause which, this time, really was applause, there were, probably, few who doubted that he was destined to go still farther. How much farther it is true that time alone could tell; but, so far as appearances went, all the prizes, which are as the crown and climax of a statesman's career, were well within his reach.

For my part, I was delighted. I had enjoyed an intellectual exercise – a species of enjoyment not so common as it might be. The Apostle had almost persuaded me that the political game was one worth playing, and that its triumphs were things to be desired. It is something, after all, to be able to appeal successfully to the passions and aspirations of your peers; to gain their plaudits; to prove your skill at the game you yourself have chosen; to be looked up to and admired. And when a woman's eyes look down on you, and her ears drink in your every word, and her heart beats time with yours – each man to his own temperament, but when that woman is the woman whom you love, to know that your triumph means her glory, and her gladness, to me that would be the best part of it all.

In that hour – the Apostle's hour! – I almost wished that I were a politician too!

The division was over. The business of the night was practically done. I was back again in the lobby! The theme of conversation was the Apostle's speech – on every side they talked of it.

Suddenly Marjorie was at my side. Her face was glowing. I never saw her look more beautiful – or happier. She seemed to be alone.

'So you have come, after all! – Wasn't it splendid? – wasn't it magnificent? Isn't it grand to have such great gifts, and to use them to such good purpose? – Speak, Sydney! Don't feign a coolness which is foreign to your nature!'

I saw that she was hungry for me to praise the man whom she delighted to honour. But, somehow, her enthusiasm cooled mine.

'It was not a bad speech, of a kind.'

'Of a kind!' How her eyes flashed fire! With what disdain she treated me! 'What do you mean by "of a kind"? My dear Sydney, are you not aware that it is an attribute of small minds to attempt to belittle those which are greater? Even if you are conscious of inferiority, it's unwise to show it. Mr

Lessingham's was a great speech, of any kind; your incapacity to recognize the fact simply reveals your lack of the critical faculty.'

'It is fortunate for Mr Lessingham that there is at least one person in whom the critical faculty is so bountifully developed. Apparently, in your judgement, he who discriminates is lost.'

I thought she was going to burst into passion. But, instead, laughing, she placed her hand upon my shoulder.

'Poor Sydney! – I understand! – It is so sad! – Do you know you are like a little boy who, when he is beaten, declares that the victor has cheated him. Never mind! As you grow older, you will learn better.'

She stung me almost beyond bearing – I cared not what I said.

'You, unless I am mistaken, will learn better before you are older.'

'What do you mean?'

Before I could have told her – if I had meant to tell; which I did not – Lessingham came up.

'I hope I have not kept you waiting; I have been delayed longer than I expected.'

'Not at all – though I am quite ready to get away; it's a little tiresome waiting here.'

This with a mischievous glance towards me – a glance which compelled Lessingham to notice me.

'You do not often favour us.'

'I don't. I find better employment for my time.'

'You are wrong. It's the cant of the day to underrate the House of Commons, and the work which it performs; don't you suffer yourself to join in the chorus of the simpletons. Your time cannot be better employed than in endeavouring to improve the body politic.'

'I am obliged to you. – I hope you are feeling better than when I saw you last.'

A gleam came into his eyes, fading as quickly as it came. He showed no other sign of comprehension, surprise, or resentment.

'Thank you. – I am very well.'

But Marjorie perceived that I meant more than met the eye, and that what I meant was meant unpleasantly.

'Come let us be off. It is Mr Atherton tonight who is not well.'

She had just slipped her arm through Lessingham's when her father approached. Old Lindon stared at her on the Apostle's arm, as if he could hardly believe that it was she.

'I thought that you were at the Duchess'?'

'So I have been, papa; and now I'm here.'

'Here!' Old Lindon began to stutter and stammer, and to grow red in the face, as is his wont when at all excited. 'W – what do you mean by here? – wh – where's the carriage?'

'Where should it be, except waiting for me outside – unless the horses have run away.'

'I – I – I'll take you down to it. I – I don't approve of y-your w-w-waiting in a place like this.'

'Thank you, papa, but Mr Lessingham is going to take me down. – I shall see you afterwards. – Good-bye.'

Anything cooler than the way in which she walked off I do not think I ever saw. This is the age of feminine advancement. Young women think nothing of twisting their mothers round their fingers, let alone their fathers; but the fashion in which that young woman walked off, on the Apostle's arm, and left her father standing there, was, in its way, a study.

Lindon seemed scarcely able to realize that the pair of them had gone. Even after they had disappeared in the crowd he stood staring after them, growing redder and redder, till the veins stood out upon his face, and I thought that an apoplectic seizure threatened. Then, with a gasp, he turned to me.

'Damned scoundrel!' I took it for granted that he alluded to the gentleman – even though his following words hardly suggested it. 'Only this morning I forbade her to have anything to do with him, and n-now he's w-walked off with her! C-confounded adventurer! That's what he is, an adventurer, and before many hours have passed I'll take the liberty to tell him so!'

Jamming his fists into his pockets, and puffing like a grampus in distress, he took himself away – and it was time he did, for his words were as audible as they were pointed, and already people were wondering what the matter was. Woodville came up as Lindon was going – just as sorely distressed as ever.

'She went away with Lessingham – did you see her?'

'Of course I saw her. When a man makes a speech like Lessingham's any girl would go away with him – and be proud to. When you are endowed with such great powers as he is, and use them for such lofty purposes, she'll walk away with you – but, till then, never.'

He was at his old trick of polishing his eyeglass.

'It's bitter hard. When I knew that she was there, I'd half a mind to make a speech myself, upon my word I had, only I didn't know what to speak about, and I can't speak anyhow – how can a fellow speak when he's shoved into the gallery?'

'As you say, how can he? – he can't stand on the railing and shout – even with a friend holding him behind.'

'I know I shall speak one day – bound to; and then she won't be there.'

'It'll be better for you if she isn't.'

'Think so? – Perhaps you're right. I'd be safe to make a mess of it, and then, if she were to see me at it, it'd be the devil! 'Pon my word, I've been wishing, lately, I was clever.'

He rubbed his nose with the rim of his eyeglass, looking the most comically disconsolate figure.

'Put black care behind you, Percy! – buck up, my boy! The division's over – you are free – now we'll go "on the fly".'

And we did 'go on the fly'.

## CHAPTER SIXTEEN

# ATHERTON'S MAGIC VAPOUR

I bore him off to supper at the Helicon. All the way in the cab he was trying to tell me the story of how he proposed to Marjorie – and he was very far from being through with it when we reached the club. There was the usual crowd of supperites, but we got a little table to ourselves, in a corner of the room, and before anything was brought for us to eat he was at it again. A good many of the people were pretty near to shouting, and as they seemed to be all speaking at once, and the band was playing, and as the Helicon supper band is not piano, Percy did not have it quite all to himself, but, considering the delicacy of his subject, he talked as loudly as was decent – getting more so as he went on. But Percy is peculiar.

'I don't know how many times I've tried to tell her – over and over again.'

'Have you now?'

'Yes, pretty near every time I met her – but I never seemed to get quite to it, don't you know.'

'How was that?'

'Why, just as I was going to say, "Miss Lindon, may I offer you the gift of my affection –"'

'Was that how you invariably intended to begin?'

'Well, not always – one time like that, another time another way. Fact is, I got off a little speech by heart, but I never got a chance to reel it off, so I made up my mind to just say anything.'

'And what did you say?'

'Well, nothing – you see, I never got there. Just as I was feeling my way, she'd ask me if I preferred big sleeves to little ones, or top hats to billycocks, or some nonsense of the kind.'

'Would she now?'

'Yes – of course I had to answer, and by the time I'd answered the chance was lost.' Percy was polishing his eyeglass. 'I tried to get there so many times, and she choked me off so often, that I can't help thinking that she suspected what it was that I was after.'

'You think she did?'

'She must have done. Once I followed her down Piccadilly, and chivied her into a glove shop in the Burlington Arcade. I meant to propose to her in there – I hadn't had a wink of sleep all night through dreaming of her, and I was just about desperate.'

'And did you propose?'

'The girl behind the counter made me buy a dozen pairs of gloves instead. They turned out to be three sizes too large for me when they came home. I believe she thought I'd gone to spoon the glove girl – she went out and left me there. That girl loaded me with all sorts of things when she was gone – I couldn't get away. She held me with her blessed eye. I believe it was a glass one.'

'Miss Lindon's? – or the glove girl's?'

'The glove girl's. She sent me home a whole cartload of green ties, and declared I'd ordered them. I shall never forget that day. I've never been up the Arcade since, and never mean to.'

'You gave Miss Lindon a wrong impression.'

'I don't know. I was always giving her wrong impressions. Once she said that she knew I was not a marrying man, that I was the sort of chap who never would marry, because she saw it in my face.'

'Under the circumstances, that was trying.'

'Bitter hard.' Percy sighed again. 'I shouldn't mind if I wasn't so gone. I'm not a fellow who does get gone, but when I do get gone, I get so beastly gone.'

'I tell you what, Percy – have a drink!'

'I'm a teetotaller – you know I am.'

'You talk of your heart being broken, and of your being a teetotaller in the same breath – if your heart were really broken you'd throw teetotalism to the winds.'

'Do you think so – why?'

'Because you would – men whose hearts are broken always do – you'd swallow a magnum at the least.'

Percy groaned.

'When I drink I'm always ill – but I'll have a try.'

He had a try – making a good beginning by emptying at a draught the glass which the waiter had just now filled. Then he relapsed into melancholy.

'Tell me, Percy – honest Indian! – do you really love her?'

'Love her?' His eyes grew round as saucers. 'Don't I tell you that I love her?'

'I know you tell me, but that sort of thing is easy telling. What does it make you feel like, this love you talk so much about?'

'Feel like? – Just anyhow – and nohow. You should look inside me, and then you'd know.'

'I see. – It's like that, is it? – Suppose she loved another man, what sort of feeling would you feel towards him?'

'Does she love another man?'

'I say, suppose.'

'I dare say she does. I expect that's it. – What an idiot I am not to have thought of that before.' He sighed – and refilled his glass. 'He's a lucky chap, whoever he is. I'd – I'd like to tell him so.'

'You'd like to tell him so?'

'He's such a jolly lucky chap, you know.'

'Possibly – but his jolly good luck is your jolly bad luck. Would you be willing to resign her to him without a word?'

'If she loves him.'

'But you say you love her.'

'Of course I do.'

'Well then?'

'You don't suppose that, because I love her, I shouldn't like to see her happy? – I'm not such a beast! – I'd sooner see her happy than anything else in all the world.'

'I see. – Even happy with another? – I'm afraid that my philosophy is not like yours. If I loved Miss Lindon, and she loved, say, Jones, I'm afraid I shouldn't feel like that towards Jones at all.'

'What would you feel like?'

'Murder. – Percy, you come home with me – we've begun the night together, let's end it together – and I'll show you one of the finest notions for committing murder on a scale of real magnificence you ever dreamed of. I should like to make use of it to show my feelings towards the supposititious Jones – he'd know what I felt for him when once he had been introduced to it.'

Percy went with me without a word. He had not had much to drink, but it had been too much for him, and he was in a condition of maundering sentimentality. I got him into a cab. We dashed along Piccadilly.

He was silent, and sat looking in front of him with an air of vacuous sullenness which ill became his cast of countenance. I bade the cabman pass through Lowndes Square. As we passed the Apostle's I pulled him up. I pointed out the place to Woodville.

'You see, Percy, that's Lessingham's house! – that's the house of the man who went away with Marjorie!'

'Yes.' Words came from him slowly, with a quite unnecessary stress on each. 'Because he made a speech. – I'd like to make a speech. – One day I'll make a speech.'

'Because he made a speech – only that, and nothing more! When a man speaks with an Apostle's tongue, he can witch any woman in the land. – Hallo, who's that? – Lessingham, is that you?'

I saw, or thought I saw, someone, or something, glide up the steps, and withdraw into the shadow of the doorway, as if unwilling to be seen. When I hailed no one answered. I called again.

'Don't be shy, my friend!'

I sprang out of the cab, ran across the pavement, and up the steps. To my surprise, there was no one in the doorway. It seemed incredible, but the place was empty. I felt about me with my hands, as if I had been playing at blind man's buff, and grasped at vacancy. I came down a step or two.

'Ostensibly, there's a vacuum – which nature abhors. – I say, driver, didn't you see someone come up the steps?'

'I thought I did, sir – I could have sworn I did.'

'So could I. – It's very odd.'

'Perhaps whoever it was has gone into the 'ouse, sir.'

'I don't see how. We should have heard the door open, if we hadn't seen it – and we should have seen it, it's not so dark as that. I've half a mind to ring the bell and inquire.'

'I shouldn't do that if I was you, sir – you jump in, and I'll get along. This is Mr Lessingham's – the great Mr Lessingham's.'

I believe the cabman thought that I was drunk – and not respectable enough to claim acquaintance with the great Mr Lessingham.

'Wake up, Woodville! Do you know I believe there's some mystery about this place – I feel assured of it. I feel as if I were in the presence of something uncanny – something which I can neither see, nor touch, nor hear.'

The cabman bent down from his seat, wheedling me.

'Jump in, sir, and we'll be getting along.'

I jumped in, and we got along – but not far. Before we had gone a dozen yards, I was out again, without troubling the driver to stop. He pulled up, aggrieved.

'Well, sir, what's the matter now? You'll be damaging yourself before you've done, and then you'll be blaming me.'

I had caught sight of a cat crouching in the shadow of the railings – a black one. That cat was my quarry. Either the creature was unusually sleepy, or slow, or stupid, or it had lost its wits – which a cat seldom does lose! – anyhow, without making an attempt to escape it allowed me to grab it by the nape of the neck.

So soon as we were inside my laboratory, I put the cat into my glass box. Percy stared.

'What have you put it there for?'

'That, my dear Percy, is what you are shortly about to see. You are about to be the witness of an experiment which, to a legislator – such as you are! – ought to be of the greatest possible interest. I am going to demonstrate, on a small scale, the action of the force which, on a large scale, I propose to employ on behalf of my native land.'

He showed no signs of being interested. Sinking into a chair, he recommenced his wearisome reiteration.

'I hate cats! – Do let it go! I'm always miserable when there's a cat in the room.'

'Nonsense – that's your fancy! What you want's a taste of whisky – you'll be as chirpy as a cricket.'

'I don't want anything more to drink! – I've had too much already!'

I paid no heed to what he said. I poured two stiff doses into a couple of tumblers. Without seeming to be aware of what it was that he was doing he disposed of the better half of the one I gave him at a draught. Putting his glass upon the table, he dropped his head upon his hands, and groaned.

'What would Marjorie think of me if she saw me now?'

'Think? – nothing. Why should she think of a man like you, when she has so much better fish to fry?'

'I'm feeling frightfully ill! – I'll be drunk before I've done!'

'Then be drunk! – only, for gracious sake, be lively drunk, not deadly doleful. – Cheer up, Percy!' I clapped him on the shoulder – almost knocking him off his seat on to the floor. 'I am now going to show you that little experiment of which I was speaking! – You see that cat?'

'Of course I see it! – the beast! – I wish you'd let it go!'

'Why should I let it go? – Do you know whose cat that is? That cat's Paul Lessingham's.'

'Paul Lessingham's?'

'Yes, Paul Lessingham's – the man who made the speech – the man whom Marjorie went away with.'

'How do you know it's his?'

'I don't know it is, but I believe it is – I choose to believe it is! – I intend to believe it is! – It was outside his house, therefore it's his cat – that's how I argue. I can't get Lessingham inside that box, so I get his cat instead.'

'Whatever for?'

'You shall see – you observe how happy it is?'

'It don't seem happy.'

'We've all our ways of seeming happy – that's its way.'

The creature was behaving like a cat gone mad, dashing itself against the sides of its glass prison, leaping to and fro, and from side to side, squealing with rage, or with terror, or with both. Perhaps it foresaw what was coming – there is no fathoming the intelligence of what we call the lower animals.

'It's a funny way.'

'We some of us have funny ways, besides, cats. Now, attention! Observe this little toy – you've seen something of its kind before. It's a spring gun; you pull the spring – drop the charge into the barrel – release the spring – and the charge is fired. I'll unlock this safe, which is built into the wall. It's a letter lock, the combination just now, is "whisky" – you see, that's a hint to you. You'll notice the safe is strongly made – it's air-tight, fire-proof, the outer casing is of triple-plated drill-proof steel – the contents are valuable – to me! – and devilish dangerous – I'd pity the thief who, in his innocent ignorance, broke in to steal. Look inside – you see it's full of balls – glass balls, each in its own little separate nest; light as feathers; transparent – you can see right through them. Here are a couple, like tiny pills. They contain neither dynamite, nor cordite, nor anything of the kind, yet, given a fair field and no favour, they'll work more mischief than all the explosives man has fashioned. Take hold of one – you say your heart is broken! – squeeze this under your nose – it wants but a gentle pressure – and in less time than no time you'll be in the land where they say there are no broken hearts.'

He shrunk back.

'I don't know what you're talking about. – I don't want the thing. – Take it away.'

'Think twice – the chance may not recur.'

'I tell you I don't want it.'

'Sure? – Consider!'

'Of course I'm sure!'

'Then the cat shall have it.'

'Let the poor brute go!'

'The poor brute's going – to the land which is so near, and yet so far. Once more, if you please, attention. Notice what I do with this toy gun. I pull back the spring; I insert this small glass pellet; I thrust the muzzle of the gun through the opening in the glass box which contains the Apostle's cat – you'll observe it fits quite close, which, on the whole, is perhaps as well for us. – I am about to release the spring. – Close attention please. – Notice the effect.'

'Atherton, let the brute go!'

'The brute's gone! I've released the spring – the pellet has been discharged – it has struck against the roof of the glass box – it has been broken by the contact – and, hey presto! the cat lies dead – and that in face of its nine lives. You perceive how still it is – how still! Let's hope that, now, it's really happy. The cat which I choose to believe is Paul Lessingham's has received its quietus; in the morning I'll send it back to him, with my respectful compliments. He'll miss it if I don't. – Reflect! think of a huge bomb, filled with what we'll call Atherton's Magic Vapour, fired, say, from a hundred and twenty ton gun, bursting at a given elevation over the heads of an opposing force. Properly managed, in less than an instant of time, a hundred thousand men – quite possibly more! – would drop down dead, as if smitten by the lightning of the skies. Isn't that something like a weapon, sir?'

'I'm not well! – I want to get away! I wish I'd never come!'

That was all Woodville had to say.

'Rubbish! – You're adding to your stock of information every second, and, in these days, when a member of Parliament is supposed to know all about everything, information's the one thing wanted. Empty your glass, man – that's the time of day for you!'

I handed him his tumbler. He drained what was left of its contents, then, in a fit of tipsy, childish temper he flung the tumbler from him. I had placed – carelessly enough – the second pellet within a foot of the edge of the table. The shock of the heavy beaker striking the board close to it, set it rolling. I was at the other side. I started forward to stop its motion, but I was too late. Before I could reach the crystal globule, it had fallen off the edge of the table on to the floor at Woodville's feet, and smashed in falling. As it smashed, he was looking down, wondering, no doubt, in his stupidity, what the pother was about – for I was shouting, and making something of a clatter in my efforts to prevent the catastrophe which I saw was coming. On the instant, as the vapour secreted in the broken pellet gained access to the air, he fell forward on to his face. Rushing to him, I snatched his senseless body from the ground, and dragged it, staggeringly, towards the door which opened on to the yard. Flinging the door open, I got him into the open air.

As I did so, I found myself confronted by someone who stood outside. It was Lessingham's mysterious Eygpto-Arabian friend, my morning's visitor.

CHAPTER SEVENTEEN

# MAGIC? – OR MIRACLE?

The passage into the yard from the electrically-lit laboratory was a passage from brilliancy to gloom. The shrouded figure standing in the shadow, was like some object in a dream. My own senses reeled. It was only because I had resolutely held my breath, and kept my face averted that I had not succumbed to the fate which had overtaken Woodville. Had I been a moment longer in gaining the open air, it would have been too late. As it was, in placing Woodville on the ground, I stumbled over him. My senses left me. Even as they went I was conscious of exclaiming – remembering the saying about the engineer being hoist by his own petard,

'Atherton's Magic Vapour!'

My sensations on returning to consciousness were curious. I found myself being supported in someone's arms, a stranger's face was bending over me, and the most extraordinary pair of eyes I had ever seen were looking into mine.

'Who the deuce are you?' I asked.

Then, understanding that it was my uninvited visitor, with scant ceremony I drew myself away from him. By the light which was streaming through the laboratory door I saw that Woodville was lying close beside me – stark and still.

'Is he dead?' I cried. 'Percy! – speak, man! – it's not so bad with you as that!'

But it was pretty bad – so bad that, as I bent down and looked at him, my heart beat uncomfortably fast lest it was as bad as it could be. His heart seemed still, – the vapour took effect directly on the cardiac centres. To revive their action, and that instantly, was indispensable. Yet my brain was in such a whirl that I could not even think of how to set about beginning. Had I been alone, it is more than probable Woodville would have died. As I stared at him, senselessly, aimlessly, the stranger, passing his arms beneath his body, extended himself at full length upon his motionless form. Putting his lips to Percy's, he seemed to be pumping life from his own body into the

535

unconscious man's. As I gazed bewildered, surprised, presently there came a movement of Percy's body. His limbs twitched, as if he was in pain. By degrees, the motions became convulsive – till on a sudden he bestirred himself to such effect that the stranger was rolled right off him. I bent down – to find that the young gentleman's condition still seemed very far from satisfactory. There was a rigidity about the muscles of his face, a clamminess about his skin, a disagreeable suggestiveness about the way in which his teeth and the whites of his eyes were exposed, which was uncomfortable to contemplate.

The stranger must have seen what was passing through my mind – not a very difficult thing to see. Pointing to the recumbent Percy, he said, with that queer foreign twang of his, which, whatever it had seemed like in the morning, sounded musical enough just then.

'All will be well with him.'

'I am not so sure.'

The stranger did not deign to answer. He was kneeling on one side of the victim of modern science, I on the other. Passing his hand to and fro in front of the unconscious countenance, as if by magic all semblance of discomfort vanished from Percy's features, and, to all appearances, he was placidly asleep.

'Have you hypnotized him?'

'What does it matter?'

If it was a case of hypnotism, it was very neatly done. The conditions were both unusual and trying, the effect produced seemed all that could be desired – the change brought about in half a dozen seconds was quite remarkable. I began to be aware of a feeling of quasi-respect for Paul Lessingham's friend. His morals might be peculiar, and manners he might have none, but in this case, at any rate, the end seemed to have justified the means. He went on.

'He sleeps. When he awakes he will remember nothing that has been. Leave him – the night is warm – all will be well.'

As he said, the night was warm – and it was dry. Percy would come to little harm by being allowed to enjoy, for a while, the pleasant breezes. So I acted on the stranger's advice, and left him lying in the yard, while I had a little interview with the impromptu physician.

## CHAPTER EIGHTEEN

# THE APOTHEOSIS OF THE BEETLE

The laboratory door was closed. The stranger was standing a foot or two away from it. I was further within the room, and was subjecting him to as keen a scrutiny as circumstances permitted. Beyond doubt he was conscious of my observation, yet he bore himself with an air of indifference, which was suggestive of perfect unconcern. The fellow was Oriental to the finger-tips – that much was certain; yet in spite of a pretty wide personal knowledge of Oriental people I could not make up my mind as to the exact part of the east from which he came. He was hardly an Arab, he was not a fellah – he was not, unless I erred, a Mohammedan at all. There was something about him which was distinctly not Mussulmanic. So far as looks were concerned, he was not a flattering example of his race, whatever his race might be. The portentous size of his beak-like nose would have been, in itself, sufficient to damn him in any court of beauty. His lips were thick and shapeless – and this, joined to another peculiarity in his appearance, seemed to suggest that, in his veins there ran more than a streak of negro blood. The peculiarity alluded to was his semblance of great age. As one eyed him one was reminded of the legends told of people who have been supposed to have retained something of their pristine vigour after having lived for centuries. As, however, one continued to gaze, one began to wonder if he really was so old as he seemed – if, indeed, he was exceptionally old at all. Negroes, and especially negresses, are apt to age with extreme rapidity. Among coloured folk one sometimes encounters women whose faces seem to have been lined by the passage of centuries, yet whose actual tale of years would entitle them to regard themselves, here in England, as in the prime of life. The senility of the fellow's countenance, besides, was contradicted by the juvenescence of his eyes. No really old man could have had eyes like that. They were curiously shaped, reminding me of the elongated, faceted eyes of some queer creature, with whose appearance I was familiar, although I could not, at the instant, recall its name. They glowed not only with the force and fire, but, also, with the frenzy of youth. More uncanny-looking eyes I had never encountered – their possessor could not be, in any sense of the word, a clubable person. Owing, probably, to some peculiar formation of the optic-nerve one felt, as one met his gaze, that he was looking right through you. More obvious danger signals never yet were placed in a creature's head. The individual who, having once caught sight of him, still sought to cultivate their owner's acquaintance, had only himself to thank if the very worst results of frequenting evil company promptly ensued.

It happens that I am myself endowed with an unusual tenacity of vision. I could, for instance, easily outstare any man I ever met. Yet, as I continued to stare at this man, I was conscious that it was only by an effort of will that I was able to resist a baleful something which seemed to be passing from his eyes to mine. It might have been imagination, but, in that sense, I am not an imaginative man; and, if it was, it was imagination of an unpleasantly vivid kind. I could understand how, in the case of a nervous, or a sensitive temperament, the fellow might exercise, by means of the peculiar quality of his glance alone, an influence of a most disastrous sort, which given an appropriate subject in the manifestation of its power might approach almost the supernatural. If ever man was endowed with the traditional evil eye, in which Italians, among modern nations, are such profound believers, it was he.

When we had stared at each other for, I daresay, quite five minutes, I began to think I had had about enough of it. So, by way of breaking the ice, I put to him a question.

'May I ask how you found your way into my back yard?'

He did not reply in words, but, raising his hands he lowered them, palms downward, with a gesture, which was peculiarly Oriental.

'Indeed? – Is that so? – Your meaning may be lucidity itself to you, but, for my benefit, perhaps you would not mind translating it into words. Once more I ask, how did you find your way into my back yard?'

Again nothing but the gesture.

'Possibly you are not sufficiently acquainted with English manners and customs to be aware that you have placed yourself within reach of the pains and penalties of the law. Were I to call in the police you would find yourself in an awkward situation – and, unless you are presently more explanatory, called in they will be.'

By way of answer he indulged in a distortion of the countenance which might have been meant for a smile – and which seemed to suggest that he regarded the police with a contempt which was too great for words.

'Why do you laugh – do you think that being threatened with the police is a joke? You are not likely to find it so. – Have you suddenly been bereft of the use of your tongue?'

He proved that he had not by using it.

'I have still the use of my tongue.'

'That, at least, is something. Perhaps, since the subject of how you got into my back yard seems to be a delicate one, you will tell me why you got there.'

'You know why I have come.'

'Pardon me if I appear to flatly contradict you, but that is precisely what I do not know.'

'You do know.'

'Do I? – Then, in that case, I presume that you are here for the reason which appears upon the surface – to commit a felony.'

'You call me thief?'

'What else are you?'

'I am no thief. – You know why I have come.'

He raised his head a little. A look came into his eyes which I felt that I ought to understand, yet to the meaning of which I seemed, for the instant, to have mislaid the key. I shrugged my shoulders.

'I have come because you wanted me.'

'Because I wanted you! – On my word! – That's sublime!'

'All night you have wanted me – do I not know? When she talked to you of him, and the blood boiled in your veins; when he spoke, and all the people listened, and you hated him, because he had honour in her eyes.'

I was startled. Either he meant what it appeared incredible that he could mean, or – there was confusion somewhere.

'Take my advice, my friend, and don't try to come the bunco-steerer over me – I'm a bit in that line myself, you know.'

This time the score was mine – he was puzzled.

'I know not what you talk of.'

'In that case, we're equal – I know not what you talk of either.'

His manner, for him, was childlike and bland.

'What is it you do not know? This morning did I not say – if you want me, then I come?'

'I fancy I have some faint recollection of your being so good as to say something of the kind, but – where's the application?'

'Do you not feel for him the same as I?'

'Who's the him?'

'Paul Lessingham.'

It was spoken quietly, but with a degree of – to put it gently – spitefulness which showed that at least the will to do the Apostle harm would not be lacking.

'And, pray, what is the common feeling which we have for him?'

'Hate.'

Plainly, with this gentleman, hate meant hate – in the solid Oriental sense. I should hardly have been surprised if the mere utterance of the words had seared his lips.

'I am by no means prepared to admit that I have this feeling which you attribute to me, but, even granting that I have, what then?'

'Those who hate are kin.'

'That, also, I should be slow to admit; but – to go a step farther – what has all this to do with your presence on my premises at this hour of the night?'

'You love her.' This time I did not ask him to supply the name – being unwilling that it should be soiled by the traffic of his lips. 'She loves him – that is not well. If you choose, she shall love you – that will be well.'

'Indeed. – And pray how is this consummation which is so devoutly to be desired to be brought about?'

'Put your hand into mine. Say that you wish it. It shall be done.'

Moving a step forward, he stretched out his hand towards me. I hesitated. There was that in the fellow's manner which, for the moment, had for me an unwholesome fascination. Memories flashed through my mind of stupid stories which have been told of compacts made with the devil. I almost felt as if I was standing in the actual presence of one of the powers of evil. I thought of my love for Marjorie – which had revealed itself after all these years; of the delight of holding her in my arms, of feeling the pressure of her lips to mine. As my gaze met his, the lower side of what the conquest of this fair lady would mean, burned in my brain; fierce imaginings blazed before my eyes. To win her – only to win her!

What nonsense he was talking! What empty brag it was! Suppose, just for the sake of the joke, I did put my hand in his, and did wish, right out, what it was plain he knew. If I wished, what harm would it do! It would be the purest jest. Out of his own mouth he would be confounded, for it was certain that nothing would come of it. Why should I not do it then?

I would act on his suggestion – I would carry the thing right through. Already I was advancing towards him, when – I stopped. I don't know why. On the instant, my thoughts went off at a tangent.

What sort of a blackguard did I call myself that I should take a woman's name in vain for the sake of playing fool's tricks with such scum of the earth as the hideous vagabond in front of me – and that the name of the woman whom I loved? Rage took hold of me.

'You hound!' I cried.

In my sudden passage from one mood to another, I was filled with the desire to shake the life half out of him. But so soon as I moved a step in his direction, intending war instead of peace, he altered the position of his hand, holding it out towards me as if forbidding my approach. Directly he did so, quite involuntarily, I pulled up dead – as if my progress had been stayed by bars of iron and walls of steel.

For the moment, I was astonished to the verge of stupefaction. The sensation was peculiar. I was as incapable of advancing another inch in his direction as if I had lost the use of my limbs – I was even incapable of attempting to attempt to advance. At first I could only stare and gape. Presently I began to have an inkling of what had happened.

The scoundrel had almost succeeded in hypnotizing me.

That was a nice thing to happen to a man of my sort at my time of life. A shiver went down my back – what might have occurred if I had not pulled up in time! What pranks might a creature of that character not have been disposed to play. It was the old story of the peril of playing with edged tools; I had made the dangerous mistake of underrating the enemy's strength. Evidently, in his own line, the fellow was altogether something out of the usual way.

I believe that even as it was he thought he had me. As I turned away, and leaned against the table at my back, I fancy that he shivered – as if this proof of my being still my own master was unexpected. I was silent – it took some seconds to enable me to recover from the shock of the discovery of the peril in which I had been standing. Then I resolved that I would endeavour to do something which should make me equal to this gentleman of many talents.

'Take my advice, my friend, and don't attempt to play that hankey pankey off on to me again.'

'I don't know what you talk of.'

'Don't lie to me – or I'll burn you into ashes.'

Behind me was an electrical machine, giving an eighteen-inch spark. It was set in motion by a lever fitted into the table, which I could easily reach from where I sat. As I spoke the visitor was treated to a little exhibition of electricity. The change in his bearing was amusing. He shook with terror. He salaamed down to the ground.

'My lord! – my lord! – have mercy, oh my lord!'

'Then you be careful, that's all. You may suppose yourself to be something of a magician, but it happens, unfortunately for you, that I can do a bit in that line myself – perhaps I'm a trifle better at the game than you are. Especially as you have ventured into my stronghold, which contains magic enough to make a show of a hundred thousand such as you.'

Taking down a bottle from a shelf, I sprinkled a drop or two of its contents on the floor. Immediately flames arose, accompanied by a blinding vapour. It was a sufficiently simple illustration of one of the qualities of phosphorous-bromide, but its effect upon my visitor was as startling as it was unexpected. If I could believe the evidence of my own eyesight, in the very act of giving utterance to a scream of terror he disappeared, how, or why, or whither, there was nothing to show – in his place, where he had been standing, there seemed to be a dim object of some sort in a state of frenzied agitation on the floor. The phosphorescent vapour was confusing; the lights appeared to be suddenly burning low; before I had sense enough to go and see if there was anything there, and, if so, what, the flames had vanished, the man himself had reappeared, and, prostrated on his knees, was salaaming in a condition of abject terror.

'My lord! my lord!' he whined. 'I entreat you, my lord, to use me as your slave!'

'I'll use you as my slave!' Whether he or I was the more agitated it would have been difficult to say – but, at least, it would not have done to betray my feelings as he did his. 'Stand up!'

He stood up. I eyed him as he did with an interest which, so far as I was concerned, was of a distinctly new and original sort. Whether or not I had been the victim of an ocular delusion I could not be sure. It was incredible to suppose that he could have disappeared as he had seemed to disappear – it was also incredible that I could have imagined his disappearance. If the thing had been a trick, I had not the faintest notion how it had been worked; and, if it was not a trick, then what was it? Was it something new in scientific marvels? Could he give me as much instruction in the qualities of unknown forces as I could him?

In the meanwhile he stood in an attitude of complete submission, with downcast eyes, and hands crossed upon his breast. I started to cross-examine him.

'I am going to ask you some questions. So long as you answer them promptly, truthfully, you will be safe. Otherwise you had best beware.'

'Ask, oh my lord.'

'What is the nature of your objection to Mr Lessingham?'

'Revenge.'

'What has he done to you that you should wish to be revenged on him?'

'It is the feud of the innocent blood.'

'What do you mean by that?'

'On his hands is the blood of my kin. It cries aloud for vengeance.'

'Who has he killed?'

'That, my lord, is for me – and for him.'

'I see. – Am I to understand that you do not choose to answer me, and that I am again to use my – magic?'

I saw that he quivered.

'My Lord, he has spilled the blood of her who has lain upon his breast.'

I hesitated. What he meant appeared clear enough. Perhaps it would be as well not to press for further details. The words pointed to what it might be courteous to call an Eastern Romance – though it was hard to conceive of the Apostle figuring as the hero of such a theme. It was the old tale re-told, that to the life of every man there is a background – that it is precisely in the unlikeliest cases that the background's darkest. What would that penny-plain-and-twopence-coloured bogey, the Nonconformist Conscience, make of such a story if it were blazoned through the land. Would Paul not come down with a run?

'"Spilling blood" is a figure of speech; pretty, perhaps, but vague. If you mean that Mr Lessingham has been killing someone, your surest and most effectual revenge would be gained by an appeal to the law.'

'What has the Englishman's law to do with me?'

'If you can prove that he has been guilty of murder it would have a great deal to do with you. I assure you that at any rate, in that sense, the Englishman's law is no respecter of persons. Show him to be guilty, and it would hang Paul Lessingham as indifferently, and as cheerfully, as it would hang Bill Brown.'

'Is that so?'

'It is so, as, if you choose, you will be easily able to prove to your own entire satisfaction.'

He had raised his head, and was looking at something which he seemed to see in front of him with a maleficent glare in his sensitive eyes which it was not nice to see.

'He would be shamed?'

'Indeed he would be shamed.'

'Before all men?'

'Before all men – and, I take it, before all women too.'

'And he would hang?'

'If shown to have been guilty of wilful murder – yes.'

His hideous face was lighted up by a sort of diabolical exultation which made it, if that were possible, more hideous still. I had apparently given him a wrinkle which pleased him most consummately.

'Perhaps I will do that in the end – in the end!' He opened his eyes to their widest limits, then shut them tight – as if to gloat on the picture which his fancy painted. Then reopened them. 'In the meantime I will have vengeance in my own fashion. He knows already that the avenger is upon him – he has good reason to know it. And through the days and the nights the knowledge shall be with him still, and it shall be to him as the bitterness of death – aye, of many deaths. For he will know that escape there is none, and that for him there shall be no more sun in the sky, and that the terror shall be with him by night and by day, at his rising up and at his lying down, wherever his eyes shall turn it shall be there – yet, behold, the sap and the juice of my vengeance is in this, in that though he shall be very sure that the days that are, are as the days of his death, yet shall he know that THE DEATH, THE GREAT DEATH, is coming – coming – and shall be on him – when I will!'

The fellow spoke like an inspired maniac. If he meant half what he said – and if he did not then his looks and his tones belied him! – then a promising future bade fair to be in store for Mr Lessingham – and, also, circumstances being as they were, for Marjorie. It was this latter reflection which gave me pause. Either this imprecatory fanatic would have to be disposed of, by Lessingham himself, or by someone acting on his behalf, and, so far as their power of doing mischief went, his big words proved empty windbags, or Marjorie would have to be warned that there was at least one passage in her suitor's life, into which, ere it was too late, it was advisable that inquiry should be made. To allow Marjorie to irrevocably link her fate with the Apostle's, without being first of all made aware that he was, to all intents and purposes, a haunted man – that was not to be thought of.

'You employ large phrases.'

My words cooled the other's heated blood. Once more his eyes were cast down, his hands crossed upon his breast.

'I crave my lord's pardon. My wound is ever new.'

'By the way, what was the secret history, this morning, of that little incident of the cockroach?'

He glanced up quickly.

'Cockroach? – I know not what you say.'

'Well – was it beetle, then?'

'Beetle!'

He seemed, all at once, to have lost his voice – the word was gasped.

'After you went we found, upon a sheet of paper, a capitally executed drawing of a beetle, which, I fancy, you must have left behind you – *Scarabæus sacer*, wasn't it?'

'I know not what you talk of.'

'Its discovery seemed to have quite a singular effect on Mr Lessingham. Now, why was that?'

'I know nothing.'

'Oh yes you do – and, before you go, I mean to know something too.'

The man was trembling, looking this way and that, showing signs of marked discomfiture. That there was something about that ancient scarab, which figures so largely in the still unravelled tangles of the Egyptian mythologies, and the effect which the mere sight of its cartouch – for the drawing had resembled something of the kind – had had on such a seasoned vessel as Paul Lessingham, which might be well worth my finding out, I felt convinced – the man's demeanour, on my recurring to the matter, told its own plain tale. I made up my mind, if possible, to probe the business to the bottom, then and there.

'Listen to me, my friend. I am a plain man, and I use plain speech – it's a kind of hobby I have. You will give me the information I require, and that at once or I will pit my magic against yours – in which case I think it extremely probable that you will come off worst from the encounter.'

I reached out for the lever, and the exhibition of electricity recommenced. Immediately his tremors were redoubled.

'My lord, I know not of what you talk.'

'None of your lies for me. – Tell me why, at the sight of the thing on that sheet of paper, Paul Lessingham went green and yellow.'

'Ask him, my lord.'

'Probably, later on, that is what I shall do. In the meantime, I am asking you. Answer – or look out for squalls.'

The electrical exhibition was going on. He was glaring at it as if he wished that it would stop. As if ashamed of his cowardice, plainly, on a sudden, he made a desperate effort to get the better of his fears – and succeeded better than I had expected or desired. He drew himself up with what, in him, amounted to an air of dignity.

'I am a child of Isis!'

It struck me that he made this remark, not so much to impress me, as with a view of elevating his own low spirits.

'Are you? – Then, in that case, I regret that I am unable to congratulate the lady on her offspring.'

When I said that, a ring came into his voice which I had not heard before.

'Silence! – You know not of what you speak! – I warn you, as I warned Paul Lessingham, be careful not to go too far. Be not like him – heed my warning.'

'What is it I am being warned against – the beetle?'

'Yes – the beetle!'

Were I upon oath, and this statement being made, in the presence of witnesses, say, in a solicitor's office, I standing in fear of pains and penalties, I think that, at this point, I should leave the paper blank. No man likes to own himself a fool, or that he ever was a fool – and ever since I have been wondering whether, on that occasion, that 'child of Isis' did, or did not, play the fool with me. His performance was realistic enough at the time, heaven knows. But, as it gets farther and farther away, I ask myself, more and more confidently, as time effluxes, whether, after all, it was not clever juggling – superhumanly clever juggling, if you will; that, and nothing more. If it was something more, then, with a vengeance! there is more in heaven and earth than is dreamed of in our philosophy. The mere possibility opens vistas which the sane mind fears to contemplate.

Since, then, I am not on oath, and, should I fall short of verbal accuracy, I do not need to fear the engines of the law, what seemed to happen was this.

He was standing within about ten feet of where I leaned against the edge of the table. The light was full on, so that it was difficult to suppose that I could make a mistake as to what took place in front of me. As he replied to my mocking allusion to the beetle by echoing my own words, he vanished – or, rather, I saw him taking a different shape before my eyes. His loose draperies all fell off him, and, as they were in the very act of falling, there issued, or there seemed to issue out of them, a monstrous creature of the beetle tribe – the man himself was gone. On the point of size I wish to make myself clear. My impression, when I saw it first, was that it was as large as the man had been, and that it was, in some way, standing up on end, the legs towards me. But, the moment it came in view, it began to dwindle, and that so rapidly that, in a couple of seconds at most, a little heap of drapery was lying on the floor, on which was a truly astonishing example of the coleoptera. It appeared to be a beetle. It was, perhaps, six or seven inches high, and about a foot in length. Its scales were of a vivid golden green. I could distinctly see where the wings were sheathed along the back, and, as they seemed to be slightly agitated, I looked, every moment, to see them opened, and the thing take wing.

I was so astonished – as who would not have been? – that for an appreciable space of time I was practically in a state of stupefaction. I could do nothing but stare. I was acquainted with the legendary transmigrations of Isis, and with the story of the beetle which issues from the woman's womb through all eternity, and with the other pretty tales, but this, of which I was an actual spectator, was something new, even in legends. If the man, with whom I had just been speaking, was gone, where had he gone to? If this glittering creature was there, in his stead, whence had it come?

I do protest this much, that, after the first shock of surprise had passed, I retained my presence of mind. I felt as an investigator might feel, who has stumbled, haphazard, on some astounding, some epoch-making, discovery. I was conscious that I should have to make the best use of my mental faculties if I was to take full advantage of so astonishing an accident. I kept my glance riveted on the creature, with the idea of photographing it on my brain. I believe that if it were possible to take a retinal print – which it some day will be – you would have a perfect picture of what it was I saw. Beyond doubt it was a lamellicorn, one of the *copridæ*. With the one exception of its monstrous size, there were the characteristics in plain view – the convex body, the large head, the projecting clypeus. More, its smooth head and throat seemed to suggest that it was a female. Equally beyond a doubt, apart from its size, there were unusual features present too. The eyes were not only unwontedly conspicuous, they gleamed as if they were lighted by internal flames – in some indescribable fashion they reminded me of my vanished visitor. The colouring was superb, and the creature appeared to have the chameleonlike faculty of lightening and darkening the shades at will. Its not least curious feature was its restlessness. It was in a state of continual agitation; and, as if it resented my inspection, the more I looked at it the more its agitation grew. As I have said, I expected every moment to see it take wing and circle through the air.

All the while I was casting about in my mind as to what means I could use to effect its capture. I did think of killing it, and, on the whole, I rather wish that I had at any rate attempted slaughter – there were dozens of things, lying ready to my hand, any one of which would have severely tried its constitution – but, on the spur of the moment, the only method of taking it alive which occurred to me, was to pop over it a big tin canister which had contained soda-lime. This canister was on the floor to my left. I moved towards it, as nonchalantly as I could, keeping an eye on that shining wonder all the time. Directly I moved, its agitation perceptibly increased – it was, so to speak, all one whirr of tremblement; it scintillated, as if its coloured scales had been so many prisms; it began to unsheath its wings, as if it had finally decided that it would make use of them. Picking up the tin, disembarrassing it of its lid, I sprang towards my intended victim. Its wings opened wide; obviously it was about to rise; but it was too late. Before it had cleared the ground, the tin was over it.

It remained over it, however, for an instant only. I had stumbled, in my haste, and, in my effort to save myself from falling face foremost on to the floor, I was compelled to remove my hands from the tin. Before I was able to replace them, the tin was sent flying, and, while I was still partially recumbent, within eighteen inches of me, that beetle swelled and swelled, until it had assumed its former portentous dimensions, when, as it seemed, it was enveloped by a human shape, and in less time than no time, there stood in front of me, naked from top to toe, my truly versatile Oriental friend. One startling fact nudity revealed – that I had been egregiously mistaken on the question of sex. My visitor was not a man, but a woman, and, judging from the brief glimpse which I had of her body, by no means old or ill-shaped either.

If that transformation was not a bewildering one, then two and two make five. The most level-headed scientist would temporarily have lost his mental equipoise on witnessing such a quick change as that within a span or two of his own nose. I was not only witless, I was breathless too – I could only gape.

And, while I gaped, the woman, stooping down, picking up her draperies, began to huddle them on her anyhow – and, also, to skedaddle towards the door which led into the yard. When I observed this last manœuvre, to some extent I did rise to the requirements of the situation. Leaping up, I rushed to stay her flight.

'Stop!' I shouted.

But she was too quick for me. Ere I could reach her, she had opened the door, and was through it – and, what was more, she had slammed it in my face. In my excitement, I did some fumbling with the handle. When, in my turn, I was in the yard, she was out of sight. I did fancy I saw a dim form disappearing over the wall at the further side, and I made for it as fast as I knew how. I clambered on to the wall, looking this way and that, but there was nothing and no one to be seen. I listened for the sound of retreating footsteps, but all was still. Apparently I had the entire neighbourhood to my own sweet self. My visitor had vanished. Time devoted to pursuit I felt would be time ill-spent.

As I returned across the yard, Woodville, who still was taking his rest under the open canopy of heaven, sat up. Seemingly my approach had roused him out of slumber. At sight of me he rubbed his eyes, and yawned, and blinked.

'I say,' he remarked, not at all unreasonably, 'where am I?'

'You're on holy – or on haunted ground – hang me if I quite know which! – but that's where you are, my boy.'

'By Jove! – I am feeling queer! – I have got a headache, don't you know.'

'I shouldn't be in the least surprised at anything you have, or haven't – I'm beyond surprise. It's a drop of whisky you are wanting – and what I'm wanting too – only, for goodness sake, drop me none of your drops! Mine is a case for a bottle at the least.'

I put my arm through his, and went with him into the laboratory. And, when we were in, I shut, and locked, and barred the door.

## CHAPTER NINETEEN

# THE LADY RAGES

Dora Grayling stood in the doorway.

'I told your servant he need not trouble to show me in – and I've come without my aunt. I hope I'm not intruding.'

She was – confoundedly; and it was on the tip of my tongue to tell her so. She came into the room, with twinkling eyes, looking radiantly happy – that sort of look which makes even a plain young woman prepossessing.

'Am I intruding? – I believe I am.'

She held out her hand, while she was still a dozen feet away, and when I did not at once dash forward to make a clutch at it, she shook her head and made a little mouth at me.

'What's the matter with you? – Aren't you well?'

I was not well – I was very far from well. I was as unwell as I could be without being positively ill, and any person of common discernment would have perceived it at a glance. At the same time I was not going to admit anything of the kind to her.

'Thank you – I am perfectly well.'

'Then, if I were you, I would endeavour to become imperfectly well; a little imperfection in that direction might make you appear to more advantage.'

'I am afraid that I am not one of those persons who ever do appear to much advantage – did I not tell you so last night?'

'I believe you did say something of the kind – it's very good of you to remember. Have you forgotten something else which you said to me last night?'

'You can hardly expect me to keep fresh in my memory all the follies of which my tongue is guilty.'

'Thank you. – That is quite enough. – Good day.'

She turned as if to go.

'Miss Grayling!'

'Mr Atherton?'

'What's the matter? – What have I been saying now?'

'Last night you invited me to come and see you this morning – is that one of the follies of which your tongue was guilty?'

The engagement had escaped my recollection – it is a fact! – and my face betrayed me.

'You had forgotten?' Her cheeks flamed; her eyes sparkled. 'You must pardon my stupidity for not having understood that the invitation was of that general kind which is never meant to be acted on.'

She was half way to the door before I stopped her – I had to take her by the shoulder to do it.

'Miss Grayling! – You are hard on me.'

'I suppose I am. – Is anything harder than to be intruded on by an undesired, and unexpected, guest?'

'Now you are harder still. – If you knew what I have gone through since our conversation of last night, in your strength you would be merciful.'

'Indeed? – What have you gone through?'

I hesitated. What I actually had gone through I certainly did not propose to tell her. Other reasons apart I did not desire to seem madder than I admittedly am – and I lacked sufficient plausibility to enable me to concoct, on the spur of the moment, a plain tale of the doings of my midnight visitor which would have suggested that the narrator was perfectly sane. So I fenced – or tried to.

'For one thing – I have had no sleep.'

I had not – not one single wink. When I did get between the sheets, 'all night I lay in agony', I suffered from that worst form of nightmare – the nightmare of the man who is wide awake. There was continually before my fevered eyes the strange figure of that Nameless Thing. I had often smiled at tales of haunted folk – here was I one of them. My feelings were not rendered more agreeable by a strengthening conviction that if I had only retained the normal attitude of a scientific observer I should, in all probability, have solved the mystery of my Oriental friend, and that his example of the genus of *copridæ* might have been pinned – by a very large pin! – on a piece – a monstrous piece! – of cork. It was galling to reflect that he and I had played together a game of bluff – a game at which civilization was once more proved to be a failure.

She could not have seen all this in my face; but she saw something – because her own look softened.

'You do look tired.' She seemed to be casting about in her own mind for a cause. 'You have been worrying.' She glanced round the big laboratory. 'Have you been spending the night in this – wizard's cave?'

'Pretty well.'

'Oh!'

The monosyllable, as she uttered it, was big with meaning. Uninvited, she seated herself in an arm-chair, a huge old thing, of shagreen leather, which would have held half a dozen of her. Demure in it she looked, like an agreeable reminiscence, alive, and a little up to date, of the women of long ago. Her dove grey eyes seemed to perceive so much more than they cared to show.

'How is it that you have forgotten that you asked me to come? – didn't you mean it?'

'Of course I meant it.'

'Then how is it you've forgotten?'

'I didn't forget.'

'Don't tell fibs. – Something is the matter – tell me what it is. – Is it that I am too early?'

'Nothing of the sort – you couldn't be too early.'

'Thank you. – When you pay a compliment, even so neat a one as that, sometimes, you should look as if you meant it. – It is early – I know it's early, but afterwards I want you to come to lunch. I told aunt that I would bring you back with me.'

'You are much better to me than I deserve.'

'Perhaps.' A tone came into her voice which was almost pathetic. 'I think that to some men women are almost better than they deserve. I don't know why. I suppose it pleases them. It is odd.' There was a different intonation – a dryness. 'Have you forgotten what I came for?'

'Not a bit of it – I am not quite the brute I seem. You came to see an illustration of that pleasant little fancy of mine for slaughtering my fellows. The fact is, I'm hardly in a mood for that just now – I've been illustrating it too much already.'

'What do you mean?'

'Well, for one thing it's been murdering Lessingham's cat.'

'Mr Lessingham's cat?'

'Then it almost murdered Percy Woodville.'

'Mr Atherton! – I wish you wouldn't talk like that.'

'It's a fact. It was a question of a little matter in a wrong place, and, if it hadn't been for something very like a miracle, he'd be dead.'

'I wish you wouldn't have anything to do with such things – I hate them.' I stared.

'Hate them? – I thought you'd come to see an illustration.'

'And pray what was your notion of an illustration?'

'Well, another cat would have had to be killed, at least.'

'And do you suppose that I would have sat still while a cat was being killed for my – edification?'

'It needn't necessarily have been a cat, but something would have had to be killed – how are you going to illustrate the death-dealing propensities of a weapon of that sort without it?'

'Is it possible that you imagine that I came here to see something killed?'

'Then for what did you come?'

I do not know what there was about the question which was startling, but as soon as it was out, she went a fiery red.

'Because I was a fool.'

I was bewildered. Either she had got out of the wrong side of bed, or I had – or we both had. Here she was, assailing me, hammer and tongs, so far as I could see, for absolutely nothing.

'You are pleased to be satirical at my expense.'

'I should not dare. Your detection of me would be so painfully rapid.'

I was in no mood for jangling. I turned a little away from her. Immediately she was at my elbow.

'Mr Atherton?'

'Miss Grayling.'

'Are you cross with me?'

'Why should I be? If it pleases you to laugh at my stupidity you are completely justified.'

'But you are not stupid.'

'No? – Nor you satirical.'

'You are not stupid – you know you are not stupid; it was only stupidity on my part to pretend that you were.'

'It is very good of you to say so. – But I fear that I am an indifferent host. Although you would not care for an illustration, there may be other things which you might find amusing.'

'Why do you keep on snubbing me?'

'I keep on snubbing you!'

'You are always snubbing me – you know you are. Sometimes I feel as if I hated you.'

'Miss Grayling!'

'I do! I do! I do!'

'After all, it is only natural.'

'That is how you talk – as if I were a child, and you were – oh, I don't know what. – Well, Mr Atherton, I am sorry to be obliged to leave you. I have enjoyed my visit very much. I only hope I have not seemed too intrusive.'

She flounced – 'flounce' was the only appropriate word! – out of the room before I could stop her. I caught her in the passage.

'Miss Grayling, I entreat you –'

'Pray do not entreat me, Mr Atherton.' Standing still she turned to me. 'I would rather show myself to the door as I showed myself in, but, if that is impossible, might I ask you not to speak to me between this and the street?'

The hint was broad enough, even for me. I escorted her through the hall without a word – in perfect silence she shook the dust of my abode from off her feet.

I had made a pretty mess of things. I felt it as I stood on the top of the steps and watched her going – she was walking off at four miles an hour; I had not even ventured to ask to be allowed to call a hansom.

It was beginning to occur to me that this was a case in which another blow upon the river might be, to say the least of it, advisable – and I was just returning into the house with the intention of putting myself into my flannels, when a cab drew up, and old Lindon got out of it.

## CHAPTER TWENTY

# A HEAVY FATHER

Mr Lindon was excited – there is no mistaking it when he is, because with him excitement means perspiration, and as soon as he was out of the cab he took off his hat and began to wipe the lining.

'Atherton, I want to speak to you – most particularly – somewhere in private.'

I took him into my laboratory. It is my rule to take no one there; it is a workshop, not a playroom – the place is private; but, recently, my rules had become dead letters. Directly he was inside, Lindon began puffing and stewing, wiping his forehead, throwing out his chest, as if he were oppressed by a sense of his own importance. Then he started off talking at the top of his voice – and it is not a low one either.

'Atherton, I – I've always looked on you as a – a kind of a son.'

'That's very kind of you.'

'I've always regarded you as a – a level-headed fellow; a man from whom sound advice can be obtained when sound advice – is – is most to be desired.'

'That also is very kind of you.'

'And therefore I make no apology for coming to you at – at what may be regarded as a – a strictly domestic crisis; at a moment in the history of the Lindons when delicacy and common sense are – are essentially required.'

This time I contented myself with nodding. Already I perceived what was coming; somehow, when I am with a man I feel so much more clear-headed than I do when I am with a woman – realize so much better the nature of the ground on which I am standing.

'What do you know of this man Lessingham?'

I knew it was coming.

'What all the world knows.'

'And what does all the world know of him? – I ask you that? A flashy, plausible, shallow-pated carpet-bagger – that is what all the world knows of

554

him. The man's a political adventurer – he snatches a precarious, and criminal, notoriety, by trading on the follies of his fellow-countrymen. He is devoid of decency, destitute of principle, and impervious to all the feelings of a gentleman. What do you know of him besides this?'

'I am not prepared to admit that I do know that.'

'Oh yes you do! – don't talk nonsense! – you choose to screen the fellow! I say what I mean – I always have said, and I always shall say. – What do you know of him outside politics – of his family – of his private life?'

'Well – not very much.'

'Of course you don't! – nor does anybody else! The man's a mushroom – or a toadstool, rather! – sprung up in the course of a single night, apparently out of some dirty ditch. – Why, sir, not only is he without ordinary intelligence, he is even without a Brummagen substitute for manners.'

He had worked himself into a state of heat in which his countenance presented a not too agreeable assortment of scarlets and purples. He flung himself into a chair, threw his coat wide open, and his arms too, and started off again.

'The family of the Lindons is, at this moment, represented by a – a young woman – by my daughter, sir. She represents me, and it's her duty to represent me adequately – adequately, sir! And what's more, between ourselves, sir, it's her duty to marry. My property's my own, and I wouldn't have it pass to either of my confounded brothers on any account. They're next door to fools, and – and they don't represent me in any possible sense of the word. My daughter, sir, can marry whom she pleases – whom she pleases! There's no one in England, peer or commoner, who would not esteem it an honour to have her for his wife – I've told her so – yes, sir, I've told her, though you – you'd think that she, of all people in the world, wouldn't require telling. Yet what do you think she does? She – she actually carries on what I – I can't help calling a – a compromising acquaintance with this man Lessingham!'

'No!'

'But I say yes! – and I wish to heaven I didn't. I – I've warned her against the scoundrel more than once; I – I've told her to cut him dead. And yet, as – as you saw yourself, last night, in – in the face of the assembled House of Commons, after that twaddling clap-trap speech of his, in which there was not one sound sentiment, nor an idea which – which would hold water, she positively went away with him, in – in the most ostentatious and – and disgraceful fashion, on – on his arm, and – and actually snubbed her father. – It is monstrous that a parent – a father! – should be subjected to such treatment by his child.'

The poor old boy polished his brow with his pocket-handkerchief.

'When I got home I – I told her what I thought of her, I promise you that – and I told her what I thought of him – I didn't mince my words with her. There are occasions when plain speaking is demanded – and that was one. I positively forbade her to speak to the fellow again, or to recognize him if she met him in the street. I pointed out to her, with perfect candour, that the fellow was an infernal scoundrel – that and nothing else! – and that he would bring disgrace on whoever came into contact with him, even with the end of a barge pole. – And what do you think she said?'

'She promised to obey you, I make no doubt.'

'Did she, sir! – By gad, did she! – That shows how much you know her! – She said, and, by gad, by her manner, and – and the way she went on, you'd – you'd have thought that she was the parent and I was the child – she said that I – I grieved her, that she was disappointed in me, that times have changed – yes, sir, she said that times have changed! – that, nowadays, parents weren't Russian autocrats – no, sir, not Russian autocrats! – that – that she was sorry she couldn't oblige me – yes, sir, that was how she put it – she was sorry she couldn't oblige me, but it was altogether out of the question to suppose that she could put a period to a friendship which she valued, simply on account of – of my unreasonable prejudices – and – and – and, in short, she – she told me to go to the devil, sir!'

'And did you –'

I was on the point of asking him if he went – but I checked myself in time.

'Let us look at the matter as men of the world. What do you know against Lessingham, apart from his politics?'

'That's just it – I know nothing.'

'In a sense, isn't that in his favour?'

'I don't see how you make that out. I – I don't mind telling you that I – I've had inquiries made. He's not been in the House six years – this is his second Parliament – he's jumped up like a Jack-in-the-box. His first constituency was Harwich – they've got him still, and much good may he do 'em! – but how he came to stand for the place – or who, or what, or where he was before he stood for the place, no one seems to have the faintest notion.'

'Hasn't he been a great traveller?'

'I never heard of it.'

'Not in the East?'

'Has he told you so?'

'No – I was only wondering. Well, it seems to me that to find out that nothing is known against him is something in his favour!'

'My dear Sydney, don't talk nonsense. What it proves is simply – that he's a nothing and a nobody. Had he been anything or anyone, something would have been known about him, either for or against. I don't want my daughter to marry a man who – who – who's shot up through a trap, simply because nothing is known against him. Ha-hang me, if I wouldn't ten times sooner she should marry you.'

When he said that, my heart leaped in my bosom. I had to turn away.

'I am afraid that is out of the question.'

He stopped in his tramping, and looked at me askance.

'Why?'

I felt that, if I was not careful, I should be done for – and, probably, in his present mood, Marjorie too.

'My dear Lindon, I cannot tell you how grateful I am to you for your suggestion, but I can only repeat that – unfortunately, anything of the kind is out of the question.'

'I don't see why.'

'Perhaps not.'

'You – you're a pretty lot, upon my word!'

'I'm afraid we are.'

'I – I want you to tell her that Lessingham is a damned scoundrel.'

'I see. – But I would suggest that if I am to use the influence with which you credit me to the best advantage, or to preserve a shred of it, I had hardly better state the fact quite so bluntly as that.'

'I don't care how you state it – state it as you like. Only – only I want you to soak her mind with a loathing of the fellow; I – I – I want you to paint him in his true colours; in – in – in fact, I – I want you to choke him off.'

While he still struggled with his words, and with the perspiration on his brow, Edwards entered. I turned to him.

'What is it?'

'Miss Lindon, sir, wishes to see you particularly, and at once.'

At that moment I found the announcement a trifle perplexing – it delighted Lindon. He began to stutter and to stammer.

'T-the very thing! – c-couldn't have been better! – show her in here! H-hide me somewhere – I don't care where – behind that screen! Y-you use your influence with her – g-give her a good talking to – t-tell her what I've told you; and at – at the critical moment I'll come in, and then – then if we can't manage her between us, it'll be a wonder.'

The proposition staggered me.

'But, my dear Mr Lindon, I fear that I cannot –'

He cut me short.

'Here she comes!'

Ere I could stop him he was behind the screen – I had not seen him move with such agility before – and before I could expostulate Marjorie was in the room. Something which was in her bearing, in her face, in her eyes, quickened the beating of my pulses – she looked as if something had come into her life, and taken the joy clean out of it.

# THE TERROR IN THE NIGHT

'Sydney!' she cried, 'I'm so glad that I can see you!'

She might be – but, at that moment, I could scarcely assert that I was a sharer of her joy.

'I told you that if trouble overtook me I should come to you, and – I'm in trouble now. Such strange trouble.'

So was I – and in perplexity as well. An idea occurred to me – I would outwit her eavesdropping father.

'Come with me into the house – tell me all about it there.'

She refused to budge.

'No – I will tell you all about it here.' She looked about her – as it struck me queerly. 'This is just the sort of place in which to unfold a tale like mine. It looks uncanny.'

'But –'

'"But me no buts!" Sydney, don't torture me – let me stop here where I am – don't you see I'm haunted?'

She had seated herself. Now she stood up, holding her hands out in front of her in a state of extraordinary agitation, her manner as wild as her words.

'Why are you staring at me like that? Do you think I'm mad? – I wonder if I'm going mad. – Sydney, do people suddenly go mad? You're a bit of everything, you're a bit of a doctor too, feel my pulse – there it is! – tell me if I'm ill!'

I felt her pulse – it did not need its swift beating to inform me that fever of some sort was in her veins. I gave her something in a glass. She held it up to the level of her eyes.

'What's this?'

'It's a decoction of my own. You might not think it, but my brain sometimes gets into a whirl. I use it as a sedative. It will do you good.'

She drained the glass.

'It's done me good already – I believe it has; that's being something like a

559

doctor. – Well, Sydney, the storm has almost burst. Last night papa forbade me to speak to Paul Lessingham – by way of a prelude.'

'Exactly. Mr Lindon –'

'Yes, Mr Lindon – that's papa. I fancy we almost quarrelled. I know papa said some surprising things – but it's a way he has – he's apt to say surprising things. He's the best father in the world, but – it's not in his nature to like a really clever person; your good high-dried old Tory never can; – I've always thought that that's why he's so fond of you.'

'Thank you. I presume that is the reason, though it had not occurred to me before.'

Since her entry, I had, to the best of my ability, been turning the position over in my mind. I came to the conclusion that, all things considered, her father had probably as much right to be a sharer of his daughter's confidence as I had, even from the vantage of the screen – and that for him to hear a few home truths proceeding from her lips might serve to clear the air. From such a clearance the lady would not be likely to come off worst. I had not the faintest inkling of what was the actual purport of her visit.

She started off, as it seemed to me, at a tangent.

'Did I tell you last night about what took place yesterday morning – about the adventure of my finding the man?'

'Not a word.'

'I believe I meant to – I'm half disposed to think he's brought me trouble. Isn't there some superstition about evil befalling whoever shelters a homeless stranger?'

'We'll hope not, for humanity's sake.'

'I fancy there is – I feel sure there is. – Anyhow, listen to my story. Yesterday morning, before breakfast – to be accurate, between eight and nine, I looked out of the window, and I saw a crowd in the street. I sent Peter out to see what was the matter. He came back and said there was a man in a fit. I went out to look at the man in the fit. I found, lying on the ground, in the centre of the crowd, a man who, but for the tattered remnants of what had apparently once been a cloak, would have been stark naked. He was covered with dust, and dirt, and blood – a dreadful sight. As you know, I have had my smattering of instruction in First Aid to the Injured, and that kind of thing, so, as no one else seemed to have any sense, and the man seemed as good as dead, I thought I would try my hand. Directly I knelt down beside him, what do you think he said?'

'Thank you.'

'Nonsense. – He said, in such a queer, hollow, croaking voice, "Paul Lessingham." I was dreadfully startled. To hear a perfect stranger, a man in his condition, utter that name in such a fashion – to me, of all people in the world! – took me aback. The policeman who was holding his head remarked, ''That's the first time he's opened his mouth. I thought he was dead.'' He opened his mouth a second time. A convulsive movement went all over him, and he exclaimed, with the strangest earnestness, and so loudly that you might have heard him at the other end of the street, ''Be warned, Paul Lessingham, be warned!'' It was very silly of me, perhaps, but I cannot tell you how his words, and his manner – the two together – affected me. – Well, the long and the short of it was, that I had him taken into the house, and washed, and put to bed – and I had the doctor sent for. The doctor could make nothing of it at all. He reported that the man seemed to be suffering from some sort of cataleptic seizure – I could see that he thought it likely to turn out almost as interesting a case as I did.'

'Did you acquaint your father with the addition to his household?'

She looked at me, quizzically.

'You see, when one has such a father as mine one cannot tell him everything, at once. There are occasions on which one requires time.'

I felt that this would be wholesome hearing for old Lindon.

'Last night, after papa and I had exchanged our little courtesies – which, it is to be hoped, were to papa's satisfaction, since they were not to mine – I went to see the patient. I was told that he had neither eaten nor drunk, moved nor spoken. But, so soon as I approached his bed, he showed signs of agitation. He half raised himself upon his pillow, and he called out, as if he had been addressing some large assembly – I can't describe to you the dreadful something which was in his voice, and on his face – "Paul Lessingham! – Beware! – The Beetle!"'

When she said that, I was startled.

'Are you sure those were the words he used?'

'Quite sure. Do you think I could mistake them – especially after what has happened since? I hear them singing in my ears – they haunt me all the time.'

She put her hands up to her face, as if to veil something from her eyes. I was becoming more and more convinced that there was something about the Apostle's connection with his Oriental friend which needed probing to the bottom.

'What sort of a man is he to look at, this patient of yours?'

I had my doubts as to the gentleman's identity – which her words dissolved; only, however, to increase my mystification in another direction.

'He seems to be between thirty and forty. He has light hair, and straggling sandy whiskers. He is so thin as to be nothing but skin and bone – the doctor says it's a case of starvation.'

'You say he has light hair, and sandy whiskers. Are you sure the whiskers are real?'

She opened her eyes.

'Of course they're real. Why shouldn't they be real?'

'Does he strike you as being a – foreigner?'

'Certainly not. He looks like an Englishman, and he speaks like one, and not, I should say, of the lowest class. It is true that there is a very curious, a weird, quality in his voice, what I have heard of it, but it is not un-English. If it is catalepsy he is suffering from, then it is a kind of catalepsy I never heard of. Have you ever seen a clairvoyant?' I nodded. 'He seems to me to be in a state of clairvoyance. Of course the doctor laughed when I told him so, but we know what doctors are, and I still believe that he is in some condition of the kind. When he said that last night he struck me as being under what those sort of people call "influence", and that whoever had him under influence was forcing him to speak against his will, for the words came from his lips as if they had been wrung from him in agony.'

Knowing what I did know, that struck me as being rather a remarkable conclusion for her to have reached, by the exercise of her own unaided powers of intuition – but I did not choose to let her know I thought so.

'My dear Marjorie! – you who pride yourself on having your imagination so strictly under control! – on suffering it to take no errant flights!'

'Is not the fact that I do so pride myself proof that I am not likely to make assertions wildly – proof, at any rate, to you? Listen to me. When I left that unfortunate creature's room – I had had a nurse sent for, I left him in her charge – and reached my own bedroom, I was possessed by a profound conviction that some appalling, intangible, but very real danger, was at that moment threatening Paul.'

'Remember – you had had an exciting evening; and a discussion with your father. Your patient's words came as a climax.'

'That is what I told myself – or, rather, that was what I tried to tell myself; because, in some extraordinary fashion, I had lost the command of my powers of reflection.'

'Precisely.'

'It was not precisely – or, at least, it was not precisely in the sense you mean. You may laugh at me, Sydney, but I had an altogether indescribable feeling, a feeling which amounted to knowledge, that I was in the presence of the supernatural.'

'Nonsense!'

'It was not nonsense – I wish it had been nonsense. As I have said, I was conscious, completely conscious, that some frightful peril was assailing Paul. I did not know what it was, but I did know that it was something altogether awful, of which merely to think was to shudder. I wanted to go to his assistance, I tried to, more than once; but I couldn't, and I knew that I couldn't – I knew that I couldn't move as much as a finger to help him. – Stop, let me finish! – I told myself that it was absurd, but it wouldn't do; absurd or not, there was the terror with me in the room. I knelt down, and I prayed, but the words wouldn't come. I tried to ask God to remove this burden from my brain, but my longings wouldn't shape themselves into words, and my tongue was palsied. I don't know how long I struggled, but, at last, I came to understand that, for some cause, God had chosen to leave me to fight the fight alone. So I got up, and undressed, and went to bed – and that was the worst of all. I had sent my maid away in the first rush of my terror, afraid, and, I think, ashamed, to let her see my fear. Now I would have given anything to summon her back again, but I couldn't do it, I couldn't even ring the bell. So, as I say, I got into bed.'

She paused, as if to collect her thoughts. To listen to her words, and to think of the suffering which they meant to her, was almost more than I could endure. I would have thrown away the world to have been able to take her in my arms, and soothe her fears. I knew her to be, in general, the least hysterical of young women; little wont to become the prey of mere delusions; and, incredible though it sounded, I had an innate conviction that, even in its wildest periods, her story had some sort of basis in solid fact. What that basis amounted to, it would be my business, at any and every cost, quickly to determine.

'You know how you have always laughed at me because of my objection to – cockroaches, and how, in spring, the neighbourhood of May-bugs has always made me uneasy. As soon as I got into bed I felt that something of the kind was in the room.'

'Something of what kind?'

'Some kind of – beetle. I could hear the whirring of its wings; I could hear its droning in the air; I knew that it was hovering above my head; that it was coming lower and lower, nearer and nearer. I hid myself; I covered myself all over with the clothes – then I felt it bumping against the coverlet. And, Sydney!' She drew closer. Her blanched cheeks and frightened eyes made my heart bleed. Her voice became but an echo of itself. 'It followed me.'

'Marjorie!'

'It got into the bed.'

'You imagined it.'

'I didn't imagine it. I heard it crawl along the sheets, till it found a way between them, and then it crawled towards me. And I felt it – against my face. – And it's there now.'

'Where?'

She raised the forefinger of her left hand.

'There! – Can't you hear it droning?'

She listened, intently. I listened too. Oddly enough, at that instant the droning of an insect did become audible.

'It's only a bee, child, which has found its way through the open window.'

'I wish it were only a bee, I wish it were. – Sydney, don't you feel as if you were in the presence of evil? Don't you want to get away from it, back into the presence of God?'

'Marjorie!'

'Pray, Sydney, pray! – I can't! – I don't know why, but I can't!'

She flung her arms about my neck, and pressed herself against me in paroxysmal agitation. The violence of her emotion bade fair to unman me too. It was so unlike Marjorie – and I would have given my life to save her from a toothache. She kept repeating her own words – as if she could not help it.

'Pray, Sydney, pray!'

At last I did as she wished me. At least, there is no harm in praying – I never heard of its bringing hurt to anyone. I repeated aloud the Lord's Prayer – the first time for I know not how long. As the divine sentences came from my lips, hesitatingly enough, I make no doubt, her tremors ceased. She became calmer. Until, as I reached the last great petition, 'Deliver us from evil,' she loosed her arms from about my neck, and dropped upon her knees, close to my feet. And she joined me in the closing words, as a sort of chorus.

'For Thine is the Kingdom, the Power, and the Glory, for ever and ever. Amen.'

When the prayer was ended, we both of us were still. She with her head bowed, and her hands clasped; and I with something tugging at my heart-strings which I had not felt there for many and many a year, almost as if it had been my mother's hand; – I daresay that sometimes she does stretch out her hand, from her place among the angels, to touch my heart-strings, and I know nothing of it all the while.

As the silence still continued, I chanced to glance up, and there was old Lindon peeping at us from his hiding-place behind the screen. The look of amazed perplexity which was on his big red face struck me with such a keen sense of the incongruous that it was all I could do to keep from laughter. Apparently the sight of us did nothing to lighten the fog which was in his brain, for he stammered out, in what was possibly intended for a whisper,

'Is – is she m-mad?'

The whisper – if it was meant for a whisper – was more than sufficiently audible to catch his daughter's ears. She started – raised her head – sprang to her feet – turned – and saw her father.

'Papa!'

Immediately her sire was seized with an access of stuttering.

'W-w-what the d-devil's the – the m-m-meaning of this?'

Her utterance was clear enough – I fancy her parent found it almost painfully clear.

'Rather it is for me to ask, what is the meaning of this! Is it possible, that, all the time, you have actually been concealed behind that – screen?'

Unless I am mistaken the old gentleman cowered before the directness of his daughter's gaze – and endeavoured to conceal the fact by an explosion of passion.

'Do-don't you s-speak to me li-like that, you un-undutiful girl! I – I'm your father!'

'You certainly are my father; though I was unaware until now that my father was capable of playing the part of eavesdropper.'

Rage rendered him speechless – or, at any rate, he chose to let us believe that that was the determining cause of his continuing silent. So Marjorie turned to me – and, on the whole, I had rather she had not. Her manner was very different from what it had been just now – it was more than civil, it was freezing.

'Am I to understand, Mr Atherton, that this has been done with your cognisance? That while you suffered me to pour out my heart to you unchecked, you were aware, all the time, that there was a listener behind the screen?'

I became keenly aware, on a sudden, that I had borne my share in playing her a very shabby trick – I should have liked to throw old Lindon through the window.

'The thing was not of my contriving. Had I had the opportunity I would have compelled Mr Lindon to face you when you came in. But your distress caused me to lose my balance. And you will do me the justice to remember that I endeavoured to induce you to come with me into another room.'

'But I do not seem to remember your hinting at there being any particular reason why I should have gone.'

'You never gave me a chance.'

'Sydney! – I had not thought you would have played me such a trick!'

When she said that – in such a tone! – the woman whom I loved! – I could have hammered my head against the wall. The hound I was to have treated her so scurvily!

Perceiving I was crushed she turned again to face her father, cool, calm, stately; – she was, on a sudden, once more, the Marjorie with whom I was familiar. The demeanour of parent and child was in striking contrast. If appearances went for aught, the odds were heavy that in any encounter which might be coming the senior would suffer.

'I hope, papa, that you are going to tell me that there has been some curious mistake, and that nothing was farther from your intention than to listen at a keyhole. What would you have thought – and said – if I had attempted to play the spy on you? And I have always understood that men were so particular on points of honour.'

Old Lindon was still hardly fit to do much else than splutter – certainly not qualified to chop phrases with this sharp-tongued maiden.

'D-don't talk to me li-like that, girl! – I – I believe you're s-stark mad!' He turned to me. 'W-what was that tomfoolery she was talking to you about?'

'To what do you allude?'

'About a rub-rubbishing b-beetle, and g-goodness alone knows what – d-diseased and m-morbid imagination – r-reared on the literature of the gutter! – I never thought that a child of mine could have s-sunk to such a depth! – Now, Atherton, I ask you to t-tell me frankly – what do you think of a child who behaves as she has done? who t-takes a nameless vagabond into the house and con-conceals his presence from her father! And m-mark the sequel! even the vagabond warns her against the r-rascal Lessingham! – Now, Atherton, tell me what you think of a girl who behaves like that?' I shrugged my shoulders. 'I – I know very well what you d-do think of her – don't be afraid to say it out because she's present.'

'No; Sydney, don't be afraid.'

I saw that her eyes were dancing – in a manner of speaking, her looks brightened under the sunshine of her father's displeasure.

'Let's hear what you think of her as a – as a m-man of the world!'

'Pray, Sydney, do!'

'What you feel for her in your – your heart of hearts!'

'Yes, Sydney, what do you feel for me in your heart of hearts?'

The baggage beamed with heartless sweetness – she was making a mock of me. Her father turned as if he would have rent her.

'D-don't you speak until you're spoken to! Atherton, I – I hope I'm not deceived in you; I – I hope you're the man I – I took you for; that you're willing and – and ready to play the part of a-a-an honest friend to this mis-misguided simpleton. T-this is not the time for mincing words, it – it's the time for candid speech. Tell this – this weakminded young woman, right out, whether this man Lessingham is, or is not, a damned scoundrel.'

'Papa! – Do you really think that Sydney's opinion, or your opinion, is likely to alter facts?'

'Do you hear, Atherton, tell this wretched girl the truth!'

'My dear Mr Lindon, I have already told you that I know nothing either for or against Mr Lessingham except what is known to all the world.'

'Exactly – and all the world knows him to be a miserable adventurer who is scheming to entrap my daughter.'

'I am bound to say, since you press me, that your language appears to me to be unnecessarily strong.'

'Atherton, I – I'm ashamed of you!'

'You see, Sydney, even papa is ashamed of you; now you are outside the pale. – My dear papa, if you will allow me to speak, I will tell you what I know to be the truth, the whole truth, and nothing but the truth. – That Mr Lessingham is a man with great gifts goes without saying – permit me, papa! He is a man of genius. He is a man of honour. He is a man of the loftiest ambitions, of the highest aims. He has dedicated his whole life to the improvement of the conditions amidst which the less fortunate of his fellow countrymen are at present compelled to exist. That seems to me to be an object well worth having. He has asked me to share his life-work, and I have told him that I will; when, and where, and how, he wants me to. And I will. I do not suppose his life has been free from peccadilloes. I have no delusion on the point. What man's life has? Who among men can claim to be without sin? Even the members of our highest families sometimes hide behind screens. But I know that he is, at least, as good a man as I ever met, I am persuaded that I shall never meet a better; and I thank God that I have found favour in his eyes. – Good-bye, Sydney. – I suppose I shall see you again, papa.'

With the merest inclination of her head to both of us she straightway left the room. Lindon would have stopped her.

'S-stay, y-y-y-you –' he stuttered.

But I caught him by the arm.

'If you will be advised by me, you will let her go. No good purpose will be served by a multiplication of words.'

'Atherton, I – I'm disappointed in you. You – you haven't behaved as I expected. I – I haven't received from you the assistance which I looked for.'

'My dear Lindon, it seems to me that your method of diverting the young lady from the path which she has set herself to tread is calculated to send her furiously along it.'

'C-confound the woman! C-confound the woman! I don't mind telling you, in c-confidence, that at – at times, her mother was the devil, and I'll be – I'll be hanged if her daughter isn't worse. – What was the tomfoolery she was talking to you about? Is she mad?'

'No – I don't think she's mad.'

'I never heard such stuff, it made my blood run cold to hear her. What's the matter with the girl?'

'Well – you must excuse my saying that I don't fancy you quite understand women.'

'I – I don't – and I – I – I don't want to either.'

I hesitated; then resolved on a taradiddle – in Marjorie's interest.

'Marjorie is high-strung – extremely sensitive. Her imagination is quickly aflame. Perhaps, last night, you drove her as far as was safe. You heard for yourself how, in consequence, she suffered. You don't want people to say you have driven her into a lunatic asylum.'

'I – good heavens, no! I – I'll send for the doctor directly I get home – I – I'll have the best opinion in town.'

'You'll do nothing of the kind – you'll only make her worse. What you have to do is to be patient with her, and let her have peace. – As for this affair of Lessingham's, I have a suspicion that it may not be all such plain sailing as she supposes.'

'What do you mean?'

'I mean nothing. I only wish you to understand that until you hear from me again you had better let matters slide. Give the girl her head.'

'Give the girl her head! H-haven't I – I g-given the g-girl her h-head all her l-life!' He looked at his watch. 'Why, the day's half gone!' He began scurrying towards the front door, I following at his heels. 'I've got a committee meeting on at the club – m-most important! For weeks they've been giving us the worst food you ever tasted in your life – p-played havoc with my digestion, and I – I'm going to tell them if – things aren't changed, they – they'll have to pay my doctor's bills. – As for that man, Lessingham –'

As he spoke, he himself opened the hall door, and there, standing on the step was 'that man Lessingham' himself. Lindon was a picture. The Apostle was as cool as a cucumber. He held out his hand.

'Good morning, Mr Lindon. What delightful weather we are having.'

Lindon put his hand behind his back – and behaved as stupidly as he very well could have done.

'You will understand, Mr Lessingham, that, in future, I don't know you, and that I shall decline to recognize you anywhere; and that what I say applies equally to any member of my family.'

With his hat very much on the back of his head he went down the steps like an inflated turkeycock.

## CHAPTER TWENTY-TWO

# THE HAUNTED MAN

To have received the cut discourteous from his future father-in-law might have been the most commonplace of incidents – Lessingham evinced not a trace of discomposure. So far as I could judge, he took no notice of the episode whatever, behaving exactly as if nothing had happened. He merely waited till Mr Lindon was well off the steps; then, turning to me, he placidly observed,

'Interrupting you again, you see. – May I?'

The sight of him had set up such a turmoil in my veins, that, for the moment, I could not trust myself to speak. I felt, acutely, that an explanation with him was, of all things, the thing most to be desired – and that quickly. Providence could not have thrown him more opportunely in the way. If, before he went away, we did not understand each other a good deal more clearly, upon certain points, the fault should not be mine. Without a responsive word, turning on my heels, I led the way into the laboratory.

Whether he noticed anything peculiar in my demeanour, I could not tell. Within he looked about him with that purely facial smile, the sight of which had always engendered in me a certain distrust of him.

'Do you always receive visitors in here?'

'By no means.'

'What is this?'

Stooping down, he picked up something from the floor. It was a lady's purse – a gorgeous affair, of crimson leather and gleaming gold. Whether it was Marjorie's or Miss Grayling's I could not tell. He watched me as I examined it.

'Is it yours?'

'No. It is not mine.'

Placing his hat and umbrella on one chair, he placed himself upon another – very leisurely. Crossing his legs, laying his folded hands upon his knees, he sat and looked at me. I was quite conscious of his observation; but endured it in silence, being a little wishful that he should begin.

Presently he had, as I suppose, enough of looking at me, and spoke.

'Atherton, what is the matter with you? – Have I done something to offend you too?'

'Why do you ask?'

'Your manner seems a little singular.'

'You think so?'

'I do.'

'What have you come to see me about?'

'Just now, nothing. – I like to know where I stand.'

His manner was courteous, easy, even graceful. I was outmanœuvred. I understood the man sufficiently well to be aware that when once he was on the defensive, the first blow would have to come from me. So I struck it.

'I, also, like to know where I stand. – Lessingham, I am aware, and you know that I am aware, that you have made certain overtures to Miss Lindon. That is a fact in which I am keenly interested.'

'As – how?'

'The Lindons and the Athertons are not the acquaintances of one generation only. Marjorie Lindon and I have been friends since childhood. She looks upon me as a brother –'

'As a brother?'

'As a brother.'

'Yes.'

'Mr Lindon regards me as a son. He has given me his confidence; as I believe you are aware, Marjorie has given me hers; and now I want you to give me yours.'

'What do you want to know?'

'I wish to explain my position before I say what I have to say, because I want you to understand me clearly. – I believe, honestly, that the thing I most desire in this world is to see Marjorie Lindon happy. If I thought she would be happy with you, I should say, God speed you both! and I should congratulate you with all my heart, because I think that you would have won the best girl in the whole world to be your wife.'

'I think so too.'

'But, before I did that, I should have to see, at least, some reasonable probability that she would be happy with you.'

'Why should she not?'

'Will you answer a question?'

'What is the question?'

'What is the story in your life of which you stand in such hideous terror?'

There was a perceptible pause before he answered.

'Explain yourself.'

'No explanation is needed – you know perfectly well what I mean.'

'You credit me with miraculous acumen.'

'Don't juggle, Lessingham – be frank!'

'The frankness should not be all on one side. – There is that in your frankness, although you may be unconscious of it, which some men might not unreasonably resent.'

'Do you resent it?'

'That depends. If you are arrogating to yourself the right to place yourself between Miss Lindon and me, I do resent it, strongly.'

'Answer my question!'

'I answer no question which is addressed to me in such a tone.'

He was as calm as you please. I recognized that already I was in peril of losing my temper – which was not at all what I desired. I eyed him intently, he returning me look for look. His countenance betrayed no sign of a guilty conscience; I had not seen him more completely at his ease. He smiled – facially, and also, as it seemed to me, a little derisively. I am bound to admit that his bearing showed not the faintest shadow of resentment, and that in his eyes there was a gentleness, a softness, which I had not observed in them before – I could almost have suspected him of being sympathetic.

'In this matter, you must know, I stand in the place of Mr Lindon.'

'Well?'

'Surely you must understand that before anyone is allowed to think of marriage with Marjorie Lindon he will have to show that his past, as the advertisements have it, will bear the fullest investigation.'

'Is that so? – Will your past bear the fullest investigation?'

I winced.

'At any rate, it is known to all the world.'

'Is it? – Forgive me if I say, I doubt it. I doubt if, of any wise man, that can be said with truth. In all our lives there are episodes which we keep to ourselves.'

I felt that that was so true that, for the instant, I hardly knew what to say.

'But there are episodes and episodes, and when it comes to a man being haunted one draws the line.'

'Haunted?'

'As you are.'

He got up.

'Atherton, I think that I understand you, but I fear that you do not understand me.' He went to where a self-acting mercurial air-pump was standing on a shelf. 'What is this curious arrangement of glass tubes and bulbs?'

'I do not think that you do understand me, or you would know that I am in no mood to be trifled with.'

'Is it some kind of an exhauster?'

'My dear Lessingham, I am entirely at your service. I intend to have an answer to my question before you leave this room, but, in the meanwhile, your convenience is mine. There are some very interesting things here which you might care to see.'

'Marvellous, is it not, how the human intellect progresses – from conquest unto conquest.'

'Among the ancients the progression had proceeded farther than with us.'

'In what respect?'

'For instance, in the affair of the Apotheosis of the Beetle; – I saw it take place last night.'

'Where?'

'Here – within a few feet of where you are standing.'

'Are you serious?'

'Perfectly.'

'What did you see?'

'I saw the legendary Apotheosis of the Beetle performed, last night, before my eyes, with a gaudy magnificence at which the legends never hinted.'

'That is odd. I once thought that I saw something of the kind myself.'

'So I understand.'

'From whom?'

'From a friend of yours.'

'From a friend of mine? – Are you sure it was from a friend of mine?'

The man's attempt at coolness did him credit – but it did not deceive me. That he thought I was endeavouring to bluff him out of his secret I perceived quite clearly; that it was a secret which he would only render with his life I was beginning to suspect. Had it not been for Marjorie, I should have cared nothing – his affairs were his affairs; though I realized perfectly well that there was something about the man which, from the scientific explorer's point of view, might be well worth finding out. Still, as I say, if it had not been for Marjorie, I should have let it go; but, since she was so intimately concerned in it, I wondered more and more what it could be.

My attitude towards what is called the supernatural is an open one. That all things are possible I unhesitatingly believe – I have, even in my short time, seen so many so-called impossibilities proved possible. That we know everything, I doubt; – that our great-great-great-great-grandsires, our fore-bears of thousands of years ago, of the extinct civilizations, knew more on some subjects than we do, I think is, at least, probable. All the legends can hardly be false.

Because men claimed to be able to do things in those days which we cannot do, and which we do not know how they did, we profess to think that their claims are finally dismissed by exclaiming – lies! But it is not so sure.

For my part, what I had seen I had seen. I had seen some devil's trick played before my very eyes. Some trick of the same sort seemed to have been played upon my Marjorie – I repeat that I write 'my Marjorie' because, to me, she will always be 'my' Marjorie! It had driven her half out of her senses. As I looked at Lessingham, I seemed to see her at his side, as I had seen her not long ago, with her white, drawn face, and staring eyes, dumb with an agony of fear. Her life was bidding fair to be knit with his – what Upas tree of horror was rooted in his very bones? The thought that her sweet purity was likely to be engulfed in a devil's slough in which he was wallowing was not to be endured. As I realized that the man was more than my match at the game which I was playing – in which such vital interests were at stake! – my hands itched to clutch him by the throat, and try another way.

Doubtless my face revealed my feelings, because, presently, he said,

'Are you aware how strangely you are looking at me, Atherton? Were my countenance a mirror I think you would be surprised to see in it your own.'

I drew back from him – I daresay, sullenly.

'Not so surprised as, yesterday morning, you would have been to have seen yours – at the mere sight of a pictured scarab.'

'How easily you quarrel.'

'I do not quarrel.'

'Then, perhaps it's I. If that is so, then, at once, the quarrel's ended – pouf! it's done. Mr Lindon, I fear, because, politically, we differ, regards me as anathema. Has he put some of his spirit into you? – You are a wiser man.'

'I am aware that you are an adept with words. But this is a case in which words only will not serve.'

'Then what will serve?'

'I am myself beginning to wonder.'

'And I.'

'As you so courteously suggest, I believe I am wiser than Lindon. I do not care for your politics, or for what you call your politics, one fig. I do not care if you are as other men are, as I am – not unspotted from the world! But I do care if you are leprous. And I believe you are.'

'Atherton!'

'Ever since I have known you I have been conscious of there being something about you which I found it difficult to diagnose; – in an unwholesome sense, something out of the common, non-natural; an atmosphere of your own. Events, so far as you are concerned, have during the last few days moved quickly. They have thrown an uncomfortably lurid light on that peculiarity of yours which I have noticed. Unless you can explain them to my satisfaction, you will withdraw your pretensions to Miss Lindon's hand, or I shall place certain facts before that lady, and, if necessary, publish them to the world.'

He grew visibly paler but he smiled – facially.

'You have your own way of conducting a conversation, Mr Atherton. – What are the events to whose rapid transit you are alluding?'

'Who was the individual, practically stark naked, who came out of your house, in such singular fashion, at dead of night?'

'Is that one of the facts with which you propose to tickle the public ear?'

'Is that the only explanation which you have to offer?'

'Proceed, for the present, with your indictment.'

'I am not so unobservant as you appear to imagine. There were features about the episode which struck me forcibly at the time, and which have struck me more forcibly since. To suggest, as you did yesterday morning, that it was an ordinary case of burglary, or that the man was a lunatic, is an absurdity.'

'Pardon me – I did nothing of the kind.'

'Then what do you suggest?'

'I suggest, and do suggest, nothing. All the suggestions come from you.'

'You went very much out of your way to beg me to keep the matter quiet. There is an appearance of suggestion about that.'

'You take a jaundiced view of all my actions, Mr Atherton. Nothing, to me, could seem more natural. – However – proceed.'

He had his hands behind his back, and rested them on the edge of the table against which he was leaning. He was undoubtedly ill at ease; but so far I had not made the impression on him, either mentally or morally, which I desired.

'Who is your Oriental friend?'

'I do not follow you.'

'Are you sure?'

'I am certain. Repeat your question.'

'Who is your Oriental friend?'

'I was not aware that I had one.'

'Do you swear that?'

He laughed, a strange laugh.

'Do you seek to catch me tripping? You conduct your case with too much animus. You must allow me to grasp the exact purport of your inquiry before I can undertake to reply to it on oath.'

'Are you not aware that at present there is in London an individual who claims to have had a very close, and a very curious, acquaintance with you in the East?'

'I am not.'

'That you swear?'

'That I do swear.'

'That is singular.'

'Why is it singular?'

'Because I fancy that that individual haunts you.'

'Haunts me?'

'Haunts you.'

'You jest.'

'You think so? – You remember that picture of the scarabæus which, yesterday morning, frightened you into a state of semi-idiocy.'

'You use strong language. – I know what you allude to.'

'Do you mean to say that you don't know that you were indebted for that to your Oriental friend?'

'I don't understand you.'

'Are you sure?'

'Certainly I am sure. – It occurs to me, Mr Atherton, that an explanation is demanded from you rather than from me. Are you aware that the purport of my presence here is to ask you how that picture found its way into your room?'

'It was projected by the Lord of the Beetle.'

The words were chance ones – but they struck a mark.

'The Lord –' He faltered – and stopped. He showed signs of discomposure. 'I will be frank with you – since frankness is what you ask.' His smile, that time, was obviously forced. 'Recently I have been the victim of delusions'; there was a pause before the word, 'of a singular kind. I have feared that they were the result of mental overstrain. Is it possible that you can enlighten me as to their source?'

I was silent. He was putting a great strain upon himself, but the twitching of his lips betrayed him. A little more, and I should reach the other side of Mr Lessingham – the side which he kept hidden from the world.

'Who is this – individual whom you speak of as my – Oriental friend?'

'Being your friend, you should know better than I do.'

'What sort of man is he to look at?'

'I did not say it was a man.'

'But I presume it is a man.'

'I did not say so.'

He seemed, for a moment, to hold his breath – and he looked at me with eyes which were not friendly. Then, with a display of self-command which did him credit, he drew himself upright, with an air of dignity which well became him.

'Atherton, consciously, or unconsciously, you are doing me a serious injustice. I do not know what conception it is which you have formed of me, or on what the conception is founded, but I protest that, to the best of my knowledge and belief, I am as reputable, as honest, and as clean a man as you are.'

'But you're haunted.'

'Haunted?' He held himself erect, looking me straight in the face. Then a shiver went all over him; the muscles of his mouth twitched; and, in an instant, he was livid. He staggered against the table. 'Yes, God knows it's true – I'm haunted.'

'So either you're mad, and therefore unfit to marry; or else you've done something which places you outside the tolerably generous boundaries of civilized society, and are therefore still more unfit to marry. You're on the horns of a dilemma.'

'I – I'm the victim of a delusion.'

'What is the nature of the delusion? Does it take the shape of a – beetle?'

'Atherton!'

Without the slightest warning, he collapsed – was transformed; I can describe the change which took place in him in no other way. He sank in a heap on the floor; he held up his hands above his head; and he gibbered – like some frenzied animal. A more uncomfortable spectacle than he presented it would be difficult to find. I have seen it matched in the padded rooms of lunatic asylums, but nowhere else. The sight of him set every nerve of my body on edge.

'In Heaven's name, what is the matter with you, man? Are you stark, staring mad? Here – drink this!'

Filling a tumbler with brandy, I forced it between his quivering fingers. Then it was some moments before I could get him to understand what it was I wanted him to do. When he did get the glass to his lips, he swallowed its contents as if they were so much water. By degrees his senses returned to him. He stood up. He looked about him, with a smile which was positively ghastly.

'It's – it's a delusion.'

'It's a very queer kind of a delusion, if it is.'

I eyed him, curiously. He was evidently making the most strenuous efforts to regain his self-control – all the while with that horrible smile about his lips.

'Atherton, you – you take me at an advantage.' I was still. 'Who – who's your Oriental friend?'

'My Oriental friend? – you mean yours. I supposed, at first, that the individual in question was a man; but it appears that she's a woman.'

'A woman? – Oh. – How do you mean?'

'Well, the face is a man's – of an uncommonly disagreeable type, of which the powers forbid that there are many! – and the voice is a man's – also of a kind! – but the body, as, last night, I chanced to discover, is a woman's.'

'That sounds very odd.' He closed his eyes. I could see that his cheeks were clammy. 'Do you – do you believe in witchcraft?'

'That depends.'

'Have you heard of Obi?'

'I have.'

'I have been told that an Obeah man can put a spell upon a person which compels a person to see whatever he – the Obeah man – may please. Do you think that's possible?'

'It is not a question to which I should be disposed to answer either yes or no.'

He looked at me out of his half-closed eyes. It struck me that he was making conversation – saying anything for the sake of gaining time.

'I remember reading a book entitled "Obscure Diseases of the Brain". It contained some interesting data on the subject of hallucinations.'

'Possibly.'

'Now, candidly, would you recommend me to place myself in the hands of a mental pathologist?'

'I don't think that you're insane, if that's what you mean.'

'No? – That is good hearing. Of all diseases insanity is the most to be dreaded. – Well, Atherton, I'm keeping you. The truth is that, insane or not, I am very far from well. I think I must give myself a holiday.'

He moved towards his hat and umbrella.

'There is something else which you must do.'

'What is that?'

'You must resign your pretensions to Miss Lindon's hand.'

'My dear Atherton, if my health is really failing me, I shall resign everything – everything!'

He repeated his own word with a little movement of his hands which was pathetic.

'Understand me, Lessingham. What else you do is no affair of mine. I am concerned only with Miss Lindon. You must give me your definite promise, before you leave this room, to terminate your engagement with her before tonight.'

His back was towards me.

'There will come a time when your conscience will prick you because of your treatment of me; when you will realize that I am the most unfortunate of men.'

'I realize that now. It is because I realize it that I am so desirous that the shadow of your evil fortune shall not fall upon an innocent girl.'

He turned.

'Atherton, what is your actual position with reference to Marjorie Lindon?'

'She regards me as a brother.'

'And do you regard her as a sister? Are your sentiments towards her purely fraternal?'

'You know that I love her.'

'And do you suppose that my removal will clear the path for you?'

'I suppose nothing of the kind. You may believe me or not, but my one desire is for her happiness, and surely, if you love her, that is your desire too.'

'That is so.' He paused. An expression of sadness stole over his face of which I had not thought it capable. 'That is so to an extent of which you do not dream. No man likes to have his hand forced, especially by one whom he regards – may I say it? – as a possible rival. But I will tell you this much. If the blight which has fallen on my life is likely to continue, I would not wish – God forbid that I should wish to join her fate with mine – not for all that the world could offer me.'

He stopped. And I was still. Presently he continued.

'When I was younger I was subject to a – similar delusion. But it vanished – I saw no trace of it for years – I thought that I had done with it for good. Recently, however, it has returned – as you have witnessed. I shall institute inquiries into the cause of its reappearance; if it seems likely to be irremovable, or even if it bids fair to be prolonged, I shall not only, as you phrase it, withdraw my pretensions to Miss Lindon's hand, but to all my other ambitions. In the interim, as regards Miss Lindon I shall be careful to hold myself on the footing of a mere acquaintance.'

'You promise me?'

'I do. – And on your side, Atherton, in the meantime, deal with me more gently. Judgement in my case has still to be given. You will find that I am not the guilty wretch you apparently imagine. And there are few things more disagreeable to one's self-esteem than to learn, too late, that one has persisted in judging another man too harshly. Think of all that the world has, at this moment, to offer me, and what it will mean if I have to turn my back on it – owing to a mischievous twist of fortune's wheel.'

He turned, as if to go. Then stopped, and looked round, in an attitude of listening.

'What's that?'

There was a sound of droning – I recalled what Marjorie had said of her experiences of the night before, it was like the droning of a beetle. The instant the Apostle heard it, the fashion of his countenance began to change – it was pitiable to witness. I rushed to him.

'Lessingham! – don't be a fool! – play the man!'

He gripped my left arm with his right hand till it felt as if it were being compressed in a vice.

'Then – I shall have to have some more brandy.'

Fortunately the bottle was within reach from where I stood, otherwise I doubt if he would have released my arm to let me get at it. I gave him the decanter and the glass. He helped himself to a copious libation. By the time that he had swallowed it the droning sound had gone. He put down the empty tumbler.

'When a man has to resort to alcohol to keep his nerves up to concert pitch, things are in a bad way with him, you may be sure of that – but then you have never known what it is to stand in momentary expectation of a tête-à-tête with the devil.'

Again he turned to leave the room – and this time he actually went. I let him go alone. I heard his footsteps passing along the passage, and the hall-door close. Then I sat in an arm-chair, stretched my legs out in front of me, thrust my hands in my trouser pockets, and – I wondered.

I had been there, perhaps, four or five minutes, when there was a slight noise at my side. Glancing round, I saw a sheet of paper come fluttering through the open window. It fell almost at my feet. I picked it up. It was a picture of a beetle – a facsimile of the one which had had such an extraordinary effect on Mr Lessingham the day before.

'If this was intended for St Paul, it's a trifle late; – unless –'

I could hear that someone was approaching along the corridor. I looked up, expecting to see the Apostle reappear; – in which expectation I was agreeably disappointed. The newcomer was feminine. It was Miss Grayling. As she stood in the open doorway, I saw that her cheeks were red as roses.

'I hope I am not interrupting you again, but – I left my purse here.' She stopped; then added, as if it were an afterthought, 'And – I want you to come and lunch with me.'

I locked the picture of the beetle in the drawer – and I lunched with Dora Grayling.

# BOOK III

# THE TERROR BY NIGHT AND THE TERROR BY DAY

*Miss Marjorie Lindon tells the Tale*

## CHAPTER TWENTY-THREE

## THE WAY HE TOLD HER

I am the happiest woman in the world! I wonder how many women have said that of themselves in their time – but I am. Paul has told me that he loves me. How long I have made inward confession of my love for him, I should be ashamed to say. It sounds prosaic, but I believe it is a fact that the first stirring of my pulses was caused by the report of a speech of his which I read in *The Times*. It was on the Eight Hours' Bill. Papa was most unflattering. He said that he was an oily spouter, an ignorant agitator, an irresponsible firebrand, and a good deal more to the same effect. I remember very well how papa fidgeted with the paper, declaring that it read even worse than it had sounded, and goodness knew that it had sounded bad enough. He was so very emphatic that when he had gone I thought I would see what all the pother was about, and read the speech for myself. So I read it. It affected me quite differently. The speaker's words showed such knowledge, charity, and sympathy that they went straight to my heart.

After that I read everything of Paul Lessingham's which I came across. And the more I read the more I was impressed. But it was some time before we met. Considering what papa's opinions were, it was not likely that he would go out of his way to facilitate a meeting. To him, the mere mention of the name was like a red rag to a bull. But at last we did meet. And then I knew that he was stronger, greater, better even than his words. It is so often the other way; one finds that men, and women too, are so apt to put their best, as it were, into their shop windows, that the discovery was as novel as it was delightful.

When the ice was once broken, we often met. I do not know how it was. We did not plan our meetings – at first, at any rate. Yet we seemed always meeting. Seldom a day passed on which we did not meet – sometimes twice or thrice. It was odd how we were always coming across each other in the most unlikely places. I believe we did not notice it at the time, but looking back I can see that we must have managed our engagements so that somewhere, somehow, we should be certain to have an opportunity of exchanging half a dozen words. Those constant encounters could not have all been chance ones.

But I never supposed he loved me – never. I am not even sure that, for some time, I was aware that I loved him. We were great on friendship, both of us – I was quite aware that I was his friend – that he regarded me as his friend; he told me so more than once.

'I tell you this,' he would say, referring to this, that, or the other, 'because I know that, in speaking to you, I am speaking to a friend.'

With him those were not empty words. All kinds of people talk to one like that – especially men; it is a kind of formula which they use with every woman who shows herself disposed to listen. But Paul is not like that. He is chary of speech; not by any means a woman's man. I tell him that is his weakest point. If legend does not lie more even than is common, few politicians have achieved prosperity without the aid of women. He replies that he is not a politician; that he never means to be a politician. He simply wishes to work for his country; if his country does not need his services – well, let it be. Papa's political friends have always so many axes of their own to grind, that, at first, to hear a member of Parliament talk like that was almost disquieting. I had dreamed of men like that; but I never encountered one till I met Paul Lessingham.

Our friendship was a pleasant one. It became pleasanter and pleasanter. Until there came a time when he told me everything; the dreams he dreamed; the plans which he had planned; the great purposes which, if health and strength were given him, he intended to carry to a great fulfilment. And, at last, he told me something else.

It was after a meeting at a Working Women's Club in Westminster. He had spoken, and I had spoken too. I don't know what papa would have said, if he had known, but I had. A formal resolution had been proposed, and I seconded it – in perhaps a couple of hundred words; but that would have been quite enough for papa to have regarded me as an Abandoned Wretch – papa always puts those sort of words into capitals. Papa regards a speechifying woman as a thing of horror – I have known him look askance at a Primrose Dame.

The night was fine. Paul proposed that I should walk with him down the Westminster Bridge Road, until we reached the House, and then he would see me into a cab. I did as he suggested. It was still early, not yet ten, and the streets were alive with people. Our conversation, as we went, was entirely political. The Agricultural Amendment Act was then before the Commons, and Paul felt very strongly that it was one of those measures which give with one hand, while taking with the other. The committee stage was at hand, and already several amendments were threatened, the effect of which would be to strengthen the landlord at the expense of the tenant. More than one of these, and they not the most moderate, were to be proposed by papa. Paul was pointing out how it would be his duty to oppose these tooth and nail, when, all at once, he stopped.

'I sometimes wonder how you really feel upon this matter.'

'What matter?'

'On the difference of opinion, in political matters, which exists between your father and myself. I am conscious that Mr Lindon regards my action as a personal question, and resents it so keenly, that I am sometimes moved to wonder if at least a portion of his resentment is not shared by you.'

'I have explained; I consider papa the politician as one person, and papa the father as quite another.'

'You are his daughter.'

'Certainly I am; – but would you, on that account, wish me to share his political opinions, even though I believe them to be wrong?'

'You love him.'

'Of course I do – he is the best of fathers.'

'Your defection will be a grievous disappointment.'

I looked at him out of the corner of my eye. I wondered what was passing through his mind. The subject of my relations with papa was one which, without saying anything at all about it, we had consented to taboo.

'I am not so sure. I am permeated with a suspicion that papa has no politics.'

'Miss Lindon! – I fancy that I can adduce proof to the contrary.'

'I believe that if papa were to marry again, say, a Home Ruler, within three weeks his wife's politics would be his own.'

Paul thought before he spoke; then he smiled.

'I suppose that men sometimes do change their coats to please their wives – even their political ones.'

'Papa's opinions are the opinions of those with whom he mixes. The reason why he consorts with Tories of the crusted school is because he fears that if he associated with anybody else – with Radicals, say – before he knew it, he would be a Radical too. With him, association is synonymous with logic.'

Paul laughed outright. By this time we had reached Westminster Bridge. Standing, we looked down upon the river. A long line of lanterns was gliding mysteriously over the waters; it was a tug towing a string of barges. For some moments neither spoke. Then Paul recurred to what I had just been saying.

'And you – do you think marriage would colour your convictions?'

'Would it yours?'

'That depends.' He was silent. Then he said, in that tone which I had learned to look for when he was most in earnest, 'It depends on whether you would marry me.'

I was still. His words were so unexpected that they took my breath away. I knew not what to make of them. My head was in a whirl. Then he addressed to me a monosyllabic interrogation.

'Well?'

I found my voice – or a part of it.

'Well? – to what?'

He came a little closer.

'Will you be my wife?'

The part of my voice which I had found, was lost again. Tears came into my eyes. I shivered. I had not thought that I could be so absurd. Just then the moon came from behind a cloud; the rippling waters were tipped with silver. He spoke again, so gently that his words just reached my ears.

'You know that I love you.'

Then I knew that I loved him too. That what I had fancied was a feeling of friendship was something very different. It was as if somebody, in tearing a veil from before my eyes, had revealed a spectacle which dazzled me. I was speechless. He misconstrued my silence.

'Have I offended you?'

'No.'

I fancy that he noted the tremor which was in my voice, and read it rightly. For he too was still. Presently his hand stole along the parapet, and fastened upon mine, and held it tight.

And that was how it came about. Other things were said; but they were hardly of the first importance. Though I believe we took some time in saying them. Of myself I can say with truth, that my heart was too full for copious speech; I was dumb with a great happiness. And, I believe, I can say the same of Paul. He told me as much when we were parting.

It seemed that we had only just come there when Paul started. Turning, he stared up at Big Ben.

'Midnight! – The House up! – Impossible!'

But it was more than possible, it was fact. We had actually been on the Bridge two hours, and it had not seemed ten minutes. Never had I supposed that the flight of time could have been so entirely unnoticed. Paul was considerably taken aback. His legislative conscience pricked him. He excused himself – in his own fashion.

'Fortunately, for once in a way, my business in the House was not so important as my business out of it.'

He had his arm through mine. We were standing face to face.

'So you call this business!'

He laughed.

He not only saw me into a cab, but he saw me home in it. And in the cab he kissed me. I fancy I was a little out of sorts that night. My nervous system was, perhaps, demoralized. Because, when he kissed me, I did a thing which I never do – I have my own standard of behaviour, and that sort of thing is quite outside of it; I behaved like a sentimental chit. I cried. And it took him all the way to my father's door to comfort me.

I can only hope that, perceiving the singularity of the occasion, he consented to excuse me.

## CHAPTER TWENTY-FOUR

## A WOMAN'S VIEW

Sydney Atherton has asked me to be his wife. It is not only annoying; worse, it is absurd.

This is the result of Paul's wish that our engagement should not be announced. He is afraid of papa; – not really, but for the moment. The atmosphere of the House is charged with electricity. Party feeling runs high. They are at each other, hammer and tongs, about this Agricultural Amendment Act. The strain on Paul is tremendous. I am beginning to feel positively concerned. Little things which I have noticed about him lately convince me that he is being overwrought. I suspect him of having sleepless nights. The amount of work which he has been getting through lately has been too much for any single human being, I care not who he is. He himself admits that he shall be glad when the session is at an end. So shall I.

In the meantime, it is his desire that nothing shall be said about our engagement until the House rises. It is reasonable enough. Papa is sure to be violent – lately, the barest allusion to Paul's name has been enough to make him explode. When the discovery does come, he will be unmanageable – I foresee it clearly. From little incidents which have happened recently I predict the worst. He will be capable of making a scene within the precincts of the House. And, as Paul says, there is some truth in the saying that the last straw breaks the camel's back. He will be better able to face papa's wild wrath when the House has risen.

So the news is to bide a wee. Of course Paul is right. And what he wishes I wish too. Still, it is not all such plain sailing for me as he perhaps thinks. The domestic atmosphere is almost as electrical as that in the House. Papa is like the terrier who scents a rat – he is always sniffing the air. He has not actually forbidden me to speak to Paul – his courage is not quite at the sticking point; but he is constantly making uncomfortable allusions to persons who number among their acquaintance 'political adventurers', 'grasping carpet-baggers', 'Radical riff-raff', and that kind of thing. Sometimes I venture to call my soul my own; but such a tempest invariably follows that I become discreet again as soon as I possibly can. So, as a rule, I suffer in silence.

Still, I would with all my heart that the concealment were at an end. No one need imagine that I am ashamed of being about to marry Paul – papa least of all. On the contrary, I am as proud of it as a woman can be. Sometimes, when he has said or done something unusually wonderful, I fear that my pride will out – I do feel it so strong within me. I should be delighted to have a trial of strength with papa; anywhere, at any time – I should not be so rude to him as he would be to me. At the bottom of his heart papa knows that I am the more sensible of the two; after a pitched battle or so he would understand it better still. I know papa! I have not been his daughter for all these years in vain. I feel like hot-blooded soldiers must feel, who, burning to attack the enemy in the open field, are ordered to skulk behind hedges, and be shot at.

One result is that Sydney has actually made a proposal of marriage – he of all people! It is too comical. The best of it was that he took himself quite seriously. I do not know how many times he has confided to me the sufferings which he has endured for love of other women – some of them, I am sorry to say, decent married women too; but this is the first occasion on which the theme has been a personal one. He was so frantic, as he is wont to be, that, to calm him, I told him about Paul – which, under the circumstances, to him I felt myself at liberty to do. In return, he was melodramatic; hinting darkly at I know not what. I was almost cross with him.

He is a curious person, Sydney Atherton. I suppose it is because I have known him all my life, and have always looked upon him, in cases of necessity, as a capital substitute for a brother, that I criticize him with so much frankness. In some respects, he is a genius; in others – I will not write fool, for that he never is, though he has often done some extremely foolish things. The fame of his inventions is in the mouths of all men; though the half of them has never been told. He is the most extraordinary mixture. The things which most people would like to have proclaimed in the street, he keeps tightly locked in his own bosom; while those which the same persons would be only too glad to conceal, he shouts from the roofs. A very famous man once told me that if Mr Atherton chose to become a specialist, to take up one branch of inquiry, and devote his life to it, his fame, before he died, would bridge the spheres. But sticking to one thing is not in Sydney's line at all. He prefers, like the bee, to roam from flower to flower.

As for his being in love with me; it is ridiculous. He is as much in love with the moon. I cannot think what has put the idea into his head. Some girl must have been ill-using him, or he imagines that she has. The girl whom he ought to marry, and whom he ultimately will marry, is Dora Grayling. She is young, charming, immensely rich, and over head and ears in love with him; –

if she were not, then he would be over head and ears in love with her. I believe he is very near it as it is – sometimes he is so very rude to her. It is a characteristic of Sydney's, that he is apt to be rude to a girl whom he really likes. As for Dora, I suspect she dreams of him. He is tall, straight, very handsome, with a big moustache, and the most extraordinary eyes; – I fancy that those eyes of his have as much to do with Dora's state as anything. I have heard it said that he possesses the hypnotic power to an unusual degree, and that, if he chose to exercise it, he might become a danger to society. I believe he has hypnotized Dora.

He makes an excellent brother. I have gone to him, many and many a time, for help – and some excellent advice I have received. I daresay I shall consult him still. There are matters of which one would hardly dare to talk to Paul. In all things he is the great man. He could hardly condescend to chiffons. Now Sydney can and does. When he is in the mood, on the vital subject of trimmings, a woman could not appeal to a sounder authority. I tell him, if he had been a dressmaker, he would have been magnificent. I am sure he would.

## CHAPTER TWENTY-FIVE

# THE MAN IN THE STREET

This morning I had an adventure.

I was in the breakfast-room. Papa, as usual, was late for breakfast, and I was wondering whether I should begin without him, when, chancing to look round, something caught my eye in the street. I went to the window to see what it was. A small crowd of people was in the middle of the road, and they were all staring at something which, apparently, was lying on the ground. What it was I could not see.

The butler happened to be in the room. I spoke to him.

'Peter, what is the matter in the street? Go and see.'

He went and saw; and, presently, he returned. Peter is an excellent servant; but the fashion of his speech, even when conveying the most trivial information, is slightly sesquipedalian. He would have made a capital cabinet minister at question time – he wraps up the smallest portions of meaning in the largest possible words.

'An unfortunate individual appears to have been the victim of a catastrophe. I am informed that he is dead. The constable asserts that he is drunk.'

'Drunk? – dead? Do you mean that he is dead drunk? – at this hour!'

'He is either one or the other. I did not behold the individual myself. I derived my information from a bystander.'

That was not sufficiently explicit for me. I gave way to a, seemingly, quite causeless impulse of curiosity. I went out into the street, just as I was, to see for myself. It was, perhaps, not the most sensible thing I could have done, and papa would have been shocked; but I am always shocking papa. It had been raining in the night, and the shoes which I had on were not so well suited as they might have been for an encounter with the mud.

I made my way to the point of interest.

'What's the matter?' I asked.

A workman, with a bag of tools over his shoulder, answered me.

'There's something wrong with someone. Policeman says he's drunk, but he looks to me as if he was something worse.'

'Will you let me pass, please?'

When they saw I was a woman, they permitted me to reach the centre of the crowd.

A man was lying on his back, in the grease and dirt of the road. He was so plastered with mud, that it was difficult, at first, to be sure that he really was a man. His head and feet were bare. His body was partially covered by a long ragged cloak. It was obvious that that one wretched, dirt-stained, sopping wet rag was all the clothing he had on. A huge constable was holding his shoulders in his hands, and was regarding him as if he could not make him out at all. He seemed uncertain as to whether it was or was not a case of shamming.

He spoke to him as if he had been some refractory child.

'Come, my lad, this won't do! – Wake up! – What's the matter?'

But he neither woke up, nor explained what was the matter. I took hold of his hand. It was icy cold. Apparently the wrist was pulseless. Clearly this was no ordinary case of drunkenness.

'There is something seriously wrong, officer. Medical assistance ought to be had at once.'

'Do you think he's in a fit, miss?'

'That a doctor should be able to tell you better than I can. There seems to be no pulse. I should not be surprised to find that he was –'

The word 'dead' was actually on my lips, when the stranger saved me from making a glaring exposure of my ignorance by snatching his wrist away from me, and sitting up in the mud. He held out his hands in front of him, opened his eyes, and exclaimed, in a loud, but painfully raucous tone of voice, as if he was suffering from a very bad cold.

'Paul Lessingham!'

I was so surprised that I all but sat down in the mud. To hear Paul – my Paul! – apostrophized by an individual of his appearance, in that fashion, was something which I had not expected. Directly the words were uttered, he closed his eyes again, sank backward, and seemingly relapsed into unconsciousness – the constable gripping him by the shoulder just in time to prevent him banging the back of his head against the road.

The officer shook him – scarcely gently.

'Now, my lad, it's plain that you're not dead! – What's the meaning of this? – Move yourself!'

Looking round I found that Peter was close behind. Apparently he had been struck by the singularity of his mistress' behaviour, and had followed to see that it did not meet with the reward which it deserved. I spoke to him.

'Peter, let someone go at once for Dr Cotes!'

Dr Cotes lives just round the corner, and since it was evident that the man's lapse into consciousness had made the policeman sceptical as to his case being so serious as it seemed, I thought it might be advisable that a competent opinion should be obtained without delay.

Peter was starting, when again the stranger returned to consciousness – that is, if it really was consciousness, as to which I was more than a little in doubt. He repeated his previous pantomime; sat up in the mud, stretched out his arms, opened his eyes unnaturally wide – and yet they appeared unseeing! – a sort of convulsion went all over him, and he shrieked – it really amounted to shrieking – as a man might shriek who was in mortal terror.

'Be warned, Paul Lessingham – be warned!'

For my part, that settled it. There was a mystery here which needed to be unravelled. Twice had he called upon Paul's name – and in the strangest fashion! It was for me to learn the why and the wherefore; to ascertain what connection there was between this lifeless creature and Paul Lessingham. Providence might have cast him there before my door. I might be entertaining an angel unawares. My mind was made up on the instant.

'Peter, hasten for Dr Cotes.' Peter passed the word, and immediately a footman started running as fast as his legs would carry him. 'Officer, I will have this man taken into my father's house. – Will some of you men help to carry him?'

There were volunteers enough, and to spare. I spoke to Peter in the hall.

'Is papa down yet?'

'Mr Lindon has sent down to say that you will please not wait for him for breakfast. He has issued instructions to have his breakfast conveyed to him upstairs.'

'That's all right.' I nodded towards the poor wretch who was being carried through the hall. 'You will say nothing to him about this unless he particularly asks. You understand?'

Peter bowed. He is discretion itself. He knows I have my vagaries, and it is not his fault if the savour of them travels to papa.

The doctor was in the house almost as soon as the stranger.

'Wants washing,' he remarked, directly he saw him.

And that certainly was true – I never saw a man who stood more obviously in need of the good offices of soap and water. Then he went through the usual medical formula, I watching all the while. So far as I could see the man showed not the slightest sign of life.

'Is he dead?'

'He will be soon, if he doesn't have something to eat. The fellow's starving.'

The doctor asked the policeman what he knew of him.

That sagacious officer's reply was vague. A boy had run up to him crying that a man was lying dead in the street. He had straightway followed the boy, and discovered the stranger. That was all he knew.

'What is the matter with the man?' I inquired of the doctor, when the constable had gone.

'Don't know. – It may be catalepsy, and it mayn't. – When I do know, you may ask again.'

Dr Cotes' manner was a trifle brusque – particularly, I believe, to me. I remember that once he threatened to box my ears. When I was a small child I used to think nothing of boxing his.

Realizing that no satisfaction was to be got out of a speechless man – particularly as regards his mysterious references to Paul – I went upstairs. I found that papa was under the impression that he was suffering from a severe attack of gout. But as he was eating a capital breakfast, and apparently enjoying it – while I was still fasting – I ventured to hope that the matter was not so serious as he feared.

I mentioned nothing to him about the person whom I had found in the street – lest it should aggravate his gout. When he is like that, the slightest thing does.

## CHAPTER TWENTY-SIX

## A FATHER'S NO

Paul has stormed the House of Commons with one of the greatest speeches which even he has delivered, and I have quarrelled with papa. And, also, I have very nearly quarrelled with Sydney.

Sydney's little affair is nothing. He actually still persists in thinking himself in love with me – as if, since last night, when he what he calls 'proposed' to me, he has not time to fall out of love, and in again, half a dozen times; and, on the strength of it, he seems to consider himself entitled to make himself as disagreeable as he can. That I should not mind – for Sydney disagreeable is about as nice as Sydney any other way; but when it comes to his shooting poisoned shafts at Paul, I object. If he imagines that anything he can say, or hint, will lessen my estimation of Paul Lessingham by one hair's breadth, he has less wisdom even than I gave him credit for. By the way, Percy Woodville asked me to be his wife tonight – which, also, is nothing; he has been trying to do it for the last three years – though, under the circumstances, it is a little trying; but he would not spit venom merely because I preferred another man – and he, I believe, does care for me.

Papa's affair is serious. It is the first clashing of the foils – and this time, I imagine, the buttons are really off. This morning he said a few words, not so much to, as at me. He informed me that Paul was expected to speak tonight – as if I did not know it! – and availed himself of the opening to load him with the abuse which, in his case, he thinks is not unbecoming to a gentleman. I don't know – or, rather, I do know what he would think, if he heard another man use, in the presence of a woman, the kind of language which he habitually employs. However, I said nothing. I had a motive for allowing the chaff to fly before the wind.

But, tonight, issue was joined.

I, of course, went to hear Paul speak – as I have done over and over again before. Afterwards, Paul came and fetched me from the cage. He had to leave me for a moment, while he gave somebody a message; and in the lobby, there was Sydney – all sneers! I could have pinched him. Just as I was coming to the conclusion that I should have to stick a pin into his arm, Paul returned – and, positively, Sydney was rude to him. I was ashamed, if Mr Atherton was not. As if it was not enough that he should be insulted by a mere popinjay, at the very moment when he had been adding another stone to the fabric of his country's glory – papa came up. He actually wanted to take me away from Paul. I should have liked to see him do it. Of course I went down with Paul to the carriage, leaving papa to follow if he chose. He did not choose – but, none the less, he managed to be home within three minutes after I had myself returned.

Then the battle began.

It is impossible for me to give an idea of papa in a rage. There may be men who look well when they lose their temper, but, if there are, papa is certainly not one. He is always talking about the magnificence, and the high breeding of the Lindons, but anything less high-bred than the head of the Lindons, in his moments of wrath, it would be hard to conceive. His language I will not attempt to portray – but his observations consisted, mainly, of abuse of Paul, glorification of the Lindons, and orders to me.

'I forbid you – I forbid you –' when papa wishes to be impressive he repeats his own words three or four times over; I don't know if he imagines that they are improved by repetition; if he does, he is wrong – 'I forbid you ever again to speak to that – that – that –'

Here followed language.

I was silent.

My cue was to keep cool. I believe that, with the exception, perhaps, of being a little white, and exceedingly sorry that papa should so forget himself, I was about the same as I generally am.

'Do you hear me? – do you hear what I say? – do you hear me, miss?'

'Yes, papa; I hear you.'

'Then – then – then promise me! – promise that you will do as I tell you! – mark my words, my girl, you shall promise before you leave this room!'

'My dear papa! – do you intend me to spend the remainder of my life in the drawing-room?'

'Don't you be impertinent! – do-do-don't you speak to me like that! – I – I – I won't have it!'

'I tell you what it is, papa, if you don't take care you'll have another attack of gout.'

'Damn gout.'

That was the most sensible thing he said; if such a tormentor as gout can be consigned to the nether regions by the mere utterance of a word, by all means let the word be uttered. Off he went again.

'The man's a ruffianly, rascally –' and so on. 'There's not such a villainous vagabond –' and all the rest of it. 'And I order you – I'm a Lindon, and I order you! I'm your father, and I order you! – I order you never to speak to such a – such a' – various vain repetitions – 'again, and – and – and I order you never to look at him!'

'Listen to me, papa. I will promise you never to speak to Paul Lessingham again, if you will promise me never to speak to Lord Cantilever again – or to recognize him if you meet him in the street.'

You should have seen how papa glared. Lord Cantilever is the head of his party. Its august, and, I presume, reverenced leader. He is papa's particular fetish. I am not sure that he does regard him as being any lower than the angels, but if he does it is certainly something in decimals. My suggestion seemed as outrageous to him as his suggestion seemed to me. But it is papa's misfortune that he can only see one side of a question – and that's his own.

'You – you dare to compare Lord Cantilever to – to that – that – that –!'

'I am not comparing them. I am not aware of there being anything in particular against Lord Cantilever – that is against his character. But, of course, I should not dream of comparing a man of his calibre, with one of real ability, like Paul Lessingham. It would be to treat his lordship with too much severity.'

I could not help it – but that did it. The rest of papa's conversation was a jumble of explosions. It was all so sad.

Papa poured all the vials of his wrath upon Paul – to his own sore disfigurement. He threatened me with all the pains and penalties of the inquisition if I did not immediately promise to hold no further communication with Mr Lessingham – of course I did nothing of the kind. He cursed me, in default, by bell, book, and candle – and by ever so many other things beside. He called me the most dreadful names – me! his only child. He warned me that I should find myself in prison before I had done – I am not sure that he did not hint darkly at the gallows. Finally, he drove me from the room in a whirlwind of anathemas.

## CHAPTER TWENTY-SEVEN

# THE TERROR BY NIGHT

When I left papa – or, rather, when papa had driven me from him – I went straight to the man whom I had found in the street. It was late, and I was feeling both tired and worried, so that I only thought of seeing for myself how he was. In some way, he seemed to be a link between Paul and myself, and as, at that moment, links of that kind were precious, I could not have gone to bed without learning something of his condition.

The nurse received me at the door.

'Well, nurse, how's the patient?'

Nurse was a plump, motherly woman, who had attended more than one odd protégé of mine, and whom I kept pretty constantly at my beck and call. She held out her hands.

'It's hard to tell. He hasn't moved since I came.'

'Not moved? – Is he still insensible?'

'He seems to me to be in some sort of trance. He does not appear to breathe, and I can detect no pulsation, but the doctor says he's still alive – it's the queerest case I ever saw.'

I went farther into the room. Directly I did so the man in the bed gave signs of life which were sufficiently unmistakable. Nurse hastened to him.

'Why,' she exclaimed, 'he's moving! – he might have heard you enter!'

He not only might have done, but it seemed possible that that was what he actually had done. As I approached the bed, he raised himself to a sitting posture, as, in the morning, he had done in the street, and he exclaimed, as if he addressed himself to someone whom he saw in front of him – I cannot describe the almost more than human agony which was in his voice.

'Paul Lessingham! – Beware! – The Beetle!'

What he meant I had not the slightest notion. Probably that was why what seemed more like a pronouncement of delirium than anything else had such an extraordinary effect upon my nerves. No sooner had he spoken than a sort of blank horror seemed to settle down upon my mind. I actually found myself trembling at the knees. I felt, all at once, as if I was standing in the immediate presence of something awful yet unseen.

As for the speaker, no sooner were the words out of his lips, than, as was the case in the morning, he relapsed into a condition of trance. Nurse, bending over him, announced the fact.

'He's gone off again! – What an extraordinary thing! – I suppose it is real.' It was clear, from the tone of her voice, that she shared the doubt which had troubled the policeman. 'There's not a trace of a pulse. From the look of things he might be dead. Of one thing I'm sure, that there's something unnatural about the man. No natural illness I ever heard of, takes hold of a man like this.'

Glancing up, she saw that there was something unusual in my face; an appearance which startled her.

'Why, Miss Marjorie, what's the matter! – You look quite ill!'

I felt ill, and worse than ill; but, at the same time, I was quite incapable of describing what I felt to nurse. For some inscrutable reason I had even lost the control of my tongue – I stammered.

'I – I – I'm not feeling very well, nurse; I – I – I think I'll be better in bed.'

As I spoke, I staggered towards the door, conscious, all the while, that nurse was staring at me with eyes wide open. When I got out of the room, it seemed, in some incomprehensible fashion, as if something had left it with me, and that It and I were alone together in the corridor. So overcome was I by the consciousness of its immediate propinquity, that, all at once, I found myself cowering against the wall – as if I expected something or someone to strike me.

How I reached my bedroom I do not know. I found Fanchette awaiting me. For the moment her presence was a positive comfort – until I realized the amazement with which she was regarding me.

'Mademoiselle is not well?'

'Thank you, Fanchette, I – I am rather tired. I will undress myself tonight – you can go to bed.'

'But if mademoiselle is so tired, will she not permit me to assist her?'

The suggestion was reasonable enough – and kindly too; for, to say the least of it, she had as much cause for fatigue as I had. I hesitated. I should have liked to throw my arms about her neck, and beg her not to leave me; but, the plain truth is, I was ashamed. In my inner consciousness I was persuaded that the sense of terror which had suddenly come over me was so absolutely causeless, that I could not bear the notion of playing the craven in my maid's eyes. While I hesitated, something seemed to sweep past me through the air, and to brush against my cheek in passing. I caught at Fanchette's arm.

'Fanchette! – Is there something with us in the room?'

'Something with us in the room? – Mademoiselle? – What does made-moiselle mean?'

She looked disturbed – which was, on the whole, excusable. Fanchette is not exactly a strong-minded person, and not likely to be much of a support when a support was most required. If I was going to play the fool, I would be my own audience. So I sent her off.

'Did you not hear me tell you that I will undress myself? – you are to go to bed.'

She went to bed – with quite sufficient willingness.

The instant that she was out of the room I wished that she was back again. Such a paroxysm of fear came over me, that I was incapable of stirring from the spot on which I stood, and it was all I could do to prevent myself from collapsing in a heap on the floor. I had never, till then, had reason to suppose that I was a coward. Nor to suspect myself of being the possessor of 'nerves'. I was as little likely as anyone to be frightened by shadows. I told myself that the whole thing was sheer absurdity, and that I should be thoroughly ashamed of my own conduct when the morning came.

'If you don't want to be self-branded as a contemptible idiot, Marjorie Lindon, you will call up your courage, and these foolish fears will fly.'

But it would not do. Instead of flying, they grew worse. I became convinced – and the process of conviction was terrible beyond words! – that there actually was something with me in the room, some invisible horror – which, at any moment, might become visible. I seemed to understand – with a sense of agony which nothing can describe! – that this thing which was with me was with Paul. That we were linked together by the bond of a common, and a dreadful terror. That, at that moment, that same awful peril which was threatening me, was threatening him and that I was powerless to move a finger in his aid. As with a sort of second sight, I saw out of the room in which I was, into another, in which Paul was crouching on the floor, covering his face with his hands, and shrieking. The vision came again and again with a degree of vividness of which I cannot give the least conception. At last the horror, and the reality of it, goaded me to frenzy.

'Paul! Paul!' I screamed.

As soon as I found my voice, the vision faded. Once more I understood that, as a matter of simple fact, I was standing in my own bedroom; that the lights were burning brightly; that I had not yet commenced to remove a particle of dress.

'Am I going mad?' I wondered.

I had heard of insanity taking extraordinary forms, but what could have caused softening of the brain in me I had not the faintest notion. Surely that

sort of thing does not come on one – in such a wholly unmitigated form! – without the slightest notice – and that my mental faculties were sound enough a few minutes back I was certain. The first premonition of anything of the kind had come upon me with the melodramatic utterance of the man I had found in the street.

'Paul Lessingham! – Beware! – The Beetle!'

The words were ringing in my ears. – What was that? – There was a buzzing sound behind me. I turned to see what it was. It moved as I moved, so that it was still at my back. I swung, swiftly, right round on my heels. It still eluded me – it was still behind. I stood and listened – what was it that hovered so persistently at my back?

The buzzing was distinctly audible. It was like the humming of a bee. Or – could it be a beetle?

My whole life long I have had an antipathy to beetles – of any sort or kind. I have objected neither to rats nor mice, nor cows, nor bulls, nor snakes, nor spiders, nor toads, nor lizards, nor any of the thousand and one other creatures, animate or otherwise, to which so many people have a rooted, and, apparently, illogical dislike. My pet – and only – horror has been beetles. The mere suspicion of a harmless, and, I am told, necessary cockroach, being within several feet has always made me seriously uneasy. The thought that a great, winged beetle – to me, a flying beetle is the horror of horrors! – was with me in my bedroom – goodness alone knew how it had got there! – was unendurable. Anyone who had beheld me during the next few moments would certainly have supposed I was deranged. I turned and twisted, sprang from side to side, screwed myself into impossible positions, in order to obtain a glimpse of the detested visitant – but in vain. I could hear it all the time; but see it – never! The buzzing sound was continually behind.

The terror returned – I began to think that my brain must be softening. I dashed to the bed. Flinging myself on my knees, I tried to pray. But I was speechless – words would not come; my thoughts would not take shape. I all at once became conscious, as I struggled to ask help of God, that I was wrestling with something evil – that if I only could ask help of Him, evil would flee. But I could not. I was helpless – overmastered. I hid my face in the bedclothes, cramming my fingers into my ears. But the buzzing was behind me all the time.

I sprang up, striking out, blindly, wildly, right and left, hitting nothing – the buzzing always came from a point at which, at the moment, I was not aiming.

I tore off my clothes. I had on a lovely frock which I had worn for the first time that night; I had had it specially made for the occasion of the Duchess' ball, and – more especially – in honour of Paul's great speech. I had said to myself, when I saw my image in a mirror, that it was the most exquisite gown I had ever had, that it suited me to perfection, and that it should continue in my wardrobe for many a day, if only as a souvenir of a memorable night. Now, in the madness of my terror, all reflections of that sort were forgotten. My only desire was to away with it. I tore it off anyhow, letting it fall in rags on the floor at my feet. All else that I had on I flung in the same way after it; it was a veritable holocaust of dainty garments – I acting as relentless executioner who am, as a rule, so tender with my things. I leaped upon the bed, switched off the electric light, hurried into bed, burying myself, over head and all, deep down between the sheets.

I had hoped that by shutting out the light, I might regain my senses. That in the darkness I might have opportunity for sane reflection. But I had made a grievous error. I had exchanged bad for worse. The darkness lent added terrors. The light had not been out five seconds before I would have given all that I was worth to be able to switch it on again.

As I cowered beneath the bedclothes I heard the buzzing sound above my head – the sudden silence of the darkness had rendered it more audible than it had been before. The thing, whatever it was, was hovering above the bed. It came nearer and nearer; it grew clearer and clearer. I felt it alight upon the coverlet; – shall I ever forget the sensations with which I did feel it? It weighed upon me like a ton of lead. How much of the seeming weight was real, and how much imaginary, I cannot pretend to say; but that it was much heavier than any beetle I have ever seen or heard of, I am sure.

For a time it was still – and during that time I doubt if I even drew my breath. Then I felt it begin to move, in wobbling fashion, with awkward, ungainly gait, stopping every now and then, as if for rest. I was conscious that it was progressing, slowly, yet surely, towards the head of the bed. The emotion of horror with which I realized what this progression might mean, will be, I fear, with me to the end of my life – not only in dreams, but too often, also, in my waking hours. My heart, as the Psalmist has it, melted like wax within me. I was incapable of movement – dominated by something as hideous as, and infinitely more powerful than, the fascination of the serpent.

When it reached the head of the bed, what I feared – with what a fear! – would happen, did happen. It began to find its way inside – to creep between the sheets; the wonder is I did not die! I felt it coming nearer and nearer, inch by inch; I knew that it was upon me, that escape there was none; I felt something touch my hair.

And then oblivion did come to my aid. For the first time in my life I swooned.

## CHAPTER TWENTY-EIGHT

# THE STRANGE STORY OF THE MAN IN THE STREET

I have been anticipating for some weeks past, that things would become exciting – and they have. But hardly in the way which I foresaw. It is the old story of the unexpected happening. Suddenly events of the most extraordinary nature have come crowding on me from the most unlooked-for quarters.

Let me try to take them in something like their proper order.

To begin with, Sydney has behaved very badly. So badly that it seems likely that I shall have to re-cast my whole conception of his character. It was nearly nine o'clock this morning when I – I cannot say woke up, because I do not believe that I had really been asleep – but when I returned to consciousness. I found myself sitting up in bed, trembling like some frightened child. What had actually happened to me I did not know – could not guess. I was conscious of an overwhelming sense of nausea, and, generally, I was feeling very far from well. I endeavoured to arrange my thoughts, and to decide upon some plan of action. Finally, I decided to go for advice and help where I had so often gone before – to Sydney Atherton.

I went to him. I told him the whole gruesome story. He saw, he could not help but see what a deep impress the events of the night had made on me. He heard me to the end with every appearance of sympathy – and then all at once I discovered that all the time papa had been concealed behind a large screen which was in the room, listening to every word I had been uttering. That I was dumbfounded, goes without saying. It was bad enough in papa, but in Sydney it seemed, and it was, such treachery. He and I had told each other secrets all our lives; it has never entered my imagination, as he very well knows, to play him false, in one jot or tittle; and I have always understood that, in this sort of matter, men pride themselves on their sense of honour being so much keener than women's. I told them some plain truths; and I fancy that I left them both feeling heartily ashamed of themselves.

One result the experience had on me – it wound me up. It had on me the revivifying effect of a cold douche. I realized that mine was a situation in which I should have to help myself.

When I returned home I learned that the man whom I had found in the street was himself again, and was as conscious as he was ever likely to be. Burning with curiosity to learn the nature of the connection which existed between Paul and him, and what was the meaning of his oracular apostrophes, I merely paused to remove my hat before hastening into his apartment.

When he saw me, and heard who I was, the expressions of his gratitude were painful in their intensity. The tears streamed down his cheeks. He looked to me like a man who had very little life left in him. He looked weak, and white, and worn to a shadow. Probably he never had been robust, and it was only too plain that privation had robbed him of what little strength he had ever had. He was nothing else but skin and bone. Physical and mental debility was written large all over him.

He was not bad-looking – in a milk and watery sort of way. He had pale blue eyes and very fair hair, and, I daresay, at one time, had been a spruce enough clerk. It was difficult to guess his age, one ages so rapidly under the stress of misfortune, but I should have set him down as being about forty. His voice, though faint enough at first, was that of an educated man, and as he went on, and gathered courage, and became more and more in earnest, he spoke with a simple directness which was close akin to eloquence. It was a curious story which he had to tell.

So curious, so astounding indeed, that, by the time it was finished, I was in such a state of mind, that I could perceive no alternative but to forgive Sydney, and, in spite of his recent, and scandalous misbehaviour, again appeal to him for assistance. It seemed, if the story told by the man whom I had found in the street was true – and incredible though it sounded, he spoke like a truthful man! – that Paul was threatened by some dreadful, and, to me, wholly incomprehensible danger; that it was a case in which even moments were precious; and I felt that, with the best will in the world, it was a position in which I could not move alone. The shadow of the terror of the night was with me still, and with that fresh in my recollection how could I hope, single-handed, to act effectually against the mysterious being of whom this amazing tale was told? No! I believed that Sydney did care for me, in his own peculiar way; I knew that he was quick, and cool, and fertile in resource, and that he showed to most advantage in a difficult situation; it was possible that he had a conscience, of a sort, and that, this time, I might not appeal to it in vain.

So I sent a servant off to fetch him, helter skelter.

As luck would have it, the servant returned with him within five minutes.

It appeared that he had been lunching with Dora Grayling, who lives just at the end of the street, and the footman had met him coming down the steps. I had him shown into my own room.

'I want you to go to the man whom I found in the street, and listen to what he has to say.'

'With pleasure.'

'Can I trust you?'

'To listen to what he has to say? – I believe so.'

'Can I trust you to respect my confidence?'

He was not at all abashed – I never saw Sydney Atherton when he was abashed. Whatever the offence of which he has been guilty, he always seems completely at his ease. His eyes twinkled.

'You can – I will not breathe a syllable even to papa.'

'In that case, come! But, you understand, I am going to put to the test the affirmations which you have made during all these years, and to prove if you have any of the feeling for me which you pretend.'

Directly we were in the stranger's room, Sydney marched straight up to the bed, stared at the man who was lying in it, crammed his hands into his trouser pockets, and whistled. I was amazed.

'So!' he exclaimed. 'It's you!'

'Do you know this man?' I asked.

'I am hardly prepared to go so far as to say that I know him, but I chance to have a memory for faces, and it happens that I have met this gentleman on at least one previous occasion. Perhaps he remembers me. – Do you?'

The stranger seemed uneasy – as if he found Sydney's tone and manner disconcerting.

'I do. You are the man in the street.'

'Precisely. I am that – individual. And you are the man who came through the window. And in a much more comfortable condition you appear to be than when first I saw you.' Sydney turned to me. 'It is just possible, Miss Lindon, that I may have a few remarks to make to this gentleman which would be better made in private – if you don't mind.'

'But I do mind – I mind very much. What do you suppose I sent for you here for?'

Sydney smiled that absurd, provoking smile of his – as if the occasion were not sufficiently serious.

'To show that you still repose in me a vestige of your confidence.'

'Don't talk nonsense. This man has told me a most extraordinary story, and I have sent for you – as you may believe, not too willingly' – Sydney bowed – 'in order that he may repeat it in your presence, and in mine.'

'Is that so? – Well! – Permit me to offer you a chair – this tale may turn out to be a trifle long.'

To humour him I accepted the chair he offered, though I should have preferred to stand; – he seated himself on the side of the bed, fixing on the stranger those keen, quizzical, not too merciful, eyes of his.

'Well, sir, we are at your service – if you will be so good as to favour us with a second edition of that pleasant yarn you have been spinning. But – let us begin at the right end! – what's your name?'

'My name is Robert Holt.'

'That so? – Then, Mr Robert Holt – let her go!'

Thus encouraged, Mr Holt repeated the tale which he had told me, only in more connected fashion than before. I fancy that Sydney's glances exercised on him a sort of hypnotic effect, and this kept him to the point – he scarcely needed a word of prompting from the first syllable to the last.

He told how, tired, wet, hungry, desperate, despairing, he had been refused admittance to the casual ward – that unfailing resource, as one would have supposed, of those who had abandoned even hope. How he had come upon an open window in an apparently empty house, and, thinking of nothing but shelter from the inclement night, he had clambered through it. How he had found himself in the presence of an extraordinary being, who, in his debilitated and nervous state, had seemed to him to be only half human. How this dreadful creature had given utterance to wild sentiments of hatred towards Paul Lessingham – my Paul! How he had taken advantage of Holt's enfeebled state to gain over him the most complete, horrible, and, indeed, almost incredible ascendency. How he actually had sent Holt, practically naked, into the storm-driven streets, to commit burglary at Paul's house – and how he – Holt – had actually gone without being able to offer even a shadow of opposition. How Paul, suddenly returning home, had come upon Holt engaged in the very act of committing burglary, and how, on his hearing Holt make a cabalistic reference to some mysterious beetle, the manhood had gone out of him, and he had suffered the intruder to make good his escape without an effort to detain him.

The story had seemed sufficiently astonishing the first time, it seemed still more astonishing the second – but, as I watched Sydney listening, what struck me chiefly was the conviction that he had heard it all before. I charged him with it directly Holt had finished.

'This is not the first time you have been told this tale.'

'Pardon me – but it is. Do you suppose I live in an atmosphere of fairy tales?'

Something in his manner made me feel sure he was deceiving me.

'Sydney! – Don't tell me a story! – Paul has told you!'

'I am not telling you a story – at least, on this occasion; and Mr Lessingham has not told me. Suppose we postpone these details to a little later. And perhaps, in the interim, you will permit me to put a question or two to Mr Holt.'

I let him have his way – though I knew he was concealing something from me; that he had a more intimate acquaintance with Mr Holt's strange tale than he chose to confess. And, for some cause, his reticence annoyed me.

He looked at Mr Holt in silence for a second or two. Then he said, with the quizzical little air of bland impertinence which is peculiarly his own.

'I presume, Mr Holt, you have been entertaining us with a novelty in fables, and that we are not expected to believe this pleasant little yarn of yours.'

'I expect nothing. But I have told you the truth. And you know it.'

This seemed to take Sydney aback.

'I protest that, like Miss Lindon, you credit me with a more extensive knowledge than I possess. However, we will let that pass – I take it that you paid particular attention to this mysterious habitant of this mysterious dwelling.'

I saw that Mr Holt shuddered.

'I am not likely ever to forget him.'

'Then, in that case, you will be able to describe him to us.'

'To do so adequately would be beyond my powers. But I will do my best.'

If the original was more remarkable than the description which he gave of him, then he must have been remarkable indeed. The impression conveyed to my mind was rather of a monster than a human being. I watched Sydney attentively as he followed Mr Holt's somewhat lurid language, and there was something in his demeanour which made me more and more persuaded that he was more behind the scenes in this strange business than he pretended, or than the speaker suspected. He put a question which seemed uncalled for by anything which Mr Holt had said.

'You are sure this thing of beauty was a man?'

'No, sir, that is exactly what I am not sure.'

There was a note in Sydney's voice which suggested that he had received precisely the answer which he had expected.

'Did you think it was a woman?'

'I did think so, more than once. Though I can hardly explain what made me think so. There was certainly nothing womanly about the face.' He paused, as if to reflect. Then added, 'I suppose it was a question of instinct.'

'I see. – Just so. – It occurs to me, Mr Holt, that you are rather strong on questions of instinct.' Sydney got off the bed. He stretched himself, as if fatigued – which is a way he has. 'I will not do you the injustice to hint that I do not believe a word of your charming, and simple, narrative. On the contrary, I will demonstrate my perfect credence by remarking that I have not the slightest doubt that you will be able to point out to me, for my particular satisfaction, the delightful residence on which the whole is founded.'

Mr Holt coloured – Sydney's tone could scarcely have been more significant.

'You must remember, sir, that it was a dark night, that I had never been in that neighbourhood before, and that I was not in a condition to pay much attention to locality.'

'All of which is granted, but – how far was it from Hammersmith Workhouse?'

'Possibly under half a mile.'

'Then, in that case, surely you can remember which turning you took on leaving Hammersmith Workhouse – I suppose there are not many turnings you could have taken.'

'I think I could remember.'

'Then you shall have an opportunity to try. It isn't a very far cry to Hammersmith – don't you think you are well enough to drive there now, just you and I together in a cab?'

'I should say so. I wished to get up this morning. It is by the doctor's orders I have stayed in bed.'

'Then, for once in a while, the doctor's orders shall be ignored – I prescribe fresh air.' Sydney turned to me. 'Since Mr Holt's wardrobe seems rather to seek, don't you think a suit of one of the men might fit him – if Mr Holt wouldn't mind making shift for the moment? – Then, by the time you've finished dressing, Mr Holt, I shall be ready.'

While they were ascertaining which suit of clothes would be best adapted to his figure, I went with Sydney to my room. So soon as we were in, I let him know that this was not a matter in which I intended to be trifled with.

'Of course you understand, Sydney, that I am coming with you.'

He pretended not to know what I meant.

'Coming with me? – I am delighted to hear it – but where?'

'To the house of which Mr Holt has been speaking.'

'Nothing could give me greater pleasure, but – might I point out? – Mr Holt has to find it yet?'

'I will come to help you to help him find it.'

Sydney laughed – but I could see he did not altogether relish the suggestion.

'Three in a hansom?'

'There is such a thing as a four-wheeled cab – or I could order a carriage if you'd like one.'

Sydney looked at me out of the corners of his eyes; then began to walk up and down the room, with his hands in his trouser pockets. Presently he began to talk nonsense.

'I need not say with what a sensation of joy I should anticipate the delights of a drive with you – even in a four-wheeled cab; but, were I in your place, I fancy that I should allow Holt and your humble servant to go hunting out this house of his alone. It may prove a more tedious business than you imagine. I promise that, after the hunt is over, I will describe the proceedings to you with the most literal accuracy.'

'I daresay. – Do you think I don't know you've been deceiving me all the time?'

'Deceiving you? – I!'

'Yes – you! Do you think I'm quite an idiot?'

'My dear Marjorie!'

'Do you think I can't see that you know all about what Mr Holt has been telling us – perhaps more about it than he knows himself?'

'On my word! – With what an amount of knowledge you do credit me.'

'Yes, I do – or discredit you, rather. If I were to trust you, you would tell me just as much as you chose – which would be nothing. I'm coming with you – so there's an end.'

'Very well. – Do you happen to know if there are any revolvers in the house?'

'Revolvers? – whatever for?'

'Because I should like to borrow one. I will not conceal from you – since you press me – that this is a case in which a revolver is quite likely to be required.'

'You are trying to frighten me.'

'I am doing nothing of the kind, only, under the circumstances, I am bound to point out to you what it is you may expect.'

'Oh, you think that you're bound to point that out, do you – then now your bounden duty's done. As for there being any revolvers in the house, papa has a perfect arsenal – would you like to take them all?'

'Thanks, but I daresay I shall be able to manage with one – unless you would like one too. You may find yourself in need of it.'

'I am obliged to you, but, on this occasion, I don't think I'll trouble. I'll run the risk. – Oh, Sydney, what a hypocrite you are!'

'It's for your sake, if I seem to be. I tell you most seriously, that I earnestly advise you to allow Mr Holt and I to manage this affair alone. I don't mind going so far as to say that this is a matter with which, in days to come, you will wish that you had not allowed yourself to be associated.'

'What do you mean by that? Do you dare to insinuate anything against – Paul?'

'I insinuate nothing. What I mean, I say right out; and, my dear Marjorie, what I actually do mean is this – that if, in spite of my urgent solicitations, you will persist in accompanying us, the expedition, so far as I am concerned, will be postponed.'

'That is what you do mean, is it? Then that's settled.' I rang the bell. The servant came. 'Order a four-wheeled cab at once. And let me know the moment Mr Holt is ready.' The servant went. I turned to Sydney. 'If you will excuse me, I will go and put my hat on. You are, of course, at liberty to please yourself as to whether you will or will not go, but, if you don't, then I shall go with Mr Holt alone.'

I moved to the door. He stopped me.

'My dear Marjorie, why will you persist in treating me with such injustice? Believe me, you have no idea what sort of adventure this is which you are setting out upon – or you would hear reason. I assure you that you are gratuitously proposing to thrust yourself into imminent peril.'

'What sort of peril? Why do you beat about the bush – why don't you speak right out?'

'I can't speak right out, there are circumstances which render it practically impossible – and that's the plain truth – but the danger is none the less real on that account. I am not jesting – I am in earnest; won't you take my word for it?'

'It is not a question of taking your word only – it is a question of something else beside. I have not forgotten my adventures of last night – and Mr Holt's story is mysterious enough in itself; but there is something more mysterious still at the back of it – something which you appear to suggest points unpleasantly at Paul. My duty is clear, and nothing you can say will turn me from it. Paul, as you are very well aware, is already overweighted with affairs of state, pretty nearly borne down by them – or I would take the tale to him, and he would talk to you after a fashion of his own. Things being as they are, I propose to show you that, although I am not yet Paul's wife, I can make his interests my own as completely as though I were. I can, therefore, only repeat that it is for you to decide what you intend to do; but, if you prefer to stay, I shall go with Mr Holt – alone.'

'Understand that, when the time for regret comes – as it will come! – you are not to blame me for having done what I advised you not to do.'

'My dear Mr Atherton, I will undertake to do my utmost to guard your spotless reputation; I should be sorry that anyone should hold you responsible for anything I either said or did.'

'Very well! – Your blood be on your own head!'

'My blood?'

'Yes – your blood. I shouldn't be surprised if it comes to blood before we're through. – Perhaps you'll oblige me with the loan of one of that arsenal of revolvers of which you spoke.'

I let him have his old revolver – or, rather, I let him have one of papa's new ones. He put it in the hip pocket in his trousers. And the expedition started – in a four-wheeled cab.

## CHAPTER TWENTY-NINE

# THE HOUSE ON THE ROAD FROM THE WORKHOUSE

Mr Holt looked as if he was in somebody else's garments. He was so thin, and worn, and wasted, that the suit of clothes which one of the men had lent him hung upon him as on a scarecrow. I was almost ashamed of myself for having incurred a share of the responsibility of taking him out of bed. He seemed so weak and bloodless that I should not have been surprised if he had fainted on the road. I had taken care that he should eat as much as he could eat before we started – the suggestion of starvation which he had conveyed to one's mind was dreadful! – and I had brought a flask of brandy in case of accidents, but, in spite of everything, I could not conceal from myself that he would be more at home in a sick-bed than in a jolting cab.

It was not a cheerful drive. There was in Sydney's manner towards me an air of protection which I instinctively resented – he appeared to be regarding me as a careful, and anxious, nurse might regard a wrong-headed and disobedient child. Conversation distinctly languished. Since Sydney seemed disposed to patronize me, I was bent on snubbing him. The result was, that the majority of the remarks which were uttered were addressed to Mr Holt.

The cab stopped – after what had appeared to me to be an interminable journey. I rejoiced at the prospect of its being at an end. Sydney put his head out of the window. A short parley with the driver ensued.

'This is 'Ammersmith Workhouse, it's a large place, sir – which part of it might you be wanting?'

Sydney appealed to Mr Holt. He put his head out of the window in his turn – he did not seem to recognize our surroundings at all.

'We have come a different way – this is not the way I went; I went through Hammersmith – and to the casual ward; I don't see that here.'

Sydney spoke to the cabman.

'Driver, where's the casual ward?'

'That's the other end, sir.'

'Then take us there.'

He took us there. Then Sydney appealed again to Mr Holt.

'Shall I dismiss the cabman – or don't you feel equal to walking?'

'Thank you, I feel quite equal to walking – I think the exercise will do me good.'

So the cabman was dismissed – a step which we – and I, in particular – had subsequent cause to regret. Mr Holt took his bearings. He pointed to a door which was just in front of us.

'That's the entrance to the casual ward, and that, over it, is the window through which the other man threw a stone. I went to the right – back the way I had come.' We went to the right. 'I reached this corner.' We had reached a corner. Mr Holt looked about him, endeavouring to recall the way he had gone. A good many roads appeared to converge at that point, so that he might have wandered in either of several directions.

Presently he arrived at something like a decision.

'I think this is the way I went – I am nearly sure it is.'

He led the way, with something of an air of dubitation, and we followed. The road he had chosen seemed to lead to nothing and nowhere. We had not gone many yards from the workhouse gates before we were confronted by something like chaos. In front and on either side of us were large spaces of waste land. At some more or less remote period attempts appeared to have been made at brickmaking – there were untidy stacks of bilious-looking bricks in evidence. Here and there enormous weather-stained boards announced that 'This Desirable Land was to be Let for Building Purposes'. The road itself was unfinished. There was no pavement, and we had the bare uneven ground for a sidewalk. It seemed, so far as I could judge, to lose itself in space, and to be swallowed up by the wilderness of 'Desirable Land' which lay beyond. In the near distance there were houses enough, and to spare – of a kind. But they were in other roads. In the one in which we actually were, on the right, at the end, there was a row of unfurnished carcases, but only two buildings which were in anything like a fit state for occupation. One stood on either side, not facing each other – there was a distance between them of perhaps fifty yards. The sight of them had a more exciting effect on Mr Holt than it had on me. He moved rapidly forward – coming to a standstill in front of the one upon our left, which was the nearer of the pair.

'This is the house!' he exclaimed.

He seemed almost exhilarated – I confess that I was depressed. A more dismal-looking habitation one could hardly imagine. It was one of those dreadful jerry-built houses which, while they are still new, look old. It had quite possibly only been built a year or two, and yet, owing to neglect, or to poverty of construction, or to a combination of the two, it was already threatening to tumble down. It was a small place, a couple of storeys high, and would have been dear – I should think! – at thirty pounds a year. The windows had surely never been washed since the house was built – those on the upper floor seemed all either cracked or broken. The only sign of occupancy consisted in the fact that a blind was down behind the window of the room on the ground floor. Curtains there were none. A low wall ran in front, which had apparently at one time been surmounted by something in the shape of an iron railing – a rusty piece of metal still remained on one end; but, since there was only about a foot between it and the building, which was practically built upon the road – whether the wall was intended to ensure privacy, or was merely for ornament, was not clear.

'This is the house!' repeated Mr Holt, showing more signs of life than I had hitherto seen in him.

Sydney looked it up and down – it apparently appealed to his æsthetic sense as little as it did to mine.

'Are you sure?'

'I am certain.'

'It seems empty.'

'It seemed empty to me that night – that is why I got into it in search of shelter.'

'Which is the window which served you as a door?'

'This one.' Mr Holt pointed to the window on the ground floor – the one which was screened by a blind. 'There was no sign of a blind when I first saw it, and the sash was up – it was that which caught my eye.'

Once more Sydney surveyed the place, in comprehensive fashion, from roof to basement – then he scrutinizingly regarded Mr Holt.

'You are quite sure this is the house? It might be awkward if you proved mistaken. I am going to knock at the door, and if it turns out that that mysterious acquaintance of yours does not, and never has lived here, we might find an explanation difficult.'

'I am sure it is the house – certain! I know it – I feel it here – and here.'

Mr Holt touched his breast, and his forehead. His manner was distinctly odd. He was trembling, and a fevered expression had come into his eyes. Sydney glanced at him, for a moment, in silence. Then he bestowed his attention upon me.

'May I ask if I may rely upon your preserving your presence of mind?'

The mere question ruffled my plumes.

'What do you mean?'

'What I say. I am going to knock at that door, and I am going to get through it, somehow. It is quite within the range of possibility that, when I am through, there will be some strange happenings – as you have heard from Mr Holt. The house is commonplace enough without; you may not find it so commonplace within. You may find yourself in a position in which it will be

in the highest degree essential that you should keep your wits about
you.'

'I am not likely to let them stray.'

'Then that's all right. – Do I understand that you propose to come in with
me?'

'Of course I do – what do you suppose I've come for? What nonsense you
are talking.'

'I hope that you will still continue to consider it nonsense by the time this
little adventure's done.'

That I resented his impertinence goes without saying – to be talked to in
such a strain by Sydney Atherton, whom I had kept in subjection ever since
he was in knickerbockers, was a little trying – but I am forced to admit that I
was more impressed by his manner, or his words, or by Mr Holt's manner, or
something, than I should have cared to own. I had not the least notion what
was going to happen, or what horrors that woebegone-looking dwelling
contained. But Mr Holt's story had been of the most astonishing sort, my
experiences of the previous night were still fresh, and, altogether, now that I
was in such close neighbourhood with the Unknown – with a capital U! –
although it was broad daylight, it loomed before me in a shape for which –
candidly! – I was not prepared.

A more disreputable-looking front door I have not seen – it was in perfect
harmony with the remainder of the establishment. The paint was off; the
woodwork was scratched and dented; the knocker was red with rust. When
Sydney took it in his hand I was conscious of quite a little thrill. As he
brought it down with a sharp rat-tat, I half expected to see the door fly open,
and disclose some gruesome object glaring out at us. Nothing of the kind took
place; the door did not budge – nothing happened. Sydney waited a second or
two, then knocked again; another second or two, then another knock. There
was still no sign of any notice being taken of our presence. Sydney turned to
Mr Holt.

'Seems as if the place was empty.'

Mr Holt was in the most singular condition of agitation – it made me
uncomfortable to look at him.

'You do not know – you cannot tell; there may be someone there who
hears and pays no heed.'

'I'll give them another chance.'

Sydney brought down the knocker with thundering reverberations. The
din must have been audible half a mile away. But from within the house
there was still no sign that any heard. Sydney came down the step.

'I'll try another way – I may have better fortune at the back.'

He led the way round to the rear, Mr Holt and I following in single file.

There the place seemed in worse case even than in the front. There were two empty rooms on the ground floor at the back – there was no mistake about their being empty, without the slightest difficulty we could see right into them. One was apparently intended for a kitchen and wash-house combined, the other for a sitting-room. There was not a stick of furniture in either, nor the slightest sign of human habitation. Sydney commented on the fact.

'Not only is it plain that no one lives in these charming apartments, but it looks to me uncommonly as if no one ever had lived in them.'

To my thinking Mr Holt's agitation was increasing every moment. For some reason of his own, Sydney took no notice of it whatever – possibly because he judged that to do so would only tend to make it worse. An odd change had even taken place in Mr Holt's voice – he spoke in a sort of tremulous falsetto.

'It was only the front room which I saw.'

'Very good; then, before very long, you shall see that front room again.'

Sydney rapped with his knuckles on the glass panels of the back door. He tried the handle; when it refused to yield he gave it a vigorous shaking. He saluted the dirty windows – so far as succeeding in attracting attention was concerned, entirely in vain. Then he turned again to Mr Holt – half mockingly.

'I call you to witness that I have used every lawful means to gain the favourable notice of your mysterious friend. I must therefore beg to stand excused if I try something slightly unlawful for a change. It is true that you found the window already open; but, in my case, it soon will be.'

He took a knife out of his pocket, and, with the open blade, forced back the catch – as I am told that burglars do. Then he lifted the sash.

'Behold!' he exclaimed. 'What did I tell you? – Now, my dear Marjorie, if I get in first and Mr Holt gets in after me, we shall be in a position to open the door for you.'

I immediately saw through his design.

'No, Mr Atherton; you will get in first, and I will get in after you, through the window – before Mr Holt. I don't intend to wait for you to open the door.'

Sydney raised his hands and opened his eyes, as if grieved at my want of confidence. But I did not mean to be left in the lurch, to wait their pleasure, while on pretence of opening the door, they searched the house. So Sydney climbed in first, and I second – it was not a difficult operation, since the window-sill was under three feet from the ground – and Mr Holt last. Directly we were in, Sydney put his hand up to his mouth, and shouted.

'Is there anybody in this house? If so, will he kindly step this way, as there is someone wishes to see him.'

His words went echoing through the empty rooms in a way which was almost uncanny. I suddenly realized that if, after all, there did happen to be somebody in the house, and he was at all disagreeable, our presence on his premises might prove rather difficult to explain. However, no one answered. While I was waiting for Sydney to make the next move, he diverted my attention to Mr Holt.

'Hollo, Holt, what's the matter with you? Man, don't play the fool like that!'

Something was the matter with Mr Holt. He was trembling all over as if attacked by a shaking palsy. Every muscle in his body seemed twitching at once. A strained look had come on his face, which was not nice to see. He spoke as with an effort.

'I'm all right. – It's nothing.'

'Oh, is it nothing? Then perhaps you'll drop it. Where's that brandy?' I handed Sydney the flask. 'Here, swallow this.'

Mr Holt swallowed the cupful of neat spirit which Sydney offered without an attempt at parley. Beyond bringing some remnants of colour to his ashen cheeks it seemed to have no effect on him whatever. Sydney eyed him with a meaning in his glance which I was at a loss to understand.

'Listen to me, my lad. Don't think you can deceive me by playing any of your fool tricks, and don't delude yourself into supposing that I shall treat you as anything but dangerous if you do. I've got this.' He showed the revolver of papa's which I had lent him. 'Don't imagine that Miss Lindon's presence will deter me from using it.'

Why he addressed Mr Holt in such a strain surpassed my comprehension. Mr Holt, however, evinced not the faintest symptoms of resentment – he had become, on a sudden, more like an automaton than a man. Sydney continued to gaze at him as if he would have liked his glance to penetrate to his inmost soul.

'Keep in front of me, if you please, Mr Holt, and lead the way to this mysterious apartment in which you claim to have had such a remarkable experience.'

Of me he asked in a whisper,

'Did you bring a revolver?'

I was startled.

'A revolver? – The idea! – How absurd you are!'

Sydney said something which was so rude – and so uncalled for! – that it was worthy of papa in his most violent moments.

'I'd sooner be absurd than a fool in petticoats.' I was so angry that I did not know what to say – and before I could say it he went on. 'Keep your eyes and ears well open; be surprised at nothing you see or hear. Stick close to me.

And for goodness sake remain mistress of as many of your senses as you conveniently can.'

I had not the least idea what was the meaning of it all. To me there seemed nothing to make such a pother about. And yet I was conscious of a fluttering of the heart as if there soon might be something. I knew Sydney sufficiently well to be aware that he was one of the last men in the world to make a fuss without reason – and that he was as little likely to suppose that there was a reason when as a matter of fact there was none.

Mr Holt led the way, as Sydney desired – or, rather, commanded, to the door of the room which was in front of the house. The door was closed. Sydney tapped on a panel. All was silence. He tapped again.

'Anyone in there?' he demanded.

As there was still no answer, he tried the handle. The door was locked.

'The first sign of the presence of a human being we have had – doors don't lock themselves. It's just possible that there may have been someone or something about the place, at some time or other, after all.'

Grasping the handle firmly, he shook it with all his might – as he had done with the door at the back. So flimsily was the place constructed that he made even the walls to tremble.

'Within there! – if anyone is in there! – if you don't open this door, I shall.'

There was no response.

'So be it! – I'm going to pursue my wild career of defiance of established law and order, and gain admission in one way, if I can't in another.'

Putting his right shoulder against the door, he pushed with his whole force. Sydney is a big man, and very strong, and the door was weak. Shortly, the lock yielded before the continuous pressure, and the door flew open. Sydney whistled.

'So! – It begins to occur to me, Mr Holt, that that story of yours may not have been such pure romance as it seemed.'

It was plain enough that, at any rate, this room had been occupied, and that recently – and, if his taste in furniture could be taken as a test, by an eccentric occupant to boot. My own first impression was that there was someone, or something, living in it still – an uncomfortable odour greeted our nostrils, which was suggestive of some evil-smelling animal. Sydney seemed to share my thought.

'A pretty perfume, on my word! Let's shed a little more light on the subject, and see what causes it. Marjorie, stop where you are until I tell you.'

I had noticed nothing, from without, peculiar about the appearance of the blind which screened the window, but it must have been made of some unusually thick material, for, within, the room was strangely dark. Sydney entered, with the intention of drawing up the blind, but he had scarcely taken a couple of steps when he stopped.

'What's that?'

'It's it,' said Mr Holt, in a voice which was so unlike his own that it was scarcely recognizable.

'It? – What do you mean by it?'

'The Beetle!'

Judging from the sound of his voice Sydney was all at once in a state of odd excitement.

'Oh, is it! – Then, if this time I don't find out the how and the why and the wherefore of that charming conjuring trick, I'll give you leave to write me down an ass – with a great, big A.'

He rushed farther into the room – apparently his efforts to lighten it did not meet with the immediate success which he desired.

'What's the matter with this confounded blind? There's no cord! How do you pull it up? – What the –'

In the middle of his sentence Sydney ceased speaking. Suddenly Mr Holt, who was standing by my side on the threshold of the door, was seized with such a fit of trembling, that, fearing he was going to fall, I caught him by the arm. A most extraordinary look was on his face. His eyes were distended to their fullest width, as if with horror at what they saw in front of them. Great beads of perspiration were on his forehead.

'It's coming!' he screamed.

Exactly what happened I do not know. But, as he spoke, I heard, proceeding from the room, the sound of the buzzing of wings. Instantly it recalled my experiences of the night before – as it did so I was conscious of a most unpleasant qualm. Sydney swore a great oath, as if he were beside himself with rage.

'If you won't go up, you shall come down.'

I suppose, failing to find a cord, he seized the blind from below, and dragged it down – it came, roller and all, clattering to the floor. The room was all in light. I hurried in. Sydney was standing by the window, with a look of perplexity upon his face which, under any other circumstances, would have been comical. He was holding papa's revolver in his hand, and was glaring round and round the room, as if wholly at a loss to understand how it was he did not see what he was looking for.

'Marjorie!' he exclaimed. 'Did you hear anything?'

'Of course I did. It was that which I heard last night – which so frightened me.'

'Oh, was it? Then, by—' in his excitement he must have been completely oblivious of my presence for he used the most terrible language, 'when I find it there'll be a small discussion. It can't have got out of the room – I know the creature's here; I not only heard it, I felt it brush against my face. – Holt, come inside and shut that door.'

Mr Holt raised his arms, as if he were exerting himself to make a forward movement – but he remained rooted to the spot on which he stood.

'I can't!' he cried.

'You can't! – Why?'

'It won't let me.'

'What won't let you?'

'The Beetle!'

Sydney moved till he was close in front of him. He surveyed him with eager eyes. I was just at his back. I heard him murmur – possibly to me.

'By George! – It's just as I thought! – The beggar's hypnotized!'

Then he said aloud,

'Can you see it now?'

'Yes.'

'Where?'

'Behind you.'

As Mr Holt spoke, I again heard, quite close to me, that buzzing sound. Sydney seemed to hear it too – it caused him to swing round so quickly that he all but whirled me off my feet.

'I beg your pardon, Marjorie, but this is of the nature of an unparalleled experience – didn't you hear something then?'

'I did – distinctly; it was close to me – within an inch or two of my face.'

We stared about us, then back at each other; there was nothing else to be seen. Sydney laughed, doubtfully.

'It's uncommonly queer. I don't want to suggest there are visions about, or I might suspect myself of softening of the brain. But – it's queer. There's a trick about it somewhere, I am convinced; and no doubt it's simple enough when you know how it's done – but the difficulty is to find that out. – Do you think our friend over there is acting?'

'He looks to me as if he were ill.'

'He does look ill. He also looks as if he were hypnotized. If he is, it must be by suggestion – and that's what makes me doubtful, because it will be the first plainly established case of hypnotism by suggestion I've encountered. – Holt?'

'Yes.'

'That,' said Sydney in my ear, 'is the voice and that is the manner of a hypnotized man, but, on the other hand, a person under influence generally responds only to the hypnotist – which is another feature about our peculiar friend which arouses my suspicions.' Then, aloud, 'Don't stand there like an idiot – come inside.'

Again Mr Holt made an apparently futile effort to do as he was bid. It was painful to look at him – he was like a feeble, frightened, tottering child, who would come on, but cannot.

'I can't.'

'No nonsense, my man! Do you think that this is a performance in a booth, and that I am to be taken in by all the humbug of the professional mesmerist? Do as I tell you – come into the room.'

There was a repetition, on Mr Holt's part, of his previous pitiful struggle; this time it was longer sustained than before – but the result was the same.

'I can't!' he wailed.

'Then I say you can – and shall! If I pick you up, and carry you, perhaps you will not find yourself so helpless as you wish me to suppose.'

Sydney moved forward to put his threat into execution. As he did so, a strange alteration took place in Mr Holt's demeanour.

CHAPTER THIRTY

# THE SINGULAR BEHAVIOUR OF MR HOLT

I was standing in the middle of the room, Sydney was between the door and me; Mr Holt was in the hall, just outside the doorway, in which he, so to speak, was framed. As Sydney advanced towards him he was seized with a kind of convulsion – he had to lean against the side of the door to save himself from falling. Sydney paused, and watched. The spasm went as suddenly as it came – Mr Holt became as motionless as he had just now been the other way. He stood in an attitude of febrile expectancy – his chin raised, his head thrown back, his eyes glancing upwards – with the dreadful fixed glare which had come into them ever since we had entered the house. He looked to me as if his every faculty was strained in the act of listening – not a muscle in his body seemed to move; he was as rigid as a figure carved in stone. Presently the rigidity gave place to what, to an onlooker, seemed causeless agitation.

'I hear!' he exclaimed, in the most curious voice I had ever heard. 'I come!'

It was as though he was speaking to someone who was far away. Turning, he walked down the passage to the front door.

'Hollo!' cried Sydney. 'Where are you off to?'

We both of us hastened to see. He was fumbling with the latch; before we could reach him, the door was open, and he was through it. Sydney, rushing after him, caught him on the step and held him by the arm.

'What's the meaning of this little caper? – Where do you think you're going now?'

Mr Holt did not condescend to turn and look at him. He said, in the same dreamy, faraway, unnatural tone of voice – and he kept his unwavering gaze fixed on what was apparently some distant object which was visible only to himself,

'I am going to him. He calls me.'

'Who calls you?'

'The Lord of the Beetle.'

Whether Sydney released his arm or not I cannot say. As he spoke, he seemed to me to slip away from Sydney's grasp. Passing through the gateway, turning to the right, he commenced to retrace his steps in the direction we had come. Sydney stared after him in unequivocal amazement. Then he looked at me.

'Well! – this is a pretty fix! – now what's to be done?'

'What's the matter with him?' I inquired. 'Is he mad?'

'There's method in his madness, if he is. He's in the same condition in which he was that night I saw him come out of the Apostle's window.' Sydney has a horrible habit of calling Paul 'the Apostle'; I have spoken to him about it over and over again – but my words have not made much impression. 'He ought to be followed – he may be sailing off to that mysterious friend of his this instant. – But, on the other hand, he mayn't, and it may be nothing but a trick of our friend the conjurer's to get us away from this elegant abode of his. He's done me twice already, I don't want to be done again – and I distinctly do not want him to return and find me missing. He's quite capable of taking the hint, and removing himself into the *Ewigkeit* – when the clue to as pretty a mystery as ever I came across will have vanished.'

'I can stay,' I said.

'You? – Alone?'

He eyed me doubtingly – evidently not altogether relishing the proposition.

'Why not? You might send the first person you meet – policeman, cabman, or whoever it is – to keep me company. It seems a pity now that we dismissed that cab.'

'Yes, it does seem a pity.' Sydney was biting his lip. 'Confound that fellow! how fast he moves.'

Mr Holt was already nearing the end of the road.

'If you think it necessary, by all means follow to see where he goes – you are sure to meet somebody whom you will be able to send before you have gone very far.'

'I suppose I shall. – You won't mind being left alone?'

'Why should I? – I'm not a child.'

Mr Holt, reaching the corner, turned it, and vanished out of sight. Sydney gave an exclamation of impatience.

'If I don't make haste I shall lose him. I'll do as you suggest – dispatch the first individual I come across to hold watch and ward with you.'

'That'll be all right.'

He started off at a run – shouting to me as he went.

'It won't be five minutes before somebody comes!'

I waved my hand to him. I watched him till he reached the end of the road.

Turning, he waved his hand to me. Then he vanished, as Mr Holt had done.

And I was alone.

## CHAPTER THIRTY-ONE

# THE TERROR BY DAY

My first impulse, after Sydney's disappearance, was to laugh. Why should he display anxiety on my behalf merely because I was to be the sole occupant of an otherwise empty house for a few minutes more or less – and in broad daylight too! To say the least, the anxiety seemed unwarranted.

I lingered at the gate, for a moment or two, wondering what was at the bottom of Mr Holt's singular proceedings, and what Sydney really proposed to gain by acting as a spy upon his wanderings. Then I turned to re-enter the house. As I did so, another problem suggested itself to my mind – what connection, of the slightest importance, could a man in Paul Lessingham's position have with the eccentric being who had established himself in such an unsatisfactory dwelling-place? Mr Holt's story I had only dimly understood – it struck me that it would require a deal of understanding. It was more like a farrago of nonsense, an outcome of delirium, than a plain statement of solid facts. To tell the truth, Sydney had taken it more seriously than I expected. He seemed to see something in it which I emphatically did not. What was double Dutch to me, seemed clear as print to him. So far as I could judge, he actually had the presumption to imagine that Paul – my Paul! – Paul Lessingham! – the great Paul Lessingham! – was mixed up in the very mysterious adventures of poor, weak-minded, hysterical Mr Holt, in a manner which was hardly to his credit.

Of course, any idea of the kind was purely and simply balderdash. Exactly what bee Sydney had got in his bonnet, I could not guess. But I did know Paul. Only let me find myself face to face with the fantastic author of Mr Holt's weird tribulations, and I, a woman, single-handed, would do my best to show him that whoever played pranks with Paul Lessingham trifled with edged tools.

I had returned to that historical front room which, according to Mr Holt, had been the scene of his most disastrous burglarious entry. Whoever had furnished it had had original notions of the resources of modern upholstery. There was not a table in the place – no chair or couch, nothing to sit down upon except the bed. On the floor there was a marvellous carpet which was apparently of eastern manufacture. It was so thick, and so pliant to the tread, that moving over it was like walking on thousand-year-old turf. It was woven in gorgeous colours, and covered with –

When I discovered what it actually was covered with, I was conscious of a disagreeable sense of surprise.

It was covered with beetles!

All over it, with only a few inches of space between each, were representations of some peculiar kind of beetle – it was the same beetle, over, and over, and over. The artist had woven his undesirable subject into the warp and woof of the material with such cunning skill that, as one continued to gaze, one began to wonder if by any possibility the creatures could be alive.

In spite of the softness of the texture, and the art – of a kind! – which had been displayed in the workmanship, I rapidly arrived at the conclusion that it was the most uncomfortable carpet I had ever seen. I wagged my finger at the repeated portrayals of the – to me! – unspeakable insect.

'If I had discovered that you were there before Sydney went I think it just possible that I should have hesitated before I let him go.'

Then there came a revulsion of feeling. I shook myself.

'You ought to be ashamed of yourself, Marjorie Lindon, to even think such nonsense. Are you all nerves and morbid imaginings – you who have prided yourself on being so strong-minded! A pretty sort you are to do battle for anyone. – Why, they're only make-believes!'

Half involuntarily, I drew my foot over one of the creatures. Of course, it was nothing but imagination; but I seemed to feel it squelch beneath my shoes. It was disgusting.

'Come!' I cried. 'This won't do! As Sydney would phrase it – am I going to make an idiot of myself?'

I turned to the window – looking at my watch.

'It's more than five minutes ago since Sydney went. That companion of mine ought to be already on the way. I'll go and see if he is coming.'

I went to the gate. There was not a soul in sight. It was with such a distinct sense of disappointment that I perceived this was so, that I was in two minds what to do. To remain where I was, looking, with gaping eyes, for the policeman, or the cabman, or whoever it was Sydney was dispatching to act as my temporary associate, was tantamount to acknowledging myself a simpleton – while I was conscious of a most unmistakable reluctance to return within the house.

Common sense, or what I took for common sense, however, triumphed, and, after loitering for another five minutes, I did go in again.

This time, ignoring, to the best of my ability, the beetles on the floor, I proceeded to expend my curiosity – and occupy my thoughts – in an examination of the bed. It only needed a very cursory examination, however, to show that the seeming bed was, in reality, none at all – or if it was a bed after the manner of the Easterns it certainly was not after the fashion of the Britons. There was no framework – nothing to represent the bedstead. It was simply a heap of rugs piled apparently indiscriminately upon the floor. A huge mass of them there seemed to be; of all sorts, and shapes, and sizes – and materials too.

The top one was of white silk – in quality, exquisite. It was of huge size, yet, with a little compression, one might almost have passed it through the proverbial wedding ring. So far as space admitted I spread it out in front of me. In the middle was a picture – whether it was embroidered on the substance or woven in it, I could not quite make out. Nor, at first, could I gather what it was the artist had intended to depict – there was a brilliancy about it which was rather dazzling. By degrees, I realized that the lurid hues were meant for flames – and, when one had got so far, one perceived that they were by no means badly imitated either. Then the meaning of the thing dawned on me – it was a representation of a human sacrifice. In its way, as ghastly a piece of realism as one could see.

On the right was the majestic seated figure of a goddess. Her hands were crossed upon her knees, and she was naked from her waist upwards. I fancied it was meant for Isis. On her brow was perched a gaily-apparelled beetle – that ubiquitous beetle! – forming a bright spot of colour against her coppery skin – it was an exact reproduction of the creatures which were imaged on the carpet. In front of the idol was an enormous fiery furnace. In the very heart of the flames was an altar. On the altar was a naked white woman being burned alive. There could be no doubt as to her being alive, for she was secured by chains in such a fashion that she was permitted a certain amount of freedom, of which she was availing herself to contort and twist her body into shapes which were horribly suggestive of the agony which she was enduring – the artist, indeed, seemed to have exhausted his powers in his efforts to convey a vivid impression of the pains which were tormenting her.

'A pretty picture, on my word! A pleasant taste in art the garnitures of this establishment suggest! The person who likes to live with this kind of thing, especially as a covering to his bed, must have his own notions as to what constitute agreeable surroundings.'

As I continued staring at the thing, all at once it seemed as if the woman on the altar moved. It was preposterous, but she appeared to gather her limbs together, and turn half over.

'What can be the matter with me? Am I going mad? She can't be moving!'

If she wasn't, then certainly something was – she was lifted right into the air. An idea occurred to me. I snatched the rug aside.

The mystery was explained!

A thin, yellow, wrinkled hand was protruding from amidst the heap of rugs – it was its action which had caused the seeming movement of the figure on the altar. I stared, confounded. The hand was followed by an arm; the arm by a shoulder; the shoulder by a head – and the most awful, hideous, wicked-looking face I had ever pictured even in my most dreadful dreams. A pair of baleful eyes were glaring up at mine.

I understood the position in a flash of startled amazement.

Sydney, in following Mr Holt, had started on a wild goose chase after all. I was alone with the occupant of that mysterious house – the chief actor in Mr Holt's astounding tale. He had been hidden in the heap of rugs all the while.

# BOOK IV

## IN PURSUIT

*The Conclusion of the Matter is Extracted from the Case-book of the Hon. Augustus Champnell, Confidential Agent*

### CHAPTER THIRTY-TWO

## A NEW CLIENT

On the afternoon of Friday, June 2, 18—, I was entering in my case-book some memoranda having reference to the very curious matter of the Duchess of Datchet's Deed-box. It was about two o'clock. Andrews came in and laid a card upon my desk. On it was inscribed 'Mr Paul Lessingham'.

'Show Mr Lessingham in.'

Andrews showed him in. I was, of course, familiar with Mr Lessingham's appearance, but it was the first time I had had with him any personal communication. He held out his hand to me.

'You are Mr Champnell?'

'I am.'

'I believe that I have not had the honour of meeting you before, Mr Champnell, but with your father, the Earl of Glenlivet, I have the pleasure of some acquaintance.'

I bowed. He looked at me, fixedly, as if he were trying to make out what sort of man I was.

'You are very young, Mr Champnell.'

'I have been told that an eminent offender in that respect once asserted that youth is not of necessity a crime.'

'And you have chosen a singular profession – one in which one hardly looks for juvenility.'

'You yourself, Mr Lessingham, are not old. In a statesman one expects grey hairs. – I trust that I am sufficiently ancient to be able to do you service.'

He smiled.

'I think it possible. I have heard of you more than once, Mr Champnell, always to your advantage. My friend, Sir John Seymour, was telling me, only the other day, that you have recently conducted for him some business, of a very delicate nature, with much skill and tact; and he warmly advised me, if ever I found myself in a predicament, to come to you. I find myself in a predicament now.'

THE BEETLE

Again I bowed.

'A predicament, I fancy, of an altogether unparalleled sort. I take it that anything I may say to you will be as though it were said to a father confessor.'

'You may rest assured of that.'

'Good. – Then, to make the matter clear to you I must begin by telling you a story – if I may trespass on your patience to that extent. I will endeavour not to be more verbose than the occasion requires.'

I offered him a chair, placing it in such a position that the light from the window would have shone full upon his face. With the calmest possible air, as if unconscious of my design, he carried the chair to the other side of my desk, twisting it right round before he sat on it – so that now the light was at his back and on my face. Crossing his legs, clasping his hands about his knee, he sat in silence for some moments, as if turning something over in his mind. He glanced round the room.

'I suppose, Mr Champnell, that some singular tales have been told in here.'

'Some very singular tales indeed. I am never appalled by singularity. It is my normal atmosphere.'

'And yet I should be disposed to wager that you have never listened to so strange a story as that which I am about to tell you now. So astonishing, indeed, is the chapter in my life which I am about to open out to you, that I have more than once had to take myself to task, and fit the incidents together with mathematical accuracy in order to assure myself of its perfect truth.'

He paused. There was about his demeanour that suggestion of reluctance which I not uncommonly discover in individuals who are about to take the skeletons from their cupboards and parade them before my eyes. His next remark seemed to point to the fact that he perceived what was passing through my thoughts.

'My position is not rendered easier by the circumstance that I am not of a communicative nature. I am not in sympathy with the spirit of the age which craves for personal advertisement. I hold that the private life even of a public man should be held inviolate. I resent, with peculiar bitterness, the attempts of prying eyes to peer into matters which, as it seems to me, concern myself alone. You must, therefore, bear with me, Mr Champnell, if I seem awkward in disclosing to you certain incidents in my career which I had hoped would continue locked in the secret depository of my own bosom, at any rate till I was carried to the grave. I am sure you will suffer me to stand excused if I frankly admit that it is only an irresistible chain of incidents which has constrained me to make of you a confidant.'

'My experience tells me, Mr Lessingham, that no one ever does come to

627

me until they are compelled. In that respect I am regarded as something worse even than a medical man.'

A wintry smile flitted across his features – it was clear that he regarded me as a good deal worse than a medical man. Presently he began to tell me one of the most remarkable tales which even I had heard. As he proceeded I understood how strong, and how natural, had been his desire for reticence. On the mere score of credibility he must have greatly preferred to have kept his own counsel. For my part I own, unreservedly, that I should have deemed the tale incredible had it been told me by Tom, Dick, or Harry, instead of by Paul Lessingham.

## CHAPTER THIRTY-THREE

# WHAT CAME OF LOOKING THROUGH A LATTICE

He began in accents which halted not a little. By degrees his voice grew firmer. Words came from him with greater fluency.

'I am not yet forty. So when I tell you that twenty years ago I was a mere youth I am stating what is a sufficiently obvious truth. It is twenty years ago since the events of which I am going to speak transpired.

'I lost both my parents when I was quite a lad, and by their death I was left in a position in which I was, to an unusual extent in one so young, my own master. I was ever of a rambling turn of mind, and when, at the mature age of eighteen, I left school, I decided that I should learn more from travel than from sojourn at a university. So, since there was no one to say me nay, instead of going either to Oxford or Cambridge, I went abroad. After a few months I found myself in Egypt – I was down with fever at Shepheard's Hotel in Cairo. I had caught it by drinking polluted water during an excursion with some Bedouins to Palmyra.

'When the fever had left me I went out one night into the town in search of amusement. I went, unaccompanied, into the native quarter, not a wise thing to do, especially at night, but at eighteen one is not always wise, and I was weary of the monotony of the sick-room, and eager for something which had in it a spice of adventure. I found myself in a street which I have reason to believe is no longer existing. It had a French name, and was called the Rue de Rabagas – I saw the name on the corner as I turned into it, and it has left an impress on the tablets of my memory which is never likely to be obliterated.

'It was a narrow street, and, of course, a dirty one, ill-lit, and, apparently, at the moment of my appearance, deserted. I had gone, perhaps, half-way down its tortuous length, blundering more than once into the kennel, wondering what fantastic whim had brought me into such unsavoury quarters, and what would happen to me, if, as seemed extremely possible, I lost my way. On a sudden my ears were saluted by sounds which proceeded from a house which I was passing – sounds of music and of singing.

'I paused. I stood awhile to listen.

'There was an open window on my right, which was screened by latticed blinds. From the room which was behind these blinds the sounds were coming. Someone was singing, accompanied by an instrument resembling a guitar – singing uncommonly well.'

Mr Lessingham stopped. A stream of recollection seemed to come flooding over him. A dreamy look came into his eyes.

'I remember it all as clearly as if it were yesterday. How it all comes back – the dirty street, the evil smells, the imperfect light, the girl's voice filling all at once the air. It was a girl's voice – full, and round, and sweet; an organ seldom met with, expecially in such a place as that. She sang a little *chansonnette*, which, just then, half Europe was humming – it occurred in an opera which they were acting at one of the Boulevard theatres – "La P'tite Voyageuse". The effect, coming so unexpectedly, was startling. I stood and heard her to an end.

'Inspired by I know not what impulse of curiosity, when the song was finished, I moved one of the lattice blinds a little aside, so as to enable me to get a glimpse of the singer. I found myself looking into what seemed to be a sort of café – one of those places which are found all over the Continent, in which women sing in order to attract custom. There was a low platform at one end of the room, and on it were seated three women. One of them had evidently just been accompanying her own song – she still had an instrument of music in her hands, and was striking a few idle notes. The other two had been acting as audience. They were attired in the fantastic apparel which the women who are found in such places generally wear. An old woman was sitting knitting in a corner, whom I took to be the inevitable *patronne*. With the exception of these four the place was empty.

'They must have heard me touch the lattice, or seen it moving, for no sooner did I glance within than the three pairs of eyes on the platform were raised and fixed on mine. The old woman in the corner alone showed no consciousness of my neighbourhood. We eyed one another in silence for a second or two. Then the girl with the harp – the instrument she was manipulating proved to be fashioned more like a harp than a guitar – called out to me.

'"*Entrez, monsieur! – Soyez le bienvenu!*"

'"I was a little tired. Rather curious as to whereabouts I was – the place struck me, even at that first momentary glimpse, as hardly in the ordinary line of that kind of thing. And not unwilling to listen to a repetition of the former song, or to another sung by the same singer.

'"On condition," I replied, "that you sing me another song."

'"Ah, monsieur, with the greatest pleasure in the world I will sing you twenty."

'She was almost, if not quite, as good as her word. She entertained me with song after song. I may safely say that I have seldom if ever heard melody more enchanting. All languages seemed to be the same to her. She sang in French and Italian, German and English – in tongues with which I was unfamiliar. It was in these Eastern harmonies that she was most successful. They were indescribably weird and thrilling, and she delivered them with a verve and sweetness which was amazing. I sat at one of the little tables with which the room was dotted, listening entranced.

'Time passed more rapidly than I supposed. While she sang I sipped the liquor with which the old woman had supplied me. So enthralled was I by the display of the girl's astonishing gifts that I did not notice what it was I was drinking. Looking back I can only surmise that it was some poisonous concoction of the creature's own. That one small glass had on me the strangest effect. I was still weak from the fever which I had only just succeeded in shaking off, and that, no doubt, had something to do with the result. But, as I continued to sit, I was conscious that I was sinking into a lethargic condition, against which I was incapable of struggling.

'After a while the original performer ceased her efforts, and, her companions taking her place, she came and joined me at the little table. Looking at my watch I was surprised to perceive the lateness of the hour. I rose to leave. She caught me by the wrist.

'"Do not go," she said; – she spoke English of a sort, and with the queerest accent. "All is well with you. Rest awhile."

'You will smile – I should smile, perhaps, were I the listener instead of you, but it is the simple truth that her touch had on me what I can only describe as a magnetic influence. As her fingers closed upon my wrist, I felt as powerless in her grasp as if she held me with bands of steel. What seemed an invitation was virtually a command. I had to say whether I would or wouldn't. She called for more liquor, and at what again was really her command I drank of it. I do not think that after she touched my wrist I uttered a word. She did all the talking. And, while she talked, she kept her eyes fixed on my face. Those eyes of hers! They were a devil's. I can positively affirm that they had on me a diabolical effect. They robbed me of my consciousness, of my power of volition, of my capacity to think – they made me as wax in her hands. My last recollection of that fatal night is of her sitting in front of me, bending over the table, stroking my wrist with her extended fingers, staring at me with her awful eyes. After that, a curtain seems to descend. There comes a period of oblivion.'

Mr Lessingham ceased. His manner was calm and self-contained enough; but, in spite of that I could see that the mere recollection of the things which he told me moved his nature to its foundations. There was eloquence in the drawn lines about his mouth, and in the strained expression of his eyes.

So far his tale was sufficiently commonplace. Places such as the one which he described abound in the Cairo of today; and many are the Englishmen who have entered them to their exceeding bitter cost. With that keen intuition which has done him yeoman's service in the political arena, Mr Lessingham at once perceived the direction my thoughts were taking.

'You have heard this tale before? – No doubt. And often. The traps are many, and the fools and the unwary are not a few. The singularity of my experience is still to come. You must forgive me if I seem to stumble in the telling. I am anxious to present my case as baldly, and with as little appearance of exaggeration as possible. I say with as little appearance, for some appearance of exaggeration I fear is unavoidable. My case is so unique, and so out of the common run of our everyday experience, that the plainest possible statement must smack of the sensational.

'As, I fancy, you have guessed, when understanding returned to me, I found myself in an apartment with which I was unfamiliar. I was lying, undressed, on a heap of rugs in a corner of a low-pitched room which was furnished in a fashion which, when I grasped the details, filled me with amazement. By my side knelt the Woman of the Songs. Leaning over, she wooed my mouth with kisses. I cannot describe to you the sense of horror and of loathing with which the contact of her lips oppressed me. There was about her something so unnatural, so inhuman, that I believe even then I could have destroyed her with as little sense of mortal turpitude as if she had been some noxious insect.

'"Where am I?" I exclaimed.

'"You are with the children of Isis," she replied. What she meant I did not know, and do not to this hour. "You are in the hands of the great goddess – of the mother of men."

'"How did I come here?"

'"By the loving kindness of the great mother."

'I do not, of course, pretend to give you the exact text of her words, but they were to that effect.

'Half raising myself on the heap of rugs, I gazed about me – and was astounded at what I saw.

'The place in which I was, though the reverse of lofty, was of considerable size – I could not conceive whereabouts it could be. The walls and roof were of bare stone – as though the whole had been hewed out of the solid rock. It seemed to be some sort of temple, and was redolent with the most extraordinary odour. An altar stood about the centre, fashioned out of a single block of stone. On it a fire burned with a faint blue flame – the fumes which rose from it were no doubt chiefly responsible for the prevailing perfumes. Behind it was a huge bronze figure, more than life size. It was in a sitting posture, and represented a woman. Although it resembled no portrayal of her I have seen either before or since, I came afterwards to understand that it was meant for Isis. On the idol's brow was poised a beetle. That the creature was alive seemed clear, for, as I looked at it, it opened and shut its wings.

'If the one on the forehead of the goddess was the only live beetle which the place contained, it was not the only representation. It was modelled in the solid stone of the roof, and depicted in flaming colours on hangings which here and there were hung against the walls. Wherever the eye turned it rested on a scarab. The effect was bewildering. It was as though one saw things through the distorted glamour of a nightmare. I asked myself if I were not still dreaming; if my appearance of consciousness were not after all a mere delusion; if I had really regained my senses.

'And, here, Mr Champnell, I wish to point out, and to emphasize the fact, that I am not prepared to positively affirm what portion of my adventures in that extraordinary, and horrible place, was actuality, and what the product of a feverish imagination. Had I been persuaded that all I thought I saw, I really did see, I should have opened my lips long ago, let the consequences to myself have been what they might. But there is the crux. The happenings were of such an incredible character, and my condition was such an abnormal one – I was never really myself from the first moment to the last – that I have hesitated, and still do hesitate, to assert where, precisely, fiction ended and fact began.

'With some misty notion of testing my actual condition I endeavoured to get off the heap of rugs on which I reclined. As I did so the woman at my side laid her hand against my chest, lightly. But, had her gentle pressure been the equivalent of a ton of iron, it could not have been more effectual. I collapsed, sank back upon the rugs, and lay there, panting for breath, wondering if I had crossed the border line which divides madness from sanity.

'"Let me get up! – let me go!" I gasped.

'"Nay," she murmured, "stay with me yet awhile, O my beloved."

'And again she kissed me.'

Once more Mr Lessingham paused. An involuntary shudder went all over him. In spite of the evidently great effort which he was making to retain his self-control his features were contorted by an anguished spasm. For some seconds he seemed at a loss to find words to enable him to continue.

When he did go on, his voice was harsh and strained.

'I am altogether incapable of even hinting to you the nauseous nature of that woman's kisses. They filled me with an indescribable repulsion. I look back at them with a feeling of physical, mental, and moral horror, across an interval of twenty years. The most dreadful part of it was that I was wholly incapable of offering even the faintest resistance to her caresses. I lay there like a log. She did with me as she would, and in dumb agony I endured.'

He took his handkerchief from his pocket, and, although the day was cool, with it he wiped the perspiration from his brow.

'To dwell in detail on what occurred during my involuntary sojourn in that fearful place is beyond my power. I cannot even venture to attempt it. The attempt, were it made, would be futile, and, to me, painful beyond measure. I seem to have seen all that happened as in a glass darkly – with about it all an element of unreality. As I have already remarked, the things which revealed themselves, dimly, to my perception, seemed too bizarre, too hideous, to be true.

'It was only afterwards, when I was in a position to compare dates, that I was enabled to determine what had been the length of my imprisonment. It appears that I was in that horrible den more than two months – two unspeakable months. And the whole time there were comings and goings, a phantasmagoric array of eerie figures continually passed to and fro before my hazy eyes. What I judge to have been religious services took place; in which the altar, the bronze image, and the beetle on its brow, figure largely. Not only were they conducted with a bewildering confusion of mysterious rites, but, if my memory is in the least degree trustworthy, they were orgies of nameless horrors. I seem to have seen things take place at them at the mere thought of which the brain reels and trembles.

'Indeed it is in connection with the cult of the obscene deity to whom these wretched creatures paid their scandalous vows that my most awful memories seem to have been associated. It may have been – I hope it was, a mirage born of my half delirious state, but it seemed to me that they offered human sacrifices.'

When Mr Lessingham said this, I pricked up my ears. For reasons of my own, which will immediately transpire, I had been wondering if he would make any reference to a human sacrifice. He noted my display of interest – but misapprehended the cause.

'I see you start, I do not wonder. But I repeat that unless I was the victim of some extraordinary species of double sight – in which case the whole business would resolve itself into the fabric of a dream, and I should indeed thank God! – I saw, on more than one occasion, a human sacrifice offered on that stone altar, presumably to the grim image which looked down on it. And, unless I err, in each case the sacrificial object was a woman, stripped to the skin, as white as you or I – and before they burned her they subjected her to every variety of outrage of which even the minds of demons could conceive. More than once since then I have seemed to hear the shrieks of the victims ringing through the air, mingled with the triumphant cries of her frenzied murderers, and the music of their harps.

'It was the cumulative horrors of such a scene which gave me the strength, or the courage, or the madness, I know not which it was, to burst the bonds which bound me, and which, even in the bursting, made of me, even to this hour, a haunted man.

'There had been a sacrifice – unless, as I have repeatedly observed, the whole was nothing but a dream. A woman – a young and lovely Englishwoman, if I could believe the evidence of my own eyes, had been outraged, and burnt alive, while I lay there helpless, looking on. The business was concluded. The ashes of the victim had been consumed by the participants. The worshippers had departed. I was left alone with the woman of the songs, who apparently acted as the guardian of that worse than slaughterhouse. She was, as usual after such an orgie, rather a devil than a human being, drunk with an insensate frenzy, delirious with inhuman longings. As she approached to offer to me her loathed caresses, I was on a sudden conscious of something which I had not felt before when in her company. It was as though something had slipped away from me – some weight which had oppressed me, some bond by which I had been bound. I was aroused, all at once, to a sense of freedom; to a knowledge that the blood which coursed through my veins was after all my own, that I was master of my own honour.

'I can only suppose that through all those weeks she had kept me there in a state of mesmeric stupor. That, taking advantage of the weakness which the fever had left behind, by the exercise of her diabolical arts, she had not allowed me to pass out of a condition of hypnotic trance. Now, for some reason, the cord was loosed. Possibly her absorption in her religious duties had caused her to forget to tighten it. Anyhow, as she approached me, she approached a man, and one who, for the first time for many a day, was his own man. She herself seemed wholly unconscious of anything of the kind. As she drew nearer to me, and nearer, she appeared to be entirely oblivious of the fact that I was anything but the fibreless, emasculated creature which, up to that moment, she had made of me.

'But she knew it when she touched me – when she stooped to press her lips to mine. At that instant the accumulating rage which had been smouldering in my breast through all those leaden torturing hours, sprang into flame. Leaping off my couch of rugs, I flung my hands about her throat – and then she knew I was awake. Then she strove to tighten the cord which she had suffered to become unduly loose. Her baleful eyes were fixed on mine. I knew that she was putting out her utmost force to trick me of my manhood. But I fought with her like one possessed, and I conquered – in a fashion. I compressed her throat with my two hands as with an iron vice. I knew that I was struggling for more than life, that the odds were all against me, that I was staking my all upon the casting of a die – I stuck at nothing which could make me victor.

'Tighter and tighter my pressure grew – I did not stay to think if I was killing her – till on a sudden –'

Mr Lessingham stopped. He stared with fixed, glassy eyes, as if the whole was being re-enacted in front of him. His voice faltered. I thought he would break down. But, with an effort, he continued.

'On a sudden, I felt her slipping from between my fingers. Without the slightest warning, in an instant she had vanished, and where, not a moment before, she herself had been, I found myself confronting a monstrous beetle – a huge, writhing creation of some wild nightmare.

'At first the creature stood as high as I did. But, as I stared at it, in stupefied amazement – as you may easily imagine – the thing dwindled while I gazed. I did not stop to see how far the process of dwindling continued – a stark raving madman for the nonce, I fled as if all the fiends in hell were at my heels.'

CHAPTER THIRTY-FOUR

## AFTER TWENTY YEARS

'How I reached the open air I cannot tell you – I do not know. I have a confused recollection of rushing through vaulted passages, through endless corridors, of trampling over people who tried to arrest my passage – and the rest is blank.

'When I again came to myself I was lying in the house of an American missionary named Clements. I had been found, at early dawn, stark naked, in a Cairo street, and picked up for dead. Judging from appearances I must have wandered for miles, all through the night. Whence I had come, or whither I was going, none could tell – I could not tell myself. For weeks I hovered between life and death. The kindness of Mr and Mrs Clements was not to be measured by words. I was brought to their house a penniless, helpless, battered stranger, and they gave me all they had to offer, without money and without price – with no expectation of an earthly reward. Let no one pretend that there is no Christian charity under the sun. The debt I owed that man and woman I was never able to repay. Before I was properly myself again, and in a position to offer some adequate testimony of the gratitude I felt, Mrs Clements was dead, drowned during an excursion on the Nile, and her husband had departed on a missionary expedition into Central Africa, from which he never returned.

'Although, in a measure, my physical health returned, for months after I had left the roof of my hospitable hosts, I was in a state of semi-imbecility. I suffered from a species of aphasia. For days together I was speechless, and could remember nothing – not even my own name. And, when that stage had passed, and I began to move more freely among my fellows, for years I was but a wreck of my former self. I was visited at all hours of the day and night, by frightful – I know not whether to call them visions, they were real enough to me, but since they were visible to no one but myself, perhaps that is the word which best describes them. Their presence invariably plunged me into a state of abject terror, against which I was unable to even make a show of fighting. To such an extent did they embitter my existence, that I voluntarily

637

placed myself under the treatment of an expert in mental pathology. For a considerable period of time I was under his constant supervision, but the visitations were as inexplicable to him as they were to me.

'By degrees, however, they became rarer and rarer, until at last I flattered myself that I had once more become as other men. After an interval, to make sure, I devoted myself to politics. Thenceforward I have lived, as they phrase it, in the public eye. Private life, in any peculiar sense of the term, I have had none.'

Mr Lessingham ceased. His tale was not uninteresting, and, to say the least of it, was curious. But I still was at a loss to understand what it had to do with me, or what was the purport of his presence in my room. Since he remained silent, as if the matter, so far as he was concerned, was at an end, I told him so.

'I presume, Mr Lessingham, that all this is but a prelude to the play. At present I do not see where it is that I come in.'

Still for some seconds he was silent. When he spoke his voice was grave and sombre, as if he were burdened by a weight of woe.

'Unfortunately, as you put it, all this has been but a prelude to the play. Were it not so I should not now stand in such pressing want of the services of a confidential agent – that is, of an experienced man of the world, who has been endowed by nature with phenomenal perceptive faculties, and in whose capacity and honour I can place the completest confidence.'

I smiled – the compliment was a pointed one.

'I hope your estimate of me is not too high.'

'I hope not – for my sake, as well as for your own. I have heard great things of you. If ever man stood in need of all that human skill and acumen can do for him, I certainly am he.'

His words aroused my curiosity. I was conscious of feeling more interested than heretofore.

'I will do my best for you. Man can do no more. Only give my best a trial.'

'I will. At once.'

He looked at me long and earnestly. Then, leaning forward, he said, lowering his voice perhaps unconsciously,

'The fact is, Mr Champnell, that quite recently events have happened which threaten to bridge the chasm of twenty years, and to place me face to face with that plague spot of the past. At this moment I stand in imminent peril of becoming again the wretched thing I was when I fled from that den of all the devils. It is to guard me against this that I have come to you. I want you to unravel the tangled thread which threatens to drag me to my doom – and, when unravelled, to sunder it – for ever, if God wills! – in twain.'

'Explain.'

To be frank, for the moment I thought him mad. He went on.

'Three weeks ago, when I returned late one night from a sitting in the House of Commons, I found, on my study table, a sheet of paper on which there was a representation – marvellously like! – of the creature into which, as it seemed to me, the woman of the songs was transformed as I clutched her throat between my hands. The mere sight of it brought back one of those visitations of which I have told you, and which I thought I had done with for ever – I was convulsed by an agony of fear, thrown into a state approximating to a paralysis both of mind and body.'

'But why?'

'I cannot tell you. I only know that I have never dared to allow my thoughts to recur to that last dread scene, lest the mere recurrence should drive me mad.'

'What was this you found upon your study table – merely a drawing?'

'It was a representation, produced by what process I cannot say, which was so wonderfully, so diabolically, like the original, that for a moment I thought the thing itself was on my table.'

'Who put it there?'

'That is precisely what I wish you to find out – what I wish you to make it your instant business to ascertain. I have found the thing, under similar circumstances, on three separate occasions, on my study table – and each time it has had on me the same hideous effect.'

'Each time after you have returned from a late sitting in the House of Commons?'

'Exactly.'

'Where are these – what shall I call them – delineations?'

'That, again, I cannot tell you.'

'What do you mean?'

'What I say. Each time, when I recovered, the thing had vanished.'

'Sheet of paper and all?'

'Apparently – though on that point I could not be positive. You will understand that my study table is apt to be littered with sheets of paper, and I could not absolutely determine that the thing had not stared at me from one of those. The delineation itself, to use your word, certainly had vanished.'

I began to suspect that this was a case rather for a doctor than for a man of my profession. And hinted as much.

'Don't you think it is possible, Mr Lessingham, that you have been overworking yourself – that you have been driving your brain too hard, and that you have been the victim of an optical delusion?'

'I thought so myself; I may say that I almost hoped so. But wait till I have finished. You will find that there is no loophole in that direction.'

He appeared to be recalling events in their due order. His manner was studiously cold – as if he were endeavouring, despite the strangeness of his story, to impress me with the literal accuracy of each syllable he uttered.

'The night before last, on returning home, I found in my study a stranger.'

'A stranger?'

'Yes. – In other words, a burglar.'

'A burglar? – I see. – Go on.'

He had paused. His demeanour was becoming odder and odder.

'On my entry he was engaged in forcing an entry into my bureau. I need hardly say that I advanced to seize him. But – I could not.'

'You could not? – How do you mean you could not?'

'I mean simply what I say. You must understand that this was no ordinary felon. Of what nationality he was I cannot tell you. He only uttered two words, and they were certainly in English, but apart from that he was dumb. He wore no covering on his head or feet. Indeed, his only garment was a long dark flowing cloak which, as it fluttered about him, revealed that his limbs were bare.'

'An unique costume for a burglar.'

'The instant I saw him I realized that he was in some way connected with that adventure in the Rue de Rabagas. What he said and did, proved it to the hilt.'

'What did he say and do?'

'As I approached to effect his capture, he pronounced aloud two words which recalled that awful scene the recollection of which always lingers in my brain, and of which I never dare to permit myself to think. Their very utterance threw me into a sort of convulsion.'

'What were the words?'

Mr Lessingham opened his mouth – and shut it. A marked change took place in the expression of his countenance. His eyes became fixed and staring – resembling the glassy orbs of the somnambulist. For a moment I feared that he was going to give me an object lesson in the 'visitations' of which I had heard so much. I rose, with a view of offering him assistance. He motioned me back.

'Thank you. – It will pass away.'

His voice was dry and husky – unlike his usual silvern tones. After an uncomfortable interval he managed to continue.

'You see for yourself, Mr Champnell, what a miserable weakling, when this subject is broached, I still remain. I cannot utter the words the stranger uttered, I cannot even write them down. For some inscrutable reason they have on me an effect similar to that which spells and incantations had on people in tales of witchcraft.'

'I suppose, Mr Lessingham, that there is no doubt that this mysterious stranger was not himself an optical delusion?'

'Scarcely. There is the evidence of my servants to prove the contrary.'

'Did your servants see him?'

'Some of them – yes. Then there is the evidence of the bureau. The fellow had smashed the top right in two. When I came to examine the contents I learned that a packet of letters was missing. They were letters which I had received from Miss Lindon, a lady whom I hope to make my wife. This, also, I state to you in confidence.'

'What use would he be likely to make of them?'

'If matters stand as I fear they do, he might make a very serious misuse of them. If the object of these wretches, after all these years, is a wild revenge, they would be capable, having discovered what she is to me, of working Miss Lindon a fatal mischief – or, at the very least, of poisoning her mind.'

'I see. – How did the thief escape – did he, like the delineation, vanish into air?'

'He escaped by the much more prosaic method of dashing through the drawing-room window, and clambering down from the verandah into the street, where he ran right into someone's arms.'

'Into whose arms – a constable's?'

'No; into Mr Atherton's – Sydney Atherton's.'

'The inventor?'

'The same. – Do you know him?'

'I do. Sydney Atherton and I are friends of a good many years' standing. – But Atherton must have seen where he came from; – and, anyhow, if he was in the state of undress which you have described, why didn't he stop him?'

'Mr Atherton's reasons were his own. He did not stop him, and, so far as I can learn, he did not attempt to stop him. Instead, he knocked at my hall door to inform me that he had seen a man climb out of my window.'

'I happen to know that, at certain seasons, Atherton is a queer fish – but that sounds very queer indeed.'

'The truth is, Mr Champnell, that, if it were not for Mr Atherton, I doubt if I should have troubled you even now. The accident of his being an acquaintance of yours makes my task easier.'

He drew his chair closer to me with an air of briskness which had been foreign to him before. For some reason, which I was unable to fathom, the introduction of Atherton's name seemed to have enlivened him. However, I was not long to remain in darkness. In half a dozen sentences he threw more light on the real cause of his visit to me than he had done in all that had gone before. His bearing, too, was more businesslike and to the point. For the first time I had some glimmerings of the politician – alert, keen, eager – as he is known to all the world.

'Mr Atherton, like myself, has been a postulant for Miss Lindon's hand. Because I have succeeded where he has failed, he has chosen to be angry. It seems that he has had dealings, either with my visitor of Tuesday night, or with some other of his acquaintance, and he proposes to use what he has gleaned from him to the disadvantage of my character. I have just come from Mr Atherton. From hints he dropped I conclude that, probably during the last few hours, he has had an interview with someone who was connected in some way with that lurid patch in my career; that this person made so-called revelations which were nothing but a series of monstrous lies; and these so-called revelations Mr Atherton has threatened, in so many words, to place before Miss Lindon. That is an eventuality which I wish to avoid. My own conviction is that there is at this moment in London an emissary from that den in the whilom Rue de Rabagas – for all I know it may be the Woman of the Songs herself. Whether the sole purport of this individual's presence is to do me injury, I am, as yet, in no position to say, but that it is proposed to work me mischief, at any rate, by the way, is plain. I believe that Mr Atherton knows more about this person's individuality and whereabouts than he has been willing, so far, to admit. I want you, therefore, to ascertain these things on my behalf; to find out what, and where, this person is, to drag her! – or him; – out into the light of day. In short, I want you to effectually protect me from the terrorism which threatens once more to overwhelm my mental and my physical powers – which bids fair to destroy my intellect, my career, my life, my all.'

'What reason have you for suspecting that Mr Atherton has seen this individual of whom you speak – has he told you so?'

'Practically – yes.'

'I know Atherton well. In his not infrequent moments of excitement he is apt to use strong language, but it goes no further. I believe him to be the last person in the world to do anyone an intentional injustice, under any circumstances whatever. If I go to him, armed with credentials from you, when he understands the real gravity of the situation – which it will be my business to make him do, I believe that, spontaneously, of his own accord, he will tell me as much about this mysterious individual as he knows himself.'

'Then go to him at once.'

'Good. I will. The result I will communicate to you.'

I rose from my seat. As I did so, someone rushed into the outer office with a din and a clatter. Andrews' voice, and another, became distinctly audible – Andrews' apparently raised in vigorous expostulation. Raised, seemingly, in vain, for presently the door of my own particular sanctum was thrown open with a crash, and Mr Sydney Atherton himself came dashing in – evidently conspicuously under the influence of one of those not infrequent 'moments of excitement' of which I had just been speaking.

## CHAPTER THIRTY-FIVE

# A BRINGER OF TIDINGS

Atherton did not wait to see who might or might not be present, but, without even pausing to take breath, he broke into full cry on the instant – as is occasionally his wont.

'Champnell! – Thank goodness I've found you in! – I want you! – At once! – Don't stop to talk, but stick your hat on, and put your best foot forward – I'll tell you all about it in the cab.'

I endeavoured to call his attention to Mr Lessingham's presence – but without success.

'My dear fellow –'

When I had got as far as that he cut me short.

'Don't "dear fellow" me! – None of your jabber! And none of your excuses either! I don't care if you've got an engagement with the Queen, you'll have to chuck it. Where's that dashed hat of yours – or are you going without it? Don't I tell you that every second cut to waste may mean the difference between life and death? – Do you want me to drag you down to the cab by the hair of your head?'

'I will try not to constrain you to quite so drastic a resource – and I was coming to you at once in any case. I only want to call your attention to the fact that I am not alone. – Here is Mr Lessingham.'

In his harum-scarum haste Mr Lessingham had gone unnoticed. Now that his observation was particularly directed to him, Atherton started, turned and glared at my latest client in a fashion which was scarcely flattering.

'Oh! – It's you, is it? – What the deuce are you doing here?'

Before Lessingham could reply to this most unceremonious query, Atherton, rushing forward, gripped him by the arm.

'Have you seen her?'

Lessingham, not unnaturally nonplussed by the other's curious conduct, stared at him in unmistakable amazement.

'Have I seen whom?'

'Marjorie Lindon!'

644

'Marjorie Lindon?'

Lessingham paused. He was evidently asking himself what the inquiry meant.

'I have not seen Miss Lindon since last night. Why do you ask?'

'Then Heaven help us! – As I'm a living man I believe he, she, or it has got her!'

His words were incomprehensible enough to stand in copious need of explanation – as Mr Lessingham plainly thought.

'What is it that you mean, sir?'

'What I say – I believe that that Oriental friend of yours has got her in her clutches – if it is a "her"; goodness alone knows what the infernal conjurer's real sex may be.'

'Atherton! – Explain yourself!'

On a sudden Lessingham's tones rang out like a trumpet call.

'If damage comes to her I shall be fit to cut my throat – and yours!'

Mr Lessingham's next proceeding surprised me – I imagine it surprised Atherton still more. Springing at Sydney like a tiger, he caught him by the throat.

'You – you hound! Of what wretched folly have you been guilty? If so much as a hair of her head is injured you shall repay it me ten thousandfold! – You mischief-making, intermeddling, jealous fool!'

He shook Sydney as if he had been a rat – then flung him from him headlong on to the floor. It reminded me of nothing so much as Othello's treatment of Iago. Never had I seen a man so transformed by rage. Lessingham seemed to have positively increased in stature. As he stood glowering down at the prostrate Sydney, he might have stood for a materialistic conception of human retribution.

Sydney, I take it, was rather surprised than hurt. For a moment or two he lay quite still. Then, lifting his head, he looked up at his assailant. Then, raising himself to his feet, he shook himself – as if with a view of learning if all his bones were whole. Putting his hands up to his neck, he rubbed it gently. And he grinned.

'By God, Lessingham, there's more in you than I thought. After all, you are a man. There's some holding power in those wrists of yours – they've nearly broken my neck. When this business is finished, I should like to put on the gloves with you, and fight it out. You're clean wasted upon politics. – Damn it, man, give me your hand!'

Mr Lessingham did not give him his hand. Atherton took it – and gave it a hearty shake with both of his.

If the first paroxysm of his passion had passed, Lessingham was still sufficiently stern.

'Be so good as not to trifle, Mr Atherton. If what you say is correct, and the wretch to whom you allude really has Miss Lindon at her mercy, then the woman I love – and whom you also pretend to love! – stands in imminent peril not only of a ghastly death, but of what is infinitely worse than death.'

'The deuce she does!' Atherton wheeled round towards me. 'Champnell, haven't you got that dashed hat of yours yet? Don't stand there like a tailor's dummy, keeping me on tenter-hooks – move yourself! I'll tell you all about it in the cab. – And, Lessingham, if you'll come with us I'll tell you too.'

## CHAPTER THIRTY-SIX

# WHAT THE TIDINGS WERE

Three in a hansom cab is not, under all circumstances, the most comfortable method of conveyance – when one of the trio happens to be Sydney Atherton in one of his 'moments of excitement' it is distinctly the opposite; as, on that occasion, Mr Lessingham and I both quickly found. Sometimes he sat on my knees, sometimes on Lessingham's, and frequently, when he unexpectedly stood up, and all but precipitated himself on to the horse's back, on nobody's. In the eagerness of his gesticulations, first he knocked off my hat, then he knocked off Lessingham's, then his own, then all three together – once, his own hat rolling into the mud, he sprang into the road, without previously going through the empty form of advising the driver of his intention, to pick it up. When he turned to speak to Lessingham, he thrust his elbow into my eye; and when he turned to speak to me, he thrust it into Lessingham's. Never, for one solitary instant, was he at rest, or either of us at ease. The wonder is that the gymnastics in which he incessantly indulged did not sufficiently attract public notice to induce a policeman to put at least a momentary period to our progress. Had speed not been of primary importance I should have insisted on the transference of the expedition to the somewhat wider limits of a four-wheeler.

His elucidation of the causes of his agitation was apparently more comprehensible to Lessingham than it was to me. I had to piece this and that together under considerable difficulties. By degrees I did arrive at something like a clear notion of what had actually taken place.

He commenced by addressing Lessingham – and thrusting his elbow into my eye.

'Did Marjorie tell you about the fellow she found in the street?' Up went his arm to force the trap-door open overhead – and off went my hat. 'Now then, William Henry! – let her go! – if you kill the horse I'll buy you another!'

We were already going much faster than, legally, we ought to have done –

but that, seemingly to him, was not a matter of the slightest consequence. Lessingham replied to his inquiry.

'She did not.'

'You know the fellow I saw coming out of your drawing-room window?'

'Yes.'

'Well, Marjorie found him in the morning after in front of her breakfast-room window – in the middle of the street. Seems he had been wandering about all night, unclothed – in the rain and the mud, and all the rest of it – in a condition of hypnotic trance.'

'Who is the – gentleman you are alluding to?'

'Says his name's Holt, Robert Holt.'

'Holt? – Is he an Englishman?'

'Very much so – City quilldriver out of a shop – stony broke absolutely! Got the chuck from the casual ward – wouldn't let him in – house full, and that sort of thing – poor devil! Pretty passes you politicians bring men to!'

'Are you sure?'

'Of what?'

'Are you sure that this man, Robert Holt, is the same person whom, as you put it, you saw coming out of my drawing-room window?'

'Sure! – Of course I'm sure! – Think I didn't recognize him? – Besides, there was the man's own tale – owned to it himself – besides all the rest, which sent one rushing Fulham way.'

'You must remember, Mr Atherton, that I am wholly in the dark as to what has happened. What has the man, Holt, to do with the errand on which we are bound?'

'Am I not coming to it? If you would let me tell the tale in my own way I should get there in less than no time, but you will keep on cutting in – how the deuce do you suppose Champnell is to make head or tail of the business if you will persist in interrupting? – Marjorie took the beggar in – he told his tale to her – she sent for me – that was just now; caught me on the steps after I had been lunching with Dora Grayling. Holt re-dished his yarn – I smelt a rat – saw that a connection possibly existed between the thief who'd been playing confounded conjuring tricks off on to me and this interesting party down Fulham way –'

'What party down Fulham way?'

'This friend of Holt's – am I not telling you? There you are, you see – won't let me finish! When Holt slipped through the window – which is the most sensible thing he seems to have done; if I'd been in his shoes I'd have slipped through forty windows! – dusky coloured charmer caught him on the hop – doctored him – sent him out to commit burglary by deputy. I said to Holt, "Show us this agreeable little crib, young man." Holt was game – then

Marjorie chipped in – she wanted to go and see it too. I said, "You'll be sorry
if you do" – that settled it! After that she'd have gone if she'd died – I never
did have a persuasive way with women. So off we toddled, Marjorie, Holt,
and I, in a growler – spotted the crib in less than no time – invited ourselves in
by the kitchen window – house seemed empty. Presently Holt became
hypnotized before my eyes – the best established case of hypnotism by
suggestion I ever yet encountered – started off on a pilgrimage of one. Like an
idiot I followed, leaving Marjorie to wait for me –'

'Alone?'

'Alone! – Am I not telling you? – Great Scott, Lessingham, in the House of
Commons they must be hazy to think you smart! I said, "I'll send the first
sane soul I meet to keep you company." As luck would have it, I never met
one – only kids, and a baker, who wouldn't leave his cart, or take it with him
either. I'd covered pretty nearly two miles before I came across a peeler – and
when I did the man was cracked – and he thought me mad, or drunk, or both.
By the time I'd got myself within nodding distance of being run in for
obstructing the police in the execution of their duty, without inducing him to
move a single one of his twenty-four-inch feet, Holt was out of sight. So,
since all my pains in his direction were clean thrown away, there was nothing
left for me but to scurry back to Marjorie – so I scurried, and I found the
house empty, no one there, and Marjorie gone.'

'But, I don't quite follow –'

Atherton impetuously declined to allow Mr Lessingham to conclude.

'Of course you don't quite follow, and you'll follow still less if you will
keep getting in front. I went upstairs and downstairs, inside and out –
shouted myself hoarse as a crow – nothing was to be seen of Marjorie – or
heard; until, as I was coming down the stairs for about the five-and-fiftieth
time, I stepped on something hard which was lying in the passage. I picked it
up – it was a ring; this ring. Its shape is not just what it was – I'm not as light
as gossamer, especially when I come jumping downstairs six at a time – but
what's left of it is here.'

Sydney held something in front of him. Mr Lessingham wriggled to one
side to enable him to see. Then he made a snatch at it.

'It's mine!'

Sydney dodged it out of his reach.

'What do you mean, it's yours?'

'It's the ring I gave Marjorie for an engagement ring. Give it me, you
hound! – unless you wish me to do you violence in the cab.'

With complete disregard of the limitations of space – or of my comfort –
Lessingham thrust him vigorously aside. Then gripping Sydney by the
wrist, he seized the gaud – Sydney yielding it just in time to save himself

from being precipitated into the street. Ravished of his treasure, Sydney turned and surveyed the ravisher with something like a glance of admiration.

'Hang me, Lessingham, if I don't believe there is some warm blood in those fishlike veins of yours. Please the piper, I'll live to fight you after all – with the bare ones, sir, as a gentleman should do.'

Lessingham seemed to pay no attention to him whatever. He was surveying the ring, which Sydney had trampled out of shape, with looks of the deepest concern.

'Marjorie's ring! – The one I gave her! Something serious must have happened to her before she would have dropped my ring, and left it lying where it fell.'

Atherton went on.

'That's it! – What has happened to her! – I'll be dashed if I know! – When it was clear that there she wasn't, I tore off to find out where she was. Came across old Lindon – he knew nothing; – I rather fancy I startled him in the middle of Pall Mall, when I left he stared after me like one possessed, and his hat was lying in the gutter. Went home – she wasn't there. Asked Dora Grayling – she'd seen nothing of her. No one had seen anything of her – she had vanished into air. Then I said to myself, "You're a first-class idiot, on my honour! While you're looking for her, like a lost sheep, the betting is that the girl's in Holt's friend's house the whole jolly time. When you were there, the chances are that she'd just stepped out for a stroll, and that now she's back again, and wondering where on earth you've gone!' So I made up my mind that I'd fly back and see – because the idea of her standing on the front doorstep looking for me while I was going off my nut looking for her, commended itself to what I call my sense of humour; and on my way it struck me that it would be the part of wisdom to pick up Champnell, because if there is a man who can be backed to find a needle in any amount of haystacks it is the great Augustus. – That horse has moved itself after all, because here we are. Now, cabman, don't go driving further on – you'll have to put a girdle round the earth if you do; because you'll have to reach this point again before you get your fare. – This is the magician's house!'

## CHAPTER THIRTY-SEVEN

# WHAT WAS HIDDEN UNDER THE FLOOR

The cab pulled up in front of a tumbledown cheap 'villa' in an unfinished cheap neighbourhood – the whole place a living monument of the defeat of the speculative builder.

Atherton leaped out on to the grass-grown rubble which was meant for a footpath.

'I don't see Marjorie looking for me on the doorstep.'

Nor did I – I saw nothing but what appeared to be an unoccupied ramshackle brick abomination. Suddenly Sydney gave an exclamation.

'Hullo! – The front door's closed!'

I was hard at his heels.

'What do you mean?'

'Why, when I went I left the front door open. It looks as if I've made an idiot of myself after all, and Marjorie's returned – let's hope to goodness that I have.'

He knocked. While we waited for a response I questioned him.

'Why did you leave the door open when you went?'

'I hardly know – I imagine that it was with some dim idea of Marjorie's being able to get in if she returned while I was absent – but the truth is I was in such a condition of helter skelter that I am not prepared to swear that I had any reasonable reason.'

'I suppose there is no doubt that you did leave it open?'

'Absolutely none – on that I'll stake my life.'

'Was it open when you returned from your pursuit of Holt?'

'Wide open – I walked straight in, expecting to find her waiting for me in the front room – I was struck all of a heap when I found she wasn't there.'

'Were there any signs of a struggle?'

'None – there were no signs of anything. Everything was just as I had left it, with the exception of the ring which I trod on in the passage, and which Lessingham has.'

'If Miss Lindon has returned, it does not look as if she were in the house at present.'

It did not – unless silence had such meaning. Atherton had knocked loudly three times without succeeding in attracting the slightest notice from within.

'It strikes me that this is another case of seeking admission through that hospitable window at the back.'

Atherton led the way to the rear. Lessingham and I followed. There was not even an apology for a yard, still less a garden – there was not even a fence of any sort, to serve as an enclosure, and to shut off the house from the wilderness of waste land. The kitchen window was open. I asked Sydney if he had left it so.

'I don't know – I dare say we did; I don't fancy that either of us stood on the order of his coming.'

While he spoke, he scrambled over the sill. We followed. When he was in, he shouted at the top of his voice,

'Marjorie! Marjorie! Speak to me, Marjorie – it is I – Sydney!'

The words echoed through the house. Only silence answered. He led the way to the front room. Suddenly he stopped.

'Hollo!' he cried. 'The blind's down!' I had noticed, when we were outside, that the blind was down at the front room window. 'It was up when I went, that I'll swear. That someone has been here is pretty plain – let's hope it's Marjorie.'

He had only taken a step forward into the room when he again stopped short to exclaim.

'My stars! – here's a sudden clearance! – Why, the place is empty – everything's clean gone!'

'What do you mean? – was it furnished when you left?'

The room was empty enough then.

'Furnished? – I don't know that it was exactly what you'd call furnished – the party who ran this establishment had a taste in upholstery which was all his own – but there was a carpet, and a bed, and – and lots of things – for the most part, I should have said, distinctly Eastern curiosities. They seem to have evaporated into smoke – which may be a way which is common enough among Eastern curiosities, though it's queer to me.'

Atherton was staring about him as if he found it difficult to credit the evidence of his own eyes.

'How long ago is it since you left?'

He referred to his watch.

'Something over an hour – possibly an hour and a half; I couldn't swear to the exact moment, but it certainly isn't more.'

'Did you notice any signs of packing up?'

'Not a sign.' Going to the window he drew up the blind – speaking as he did so. 'The queer thing about this business is that when we first got in this blind wouldn't draw up a little bit, so, since it wouldn't go up I pulled it down, roller and all, now it draws up as easily and smoothly as if it had always been the best blind that ever lived.'

Standing at Sydney's back I saw that the cabman on his box was signalling to us with his outstretched hand. Sydney perceived him too. He threw up the sash.

'What's the matter with you?'

'Excuse me, sir, but who's the old gent?'

'What old gent?'

'Why, the old gent peeping through the window of the room upstairs?'

The words were hardly out of the driver's mouth when Sydney was through the door and flying up the staircase. I followed rather more soberly – his methods were a little too flighty for me. When I reached the landing, dashing out of the front room he rushed into the one at the back – then through a door at the side. He came out shouting.

'What's the idiot mean! – with his old gent! I'd old gent him if I got him! – There's not a creature about the place!'

He returned into the front room – I at his heels. That certainly was empty – and not only empty, but it showed no traces of recent occupation. The dust lay thick upon the floor – there was that mouldy, earthy smell which is so frequently found in apartments which have been long untenanted.

'Are you sure, Atherton, that there is no one at the back?'

'Of course I'm sure – you can go and see for yourself if you like; do you think I'm blind? Jehu's drunk.' Throwing up the sash he addressed the driver. 'What do you mean with your old gent at the window? – what window?'

'That window, sir.'

'Go to! – you're dreaming, man! – there's no one here.'

'Begging your pardon, sir, but there was someone there not a minute ago.'

'Imagination, cabman – the slant of the light on the glass – or your eyesight's defective.'

'Excuse me, sir, but it's not my imagination, and my eyesight's as good as any man's in England – and as for the slant of the light on the glass, there ain't much glass for the light to slant on. I saw him peeping through that bottom broken pane on your left hand as plainly as I see you. He must be somewhere about – he can't have got away – he's at the back. Ain't there a cupboard nor nothing where he could hide?'

The cabman's manner was so extremely earnest that I went myself to see. There was a cupboard on the landing, but the door of that stood wide open, and that obviously was bare. The room behind was small, and, despite the splintered glass in the window frame, stuffy. Fragments of glass kept company with the dust on the floor, together with a choice collection of stones, brickbats, and other missiles – which not improbably were the cause of their being there. In the corner stood a cupboard – but a momentary examination showed that that was as bare as the other. The door at the side, which Sydney had left wide open, opened on to a closet, and that was empty. I glanced up – there was no trap door which led to the roof. No practicable nook or cranny, in which a living being could lie concealed, was anywhere at hand.

I returned to Sydney's shoulder to tell the cabman so.

'There is no place in which anyone could hide, and there is no one in either of the rooms – you must have been mistaken, driver.'

The man waxed wroth.

'Don't tell me! How could I come to think I saw something when I didn't?'

'One's eyes are apt to play us tricks; – how could you see what wasn't there?'

'That's what I want to know. As I drove up, before you told me to stop, I saw him looking through the window – the one at which you are. He'd got his nose glued to the broken pane, and was staring as hard as he could stare. When I pulled up, off he started – I saw him get up off his knees, and go to the back of the room. When the gentleman took to knocking, back he came – to the same old spot, and flopped down on his knees. I didn't know what caper you was up to – you might be bum bailiffs for all I knew! – and I supposed that he wasn't so anxious to let you in as you might be to get inside, and that was why he didn't take no notice of your knocking, while all the while he kept a eye on what was going on. When you goes round to the back, up he gets again, and I reckoned that he was going to meet yer, and perhaps give yer a bit of his mind, and that presently I should hear a shindy, or that something would happen. But when you pulls up the blind downstairs, to my surprise back he come once more. He shoves his old nose right through the smash in the pane, and wags his old head at me like a chattering magpie. That didn't seem to me quite the civil thing to do – I hadn't done no harm to him; so I gives you the office, and lets you know that he was there. But for you to say that he wasn't there, and never had been – blimey! that cops the biscuit. If he wasn't there, all I can say is I ain't here, and my 'orse ain't here, and my cab ain't neither – damn it! – the house ain't here, and nothing ain't!'

He settled himself on his perch with an air of the most extreme ill usage – he had been standing up to tell his tale. That the man was serious was unmistakable. As he himself suggested, what inducement could he have had to tell a lie like that? That he believed himself to have seen what he declared he saw was plain. But, on the other hand, what could have become – in the space of fifty seconds! – of his 'old gent'?

Atherton put a question.

'What did he look like – this old gent of yours?'

'Well, that I shouldn't hardly like to say. It wasn't much of his face I could see, only his face and his eyes – and they wasn't pretty. He kept a thing over his head all the time, as if he didn't want too much to be seen.'

'What sort of a thing?'

'Why – one of them cloak sort of things, like them Arab blokes used to wear what used to be at Earl's Court Exhibition – you know!'

This piece of information seemed to interest my companions more than anything he had said before.

'A burnoose do you mean?'

'How am I to know what the thing's called? I ain't up in foreign languages – 'tain't likely! All I know that them Arab blokes what was at Earl's Court used to walk about in them all over the place – sometimes they wore them over their heads, and sometimes they didn't. In fact if you'd asked me, instead of trying to make out as I sees double, or things what was only inside my own noddle, or something or other, I should have said this here old gent what I've been telling you about was a Arab bloke – when he gets off his knees to sneak away from the window, I could see that he had his cloak thing, what was over his head, wrapped all round him.'

Mr Lessingham turned to me, all quivering with excitement.

'I believe that what he says is true!'

'Then where can this mysterious old gentleman have got to – can you suggest an explanation? It is strange, to say the least of it, that the cabman should be the only person to see or hear anything of him.'

'Some devil's trick has been played – I know it, I feel it! – my instinct tells me so!'

I stared. In such a matter one hardly expects a man of Paul Lessingham's stamp to talk of 'instinct'. Atherton stared too. Then, on a sudden, he burst out,

'By the Lord, I believe the Apostle's right – the whole place reeks to me of hankey-pankey – it did as soon as I put my nose inside. In matters of prestidigitation, Champnell, we Westerns are among the rudiments, we've everything to learn – Orientals leave us at the post. If their civilization's what we're pleased to call extinct, their conjuring – when you get to know it! – is all alive oh!'

He moved towards the door. As he went he slipped, or seemed to, all but stumbling on to his knees.

'Something tripped me up – what's this?' He was stamping on the floor with his foot. 'Here's a board loose. Come and lend me a hand, one of you fellows, to get it up. Who knows what mystery's beneath?'

I went to his aid. As he said, a board in the floor was loose. His stepping on it unawares had caused his stumble. Together we prised it out of its place – Lessingham standing by and watching us the while. Having removed it, we peered into the cavity it disclosed.

There was something there.

'Why,' cried Atherton, 'it's a woman's clothing!'

CHAPTER THIRTY-EIGHT

# THE REST OF THE FIND

It was a woman's clothing, beyond a doubt, all thrown in anyhow – as if the person who had placed it there had been in a desperate hurry. An entire outfit was there, shoes, stockings, body linen, corsets, and all – even to hat, gloves, and hairpins; – these latter were mixed up with the rest of the garments in strange confusion. It seemed plain that whoever had worn those clothes had been stripped to the skin.

Lessingham and Sydney stared at me in silence as I dragged them out and laid them on the floor. The dress was at the bottom – it was an alpaca, of a pretty shade in blue, bedecked with lace and ribbons, as is the fashion of the hour, and lined with sea-green silk. It had perhaps been a 'charming confection' once – and that a very recent one! – but now it was all soiled and creased and torn and tumbled. The two spectators made a simultaneous pounce at it as I brought it to the light.

'My God!' cried Sydney, 'it's Marjorie's! – she was wearing it when I saw her last!'

'It's Marjorie's!' gasped Lessingham – he was clutching at the ruined costume, staring at it like a man who has just received sentence of death. 'She wore it when she was with me yesterday – I told her how it suited her, and how pretty it was!'

There was silence – it was an eloquent find; it spoke for itself. The two men gazed at the heap of feminine glories – it might have been the most wonderful sight they ever had seen. Lessingham was the first to speak – his face had all at once grown grey and haggard.

'What has happened to her?'

I replied to his question with another.

'Are you sure this is Miss Lindon's dress?'

'I am sure – and were proof needed, here it is.'

He had found the pocket, and was turning out the contents. There was a purse which contained money and some visiting cards on which were her name and address; a small bunch of keys, with her nameplate attached; a

657

handkerchief, with her initials in a corner. The question of ownership was placed beyond a doubt.

'You see,' said Lessingham, exhibiting the money which was in the purse, 'it is not robbery which has been attempted. Here are two ten-pound notes, and one for five, besides gold and silver – over thirty pounds in all.'

Atherton, who had been turning over the accumulation of rubbish between the joists, proclaimed another find.

'Here are her rings, and watch, and a bracelet – no, it certainly does not look as if theft had been an object.'

Lessingham was glowering at him with knitted brows.

'I have to thank you for this.'

Sydney was unwontedly meek.

'You are hard on me, Lessingham, harder than I deserve – I had rather have thrown away my own life than have suffered misadventure to have come to her.'

'Yours are idle words. Had you not meddled this would not have happened. A fool works more mischief with his folly than of malice prepense. If hurt has befallen Marjorie Lindon you shall account for it to me with your life's blood.'

'Let it be so,' said Sydney. 'I am content. If hurt has come to Marjorie, God knows that I am willing enough that death should come to me.'

While they wrangled, I continued to search. A little to one side, under the flooring which was still intact, I saw something gleam. By stretching out my hand, I could just manage to reach it – it was a long plait of woman's hair. It had been cut off at the roots – so close to the head in one place that the scalp itself had been cut, so that the hair was clotted with blood.

They were so occupied with each other that they took no notice of me. I had to call their attention to my discovery.

'Gentlemen, I fear that I have here something which will distress you – is not this Miss Lindon's hair?'

They recognized it on the instant. Lessingham, snatching it from my hands, pressed it to his lips.

'This is mine – I shall at least have something.' He spoke with a grimness which was a little startling. He held the silken tresses at arm's length. 'This points to murder – foul, cruel, causeless murder. As I live, I will devote my all – money, time, reputation! – to gaining vengeance on the wretch who did this deed.'

Atherton chimed in.

'To that I say, Amen!' He lifted his hand. 'God is my witness!'

'It seems to me, gentlemen, that we move too fast – to my mind it does not by any means of necessity point to murder. On the contrary, I doubt if murder has been done. Indeed, I don't mind owning that I have a theory of my own which points all the other way.'

Lessingham caught me by the sleeve.

'Mr Champnell, tell me your theory.'

'I will, a little later. Of course it may be altogether wrong; – though I fancy it is not; I will explain my reasons when we come to talk of it. But, at present, there are things which must be done.'

'I vote for tearing up every board in the house!' cried Sydney. 'And for pulling the whole infernal place to pieces. It's a conjurer's den – I shouldn't be surprised if cabby's old gent is staring at us all the while from some peephole of his own.'

We examined the entire house, methodically, so far as we were able, inch by inch. Not another board proved loose – to lift those which were nailed down required tools, and those we were without. We sounded all the walls – with the exception of the party walls they were the usual lath and plaster constructions, and showed no signs of having been tampered with. The ceilings were intact; if anything was concealed in them it must have been there some time – the cement was old and dirty. We took the closet to pieces; examined the chimneys; peered into the kitchen oven and the copper – in short, we pried into everything which, with the limited means at our disposal, could be pried into – without result. At the end we found ourselves dusty, dirty, and discomfited. The cabman's 'old gent' remained as much a mystery as ever, and no further trace had been discovered of Miss Lindon.

Atherton made no effort to disguise his chagrin.

'Now what's to be done? There seems to be just nothing in the place at all, and yet that there is, and that it's the key to the whole confounded business I should be disposed to swear.'

'In that case I would suggest that you should stay and look for it. The cabman can go and look for the requisite tools, or a workman to assist you, if you like. For my part it appears to me that evidence of another sort is, for the moment, of paramount importance; and I propose to commence my search for it by making a call at the house which is over the way.'

I had observed, on our arrival, that the road only contained two houses which were in anything like a finished state – that which we were in, and another, some fifty or sixty yards further down, on the opposite side. It was to this I referred. The twain immediately proffered their companionship.

'I will come with you,' said Mr Lessingham.

'And I,' echoed Sydney. 'We'll leave this sweet homestead in charge of the cabman – I'll pull it to pieces afterwards.' He went out and spoke to the driver. 'Cabby, we're going to pay a visit to the little crib over there – you keep an eye on this one. And, if you see a sign of anyone being about the place – living, or dead, or anyhow – you give me a yell. I shall be on the lookout, and I'll be with you before you can say Jack Robinson.'

'You bet I'll yell – I'll raise the hair right off you.' The fellow grinned. 'But I don't know if you gents are hiring me by the day – I want to change my horse; he ought to have been in his stable a couple of hours ago.'

'Never mind your horse – let him rest a couple of hours extra tomorrow to make up for those he has lost today. I'll take care you don't lose anything by this little job – or your horse either. – By the way, look here – this will be better than yelling.'

Taking a revolver out of his trousers' pocket he handed it up to the grinning driver.

'If that old gent of yours does appear, you have a pop at him – I shall hear that easier than a yell. You can put a bullet through him if you like – I give you my word it won't be murder.'

'I don't care if it is,' declared the cabman, handling the weapon like one who was familiar with arms of precision. 'I used to fancy my revolver shooting when I was with the colours, and if I do get a chance I'll put a shot through the old hunks, if only to prove to you that I'm no liar.'

Whether the man was in earnest or not I could not tell – nor whether Atherton meant what he said in answer.

'If you shoot him I'll give you fifty pounds.'

'All right!' The driver laughed. 'I'll do my best to earn that fifty!'

## CHAPTER THIRTY-NINE

## MISS LOUISA COLEMAN

That the house over the way was tenanted was plain to all the world – at least one occupant sat gazing through the window of the first floor front room. An old woman in a cap – one of those large old-fashioned caps which our grandmothers used to wear, tied with strings under the chin. It was a bow window, and as she was seated in the bay looking right in our direction she could hardly have failed to see us as we advanced – indeed she continued to stare at us all the while with placid calmness. Yet I knocked once, twice, and yet again without the slightest notice being taken of my summons.

Sydney gave expression to his impatience in his own peculiar vein.

'Knockers in this part of the world seem intended for ornament only – nobody seems to pay any attention to them when they're used. The old lady upstairs must be either deaf or dotty.' He went out into the road to see if she still was there. 'She's looking at me as calmly as you please – what does she think we're doing here, I wonder; playing a tune on her front door by way of a little amusement? – Madam!' He took off his hat and waved it to her. 'Madam! might I observe that if you won't condescend to notice that we're here your front door will run the risk of being severely injured! – She don't care for me any more than if I was nothing at all – sound another tattoo upon that knocker. Perhaps she's so deaf that nothing short of a cataclysmal uproar will reach her auditory nerves.'

She immediately proved, however, that she was nothing of the sort. Hardly had the sounds of my further knocking died away than, throwing up the window, she thrust out her head and addressed me in a fashion which, under the circumstances, was as unexpected as it was uncalled for.

'Now, young man, you needn't be in such a hurry!'

Sydney explained.

'Pardon me, madam, it's not so much a hurry we're in as pressed for time – this is a matter of life and death.'

She turned her attention to Sydney – speaking with a frankness for which, I imagine, he was unprepared.

'I don't want none of your imperence, young man. I've seen you before – you've been hanging about here the whole day long! – and I don't like the looks of you, and so I'll let you know. That's my front door, and that's my knocker – I'll come down and open when I like, but I'm not going to be hurried, and if the knocker's so much as touched again, I won't come down at all.'

She closed the window with a bang. Sydney seemed divided between mirth and indignation.

'That's a nice old lady, on my honour – one of the good old crusty sort. Agreeable characters this neighbourhood seems to grow – a sojourn hereabouts should do one good. Unfortunately I don't feel disposed just now to stand and kick my heels in the road.' Again saluting the old dame by raising his hat he shouted to her at the top of his voice. 'Madam, I beg ten thousand pardons for troubling you, but this is a matter in which every second is of vital importance – would you allow me to ask you one or two questions?'

Up went the window; out came the old lady's head.

'Now, young man, you needn't put yourself out to holler at me – I won't be hollered at! I'll come down and open that door in five minutes by the clock on my mantelpiece, and not a moment before.'

The fiat delivered, down came the window. Sydney looked rueful – he consulted his watch.

'I don't know what you think, Champnell, but I really doubt if this comfortable creature can tell us anything worth waiting another five minutes to hear. We mustn't let the grass grow under our feet, and time is getting on.'

I was of a different opinion – and said so.

'I'm afraid, Atherton, that I can't agree with you. She seems to have noticed you hanging about all day; and it is at least possible that she has noticed a good deal which would be well worth our hearing. What more promising witness are we likely to find? – her house is the only one which overlooks the one we have just quitted. I am of opinion that it may not only prove well worth our while to wait five minutes, but also that it would be as well, if possible, not to offend her by the way. She's not likely to afford us the information we require if you do.'

'Good. If that's what you think I'm sure I'm willing to wait – only it's to be hoped that that clock upon her mantelpiece moves quicker than its mistress.'

Presently, when about a minute had gone, he called to the cabman.

'Seen a sign of anything?'

The cabman shouted back.

'Ne'er a sign – you'll hear a sound of popguns when I do.'

Those five minutes did seem long ones. But at last Sydney, from his post of vantage in the road, informed us that the old lady was moving. 'She's getting up; – she's leaving the window; – let's hope to goodness she's coming down to open the door. That's been the longest five minutes I've known.'

I could hear uncertain footsteps descending the stairs. They came along the passage. The door was opened – 'on the chain'. The old lady peered at us through an aperture of about six inches.

'I don't know what you young men think you're after, but have all three of you in my house I won't. I'll have him and you' – a skinny finger was pointed to Lessingham and me; then it was directed towards Atherton – 'but have him I won't. So if it's anything particular you want to say to me, you'll just tell him to go away.'

On hearing this Sydney's humility was abject. His hat was in his hand – he bent himself double.

'Suffer me to make you a million apologies, madam, if I have in any way offended you; nothing, I assure you, could have been farther from my intention, or from my thoughts.'

'I don't want none of your apologies, and I don't want none of you neither; I don't like the looks of you, and so I tell you. Before I let anybody into my house you'll have to sling your hook.'

The door was banged in our faces. I turned to Sydney.

'The sooner you go the better it will be for us. You can wait for us over the way.'

He shrugged his shoulders, and groaned – half in jest, half in earnest.

'If I must I suppose I must – it's the first time I've been refused admittance to a lady's house in all my life! What have I done to deserve this thing? – If you keep me waiting long I'll tear that infernal den to pieces!'

He sauntered across the road, viciously kicking the stones as he went. The door reopened.

'Has that other young man gone?'

'He has.'

'Then now I'll let you in. Have him inside my house I won't.'

The chain was removed. Lessingham and I entered. Then the door was refastened and the chain replaced. Our hostess showed us into the front room on the ground floor; it was sparsely furnished and not too clean – but there were chairs enough for us to sit upon; which she insisted on our occupying.

'Sit down, do – I can't abide to see folks standing, it gives me the fidgets.'

So soon as we were seated, without any overture on our parts she plunged in *medias res*.

'I know what it is you've come about – I know! You want me to tell you who it is as lives in the house over the road. Well, I can tell you – and I dare bet a shilling that I'm about the only one who can.'

I inclined my head.

'Indeed. Is that so, madam?'

She was huffed at once.

'Don't madam me – I can't bear none of your lip service. I'm a plain-spoken woman, that's what I am, and I like other people's tongues to be as plain as mine. My name's Miss Louisa Coleman; but I'm generally called Miss Coleman – I'm only called Louisa by my relatives.'

Since she was apparently between seventy and eighty – and looked every year of her apparent age – I deemed that possible. Miss Coleman was evidently a character. If one was desirous of getting information out of her it would be necessary to allow her to impart it in her own manner – to endeavour to induce her to impart it in anybody else's would be time clean wasted. We had Sydney's fate before our eyes.

She started with a sort of roundabout preamble.

'This property is mine; it was left me by my uncle, the late George Henry Jobson – he's buried in Hammersmith Cemetery just over the way – he left me the whole of it. It's one of the finest building sites near London, and it increases in value every year, and I'm not going to let it for another twenty, by which time the value will have more than trebled – so if that is what you've come about, as heaps of people do, you might have saved yourselves the trouble. I keep the boards standing, just to let people know that the ground is to let – though, as I say, it won't be for another twenty years, when it'll be for the erection of high-class mansions only, same as there is in Grosvenor Square – no shops or public houses, and none of your shanties. I live in this place just to keep an eye upon the property – and as for the house over the way, I've never tried to let it, and it never has been let, not until a month ago, when, one morning, I had this letter. You can see it if you like.'

She handed me a greasy envelope which she ferreted out of a capacious pocket which was suspended from her waist, and which she had to lift up her skirt to reach. The envelope was addressed, in unformed characters, 'Miss Louisa Coleman, The Rhododendrons, Convolvulus Avenue, High Oaks Park, West Kensington' – I felt, if the writer had not been of a humorous turn of mind, and drawn on his imagination, and this really was the lady's correct address, then there must be something in a name.

The letter within was written in the same straggling characterless caligraphy – I should have said, had I been asked offhand, that the whole thing was the composition of a servant girl. The composition was about on a par with the writing.

The undersigned would be obliged if Miss Coleman would let her emptey house. I do not know the rent but send fifty pounds. If more will send. Please address, Mohamed el Kheir, Post Office, Sligo Street, London.

It struck me as being as singular an application for a tenancy as I remembered to have encountered. When I passed it on to Lessingham, he seemed to think so too.

'This is a curious letter, Miss Coleman.'

'So I thought – and still more so when I found the fifty pounds inside. There were five ten-pound notes, all loose, and the letter not even registered. If I had been asked what was the rent of the house, I should have said, at the most, not more than twenty pounds – because, between you and me, it wants a good bit of doing up, and is hardly fit to live in as it stands.'

I had had sufficient evidence of the truth of this altogether apart from the landlady's frank admission.

'Why, for all he could have done to help himself I might have kept the money, and only sent him a receipt for a quarter. And some folks would have done – but I'm not one of that sort myself, and shouldn't care to be. So I sent this here party – I never could pronounce his name, and never shall – a receipt for a year.'

Miss Coleman paused to smooth her apron, and consider.

'Well, the receipt should have reached this here party on the Thursday morning, as it were – I posted it on the Wednesday night, and on the Thursday, after breakfast, I thought I'd go over the way to see if there was any little thing I could do – because there wasn't hardly a whole pane of glass in the place – when I all but went all of a heap. When I looked across the road, blessed if the party wasn't in already – at least as much as he ever was in, which, so far as I can make out, never has been anything particular – though how he had got in, unless it was through a window in the middle of the night, is more than I should care to say – there was nobody in the house when I went to bed, that I could pretty nearly take my Bible oath – yet there was the blind up at the parlour, and, what's more, it was down, and it's been down pretty nearly ever since.

'"Well," I says to myself, "for right down imperence this beats anything – why he's in the place before he knows if I'll let him have it. Perhaps he thinks I haven't got a word to say in the matter – fifty pounds or no fifty pounds, I'll soon show him." So I slips on my bonnet, and I walks over the road, and I hammers at the door.

'Well, I have seen people hammering since then, many a one, and how they've kept it up has puzzled me – for an hour, some of them – but I was the first one as begun it. I hammers, and I hammers, and I kept on hammering, but it wasn't no more use than if I'd been hammering at a tombstone. So I starts rapping at the window, but that wasn't no use neither. So I goes round behind, and I hammers at the back door – but there, I couldn't make anyone hear no-how. So I says to myself, "Perhaps the party as is in, ain't in, in a manner of speaking; but I'll keep an eye on the house, and when he is in I'll take care that he ain't out again before I've had a word to say.''

'So I come back home, and as I said I would, I kept an eye on the house the whole of that livelong day, but never a soul went either out or in. But the next day, which it was a Friday, I got out of bed about five o'clock, to see if it was raining, through my having an idea of taking a little excursion if the weather was fine, when I see a party coming down the road. He had on one of them dirty-coloured bed-cover sort of things, and it was wrapped all over his head and round his body, like, as I have been told, them there Arabs wear – and, indeed, I've seen them in them myself at West Brompton, when they was in the exhibition there. It was quite fine, and broad day, and I see him as plainly as I see you – he comes skimming along at a tear of a pace, pulls up at the house over the way, opens the front door, and lets himself in.

'''So,'' I says to myself, ''there you are. Well, Mr Arab, or whatever, or whoever, you may be, I'll take good care that you don't go out again before you've had a word from me. I'll show you that landladies have their rights, like other Christians, in this country, however it may be in yours.'' So I kept an eye on the house, to see that he didn't go out again, and nobody never didn't, and between seven and eight I goes and I knocks at the door – because I thought to myself that the earlier I was the better it might be.

'If you'll believe me, no more notice was taken of me than if I was one of the dead. I hammers, and I hammers, till my wrist was aching, I daresay I hammered twenty times – and then I went round to the back door, and I hammers at that – but it wasn't the least good in the world. I was that provoked to think I should be treated as if I was nothing and nobody, by a dirty foreigner, who went about in a bed-gown through the public streets, that it was all I could do to hold myself.

'I comes round to the front again, and I starts hammering at the window, with every knuckle on my hands, and I calls out, ''I'm Miss Louisa Coleman, and I'm the owner of this house, and you can't deceive me – I saw you come in, and you're in now, and if you don't come and speak to me this moment I'll have the police.''

'All of a sudden, when I was least expecting it, and was hammering my very hardest at the pane, up goes the blind, and up goes the window too, and the most awful-looking creature ever I heard of, not to mention seeing, puts his head right into my face – he was more like a hideous baboon than anything else, let alone a man. I was struck all of a heap, and plumps down on the little wall, and all but tumbles head over heels backwards. And he starts shrieking, in a sort of a kind of English, and in such a voice as I'd never heard the like – it was like a rusty steam engine.

'''Go away! go away! I don't want you! I will not have you – never! You have your fifty pounds – you have your money – that is the whole of you – that is all you want! You come to me no more! – never! – never no more! – or you be sorry! – Go away!''

'I did go away, and that as fast as ever my legs would carry me – what with his looks, and what with his voice, and what with the way that he went on, I was nothing but a mass of trembling. As for answering him back, or giving him a piece of my mind, as I had meant to, I wouldn't have done it not for a thousand pounds. I don't mind confessing, between you and me, that I had to swallow four cups of tea, right straight away, before my nerves was steady.

'"Well,'' I says to myself, when I did feel, as it might be, a little more easy, ''you never have let that house before, and now you've let it with a vengeance – so you have. If that there new tenant of yours isn't the greatest villain that ever went unhung it must be because he's got near relations what's as bad as himself – because two families like his I'm sure there can't be. A nice sort of Arab party to have sleeping over the road he is!''

'But after a time I cools down, as it were – because I'm one of them sort as likes to see on both sides of a question. ''After all,'' I says to myself, ''he has paid his rent, and fifty pounds is fifty pounds – I doubt if the whole house is worth much more, and he can't do much damage to it whatever he does.''

'I shouldn't have minded, so far as that went, if he'd set fire to the place, for, between ourselves, it's insured for a good bit over its value. So I decided that I'd let things be as they were, and see how they went on. But from that hour to this I've never spoken to the man, and never wanted to, and wouldn't, not of my own free will, not for a shilling a time – that face of his will haunt me if I live till Noah, as the saying is. I've seen him going in and out at all hours of the day and night – that Arab party's a mystery if ever there was one – he always goes tearing along as if he's flying for his life. Lots of people have come to the house, all sorts and kinds, men and women – they've been mostly women, and even little children. I've seen them hammer and hammer at that front door, but never a one have I seen let in – or yet seen taken any notice of, and I think I may say, and yet tell no lie, that I've scarcely took my eye off the house since he's been inside it, over and over again in the middle of the night have I got up to have a look, so that I've not missed much that has took place.

'What's puzzled me is the noises that's come from the house. Sometimes for days together there's not been a sound, it might have been a house of the dead; and then, all through the night, there've been yells and screeches, squawks and screams – I never heard nothing like it. I have thought, and more than once, that the devil himself must be in that front room, let alone all the rest of his demons. And as for cats! – where they've come from I can't think. I didn't use to notice hardly a cat in the neighbourhood till that there Arab party came – there isn't much to attract them; but since he came there's been regiments. Sometimes at night there's been troops about the place screeching like mad – I've wished them farther, I can tell you. That Arab party must be fond of 'em. I've seen them inside the house, at the windows, upstairs and downstairs, as it seemed to me, a dozen at a time.'

## CHAPTER FORTY

# WHAT MISS COLEMAN SAW THROUGH THE WINDOW

As Miss Coleman had paused, as if her narrative was approaching a conclusion, I judged it expedient to make an attempt to bring the record as quickly as possible up to date.

'I take it, Miss Coleman, that you have observed what has occurred in the house today.'

She tightened her nut-cracker jaws and glared at me disdainfully – her dignity was ruffled.

'I'm coming to it, aren't I? – if you'll let me. If you've got no manners I'll learn you some. One doesn't like to be hurried at my time of life, young man.'

I was meekly silent; – plainly, if she was to talk, everyone else must listen.

'During the last few days there have been some queer goings on over the road – out of the common queer, I mean, for goodness knows that they always have been queer enough. That Arab party has been flitting about like a creature possessed – I've seen him going in and out twenty times a day. This morning –'

She paused – to fix her eyes on Lessingham. She apparently observed his growing interest as she approached the subject which had brought us there – and resented it.

'Don't look at me like that, young man, because I won't have it. And as for questions, I may answer questions when I'm done, but don't you dare to ask me one before, because I won't be interrupted.'

Up to then Lessingham had not spoken a word – but it seemed as if she was endowed with the faculty of perceiving the huge volume of the words which he had left unuttered.

'This morning – as I've said already –' she glanced at Lessingham as if she defied his contradiction – 'when that Arab party came home it was just on the stroke of seven. I know what was the exact time because, when I went to the door to the milkman, my clock was striking the half hour, and I always keep it thirty minutes fast. As I was taking the milk, the man said to me, "Hollo,

Miss Coleman, here's your friend coming along." "What friend?" I says –
for I ain't got no friends, as I know, round here, nor yet, I hope no enemies
neither.

'And I looks round, and there was the Arab party coming tearing down the
road, his bedcover thing all flying in the wind, and his arms straight out in
front of him – I never did see anyone go at such a pace. "My goodness," I
says, "I wonder he don't do himself an injury." "I wonder someone else
don't do him an injury," says the milkman. "The very sight of him is enough
to make my milk go sour." And he picked up his pail and went away quite
grumpy – though what that Arab party's done to him is more than I can say. –
I have always noticed that milkman's temper's short like his measure. I
wasn't best pleased with him for speaking of that Arab party as my friend,
which he never has been, and never won't be, and never could be neither.

'Five persons went to the house after the milkman was gone, and that there
Arab party was safe inside – three of them was commercials, that I know,
because afterwards they came to me. But of course they none of them got no
chance with that there Arab party except of hammering at his front door,
which ain't what you might call a paying game, nor nice for the temper, but
for that I don't blame him, for if once those commercials do begin talking
they'll talk for ever.

'Now I'm coming to this afternoon.'

I thought it was about time – though for the life of me, I did not dare to hint
as much.

'Well, it might have been three, or it might have been half past, anyhow it
was thereabouts, when up there comes two men and a woman, which one of
the men was that young man what's a friend of yours. "Oh," I says to
myself, "here's something new in callers, I wonder what it is they're
wanting." That young man what was a friend of yours, he starts hammering,
and hammering, as the custom was with everyone who came, and, as usual,
no more notice was taken of him than nothing – though I knew that all the
time the Arab party was indoors.'

At this point I felt that all hazards I must interpose a question.

'You are sure he was indoors?'

She took it better than I feared she might.

'Of course I'm sure – hadn't I seen him come in at seven, and he never
hadn't gone out since, for I don't believe that I'd taken my eyes off the place
not for two minutes together, and I'd never had a sight of him. If he wasn't
indoors, where was he then?'

For the moment, so far as I was concerned, the query was unanswerable.
She triumphantly continued:

'Instead of doing what most did, when they'd had enough of hammering, and going away, these three they went round to the back, and I'm blessed if they mustn't have got through the kitchen window, woman and all, for all of a sudden the blind in the front room was pulled not up, but down – dragged down it was, and there was that young man what's a friend of yours standing with it in his hand.

'"Well," I says to myself, "if that ain't cool I should like to know what is. If, when you ain't let in, you can let yourself in, and that without so much as saying by your leave, or with your leave, things is coming to a pretty pass. Wherever can that Arab party be, and whatever can he be thinking of, to let them go on like that because that he's the sort to allow a liberty to be took with him, and say nothing, I don't believe."

'Every moment I expects to hear a noise and see a row begin, but, so far as I could make out, all was quiet and there wasn't nothing of the kind. So I says to myself, "There's more in this than meets the eye, and them three parties must have right upon their side, or they wouldn't be doing what they are doing in the way they are, there'd be a shindy."

'Presently, in about five minutes, the front door opens, and a young man – not the one what's your friend, but the other – comes sailing out, and through the gate, and down the road, as stiff and upright as a grenadier – I never see anyone walk more upright, and few as fast. At his heels comes the young man what is your friend, and it seems to me that he couldn't make out what this other was a-doing of. I says to myself, "There's been a quarrel between them two, and him as has gone has hooked it." This young man what is your friend he stood at the gate, all of a fidget, staring after the other with all his eyes, as if he couldn't think what to make of him, and the young woman, she stood on the doorstep, staring after him too.

'As the young man what had hooked it turned the corner, and was out of sight, all at once your friend he seemed to make up his mind, and he started off running as hard as he could pelt – and the young woman was left alone. I expected, every minute, to see him come back with the other young man, and the young woman by the way she hung about the gate, she seemed to expect it too. But no, nothing of the kind. So when, as I expect, she'd had enough of waiting, she went into the house again, and I see her pass the front room window. After a while, back she comes to the gate, and stands looking and looking, but nothing was to be seen of either of them young men. When she'd been at the gate, I daresay five minutes, back she goes into the house – and I never saw nothing of her again.'

'You never saw anything of her again? – Are you sure she went back into the house?'

'As sure as I am that I see you.'

'I suppose that you didn't keep a constant watch upon the premises?'

'But that's just what I did do. I felt something queer was going on, and I made up my mind to see it through. And when I make up my mind to a thing like that I'm not easy to turn aside. I never moved off the chair at my bedroom window, and I never took my eyes off the house, not till you come knocking at my front door.'

'But, since the young lady is certainly not in the house at present, she must have eluded your observation, and, in some manner, have left it without your seeing her.'

'I don't believe she did, I don't see how she could have done – there's something queer about that house, since that Arab party's been inside it. But though I didn't see her, I did see someone else.'

'Who was that?'

'A young man.'

'A young man?'

'Yes, a young man, and that's what puzzled me, and what's been puzzling me ever since, for see him go in I never did do.'

'Can you describe him?'

'Not as to the face, for he wore a dirty cloth cap pulled down right over it, and he walked so quickly that I never had a proper look. But I should know him anywhere if I saw him, if only because of his clothes and his walk.'

'What was there peculiar about his clothes and his walk?'

'Why, his clothes were that old, and torn, and dirty, that a ragman wouldn't have given a thank you for them – and as for fit – there wasn't none, they hung upon him like a scarecrow – he was a regular figure of fun; I should think the boys would call after him if they saw him in the street. As for his walk, he walked off just like the first young man had done, he strutted along with his shoulders back, and his head in the air, and that stiff and straight that my kitchen poker would have looked crooked beside of him.'

'Did nothing happen to attract your attention between the young lady's going back into the house and the coming out of this young man?'

Miss Coleman cogitated.

'Now you mention it there did – though I should have forgotten all about it if you hadn't asked me – that comes of your not letting me tell the tale in my own way. About twenty minutes after the young woman had gone in someone put up the blind in the front room, which that young man had dragged right down. I couldn't see who it was for the blind was between us, and it was about ten minutes after that that young man came marching out.'

'And then what followed?'

'Why, in about another ten minutes that Arab party himself comes scooting through the door.'

'The Arab party?'

'Yes, the Arab party! The sight of him took me clean aback. Where he'd been, and what he'd been doing with himself while them there people played hi-spy-hi about his premises I'd have given a shilling out of my pocket to have known, but there he was, as large as life, and carrying a bundle.'

'A bundle?'

'A bundle, on his head, like a muffin-man carries his tray. It was a great thing, you never would have thought he could have carried it, and it was easy to see that it was as much as he could manage; it bent him nearly double, and he went crawling along like a snail – it took him quite a time to get to the end of the road.'

Mr Lessingham leaped up from his seat, crying,

'Marjorie was in that bundle!'

'I doubt it,' I said.

He moved about the room distractedly, wringing his hands.

'She was! she must have been! God help us all!'

'I repeat that I doubt it. If you will be advised by me you will wait awhile before you arrive at any such conclusion.'

All at once there was a tapping at the window pane. Atherton was staring at us from without.

He shouted through the glass.

'Come out of that, you fossils! – I've news for you!'

## CHAPTER FORTY-ONE

# THE CONSTABLE – HIS CLUE – AND THE CAB

Miss Coleman, getting up in a fluster, went hurrying to the door.

'I won't have that young man in my house. I won't have him! Don't let him dare to put his nose across my doorstep.'

I endeavoured to appease her perturbation.

'I promise you that he shall not come in, Miss Coleman. My friend here, and I, will go and speak to him outside.'

She held the front door open just wide enough to enable Lessingham and me to slip through, then she shut it after us with a bang. She evidently had a strong objection to any intrusion on Sydney's part.

Standing just without the gate he saluted us with a characteristic vigour which was scarcely flattering to our late hostess. Behind him was a constable.

'I hope you two have been mewed in with that old pussy long enough. While you've been tittle-tattling I've been doing – listen to what this bobby's got to say.'

The constable, his thumbs thrust inside his belt, wore an indulgent smile upon his countenance. He seemed to find Sydney amusing. He spoke in a deep bass voice – as if it issued from his boots.

'I don't know that I've got anything to say.'

It was plain that Sydney thought otherwise.

'You wait till I've given this pretty pair of gossips a lead, officer, then I'll trot you out.' He turned to us.

'After I'd poked my nose into every dashed hole in that infernal den, and been rewarded with nothing but a pain in the back for my trouble, I stood cooling my heels on the doorstep, wondering if I should fight the cabman, or get him to fight me, just to pass the time away – for he says he can box, and he looks it – when who should come strolling along but this magnificent example of the metropolitan constabulary.' He waved his hand towards the policeman, whose grin grew wider. 'I looked at him, and he looked at me, and then when we'd had enough of admiring each other's fine features and

striking proportions, he said to me, "Has he gone?" I said, "Who? – Baxter? – or Bob Brown?" He said, "No, the Arab." I said, "What do you know about any Arab?" He said, "Well, I saw him in the Broadway about three-quarters of an hour ago, and then, seeing you here, and the house all open, I wondered if he had gone for good." With that I almost jumped out of my skin, though you can bet your life I never showed it. I said, "How do you know it was he?" He said, "It was him right enough, there's no doubt about that. If you've seen him once, you're not likely to forget him." "Where was he going?" "He was talking to a cabman – four-wheeler. He'd got a great bundle on his head – wanted to take it inside with him. Cabman didn't seem to see it." That was enough for me – I picked this most deserving officer up in my arms, and carried him across the road to you two fellows like a flash of lightning.'

Since the policeman was six feet three or four, and more than sufficiently broad in proportion, he scarcely seemed the kind of figure to be picked up in anybody's arms and carried like a 'flash of lightning', which – as his smile grew more indulgent, he himself appeared to think.

Still, even allowing for Atherton's exaggeration, the news which he had brought was sufficiently important. I questioned the constable upon my own account.

'There is my card, officer, probably, before the day is over, a charge of a very serious character will be preferred against the person who has been residing in the house over the way. In the meantime it is of the utmost importance that a watch should be kept upon his movements. I suppose you have no sort of doubt that the person you saw in the Broadway was the one in question?'

'Not a morsel. I know him as well as I do my own brother – we all do upon this beat. He's known amongst us as the Arab. I've had my eye on him ever since he came to the place. A queer fish he is. I always have said that he's up to some game or other. I never came across one like him for flying about in all sorts of weather, at all hours of the night, always tearing along as if for his life. As I was telling this gentleman I saw him in the Broadway – well, now it's about an hour since, perhaps a little more. I was coming on duty when I saw a crowd in front of the District Railway Station – and there was the Arab, having a sort of argument with the cabman. He had a great bundle on his head, five or six feet long, perhaps longer. He wanted to take this great bundle with him into the cab, and the cabman, he didn't see it.'

'You didn't wait to see him drive off.'

'No – I hadn't time. I was due at the station – I was cutting it pretty fine as it was.'

'You didn't speak to him – or to the cabman?'

'No, it wasn't any business of mine you understand. The whole thing just caught my eye as I was passing.'

'And you didn't take the cabman's number?'

'No, well, as far as that goes it wasn't needful. I know the cabman, his name and all about him, his stable's in Bradmore.'

I whipped out my note-book.

'Give me his address.'

'I don't know what his Christian name is, Tom, I believe, but I'm not sure. Anyhow his surname's Ellis and his address is Church Mews, St John's Road, Bradmore – I don't know his number, but anyone will tell you which is his place, if you ask for Four-Wheel Ellis – that's the name he's known by among his pals because of his driving a four-wheeler.'

'Thank you, officer. I am obliged to you.' Two half-crowns changed hands. 'If you will keep an eye on the house and advise me at the address which you will find on my card, of any thing which takes place there during the next few days, you will do me a service.'

We had clambered back into the hansom, the driver was just about to start, when the constable was struck by a sudden thought.

'One moment, sir – blessed if I wasn't going to forget the most important bit of all. I did hear him tell Ellis where to drive him to – he kept saying it over and over again, in that queer lingo of his. "Waterloo Railway Station, Waterloo Railway Station." "All right," said Ellis, "I'll drive you to Waterloo Railway Station right enough, only I'm not going to have that bundle of yours inside my cab. There isn't room for it, so you put it on the roof." "To Waterloo Railway Station," said the Arab, "I take my bundle with me to Waterloo Railway Station – I take it with me." "Who says you don't take it with you?" said Ellis. "You can take it, and twenty more besides, for all I care, only you don't take it inside my cab – put it on the roof." "I take it with me to Waterloo Railway Station," said the Arab, and there they were, wrangling and jangling, and neither seeming to be able to make out what the other was after, and the people all laughing.'

'Waterloo Railway Station – you are sure that was what he said?'

'I'll take my oath to it, because I said to myself when I heard it, "I wonder what you'll have to pay for that little lot, for the District Railway Station's outside the four-mile radius."'

As we drove off I was inclined to ask myself, a little bitterly – and perhaps unjustly – if it were not characteristic of the average London policeman to almost forget the most important part of his information – at any rate to leave it to the last and only to bring it to the front on having his palm crossed with silver.

As the hansom bowled along we three had what occasionally approached a warm discussion.

'Marjorie was in that bundle,' began Lessingham, in the most lugubrious of tones, and with the most woebegone of faces.

'I doubt it,' I observed.

'She was – I feel it – I know it. She was either dead and mutilated, or gagged and drugged and helpless. All that remains is vengeance.'

'I repeat that I doubt it.'

Atherton struck in.

'I am bound to say, with the best will in the world to think otherwise, that I agree with Lessingham.'

'You are wrong.'

'It's all very well for you to talk in that cocksure way, but it's easier for you to say I'm wrong than to prove it. If I am wrong, and if Lessingham's wrong, how do you explain his extraordinary insistance on taking it inside the cab with him, which the bobby describes? If there wasn't something horrible, awful in that bundle of his, of which he feared the discovery, why was he so reluctant to have it placed upon the roof?'

'There probably was something in it which he was particularly anxious should not be discovered, but I doubt if it was anything of the kind which you suggest.'

'Here is Marjorie in a house alone – nothing has been seen of her since – her clothing, her hair, is found hidden away under the floor. This scoundrel sallies forth with a huge bundle on his head – the bobby speaks of it being five or six feet long, or longer – a bundle which he regards with so much solicitude that he insists on never allowing it to go, for a single instant, out of his sight and reach. What is in the thing? Don't all the facts most unfortunately point in one direction?'

Mr Lessingham covered his face with his hands, and groaned.

'I fear that Mr Atherton is right.'

'I differ from you both.'

Sydney at once became heated.

'Then perhaps you can tell us what was in the bundle?'

'I fancy I could make a guess at the contents.'

'Oh you could, could you, then, perhaps, for our sakes, you'll make it – and not play the oracular owl! – Lessingham and I are interested in this business, after all.'

'It contained the bearer's personal property: that, and nothing more. Stay! before you jeer at me, suffer me to finish. If I am not mistaken as to the identity of the person whom the constable describes as the Arab, I apprehend that the contents of that bundle were of much more importance to him than if they had consisted of Miss Lindon, either dead or living. More, I am inclined to suspect that if the bundle was placed on the roof of the cab, and if the driver did meddle with it, and did find out the contents, and understand them, he would have been driven, out of hand, stark staring mad.'

Sydney was silent, as if he reflected. I imagine he perceived there was something in what I said.

'But what has become of Miss Lindon?'

'I fancy that Miss Lindon, at this moment, is – somewhere; I don't, just now, know exactly where, but I hope very shortly to be able to give you a clearer notion – attired in a rotten, dirty pair of boots; a filthy, tattered pair of trousers; a ragged, unwashed apology for a shirt; a greasy, ancient, shapeless coat; and a frowsy peaked cloth cap.'

They stared at me, open eyed. Atherton was the first to speak.

'What on earth do you mean?'

'I mean that it seems to me that the facts point in the direction of my conclusions rather than yours – and that very strongly too. Miss Coleman asserts that she saw Miss Lindon return into the house; that within a few minutes the blind was replaced at the front window; and that shortly after a young man, attired in the costume I have described, came walking out of the front door. I believe that young man was Miss Marjorie Lindon.'

Lessingham and Atherton both broke out into interrogations, with Sydney, as usual, loudest.

'But – man alive! what on earth should make her do a thing like that? Marjorie, the most retiring, modest girl on all God's earth, walk about in broad daylight, in such a costume, and for no reason at all! My dear Champnell, you are suggesting that she first of all went mad.'

'She was in a state of trance.'

'Good God! – Champnell!'

'Well?'

'Then you think that – juggling villain did get hold of her?'

'Undoubtedly. Here is my view of the case, mind it is only a hypothesis and you must take it for what it is worth. It seems to me quite clear that the Arab, as we will call the person for the sake of identification, was somewhere about the premises when you thought he wasn't.'

'But – where? We looked upstairs, and downstairs, and everywhere – where could he have been?'

'That, as at present advised, I am not prepared to say, but I think you may take it for granted that he was there. He hypnotized the man Holt, and sent him away, intending you to go after him, and so being rid of you both –'

'The deuce he did, Champnell! You write me down an ass!'

'As soon as the coast was clear he discovered himself to Miss Lindon, who, I expect, was disagreeably surprised, and hypnotized her.'

'The hound!'

'The devil!'

The first exclamation was Lessingham's, the second Sydney's.

'He then constrained her to strip herself to the skin —'

'The wretch!'

'The fiend!'

'He cut off her hair; he hid it and her clothes under the floor where we found them — where I think it probable that he had already some ancient masculine garments concealed —'

'By Jove! I shouldn't be surprised if they were Holt's. I remember the man saying that that nice joker stripped him of his duds — and certainly when I saw him — and when Marjorie found him! — he had absolutely nothing on but a queer sort of cloak. Can it be possible that that humorous professor of hankey-pankey — may all the maledictions of the accursed alight upon his head! — can have sent Marjorie Lindon, the daintiest damsel in the land! — into the streets of London rigged out in Holt's old togs!'

'As to that, I am not able to give an authoritative opinion, but, if I understand you aright, it at least is possible. Anyhow I am disposed to think that he sent Miss Lindon after the man Holt, taking it for granted that he had eluded you —'

'That's it. Write me down an ass again!'

'That he did elude you, you have yourself admitted.'

'That's because I stopped talking with that mutton-headed bobby — I'd have followed the man to the ends of the earth if it hadn't been for that.'

'Precisely; the reason is immaterial, it is the fact with which we are immediately concerned. He did elude you. And I think you will find that Miss Lindon and Mr Holt are together at this moment.'

'In men's clothing?'

'Both in men's clothing, or, rather, Miss Lindon is in a man's rags.'

'Great Potiphar! To think of Marjorie like that!'

'And where they are, the Arab is not very far off either.'

Lessingham caught me by the arm.

'And what diabolical mischief do you imagine that he proposes to do to her?'

I shirked the question.

'Whatever it is, it is our business to prevent his doing it.'

'And where do you think they have been taken?'

'That it will be our immediate business to endeavour to discover — and here, at any rate, we are at Waterloo.'

## CHAPTER FORTY-TWO

# THE QUARRY DOUBLES

.I turned towards the booking-office on the main departure platform. As I went, the chief platform inspector, George Bellingham, with whom I had some acquaintance, came out of his office. I stopped him.

'Mr Bellingham, will you be so good as to step with me to the booking-office, and instruct the clerk in charge to answer one or two questions which I wish to put to him. I will explain to you afterwards what is their exact import, but you know me sufficiently to be able to believe me when I say that they refer to a matter in which every moment is of the first importance.'

He turned and accompanied us into the interior of the booking-case.

'To which of the clerks, Mr Champnell, do you wish to put your questions?'

'To the one who issues third-class tickets to Southampton.'

Bellingham beckoned to a man who was counting a heap of money, and apparently seeking to make it tally with the entries in a huge ledger which lay open before him – he was a short, slightly-built young fellow, with a pleasant face and smiling eyes.

'Mr Stone, this gentleman wishes to ask you one or two questions.'

'I am at his service.'

I put my questions.

'I want to know, Mr Stone, if, in the course of the day, you have issued any tickets to a person dressed in Arab costume?'

His reply was prompt.

'I have – by the last train, the 7.25 – three singles.'

Three singles! Then my instinct had told me rightly.

'Can you describe the person?'

Mr Stone's eyes twinkled.

'I don't know that I can, except in a general way – he was uncommonly old and uncommonly ugly, and he had a pair of the most extraordinary eyes I ever saw – they gave me a sort of all-overish feeling when I saw them glaring at me through the pigeon hole. But I can tell you one thing about him, he had a great bundle on his head, which he steadied with one hand, and as it bulged out in all directions its presence didn't make him popular with other people who wanted tickets too.'

Undoubtedly this was our man.

'You are sure he asked for three tickets?'

'Certain. He said three tickets to Southampton; laid down the exact fare – nineteen and six – and held up three fingers – like that. Three nasty looking fingers they were, with nails as long as talons.'

'You didn't see who were his companions?'

'I didn't – I didn't try to look. I gave him his tickets and off he went – with the people grumbling at him because that bundle of his kept getting in their way.'

Bellingham touched me on the arm.

'I can tell you about the Arab of whom Mr Stone speaks. My attention was called to him by his insisting on taking his bundle with him into the carriage – it was an enormous thing, he could hardly squeeze it through the door; it occupied the entire seat. But as there weren't as many passengers as usual, and he wouldn't or couldn't be made to understand that his precious bundle would be safe in the luggage van along with the rest of the luggage, and as he wasn't the sort of person you could argue with to any advantage, I had him put into an empty compartment, bundle and all.'

'Was he alone then?'

'I thought so at the time, he said nothing about having more than one ticket, or any companions, but just before the train started two other men – English men – got into his compartment; and as I came down the platform, the ticket inspector at the barrier informed me that these two men were with him, because he held tickets for the three, which, as he was a foreigner, and they seemed English, struck the inspector as odd.'

'Could you describe the two men?'

'I couldn't, not particularly, but the man who had charge of the barrier might. I was at the other end of the train when they got in. All I noticed was that one seemed to be a commonplace-looking individual and that the other was dressed like a tramp, all rags and tatters, a disreputable looking object he appeared to be.'

'That,' I said to myself, 'was Miss Marjorie Lindon, the lovely daughter of a famous house; the wife-elect of a coming statesman.'

To Bellingham I remarked aloud:

'I want you to strain a point, Mr Bellingham, and to do me a service which I assure you you shall never have any cause to regret. I want you to wire instructions down the line to detain this Arab and his companions and to keep them in custody until the receipt of further instructions. They are not wanted by the police as yet, but they will be as soon as I am able to give certain information to the authorities at Scotland Yard – and wanted very badly. But, as you will perceive for yourself, until I am able to give that information every moment is important. – Where's the Station Superintendent?'

'He's gone. At present I'm in charge.'

'Then will you do this for me? I repeat that you shall never have any reason to regret it.'

'I will if you'll accept all responsibility.'

'I'll do that with the greatest pleasure.'

Bellingham looked at his watch.

'It's about twenty minutes to nine. The train's scheduled for Basingstoke at 9.6. If we wire to Basingstoke at once they ought to be ready for them when they come.'

'Good!'

The wire was sent.

We were shown into Bellingham's office to await results. Lessingham paced agitatedly to and fro; he seemed to have reached the limits of his self-control, and to be in a condition in which movement of some sort was an absolute necessity. The mercurial Sydney, on the contrary, leaned back in a chair, his legs stretched out in front of him, his hands thrust deep into his trouser pockets, and stared at Lessingham, as if he found relief to his feelings in watching his companion's restlessness. I, for my part, drew up as full a précis of the case as I deemed advisable, and as time permitted, which I despatched by one of the company's police to Scotland Yard.

Then I turned to my associates.

'Now, gentlemen, it's past dinner time. We may have a journey in front of us. If you take my advice you'll have something to eat.'

Lessingham shook his head.

'I want nothing.'

'Nor I,' echoed Sydney.

I started up.

'You must pardon my saying nonsense, but surely you of all men, Mr Lessingham, should be aware that you will not improve the situation by rendering yourself incapable of seeing it through. Come and dine.'

I haled them off with me, willy nilly, to the refreshment room. I dined – after a fashion; Mr Lessingham swallowed, with difficulty, a plate of soup; Sydney nibbled at a plate of the most unpromising looking 'chicken and ham' – he proved, indeed, more intractable than Lessingham, and was not to be persuaded to tackle anything easier of digestion.

I was just about to take cheese after chop when Bellingham came hastening in, in his hand an open telegram.

'The birds have flown,' he cried.

'Flown! – How?'

In reply he gave me the telegram. I glanced at it. It ran:

Persons described not in the train. Guard says they got out at Vauxhall. Have wired Vauxhall to advise you.

'That's a level-headed chap,' said Bellingham. 'The man who sent that telegram. His wiring to Vauxhall should save us a lot of time – we ought to hear from there directly. Hollo! what's this? I shouldn't be surprised if this is it.'

As he spoke a porter entered – he handed an envelope to Bellingham. We all three kept our eyes fixed on the inspector's face as he opened it. When he perceived the contents he gave an exclamation of surprise.

'This Arab of yours, and his two friends, seem rather a curious lot, Mr Champnell.'

He passed the paper on to me. It took the form of a report. Lessingham and Sydney, regardless of forms and ceremonies, leaned over my shoulder as I read it.

Passengers by 7.30 Southampton, on arrival of train, complained of noises coming from a compartment in coach 8964. Stated that there had been shrieks and yells ever since the train left Waterloo, as if someone was being murdered. An Arab and two Englishmen got out of the compartment in question, apparently the party referred to in wire just to hand from Basingstoke. All three declared that there was nothing the matter. That they had been shouting for fun. Arab gave up three third singles for Southampton, saying, in reply to questions, that they had changed their minds, and did not want to go any farther. As there were no signs of a struggle or of violence, nor, apparently, any definite cause for detention, they were allowed to pass. They took a four-wheeler, No. 09435. The Arab and one man went inside, and the other man on the box. They asked to be driven to Commercial Road, Limehouse. The cab has since returned. Driver says he put the three men down, at their request, in Commercial Road, at the corner of Sutcliffe Street, near the East India Docks. They walked up Sutcliffe Street, the Englishmen in front, and the Arab behind, took the first turning to the right, and after that he saw nothing of them. The driver further states that all the way the Englishman inside, who was so ragged and dirty that he was reluctant to carry him, kept up a sort of wailing noise which so attracted his attention that he twice got off his box to see what was the matter, and each time he said it was nothing. The cabman is of opinion that both the Englishmen were of weak intellect. We were of the same impression here. They said nothing, except at the seeming instigation of the Arab, but when spoken to stared and gaped like lunatics.

It may be mentioned that the Arab had with him an enormous bundle, which he persisted, in spite of all remonstrances, on taking with him inside the cab.

As soon as I had mastered the contents of the report, and perceived what I believed to be – unknown to the writer himself – its hideous inner meaning, I turned to Bellingham.

'With your permission, Mr Bellingham, I will keep this communication – it will be safe in my hands, you will be able to get a copy, and it may be necessary that I should have the original to show to the police. If any inquiries are made for me from Scotland Yard, tell them that I have gone to the Commercial Road, and that I will report my movements from Limehouse Police Station.'

In another minute we were once more traversing the streets of London – three in a hansom cab.

## CHAPTER FORTY-THREE

# THE MURDER AT MRS 'ENDERSON'S

It is something of a drive from Waterloo to Limehouse – it seems longer when all your nerves are tingling with anxiety to reach your journey's end; and the cab I had hit upon proved to be not the fastest I might have chosen. For some time after our start, we were silent. Each was occupied with his own thoughts.

Then Lessingham, who was sitting at my side, said to me,

'Mr Champnell, you have that report.'

'I have.'

'Will you let me see it once more?'

I gave it to him. He read at once, twice – and I fancy yet again. I purposely avoided looking at him as he did so. Yet all the while I was conscious of his pallid cheeks, the twitched muscles of his mouth, the feverish glitter of his eyes – this Leader of Men, whose predominate characteristic in the House of Commons was immobility, was rapidly approximating to the condition of a hysterical woman. The mental strain which he had been recently undergoing was proving too much for his physical strength. This disappearance of the woman he loved bade fair to be the final straw. I felt convinced that unless something was done quickly to relieve the strain upon his mind he was nearer to a state of complete mental and moral collapse than he himself imagined. Had he been under my orders I should have commanded him to at once return home, and not to think; but conscious that, as things were, such a direction would be simply futile, I decided to do something else instead. Feeling that suspense was for him the worst possible form of suffering I resolved to explain, so far as I was able, precisely what it was I feared, and how I proposed to prevent it.

Presently there came the question for which I had been waiting, in a harsh, broken voice which no one who had heard him speak on a public platform, or in the House of Commons, would have recognized as his.

'Mr Champnell – who do you think this person is of whom the report from Vauxhall Station speaks as being all in rags and tatters?'

He knew perfectly well – but I understood the mental attitude which induced him to prefer that the information should seem to come from me.

'I hope that it will prove to be Miss Lindon.'

'Hope!' He gave a sort of gasp.

'Yes, hope – because if it is I think it possible, nay probable, that within a few hours you will have her again enfolded in your arms.'

'Pray God that it may be so! pray God! – pray the good God!'

I did not dare to look round for, from the tremor which was in his tone, I was persuaded that in the speaker's eyes were tears. Atherton continued silent. He was leaning half out of the cab, staring straight ahead, as if he saw in front a young girl's face, from which he could not remove his glance, and which beckoned him on.

After a while Lessingham spoke again, as if half to himself and half to me.

'This mention of the shrieks on the railway, and of the wailing noise in the cab – what must this wretch have done to her? How my darling must have suffered!'

That was a theme on which I myself scarcely ventured to allow my thoughts to rest. The notion of a gently-nurtured girl being at the mercy of that fiend incarnate, possessed – as I believed that so-called Arab to be possessed – of all the paraphernalia of horror and of dread, was one which caused me tangible shrinkings of the body. Whence had come those shrieks and yells, of which the writer of the report spoke, which had caused the Arab's fellow-passengers to think that murder was being done? What unimaginable agony had caused them? what speechless torture? And the 'wailing noise', which had induced the prosaic, indurated London cabman to get twice off his box to see what was the matter, what anguish had been provocative of that? The helpless girl who had already endured so much, endured, perhaps, that to which death would have been preferred! – shut up in that rattling, jolting box on wheels, alone with that diabolical Asiatic, with the enormous bundle, which was but the lurking place of nameless terrors – what might she not, while being borne through the heart of civilized London, have been made to suffer? What had she not been made to suffer to have kept up that continued 'wailing noise'?

It was not a theme on which it was wise to permit one's thoughts to linger – and particularly was it clear that it was one from which Lessingham's thoughts should have been kept as far as possible away.

'Come, Mr Lessingham, neither you nor I will do himself any good by permitting his reflections to flow in a morbid channel. Let us talk of something else. By the way, weren't you due to speak in the House tonight?'

'Due! – Yes, I was due – but what does it matter?'

'But have you acquainted no one with the cause of your non-attendance?'

'Acquaint! – whom should I acquaint?'

'My good sir! Listen to me, Mr Lessingham. Let me entreat you very earnestly, to follow my advice. Call another cab – or take this! and go at once to the House. It is not too late. Play the man, deliver the speech you have undertaken to deliver, perform your political duties. By coming with me you will be a hindrance rather than a help, and you may do your reputation an injury from which it never may recover. Do as I counsel you, and I will undertake to do my very utmost to let you have good news by the time your speech is finished.'

He turned on me with a bitterness for which I was unprepared.

'If I were to go down to the House, and try to speak in the state in which I am now, they would laugh at me, I should be ruined.'

'Do you not run an equally great risk of being ruined by staying away?'

He gripped me by the arm.

'Mr Champnell, do you know that I am on the verge of madness? Do you know that as I am sitting here by your side I am living in a dual world? I am going on and on to catch that – that fiend, and I am back again in that Egyptian den, upon that couch of rugs, with the Woman of the Songs beside me, and Marjorie is being torn and tortured, and burnt before my eyes! God help me! Her shrieks are ringing in my ears!'

He did not speak loudly, but his voice was none the less impressive on that account. I endeavoured my hardest to be stern.

'I confess that you disappoint me, Mr Lessingham. I have always understood that you were a man of unusual strength; you appear, instead, to be a man of extraordinary weakness; with an imagination so ill-governed that its ebullitions remind me of nothing so much as feminine hysterics. Your wild language is not warranted by circumstances. I repeat that I think it quite possible that by tomorrow morning she will be returned to you.'

'Yes – but how? as the Marjorie I have known, as I saw her last – or how?'

That was the question which I had already asked myself, in what condition would she be when we had succeeded in snatching her from her captor's grip? It was a question to which I had refused to supply an answer. To him I lied by implication.

'Let us hope that, with the exception of being a trifle scared, she will be as sound and hale and hearty as ever in her life.'

'Do you yourself believe that she'll be like that – untouched, unchanged, unstained?'

Then I lied right out – it seemed to me necessary to calm his growing excitement.

'I do.'

'You don't!'

'Mr Lessingham!'

'Do you think that I can't see your face and read in it the same thoughts which trouble me? As a man of honour do you care to deny that when Marjorie Lindon is restored to me – if she ever is! – you fear she will be but the mere soiled husk of the Marjorie whom I knew and loved?'

'Even supposing that there may be a modicum of truth in what you say – which I am far from being disposed to admit – what good purpose do you propose to serve by talking in such a strain?'

'None – no good purpose – unless it be the desire of looking the truth in the face. For, Mr Champnell, you must not seek to play with me the hypocrite, nor try to hide things from me as if I were a child. If my life is ruined – it is ruined – let me know it, and look the knowledge in the face. That, to me, is to play the man.'

I was silent.

The wild tale he had told me of that Cairene inferno, oddly enough – yet why oddly, for the world is all coincidence! – had thrown a flood of light on certain events which had happened some three years previously and which ever since had remained shrouded in mystery. The conduct of the business afterwards came into my hands – and briefly, what had occurred was this:

Three persons – two sisters and their brother, who was younger than themselves, members of a decent English family, were going on a trip round the world. They were young, adventurous, and – not to put too fine a point on it – foolhardy. The evening after their arrival in Cairo, by way of what is called 'a lark', in spite of the protestations of people who were better informed than themselves, they insisted on going, alone, for a ramble through the native quarter.

They went – but they never returned. Or, rather the two girls never returned. After an interval the young man was found again – what was left of him. A fuss was made when there were no signs of their reappearance, but as there were no relations, nor even friends of theirs, but only casual acquaintances on board the ship by which they had travelled, perhaps not so great a fuss as might have been was made. Anyhow, nothing was discovered. Their widowed mother, alone in England, wondering how it was that beyond the receipt of a brief wire, acquainting her with their arrival at Cairo, she had heard nothing further of their wanderings, placed herself in communication with the diplomatic people over there – to learn that, to all appearances, her three children had vanished from off the face of the earth.

Then a fuss was made – with a vengeance. So far as one can judge the whole town and neighbourhood was turned pretty well upside down. But nothing came of it – so far as any results were concerned, the authorities might just as well have left the mystery of their vanishment alone. It continued where it was in spite of them.

However, some three months afterwards a youth was brought to the British Embassy by a party of friendly Arabs who asserted that they had found him naked and nearly dying in some remote spot in the Wady Halfa desert. It was the brother of the two lost girls. He was as nearly dying as he very well could be without being actually dead when they brought him to the Embassy – and in a state of indescribable mutilation. He seemed to rally for a time under careful treatment, but he never again uttered a coherent word. It was only from his delirious ravings that any idea was formed of what had really occurred.

Shorthand notes were taken of some of the utterances of his delirium. Afterwards they were submitted to me. I remembered the substance of them quite well, and when Mr Lessingham began to tell me of his own hideous experiences they came back to me more clearly still. Had I laid those notes before him I have little doubt but that he would have immediately perceived that seventeen years after the adventure which had left such an indelible scar upon his own life, this youth – he was little more than a boy – had seen the things which he had seen, and suffered the nameless agonies and degradations which he had suffered. The young man was perpetually raving about some indescribable den of horror which was own brother to Lessingham's temple and about some female monster, whom he regarded with such fear and horror that every allusion he made to her was followed by a convulsive paroxysm which taxed all the ingenuity of his medical attendants to bring him out of. He frequently called upon his sisters by name, speaking of them in a manner which inevitably suggested that he had been an unwilling and helpless witness of hideous tortures which they had undergone; and then he would rise in bed, screaming, 'They're burning them! they're burning them! Devils! devils!' And at those times it required all the strength of those who were in attendance to restrain his maddened frenzy.

The youth died in one of these fits of great preternatural excitement, without, as I have previously written, having given utterance to one single coherent word, and by some of those who were best able to judge it was held to have been a mercy that he did die without having been restored to consciousness. And, presently, tales began to be whispered, about some idolatrous sect, which was stated to have its headquarters somewhere in the interior of the country – some located it in this neighbourhood, and some in that – which was stated to still practise, and to always have practised, in unbroken historical continuity, the debased, unclean, mystic, and bloody rites, of a form of idolatry which had had its birth in a period of the world's story which was so remote, that to all intents and purposes it might be described as prehistoric.

While the ferment was still at its height, a man came to the British Embassy who said that he was a member of a tribe which had its habitat on the banks of the White Nile. He asserted that he was in association with this very idolatrous sect – though he denied that he was one of the actual sectaries. He did admit, however, that he had assisted more than once at their orgies, and declared that it was their constant practice to offer young women as sacrifices – preferably white Christian women, with a special preference, if they could get them, to young English women. He vowed that he himself had seen with his own eyes English girls burnt alive. The description which he gave of what preceded and followed these foul murders appalled those who listened. He finally wound up by offering, on payment of a stipulated sum of money, to guide a troop of soldiers to this den of demons, so that they should arrive there at a moment when it was filled with worshippers, who were preparing to participate in an orgie which was to take place during the next few days.

His offer was conditionally accepted. He was confined in an apartment with one man on guard inside and another on guard outside the room. That night the sentinel without was startled by hearing a great noise and frightful screams issuing from the chamber in which the native was interned. He summoned assistance. The door was opened. The soldier on guard within was stark, staring mad – he died within a few months, a gibbering maniac to the end. The native was dead. The window, which was a very small one, was securely fastened inside and strongly barred without. There was nothing to show by what means entry had been gained. Yet it was the general opinion of those who saw the corpse that the man had been destroyed by some wild beast. A photograph was taken of the body after death, a copy of which is still in my possession. In it are distinctly shown lacerations about the neck and the lower portion of the abdomen, as if they had been produced by the claws of some huge and ferocious animal. The skull is splintered in half-a-dozen places, and the face is torn to rags.

That was more than three years ago. The whole business has remained as great a mystery as ever. But my attention has once or twice been caught by trifling incidents, which have caused me to more than suspect that the wild tale told by that murdered native had in it at least the elements of truth; and which have even led me to wonder if the trade in kidnapping was not being carried on to this very hour, and if women of my own flesh and blood were not still being offered up on that infernal altar. And now, here was Paul Lessingham, a man of world-wide reputation, of great intellect, of undoubted

THE BEETLE

honour, who had come to me with a wholly unconscious verification of all my worst suspicions!

That the creature spoken of as an Arab – and who was probably no more an Arab than I was, and whose name was certainly not Mohamed el Kheir! – was an emissary from that den of demons, I had no doubt. What was the exact purport of the creature's presence in England was another question. Possibly part of the intention was the destruction of Paul Lessingham, body, soul and spirit; possibly another part was the procuration of fresh victims for that long-drawn-out holocaust. That this latter object explained the disappearance of Miss Lindon I felt persuaded. That she was designed by the personification of evil who was her captor, to suffer all the horrors at which the stories pointed, and then to be burned alive, amidst the triumphant yells of the attendant demons, I was certain. That the wretch, aware that the pursuit was in full cry, was tearing, twisting, doubling, and would stick at nothing which would facilitate the smuggling of the victim out of England, was clear.

My interest in the quest was already far other than a merely professional one. The blood in my veins tingled at the thought of such a woman as Miss Lindon being in the power of such a monster. I may assuredly claim that throughout the whole business I was urged forward by no thought of fee or of reward. To have had a share in rescuing that unfortunate girl, and in the destruction of her noxious persecutor, would have been reward enough for me.

One is not always, even in strictly professional matters, influenced by strictly professional instincts.

The cab slowed. A voice descended through the trap door.

'This is Commercial Road, sir – what part of it do you want?'

'Drive me to Limehouse Police Station.'

We were driven there. I made my way to the usual inspector behind the usual pigeon-hole.

'My name is Champnell. Have you received any communication from Scotland Yard tonight having reference to a matter in which I am interested?'

'Do you mean about the Arab? We received a telephonic message about half an hour ago.'

'Since communicating with Scotland Yard this has come to hand from the authorities at Vauxhall Station. Can you tell me if anything has been seen of the person in question by the men of your division?'

I handed the Inspector the 'report'. His reply was laconic.

'I will inquire.'

He passed through a door into an inner room and the 'report' went with him.

691

'Beg pardon, sir, but was that a Harab you was a-talking about to the Hinspector?'

The speaker was a gentleman unmistakably of the guttersnipe class. He was seated on a form. Close at hand hovered a policeman whose special duty it seemed to be to keep an eye upon his movements.

'Why do you ask?'

'I beg your pardon, sir, but I saw a Harab myself about a hour ago – leastways he looked like as if he was a Harab.'

'What sort of a looking person was he?'

'I can't 'ardly tell you that, sir, because I didn't never have a proper look at him – but I know he had a bloomin' great bundle on 'is 'ead . . . It was like this, 'ere. I was comin' round the corner, as he was passin', I never see 'im till I was right atop of 'im, so that I haccidentally run agin' 'im – my heye! didn't 'e give me a downer! I was down on the back of my 'ead in the middle of the road before I knew where I was and 'e was at the other end of the street. If 'e 'adn't knocked me more'n 'arf silly I'd been after 'im, sharp – I tell you! and hasked 'im what 'e thought 'e was a-doin' of but afore my senses was back agin 'e was out o' sight – clean!'

'You are sure he had a bundle on his head?'

'I noticed it most particular.'

'How long ago do you say this was? and where?'

'About a hour ago – perhaps more, perhaps less.'

'Was he alone?'

'It seemed to me as if a cove was a-follerin' 'im, leastways there was a bloke as was a-keepin' close at 'is 'eels – though I don't know what 'is little game was, I'm sure. Ask the pleesman – he knows, he knows everythink, the pleesman do.'

I turned to the 'pleesman'.

'Who is this man?'

The 'pleesman' put his hands behind his back, and threw out his chest. His manner was distinctly affable.

'Well – he's being detained upon suspicion. He's given us an address at which to make inquiries, and inquiries are being made. I shouldn't pay too much attention to what he says if I were you. I don't suppose he'd be particular about a lie or two.'

This frank expression of opinion re-aroused the indignation of the gentleman on the form.

'There you hare! at it again! That's just like you peelers – you're all the same! What do you know about me? – Nuffink! This gen'leman ain't got no call to believe me, not as I knows on – it's all the same to me if 'e do or don't, but it's trewth what I'm sayin', all the same.'

At this point the Inspector re-appeared at the pigeon-hole. He cut short the flow of eloquence.

'Now then, not so much noise outside there!' He addressed me. 'None of our men have seen anything of the person you're inquiring for, so far as we're aware. But, if you like, I will place a man at your disposal, and he will go round with you, and you will be able to make your own inquiries.'

A capless, wildly excited young ragamuffin came dashing in at the street door. He gasped out, as clearly as he could for the speed which he had made:

'There's been murder done, Mr Pleesman – a Harab's killed a bloke.'

'Mr Pleesman' gripped him by the shoulder.

'What's that?'

The youngster put up his arm, and ducked his head, instinctively, as if to ward off a blow.

'Leave me alone! I don't want none of your 'andling! – I ain't done nuffink to you! I tell you 'e 'as!'

The Inspector spoke through the pigeon-hole.

'He has what, my lad? What do you say has happened?'

'There's been murder done – it's right enough! – there 'as! – up at Mrs 'Enderson's, in Paradise Place – a Harab's been and killed a bloke!'

## CHAPTER FORTY-FOUR

# THE MAN WHO WAS MURDERED

The Inspector spoke to me.

'If what the boy says is correct it sounds as if the person whom you are seeking may have had a finger in the pie.'

I was of the same opinion, as, apparently, were Lessingham and Sydney. Atherton collared the youth by the shoulder which Mr Pleesman had left disengaged.

'What sort of looking bloke is it who's been murdered?'

'I dunno! I 'aven't seen 'im! Mrs 'Enderson, she says to me! "'Gustus Barley," she says, "a bloke's been murdered. That there Harab what I chucked out 'alf a hour ago been and murdered 'im, and left 'im behind up in my back room. You run as 'ard as you can tear and tell them there dratted pleese what's so fond of shovin' their dirty noses into respectable people's 'ouses." So I comes and tells yer. That's all I knows about it.'

We went four in the hansom which had been waiting in the street to Mrs Henderson's in Paradise Place – the Inspector and we three. 'Mr Pleesman' and ''Gustus Barley' followed on foot. The Inspector was explanatory.

'Mrs Henderson keeps a sort of lodging-house – a "Sailors' Home" she calls it, but no one could call it sweet. It doesn't bear the best of characters, and if you asked me what I thought of it, I should say in plain English that it was a disorderly house.'

Paradise Place proved to be within three or four hundred yards of the Station House. So far as could be seen in the dark it consisted of a row of houses of considerable dimensions – and also of considerable antiquity. They opened on to two or three stone steps which led directly into the street. At one of the doors stood an old lady with a shawl drawn over her head. This was Mrs Henderson. She greeted us with garrulous volubility.

'So you 'ave come, 'ave you? I thought you never was a-comin' that I did.' She recognized the Inspector. 'It's you, Mr Phillips, is it?' Perceiving us, she drew a little back. 'Who's them 'ere parties? They ain't coppers?'

Mr Phillips dismissed her inquiry, curtly.

'Never you mind who they are. What's this about someone being murdered.'

'Ssh!' The old lady glanced round. 'Don't you speak so loud, Mr Phillips. No one don't know nothing about it as yet. The parties what's in my 'ouse is most respectable – most! and they couldn't abide the notion of there being police about the place.'

'We quite believe that, Mrs Henderson.'

The Inspector's tone was grim.

Mrs Henderson led the way up a staircase which would have been distinctly the better for repairs. It was necessary to pick one's way as one went, and as the light was defective stumbles were not infrequent.

Our guide paused outside a door on the topmost landing. From some mysterious recess in her apparel she produced a key.

'It's in 'ere. I locked the door so that nothing mightn't be disturbed. I knows 'ow particular you pleesmen is.'

She turned the key. We all went in – we, this time in front, and she behind.

A candle was guttering on a broken and dilapidated single washhand stand. A small iron bedstead stood by its side, the clothes on which were all tumbled and tossed. There was a rush-seated chair with a hole in the seat – and that, with the exception of one or two chipped pieces of stoneware, and a small round mirror which was hung on a nail against the wall, seemed to be all that the room contained. I could see nothing in the shape of a murdered man. Nor, it appeared, could the Inspector either.

'What's the meaning of this, Mrs Henderson? I don't see anything here.'

'It's be'ind the bed, Mr Phillips. I left 'im just where I found 'im, I wouldn't 'ave touched 'im not for nothing, nor yet 'ave let nobody else 'ave touched him neither, because, as I say, I know 'ow particular you pleesmen is.'

We all four went hastily forward. Atherton and I went to the head of the bed, Lessingham and the Inspector, leaning right across the bed, peeped over the side. There, on the floor in the space which was between the bed and the wall, lay the murdered man.

At sight of him an exclamation burst from Sydney's lips.

'It's Holt!'

'Thank God!' cried Lessingham. 'It isn't Marjorie!'

The relief in his tone was unmistakable. That the one was gone was plainly nothing to him in comparison with the fact that the other was left.

Thrusting the bed more into the centre of the room I knelt down beside the man on the floor. A more deplorable spectacle than he presented I have seldom witnessed. He was decently clad in a grey tweed suit, white hat, collar and necktie, and it was perhaps that fact which made his extreme attenuation the more conspicuous. I doubt if there was an ounce of flesh on the whole of his body. His cheeks and the sockets of his eyes were hollow. The skin was drawn tightly over his cheek bones – the bones themselves were staring through. Even his nose was wasted, so that nothing but a ridge of cartilage remained. I put my arm beneath his shoulder and raised him from the floor; no resistance was offered by the body's gravity – he was as light as a little child.

'I doubt,' I said, 'if this man has been murdered. It looks to me like a case of starvation, or exhaustion – possibly a combination of both.'

'What's that on his neck?' asked the Inspector – he was kneeling at my side.

He referred to two abrasions of the skin – one on either side of the man's neck.

'They look to me like scratches. They seem pretty deep, but I don't think they're sufficient in themselves to cause death.'

'They might be, joined to an already weakened constitution. Is there anything in his pockets? – let's lift him on to the bed.'

We lifted him on to the bed – a featherweight he was to lift. While the Inspector was examining his pockets – to find them empty – a tall man with a big black beard came bustling in. He proved to be Dr Glossop, the local police surgeon, who had been sent for before our quitting the Station House.

His first pronouncement, made as soon as he commenced his examination, was, under the circumstances, sufficiently startling.

'I don't believe the man's dead. Why didn't you send for me directly you found him?'

The question was put to Mrs Henderson.

'Well, Dr Glossop, I wouldn't touch 'im myself, and I wouldn't 'ave 'im touched by no one else, because, as I've said afore, I know 'ow particular them pleesmen is.'

'Then in that case, if he does die you'll have had a hand in murdering him – that's all.'

The lady sniggered. 'Of course Dr Glossop, we all knows that you'll always 'ave your joke.'

'You'll find it a joke if you have to hang, as you ought to, you—' The doctor said what he did say to himself, under his breath. I doubt if it was flattering to Mrs Henderson. 'Have you got any brandy in the House?'

'We've got everythink in the 'ouse for them as likes to pay for it – everythink.' Then suddenly remembering that the police were present, and that hers were not exactly licensed premises, 'Leastways we can send out for it for them parties as gives us the money, being, as is well known, always willing to oblige.'

'Then send for some – to the tap downstairs, if that's the nearest! If this man dies before you've brought it I'll have you locked up as sure as you're a living woman.'

The arrival of the brandy was not long delayed – but the man on the bed had regained consciousness before it came. Opening his eyes he looked up at the doctor bending over him.

'Hollo, my man! that's more like the time of day! How are you feeling?'

The patient stared hazily up at the doctor, as if his sense of perception was not yet completely restored – as if this big bearded man was something altogether strange. Atherton bent down beside the doctor.

'I'm glad to see you looking better, Mr Holt. You know me, don't you? I've been running about after you all day long.'

'You are – you are –' The man's eyes closed, as if the effort at recollection exhausted him. He kept them closed as he continued to speak.

'I know who you are. You are – the gentleman.'

'Yes, that's it, I'm the gentleman – name of Atherton. – Miss Lindon's friend. And I daresay you're feeling pretty well done up, and in want of something to eat and drink – here's some brandy for you.'

The doctor had some in a tumbler. He raised the patient's head, allowing it to trickle down his throat. The man swallowed it mechanically, motionless, as if unconscious what it was that he was doing. His cheeks flushed, the passing glow of colour caused their condition of extraordinary and, indeed, extravagant attenuation to be more prominent than ever. The doctor laid him back upon the bed, feeling his pulse with one hand, while he stood and regarded him in silence.

Then, turning to the Inspector, he said to him in an undertone:

'If you want him to make a statement he'll have to make it now, he's going fast. You won't be able to get much out of him – he's too far gone, and I shouldn't bustle him, but get what you can.'

The Inspector came to the front, a notebook in his hand.

'I understand from this gentleman –' signifying Atherton – 'that your name's Robert Holt. I'm an Inspector of police, and I want you to tell me what has brought you into this condition. Has anyone been assaulting you?'

Holt, opening his eyes, glanced up at the speaker mistily, as if he could not see him clearly – still less understand what it was that he was saying. Sydney, stooping over him, endeavoured to explain.

'The Inspector wants to know how you got here, has anyone been doing anything to you? Has anyone been hurting you?'

The man's eyelids were partially closed. Then they opened wider and wider. His mouth opened too. On his skeleton features there came a look of panic fear. He was evidently struggling to speak. At last words came.

'The beetle!' He stopped. Then, after an effort, spoke again. 'The beetle!'

'What's he mean?' asked the Inspector.

'I think I understand,' Sydney answered; then turning again to the man in the bed. 'Yes, I hear what you say – the beetle. Well, has the beetle done anything to you?'

'It took me by the throat!'

'Is that the meaning of the marks upon your neck?'

'The beetle killed me.'

The lids closed. The man relapsed into a state of lethargy. The Inspector was puzzled; – and said so.

'What's he mean about a beetle?'

Atherton replied.

'I think I understand what he means – and my friends do too. We'll explain afterwards. In the meantime I think I'd better get as much out of him as I can – while there's time.'

'Yes,' said the doctor, his hand upon the patient's pulse, 'while there's time. There isn't much – only seconds.'

Sydney endeavoured to rouse the man from his stupor.

'You've been with Miss Lindon all the afternoon and evening, haven't you, Mr Holt?'

Atherton had reached a chord in the man's consciousness. His lips moved – in painful articulation.

'Yes – all the afternoon – and evening – God help me!'

'I hope God will help you my poor fellow; you've been in need of His help if ever man was. Miss Lindon is disguised in your old clothes, isn't she?'

'Yes – in my old clothes. My God!'

'And where is Miss Lindon now?'

The man had been speaking with his eyes closed. Now he opened them wide; there came into them the former staring horror. He became possessed by uncontrollable agitation – half raising himself in bed. Words came from his quivering lips as if they were only drawn from him by the force of his anguish.

'The beetle's going to kill Miss Lindon.'

A momentary paroxysm seemed to shake the very foundations of his being. His whole frame quivered. He fell back on to the bed – ominously. The doctor examined him in silence – while we too were still.

'This time he's gone for good, there'll be no conjuring him back again.'

I felt a sudden pressure on my arm, and found that Lessingham was clutching me with probably unconscious violence. The muscles of his face were twitching. He trembled. I turned to the doctor.

'Doctor, if there is any of that brandy left will you let me have it for my friend?'

Lessingham disposed of the remainder of the 'shillingsworth'. I rather fancy it saved us from a scene.

The Inspector was speaking to the woman of the house.

'Now, Mrs Henderson, perhaps you'll tell us what all this means. Who is this man, and how did he come in here, and who came in with him, and what do you know about it altogether? If you've got anything to say, say it, only you'd better be careful, because it's my duty to warn you that anything you do say may be used against you.'

## CHAPTER FORTY-FIVE

# ALL THAT MRS 'ENDERSON KNEW

Mrs Henderson put her hands under her apron and smirked.

'Well, Mr Phillips, it do sound strange to 'ear you talkin' to me like that. Anybody'd think I'd done something as I didn't ought to 'a' done to 'ear you going on. As for what's 'appened, I'll tell you all I know with the greatest willingness on earth. And as for bein' careful, there ain't no call for you to tell me to be that, for that I always am, as by now you ought to know.'

'Yes – I do know. Is that all you have to say?'

'Rilly, Mr Phillips, what a man you are for catching people up, you rilly are. O' course that ain't all I've got to say – ain't I just a-comin' to it?'

'Then come.'

'If you presses me so you'll muddle of me up, and then if I do 'appen to make a herror, you'll say I'm a liar, when goodness knows there ain't no more truthful woman not in Limehouse.'

Words plainly trembled on the Inspector's lips – which he refrained from uttering. Mrs Henderson cast her eyes upwards, as if she sought for inspiration from the filthy ceiling.

'So far as I can swear it might 'ave been a hour ago, or it might 'ave been a hour and a quarter, or it might 'ave been a hour and twenty minutes –'

'We're not particular as to the seconds.'

'When I 'ears a knockin' at my front door, and when I comes to open it, there was a Harab party, with a great bundle on 'is 'ead, bigger nor 'isself, and two other parties along with him. This Harab party says, in that queer foreign way them Harab parties 'as of talkin', "A room for the night, a room." Now I don't much care for foreigners, and never did, especially them Harabs, which their 'abits ain't my own – so I as much 'ints the same. But this 'ere Harab party, he didn't seem to quite foller of my meaning, for all he done was to say as he said afore, "A room for the night, a room." And he shoves a couple of 'arf crowns into my 'and. Now it's always been a motter o' mine, that money is money, and one man's money is as good as another man's. So, not wishing to be disagreeable – which other people would have taken 'em if I 'adn't, I shows 'em up 'ere. I'd been downstairs it might 'ave been 'arf a hour, when I 'ears a shindy a-coming from this room –'

'What sort of a shindy?'

'Yelling and shrieking – oh my gracious, it was enough to set your blood all curdled – for ear-piercingness I never did 'ear nothing like it. We do 'ave troublesome parties in 'ere, like they do elsewhere, but I never did 'ear nothing like that before. I stood it for about a minute, but it kep' on, and kep' on, and every moment I expected as the other parties as was in the 'ouse would be complainin', so up I comes and I thumps at the door, and it seemed that thump I might for all the notice that was took of me.'

'Did the noise keep on?'

'Keep on! I should think it did keep on! Lord love you! shriek after shriek, I expected to see the roof took off.'

'Were there any other noises? For instance, were there any sounds of struggling, or of blows?'

'There weren't no sounds except of the party hollering.'

'One party only?'

'One party only. As I says afore, shriek after shriek – when you put your ear to the panel there was a noise like some other party blubbering, but that weren't nothing, as for the hollering you wouldn't have thought that nothing what you might call 'umin could 'ave kep' up such a screechin'. I thumps and thumps and at last when I did think that I should 'ave to 'ave the door broke down, the Harab says to me from inside, "Go away! I pay for the room! go away!" I did think that pretty good, I tell you that. So I says, "Pay for the room or not pay for the room, you didn't pay to make that shindy!" And what's more I says, "If I 'ear it again," I says, "out you goes! And if you don't go quiet I'll 'ave somebody in as'll pretty quickly make you!"'

'Then was there silence?'

'So to speak there was – only there was this sound as if some party was a-blubbering, and another sound as if a party was a-panting for his breath.'

'Then what happened?'

'Seeing that, so to speak, all was quiet, down I went again. And in another quarter of a hour, or it might 'ave been twenty minutes, I went to the front door to get a mouthful of hair. And Mrs Barker, what lives over the road, at No. 24, she comes to me and says, "That there Arab party of yours didn't stop long." I looks at 'er, "I don't quite foller you," I says – which I didn't. "I saw him come in," she says, "and then, a few minutes back, I see 'im go again, with a great bundle on 'is 'ead he couldn't 'ardly stagger under!" "Oh," I says, "that's news to me, I didn't know 'e'd gone, nor see him neither –" which I didn't. So, up I comes again, and, sure enough, the door

701

was open, and it seems to me that the room was empty, till I come upon this pore young man what was lying be'ind the bed.'

There was a growl from the doctor.

'If you'd had any sense, and sent for me at once, he might have been alive at this moment.'

''Ow was I to know that, Dr Glossop? I couldn't tell. My finding 'im there murdered was quite enough for me. So I runs downstairs, and I nips 'old of 'Gustus Barley, what was leaning against the wall, and I says to him, "'Gustus Barley, run to the station as fast as you can and tell 'em that a man's been murdered – that Harab's been and killed a bloke." And that's all I know about it, and I couldn't tell you no more Mr Phillips, not if you was to keep on asking me questions not for hours and hours.'

'Then you think it was this man' – with a motion towards the bed – 'who was shrieking?'

'To tell you the truth, Mr Phillips, about that I don't 'ardly know what to think. If you 'ad asked me I should 'ave said it was a woman. I ought to know a woman's holler when I 'ear it, if any one does, I've 'eard enough of 'em in my time, goodness knows. And I should 'ave said that only a woman could 'ave hollered like that and only 'er when she was raving mad. But there weren't no woman with him. There was only this man what's murdered, and the other man – and as for the other man I will say this, that 'e 'adn't got twopennyworth of clothes to cover 'im. But, Mr Phillips, howsomever that may be, that's the last Harab I'll 'ave under my roof, no matter what they pays, and you may mark my words I'll ave no more.'

Mrs Henderson, once more glancing upward, as if she imagined herself to have made some declaration of a religious nature, shook her head with much solemnity.

## CHAPTER FORTY-SIX

# THE SUDDEN STOPPING

As we were leaving the house a constable gave the Inspector a note. Having read it he passed it to me. It was from the local office.

> Message received that an Arab with a big bundle on his head has been noticed loitering about the neighbourhood of St Pancras Station. He seemed to be accompanied by a young man who had the appearance of a tramp. Young man seemed ill. They appeared to be waiting for a train, probably to the North. Shall I advise detention?

I scribbled on the flyleaf of the note.

> Have them detained. If they have gone by train have a special in readiness.

In a minute we were again in the cab. I endeavoured to persuade Lessingham and Atherton to allow me to conduct the pursuit alone – in vain. I had no fear of Atherton's succumbing, but I was afraid for Lessingham. What was more almost than the expectation of his collapse was the fact that his looks and manner, his whole bearing, so eloquent of the agony and agitation of his mind, was beginning to tell upon my nerves. A catastrophe of some sort I foresaw. Of the curtain's fall upon one tragedy we had just been witnesses. That there was worse – much worse, to follow I did not doubt. Optimistic anticipations were out of the question – that the creature we were chasing would relinquish the prey uninjured, no one, after what we had seen and heard, could by any possibility suppose. Should a necessity suddenly arise for prompt and immediate action, that Lessingham would prove a hindrance rather than a help I felt persuaded.

But since moments were precious, and Lessingham was not to be persuaded to allow the matter to proceed without him, all that remained was to make the best of his presence.

The great arch of St Pancras was in darkness. An occasional light seemed to make the darkness still more visible. The station seemed deserted. I thought, at first, that there was not a soul about the place, that our errand was in vain, that the only thing for us to do was to drive to the police station and to pursue our inquiries there. But as we turned towards the booking-office, our footsteps ringing out clearly through the silence and the night, a door opened, a light shone out from the room within, and a voice inquired:

'Who's that?'

'My name's Champnell. Has a message been received from me from the Limehouse Police Station?'

'Step this way.'

We stepped that way – into a snug enough office, of which one of the railway inspectors was apparently in charge. He was a big man, with a fair beard. He looked me up and down, as if doubtfully. Lessingham he recognized at once. He took off his cap to him.

'Mr Lessingham, I believe?'

'I am Mr Lessingham. Have you any news for me?'

I fancy, by his looks – that the official was struck by the pallor of the speaker's face – and by his tremulous voice.

'I am instructed to give certain information to a Mr Augustus Champnell.'

'I am Mr Champnell. What's your information?'

'With reference to the Arab about whom you have been making inquiries. A foreigner, dressed like an Arab, with a great bundle on his head, took two single thirds for Hull by the midnight express.'

'Was he alone?'

'It is believed that he was accompanied by a young man of very disreputable appearance. They were not together at the booking-office, but they had been seen together previously. A minute or so after the Arab had entered the train this young man got into the same compartment – they were in the front waggon.'

'Why were they not detained?'

'We had no authority to detain them, nor any reason. Until your message was received a few minutes ago we at this station were not aware that inquiries were being made for them.'

'You say he booked to Hull – does the train run through to Hull?'

'No – it doesn't go to Hull at all. Part of it's the Liverpool and Manchester Express, and part of it's for Carlisle. It divides at Derby. The man you're looking for will change either at Sheffield or at Cudworth Junction and go on to Hull by the first train in the morning. There's a local service.'

I looked at my watch.

'You say the train left at midnight. It's now nearly five-and-twenty past. Where's it now?'

'Nearing St Albans, it's due there 12.35.'

'Would there be time for a wire to reach St Albans?'

'Hardly – and anyhow there'll only be enough railway officials about the place to receive and despatch the train. They'll be fully occupied with their ordinary duties. There won't be time to get the police there.'

'You could wire to St Albans to inquire if they were still in the train?'

'That could be done – certainly. I'll have it done at once if you like.'

'Then where's the next stoppage?'

'Well, they're at Luton at 12.51. But that's another case of St Albans. You see there won't be much more than twenty minutes by the time you've got your wire off, and I don't expect there'll be many people awake at Luton. At these country places sometimes there's a policeman hanging about the station to see the express go through, but, on the other hand, very often there isn't, and if there isn't, probably at this time of night it'll take a good bit of time to get the police on the premises. I tell you what I should advise.'

'What's that?'

'The train is due at Bedford at 1.29 – send your wire there. There ought to be plenty of people about at Bedford, and anyhow there'll be time to get the police to the station.'

'Very good. I instructed them to tell you to have a special ready – have you got one?'

'There's an engine with steam up in the shed – we'll have all ready for you in less than ten minutes. And I tell you what – you'll have about fifty minutes before the train is due at Bedford. It's a fifty mile run. With luck you ought to get there pretty nearly as soon as the express does. – Shall I tell them to get ready?'

'At once.'

While he issued directions through a telephone to what, I presume, was the engine shed, I drew up a couple of telegrams. Having completed his orders he turned to me.

'They're coming out of the siding now – they'll be ready in less than ten minutes. I'll see that the line's kept clear. Have you got those wires?'

'Here is one – this is for Bedford.'

It ran:

'Arrest the Arab who is in train due at 1.29. When leaving St Pancras he was in a third-class compartment in front waggon. He has a large bundle, which detain. He took two third singles for Hull. Also detain his companion, who is dressed like a tramp. This is a young lady whom the Arab has disguised and kidnapped while in a condition of hypnotic trance. Let her have medical assistance and be taken to a hotel. All expenses will be paid on the arrival of the undersigned who is following by special train. As the Arab will probably be very violent a sufficient force of police should be in waiting.

'AUGUSTUS CHAMPNELL.'

'And this is the other. It is probably too late to be of any use at St Albans – but send it there, and also to Luton.'

'Is Arab with companion in train which left St Pancras at 12.0? If so, do not let them get out till train reaches Bedford, where instructions are being wired for arrest.'

The Inspector rapidly scanned them both.

'They ought to do your business, I should think. Come along with me – I'll have them sent at once, and we'll see if your train's ready.'

The train was not ready – nor was it ready within the prescribed ten minutes. There was some hitch, I fancy, about a saloon. Finally we had to be content with an ordinary old-fashioned first-class carriage. The delay, however, was not altogether time lost. Just as the engine with its solitary coach was approaching the platform someone came running up with an envelope in his hand.

'Telegram from St Albans.'

I tore it open. It was brief and to the point.

'Arab with companion was in train when it left here. Am wiring Luton.'

'That's all right. Now unless something wholly unforeseen takes place, we ought to have them.'

That unforeseen!

I went forward with the Inspector and the guard of our train to exchange a few final words with the driver. The Inspector explained what instructions he had given.

'I've told the driver not to spare his coal but to take you into Bedford within five minutes after the arrival of the express. He says he thinks that he can do it.'

The driver leaned over his engine, rubbing his hands with the usual oily rag. He was a short, wiry man with grey hair and a grizzled moustache, with about him that bearing of semi-humorous, frank-faced resolution which one notes about engine-drivers as a class.

'We ought to do it, the gradients are against us, but it's a clear night and there's no wind. The only thing that will stop us will be if there's any shunting on the road, or any luggage trains; of course, if we are blocked, we are blocked, but the Inspector says he'll clear the way for us.'

'Yes,' said the Inspector, 'I'll clear the way. I've wired down the road already.'

Atherton broke in.

'Driver, if you get us into Bedford within five minutes of the arrival of the mail there'll be a five-pound note to divide between your mate and you.'

The driver grinned.

'We'll get you there in time, sir, if we have to go clear through the shunters. It isn't often we get a chance of a five-pound note for a run to Bedford, and we'll do our best to earn it.'

The fireman waved his hand in the rear.

'That's right, sir!' he cried. 'We'll have to trouble you for that five-pound note.'

So soon as we were clear of the station it began to seem probable that, as the fireman put it, Atherton would be 'troubled'. Journeying in a train which consists of a single carriage attached to an engine which is flying at topmost speed is a very different business from being an occupant of an ordinary train which is travelling at ordinary express rates. I had discovered that for myself before. That night it was impressed on me more than ever. A tyro – or even a nervous 'season' – might have been excused for expecting at every moment we were going to be derailed. It was hard to believe that the carriage had any springs – it rocked and swung, and jogged and jolted. Of smooth travelling had we none. Talking was out of the question – and for that, I, personally, was grateful. Quite apart from the difficulty we experienced in keeping our seats – and when every moment our position was being altered and we were jerked backwards and forwards, up and down, this way and that, that was a business which required care – the noise was deafening. It was as though we were being pursued by a legion of shrieking, bellowing, raging demons.

'George!' shrieked Atherton, 'he does mean to earn that fiver. I hope I'll be alive to pay it him!'

He was only at the other end of the carriage, but though I could see by the distortion of his visage that he was shouting at the top of his voice – and he has a voice – I only caught here and there a word or two of what he was saying. I had to make sense of the whole.

Lessingham's contortions were a study. Few of that large multitude of persons who are acquainted with him only by means of the portraits which have appeared in the illustrated papers, would then have recognized the rising statesman. Yet I believe that few things could have better fallen in with his mood than that wild travelling. He might have been almost shaken to pieces – but the very severity of the shaking served to divert his thoughts from the one dread topic which threatened to absorb them to the exclusion of all else beside. Then there was the tonic influence of the element of risk. The pick-me-up effect of a spice of peril. Actual danger there quite probably was none; but there very really seemed to be. And one thing was absolutely certain, that if we did come to smash while going at that speed we should come to as everlasting smash as the heart of man could by any possibility desire. It is probable that the knowledge that this was so warmed the blood in Lessingham's veins. At any rate as – to use what, in this case, was simply a form of speech – I sat and watched him, it seemed to me that he was getting a firmer hold of the strength which had all but escaped him, and that with every jog and jolt he was becoming more and more of a man.

On and on we went dashing, crashing, smashing, roaring, rumbling. Atherton, who had been endeavouring to peer through the window, strained his lungs again in the effort to make himself audible.

'Where the devil are we?'

Looking at my watch I screamed back at him.

'It's nearly one, so I suppose we're somewhere in the neighbourhood of Luton. – Hollo! What's the matter?'

That something was the matter seemed certain. There was a shrill whistle from the engine. In a second we were conscious – almost too conscious – of the application of the Westinghouse brake. Of all the jolting that was ever jolted! the mere reverberation of the carriage threatened to resolve our bodies into their component parts. Feeling what we felt then helped us to realize the retardatory force which that vacuum brake must be exerting – it did not seem at all surprising that the train should have been brought to an almost instant standstill.

Simultaneously all three of us were on our feet. I let down my window and Atherton let down his – he shouting out,

'I should think that Inspector's wire hasn't had its proper effect, looks as if we're blocked – or else we've stopped at Luton. It can't be Bedford.'

It wasn't Bedford – so much seemed clear. Though at first from my window I could make out nothing. I was feeling more than a trifle dazed – there was a singing in my ears – the sudden darkness was impenetrable. Then I became conscious that the guard was opening the door of his compartment. He stood on the step for a moment, seeming to hesitate. Then, with a lamp in his hand, he descended on to the line.

'What's the matter?' I asked.

'Don't know, sir. Seems as if there was something on the road. What's up there?'

This was to the man on the engine. The fireman replied:

'Someone in front there's waving a red light like mad – lucky I caught sight of him, we should have been clean on top of him in another moment. Looks as if there was something wrong. Here he comes.'

As my eyes grew more accustomed to the darkness I became aware that someone was making what haste he could along the six-foot way swinging a red light as he came. Our guard advanced to meet him, shouting as he went:

'What's the matter! Who's that?'

A voice replied,

'My God! Is that George Hewett? I thought you were coming right on top of us!'

Our guard again.

'What! Jim Branson! What the devil are you doing here, what's wrong? I thought you were on the twelve out, we're chasing you.'

'Are you? Then you've caught us. Thank God for it! – We're a wreck.'

I had already opened the carriage door. With that we all three clambered out on to the line.

CHAPTER FORTY-SEVEN

# THE CONTENTS OF THE THIRD-CLASS CARRIAGE

I moved to the stranger who was holding the lamp. He was in official uniform.

'Are you the guard of the 12.0 out from St Pancras?'

'I am.'

'Where's your train? What's happened?'

'As for where it is, there it is, right in front of you, what's left of it. As to what's happened, why, we're wrecked.'

'What do you mean by you're wrecked?'

'Some heavy loaded trucks broke loose from a goods in front and came running down the hill on top of us.'

'How long ago was it?'

'Not ten minutes. I was just starting off down the road to the signal box, it's a good two miles away, when I saw you coming. My God! I thought there was going to be another smash.'

'Much damage done?'

'Seems to me as if we're all smashed up. As far as I can make out they're match-boxed up in front. I feel as if I was all broken up inside of me. I've been in the service going on for thirty years, and this is the first accident I've been in.'

It was too dark to see the man's face, but judging from his tone he was either crying or very near to it.

Our guard turned and shouted back to our engine.

'You'd better go back to the box and let 'em know!'

'All right!' came echoing back.

The special immediately commenced retreating, whistling continually as it went. All the country side must have heard the engine shrieking, and all who did hear must have understood that on the line something was seriously wrong.

The smashed train was all in darkness, the force of the collision had put out all the carriage lamps. Here was a flickering candle, there the glimmer of a match, these were all the lights which shone upon the scene. People were piling up débris by the side of the line, for the purpose of making a fire – more for illumination than for warmth.

Many of the passengers had succeeded in freeing themselves, and were moving hither and thither about the line. But the majority appeared to be still imprisoned. The carriage doors were jammed. Without the necessary tools it was impossible to open them. Every step we took our ears were saluted by piteous cries. Men, women, children, appealed to us for help.

'Open the door, sir!' 'In the name of God, sir, open the door!'

Over and over again, in all sorts of tones, with all degrees of violence, the supplication was repeated.

The guards vainly endeavoured to appease the, in many cases, half-frenzied creatures.

'All right, sir! If you'll only wait a minute or two, madam! We can't get the doors open without tools, a special train's just started off to get them. If you'll only have patience there'll be plenty of help for everyone of you directly. You'll be quite safe in there, if you'll only keep still.'

But that was just what they found it most difficult to do – keep still!

In the front of the train all was chaos. The trucks which had done the mischief – there were afterwards shown to be six of them, together with two guards' vans – appeared to have been laden with bags of Portland cement. The bags had burst, and everything was covered with what seemed gritty dust. The air was full of the stuff, it got into our eyes, half blinding us. The engine of the express had turned a complete somersault. It vomited forth smoke, and steam, and flames – every moment it seemed as if the woodwork of the carriages immediately behind and beneath would catch fire.

The front coaches were, as the guard had put it, 'match-boxed'. They were nothing but a heap of débris – telescoped into one another in a state of apparently inextricable confusion. It was broad daylight before access was gained to what had once been the interiors. The condition of the first third-class compartment revealed an extraordinary state of things.

Scattered all over it were pieces of what looked like partially burnt rags, and fragments of silk and linen. I have those fragments now. Experts have assured me that they are actually neither of silk nor linen! but of some material – animal rather than vegetable – with which they are wholly unacquainted. On the cushions and woodwork – especially on the woodwork of the floor – were huge blotches – stains of some sort. When first noticed they were damp, and gave out a most unpleasant smell. One of the pieces of woodwork is yet in my possession – with the stain still on it. Experts have pronounced upon it too – with the result that opinions are divided. Some maintain that the stain was produced by human blood, which had been subjected to a great heat, and, so to speak, parboiled. Others declare that it is the blood of some wild animal – possibly of some creature of the cat species. Yet others affirm that it is not blood at all, but merely paint. While a fourth describes it as – I quote the written opinion which lies in front of me – 'caused apparently by a deposit of some sort of viscid matter, probably the excretion of some variety of lizard'.

In a corner of the carriage was the body of what seemed a young man costumed like a tramp. It was Marjorie Lindon.

So far as a most careful search revealed that was all the compartment contained.

## CHAPTER FORTY-EIGHT

# THE CONCLUSION OF THE MATTER

It is several years since I bore my part in the events which I have rapidly sketched – or I should not have felt justified in giving them publicity. Exactly how many years, for reasons which should be sufficiently obvious, I must decline to say.

Marjorie Lindon still lives. The spark of life which was left in her, when she was extricated from among the débris of the wrecked express, was fanned again into flame. Her restoration was, however, not merely an affair of weeks or months, it was a matter of years. I believe that, even after her physical powers were completely restored – in itself a tedious task – she was for something like three years under medical supervision as a lunatic. But all that skill and money could do was done, and in course of time – the great healer – the results were entirely satisfactory.

Her father is dead – and has left her in possession of the family estates. She is married to the individual who, in these pages, has been known as Paul Lessingham. Were his real name divulged she would be recognized as the popular and universally reverenced wife of one of the greatest statesmen the age has seen.

Nothing has been said to her about the fateful day on which she was – consciously or unconsciously – paraded through London in the tattered masculine habiliments of a vagabond. She herself has never once alluded to it. With the return of reason the affair seems to have passed from her memory as wholly as if it had never been, which, although she may not know it, is not the least cause she has for thankfulness. Therefore what actually transpired will never, in all human probability, be certainly known and particularly what precisely occurred in the railway carriage during that dreadful moment of sudden passing from life unto death. What became of the creature who all but did her to death; who he was – if it was a 'he', which is extremely doubtful; whence he came; whither he went; what was the purport of his presence here – to this hour these things are puzzles.

Paul Lessingham has not since been troubled by his old tormentor. He has ceased to be a haunted man. None the less he continues to have what seems to be a constitutional disrelish for the subject of beetles, nor can he himself be induced to speak of them. Should they be mentioned in a general conversation, should he be unable to immediately bring about a change of theme, he will, if possible, get up and leave the room. More, on this point he and his wife are one.

The fact may not be generally known, but it is so. Also I have reason to believe that there still are moments in which he harks back, with something like physical shrinking, to that awful nightmare of the past, and in which he prays God, that as it is distant from him now so may it be kept far off from him for ever.

Before closing, one matter may be casually mentioned. The tale has never been told, but I have unimpeachable authority for its authenticity.

During the recent expeditionary advance towards Dongola, a body of native troops which was encamped at a remote spot in the desert was aroused one night by what seemed to be the sound of a loud explosion. The next morning, at a distance of about a couple of miles from the camp, a huge hole was discovered in the ground – as if blasting operations, on an enormous scale, had recently been carried on. In the hole itself, and round about it, were found fragments of what seemed bodies; credible witnesses have assured me that they were bodies neither of men nor women, but of creatures of some monstrous growth. I prefer to believe, since no scientific examination of the remains took place, that these witnesses ignorantly, though innocently, erred.

One thing is sure. Numerous pieces, both of stone and of metal, were seen, which went far to suggest that some curious subterranean building had been blown up by the force of the explosion. Especially were there portions of moulded metal which seemed to belong to what must have been an immense bronze statue. There were picked up also, more than a dozen replicas in bronze of the whilom sacred scarabæus.

That the den of demons described by Paul Lessingham, had, that night, at last come to an end, and that these things which lay scattered, here and there, on that treeless plain, were the evidences of its final destruction, is not a hypothesis which I should care to advance with any degree of certainty. But, putting this and that together, the facts seem to point that way – and it is a consummation devoutly to be desired.

By-the-bye, Sydney Atherton has married Miss Dora Grayling. Her wealth has made him one of the richest men in England. She began, the story goes, by loving him immensely; I can answer for the fact that he has ended by loving her as much. Their devotion to each other contradicts the pessimistic nonsense which supposes that every marriage must be of necessity a failure.

He continues his career of an inventor. His investigations into the subject of aërial flight, which have brought the flying machine within the range of practical politics, are on everybody's tongue.

The best man at Atherton's wedding was Percy Woodville, now the Earl of Barnes. Within six months afterwards he married one of Mrs Atherton's bridesmaids.

It was never certainly shown how Robert Holt came to his end. At the inquest the coroner's jury was content to return a verdict of 'Died of exhaustion'. He lies buried in Kensal Green Cemetery, under a handsome tombstone, the cost of which, had he had it in his pockets, might have indefinitely prolonged his days.

It should be mentioned that that portion of this strange history which purports to be The Surprising Narration of Robert Holt was compiled from the statements which Holt made to Atherton, and to Miss Lindon, as she then was, when, a mud-stained, shattered derelict he lay at the lady's father's house.

Miss Lindon's contribution towards the elucidation of the mystery was written with her own hand. After her physical strength had come back to her, and, while mentally, she still hovered between the darkness and the light, her one relaxation was writing. Although she would never speak of what she had written, it was found that her theme was always the same. She confided to pen and paper what she would not speak of with her lips. She told, and re-told, and re-told again, the story of her love, and of her tribulation so far as it is contained in the present volume. Her MSS invariably began and ended at the same point. They have all of them been destroyed, with one exception. That exception is herein placed before the reader.

On the subject of the Mystery of the Beetle I do not propose to pronounce a confident opinion. Atherton and I have talked it over many and many a time, and at the end we have got no 'forrarder'. So far as I am personally concerned, experience has taught me that there are indeed more things in heaven and earth than are dreamed of in our philosophy, and I am quite prepared to believe that the so-called Beetle, which others saw, but I never, was – or is, for it cannot be certainly shown that the Thing is not still exist-ing – a creature born neither of God nor man.